"Pilot," he said, "I believe I gave you an order. If Lanoe thinks he can make it through, so can we. And I will *not* allow him to get away from me. This battle is not over until I say it is!"

No one on the bridge said a word. None of them moved, except the pilot. And she only stirred far enough to get the ship moving.

Gravity pushed them all down into their seats as the carrier surged forward, toward the wormhole throat.

Praise for D. Nolan Clark

FORSAKEN SKIES

"Unforgettable characters and is jam-packed with action [and] adventure...one readers will not want to miss."

—Booklist

"About as exciting an action story set in space as any this reviewer has seen in print in quite some time. It is worth the read...a terrific and thrilling novel."

—SciFi magazine

"Gripping writing, a brilliantly realised future culture and sympathetic characters...an entertaining and compelling read."

—SFX

FORGOTTEN WORLDS

"No less intriguing and action-packed than its predecessor. Here, sci-fi tropes such as AI and space aliens are turned into something entirely thoughtful and original."

—RT Book Reviews

FORBIDDEN SUNS

By D. Nolan Clark

THE SILENCE

Forsaken Skies
Forgotten Worlds
Forbidden Suns

FORBIDDEN SUNS

BOOK THREE OF THE SILENCE

WITHDRAWN

D. NOLAN CLARK

www.orbitbooks.net

Copyright © 2017 by David Wellington
Excerpt from *The Eternity War: Pariah* copyright © 2017 by Jamie Sawyer
Excerpt from *Tracer* copyright © 2015 by Rob Boffard

Cover design by Lauren Panepinto
Cover illustration by Victor Mosquera
Cover copyright © 2017 by Hachette Book Group, Inc.

Orbit
Hachette Book Group
1290 Avenue of the Americas
New York, NY 10104
orbitbooks.net

First Edition: October 2017

Orbit is an imprint of Hachette Book Group.
The Orbit name and logo are trademarks of Little, Brown Book Group Limited.

The publisher is not responsible for websites (or their content) that are not owned by the publisher.

The Hachette Speakers Bureau provides a wide range of authors for speaking events. To find out more, go to www.hachettespeakersbureau.com or call (866) 376-6591.

Library of Congress Cataloging-in-Publication Data:

Names: Clark, D. Nolan, author.
Title: Forbidden suns / D. Nolan Clark.
Description: First edition. | New York : Orbit, 2017. | Series: The silence trilogy ; 3
Identifiers: LCCN 2017025899| ISBN 9780316355810 (softcover) | ISBN 9780316355803 (ebook)
Subjects: | BISAC: FICTION / Science Fiction / Adventure. | FICTION / Science Fiction / High Tech. | FICTION / Science Fiction / Military. | FICTION / Science Fiction / Space Opera. | GSAFD: Science fiction. | War stories.
Classification: LCC PS3603.L3568 F67 2017 | DDC 813/.6—dc23 LC record available at https://lccn.loc.gov/2017025899

ISBNs: 978-0-316-35581-0 (trade paperback), 978-0-316-35580-3 (ebook)

Printed in the United States of America

LSC-C

10 9 8 7 6 5 4 3 2 1

For Alex

PART I

DISTANT DETACHED OBJECT

Chapter One

The Hipparchus-class carrier rocked from side to side, and somewhere, down a long corridor, Ashlay Bullam could hear an explosion and a muffled scream. They were under attack—which meant they must have found their quarry.

At the worst possible moment, of course. Her disease had come back with a vengeance, and she could barely move. She turned desperate eyes toward the man next to her.

"Get me to the bridge," she said.

"Nothing would give me more pleasure." Auster Maggs had an elegantly sculpted mustache and a sarcastic leer that seemed to be a permanent part of his face. Less than eight hours ago, he'd been a Navy pilot and her sworn enemy. Then he'd seen the writing on the wall—that the Navy couldn't win this fight. He'd immediately defected to Centrocor's side.

Now he was her new best friend.

He wrapped an arm around her waist and lifted her gently from her bed. The carrier was under slight acceleration, which meant there was a little gravity to contend with, but not much. He had no trouble half carrying, half walking her the short distance. He touched the release for her and the bridge hatch slid open on a scene of utter chaos.

Displays all around the bridge showed the state of the battle.

Fighters wheeled and struck, guns flashing as they twisted in for quick attack runs, thrusters flaring as they raced away again, missing deadly shots by a matter of centimeters. A Yk.64 fighter—one of their own—exploded just off the bow of the carrier and the bridge was washed with orangish-white light. The carrier swayed and Bullam lunged for something to hold on to as she was knocked from her feet.

"Are we winning, at least?" she demanded.

Captain Shulkin, the carrier's commanding officer, turned in his seat to glare at her. "Victory is inevitable," he said. "Which does not mean we can afford to grow complacent. Information Officer—give me the status of the enemy's guns."

"Weapons hot, sir—I register all sixteen of their coilguns ready to fire."

Bullam's blood ran cold. The last time they'd fought the Hoplite-class cruiser, it had fired one shot from just one of its guns, and Shulkin had been forced to make a terrible sacrifice to keep them all from being killed. Now all of the cruiser's guns were active—

"Except—sir," the IO said, his face crinkled up with bewilderment, "they aren't aiming at us. The guns are pointed at the city."

City? Bullam had no idea what the man was talking about. The last she'd heard, the carrier was transiting through a wormhole throat. They could be anywhere in the galaxy by now. She slid into her seat at the back of the bridge and tapped her wrist minder to bring up a tactical display.

What she saw answered very few of her questions. Instead it raised many, many more.

The carrier wasn't in outer space. It was in a vast cavern, perhaps a hundred kilometers in diameter, with walls of pure ghostlight. The same eerie phosphorescence you saw lining the interior of a wormhole. But this couldn't be a wormhole—they didn't come this big, not by a power of ten. Moreover, wormholes were tunnels, linking two points in space. This cavern had only one entrance, the one they'd come through. It was like a bubble of higher-dimensional space carved out of the very wall of the universe.

Floating in the middle of the bubble, quite impossibly, was a city a few kilometers across. A ball of gothic architecture, spires and towers radiating outward from a hidden center. From the tops of the highest buildings brilliant searchlights swept across the bubble, lighting up Centrocor and Navy ships alike.

Bullam could hardly believe it. But she knew, instantly—this was what they'd come to find. This was why they'd chased the cruiser across hundreds of light-years of space.

"Captain!" she called. "You have to stop them! We can't let them destroy that city."

Shulkin twisted his mouth over to one side of his cadaverous face. "I assume the civilian observer has a good reason to issue orders on my damned bridge?" he asked.

"We can't let them fire on the city," she said. "Those are potential *customers* down there!"

~~~~~

It had been a long journey to get here—wherever they were.

Bullam worked for Centrocor, one of the interplanetary monopolies, or polys, which effectively owned all planets outside the original solar system. Centrocor was in a constant state of cold warfare with the Navy of Earth. The balance of power shifted endlessly, but never so far as to reach a tipping point. Until, perhaps, now.

Centrocor had spies inside the Navy. Those spies had reported that the very top level of Naval command had approved a mission of utmost secrecy. The admirals had sent one of their officers— Aleister Lanoe—to meet with some unknown group, some third party, in the hope of creating an alliance. Centrocor couldn't allow that to happen—anything that gave new strength to the Navy would harm the polys, perhaps fatally.

So the poly had sent Bullam to capture Lanoe, or at the very least to find out what he was up to. She had been given an enormous amount of support. A Hipparchus-class carrier half a kilometer long, which held a crew of over a hundred people and fifty smaller

Yk.64 fighter craft. Two Peltast-class destroyers, only a hundred meters long each but so covered in guns they looked shaggy. Powerful, extremely fast, very deadly.

Perhaps most important, they'd given her Captain Shulkin. An ex-Navy officer who, for all his limitations, was a brilliant tactician and a ruthless leader.

Lanoe only had one ship, a Hoplite-class cruiser, and a handful of fighters. He was working with a skeleton crew and a tiny number of pilots.

He was also the luckiest bastard who'd ever lived. Lanoe had fought in every major war since Mars rebelled against Earth three hundred years ago. He'd always been on the winning side. He was the most decorated pilot in Navy history, having survived more dogfights and attack runs than should be possible for one man. He was smart, quick, and sneaky, and somehow he had kept his people alive and his cruiser intact despite everything Centrocor had thrown at him.

That couldn't last. The odds were undeniably in Centrocor's favor—they outnumbered him in every statistic that mattered. In previous encounters, it had been considered crucial to capture Lanoe alive. Now that they had reached this mysterious city, that was no longer necessary. They could throw everything they had at him.

It was just a matter of time. Lanoe was going to die. Centrocor was going to win. Bullam would gain unfettered access to the city and she would make a deal with its inhabitants. Steal the Navy's new ally for the poly. She would return home to a promotion, to stock options, to guaranteed medical care. All she had to do was sit back and watch the battle play itself out.

We've already won.

She kept telling herself that. Repeating it over and over like a mantra. She was certain that eventually she would start to believe it.

"Where the hell is Lanoe?" Shulkin demanded. The IO didn't even bother to answer out loud, he just brought up a subdisplay that showed the Navy cruiser, twenty kilometers away. The Hoplite was three hundred meters long, nearly a third of that taken up by its massive fusion engines, much of the rest comprising its deadly coil-guns and a large vehicle bay that could hold a dozen fighters. The ship was scarred by explosions, scorched by dozens of hits from particle beam weapons—PBWs. Portions of its armor were missing altogether. Its vehicle bay was open to the elements, its hatch torn away.

It was not, however, undefended. A single BR.9 fighter—a Navy ship—spun circles around the big ship, a minnow twisting around the body of a wounded shark. Centrocor Yk.64 fighters darted in wherever they saw an opening, but, incredibly, impossibly, the BR.9 was always there to drive them back with salvos from its twin PBWs. The view magnified still further and Bullam saw that the enemy fighter's canopy had been blasted away, that its fuselage had been stripped down to exposed wiring and burnt-out components, but still it fought on. Through the damage she could actually see the helmet of the pilot—could even get a glimpse of short gray hair.

"It's him," Shulkin breathed. "Put a call in to the Batygin brothers."

A pair of holographic images appeared on either side of the magnified view, showing the commanders of the two Peltast-class destroyers. Identical twins, their hair combed in opposite directions as if that would allow someone to tell them apart. Their pupils were enormous because they were both drugged with a vasodilator that supposedly enhanced their response time and combat effectiveness. It also let them speak almost in unison.

"Ready, Captain."

"Ready, Captain."

Shulkin didn't look at them—he only had eyes for Lanoe. "Focus your attack on that BR.9. As long as he's alive we haven't won anything."

"Understood."

"Understood…"

"What?" Shulkin demanded. "Why are you hesitating?"

"We're currently under attack ourselves."

"We *are* currently under attack ourselves."

"There!" Bullam said, jabbing a finger at the display no one else was watching. The one that showed the battle raging just outside the carrier's hull.

A second BR.9 had been streaking toward them the whole time, virtually ignoring every Sixty-Four Centrocor had in play. Even as whole squads of the poly's fighters plunged toward it, the BR.9 kept coming, burning hard in a blatantly suicidal charge.

"That's Candless," Maggs said from behind Bullam's shoulder.

She swiveled around. She'd nearly forgotten he was there.

"Who?" she asked.

"Marjoram Candless. She's Lanoe's executive officer. Until recently she worked as an instructor at the Navy's flight school, but don't let that fool you. The old adage that those who can't, teach? Not frightfully accurate in this case. She's a real devil behind a control stick."

"She can't hope to achieve anything by herself," Bullam insisted.

"Ah, well, there's the rub," Maggs said, and nodded at the display.

Out of nowhere eight more BR.9s came swinging into the battle, their PBWs blazing away indiscriminately. Sixty-Fours burned and exploded left and right, and suddenly there was a hole in their defense, a vulnerability big enough for Candless to punch right through. She continued on her course, straight toward one of the destroyers, not deviating so much as a fraction of a degree.

"No," Bullam said. "No—our intelligence said Lanoe only had five pilots left. Who the hell are these eight?"

"Tannis Valk," Maggs told her, stroking his mustache.

"Valk—he's one of the five," Bullam said, "but—"

Even Maggs looked worried now. "I'll save you the trouble of asking how one man can fly eight ships at the same time. He isn't. A man, that is. He's an artificial intelligence loaded into a space suit."

No. No, no, no. That wasn't...for one thing, that was illegal. Just allowing an AI to exist was a capital crime. Giving one access to weapons and military hardware was so incredibly unlawful, so incredibly unethical, that Bullam couldn't even imagine someone doing it. Not even a devious bastard like Aleister Lanoe. "No," she said.

"I'm afraid the answer is yes. And now—"

"Sir!" the IO shouted. "Sir, the enemy BR.9 has loaded a disruptor. It's within range of one of our destroyers."

One of the Batygin brothers opened his mouth as if to speak. The other mirrored the gesture a split second later. "Brace for impact," he said.

"Brace for impact!"

In the display, Bullam could actually watch it happen. A panel in the undercarriage of Candless's BR.9 slid open, and the missile extended outward on a boom. A meter-long spear with multiple warheads—one round like that could tear a destroyer to pieces.

And at the last minute, the very last second, Candless pulled a snap turn—and fired the missile not at the destroyer, but right at the carrier.

Bullam could see it coming right at her, head-on.

The destroyers had already started to turn, hopelessly attempting to outmaneuver the disruptor. They ended up having to burn all their jets in an attempt not to collide with each other—or with the carrier.

The pilot of the carrier was far too busy to do any fancy flying. Everyone on board the giant ship was simply trying to hold on.

The disruptor round detonated just before it touched the carrier's outer hull, the shock wave of the blast peeling the ship's armor back like the rind of a fruit. It kept exploding as it plunged through power relays, crew spaces, cable junctions, computer systems. It passed through the cavernous vehicle bay without meeting much resistance. Still exploding, it tore apart a pair of reserve fighters, a maintenance cradle, and three engineers—and kept going.

On the bridge every display flashed red and the air was full of screaming chimes. Damage control boards popped up automatically and the pilot, the navigator, and the IO tried desperately to issue commands to the crew, tried to lock down vital systems or bring up blast doors to keep fires from raging through the life support system.

Then the carrier turned on its side, rolling with the blast, and everyone was thrown over in their seats. Bullam's body bent the wrong way and she felt her bones twist in their sockets as she was tossed around, her neck whipping around and her arms flying in the air. Behind her Maggs smashed into one wall, his hands grabbing at anything he could reach, anything that would hold his weight.

The disruptor kept bursting its way through compartment after compartment of the ship, still exploding as it went, bursting the eardrums and lungs of Centrocor crew members as it passed them by, flash-frying sensitive electronics as it dug its way ever deeper into the mass of the carrier.

It was over in the space of a few seconds. It left Bullam's head ringing like a bell and blood dripping from her nose. She grabbed a brocaded handkerchief from a pocket of her suit and pressed it—hard—against her face. "Captain," she called. "Captain Shulkin!"

Smoke drifted across the bridge. The only light came from a single display that looked like a jigsaw puzzle—some of its emitters must have been smashed. In the fitful light, she saw Shulkin floating in the middle of the bridge, holding on to his chair with the long, skeletal fingers of one hand.

He was smiling.

"Well done," he said, a throaty whisper.

Then he flipped around to face the navigator. "Take us closer to the cruiser," he said.

"Captain, sir," the IO said. Blood slicked the left arm of the man's suit. "We need to do some damage control, we need to make sure we haven't lost—"

"The battle," Shulkin insisted, "isn't over yet. Move us closer. Tell the Batygin brothers to engage with everything they have."

Bullam rubbed her neck with one hand—she was relatively sure it wasn't broken—and tapped anxiously at her wrist minder.

It brought up a new display, showing her the city below. Fighters banked and soared over its spires, individual ships now caught up in lethal dogfights. She saw one of the enemy BR.9s break into pieces, debris twisting and streaming away from it even as inertia carried it down into the city streets. Debris from collisions and explosions and general destruction was cascading onto the dark stone towers, a dangerous rain of burnt titanium and shredded carbon fiber.

A single BR.9 flashed across her view, momentarily filling the entire display. She backed up frame by frame until she could see the pilot's face. Sharp features, hair pulled back in a severe bun, prim, pursed lips. Maggs had said this Candless was a teacher. She'd come very close to killing every human being on the carrier.

The damage done, Candless was streaking away, swinging back and forth to avoid Centrocor fire. She was breaking free of the fight, headed back toward the cruiser. Not to defend it, Bullam thought. No.

"They're retreating," she said.

"Don't be a fool," Shulkin told her. "Where could they go? There's only one exit from this cavern, and we're blocking their way."

Bullam shook her head. "That attack—it wasn't meant to kill us. Just tie us up with damage control. She was playing for time."

"Time for what?" Shulkin demanded.

They didn't have to wait long to get an answer.

Bullam was probably the only one on the bridge who was looking at the city, not at the battle still raging all around them. She was the first to notice when the searchlights down there began to pivot around until they were all facing the same direction. A surge of white plasma poured out of them, beam after beam twisting around toward a common target. Though she couldn't see what they were pointing at—they seemed to be converging on thin air.

"What are they doing?" she demanded, not really expecting an answer. Nor did she receive one. None of the bridge crew were even paying attention to her. Valk's drone ships were tearing away at one of the destroyers, targeting its many guns, scoring its hull with burst after burst of concentrated PBW fire. Candless was halfway back to the cruiser already, where Lanoe was still defending his ship against all comers.

"There's something…happening," she said. "Damn you, Shulkin! Look at this!"

The captain finally twisted around in his seat to look at her. She held up her wrist minder so he could see the display.

The beams from the city were coalescing into a cloud of radiance, a sort of nebulous, formless glob of plasma.

"You there! Traitor!" Shulkin called.

Maggs looked deeply hurt, but he refrained from saying anything in his own defense. The charge was, after all, irrefutable. "How may I assist?"

"You were with Lanoe before we got here. What the devil is he doing? What are those beams? Some kind of weapon?"

"I'm afraid I wasn't privy to his negotiations with the people of the city," Maggs said. "I haven't the faintest. Many apologies."

Shulkin's face was fleshless and pale at the best of times. At that moment he looked like nothing more than a skull with lips. "IO! Give me data on that weapon!"

"Sir, it's…a series of collimated plasma beams, and, well…yes," the poor information officer said. "I suppose it could be used as a…as a weapon, but—"

"Stop stammering and tell me what I need to know," Shulkin said. "Or I will replace you with someone who can."

The navigator and pilot looked away. They knew perfectly well what Shulkin meant. He'd shot the previous navigator for hesitation in following an order. There was no question he would do the same thing again.

"The beams are hot enough to cut through armor plate, yes, sir," the IO said. "I'm getting some anomalous readings from them, though—the plasma seems to have negative mass."

"*Negative*? Negative *mass*?"

"It's not as impossible as it sounds, sir. It's called exotic matter, and hypothetically you could use it to create a—"

On the display, the beams wove together into a ring of coruscating light. It flared bright enough that Bullam started to look away—but then the ring collapsed inward, into itself, and seemed to pop out of existence as quickly as it had appeared.

"—to create a wormhole throat," the IO finished, in a near whisper.

Where the ring had been, where the beams had crossed, there was nothing now except a strange spherical distortion in the air, as if a globe of perfect glass hung there.

Every single one of them knew what that meant. A wormhole throat. A passageway through the belly of the universe. It could go anywhere—literally anywhere.

And it was right where the cruiser needed it to be.

"They're going to escape," Bullam said, hardly believing it. "They're going to get away from us—*again*."

BR.9s started streaming into the cruiser's open vehicle bay, one by one. Static guns mounted on the hull of the Hoplite blazed away at those few Sixty-Fours that were still in range, still trying to get close enough to the cruiser to launch disruptors.

"Their engines are warming up," the IO called out. "They're going to move."

"Of course they are," Shulkin said. He sat down in his chair and pulled a strap across his waist. Then he steepled his fingers together before his face.

"Batygins," he called.

"A bit busy right now."

"A *bit* busy right now," the twins replied.

"I don't care," Shulkin said, though his voice was oddly soft. "Maneuver on your own time. Right now I need you to pour every ounce of fire you can into that cruiser. I want every missile, every flak gun firing. If this is our only chance, we *will* kill Aleister Lanoe. Am I understood?"

The brothers didn't even take the time to respond. Their guns opened fire almost instantly, heavy PBW salvos lancing across the sky, missiles firing in quick succession out of their pods. A few shots even found their target, burning long streaks down the engine modules of the Hoplite. Missiles locked on and flared with light as they accelerated toward the cruiser's thrusters. Anything in the way of that torrent of destruction would have been vaporized.

But it was too late. Even Bullam—who had no training in space combat—could see that. The cruiser's nose was already disappearing into the new wormhole throat, even as a final BR.9 raced for safety inside its vehicle bay. Lanoe's ship vanished into thin air, a little at a time. On the display it looked like it was moving with glacial slowness, like it had all the time in the world. But it kept disappearing, bit by bit.

"Keep firing!" Shulkin said.

A missile hit home—but only one. It burst against a thick plate of armor on the cruiser's side, light and debris spreading outward in a deadly cloud. But the Hoplite was half-gone now, its coilguns blinking out of existence one by one. The vehicle bay disappeared, and then the thrusters were all that remained, just a dull glow of heat and ionized gas, and then, finally, even that was gone.

The missiles lost their lock and could no longer home in on their targets. Rudderless, they twisted off, away from the wormhole throat, losing speed as they twirled pointlessly in the air. A few blasts of heavy PBW fire followed the cruiser through the throat, but it was impossible to see if they hit anything.

Eventually the destroyers stopped firing. What was the point?

Shulkin lifted his hands to his face, covering his eyes.

Bullam held her breath. She knew that something was coming. The captain was insane. Neurologically impaired. Back when he'd still been with the Navy, he'd developed a suicidal mania brought on by extreme combat stress. The Navy had fixed him, as best they could, with extensive brain surgery. They'd left him nearly catatonic, able to do nothing but fight.

Cheated of his prey now, how would he react? Would he pull out a pistol and blow his own brains out? Or maybe he would shoot everyone else first.

"Maggs," Bullam whispered. "Maggs, get ready to run if—"

"Send the recall," Shulkin said.

"Sir?" the IO asked.

"Send the recall order. I want every fighter back here, in our vehicle bay. I want the destroyers lined up and ready to maneuver. Have all crew aboard this ship report to stations, or to their bunks if they have no immediate duties."

"Yes, sir," the IO said.

Then Shulkin started to scrape at his eye sockets. Digging his nails deep into the skin around his eyelids. Rubbing at his brows with the balls of his thumbs.

"Captain?" Bullam asked. "Are you ...?"

"Navigator," Shulkin said. "Give me a course that takes us through that wormhole as fast as possible."

"Wait," Bullam said.

"If the civilian observer wishes to comment on my orders, she can do so in writing at some future time," Shulkin said. "Navigator?"

"Course entered, sir."

"Pilot," Shulkin said. "Take us—"

"No," Bullam said. "No! That won't be necessary. Our mission was to find out what Lanoe was up to. To find these allies he was looking for, and, well, here we are." She opened a display to show the city below them. "We've done it, Captain. We've reached our objective and we no longer need to capture Lanoe, we can—"

"Ignore her," Shulkin said. "If anyone on this bridge so much as looks at her, they will be disciplined. This is my ship. Pilot, take us through that wormhole."

"Sir, I'm sorry to interrupt," the IO said, "but there's something you should know. That wormhole isn't stable." On his display a schematic of the wormhole appeared. It dwindled even as Bullam watched, the throat tightening down to nothing. "It's shrinking. If we get caught in there when it collapses, we'll be annihilated. Every one of us will die. And we, uh ... we won't be able to ... kill Lanoe."

"Noted," Shulkin said. He scratched along the side of his nose as if he were trying to peel off a mask. "Pilot," he said, "I believe I gave you an order. If Lanoe thinks he can make it through, so can we.

And I will *not* allow him to get away from me. This battle is not over until I say it is!"

No one on the bridge said a word. None of them moved, except the pilot. And she only stirred far enough to get the ship moving.

Gravity pushed them all down into their seats as the carrier surged forward, toward the wormhole throat.

Chapter Two

Too many stars.

Aleister Lanoe stood on the surface of his cruiser, his boots adhering to the armor plates and keeping him from just drifting off into nothingness. He folded his arms behind him, tilted his head back, and tried to take it all in.

Too many stars here. The sky was packed with them. Paved with light.

They'd come ten thousand light-years in the space of an hour. Ten thousand light-years closer to the center of the galaxy.

In the spiral arm where Earth lay, in the tiny zone of worlds colonized and inhabited by human beings, stars were far apart. So distant from one another they looked like white dots on black velvet. As you traveled inward, though, toward the center, the stars grew thicker, more closely packed. Valk had told him the stars here were on average less than a light-year apart.

Arcing across Lanoe's view was the Milky Way itself. Whereas before he'd always known it as a vague pale streak across the sky, here it was a solid blur of light, a band of fierce energy that was hard to look at.

He felt exposed. Pinned down by all that hard light, like every star was an eye watching him, studying him. He knew that was just the anthropic fallacy at work. The ludicrous idea that in a universe as big as this one, as mind-freezingly gigantic, anything a human being could ever do would make one whit of difference. That in the scale of stars and globular clusters and galaxies, of deep time, the entire human race could make so much as one tiny dent in the attention of the cosmos. Nonsense, of course.

Still, he couldn't shake the feeling.

Dead ahead lay a single orangish-white sun, a K-type red dwarf. From here, fifty astronomical units away, it looked like just another of the great multitude of stars. This one, though, was what he'd come for.

This star belonged to the Blue-Blue-White. The bastards who had wiped out almost all life in the galaxy. The bastards who had killed Zhang—the only human being Lanoe had ever truly loved.

Lanoe had moved heaven and earth to get this close. To get his chance at revenge.

Just a little farther now. They would arrive soon enough.

For now, he walked across the hull of his ship, feeling it vibrate beneath the soles of his feet. The powerful engines were burning, pushing them closer. He saw the ship's scars. He saw the missing sections of hull plating, saw the scorched and burnt-out components. Already the ship and its crew had suffered. What lay ahead was going to test their limits. He hoped they would be strong enough.

As he came to the missing hatch over the vehicle bay, he stopped and looked up at the busy sky. Knowing what he would face once he stepped back inside, into air and warmth and human companionship.

He spent one last moment enduring the cyclopean gaze of the orange star dead ahead. And then he nodded in acknowledgment.

That's right, you bastards, he thought. *I'm coming for you.*

In the cruiser's tiny sick bay, Marjoram Candless considered her failures.

Bury hadn't regained consciousness. He lay strapped into a bed, the long arms of a medical drone tending to his injuries. He was one of her former students, brought along on this mission without any idea of what he was getting into. He had been born on the planet Hel, a very dry place, and like all the people of that world he was hairless and his skin had been infused with polymers to trap his sweat so it could be recycled. It made his skin shiny and smooth, as if he were just an infant.

If he knew she was thinking that, he would have flown into a rage. He would have insisted he was a *man*, an adult. Well. He'd proven his right to that, she supposed.

In the last battle with Centrocor his fighter had been nearly obliterated by an enemy missile. He'd barely made it back to the cruiser, even with her help. His shiny face was scarred now, burned in patches. The medical drone scrubbed at the injured flesh, rebuilding what it could, fusing together wounds that were too grievous to be erased.

He looked so very pale.

Candless checked the sensors that listed out his pulse, his respiration, his blood oxygen levels. He had stabilized but he was far from whole. Candless had been monitoring his condition quite closely, and she knew he was improving, but very slowly. She didn't know how long it would be before he regained consciousness. Even then he would need extensive therapy if he was going to return to his duties.

She touched his cold hand. She refrained from squeezing it—he needed to sleep. She closed her eyes. Candless had never been a religious woman, and she did not pray now, but she visualized him healing, getting better. She had a responsibility to him, one she had failed to carry out. A responsibility to keep him safe.

"I expect you to make a full recovery, young man," she told him, whispering. "I will accept nothing less. I intend to bring you home in the same shape I found you."

Sometimes it helped, saying things like that aloud. Sometimes, if she said them in just the right tone, with just enough authority, she thought they actually sounded believable.

Lanoe moved quietly through the ship. There was no one he particularly wanted to talk to at that moment. He passed through the vehicle bay and then into the axial corridor that ran the length of the ship, from the ruined bridge down to the engineering section.

A starship under acceleration is not like a yacht sailing on a placid ocean. Gravity pulls in the opposite direction of thrust, so the engines of the cruiser were down and everything else was up. The axial corridor ran through all the crew spaces of the Hoplite, a hundred meters and more. When the ship was moving it was essentially a very, very long ladder. Lanoe had to climb through the gun decks, where a dozen side passages branched off from the main corridor. As he hauled himself past, he heard raised voices, and he stopped for a moment to listen.

"We didn't sign up for this!"

"Where the hell are we?"

"When are we going home?"

Lanoe spent most of his time on the ship in the company of its officers: Candless, his executive officer; Paniet, his chief engineer; Valk, his...everything else. The enlisted men and women onboard never came into his orbit. There were twenty marines and three engineers aboard and he'd barely managed to memorize their names.

A good commander should be constantly aware of how his people are doing, at least so that he knows how close they are to open mutiny. Lanoe had never been a very good commander—his skills lay in other areas. He could hear the anger and the desperate confusion in their voices, though, and he knew he ought to at least hear them out.

He stepped into one of the side passages and poked his head into the gun decks, a cavernous space in the middle of the ship dominated by the hulking masses of the sixteen coilguns. He was surprised to see how many of the enlisted were there, perched on the huge barrels, slumped against the electromagnetic firing chambers. Surprised to see that they weren't at their stations, doing their jobs.

Caroline Ehta, his warrant officer, paced in front of them, occasionally chewing on a fingernail and spitting out the fragments. Lanoe could see she wasn't looking any of them in the eye.

Ehta had been a pilot once, until she got a bad case of the nerves. Then she'd volunteered for the Planetary Brigade Marines because she didn't know what else to do. The average life expectancy of a PBM in the field could be measured in weeks, but somehow she'd survived for years. Long enough to be promoted to sergeant. He'd made her a lieutenant so she could command his marines.

"I don't know," she said. She bit down hard on a hangnail, hard enough to draw blood. "I don't know *any* of that stuff. You think they tell me everything? That's a laugh. I don't know where we are. I don't know what we're doing here. As soon as I find out, I'll tell you guys. For now I need you to hang in there. I need you to keep working. Look, do any of you doubt I have your back?"

There were a few murmurs. No direct answers, yes or no.

"I fought with all of you on Tuonela. We went through hell back there, together."

That, at least, garnered some assent.

"You remember what the officers there were like, right? Happy to send us out to be targets for enemy artillery, or hit with biologicals, or to just spend a week crawling through the mud looking for something that wasn't there. And all the time they'd be back in their tents, drinking tea and polishing their boots and arguing about how many medals they should give each other."

Some of the marines laughed. Most of them nodded.

"So when I tell you I trust Commander Lanoe, that oughta mean something. I've known him a long time, and he's saved my ass more than once. You give him the benefit of the doubt now—it'll pay off. We'll come through this okay. You just gotta trust me. For now."

Some of the marines nodded and got up from where they sat. They headed off into the deep recesses of the ship, presumably to get back to work. Others lingered behind to slap Ehta on the back or the shoulders, which she answered invariably with a nod.

She still wasn't meeting their eyes.

Lanoe hung back near the axial corridor until she'd spoken with the last of them, made her final reassurances. When she was alone on the gun decks, he stepped inside and waved a hand to get her attention. She jumped when she saw him, but recovered herself quickly.

"Sir," she said.

"I hope I can live up to that speech," he told her.

"You...you heard that?"

"That's right. Tell me something, Ehta. All those nice things you just said about me, all that faith you put in me—how much of that did you actually mean?"

Her eyes went wide. "...Sir. I meant all of it." She licked her lips. "Every word."

She looked him right in the eye, without blinking. Clearly she wanted him to believe her.

Lanoe had lived a long time, though. More than three hundred years. After that long you learned to read people pretty well. He hadn't missed the slight hesitation before she answered.

＊

Candless left the sick bay and made her way back to the brig. There was supposed to be an armed guard stationed there, but the marines apparently had more important things to do. Candless supposed it didn't matter. The brig was no longer being used as a detention center. Instead, the chorister, Rain-on-Stones, was sleeping in one of the cells. The aliens known collectively as the Choir were three meters tall, which limited the number of places where Rain-on-Stones could be quartered. The cells of the brig were just large enough.

Candless touched the display built into the door of the cell and it came to life, giving her a view of the interior. The chorister took up much of the space, an enormous monstrosity. Just seeing the alien still gave Candless the chills. They were just so inhuman...From the cylindrical head that lacked any features except a ring of silver eyes, to the four arms that radiated outward from the torso, to the many jointed legs hidden beneath the alien's black dress, none of it made sense, none of it resonated with her idea of what an intelligent being should look like. Conceptually she could understand that Rain-on-Stones was as intelligent as herself, perhaps even more so. The chorister was a trained surgeon who had saved Bury's life. Still, Candless could never think of anything but crabs and silverfish when she looked at it.

Not *it*, of course. *Her.* Rain-on-Stones was female. Candless had to remind herself of that constantly. The Choir were all female. The males of their species were stunted, many-legged things, no smarter or bigger than spiders. Several of them were visible even as she watched the alien. One crawled out of Rain-on-Stones's collar and ran across her neck, then slipped between two plates of armor on the side of the chorister's head. Others roamed across her claws, or picked their way along her dress. Rain-on-Stones was positively crawling with the things. She had dozens, perhaps hundreds of males secreted around her body, hiding anywhere they could find warmth and safety. Normally you saw only one of them at a time, if that. Now they were swarming, perhaps troubled, stirred up by their host's uneasy sleep.

Candless's skin crawled with revulsion.

"Lieutenant?" Ginger asked, coming up behind her. Ginger lived in the brig, too, now, never very far from the alien.

Candless turned and looked at the girl. Saw the red hair, the first thing anyone noticed about her—the thing that had given Ginger her name. Saw the soft, sad eyes, the trembling mouth. She saw the place on Ginger's left temple where the hair had been shaved away. There was a short, mostly healed scar there.

"I've come to see how you are," Candless said. "Whether you need anything."

"We're fine," Ginger said. She turned to look at the display that showed Rain-on-Stones. "We will be for a while longer. Until I run out of her sedative. We have a week or two, maybe."

Candless frowned. "And what happens then? When you do run out?"

"I don't know, exactly. I imagine she'll wake up screaming. Terrified, and maybe righteously pissed off. You did kidnap her, after all."

The obscenity took Candless aback a little, but she forced herself not to show it. Naval officers were not supposed to use that word. Of course, Ginger had been relieved of duty—she was all but a civilian now. She'd proved that she was incapable of flying combat missions. Instead, she'd taken on a different role.

The scar on Ginger's head marked where Rain-on-Stones had implanted an antenna in the girl's brain. The Choir did not have a spoken language—instead they communicated by a form of telepathy. Ginger's implant allowed her to speak with them, but that had turned out to mean much more than just simple communication. As the Choir saw it, Ginger was now part of their community— part of the harmony, the gestalt formed of all their thoughts and emotions.

Sometimes Ginger seemed to think they were right. Sometimes now, when Candless spoke with the girl, she seemed more alien than human.

Candless did not claim to understand it at all. She did know that Ginger had agreed to join the Choir in exchange for the unstable wormhole that had brought them here. The deal she had struck was that she would go among them and live with them for the rest of her life, as one of them. She had assumed that Lanoe would allow her and Rain-on-Stones to return to the Choir's city before the cruiser entered the wormhole.

Lanoe had chosen not to fulfill that part of the agreement. Instead he'd brought Ginger and Rain-on-Stones along for the ride, against their will. He had not shared his reasoning with Candless. Perhaps he just couldn't bear to part with Ginger, one of his crew.

Or maybe he wanted Rain-on-Stones as a hostage, to guarantee the Choir wouldn't collapse the wormhole as soon as he was inside. He'd given the Choir plenty of reason to hate him. He'd threatened their city, turned the cruiser's guns on their only home. He'd been prepared to kill them all to get his wormhole. In the end, Ginger had reasoned with them and got Lanoe what he wanted. Nobody doubted he would have followed through on his ultimatum, though.

"When she wakes up she'll be so alone," Ginger said, her face heavy with grief. "She won't know what to do. They're surrounded by others like them from birth—they can't imagine a world where they can't hear each other's thoughts all the time." Ginger shook her head. "I can...hear her dreaming. It's just, I don't know. Shapes and colors and sounds that don't make any sense. It's terrible. She's lost, frightened...It's going to be much worse when she understands what's happened to her."

"We need to keep her healthy, and stable," Candless pointed out. "She may be our only way to get home." No human had the capacity to open a wormhole. Only the Choir knew how to do that. The wormhole that had brought them this far was gone now—it had been unstable, and now it had collapsed. If they were ever going to return to human worlds, Rain-on-Stones would have to open the way for them.

Ginger's eyes flashed sideways for a moment, and her mouth opened as if she might say something. But then she closed it again and shook her head. "I'll do what I can," she said. "I'll help her, any way that I can."

"Very good," Candless said. She sensed there was something there, something Ginger wasn't telling her. She didn't want to push, though. "You look tired. When was the last time you slept?"

Ginger just shrugged. She didn't take her eyes off the display.

"I hope you'll take care of yourself as well."

"Of course. You need me, too. I'm the only one who can talk to her."

"That isn't what I meant," Candless said. She reached for the girl's arm, but Ginger pulled away. "Ginger—I'm here for you, if you need me."

The girl didn't look up.

The cruiser had taken a bad hit during an early battle with Centrocor. A disruptor round had torn through the forward section, obliterating the bridge and the officers' quarters. Hoplite-class cruisers had a reputation for being indestructible, and this one had proved that out, but they'd been forced to make certain compromises. Now the ship was controlled not from a bridge but from a workstation built into the wall of an old wardroom—a space that had once been the marines' dining facility.

Tannis Valk, or rather the artificial intelligence that had once believed itself to be a man named Tannis Valk, was permanently stationed there, strapped into an uncomfortable chair in front of a massive and ever-changing suite of displays. He still looked mostly human. He wore a heavy pilot's suit with the helmet up and tuned until it was a solid, opaque black—hiding the fact that there was nothing inside, no head, no skull, no trace of the man whose memories the suit contained. He was taller than most people, well over two meters, but somehow that had always made Lanoe think he looked more human rather than less. Why would an AI need to be so big?

"You said you had new information," Lanoe said as he came into the wardroom, with Ehta trailing behind. Candless and Paniet were already there, staring intently at one of Valk's displays.

"There's no shortage of that, dearie," Paniet said. The engineer had been injured during maneuvers less than twenty-four hours before. He'd mostly recovered, though the ring of circuitry around his left eye was completely destroyed. He'd had most of it pulled out except for a few shards of metal where his eyebrow had once been. "We've been working our little telescopes to the bone, just trying to figure out exactly where we are. We must have logged a couple dozen terabytes of low-resolution imagery of star charts, and that's just the start."

"I still can't get an exact fix on our location," Valk said. "I don't have an explanation for it...I've been looking for landmarks, the standard candles that let you find your way around the galaxy. But they aren't showing up. At least not in the right places."

"Maybe we're just too close to the center of the galaxy," Paniet offered. "Too many other stars in the way. We can't see the forest for the trees, hmm?" Lanoe didn't think Paniet sounded convinced that was it, though.

Maybe Valk's malfunctioning, Lanoe thought. There was a terrifying prospect. They relied on the AI to keep the ship moving, among other things.

He put the thought aside for the moment. "There's only one star I'm really interested in," he said. "The red dwarf straight ahead of us."

Valk gestured at the displays. "We've been scanning that pretty closely, yeah. And we've learned a couple of things. Not what we expected, though. You want the bad news first, or the weird news?"

Lanoe scowled. "Weird," he said.

"I've checked the system from top to bottom," Valk said, pointing at the vaguely orange dot in the center of his main display. The view zoomed in until it grew big enough to actually look spherical. "Looking for planets, or at least any sign that the Blue-Blue-White really live here."

Lanoe nodded. In the entire galaxy, only three intelligent species were still in existence. Humanity and the Choir were equally afraid of the third—giant jellyfish who had wiped out all other life. Lanoe had forced the Choir to send him here so he could finally get some justice for all the species that hadn't made it. He had to assume they had sent him to the right place, to the homeworld of the Blue-Blue-White.

"What did you find?" Lanoe asked.

"It's what we didn't find that makes it weird. No planets."

Lanoe dropped to one knee down in front of the display, as if by physically getting closer to it he could spot what Valk had missed. "That can't be right," he said. "The Choir sent us here for a reason."

Valk lifted his arms and let them fall again. "I'm just reporting what we've seen. There's a lot of gas and dust in the system—way more than we'd expect, actually. Plenty of asteroids and comets, but nothing bigger than about two thousand kilometers across."

Lanoe inhaled sharply. Earth's moon was bigger than that. You couldn't even build a proper colony on a rock that small—it wouldn't support a thick atmosphere, for one thing. "The Blue-Blue-White live in the atmospheres of gas giants. We know that, right? And you're telling me—"

"Nothing," Valk said. "Giants are the easiest kind of planets to find. If there were any here...Well, there aren't. I'm sorry, Lanoe. I'm not sure we're in the right place at all. Or at least—this isn't what we expected."

Lanoe stood back up, his old knees creaking just a little. "You've missed it somehow. I'm not criticizing your skills, just—"

Paniet clucked his tongue. "We've had most of our sensors working on this since we arrived, Commander. Criticize us all you like, but the data doesn't lie."

"Hold on. Most of your sensors, you said. Not all."

"That's where the bad news comes in," Valk told him.

Lanoe nodded. "Go ahead."

Valk brought up a new display, this one showing the volume of space directly behind the cruiser. "This is a recording we captured just after we arrived in this system, a couple of hours ago," the AI said. "I've magnified it to the limit of this display's resolution so you can see...there."

On the display, the wormhole throat they'd emerged from was just visible. A bead of glass hanging in that starry sky, a perfectly spherical distortion of spacetime. It shrank as Lanoe watched, until eventually it evaporated into nothingness.

Valk wasn't showing him this just to remind him that they'd lost their only way home, however. There was something odd about the video. It took Lanoe a while to figure out what it was.

Just before it winked out of existence altogether, it grew darker, just for a split second. Lanoe squinted at the view. "Run that back."

Valk set the video to play on a loop. The quality of the image was maddening. It showed just enough detail for Lanoe to be certain there was something there. Maybe something dark had passed in front of the camera, or maybe it was a fault with the equipment. He didn't think so, though.

No, he thought it looked like something was emerging from the throat, in the last few seconds before it collapsed.

"Something followed us," Valk said. "Something—somebody—chased us through that wormhole."

"By which, of course, you mean Centrocor," Candless said.

"Sure," Lanoe said. It was the only possibility that made sense. He had been crazy enough to fly through the wormhole without knowing where it went. Centrocor had been even crazier—following him in the hope they could make it through before the wormhole collapsed. If they'd still been inside the tunnel when it shrank down to nothing they would have been annihilated utterly.

They'd made it. Just. But they'd made it. Which meant that the Hoplite hadn't escaped its pursuers after all.

"Damn," Lanoe said. "This kind of distraction is the last thing we need."

"Distraction?" Ehta said, snorting in derision. "That's what you call a half a carrier group chasing us across ten thousand light-years? Boss, if they're still after us, we could be sunk before we even find this mythical planet of yours."

"Mythical?" Lanoe demanded.

Ehta lifted her hands for peace. "I just meant..."

"Perhaps you might think more, and speak less," Candless said, glaring at her. There had never been any love lost between the two women. The XO turned to face Lanoe. "Though she does have a point, as loath as I am to admit it. If Centrocor is here, still chasing us—that'll have to be our first priority."

Lanoe shook his head. "Valk, how far are we from the throat? Where the throat used to be, I mean?"

"We were moving pretty fast when we arrived here, and we never slowed down," Valk told him. "We're about a hundred million kilometers from there."

Lanoe nodded. "That might be good." Finding an enemy ship in deep space was one of the hardest parts of space combat. The distances involved tended to be enormous, and even the most barren system provided plenty of rocks to hide behind. "At that distance, Centrocor won't be able to see us. They know we're here, somewhere, but it'll be like searching for a needle in a swimming pool full of ink. That gives us some time."

"Some," Candless said. "Almost assuredly not as much as we'd like."

She was right. Centrocor had no mission here except to find and destroy them. They could put all their resources into that one goal. And once they caught sight of the cruiser, they would resume their attack without hesitation. There was more room to maneuver out here than they'd had inside the bubble, but the odds weren't much better. If it came down to a pitched battle, the cruiser would lose.

"We can hedge our bets, a little. Valk, switch off the engines. They've taken some damage, so they're probably blazing like signal beacons in the infrared. Turn off all of our exterior lights, too. Paniet, I want you to put some insulating foil over that missing hatch in the vehicle bay." There was no way to make the cruiser invisible, but they could make it as hard to find as possible. "Candless—get down there and run diagnostics on all our fighters."

"We lost several in the last battle," she pointed out. "You and Bury both brought your BR.9s back fit for nothing but the scrapyard."

Lanoe nodded. He remembered. "See how many of them can be repaired, then." It was going to come down to a fight, eventually, of that he was sure. But he intended to make it a short one. He had far more important work to do.

Chapter Three

The cruiser's telescopes moved from one object to another, each rock in the system getting a few seconds of observation time. The data thus recorded was fed directly to Valk, the candidates spooling through his consciousness. He didn't see the objects except as numbers: diameter, average orbital distance, albedo, spectroscopic profile. Each object in the system had to be evaluated, cataloged, rejected. "Object number 6020," he said. "Four hundred and fifty-one kilometers across its major axis. Twenty-one AU from the star. Albedo point seven one, indicating an icy but dynamic surface. Spectral lines indicate no atmosphere. No satellites."

"Uh-huh," Paniet replied. "Dearie, do you know I could be working on actually repairing this ship just now? Oh, how I would adore to be tracing circuits and welding bulkheads just now. Compared to this snipe hunt."

"Lanoe needs a planet," Valk said. "Let's move on. Object number 6021. Five hundred and twelve kilometers across its major axis. Twenty-one AU. Albedo point zero four, indicates a carbon/silicate hybrid composition, which is backed up by spectral lines. No atmosphere. One satellite, listed as 6021-a, one point six kilometers across major—"

"Enough," Paniet said. "Enough. I'm headed back to the engines.

If I can get a patch on the damaged shielding down there, it'll make us harder to track."

"That's fine," Valk said. "We don't need to be in the same place to keep running down the planetary candidates."

"Valk, my friend," Paniet said. "Look at me a moment."

Valk hadn't even been aware that his visual sensors were switched off. He brought them back online and trained them on Paniet. Anyone else would have noticed no change in him—he was still motionless in the seat by the ship's controls. Somehow, though, Paniet must have sensed it. "How did you know I wasn't looking at you?" he asked.

"How did I know you were sitting there blind as a bat? Because you didn't have any displays active."

Valk looked around and saw it was true. Normally he kept at least one visual display going—a view of what was directly ahead of the cruiser. He maintained that display for the sake of anyone who happened to be standing nearby. He must have shut it down by reflex, to save power. He switched it back on now, even though there was nothing to be seen but the multitude of crowded stars.

"I...I don't need a display to fly this crate," he said. Trying to make it sound like a joke.

"I know you don't," Paniet said. The engineer sighed. "There are a lot of things you don't need anymore, hmm?"

Valk had no ability to look ashamed or embarrassed. He had no face, and his body language was limited by what he could do with his arms in his bulky suit. "You're suggesting that maybe I don't need the human crew of this ship."

There had been a time when he thought he was a human being. Tannis Valk, the Blue Devil, the hero pilot of the Establishment. The legend was that Tannis had been flying a routine patrol in an FA.6 one day when he was ambushed by an enemy destroyer. He was struck by an antivehicle round that turned his cockpit into a hell of fire. Even as his skin crisped and his muscles burned, Tannis had continued to fight, getting two more confirmed kills before he flew back to his base. Afterward he'd become a legend—the pilot so tough he refused to die. Though he had suffered third-degree burns over his entire body, he could still fight on for the great cause. In public, after that day, he'd only ever appeared in his suit with his helmet up and tuned to an opaque black. Supposedly to spare anyone from having to see what was left of his face.

The real reason was that the suit—and the helmet—was completely empty. Tannis Valk had died instantly when the fireball tore through his ship. The FA.6 had been smart enough to get the two kills and fly home on its own. The Establishment had a bad need for heroes, though. At the time it was fighting the combined fleets of Earth and the polys, and it was losing. So Tannis's consciousness had been scanned from the charred ruin of his skull. Downloaded into a computer and made to think and see again. Not as a man, but as an artificial intelligence.

Creating an AI capable of independent thought and action was a serious crime. Giving such a being access to weapons—like, say, a cataphract-class fighter—was one of the worst crimes imaginable. The last time an AI had been armed, half the human race had died as a result. It was just assumed that any artificial intelligence would eventually turn on its creators and try to wipe them out.

The Establishment had been desperate enough to try it anyway. They had thought that if they told Valk he was still alive, still human, they could keep him on their side. Their plan had been to dismantle him and quietly erase his programming just as soon as they won the war. The problem was that they lost.

Valk had been left thinking he was a human being until shortly after he met Lanoe. When he'd discovered the truth, it had nearly driven him insane. He was only now starting to come to terms with what he really was. What he had always been.

"You're afraid that I'm going to go rogue and kill you all," Valk said.

"I'll admit it's a worry," Paniet told him. "But not a significant one. I've worked with you long enough to know how loyal you are to Lanoe. I don't think you would ever betray him."

Valk was surprised to find how much relief he felt, hearing that. He knew there were others in the crew who didn't trust him at all.

"Don't forget," Paniet went on, "I know computers better than anyone else here—except you. I know how computers think. I'm much more worried that you'll just shut down on us. That you'll get stuck on some impossible problem. Something that a human being could just shrug and put aside—but instead you'll be unable to let it go, and so you'll devote more and more processing power to it until you stop communicating with us altogether."

"What, like calculating pi to the last digit or something?"

"Or, say, pointlessly cataloging every chunk of matter in this system, looking for a planet that isn't there," Paniet said.

"No. That can't be right. Lanoe said the Choir wouldn't have sent us here for no reason. There has to be something."

"We would have seen it by now," Paniet replied. "We've run so many sensor sweeps—a big planet couldn't hide from us, not like this."

"Most of our scans have been in the visual portion of the spectrum," Valk pointed out. "If the planet was exceptionally dark, say, with an albedo below point zero one—"

"Ahem," Paniet said. "You think I hadn't considered that? But to have an albedo that low, the planet would have to be made of nothing but carbon nanotubes. We're looking for a gas giant with a hydrogen atmosphere."

"We don't know *what* we're looking for. It might not even be a planet."

"I suppose that's true, but—"

"I want to start running a series of transit photometry scans. If an exceptionally dark object passed in front of the star, we would see a dip in its light output," Valk said. "Anyway. You don't need to worry about me climbing up my own posterior and disappearing. I have a safeguard built in to prevent that."

"You do?" Paniet asked. Valk thought he sounded skeptical.

"Yes. Pain."

"I'm not sure I understand how that tracks."

Valk couldn't sigh, or snort in derision, or laugh. You needed lungs for those things. He could simulate them just fine, create sound files he could play when he needed to express an emotion. It didn't feel the same, though. "I hurt. Just all over. Back when I believed I was a human, I thought it was pain from my injuries. Now I know better—it was something like phantom limb syndrome, except everywhere at once. I call it phantom body syndrome. My simulated brain expects to get constant signals from my nonexistent nerves, and when that input doesn't show up, it assumes something is very wrong. So it tries to tell me that—by making me hurt."

"Is it...bad?" Paniet asked.

"Excruciating," Valk told him. "Worse when I move around, because I'm more aware of the fact that my joints aren't there."

"The devil you say," Paniet swore. "I—I didn't know."

"It's fine. I've lived with that pain for, well, the entire time I've existed. I know how to ride it out."

"Couldn't you just turn it off?" Paniet asked him.

"Of course. Easiest thing in the world—I just need to edit a one and make it a zero. But I won't."

"Why in Earth's name not?"

Valk couldn't smile. He had no mouth. "Because it's the last part of me that still feels human," he said. "You're worried I'm going to turn into a pure computer and stop thinking like a human being. That won't happen, you see? Because if I started down that road, the pain would bring me back. It would remind me of what I used to be."

The emotion that crossed Paniet's face then was difficult to parse. Valk chose to ignore it.

"Candidate number 6022," he said. "Thirty-seven kilometers along its major axis..."

Four.

Numbers were easy. Especially the number four. He saw it in his head, rotating in empty space. *Four four four four.* The number was always there.

There were words, too, thoughts spooling through his head, what felt like whole sentences, memories of things said, things other people had said. When he tried to catch them, though, they turned to nonsense, melted in his hands. Turned into a ringing sound, the ringing sound, the ringing noise that filled his head and turned him inside out and—

And—

"Gah," he said.

A word. A real word, in the oldest language. In baby talk. In the primal cry.

"Gah."

It made sense. It was the first word that had made sense to him in a long time. It meant something.

It meant "get this thing off of me." Except not quite. The word was missing something. Oh, right. It was emphatic. It needed an exclamation mark.

Get this thing off of me!

"Gah!" he said, thrashing against the mass on his face, against the intruder in his throat, *inside* of him—

"Hold on," someone told him. A woman, and then he felt soft hands on his face, on his chest, and then a hundred-meter-long snake came slithering out of him, biting and tearing at his insides as it came, and he tried to scream but the woman shushed him and he couldn't resist, couldn't resist that oldest and first maternal command, and then he gagged and spat up the last of the snake, its twisting tail, and saw it was a length of plastic tubing no more than twenty centimeters long.

There was blood on it. Blood and spit.

That thing had been inside him. He was—he was hurt, he'd been—

"Wah," he said, more baby talk, but now he was conscious enough, aware enough to feel shame. He was better than this, he was a Hellion, and that meant something, it meant he was tough, tough enough for real words—

"Wat!" he cried.

And because it was almost a word, because it almost made sense, he was rewarded. The woman pressed a squeeze tube of water to his mouth and he sucked at it, just like an infant sucking at a bottle—

No, damn it. He was an adult, a man, but—but the water in the tube was so perfect, so cool and soothing and clean. He sucked and sucked until it was taken away.

"Muh," he said.

"In a minute. You don't want to overdo it yet. Shh."

The soft hand stroked his forehead. Eased away the tension there, the taut agony of straining muscles, of a pounding headache, and it felt so, so good.

"Ginj," he whispered.

Which was not just a real word, but an actual name. Ginger. It had to be her—the only woman who'd ever shown him any kindness or understanding since he left his mother's home back on Hel. The only friend he had in the world—

"No," the woman said. "It's Lieutenant Candless."

Bury opened his eyes. Stared at her.

His old instructor, from flight school. Now his superior officer, the second in command of his ship. Bury stared at her with wide, terrified eyes. She'd been hard on him, so hard back in school, always pushing him, needling him, insulting him. She'd treated him like a child, like a petulant brat. He'd hated her, hated her like poison even when he'd respected her, even when he'd felt—when he felt—

"Off," he said. "Get off!"

Her hands, those hands that a moment before had felt so comforting, pulled back. He couldn't stand to have her touch him like that, it was just wrong, so wrong. He reached out and grabbed the side of the bed, hauled at it with both hands until he swung around.

"Bury, no—don't move, you can't move yet, you're still—"

He ignored her. He needed to get away, needed to...to...Oh, by all the chapels in hell, he'd thought she was Ginger, he'd let her touch him like that, let her—

"Get away from me!" he howled, and tried to put his feet down, tried to put his bare feet on what he expected to be a cold, hard floor, except he wasn't prepared for the fact that there was no gravity and he launched himself out of the bed, launched himself up into one corner of the room, behind the segmented arms of a medical drone. Grabbed on to anything he could and curled himself into a corner, staring down at her.

At her maddening, prim face. At her severe and demanding and unbearably smug face. Oh, by hell, by bloody, bloody hell, he'd thought she was Ginger, thought—

"Get out of here!" he screamed at her. "Get out!"

———※———

"Oh," Valk said. "It looks like Bury's woken up. That's some good news."

Lanoe scowled at him. "Sure," he said. "Is that why you called me down here?"

Valk knew that Lanoe could come across as callous sometimes, but that the commander truly cared about his crew. He was just distracted by everything else that was going on.

It looked like Paniet didn't understand that. The engineer visibly flinched. "When I got dropped on my head and went into a little coma, were you this angry about it?" he asked.

"Sorry," Lanoe told him. He let out a long sigh of impatience. "Yeah, it's good. I'm glad Bury's going to be okay. Just—tell me what you wanted to say."

Valk brought up a display and spooled through page after page of dense text. "We've cataloged eighty-six thousand seven hundred and ninety-one objects in this system. There may be a few we've missed, but they're likely to be very small."

"You counted eighty thousand rocks here?" Lanoe interrupted.

"Every star system is just littered with bits and pieces left over from its formation," Paniet said. "Even a small one like this. Comets and asteroids, dwarf planets and scattered disk objects and meteoroids in vast profusion. Eighty thousand is probably just scratching the surface. The asteroid belt around Earth's sun contains millions of objects more than half a kilometer across, and the Oort cloud out past the orbit of Neptune probably has *trillions*. No one has ever bothered to count them all. Such a thing might not even be possible."

Lanoe shook his head. "I'm aware of how crowded the solar system is. What surprised me is that you scanned eighty thousand rocks and none of them were planet-sized. Because I'm assuming if you had found a planet you would have led with that."

Paniet rolled his eyes. "Oh, indeed. And no, we didn't find any planets. But it's possible our survey wasn't completely in vain. We did find one candidate mass that intrigued us. M. Valk, if you please?"

Valk brought up a new display. This one showed a light-enhanced view of the object they called 82312, an icy mass about three hundred kilometers in diameter. Its surface was mostly flat, a skin of sheer ice broken only by very deep craters. Paniet had said it looked like a hollow skull, if one were feeling poetic. When Valk looked at it, it just looked like a big chunk of frozen rock.

"Okay," Lanoe said. "Now's the part where you tell me why I should care about this thing."

"Look at the metadata in the corner of the display," Valk said. A list of numbers was printed there, showing 82312's orbital parameters, its surface gravity, its hypothesized composition, its rotational period and values for its perturbation and precession—

"Just tell me, Paniet," Lanoe said.

"It's exactly what it looks like, a big chunk of dirty ice, but contain your disappointment. It's only a few million kilometers away from our present position. We could hide the cruiser behind it so that Centrocor could never find us. If we're feeling cheeky, we could even harvest an enormous quantity of deuterium and tritium from its ice."

"Fuel. For the engines," Lanoe said, giving Paniet a shrewd look. "Is that something we need?"

"Not immediately," Paniet admitted. "Though if we're going to be operating in this system for a long time, or if, say, we wanted to relocate to another star, one that might actually have planets—"

Lanoe nodded. "Understood. You're saying this place would

make a good base of operations. I agree. There's just one problem, though. A couple million kilometers away is still a pretty significant distance when we can't risk running our engines. The second we turn them on, Centrocor will know exactly where we are."

"They would see the light generated by our main thrusters, yes," Paniet said. "We can run our maneuvering and positioning jets without too much of a worry, though. Centrocor would have to have telescopes trained right on us already to see them firing. It'll be slow going, but safe."

"How slow?"

"We can be at 82312 in sixteen hours," Valk told Lanoe.

"Sure." Lanoe studied the image of the iceball and nodded for a while. "Sure. If Centrocor doesn't find us by then . . . All right. Let's do it." He nodded one more time, definitively. Then his eyes narrowed and Valk knew he'd just thought of something. "One thing. If we burned our main engines just for a couple seconds, how much quicker could we get there?"

"Half the time," Paniet said.

"Do that," Lanoe told the engineer.

"But Centrocor—"

"Will see it and come investigate, yes. They'll come look for us right here, where we are right now. By then we'll be long gone." And with that Lanoe departed the makeshift bridge, leaving the two of them alone with their instructions.

"I suppose he has a point," Paniet said once he was gone. "But he's taking a largish risk there, isn't he?"

Valk cleared the displays and brought up the ship's drive controls. "This is Lanoe we're talking about. The man's a master strategist. Did you see the look on his face just then?" he asked the engineer. "He gets that look every time he has a brilliant idea."

⤳⤙

If Bury pushed off one wall of the sick bay as hard as he could, it took exactly three-tenths of a second to fly to the far wall. He caught himself against the impact with both hands, then twisted around and launched himself through the air again, careful not to get tangled in the arms of the medical drone. Point two nine eight seconds, according to his wrist display. He turned around and got his feet against the wall and launched himself across the room one more time.

When the hatch opened, he barely had time to stick out a leg and catch the edge of the bed before he went sprawling into Ginger. Her eyes went wide as he bounced back, laughing. "Ginj!" he said. "Ginj! Hey!"

"You should be in bed," she told him.

He shrugged and grasped the edge of the bed. He had no intention of getting back into that thing as long as he lived. "I feel fine," he told her.

"The last time I came in here you were comatose." She pushed her way inside the room and let the hatch close behind her. "You never were very bright, Bury. You could have *died*. Do you understand that? I talked to Engineer Paniet a little while ago. He says your fighter was a total loss—he couldn't even rebuild it after it got hit by that missile. You—"

"I said I feel fine," Bury told her, his voice sounding a little higher pitched than he'd intended. He took a deep breath and tried to calm himself. "Look, you're worried about me, and I appreciate it. I really do, Ginj. If it makes you happy, I'll sit down. But I'm *fine*."

She frowned and looked away. "We need to run a bunch more tests. You lost a lot of blood, and there was some pretty severe organ damage. Rain-on-Stones fixed you up as best she could, but—"

"Who?" he asked.

"Oh, hellfire," Ginger said. "That's right. You don't know anything about the Choir. About what we found in the bubble. You probably don't even know where we are."

"I've been napping," he said, and smiled at her, but she didn't smile back.

What was going on?

"You want to get out of this room for a while? See some things?"

"Hellfire, yes," he told her.

She nodded. For the first time he noticed that the red hair on one side of her head had been shaved away. She had a thin scar running across her temple. Had she been hurt?

What the ruddy hell was going on?

Valk launched a flight of microdrones—tiny robots no bigger than a human thumb, each carrying nothing but a camera, an antenna, and a miniscule thruster package. They spread out away from the cruiser in every direction, moving fast. They would let him closely monitor the volume of space near the cruiser—and hopefully, eventually, give them some sense of Centrocor's movements.

"I don't care for this one bit, ducks," Paniet said. "We don't know where the enemy are, any more than they can find us. They could be sitting close by right now—and your little friends there could be the thing that gives away our position."

"Not very likely," Valk said. "I'm of the opinion that more information is always better."

"You would say that, wouldn't you?" Paniet asked. "Oh, don't give me that look. I was only kidding."

"What look?" Valk asked. "I'm not physically capable of having an expression, much less an objectionable—"

"Don't forget that having a sense of humor is a sign of functional intelligence," Paniet told him.

Valk laughed. He played a sound file of a human laugh. For a moment he wondered if he was genuinely amused, or if some deep-buried subroutine in his programming had simply recognized that a joke had been told and responded accordingly. Or if that was even a valid question.

He never used to have thoughts like that.

The display in front of him split in two, then four, then sixteen as the microdrones came online. Soon one hundred and twenty-eight different camera views floated around him. He closed the subdisplays, because of course he didn't need them. He could query each microdrone independently or call up a composite view as necessary.

As the tiny cameras maneuvered to spread as far from each other as possible, they gave Valk a good view of the cruiser. He hadn't realized how badly damaged it was. Half the armor had been stripped from one side. The forward section, where the bridge used to be, was nothing but wreckage and skeletal girders. The damage to the thrusters looked the worst—one of the big cones looked like it had been chewed on by some enormous dog, and there was a deep gouge in the shielding back there. Paniet had completed all the repairs he could manage—if the Hoplite was ever going to be whole again, he'd told Lanoe, it needed to put in at a repair dock, and the nearest of those was ten thousand light-years away. Lanoe, being Lanoe, had simply told him to do what he could. Paniet had worked endless shifts putting the cruiser back together, but he couldn't make carbon fiber sheathing or armor plate just appear out of thin air.

Valk brought up a display so Paniet could see how ragged the ship looked. "You missed a spot," he said.

It was Paniet's turn to laugh. "All right, all right. Are you ready for the burn?"

"Yeah." Valk activated alarm chimes and flashing lights throughout the ship to let everyone know they were about to be subjected to significant gravity, if only for a few seconds. He called up a control board and lifted a finger toward the virtual key that would activate the engines. He didn't really need the board—he could have made the maneuver as easily as thinking about it—but he thought maybe Paniet would appreciate the gesture.

The engineer strapped himself into a chair and gave Valk the nod.

The engines roared to life, ionized exhaust flooding out through the cones. The microdrones were programmed to turn to follow any moving body in their vicinity, so in the composite display the cruiser didn't seem to move at all. Valk switched to an infrared view and saw the brilliant plume of heat they left in their wake, like a giant arrow pointing right at them.

Valk let the engines burn for five seconds, then switched them back off. He sounded the gravity alarm again, then let his arm fall back at his side.

"It needs a name," Paniet said.

"What?"

"The iceball. The one we're going to hide behind. We can't just keep calling it 82312. At least I can't. What do you think?"

Valk consulted a database, looking for a suitable name. "Caina," he said, after considering and rejecting several hundred possibilities.

Paniet frowned. "I don't get the reference."

"Caina," Valk said, "was one of the lowest levels of Dante's Inferno. Because this is one of the farthest objects from the red dwarf." He brought up a text display about the name, and Paniet scanned a few lines.

"A place of horrible cold and ice. Where only the very worst of sinners end up after they leave the world behind," the engineer mused. "Sounds familiar."

"Sinners," Valk said. "We're not that bad, are we?"

"We just got here," Paniet responded. "Give us time."

⊰―⊱

Bury hardly noticed when gravity returned. He reached out reflexively and grabbed a nylon strap hanging from the brig's wall. When the gravity went away again, he let go. He never moved his eyes from the display on the cell's hatch.

"That...thing...operated on me," he said, very quietly.

"She's a gifted surgeon," Ginger told him.

"She's a giant crab alien covered in bugs. Putting her in a black dress doesn't help much."

"We didn't put that on her. That's how the Choir all dress. They believe in living harmoniously—they all dress the same, eat the same food."

"Sounds kind of, I don't know. Dull," Bury said.

"They govern by consensus. They're telepaths. They share everything, their thoughts, their emotions... You can't understand."

"But you can," he said.

It was the hardest part for him to accept. Not the existence of aliens—he'd heard all about the evil Blue-Blue-White, so another species of intelligent life wasn't wrecking his brain. The fact that these new aliens could create wormholes and share thoughts across distances was all so abstract and weird he didn't even try to process it. No, what sent shivers down his spine was that this alien had cut both of them open. The chorister had performed surgery on Ginger and himself. Those wicked-looking claws had been inside their bodies. The thing had put an antenna in Ginger's head so they could talk. And it had performed surgery on him, cut him open and clacked away in his guts.

Commander Lanoe had let that happen to them. He'd ordered it to cut into them. To change them.

Bury pushed back away from the hatch of the cell. The thing sleeping in there—he couldn't bring himself to call it a person—disgusted him.

He ran a hand down his chest. They'd taken him out of his suit and put him in a thermal comfort garment, the first piece of fabric clothing he'd worn since he entered flight school. Through the thin cloth he could feel the puckered scar that ran from his sternum down to his groin.

He knew he should be grateful. By all accounts, if the alien hadn't patched him up he would have died in the sick bay. But he wasn't grateful. All he could think about was those little spider things crawling all over Rain-on-Stones's body. All he could imagine was bugs like that inside of him, their tiny legs wiggling in the dark of his abdominal cavity.

"I feel sick. I feel so sick right now," he said. "I'm sorry, Ginj. I mean, I get it, you have a connection to that thing. But I can't... Oh, hellfire." An acidic belch worked its way up his throat. He tried to suppress it but there was no way to keep it down.

"Bury?" Ginger said. "Bury?"

He kicked his way out of the brig and back toward the sick bay. It wasn't far, but he barely managed to get inside before he started heaving. There was nothing in his stomach, but his body kept trying to throw up anyway.

He could feel his heart pounding in his chest like a piston. The muscles in his arms and legs turned rubbery and weak. He crawled back into the bed and pulled a strap across himself. The effort of doing just that left him feeling drained and half-dead. He pressed his face against the pillow and clamped his eyes shut, even as his stomach twitched and spasmed inside of him.

"Bury," Ginger called as she came inside the little room. "Your pulse is through the roof. You're in shock, I think—I don't know. I don't know how any of these displays work. I'll go and get Lieutenant Candless, she—"

"No!" he said. "No. Please, Ginger. Don't—don't tell her about this. I'm fine. I'm going to be fine."

"You really scared her when you woke up and had your panic attack. She gave me strict orders to keep her informed about your health. I need to tell her."

"No, you don't. Four, Ginger. Four."

She looked deeply confused.

"Four confirmed kills. I have four confirmed kills already. I have to get better so I can fight again. So I can get to five. If you tell her I'm sick, she won't let me fly. Just—just let me sleep a little, and I'll be fine. Four. One more and I'll be an ace. I'll get my blue star."

"Even if it kills you," she said.

He shook his head. "I'm going to be fine. I just need to rest, okay? I just need to rest a little. Please."

"All right," she said, with a sigh. "But if I see any sign that you're not okay—"

"Of course. But I just need to rest."

She nodded.

He waited until she was gone before he let himself heave again. This time something did come up. A thin trickle of acidic spit squeezed out between his lips before he could catch it. The medical drone reached down with a suction arm to vacuum it away.

Chapter Four

Does it ever occur to you, son, that you might have acted in a not entirely ethical manner?

Auster Maggs was the son of a famous admiral—Father had been a hero and a casualty of the Uhlan Belt, one of the last battles of the Establishment Crisis. He had left his darling baby boy Auster with two great legacies. The first was a commission. The Navy had become such an aristocratic institution by the time of the Crisis that the children of ranking officers inherited their parents' status as officers. It was purely through this near-feudal policy of nepotism that Maggs *fils* had been able to rise so quickly to the rank of lieutenant.

I'll hardly call you out on cleverness, Maggsy. But betraying one's own commander, in the very midst of a battle, never feels...decorous, what?

The second inheritance he had from the admiral was a wealth of experience, of advice and counsel, learned at the knee of a man who could not resist telling the same stories over and over again. Young Maggs had absorbed these pearls of wisdom so thoroughly that now he could not but hear his father's voice in his head, an eternal internal monologue that sometimes drove him quite mad.

Perhaps next time you'll look before you leap. Although, to be fair, I never did.

"Enough," he said aloud.

The marines climbing past him in one of the carrier's more heavily trafficked companionways did not turn and stare. They were too disciplined for that. All the same he felt a distinct prickling on the back of his neck, and knew he'd been observed.

Bloody enlisted chaps. They saw so much more than you wanted them to. He forced a bright smile on his face and climbed the last few dozen meters to the very top of the carrier, to a small observation cupola in its bows.

In shape the carrier was a cylinder five hundred meters long and a hundred meters across. At its aft end lay the massive engines, powered by dozens of tokamak reactors. Its fore end was the flight deck, open to space—the fifty fighters lay nestled inside like bats hanging from the walls of a cave. The vessel's bridge was in its most protected spot, between engines and flight deck. There were no windows there.

Thus if you wanted to look outside, to see where you were with your natural human eyes, you had to climb to the very tip-top of the cylinder, where three observation lounges sat evenly spaced around the circular rim. They looked like miniature round greenhouses, their thick carbonglas panes mounted in a web of reinforced titanium.

In the last fight with Lanoe, the harridan Candless had successfully wounded the carrier with a disruptor round that tore through the ship quite indiscriminately. As a result several crew spaces—including one of the observation cupolas—were now off-limits until they could be repaired. Which might take a while, as fixing up an observation lounge was very low on the list of things that needed to be done. Perhaps because of this—because she could expect a certain degree of privacy there—Ashlay Bullam had requested his presence in the damaged cupola so that they could discuss strategy.

He found her sitting on a low bench, surrounded by her omnipresent drones. One of them turned toward him as he entered. Lights burned on its vacant face, looking not unlike eyes. The drone regarded him in silence for a moment, then turned back toward its customary adoration of its mistress.

There was no air in the cupola, making normal speech impossible. Making it impossible for anyone to eavesdrop on them as well. A green pearl appeared in the corner of Maggs's vision, telling him he had an incoming transmission. He flicked his eyes across the pearl to accept the connection.

"Rather beautiful, isn't it?" Bullam asked.

She was facing away from him, looking up through the cracked windows. Her helmet was up, of course. Through the flowglas he could see that her frost-blue hair was gathered and held by a fine net of interlocking golden hexagons.

"I beg your pardon?" Maggs inquired.

"All these stars. On the world where I was born the clouds are so thick we never see the night sky. As a child I read about stars, of course, but I could only imagine them. The first time I went above the atmosphere—when I was at school—I stayed awake the night before, wondering what space would be like."

"Was it everything you'd dreamed of?"

"Hardly," Bullam told him. "I was deeply disappointed. From the shuttle's windows we couldn't see any but the brightest stars. Their light was overwhelmed by the light from our sun. The paltry handful I could see just looked like pinpricks in a sheet of black paper. This," she said, and gestured at the view, "is what I imagined."

Maggs spared the universe a glance. It was, he had to admit, arrayed in gaudy splendor. Wherever they were now, wherever the wormhole had brought them, there was no shortage of bright, colorful stars. "This must be quite the sentimental moment for you, then."

Bullam turned and faced him with narrowed eyes. "It might. If I wasn't so frightened of what they mean. Lanoe ran a very long way. And it wasn't just to escape us, was it? I think we both know why we're here."

Maggs knew because he had fought alongside Lanoe at the battle of Niraya—the first world the Blue-Blue-White had tried to sterilize of human life. He had, of course, been instrumental in driving the aliens back, not that Lanoe would ever admit he'd needed Maggs's help.

"Lanoe brought us here because this is where he thinks he can get his revenge," Maggs said. He wished he could stroke his mustache in a pensive manner, but of course that was impossible with his helmet up. "The Blue-Blue-White killed his lover, Bettina Zhang."

"And Shulkin brought us here because there is nothing left of him except the burning need to kill Lanoe," Bullam said. "The two of them are madmen. Obsessed." Her mouth twisted up for a moment, then relaxed. "I imagine you share Shulkin's desire. You'd like to see Lanoe killed."

"I don't care for the man, no. Not one whit. Killed? Well. I suppose it would be expedient." Maggs knew for a fact that if he was ever in the same room with Lanoe again, the Navy commander would not hesitate to strangle him with his bare hands. If Lanoe were dead, he could sleep easier. Still. "I wouldn't go out of my way to do it, though."

"Good. That's what I wanted to hear—that you're still capable of thinking rationally. That's a rare enough quality here. I need logical people on my side."

"You may trust me implicitly," Maggs assured her, and sketched a bow.

"Hardly. Oh, don't look like that, Auster. I don't trust anyone. I'm too good a businesswoman to believe in loyalty or even courtesy. People act in their own self-interest ninety-nine percent of the time. The only way to secure someone's loyalty is to make sure their goals align with yours. And I believe we—you and I— have the same priority right now."

"To go home," Maggs said, without hesitation.

Bullam's eyes sparkled. "It's always a pleasure to see that you've sized someone up correctly. Yes."

She looked up through the windows of the cupola. "There are no wormholes in this system. If Shulkin kills Lanoe, we'll be stranded here forever."

"The fact has not escaped me."

She sighed and leaned back on the bench until she was lying prone, looking up at the bright sky. "Lanoe must know some way to get back. He's no fool. But I can guarantee you that Shulkin hasn't given it a moment's thought. Clearly we're at odds with him. He'll kill Lanoe the very next chance he gets, even if that means sacrificing our only way home."

Maggs clasped his hands behind his back and walked over to the wall of carbonglas. He studied the welter of light in front of them. The carrier was in motion but because of parallax even the closest stars seemed fixed to the sky, jewels encrusting a black glass dome.

"We can't let that happen," Bullam said. "We need Lanoe alive."

"You're suggesting insurrection."

"Am I? This isn't a Navy ship. It belongs to Centrocor. I'm an executive of Centrocor. In the corporate hierarchy I outrank Shulkin by a considerable margin."

"Hmm," Maggs said, and gave her one of his best smiles.

Bullam's face was set, expressionless. "As far as I'm concerned, I gave Shulkin a direct order back…wherever that was, in that bubble of space, and he disobeyed it. By entering the wormhole that brought us here, he committed a gross act of insubordination. I intend to discipline him, as I would any unruly employee. This isn't a mutiny I'm proposing. I'm going to fire him, not usurp him."

"And you want my help with that. Even though I have no official position in your org chart."

"That's what makes you useful. The crew of this ship is afraid of Shulkin. With good enough reason, I suppose. You, on the other hand, are outside of his command, and I doubt there's anyone you're afraid of. If you were willing to betray Aleister Lanoe, I imagine you'll have no trouble turning on Shulkin. Furthermore, once our psychopathic captain is gone I'm going to need someone to replace him. Someone to take charge of this vessel."

That's how you make your bones, Maggsy. By proving your indispensability, his father's voice told him.

She was offering him command of the ship. How delightful.

"Consider me your obedient servant, M. Bullam," Maggs said.

"Forget that. As of now, you're my personal assistant." One of her drones lifted from the floor and came over to him. A biometric panel on its face lit up. "Let it scan your retinas and we'll have a contract. Just a formality, of course, but I like to be protected."

Maggs leaned over and peered into the panel. The drone swept a laser across the backs of his eyes, recording the unique pattern of the veins in his retinas, more unique than any fingerprint or signature. It only took a moment.

"Congratulations," Bullam said. "You're now an official Centrocor employee. When we get back to civilization, we can discuss your compensation and benefits package."

Then the die is cast, Maggs senior said. *You've picked a side, for good or ill.*

A side? Maggs thought—in his own voice. *Why, yes. My own.*

All of the cruiser's officers had been gathered together in the makeshift bridge as they approached final maneuvers. Candless was just glad there was finally something to see. The iceball they'd dubbed Caina filled half of the big display, a blindingly white mass that flooded the wardroom with light. Candless studied the planetoid's surface with pursed lips, mostly out of nervous habit. If one was about to get into a pitched battle, it behooved one to know the lay of the land, she supposed.

Caina was a protocomet—an icy mass that never got close enough to its star to actually grow a tail. Spectroscope and mass density scans showed it was a vaguely spherical agglomeration of frozen water, frozen nitrogen, and dust, barely held together by its own gravity. Its surface was a glossy white except where it had been punctured by craters full of shadow. To Candless those deep pits looked like the mouths of animal warrens. She would not have been surprised if some massive space beast stuck its head out of one of the holes and snapped at the cruiser with its toothy maw. Ejecta from the craters spread outward in long triangular rays, the roughest terrain visible on the surface. Between the craters were broad plains of perfectly flat ground, so devoid of features they glistened in the light of the distant sun.

"What makes it so smooth?" she asked.

"My best model suggests resurfacing," Valk told her. "The surface is solid ice, but only for the first ten or twenty meters down. Below that it's a sort of half-liquid slush right to the core. When a meteoroid or something hits Caina it punches straight through the crust. Heat from the impact liquefies the slush below and sends it geysering out into space. The liquid falls back to the ground and freezes almost instantly, burying any surface features. Eventually that process even fills in the craters. That's why you see so few of them on an object this old."

"How can you tell how old it is?" Ehta, the head of the marines, asked.

"You look for traces of radioactive decay," Valk explained to her. "Stuff like radium and uranium breaks down over time, turning into lead. The younger an object is, the more radioactive it'll be."

"How much radiation is this thing putting out?"

"None," Valk told the marine. "Not so much as a blip on the scintillator. This place could be older than Earth's solar system, maybe a lot older. It doesn't look like it's ever been touched by intelligent hands. We could be the first living things to even see it."

Candless glanced over at Lanoe, though she did so discreetly. He was still under the impression that this system was the home of the Blue-Blue-White, despite its lack of any planets. Caina's uncharted nature didn't prove him wrong, but it certainly wasn't evidence to back up his claim.

"I'm ready to use the maneuvering jets to put us in close orbit," Valk said. "Just say the word, Lanoe."

"Ooh! I think I've guessed your plan," Paniet said, surprising her. "Tell me if I'm right, will you?"

Lanoe nodded absentmindedly.

"You're going to be clever," the engineer said. "You had us fire up the engines just for a few seconds, knowing perfectly well that Centrocor would see it. They'll come investigate, of course—they'll head right for the last place they saw us. Meanwhile you'll be waiting for them behind Caina, ready to pop out and hit them with all our guns blazing at once. That's it, yes? You asked for that burn so we could lure them in?"

"That's an old Navy trick, sure," Lanoe said. "Standard stratagem for use in a situation like this, where you're outnumbered." He leaned close to the display until its white light blazed in his eyes. "Which is exactly why we're not going to do it."

"Wait—what?" Paniet asked.

"Whoever they've got commanding the carrier, he or she is ex-Navy," Lanoe explained. "A campaign veteran, definitely—I could tell the last time we fought them. Don't ask me what somebody like that is doing working for a poly, but I'm sure of it. And that means they learned the same tricks I did back in flight school. So they'll be expecting an ambush like that. They'll already have thought of how to counter it, too. So, no, we're going to do something else. Something unexpected. Valk, I've got a new bearing for you." He tapped a few virtual keys on his wrist display. Valk stirred as if he was surprised by his new orders.

Next Lanoe turned to Candless. "I need you in the vehicle bay. I'll meet you there in a few minutes. Ehta, you, too."

"Me?" Ehta asked. Candless knew the marine had been a pilot once, but that she'd lost her nerve and could no longer fly. "You want *me* there?"

"Yes," Lanoe said. "Now. Let's go."

＊

Maggs had no illusions about what Bullam had in mind for Captain Shulkin. She hadn't said it outright, but it was clear that "firing" the old fool wasn't going to be as easy as sending him a message to clear out his bunk.

What she really wanted was...somewhat distasteful. It was also the one thing standing between Maggs and command of a Hipparchus-class carrier. When he left the cupola, he headed directly for the aft section of the carrier where stores were kept. The ship's quartermaster had a small workstation amidst the low-ceilinged cargo compartments that served both as a general dispensary and as the arsenal for the carrier's marines.

Maggs had been aboard carriers like this before—he'd lived on one for several months back during the Establishment Crisis. He knew perfectly well what obstacles he was about to face. Nothing for it, sadly.

A fleet travels on its belly, his father said inside the dark chambers of his skull. *Can't remember who said that first, but it's true. Proper accounting of supplies is vital to any military operation.*

Is that why it's always so bloody difficult to get a replacement every time you lose a toothbrush? Maggs asked his father.

Maggs was given to sarcasm almost habitually, and he often asked such pointed questions of the memory of his father that lived in his head. The old man very rarely answered.

The quartermaster turned out to be a woman with a scar across her face that made rather a ruin of her nose. The collar ring of her suit was engraved with a pattern of interlocking gears, which meant she'd been a neddy once—an officer of the Naval Engineering Division. The hexagons painted on her shoulders marked her as currently belonging to Centrocor. She was neck-deep in a dozen displays when he arrived, and she failed to look up even when he'd cleared his throat several times.

"I truly do beg your pardon," he told her, "but I have a need only you can fill."

One of the quartermaster's eyebrows lifted in suspicion. The other one, Maggs noticed, had been neatly erased from her head by her scar. Lovely.

"My name," he said, "is Auster Maggs, and I—"

"I know who you are," she said, and looked back down at her displays. "The traitor."

Maggs refused to let her get under his skin. "That's as may be.

We're on the same side now, though, and perhaps you could see your way clear to—"

"You want something? Maybe you can switch sides again, and maybe they'll give it to you over there. I've got clear orders concerning you, and they basically boil down to one word."

"I hope it's a nice one," Maggs said.

"The word is 'no.'"

"No?"

"No. You come in here asking for equipment, for supplies, I'm supposed to say no. You aren't cleared for so much as a roll of razor paper. Captain Shulkin doesn't trust you."

"Are you so sure of that?" Maggs asked. "Perhaps we should call him up and—"

"He sent me a personal message when you came aboard. I'm going to paraphrase, but the message essentially said, 'I do not trust this man. If he asks for any item or supply, the answer is no. Especially no weapons.'"

"Ah. Well," Maggs said, "then perhaps—"

"No."

Maggs nodded. "The thing of it is—"

"No."

"—I'm not actually asking for anything."

The single eyebrow went marching up the woman's face again.

"Nothing that doesn't belong to me, at any rate. It happens that when I came aboard, I was thoroughly searched and everything in my possession was confiscated. Before you tell me that that's standard operating procedure, please don't, because I know that. Even my suit was taken from me, perhaps in the thought it might contain some tracking device or other instrument of sabotage. All perfectly normal and understandable. Centrocor was even kind enough to furnish me with a replacement suit. The one I am currently wearing."

"Did you come down here to thank me for that piece of junk? It's at least twenty years old. The last guy who wore that suit died in it. He was shot to death. I can see the patch where they covered over the puncture."

Maggs looked down and saw the brighter spot of fabric in the middle of the suit's chest. He ran an idle finger around the seam of the patch.

"Do you know the provenance of every piece of gear in your charge so well?"

"The suits, yeah," the quartermaster replied. "That way when somebody comes down here asking for one, I can decide which one they get based on how much I like them." She gave him a rather ghastly smile. There were teeth missing from it. "I picked that suit out for you personally."

"How kind. But I can see I've taken up enough of your time. If you'll simply return my old suit and my personal effects, I'll be on my way, and—"

"No."

"Back to this, then," Maggs said. He even permitted himself a tiny sigh. He'd really hoped his next gambit would have been unncessary. Partly because he wasn't sure if it was going to work. If it didn't, he was out of ideas. "I suppose I'll just have to pull rank."

"I'm a major. You're a lieutenant. A major in the Neddies beats a lieutenant in the Navy."

"You're ex-Neddy," Maggs said. He knew that the vast majority of the carrier's crew had originally served in the NEF, the PBM, or the NED—in other words, for Earth. Either they'd been discharged from duty, wounded and invalided out, or they had quit the service for their own reasons, only to discover they had no skills that would allow them to thrive in the civilian job market. Centrocor had been hiring such people for years, as a way of building up their own armed forces. "I also once served the triple-headed eagle. But those days are gone. Now we're both Centrocor. Are you an executive-level employee?"

The eyebrow lowered itself to half-mast. Clearly the woman was confused.

"As of half an hour ago, *I* am," Maggs said.

"You can't—that's not—"

"Check my Centrocor employee number. While we wait, perhaps you'd like to consider how much you enjoy working for our mutual employer. We're all in this together, you know."

A great silence fell between them, as the quartermaster checked the veracity of his claim. For a bad moment he thought perhaps she would still refuse him on principle. Yet finally she grumbled out something that might sound, to a charitable ear, like an apology.

His plan had worked.

A few minutes later he was handed his personal gear, which had been neatly folded and sealed in a rapidly degradable bag. He carried it back to his bunk and pulled the thin quickplastic away from the suit and his few personal possessions. The quickplastic, released from its stable configuration, dissolved into twists of vapor all around him as he shook out the suit and laid it carefully across his bed to get the wrinkles out.

It would be pleasant, he thought, to get out of the ill-fitting loaner suit he'd been issued and back into his perfectly tailored and quite expensive Naval-issue heavy pilot suit. That measure of comfort had not, however, been the main point of this laborious exercise. He hadn't gone to such trouble to secure the entire suit. Just one of its accessories.

Mounted on the hip of the heavy suit was a long thin pouch with a quick-release catch. Maggs flipped it open and drew forth its contents: one dirk, twenty-centimeter blade, ceremonial.

He took the knife from its sheath and held it up to the light. Tested its edge by slicing through a tenacious length of quickplastic that was still hovering on an air current.

Naval uniform regulations required all pilots to carry a dirk during inspections and parades. Technically there was nothing in the regs that said one had to keep the blade razor sharp. Maggs had just always been a stickler for proper dress.

＊

Candless looked over the fighters in the vehicle bay while she waited for Lanoe to arrive. There had been a dozen of them once. Eleven

BR.9s, and Maggs's personal Z.XIX. Time and war had reduced the ship's complement considerably. Maggs had taken his sleek machine with him when he defected. In the last battle with Centrocor, Bury and Lanoe had both reduced their fighters to heaps of slag. Both of those ships were useless now except for the spare parts Paniet might cannibalize from them. In that same battle, Valk had flown eight of the remaining ships simultaneously—but only five had made it back.

Which left six intact BR.9s, one of which—her own—was damaged, but only superficially. Six fighters against the carrier's complement, and the massed guns of the two destroyers. With odds like those, most admirals of Candless's experience would have seen no option but to surrender to the enemy.

Lanoe, of course, was famous for getting out of bad scrapes and winning the day against all odds. The man had fought in six wars and a hundred battles and he was still alive. There had been a time when that was enough for Candless. There had been a time when she would have followed Lanoe through the gates of hell, knowing he would get her back out in one piece. In a way, wasn't that exactly what she'd done, coming here?

Yet her faith had been strained. Bury could have been killed—and Lanoe had done nothing to stop it. That had been enough to make her remember a simple fact: Lanoe always got out of a battle intact. Those who flew beside him weren't always so lucky.

Now he was going to ask her to fly into the face of certain death once again. She would go, of course. Because it was her duty. Because it was the only way to protect Bury and Ginger.

She wasn't going because she believed, though. It wasn't because of Lanoe's legend, not anymore.

He came gliding into the vehicle bay with a large bundle under one arm, wrapped up in a piece of cloth. He stashed it against one wall and kicked over to where she waited. "We're going to have gravity in a minute. Is everything lashed down?"

"Of course," she told him. "Are you questioning my discipline? I run a tight ship."

"Never doubted it," he said. "Any word from Ehta?"

"On her way, when last I checked," Candless said. "Are you going to tell me exactly why you called her down here? She can't fly, and you know it."

"Sure," Lanoe said. "She's good at other things, though. Don't worry. I'm not sending you out there alone."

"I should think not. In fact—wait." Why would he even suggest such a thing? Obviously he was going to be flying one of the BR.9s. He'd never been able to resist a chance to get into the cockpit of a fighter before, even after he reached command rank, even after he was theoretically barred from engaging in close combat because he was too valuable to the Navy to risk his life. He'd always ignored that general order and flown point anyway. "Are you telling me—"

"You'll have Valk. He's going to make copies of himself and download them into the other five fighters. So you'll have plenty of backup."

"You're not coming with us," she said.

"I'll be too busy," he told her.

Ehta came in, then, leading five marines in heavy combat armor. She looked a bit ill, a little green in the face. Candless did not care for the marine lieutenant, not in the slightest, but you never wanted to see your compatriots at anything less than their best just before a battle.

"You . . . sure about this, boss?" Ehta asked.

"I'm sure," Lanoe told her. "Have your people gear up. I checked all of these personally, they're good." He pulled the cloth off of the bundle he'd brought with him, revealing a pile of long, wicked-looking particle rifles and handguns. The marines dove on them like pigeons on a bag of bread crumbs.

"No offense, but I want my people checking their own weapons," Ehta said. "It's just good practice, right?"

"Sure," Lanoe said. "When we're ready, start loading up the cutter. And everybody find something to grab—we're about to get gravity."

"The cutter," Candless said. She looked over at a seventh space-craft in the vehicle bay. One she hadn't bothered to count, because it was completely unarmed. A large, crescent-shaped ship covered in dull black cladding.

Suddenly Candless understood Lanoe's plan.

She didn't care for it one bit.

The gravity alarm chimed and a yellow light flashed by the vehicle bay's hatch. Candless reached down, grasped a fairing of one of the BR.9s, and settled gently to the floor. It felt like Valk had engaged the main drives.

"We're behind Caina right now, where Centrocor can't see us," Lanoe told her. Not that she'd asked why he was risking all their lives by using the ship's engines again. He turned to his warrant officer. "Ehta, you ready?"

Ehta picked up the last rifle from the pile, the one none of the other marines had claimed for themselves. It was a massive steadygun, a kind of recoilless rifle designed for use in microgravity conditions. She flipped a catch and slipped the magazine out of the weapon, checked the rounds inside, slammed it back into place.

"As long as I don't throw up on the way over, I'm good," she said.

Make no move until I give you the signal.

The message appeared on Maggs's wrist display without a signature, without any indication of where it had originated—not that he needed any. Even as he looked at the words, they faded and disappeared.

He glanced over at Bullam—discreetly—and gave her a wink. She did not react. He was unclear what exactly her official job title might be, but he had gotten a very clear sense that skullduggery was at the top of the skills she would list on her résumé. He had every faith in her ability to stay cool until the precisely correct moment.

The two of them had been summoned to the bridge of the carrier. Rather, Bullam had been summoned. When Shulkin saw Maggs enter, he scowled.

"Your pet traitor may remain here," the captain said, "as long as he's quiet."

"I shall be as silent as the proverbial mouse," Maggs said, and clicked his heels together.

Shulkin didn't look amused.

Shulkin. Shulkin. I know that name's familiar, Maggsy. Let me try to remember what I know about the beggar, Maggs's father said inside his head.

The bridge crew didn't even look up. They had the harried look of soldiers who'd been down in the trenches too long, that dogged exhausted stare Maggs knew from his brief and infrequent associations with PBMs. Their fatigue was understandable, of course. None of the bridge crew had left the room in more than twenty-four hours, as Shulkin pushed them to find Lanoe.

"I called you down here," the captain told Bullam, "because they finally made a mistake. I wouldn't want you to miss the moment when I defeat Aleister Lanoe."

"I'll be sure to make a note of it for your next performance review," Bullam said.

"My IO caught a glimpse of the Hoplite in motion. They were foolish enough to use their main thrusters. Now we have them. You'll have noticed we've been accelerating for a while now. We're approaching their last known position. Of course, they won't be there when we arrive. But I know Lanoe well enough to guess his next move. It's a good one, but if we're smart we won't fall into his trap."

Maggs couldn't help but note the change in Shulkin's manner. Normally the captain was a dead-eyed zombie, cut off from the world around him. The only thing that brought him back to life was combat. Just now the man seemed positively gleeful. Like he might break out in a fit of giggles with no notice.

"Batygins," the captain shouted.

The holographic images of the twin brothers appeared flanking the main view. Their eyes were almost solid black, because of the dilation of their pupils—clearly they'd partaken of their drug to be ready for the coming battle.

Maggs checked a subdisplay and saw that the two destroyers were quite close, no more than ten kilometers away. They flanked the carrier, running a little behind. It was a standard formation for a carrier group. Back there they wouldn't get in the way if the carrier scrambled its fighters, but they were still close enough that they could surge forward to protect it if the need arose.

"Ready for orders, Captain," Rhys Batygin said. Or was it Oritt? Maggs had never learned—nor cared enough to learn—to tell the two of them apart.

"Ready for orders, Captain," the other said, almost in synchrony. Almost but not quite. The slight discrepancy set Maggs's teeth on edge. It was all very well and good to adopt an unsettling mannerism in order to intimidate people. In his estimation, though, one should at least fully commit to the act.

"I assume," Shulkin said, "that the two of you have noticed the icy body ten million kilometers from our current location. That's going to be our target. Lanoe is hiding behind it right now."

The navigator stirred in his chair. He brought up a large display to show them all a protocomet scored with the dark holes of deep craters. Maggs thought it looked a spectacularly uninteresting place. Lanoe had never had much of a sense of drama, of course, but if one were going to pick the place where one was likely to die, surely there were better options.

"Lanoe knows we'll investigate. He's set up an ambush—he hopes to lure us into the range of his coilguns, so he can blast us before we even have a chance to strike. I do not intend to let that happen."

Shulkin turned to face the twins. "The two of you are going to close in on that rock at full speed. Lanoe is likely to poke his head out once he realizes his plan has failed. You'll be ready, with guns hot, and you will carve him to pieces. We will provide a screen of fighters to assist and to protect you from his pilots. You may begin your attack now."

"Of course, sir."

"Of *course*, sir," the Batygins said.

Shulkin went and sat back down in his chair, strapping himself in. "Pilot. Bring us to zero delta vee."

The carrier's engines cut out, and Maggs had to hurry to grab a handhold on the wall of the bridge before his feet left the floor.

Bullam glanced over at him as she strapped herself into her own chair. She did not shake her head, or give any indication of what she wanted him to do. She was simply checking in, making sure he knew to be ready.

Maggs resisted the urge to touch the dagger in its pouch at his hip.

Shulkin, his father said. *Served in the Crisis, of that I'm sure. At Sheol? No, no, it was Jehannum. Right! I remember now. A fair tactician. Bit unhinged, perhaps.*

Maggs allowed himself a bit of an eye roll. That much, he thought, was patently obvious.

"This is all very exciting," Bullam said. "Will it be a long battle, do you think?"

"It will take," Shulkin replied, "exactly as long as it takes. But the ending is inevitable."

Minutes ticked by. On the tactical board the Batygins ate up the distance to the protocomet, their weapons warmed up and ready to fire as soon as an enemy presented itself. None did for rather the longest time.

More minutes ticked by. Just numbers changing on a display. Maggs considered making the grand move, assassinating Shulkin, just for something to do. He held off, satisfying himself with the notion that, eventually, command of the Hipparchus would be his. Eventually. *It will take,* he thought to himself, *exactly as long as it takes.*

As always, the beginning of the battle came without warning. Just when Maggs was about to fall asleep.

"Movement near the protocomet," the IO said. "I register an engine flare."

"How many?" Shulkin asked.

"Just one, sir…No, two now…Four! I'll put them on the board."

"Batygins!" Shulkin bellowed.

"In position."

"In position," the twins answered.

"Fire at will!"

Though Shulkin was not, if I recall correctly, the sharpest knife in the shed, Maggs's father said inside his skull.

Chapter Five

Flak exploded off to Candless's left, like a firework in space—a fizzing bloom of light that dazzled her as submunitions cooked off in the vacuum. She looked away. You couldn't worry too much about flak. Either you saw it in time and veered to avoid it, or you didn't see it and then nothing mattered. She pulled right into a wide banking curve and then switched into a barrel roll as PBW fire came stretching toward her, bright lines drawn against the dark.

Up ahead one of the destroyers turned its nose toward her, swinging around slowly enough that it was easy to dip under its main cone of fire. She was still well out of range of its biggest guns. The real danger was its missile batteries, but so far it had failed to bring those to bear. Maybe it was saving them for the cruiser.

"Fighters inbound, looks like a full squadron," Valk said. One of the Valks.

Because he was in essence a fantastically complex computer program, Valk could make copies of himself, as many as he wished. Just like copying a data file—he had duplicated his mind and downloaded it into the computers of five BR.9s. They showed up on Candless's tactical board as yellow dots.

Centrocor's fighters showed up as blue dots. There were more blue dots than yellow dots.

"I see them. Burning to intercept," she called back.

The destroyer in front of her was moving, accelerating hard toward Caina. It wasn't paying her as much attention as it should—perhaps it expected its screen of fighters to protect it. Her hand hovered over her weapons panel, her fingers twitching. She could load a disruptor round right now, swing in fast from the destroyer's blind spot, line up a perfect shot, and let the disruptor tear through the big ship's bridge…

But no. She had her orders. She twisted away, burning for deep space, toward the incoming fighters. They weren't hard to find. Centrocor Yk.64s, twelve of them in a tight formation, a knot of canopies and airfoils and PBWs. They opened fire long before she was in range, perhaps hoping for a lucky shot. Candless spun around in a loose corkscrew, refusing to give them a target. Pouring on speed to close the distance.

Behind her the destroyer banked around the curve of Caina, hunting for the cruiser. She saw a flash of light along the destroyer's flank and knew one of the Valks had moved in to harry it, to keep its crew on their toes. Guns all along the front of the destroyer lit up, chewing at empty space where the Valk had been just a moment before.

She had her own job to do. She nudged her control stick until her nose was pointed right at the middle of the formation of Sixty-Fours, then shoved open her throttle and dove right into them, a cat pouncing on a flock of pigeons.

The pilots of the Sixty-Fours were ex-Navy, which meant they'd had some training—though not much, from what she saw. They knew enough to scatter—if only to avoid a collision—but while they maneuvered they were too busy to get a lock on her. Candless didn't have that problem. She picked one of the fighters at random and raked its canopy with PBW fire. Her shots sparked off the fighter's vector field, failing to do any damage, but the pilot lost his cool and broke away, burning hard to escape her. The others were trying to regroup but she'd already shot past them. She twisted around on her long axis until she was flying backward, and suddenly she could see their vulnerable thrusters.

She did not hesitate. She blasted the cones right off one fighter, leaving it spinning helplessly in the void. She hit another one from the side, most of her shots shunted off by its vector field but a few striking home, perforating the fairings around its engine shielding.

The Centrocor pilots started to regroup. They wheeled on her, turning in a looser formation. Their main advantage was their numbers, and they were smart enough to know it. Instead of breaking off to engage her one by one, they flanked her on three sides, trying to pin her down and keep her from running away. PBW fire lanced through space all around her and sparks jumped from her canopy as stray shots came close to actually touching her. Their aim would only improve with time, she knew. If she couldn't escape this snare she was done for.

"Got you," a Valk said, screaming in from on high. One of the Sixty-Fours that had her pinned burst into a welter of sparks as the Valk's PBW fire lit up its vector field. She could see right through the bubble-like canopy, see the pilot lift an arm over his head, as if he were warding off an attacking bird.

It was all the distraction she needed. Candless pointed herself right at him and punched her main thrusters, launching herself forward. Microseconds before she would have smashed right into him she rolled over on her side, her airfoils just avoiding clipping his undercarriage, and then she was free.

"It never hurts to say thank you," the Valk called.

"I've never felt the need to be courteous to a drone," Candless shot back.

"I'm not a drone," the Valk replied, laughing a little, "I'm a—"

He didn't get the chance to finish his thought. Three Centrocor fighters were hot on his tail, their weapons blazing away. Candless moved to intercept them but the Valk simply spun around and started firing back. He made no attempt to evade their fire—he simply lined up a shot as if he had all the time in the world and then loosed a devastating salvo right through a bubble canopy, impaling the pilot with a beam of particles.

The other two pilots were smart enough to veer off, burning to put distance between them and a pilot that cold-blooded.

Whatever she might think of Valk—and Candless was no great admirer of the AI—she could not say he lacked courage.

⟶〜

Caroline Ehta was having a very hard time remembering why she'd ever agreed to this mission.

She was sitting in the cutter with five of her best marines and Lanoe—probably the six people she trusted most, anywhere. The cutter was big enough for all of them. There was plenty of air to breathe, and it was warm enough inside, whatever the outside temperature.

The cutter had no viewports. No portholes, no gun slits—nothing to look through. Those would have interfered with the vehicle's aerodynamic and stealth properties. Its designers had come up with a solution to that problem—one that left Ehta unable to breathe properly. They had coated every square centimeter of the interior walls of the cutter with display surfaces that showed a real-time view from outside. The cutter might as well have been made of glass. Ehta felt like she was sitting in a crew seat unsupported in empty space, exposed entirely to the void.

Right now the displays showed the smooth, almost vertical walls of one of Caina's smaller craters. The walls were only a few dozen meters away, and rose like crystalline curtains on every side. Below them was the slushy dark floor of the crater, which undulated slowly according to some unknowable internal stress on the protocomet's core. Above her were a million stars.

In front of Lanoe a basic display lit up to show tactical and navigational data. Yellow and blue dots flickered across empty three-dimensional space. If you knew how to read that board—and Ehta did—you could see a space battle going on there, but it was so abstract as to be meaningless. It was all happening on the far side of the little world. If Lanoe was a careful pilot—and he always was—they would never see any of it with their own eyes.

"Okay," Lanoe said. "They're busy. I'm taking us up."

Ehta nodded, though she knew he hadn't been speaking to her directly. She gripped the sides of her seat and held on as Lanoe touched the throttle and the cutter rose through the shaft of the crater. Soon they were out and away and Ehta had to clamp her eyes shut to avoid seeing the ground fall away.

Closing her eyes was a problem all on its own, though. In her head, she started to see red lights flicker into life. Heard alarm chimes she knew didn't exist outside of her own skull.

Ehta had been a pilot once. She'd been a member of Lanoe's 94th Squadron, back during the Establishment Crisis. When he'd retired his commission she'd stayed on with the Naval Expeditionary Force, fighting in any number of little wars for various polys, running endless patrols in a BR.9. The polys had pushed their fighter pilots hard, making them work ridiculously long hours, endless and increasingly dangerous patrols. Their corporate masters hadn't cared about pilots—they were happy to throw away whole squadrons to take the smallest and least strategically important objectives. Ehta had pushed through it, because she'd never known anything except flying.

Over time, it took a toll on her. When she came back after a long patrol she would find it hard to sleep. She would feel like she was still moving at a good fraction of the speed of light, even lying in bed on a solid planet. That was when the red lights had started appearing— red lights like the ones you got on a damage control board when something went wrong with your fighter. Just one red light at first, but it was always there when she closed her eyes, when she tried to stop her mind. Just one—at first. More of them came later.

It had reached a point where she couldn't sleep at all. It reached a point where she couldn't fly anymore. The Navy had wanted to fix her with invasive brain surgery. Ehta had chosen a different path. She'd enlisted in the PBMs. The Planetary Brigade Marines, or as they were also commonly known, the Poor Bloody Marines.

Life in the marines was just as hazardous as life in the cockpit— even more so, depending on the campaign. Marines had an average life span of only a few weeks. Ehta had never been afraid of dying.

Not the way she was afraid of red lights.

She forced herself to open her eyes, to look around. Caina had shrunk behind them, only the size of a coin now, and it was dwindling fast. She craned her head around, trying to find any sign of the battle raging nearby.

She almost didn't see the burst of flak until the cutter rocked in the shock wave of a near miss. Until the twisting comet trails of exploding submunitions burned her eyes and she had to turn her head. She let out a tiny yelp, despite herself.

"Ma'am?" Binah asked, putting a hand on her shoulder.

She knocked it away. Binah was a friend. The two of them had been through real hell together in the fighting at Tuonela—but Ehta couldn't bear the thought of being comforted just then. She was too embarrassed.

"It was just a stray round, ma'am. They're not aiming at us. They don't even know we're here," Gutierrez said. Gutierrez who'd been her corporal once.

"Lieutenant Ehta's just anxious to get this mission started," Lanoe said, not looking back over his shoulder. He was too busy veering around the expanding cloud of flak. Ehta tried not to feel sick as the cutter rolled over on its side. "She's ready to get fighting again."

"Is that it, ma'am?" Gutierrez asked. There was no sarcasm in her voice. She was giving Ehta a chance to save face.

As galling as it was to think she needed such a thing, Ehta took it. "That's right. Just excited about getting to pop some hexagon ass."

The marines laughed at the profanity—even marines didn't use words like that in mixed company, especially not marine officers. They slapped each other on the shoulders, whooped to build the excitement. If their merriment seemed a little strained, Ehta decided maybe they all needed a little bravado just then.

Maybe she wasn't the only one petrified by this mission. Maybe they all had the wind up them, and she just had it the worst. What Lanoe had in mind for them was enough to scare the hell out of anybody.

Candless swung away from a pair of Centrocor fighters that had been trying to sandwich her and let loose a wild shot that didn't even come close to hitting either of them. One of them veered away anyway and boosted off into deep space.

She pulled back on her stick and up into a tight controlled loop, coming out of it right behind the other Sixty-Four before its pilot could even begin to react. She disabled the enemy's engines with a few carefully placed shots, leaving the fool alive but drifting, far from the carrier. She supposed the Sixty-Four could limp home on its maneuvering jets. She let it go—no need to actually kill someone if they were no longer a threat.

She turned, looking for another target, but found none. Centrocor's fighters had pulled away from Caina. Maybe they'd sustained too many losses to continue the fight.

That, of course, would be far too convenient. Most likely they would pull back and regroup, then come at her twice as hard the next time. But for a moment, at least, there was a lull in the fighting. She looked for Valk and found two of him flying together, not a hundred kilometers away. She banked over to meet them. "They're losing cohesion," she said. "Their formations are broken—I daresay they're afraid of us. I suppose one expects nothing better of half-trained poly militia, but these pilots are ex-Navy."

"It feels like they're holding back. Like maybe they know we're just here as a distraction," one of the Valks suggested.

"For Lanoe's sake, I very much hope that isn't the case."

Candless wondered idly which of the two Valks was speaking to her. Without checking her boards it would be impossible to tell, even if she were right next to them. There were no pilots in those BR.9s, just empty cockpits.

A bad chill ran down her spine, just thinking about it.

The idea of a fighter being run strictly by a computer program, with no human hand on the stick, was loathsome to her. It had been drilled into her since childhood that one could never trust a machine with a gun. It was possible, sometimes, to look at Valk—the space suit at the helm of the cruiser—and forget what he really was. This was something completely different.

Yet she had to admit the five Valks had fought admirably. Three of them had far exceeded her own score in this battle, chopping down Sixty-Fours left and right. The other two had worked hard at corralling the enemy, keeping them from getting too far around the horizon of Caina. Candless almost felt as if they could have done it all without her.

She cleared her throat. Perhaps it was time to accept that this was how things were going to be. Clearly Lanoe intended to use the Valks in every battle he fought henceforth. She might attempt to be civil to them.

"You've done very well," she said.

"Thanks. Just doing our job. I'll be glad when this is over."

Candless scowled, where they couldn't see her. "You don't enjoy fighting, then? Your...I don't know the right term. Your inceptor. Your original, your ectype—"

"You mean the Valk back on the cruiser, the one who made us? We call him Valk Prime," the copy told her.

"Quite," Candless said. "He always seemed happy enough at the control stick. Is there some reason you differ from him in this?"

"It...hurts. It hurts to fly these things. I don't know if I can explain," the Valk said. "Like being stuffed in a coffin that's too big and too small at the same time. One that's an awkward shape. The wrong shape."

"I'll admit I don't entirely understand."

The Valk grunted in frustration. "I've got cameras and sensors instead of eyes and ears. Airfoils and thrusters instead of arms and legs. But I'm based on a human body plan, just like Valk Prime. My nervous system is just a bunch of lines of code, but it knows when something's wrong."

"That sounds dreadful," Candless said. "Is that why you take so many risks?"

"Yeah. Yeah—I don't want to do this forever. I've got a root directory file saying I can't just crash myself into Caina and be done with it. I've got to fight to the best of my ability, if I want Valk Prime to keep his promise. He— Hold on. You seeing this?"

Candless had not in fact noticed anything. Now, just out of the corner of her eye, she did become aware of a blue dot on her tactical board. She swiped it back into the center of her view and bit her lip. There was just one blue dot there, a single enemy approaching. It was not, however, a fighter. It was far too big for that.

"One of the destroyers," she said.

"Yeah. They must have finished their sweep of Caina. Noticed—"

"—that the cruiser isn't actually here," she said, finishing the thought. "Indeed."

Lanoe had known that Centrocor would attack Caina, intending to destroy the cruiser for once and for all. He had known the battered Hoplite could not stand up to the combined onslaught of a carrier and two destroyers. So he had sent the cruiser onward, into deeper space, where it couldn't be found. He'd left Candless and the Valks at Caina as a decoy, and of course Centrocor had fallen for it.

If they'd figured out the deception, though—

"They're going to be mad as hell," the Valk said.

"Rather," Candless said. "And they'll want to take out their frustrations on someone. Too bad we're the only ones around."

⤙⤚

The cutter had five million kilometers to cross, most of it through perfectly empty space. Ehta worked very hard at not whimpering the whole way. She just about managed.

She focused on her breathing. Focused on listening to the small sounds of the vehicle, the sigh of the air recirculators, the grumble of the engines. Lanoe used the drive very sparingly— they did not want to draw any attention to themselves. That left them in freefall almost the whole way, which was strangely comforting. Ehta's triggers all had to do with being in the cockpit of a fighter as it weaved and darted through combat, and in a battle you were constantly under acceleration, zooming in one direction or another. The absence of gravity, and the lack of a meaningful view once they were away from Caina, made it easier to pretend she wasn't flying at all, that she was simply floating between the stars.

Her marines spent the trip talking in low tones. At first they kept glancing at the back of Lanoe's head, perhaps expecting him to turn around and tell them to shut up. He was a good enough commander to know not to do that. Marines were a chatty bunch, born gossips every one of them. They needed to socialize. It helped them form the bonds of camaraderie that would hold them together as a unit once the shooting started.

It was an unspoken tradition in the PBMs that before a fight you could talk about anything—any subject, no matter how grotesque or risqué—as long as you did not mention guns or bombs or any weapon of war. Typically that meant they talked about sex. About who had snuck away after lights-out with whom, about what video stars were like with their clothes off. They loved to discuss and especially to rate former lovers.

There'd been a time when Ehta had loved those dirty talks, when it had been her favorite part of being a marine. Her first year as a PBM she'd memorized hundreds of dirty jokes and learned to twist anything anybody said into the nastiest, most sexually depraved innuendo. Then she'd made a terrible mistake. She'd lived long enough to get promoted.

Marine sergeants did not talk to their people like that, except on very special occasions. Typically when they were all being shipped home. Marine lieutenants—her current rank—did not so much as acknowledge the existence of ribaldry. They were supposed to be sexless, humorless beings from some higher plane of existence where decorum was everything.

So she couldn't turn around and leer, much less comment, when Binah talked about the birthmark that Mestlez had in a very special place. Nor even when Gutierrez talked about the cat she'd had as a child, and its very soft fur.

She could only bite her lip and pretend like she hadn't heard.

Still, listening in helped her. It kept her from feeling like she was going to jump out of her own skin. Even when Lanoe touched the control stick for the first time in an hour and she was pressed back into her seat by a gentle acceleration.

"Close now," he said, glancing over at her. "You ever done this before?"

"Me? Hell no. I do my best fighting on the ground," she told him. "Find me a trench full of mud, and I'll show you some things."

She had to act as if she did not hear what Binah thought of that. She allowed herself a tiny smile.

It faded very quickly when she realized that the patch of darkness up ahead was not just empty space between stars. That it was an object, a vessel, in fact, and they were approaching it at speed.

The cutter had been built for clandestine work. It absorbed radar and lidar scans instead of reflecting them. Its drives and exhausts were fed through special ducts that left almost no trail behind and hid the light they gave off. Even the cutter's skin had been constructed of a special chromatophoric polymer that could change color thousands of times a second. Right now it was tuned to the colors of deep space—black void and bright white stars. Anyone who saw the cutter pass by, even with their naked eyes, would have a hard time realizing it was there.

Thank the devil for small favors, she thought. That was the carrier up there, Centrocor's main ship. It had stayed well clear of Caina, probably because its commander expected Lanoe to stage an ambush there. Now it was far removed from its own defensive screen. The two destroyers and most of its fighters had been sent forward to the protocomet, while the carrier hung back at a safe distance. All alone.

"You must have been trained for this, though," Lanoe said.

"Yeah, absolutely," Ehta said. "The PBMs taught me how to

infiltrate all kinds of things. But I've never actually had call to *do* it. I'm not a commando, boss. I'm a ground-pounder." Ehta sighed and ran her fingertips over the short growth of fuzz on her scalp. It sent tiny shivers through her brain. "Okay, okay. I remember— something. Some mention of this, yeah."

"Go ahead," he told her.

She scowled. She was almost certain he knew the answer a lot better than she did. He'd been around so long he'd probably even done it before. He just wanted her to feel needed, maybe. Or perhaps he wanted to help her impress her troops.

"Okay," she said again. "So you want to break into a Hipparchus-class carrier, without anybody noticing. The first step is..."

The Peltast class of destroyers had been built for one role: to hunt down and obliterate big ships. They were covered in devastating weapon systems—missile packs, flak cannons, and heavy PBWs, as well as a full suite of information-war and dismantler equipment, and coated from stem to stern in reactive armor plating. Though they were a hundred meters long, most of their mass was taken up by weapons and drives, leaving only a small space inside for crew.

They were theoretically vulnerable to an attack by a cataphract pilot. A fighter's vector field could hold up, for a little while, against all that withering firepower. This one didn't look particularly afraid of her.

It had come straight for Candless, burning hard to close the distance. She'd tried to outrun it—her orders here were simply to distract Centrocor, not engage them in any meaningful way. In the end, though, there was one problem. She might be faster than the destroyer—but she wasn't faster than its weapon systems.

"Missiles loose," one of the Valks said.

She gave her tactical board a split-second glance and saw the missiles. Four of them. Moving slowly, for the moment, but accelerating hard. Well outside the range of her PBWs.

All of them headed right for her.

Panic wasn't justified. Not immediately, anyway. "Evading now," Candless said. She twisted her stick over to one side, throwing herself into a tight corkscrew to make it difficult for the missiles to get a lock on her. It wouldn't work, but it might buy her a few milliseconds to think of something better.

"I'll move to intercept," Valk called.

Her tactical board told her that was a bad move. "If you do, you'll be in range of their heavy guns. Stay clear—that's an order!"

The Valks did not argue with her. "Dive for Caina," the AI said instead. "The bright surface might spoof their optical guidance."

Candless knew a good idea when she heard one. She cut out of her corkscrew in a flat spin, then burned hard toward the protocomet. The missiles were closing the distance fast—only thirty thousand kilometers now. They would be on her in a few seconds. She let fly a volley of PBW shots in their direction, knowing how unlikely it was she would hit any of them. There was always room for blind luck in space combat. Without even checking if she'd hit the missiles, she poured on the thrust until Caina grew to fill half her forward view.

There was nothing down there to use for real cover, no mountains, no canyons to fly down. She could duck inside one of the craters, but then she'd be stuck, unable to move. Speed was always the fighter pilot's best ally. She couldn't afford to slow down.

The missiles were ten thousand kilometers away.

The ground rushed at her in a white blur. Candless brought up her engine board and readied her maneuvering jets. Set her secondary thrusters for gimbaled propulsion. She would have to cut this very close.

Four thousand kilometers.

Seven hundred kilometers, and her brain, her nerves, every fiber of her being, screamed at her to pull up, to avoid crashing into the protocomet. A moment later her collision alarm started chiming, and the stick jumped in her hand—the fighter trying to take control of itself, to avoid a crash. She shot out her left hand and disabled the collision avoidance system. The computer demanded to know if she was sure. She was sure.

One hundred kilometers. Fifty. She was seconds away from plowing into the icy crust of Caina. She could fool the optical guidance systems of the missiles all she wanted. They still had heat-seeking capability, and her engines were by far the hottest things around.

She cut her main thrusters, yanked backward on her control stick. Her secondaries and her maneuvering jets roared, but for a bad moment, the space of a single heartbeat, nothing happened. She'd been moving so fast, built up so much momentum, that her jets were having a hard time hauling her out of her death dive.

The missiles were less than a kilometer behind her. Eating up the distance *fast*.

The view through her canopy swung crazily as she suddenly shot forward instead of down, her secondaries shoving her away from certain death. One of the missiles, the one closest to her, couldn't make the turn. It smashed into the ice beneath her and detonated, sending up a massive geyser of sublimated water vapor, a wall of steam right behind her.

A wall of superheated water, between her and the three remaining missiles. Suddenly she wasn't the hottest thing they could see. They veered away in random directions, hunting for her, unable to find her again—for the moment.

She let herself exhale.

Beneath her the smooth surface of Caina flew by, white broken only sporadically by the deep mouths of craters. She punched her primary thrusters back to life and poured on the speed, knowing she wasn't done. When she'd maxed out her velocity, she twisted around on her long axis so she was flying backward, just meters above the protocomet's surface.

The three missiles were blurred shadows, racing toward her. They'd reacquired their lock and were accelerating to regain the speed they'd lost.

She brought up a virtual Aldis sight, a set of crosshairs that drifted across her canopy as her systems tried to get a bead on the missiles. She was not surprised in the slightest when they failed. She took over manual control and tried to keep the sight steady, tried to line up the shot perfectly. Because the missiles were coming straight at her, she only had the cross sections of their nosecones to target, tiny dots in the distance. She could fire all she wanted, but she needed to score three bull's-eyes under an extraordinarily tight timeframe.

She'd seen Lanoe do this once. She'd watched—and tried to help—as he shot down missiles that were streaking toward Bury's fighter. He'd got some of them. Not enough. Bury had taken a direct hit from one and nearly died.

Now it was her turn.

One of the Valks signaled her. "Candless—"

"Not bloody now!" she howled, and squeezed her trigger.

Her shots went wide. She tried to walk them back, tried to center the sight. She ignored completely the readout that told her the missiles were less than ten kilometers away, that she had at best a solid second before they touched her—fired again, and again, and—

Yes! One of them exploded under her fire, its fuselage bursting into twists of carbon fiber that smoldered with the energy of her shot. She wasted no time in twitching the sight over to the next one, lined up a shot on the nosecone and fired, and fired, and fired. The Aldis swung back and forth, the tiniest vibration in her ship making it jump. Through sheer effort of will she forced the sight and the shadowed nose of the missile to converge, forced her shot home and—there! The missile all but evaporated in a puff of dark smoke. She must have ignited its propellant.

One last missile, less than three kilometers back now, and she fired, and fired, and fired, but couldn't hit it. She lanced out with PBW rounds that cut through space like perfectly straight strings of glowing pearls. She tried to find the magic again, tried to get a direct hit but—damnation! Hellfire! Her shots kept going wide, the missile got bigger and bigger and—seven hundred meters, five, it wasn't going to work—

PBW rounds came down from on high, shaft after shaft of

golden fire spearing into the ice below, all around the missile. Gifts from some hypothetical archer god, but none of them struck home.

"Candless!" Valk shouted, one of the Valks shouted. "I'm inbound, watch your head!"

A dark shape swooped out of the brilliant sky, a ton and a half of cataphract-class fighter dropping like a stone. Candless let go of her stick, her hands reflexively coming up to protect her head as one of the Valks burned straight toward the ground, just as she had a few seconds before, coming down with incredible speed. *Pull up, pull up,* she thought—she didn't have time to say the words aloud.

But the Valk didn't pull up. He smashed right into the ice, as fast and as hard as a meteoroid. On the way down he collided with the missile, smashing it to scrap instantly, and kept going, punching through the ice deep into the slushy mantle below. Water so hot it glowed shot straight upward, a column of light and bubbles, a stream of water that started to gel, to freeze, even as it cascaded downward again, even as it succumbed to Caina's mild gravity. It would take a while for the vapor and mist to clear, but Candless knew that when it did the protocomet would have a new crater.

"Valk," she called. "Valk—"

"Here," he said.

One of them did. One of the four that remained. The fighter that had crashed into Caina didn't even show up on her tactical board anymore. It was gone—utterly annihilated by the impact.

"What did he do—what did—you're programmed not to self-destruct, you said. You told me that!"

"Yeah. We can't suicide. At least not without a good reason."

Candless chewed on her lower lip. What had Valk become? Valk Prime, she meant—how had he brought himself to make these things? "You said before he'd made you a promise. You didn't have a chance to tell me what it was."

"Yeah. The promise is, we fight, we do our best. And the second we get back to the cruiser, he deletes us. Wipes us clean."

Candless bit back what she wanted immediately to say. Instead she took a moment to think of the proper words. "I shall be having a quite stern word with your original, if I make it back to the cruiser."

The remaining Valks had nothing to say to that.

Candless sighed and pulled back on her stick, shooting back up into the sky. "For now," she said, "it would appear we have the attention of this destroyer. Let's see how long we can keep it distracted. Lanoe, I'm sure, will need as much time as he can get."

Lanoe moved the cutter into the exhaust trail of the carrier. The last place anyone would think to look for them.

The cones of the main thrusters were big enough to swallow the cutter whole. The empty space around them wavered with subtle distortions. Though the engines were currently switched off, they were still producing enough hot ion flux to raise the outside temperature to nearly five hundred degrees.

"If those engines come online. If they decide to maneuver, while we're sitting here," Ehta said. "If they even just need to make a positional correction—"

"No one volunteered for this job thinking it would be *safe*," Lanoe said. "Now. Where's this airlock?"

"There," Ehta said, pointing at a hatch just to one side of the tertiary thrusters. "It's a maintenance hatch. It won't be guarded, but we'll need a Centrocor employee number to open it."

"I just happen to have one," Lanoe said.

Ehta nodded. Of course he did. Lanoe knew exactly what he was doing. He'd thought out all the angles in advance. She figured that gave them a very small chance of getting through this alive. "Maggs, right?"

"Maggs," Lanoe said. It sounded like he'd just bitten into an excrement pie. "It was right there in his service record. He used to work as an attaché between the Navy and Centrocor. I guess that's why he figured when he betrayed us he could just jump onboard with Big Hexagon and be sure of a warm welcome."

"Okay," Ehta said. She turned around to look at her people. "Corporal Gutierrez, are your troops ready to do this?"

"Ma'am, yes, ma'am," the marine shouted, her voice echoing in the enclosed space. She reached up and touched the recessed key at her throat. Her helmet flowed up over her face, opaque and silvered. The others followed suit. Binah and Mestlez, Malcolm and Yi. All veterans from Ehta's old squad on Tuonela. Good people.

She thought what a shame it would be, to throw them away on such a stupid, suicidal mission as this.

She had that thought every time she ordered people over the top of a trench, or to rush an artillery position, or just to move out of cover during a firefight. That was the curse of command. You had to love the people you ordered around. And you had to tell them to go get themselves killed for reasons you barely understood yourself.

You did it. You did it anyway.

"Let's go," she said, and raised her own helmet. They dove out through the hatch in the floor of the cutter, one after another, exactly by the numbers. Lanoe coming last, his helmet up and opaque black—Navy style. It made him look a little like Valk.

"Go, go, go!" Gutierrez shouted over the shared radio channel.

Their suit jets activated automatically once they hit the vacuum. Once there was nothing for them to stand on.

There was no way to dock the cutter to the carrier, not without setting off about a million alarms. They had to do this the old-fashioned way—by spacewalk. Ehta half expected to have a panic attack the second she was out of the cutter with nothing underneath her, nothing but the wall of the universe however many billions of light-years away. She'd thought the red lights would flash so bright in her head she wouldn't be able to see.

Instead—she didn't panic. She didn't scream in terror. She just...floated.

She felt...nothing, really. Peace, but, no—not even that. She didn't feel a Zen-like calm or anything, just…okay. She could hear nothing but the sound of her own breathing. She was neither hot nor cold. She held up one hand in front of her face, and saw it was holding steady. Not shaking at all.

Being a pilot had nearly killed her. It had driven her crazy. Being a marine was like…like something she was born to do.

She came around a big thruster cone, so big its curve was like the limb of a planet at dawn. She reached out her hands and touched the side of the carrier, its hull, its skin.

Marines slammed into the hull all around her, one after the other, Lanoe bringing up the rear. The heavy weapons slung over their shoulders made them look a little like they had wings. Like devils falling.

She moved along the hull, hand over hand. Every piece of armor plate, every junction box, every maintenance panel they passed had a little neat hexagon painted on it. Centrocor was in love with its own logo. She dug her fingers into a seam between two armor sections and pushed herself along until she reached the maintenance airlock.

She glanced back at Lanoe. He gave her a thumbs-up. She nodded, even if he couldn't see her through her silvered helmet, and turned to the hatch. She touched the edges of the keypad there, flexed her fingers to loosen them up. Lanoe read off a string of numbers and letters—Maggs's employee number—and she typed them in, careful not to make any mistakes. Her index finger hovered over the ENTER key.

When they opened this hatch, no alarms would sound inside the ship. No red lights would show up on the bridge. This would be an authorized entry, as far as the ship knew. Still, the access would show up on a log somewhere. If someone was looking at that log just now—

It wasn't worth worrying about. She jabbed the key. The hatch slid open, air from inside buffeting her for a moment, threatening to rip her free from her handhold. She'd used an airlock before. She was fine.

She pointed at Gutierrez and motioned her into the airlock. One by one the marines crowded inside, piling in until they filled the not exactly large space. She shoved herself into the mass of suited bodies, then helped Lanoe pull himself in as well. The seven of them filled every cubic centimeter of the airlock. But they fit.

Lanoe cycled the airlock the second he was inside. The outer hatch slid closed and then the tiny space filled up with air and suddenly Ehta could hear them, could hear her people moving, shifting, laughing as someone got an elbow in the crotch, griping as someone else got a good view of Mestlez's posterior.

"Quiet," Ehta barked.

They obeyed her.

The inner hatch slid open and they pushed out into the carrier, silent, watchful.

They were in.

Chapter Six

The carrier's bridge was full of displays large and small—some showing the view dead ahead of a field of unbroken stars, some showing the protocomet so many millions of kilometers away. Dozens of little ones showed graphs and infometrics that meant nothing to Bullam. She had been through enough space battles now to know to ignore ninety percent of the information she could see. She watched the tactical board like an old campaign veteran.

Even if it didn't make any sense.

"Give me some information I can actually use, IO," Shulkin bellowed.

The carrier's information officer was a very young, very nervous man whose name she'd never managed to remember. "Sir, the numbers have been checked and rechecked. I've spoken personally with the Batygins. The data is accurate."

"Meaning?" Shulkin demanded.

"The destroyers have scanned every square centimeter of the protocomet. The Hoplite-class cruiser isn't there."

Shulkin growled like an animal.

She could smell the frustration wafting off his thin, papery skin. Aleister Lanoe had gotten the best of him—yet again. *It must be eating at his guts,* she thought.

She could take a certain perverse pleasure in that. She'd never liked Shulkin. She had tried, when the mission depended on it, to work with him in a civil and courteous fashion. It was like trying to seduce a brick wall. You got nowhere, and you ended up with scrapes in all the wrong places.

Under Shulkin's command she'd even sustained a grievous injury. He had ordered the carrier through a series of maneuvers that had nearly shaken her apart. Bullam had a rare disease called Ehlers-Danlos syndrome that meant her body couldn't produce necessary collagens. As a result, under severe physical stress her veins and arteries could, and did, shred like paper, leaving her covered in ugly bruises and, far worse, letting her blood pool in her tissues and form free-floating blood clots. She might have a clot roaming around her body right now, and she wouldn't know it until it reached her brain and gave her a stroke.

The carrier didn't have the right medical equipment to fix that. If she could have gotten back to a civilized planet, she could have a treatment at any hospital that would break up any and all clots and protect her. Because of Shulkin that was impossible. He had dragged her out here to the literal middle of nowhere, just because of his mad need to kill Aleister Lanoe.

Now he couldn't even do that.

She glanced over at Maggs where he hung from a wall at the aft end of the bridge. She could not, of course, wink at him—that would be indecorous—nor could she give him any instructions. Someone might overhear. But she was sure he was ready, that he would strike as soon as she gave the signal.

It was always good to have a pet killer on your side. You never knew when they might come in handy.

"He's there. He's there somewhere," Shulkin said. "He's smart. I'll give him that. Smart enough to know where we would look. Maybe...maybe he's hiding in one of those craters."

"Sir, there are only a few craters big enough to hold a Hoplite, and the Batygins have searched all of them," the IO insisted.

Shulkin didn't even seem to hear the man. "Tell the Batygins to start a carpet bombardment of that iceball. I want it broken down to rubble."

"Sir—" the IO tried. Brave man, Bullam thought.

Shulkin stared at him with eyes like welding lasers. The IO wilted visibly under that glare.

"Yes, sir," he said, and turned back to his boards.

"Lanoe is close," Shulkin said, pounding his fist on the arm of his chair, his arm moving up and down like a triphammer. "He's close. And he won't get away, not this time."

Lanoe peered around a corner and down a long, empty companionway. The padded walls and the shapes of the hatches were all familiar to him. Not exactly surprising. They were regulation Navy design, exactly the same as those he'd seen every day for weeks now onboard the cruiser.

He frowned behind his black helmet. Centrocor built their own spacecraft—usually cheap knockoffs designed around obsolete Navy technology. That was how they got the inferior Yk.64s that his own BR.9s could fly rings around. This carrier, though—this wasn't some lowest-bidder copy of a Hipparchus-class. This was the real deal. Somehow Centrocor had gotten their hands on a prime example of the Navy's most advanced and most powerful starship. That was illegal, of course—the Navy would never let a poly own a Hipparchus if they could help it.

Well, add that to the long list of reasons he had not to like Centrocor. It was pretty low in the ranking just then. Number one was the fact that anyone who spotted them here would try to kill them on sight.

A message came in from Ehta—text only. He glanced down at the display on his wrist.

How do you want this done, boss? Neat and clean, by Navy regs? Or do we do it marine style?

He typed back his reply without having to give it any thought. *Quick and dirty,* he told her.

This was no time for fair play or nice behavior.

Ehta touched each of her marines on the shoulder, then flashed some quick hand signals at them. She tucked her heavy steadygun under one arm and kicked down the hallway, her people falling into perfect formation behind her. They moved fast, twisting around a corner into a main corridor so deftly Lanoe had to hurry to keep up.

The main corridor was empty—at first. As the marines shot down its length, Lanoe just had time to register a hatch opening to one side. A neddy in a thinsuit came through, looking back over his shoulder. He was laughing, sharing a joke with somebody Lanoe couldn't see.

Binah was closest. The marine grabbed the neddy's arm and pulled him into the corridor, then brought up a combat knife and stabbed down into the neddy's brain. The poor engineer's helmet tried to flow up around his face to protect him, but Binah knew what he was doing and yanked his hand back before it could be encased in flowglas. He left the knife inside the helmet.

The neddy still had one foot inside the hatch. Binah pulled the corpse free and the hatch slid closed. There was no cry of alarm from inside. Whoever the neddy had been joking with, they had no idea what had just happened.

Good.

Binah pulled a tube of adhesive from his suit and glued the body to the wall, where it wouldn't float around and make a mess. As soon as that was done he was moving again, following Ehta around another corner.

Then everything went to hell.

Before Lanoe could even get there to see what was happening, he heard shots. The wicked chatter of a machine rifle and then the low, burping roar of Ehta's steadygun. As he came up beside her he saw little jets puffing from vents on the chunky gun, holding it perfectly still in midair, defying the physics of microgravity. Ehta rested one hand on the trigger, keeping the rest of her body behind the cover of the corner.

Up ahead, Lanoe saw the bodies of three Centrocor marines floating in midair, drops of blood orbiting around them like tiny red moons. Two more were down at the end of the hall, their bodies mostly behind cover, their guns flaring as they returned fire.

Lanoe grabbed his own pistol from the holster at his hip and brought it up to snap off a shot. It went wide, but the Centrocor marine he'd been aiming at didn't get a chance to fire back. The steadygun belched again and fire burst all around the poor bastard, his arms jerking as an explosive shock wave pulverized his internal organs.

Yi brought up her particle rifle and sprayed down the end of the hall, cutting one Centrocor soldier in half. Neat holes perforated the silver helmet of another and they were clear. There was no one left alive down there. Ehta got her people moving right away. "They'll have heard that," she said. "Double time now, marines! Go, go, go now!" She grabbed the steadygun and pulled it out of its static position, then kicked hard down the hall. Lanoe followed, pistol still in hand.

Mestlez—Ehta's information specialist—checked his wrist display as they shot down the corridor. "They're moving, responding. Looks like six bad guys headed our way right now, lots more starting to figure out something's up."

"One hundred and ten meters to target," Malcolm said, bracing his feet against a wall and then kicking off, hard. Blood drops shook loose from his sleeve. Not his own.

"We've got emergency hatches closing all over the place," Mestlez said. "Don't worry, boss, I'm on it." His fingers danced across his wrist display, even as he kicked down the hall to keep up. "Running a denial of service attack right now."

"Get it done, or we're rats in a cage here," Ehta screamed at him. "People, did I say move? Because it looks like I accidentally said, 'Let's stop here for a picnic.' Damn your damned eyes to hell, you *move* when I say *move*!"

Lanoe sensed rather than saw someone coming up behind him. He wheeled around and saw a Centrocor pilot bending over the dead body of the neddy they'd left glued to the wall. Maybe the pilot was armed. Maybe he wasn't.

Lanoe didn't care. He lifted his pistol and fired three rounds into the bastard's chest. The pilot reared back, then splattered, as the explosive rounds detonated inside his body cavity. Blood and gore fountained from the collar ring of his suit.

Lanoe turned back around and saw Binah watching him.

"She said move, damn you," he told the marine.

———

"Something's wrong," Bullam said. She'd heard a noise, a rumbling sound like a distant explosion. Her chair vibrated, just for a moment. "Something—"

Red lights flared all over the IO's position. A warning chime sounded, pulsing fast. Shulkin didn't move, didn't so much as look up, but every other person on the bridge tensed and looked around, desperate to find out what was going on.

"Security is reporting a...a..." The IO shook his head. "It's not clear, sir, but there are reports of explosions, of weapons fire—"

"Lock us down," Shulkin said. As if he was ordering breakfast.

The navigator turned around to stare at him. "Sir—there's only one exit from this room, protocol suggests...I mean, perhaps we should consider evacuating—"

"This is the safest compartment on the ship," the pilot interjected. "If we seal the hatch, we can—"

"Lock us down," Shulkin said again. He was not in the habit of repeating his orders, and did not look pleased to have to do so now.

Bullam twisted around and saw thick armor plating slide over the hatch behind her. Bolts clunked into place, clamping the armor down. The air recirculators hissed and died and new displays popped up all around the IO until he was surrounded by them, walled in by light. Data streams spooled across those displays far too fast for any human eye to make sense of them.

"They're running an electronic attack on our systems," the IO said. "Trying to force open the safety hatches—"

"Who?" Bullam demanded. "Who's running the attack? Who's here?"

"Presumably someone who wants to kill us," Shulkin said.

Bullam looked for Maggs, found him. His mouth was pursed. He lifted his shoulders, then let them drop again.

She mouthed the words "protect me" at him, and he nodded.

"What are we seeing?" the navigator demanded. "Is this sabotage? Did they have spies on board, are we—"

"Biometrics are...confusing," the IO said, his face hidden behind three new displays that had just popped up. "We have casualties, lots of them, but I'm also seeing unknown IDs, people I can't account for, we..."

He swiped a number of displays away from himself, as if he were climbing out of his well of light.

"Captain," he said, "we've been boarded."

An explosion went off right next to Lanoe's head. No, that couldn't be...couldn't be right, if it had been that close he would be—he would be dead—

His ears rang and his eyes swam. Something was moving toward him through smoke, through flickering light. Half of a particle rifle, the stock blown off, spinning right toward his face. He batted it away with his free hand.

He raised his pistol and fired into the smoke, one shot, two, three. He had ten rounds left, and two clips in pouches on his suit. Ehta's steadygun burped and his head reeled as another explosion rocked the corridor.

He couldn't see anything useful—stabs of light, reefs of smoke that stank of burning insulation. He realized his helmet was down. He reached up and fumbled for the key that would bring it back up. Why had he lowered it? He couldn't remember.

One of the marines screamed and his arm came off, spinning fast as it bounced off the walls, leaving spots of blood everywhere it touched. Lanoe grabbed him and pushed him up against a wall, then grabbed an adhesive patch from his pocket and slammed it over the spurting wound, the raw meat of the marine's shoulder. He brought the marine's helmet down and saw the man had gone into shock already, his eyes rolling back in his head. His suit would pump him full of painkillers and stabilizers. There was nothing else Lanoe could do for him.

"Give me that," Ehta said, scooping up the rifle. The poor beggar didn't need it anymore. "He'll live," she told Lanoe. "Let him go. Leave him! Malcolm's dead. I've got Binah talking to their computers, but he's not trained for that and it's not working. Doesn't matter. Yi's got a dismantler. We're almost there, boss. Stay with me!"

"I'm—I'm fine," Lanoe told her, wondering if he really was. Wondering if she'd seen something in his face, if he'd just lost his reputation for having icewater for blood. "Where's the hatch? Where's the hatch for the bridge?"

"There," Ehta said, stabbing a finger down the hall. "We're holding it, we're in position, but they keep throwing more people at us. Come on, get up to where Yi is, we can use somebody who knows how to aim a gun."

Lanoe nodded and pushed past her, careening through the smoke to reach a wide hatch where her three remaining intact marines were pressed up against the wall. The steadygun hovered in midair in front of them in turret mode, twisting now this way, now that as it launched its heavy explosive rounds. Gutierrez was injured, but it wasn't slowing her down. Binah and Yi looked unhurt.

Yi had a wet-looking red ball in one hand. Even as Lanoe arrived, she slapped it against the hatch. It was a dismantler, and Lanoe knew to stay well clear of it. Yi tore off her glove and threw it away from her, even as the red ball started to smoke.

The dismantler flattened against the metal surface, red veins growing outward from its central mass, veins that branched and twisted across the full length of the hatch. They steamed and hissed wherever they touched metal, and intense heat radiated from the hatch as it started to melt. Lanoe pushed away into the corridor and fired off two shots at a vague shadow he saw approaching their position. Gutierrez shoved him aside as the steadygun lobbed an explosive round down that way.

Particle rifle fire streaked across Lanoe's vision, dazzling him. He turned his face away, just in time to see Binah scream as perfectly straight lines of blood welled up across his cheek. He looked more embarrassed than truly hurt, and he scowled as he leaned out into the smoke and shot back, his own particle beams like needles of fire diving through the murk. Down there someone howled, a sound that was cut off almost instantly by an explosion.

"Boss!" Ehta said. "Grenade!"

In the absence of gravity, the grenade came speeding toward Lanoe in a straight line, shiny sensor plates on its forward end winking as they caught flashes of light. There was no time to think. Lanoe threw himself at it in a forward flip, one boot shooting out to intercept the grenade. He smacked it with his toes and sent it flying farther down the corridor. It exploded far enough away that the burst merely showered him with blood and torn shreds of carbon fiber.

The dismantler hissed and spat big fat sparks of molten metal, and suddenly the hatch sagged in its frame, sagged and bent outward as chunks of it came free. Before the dismantler could even cool down, Binah got his shoulder against a red-hot part of the hatch and shoved, *hard*. The hatch shattered, broken shards of metal flashing out into the hallway, right in their faces. Lanoe knocked one of the shards away with his wrist and felt the skin there sear and crisp, even through layer on layer of carbon fiber and suit armor. It didn't matter.

It was done. The bridge was open.

Behind them, down the hall, came the shouts of a whole new squad of Centrocor marines advancing on their position.

Bullam was the first to see the glowing cracks spread through the hatch. "They're coming in!" she shouted.

"Hellfire," the navigator shrieked. "None of us are armed—they'll slaughter us!"

The pilot kicked away from her seat, as if there was somewhere to run. Shulkin barked at her to return to her position, a snarl of noise that barely sounded like words. The pilot pushed herself up against a wall as if she could squeeze through it, her eyes fixed on the glowing hatch.

No, Bullam thought. *No. I will not die here just because Aleister Lanoe is a clever bastard, not because Shulkin is a maniac who doesn't know when to quit, not because—*

The hatch shattered before she could finish that thought, triangular sections of it spinning wildly as they flew into the bridge. A man in a heavy Navy suit with campaign flags painted on the sleeves kicked inside, an enormous pistol in his hand. He waved it over his head, shouting a command she couldn't hear over the sound of her own heart thundering in her chest.

Behind him, marines crowded the hatch, shoving their way inside. Particle rifle fire shot through the room, and some of the IO's displays blinked out as his console erupted in sparks.

It happened slowly, time turning fluid. It felt like they were all underwater, all sounds distorted, every motion exaggerated into a long, painful arc. The Navy man—it had to be Lanoe, it had to be—moved on a perfectly flat trajectory, headed straight toward Shulkin's back, toward the chair where the mad captain sat still craning forward, staring at a display.

Before Lanoe could reach him, however, Shulkin moved, far faster than Bullam would have thought possible if she hadn't seen it herself. In one simple, economic motion he twisted around, his seat turning on its pivot, and brought up his own weapon. An enormous silver pistol of the old style, like something you would use in a duel. Its round barrel was full of bullets the size of Bullam's thumbs, bullets made of lead. She'd seen it before. She'd seen him use it before.

The arm holding that ancient pistol swung up as if it were being pulled on wires, even as Lanoe covered the last meter to Shulkin's position. The muzzle of the pistol clinked against Lanoe's helmet, stopping him in midair.

If time had slowed before, now it froze. The marines in the hatch lifted their rifles, rifles that hummed and buzzed—particle weapons, more than capable of cutting Shulkin into slices. They didn't fire. The pilot turned her face against the wall. The navigator whimpered. The IO swiped displays away from himself so he could see.

And Maggs—Maggs was there, right behind Shulkin. When had he moved over there? Bullam hadn't been aware of him at all. *He shouldn't be there,* she thought. He should be at her side, protecting her—

"Commander Lanoe," Shulkin said. His pistol's barrel was centimeters from Lanoe's nose. "A pleasure to meet you."

The helmet had been polarized before, an opaque black. Now it changed, becoming transparent. As if Lanoe wanted Shulkin to see his face. He tossed away his own pistol, throwing it back toward the marines in the hatch. One of them caught it.

"I don't know you," Lanoe said. "Ex-Navy?"

A veritable rictus of a grin spread across Shulkin's face, creasing the flesh around his eyes. "That's right. They forced me to retire. But I've got a little fight left in me."

No one on the bridge so much as breathed.

"I would suggest you tell your people to hold their fire," Shulkin said. "They have no way of killing me before I pull this trigger."

Maggs looked in Bullam's direction. His mouth was a straight line beneath his mustache. His right hand touched the pouch at his waist, the one she knew contained some kind of weapon. He reached inside and pulled out what looked like a dagger.

Still the marines in the hatch didn't shoot. No one moved any more than they absolutely had to.

"We need him alive," Bullam said, but it came out as a whisper. She forced herself to raise her voice. "Lanoe's the only one who can get us home."

"I don't care," Shulkin said.

She hadn't been speaking to the captain. She'd been speaking to Maggs. Who moved his arm just a little, changed his grip on his dagger just a hair. Could he do it? The back of Shulkin's neck was exposed. Maybe Maggs could kill him with one very fast blow—before the maniac could pull the trigger.

Of course, the marines might shoot Maggs first, if they saw the dagger. And there was no guarantee that Maggs was that good with a knife.

"Time for you to stand down," Lanoe said.

"Or...?" Shulkin asked.

"By the authority of the Council of Sector Wardens, and the Naval Expeditionary Force, I'm commandeering this vehicle. Under section fourteen of the Los Angeles Convention, no poly is allowed to own a Naval spacecraft, either decommissioned, disarmed, or otherwise. You will cede command to me, now. It's not a request."

He's just as mad as Shulkin, Bullam thought. Quoting archaic law, with a gun pointed in his face? What did he hope to achieve?

And yet—there was some kind of effect. Some subtle change in Shulkin's face. His grin didn't falter, but a dry gray tongue extruded from one corner of his mouth and he licked his lips.

Behind him Maggs lifted the dagger another few centimeters, closer to the back of Shulkin's head.

"I..." Shulkin blinked. "I..."

Lanoe said nothing. He was clearly waiting for an answer.

Now, Bullam thought. *Maggs, do it now, or we're both damned—Shulkin will shoot, because that's all he has left, it's suicide of course, but he doesn't have the imagination for anything else, he's going to shoot, he's going to—*

Maggs lifted the dagger a bit higher. Then he frowned.

"I..." Shulkin said.

"Captain," Maggs said, leaning in close as if he were whispering into Shulkin's ear. "I believe the *commander* has given you an order. Your superior, sir. He's a *superior officer.*"

"An...order," Shulkin said. He swallowed—his whole neck distending and then relaxing, as if he were a snake who'd swallowed a poisoned rat. "Orders. You—you—"

He couldn't seem to finish the thought. Instead, he looked down at his own hands.

Then he turned his pistol around, until he was holding it by the barrel. For a moment he stroked its shiny metal surface. Bullam thought he might put it in his mouth and blow his own head off.

"Sir," Shulkin said. He handed the pistol to Lanoe, who took it and shoved it into a pouch on the front of his suit. "Sir. The bridge is yours."

The marines flooded into the bridge then, swarming around Bullam, shoving her up against a wall, binding her hands with plastic that tore into her wrists. They shouted and fired a couple more shots as they secured the bridge crew, as they pulled the dagger out of Maggs's unresisting hand, and someone smacked Shulkin across the temple with the butt of a rifle, which just made his eyes flutter and his nasty grin come back, made him cackle in mad joy, so they did it again, and again, but he wouldn't stop laughing.

Chapter Seven

Valk did not have a head. He did not have a body, outside of the suit he'd worn since he was created. He didn't have eyes—instead he had cameras built into the suit, cameras that allowed him three-hundred-and-sixty-degree vision. He could see how crowded the wardroom had become. Bury and Ginger were there, close together right behind him. The marines who had not gone on the boarding mission and the three enlisted neddies were crowded around the room, perched wherever they could find space. Paniet floated directly in front of Valk, his legs tucked up into a zero-gravity lotus position.

"Are you sure everybody should be up here?" Valk asked. "Instead of, you know, at their battle stations?"

Paniet snorted. "As hilarious as I find the fact, ducky, I'm the ranking officer on this tub right now. Until Lieutenant Candless gets back, what I say goes. And I say everyone has a right to see this."

"Okay," Valk said. "Coming up on Caina now—we're about ten thousand kilometers out, still, but we should be able to see them."

On the main display the image of the protocomet expanded until white light washed out all the stars. Valk could see the new crater down there, its edges sharp and shiny. One of his copied selves was buried down there.

He found, with slight surprise, that the thought didn't bother him.

"Look, there," Bury said, pointing. He'd indicated a shadow moving across the surface, little more than a blip. Just big enough that they could make out its furry edges. A second, identical shadow moved into view just behind and to the left of the first.

"I really hope Lanoe's transmission was accurate," Paniet said. "Otherwise it's the devil himself to pay."

"Lanoe knows what he's doing," Valk said.

"You *would* think that," Paniet replied. The engineer didn't look at Valk directly. Instead he glanced up at a camera mounted in the ceiling. He must know that Valk could see through that one, too. Paniet gave the camera a wry look, his mouth twisted over to one side.

Valk had no idea what that was supposed to mean.

"I'll step up the magnification," Valk said.

On the main display the two shadows grew until actual details could be made out. The twin destroyers were revealed in all their wicked glory—long, thin ships so covered with guns and missile packs and thrusters that you couldn't even see their viewports, or any sign at all that there were people onboard.

The cruiser was well inside the range of the destroyers' missiles now, and drifting closer every second. Valk would never have dared to get so close if Lanoe hadn't insisted it was safe. Still, he worked up a series of calculations as to how he would run for deep space if the destroyers showed any sign of aggression.

For the moment, at least, they were quiescent. "I'm scanning their guns...looks like all their weapons are cold. I'm pinging them now to establish a datalink. Getting good telemetry and sensor data. They're making no attempt to keep me out of their systems."

Paniet nodded. "Let's all be good sports, now. Take us in closer, as a sign of good faith. Where's Lieutenant Candless?"

"Inbound now, with my four cataphracts," Valk said. He could hear his other selves whispering in the dark, feeding him data and logs of everything they'd done while they were away. Reminding him of the promise he'd made them, that as soon as they returned he would erase them, delete them thoroughly. "She said she wanted to stay outside until we were sure about this."

"Understood," Paniet said. "Distance?"

"We're nine thousand kilometers out," Valk told him. "Closing the gap."

The cruiser's engines powered up and Valk accelerated toward the protocomet, ramping up the power so gently that Paniet merely settled to the floor, rather than falling out of the air. The engineer didn't seem surprised by the return of gravity. "Eight thousand kilometers," Valk said. A minute ticked by. "Six."

"Close enough," Paniet told him. "Send a request to speak with the commander of one of them."

"Which one?"

"It doesn't matter. Surprise me, love," Paniet said.

There was no delay in establishing the connection—the destroyers must have been waiting for the request. "They're receiving," Valk told the engineer.

Paniet nodded and jumped up to his feet. "My name is Hassan Paniet, a lieutenant of the Naval Engineering Division. I am the acting captain of the Hoplite-class cruiser in orbit above you. May I ask whom I am addressing?"

"Oritt Batygin here," the reply came. The connection was audio only, the quality stepped down until the destroyer captain's voice sounded tinny and distant. It was possible, on an open connection like this, to send signals that could kill or incapacitate anyone who listened to them—earworms and hypnodelic pulses. Valk wasn't taking any chances. He'd intentionally kept the connection quality poor to rule out such things.

"Well, M. Batygin, it's a pleasure to make your acquaintance," Paniet said. "I'd like to say that you and your compatriots gave us quite a run for our money. You fought admirably and you have the respect of the Navy of Earth."

Batygin laughed. "That's very kind of you," he replied. "And may I say, you got extremely lucky. There is no way you should have survived all we threw at you."

"Oh, don't I know it," Paniet said. "There were times there when I started designing my own coffin in my head, because I was sure I would need one. Well. Glad we can put all of that behind us. I'm sure we'll all be great friends from now on. Hmm?"

"That's ... one way of describing the current state of play," Batygin responded.

"So let's make it official," Paniet told him. "Will you do the honors?"

"One moment," Batygin said.

Paniet drew a finger across his throat. Valk muted the connection.

"This is the part," Paniet said, "where we find out if Lanoe actually does live up to his legend." He craned his head around and looked at the crowd gathered in the wardroom. "You all might take a moment to brace yourselves."

On the display, the two destroyers moved closer together, pulling into a standard maneuvering formation. Then, almost in unison, they began to display a string of lights all along their lengths, from nose to engines. An unbroken line of white lamps.

"Back during basic training," Paniet said, "I might have slept through the class on visual signaling. Can someone remind me what that means?"

It was Bury who answered. "A string of white lights means unconditional surrender," the kid said.

A cheer went up in the wardroom, and great whoops of joy. Valk raised one arm over his head and waved it in a simulacrum of jubilation.

☇

Maggs's hands were bound behind his back and someone pulled a sack over his helmet. He could see nothing, hear nothing but meaningless shouts as he was pushed down a corridor. He could feel himself flying, and had a vague sense of hard walls all around him, but couldn't see anything but the little light that came through the sack. They could be throwing him headfirst down the longest corridor on the carrier and he would have no way of knowing until he collided with the far end.

He refused to scream. He refused to beg for mercy.

Mostly because he knew that with this bunch, that was likely to elicit nothing but peals of mocking laughter.

Maggsy, you've been in some hot water in your time, but—

Father, Maggs told the voice in his head, *with all due filial respect, shut up or go to the devil. The choice is yours.*

Rough hands caught him and shoved him sideways. He was moved now left, now straight, now right.

At one point, with no warning, a fist smashed into his midsection. Even through the layers of his suit he felt like he'd been hit with a hammer. The breath exploded out of him, fogging his helmet, and stars burst behind his eyes.

Eventually he was shoved through some kind of a hatch and then strapped down into a chair. He could hear other people being given the same treatment, though to his ears it sounded like they were having a gentler time of it. There was a long time when he was left with nothing but his thoughts.

He found very little consolation there.

He felt motion—the return of some measure of gravity. He must be on a vehicle of some kind, a ship. His destination, and his fate when he should arrive there, was as great and profound a mystery as the question of what lay outside the bound of the universe.

Even with the sack over his head, he endeavored to maintain the stiff upper lip. He had to admit—if only to himself—that he was not completely successful.

"Maggs," someone said. Just a whisper. He thought perhaps it sounded like Ashlay Bullam. "Maggs. Can you speak?"

"It is the one faculty that remains mine to use," he said, speaking as softly as she.

"What are they going to do to us? Where are we going?"

He spent a moment thinking of how to answer. He could be kind and lie, but that seemed entirely pointless, and it was unlikely a woman like Bullam would appreciate being cozened at this particular pass. He considered that what he was about to say might be his final words, and he pondered on some line of poesy, some grandiloquent oration that would cement his place in the annals of myth. Then he realized that there was no one there to record what he said. Even if there were, true eloquence would be utterly lost in the vacuous well that was the mind of the average Poor Bloody Marine.

No, in the end, he was forced to fall back on his least favorite rhetorical strategy. He settled on speaking the absolute, unvarnished truth.

"They're going to take us somewhere undignified and then they're going to execute us, one by one. We're going to the firing squad," he told her.

"M. Valk, are you receiving my transmission?"

Valk was more than capable of paying attention to more than one thing at a time. He partitioned a section of his consciousness to respond to Candless, who had granted him access to the sensors built into her suit.

"Yeah, I've got visual and audio," he told her. It was a little odd, looking at things from her perspective, but nothing he hadn't done before. Currently she was in the cockpit of her fighter, orbiting Caina just a few hundred meters from one of the destroyers. As he watched, she lowered her canopy and pushed her way out of her seat, gliding over toward the main hatch of the enemy ship. *Former* enemy ship, he reminded himself.

"It falls on me to perform an inspection of our new allies," Candless told him. "Do me the favor, if you will, of scanning them for explosives or informational hazards."

"Got it." Twelve people in suits were floating just outside the destroyer. The entire crew of the ship. "I'm showing the captain, the pilot, and ten gunners," Valk said. He pinged their cryptabs—small data plaques on the fronts of their suits that contained their service records and vital statistics. "All but a couple of them have Navy records," he told her. "Two of the gunners are just Centrocor militia."

"Explosives?" she asked. "Informational hazards? Or did you forget?"

Candless appreciated precision and thoroughness. She and Valk had never got along, but he'd developed a real respect for her. "No, I already did the scan. I would have told you if I found anything. Promise."

One of the destroyer's crew—the captain—moved forward on tiny puffs of gas from his suit jets. He lifted his hands in a gesture of peace, but Valk could feel Candless edging her hand down toward the sidearm she kept at her hip.

"Rhys Batygin," he said, introducing himself. Valk had already gotten the name from the man's cryptab. "Let me be the first to welcome you aboard, Lieutenant."

"I imagine you might wish it was under different circumstances," she said.

Batygin laughed. "I'm still alive. I haven't been put down like a mad dog. I'd say things are working out for me and my brother."

"One might be forgiven," Candless said, "for expecting a more bitter reaction. Even a vengeful one."

"Of course," Batygin told her. "Yet I think you'll find us good losers. Really, we aren't much concerned with who commands us—Centrocor, the Navy." He fluttered one hand dismissively. "It's flying and fighting we love, not politics."

Hellfire, Valk thought. *Officers sure do like to talk fancy to each other.*

Tannis Valk, the man whose memories Valk carried, had never been a big believer in putting on airs.

There was something wrong with the man's eyes. Valk checked his biometrics. "You should know this guy is scared," Valk told

Candless. "He's trying to hide it, but his heart rate is really high, and he's sweating profusely. The drugs in his system probably aren't helping. He's terrified of what you're going to do to him. What in the devil's name did Lanoe get up to over on the carrier?"

Candless did not answer his question. "I'll need to take a look inside," she said to the Batygin. "I would apologize for violating your privacy, if the necessity wasn't manifestly obvious."

"I understand. Please, be my guest," Batygin told her.

Candless jetted over to the main hatch and wriggled inside. For a moment Valk could see nothing but a shadowy bulkhead and the edge of a hatch—the airlock was a tight enough squeeze that Candless's cameras were pressed up against the walls. She cycled the lock and moved inside, into the ship.

"This'll be interesting," Valk told her. "I've never seen the inside of a Peltast-class destroyer before."

"I doubt it will impress you," Candless said. The airlock was located near the aft end of the ship, back in the engine shielding. She glanced quickly at the engineering section, which amounted to a single cramped workstation. "Valk, I'm relying on you here. If there are any booby traps you're likely to notice them before I do. In fact, I'm only likely to notice them at all if I trigger them. Please keep your eyes open." She paused for a moment. "I meant that metaphorically, of course."

"Got it," Valk said.

She moved forward through a narrow corridor lined with utilitarian bunks—six of them in total. Although the destroyer was a hundred meters long, so much of its mass was taken up by overpowered engines and piles of ship-to-ship guns and weapon systems that there wasn't a lot of room left for the crew. There was no wardroom, or any kind of common space. Only half the crew could sleep at a given time, so they would have to do it in shifts. "Hotbedding," they called it. Valk remembered the practice—with no fondness whatsoever—from his own days as a pilot.

"Are you seeing anything that should concern me?" Candless asked.

"Only that I don't ever want to crew one of these things," Valk said. "Back at Niraya, we had a Peryton-class fighter tender. Twenty meters long and it was roomier than this." Missions aboard destroyers could last for months. You would have to really like your fellow crew members or life on the ship would quickly get hellish.

"Be glad," Candless said, "that you don't have to experience the smell."

Valk activated a spectroscopic analyzer on the front of Candless's suit. "I see what you mean. Lots of butyric acid and thioalcohols in the air."

"I beg your pardon?"

"Body odor," he told her.

"Quite." Candless moved forward through a passageway so narrow she had to go headfirst. It passed through a rank of canister-shaped gunnery pods—basically armored workstations where a gunner could operate several weapons systems simultaneously. The positions took up a huge amount of space, and they seemed completely unnecessary to Valk. Computers could run the guns much better than human beings, and take up a lot less room. The same law that forbade his very existence prohibited any computerized system to have access to weaponry, though, so the destroyer's crew had to operate all the guns manually.

Up near the front of the destroyer the passageway widened a little and split off in two directions. There was no actual bridge. Instead there were a pair of awkwardly shaped workstations, separated by more of the armored pods. "One of those is for the pilot," Valk guessed. "Where does everybody else sit?"

"The captain of the ship is also the information officer and the navigator," Candless replied. "It takes a rather focused and talented person to captain a destroyer."

"Or one who's high on speed all the time," Valk pointed out.

Candless did not favor that with a reply. Instead she sighed and poked her head into the pilot's position. Took a quick look through the viewport, a narrow slit of carbonglas that currently showed a huge number of stars and one edge of Caina.

"There's nothing here. This was a pointless exercise, of course," she said.

"Had to be done."

"Hmm. If we had more officers on the cruiser, it might have been done by someone other than the XO. Rank, I am told, has its privileges. I have yet to actually experience any of them."

"Lanoe really leans on you, I know," Valk told her. "You know it's because he believes in you. That you're capable of everything he hands you."

"I suppose that's a sort of compliment. Very well. We need to repeat this futile performance for the other destroyer. But first— Valk. I need to discuss something with you."

"Yeah? Okay, well, I guess we have time."

Candless inhaled sharply through her nose. "I spoke with your other selves, before. The copies of yourself that you wedged into our BR.9s."

"A bunch of charming guys, I bet," Valk said.

"Hmm. One of them sacrificed himself to save my life."

"Oh," Valk said. "Listen, before this gets awkward, I mean, I get you want to thank me, but—"

"Thank you?" Candless said. "Hardly."

"Okay, so then . . ."

"I was disgusted," she said. "You put them in those fighters like it was a Procrustean bed. Tortured them. You tortured versions of your self."

"Limited versions," Valk said. "A BR.9 doesn't have the memory capacity to hold all of my files."

"That makes it better somehow? Stunted reflections of your self are less worthy of existence? They can be thrown away with abandon?"

"You don't understand," he told her.

He'd always known it would come to this. Candless had never hidden her feelings about artificial intelligences—or Valk personally. Her antipathy was hardly surprising. Possession of an AI, or simply harboring one, was a capital crime on every human world. Giving an AI access to weaponry was an automatic death sentence.

The Martians had built an AI, back during the Century War. They'd installed it on a dreadnought, a kind of super-battleship. They'd given it the mission to win that war and bring Earth to heel. It had acted according to pure logic—flying to Earth and shelling the homeworld until half the human race was dead. It only stopped because it needed to reload. It made perfect sense, of course. If everyone on Earth was dead, Mars would win the war by default.

Candless hadn't even been alive back when it happened. As far as Valk knew, he was the only artificial intelligence built since that time. Yet something in the ancestral memory of humanity had kept that fear—and thus that hatred—alive. Lanoe had forbidden Candless from confronting Valk directly, but she'd never grown to like him.

"What are you?" she demanded now.

"A ghost," he told her. "The memories of a man named Tannis Valk."

"I know about the Blue Devil. The hero pilot of the Establishment. That's not what I'm asking," she replied. "I'm asking who *you* are. I've spoken with Engineer Paniet. He tells me you're changing. Becoming less human over time."

What could he do? Valk decided he would be honest with her. She already hated him. Nothing he could say would change that. "It's been a process of discovery. That is, I keep discovering things I don't have anymore. Things I don't have to do anymore, too. I don't have to eat. I don't have to sleep. One day I realized I didn't need to breathe. That was a real shock."

He looked for Candless's reflection in one of the destroyer's carbonglas viewports. He saw her shake her head in confusion.

"Are you...are you more intelligent than we are? Humans, I mean."

"No. I don't think so," Valk said. "I can do some things better than you can. I can talk to computers without needing an interface. I have better reaction times. But smarter? I feel about as smart as Tannis Valk was. I guess."

"You could be, though. You could make yourself smarter."

It was an old belief about AI that because its mental processes could be understood, they could be improved upon. That the first action any AI would take would be to search out additional processor power, faster file handling protocols, ways to overclock its processes. That if left unchecked, any AI would increase its intelligence exponentially, until human beings could no longer comprehend its thoughts. That it would become something better, bigger, than the people who created it.

"I've never tried. I won't," Valk said. "You—and I mean people in general—hate me enough already. All of you except Lanoe."

"I don't understand it," Candless told him. "How he thinks he can trust you. If you wanted to kill me right now, you could. Couldn't you?"

It would be pretty easy, actually. Candless's suit was protecting her in all kinds of ways. It gave her the oxygen she needed, it regulated her body's temperature. It shielded her from radiation. He could change any number of parameters in the suit's software and she would be dead within minutes.

"Yes," he told her. "But I wouldn't do that."

"And one is expected to believe you. Simply because you say so."

"Because—because the same reasons you don't just walk up to Ehta and strangle her with your bare hands. I know you've considered that." The two lieutenants, one the cruiser's executive officer and the other its warrant officer, had been at odds since they first met. "You don't do it for one simple reason, because there are consequences to actions. Lanoe wouldn't like it if I hurt you. He would never forgive me."

"His opinion means that much to you?"

Valk lacked the ability to sigh. He could only play an audio file of what it sounded like when Tannis Valk used to sigh. Before he died.

"Lanoe's the only reason I'm still here," Valk told her. "You think I'm an abomination, and you know what? I get it. I do. I think the same thing. Tannis Valk hated AI as much as you do."

"Oh," Candless said. "But then—"

"I want to die," Valk told her. "I want to be deleted. I'm not allowed to. Not until Lanoe is done with me. Not as long as I'm still useful."

Air rushed past Maggs's head, rustling the sack that obscured his vision. All external sounds went away and he understood. Someone had just opened a hatch onto hard vacuum. His straps were undone and he was hauled out of his seat. Someone kicked his legs until he jerked them forward and found his feet planted on solid deck plates.

Gravity. They'd taken him somewhere with gravity. That meant either he was onboard a ship that was undergoing acceleration, or he was on actual terra firma. The gravity didn't waver or feel unsteady at all, which suggested the latter.

The protocomet, then. They'd taken him to the protocomet. As good a place as any. It was a tradition that when the Navy executed someone, they had to be buried or ejected into space immediately afterward. Most likely this tradition had begun because there was so little room on Navy ships for the storage of corpses.

Maggs also thought that Lanoe might want to carry out the executions somewhere other than on the carrier for another reason. He wouldn't want all the Centrocor employees there to witness the deaths of their former officers. It could be bad for morale.

Hands grabbed his arms and legs and he was pushed through a narrow opening, then hauled back up to his feet. Someone stood on either side of him, holding him, forcing him to march forward. There was so little gravity on the protocomet that Maggs was forced to shuffle along, careful to keep from bounding off into the sky.

They didn't go very far. Maggs was forced to his knees. He felt as light as a feather, no doubt due to the low gravity of the protocomet—it couldn't possibly be fear that made him feel so empty and sick.

Maggs had a bad habit of being sarcastic even in his own internal monologue.

For what felt like a very, very long time he was left there, kneeling on smooth ice. He attempted to use his suit's communications faculties but soon discovered—with not a shred of surprise—that they'd been blocked. He was left unable to speak to anyone, unable to see anything, unable to think of anything but what was about to happen.

He supposed that keeping a stiff upper lip had its limits. And surely he could be excused for breaking down a little, now, when no one could see him.

"Dad," he said. His voice sounded, to his own ears, hoarse and weak. "Father. I beg your pardon for what I said before. I'd very much like to speak with you again now. I don't want to be alone."

There was no response. The voice that had lived in his head for years failed to manifest itself.

"Please, Admiral," he said to his decorated father. "Please. You always have such good advice. Especially when I don't want it. I could really use some now."

He felt a distant rhythmic vibration, perhaps footfalls coming toward him. Perhaps that was the step of the executioner.

"Daddy!" he shrieked. "I'm begging you! I'm your son, your only son! Please—please come speak with me. Please, just—just tell me it's going to be all right. It doesn't matter that it's a lie. It would make me feel so much better. Please, Dad."

He closed his eyes to hold back the tears that pooled in his eye sockets, surface tension overcoming the miniscule gravity.

"Please," he begged.

Someone pulled the sack off his head. He saw a human form, silhouetted against so many, many stars.

He blinked rapidly to clear away the tears. Looked left and right, and saw he was kneeling in a line of people, some of whom he recognized—Shulkin and Bullam, and the IO from the bridge—and some he didn't. They were grouped in a very shallow semicircle, a meter away from the rim of a deep crater with steep walls.

Maggs craned his head around, trying to see more. He quickly located Lieutenant Ehta, the warrant officer from the cruiser. He saw several marines he vaguely recognized from the Hoplite, people whose names he'd never bothered to learn. Weapons slung loose in their arms.

Then he looked up again and saw Lanoe. It was Lanoe who'd taken the sack away. Lanoe who was holding a pistol in one hand.

And smiling at him.

Candless took her fighter over to the carrier, a few million kilometers away. Valk stayed with her, linked in through her suit. "We will have further words, you and I," she told him as she flew.

He didn't doubt it.

"For the moment, however, we have to stay alert. We can't very well make the entire crew of the carrier wait outside while we perform our inspection. Nor will I be able to complete this task on my own—the vehicle is just too large. It looks like I need your help now. I worry I'll find you as convenient as Lanoe does."

"Always glad to be of service," Valk said. Tweaking the tone of his voice to convey some sarcasm.

As they approached the round maw of the big ship, Valk couldn't help but feel a little apprehensive, even after the carrier's flight deck crew signaled that they were cleared for approach. He could see the old scar along the hull of the ship where Candless had struck it with a disruptor round. The damage was severe and only partially repaired. Still, compared to the cruiser the carrier looked to be in far better condition. If Lanoe hadn't taken the chance of infiltrating it, Valk knew that they never would have stood a chance. Centrocor would have killed them all.

Candless eased her BR.9 inside the carrier's flight deck, a vast steel cave lined with docking berths for fifty fighters. Only about two-thirds of that complement remained now—repeated battles had thinned their numbers considerably—but still there were enough Sixty-Fours and carrier scouts to make the flight deck a place of long, sharp shadows.

"They want you to put down over there," Valk said, indicating the approved berth by superimposing a yellow rectangle on her canopy.

"I'll dock where I wish to," Candless told him. She called over to the flight controllers and indicated she would use a berth she must have chosen at random. "It's important to remind them who's in charge now, I think," she told Valk. "As for you, please do not interface with my craft's computers any further. I don't care for it."

"Okay," Valk said.

Candless was an excellent pilot. She set down without so much as a thump. Long metal restraining bars craned down over the fighter to hold it in place, and a narrow hatch opened up next to the berth, spilling light into the gloom. Candless lowered her canopy and then pushed her way into the hatch, which closed behind her with a hiss.

Every berth in the flight deck had its own dedicated airlock. That way the pilots could get to their ships faster when it was time to scramble. "Have you been on a Hipparchus-class carrier before?" Candless asked him.

"A couple times," Valk said. "Once as a pilot, during some campaign or other. Once as a prisoner, at the end of the Establishment Crisis. They made us turn our fighters in so we could be processed in the demobilization. There were so many of us they had to bring in a bunch of carriers just to hold us all. We were worried we were boarding prison ships, but the Navy treated us okay. Right up until they stripped our service records and cut us loose to try to find jobs where we could."

"That wasn't the Navy's decision, to leave you out in the cold," Candless suggested. "That was the Sector Wardens."

"I guess that ought to make a difference."

He felt Candless's irritation through her suit sensors. There was still some bad blood between the Navy and the pilots who had fought for the Establishment. This wasn't the time for dredging up bad history, though.

The airlock opened into a maze of corridors inside the hull of the carrier. At first no one was there to greet them, but soon a PBM with hexagons painted on his shoulders came puffing up toward them, kicking off the walls.

"Lieutenant?" he asked. "Ma'am? I'm, uh, I'm Sergeant Foulkes. I'm supposed to help you with . . . with your . . ."

"Inspection," Candless told the young man. He couldn't be over twenty-five. "In the future, when you announce yourself, simply state your name and rank. When you hem and haw like that it makes you sound like you have something to hide."

"Yes, ma'am," the marine said. His eyes were trembling in their sockets, he was so scared.

"Ease up," Valk told Candless. "We have to work with these people."

Candless did not respond. Perhaps she didn't want Foulkes to know she had a passenger riding on her shoulder, so to speak.

"Take me to the bridge, Sergeant. Now."

Foulkes didn't even say "Yes, ma'am." He twisted around in the corridor and kicked off the wall, his hands out in front of him to catch the edge of a hatch up ahead. He led Candless into a much larger passage, one lined with hatches. Most of those hatches were open, and people were poking their heads out of them, staring at the newcomer.

Candless didn't look at them.

"They're worried, ma'am," Foulkes said, as if she'd asked. "Worried about what's going to happen to them."

"Just a couple kind words now," Valk suggested, "and—"

"With any change of command," Candless told Foulkes, "there will be uncomfortable transitions."

The bridge wasn't much farther. Foulkes brought them up short at another hatch that opened into a broad space where several corridors came together. At the exact center of the space was one very large hatch.

Or at least there used to be a very large hatch there. Shards of it remained in the frame, triangular lengths of metal with bright, smooth edges. A dismantler had dissolved the rest.

The walls around the broken hatch were stained. Ribbons and splotches of pink had soaked into the padding. There were scorch marks and bullet holes all around, and the air was full of semitoxic chemicals. Complex organic compounds, the residue left over when very nasty weapons went off in an enclosed space full of bodies.

Candless passed it all by, kicking her way into the bridge beyond. The room wasn't in bad shape, considering. There were a few ruined displays, and one wall looked like it had been scratched by a very large, very ferocious tiger. Valk recognized the trails left behind by the rounds of a particle rifle. Otherwise the bridge was intact.

And almost empty. A pilot and a navigator were seated at their respective positions. There was no one in the captain's chair.

"Thank you, Sergeant," Candless said. "Please leave me alone now."

Valk expected Candless to take the captain's chair, but instead she went to the IO's position and strapped herself into the seat. She tried to bring up some displays—schematics of the carrier, personnel manifests, damage reports. Only a few of the displays she requested actually appeared. She leaned forward, over the IO's console. The display surface there was cracked and riddled with bullet holes. Candless reached inside the broken gray plastic of the console. Valk looked inside along with her and saw smashed and burnt-out emitters.

Candless sighed, long and deep.

"I can bring up all that information for you, if you want," Valk said.

"Very well. Again, the convenience of your abilities trumps my disgust."

Valk tried to ignore that. "You could have been nicer to Foulkes," he said.

"Not if I expect these people to respect me. They lost a battle. However, because Lanoe was very clever, it didn't look like a battle. Most of them didn't even know it was going on at the time. It wasn't real to them—they woke up this morning working for Centrocor, and now, without so much as having had a chance to fire a shot in their defense, they are prisoners of the Navy. They need to know something serious happened here. They need to know they lost."

"I guess that's one way of looking at it," Valk said. "Did you... did you see all the blood out there?"

"The reports, please," Candless said.

"Yeah." Valk worked with what emitters he could find, any console that was still functional. The displays popped up in the air around her. While she studied the reports, he scanned the room, and then the corridors around them, looking for booby traps.

"Hold on," he said, because he'd found something. Though not what he expected. "Under the navigator's position. There." She got up and moved across the room, following his directions. "There's something lodged against an air intake there. I don't know if—"

Candless reached under the navigator's console. The thing Valk had detected was oblong, about six centimeters in length. Pale in color, mostly soft, but with a harder section at one end. He thought it might be some kind of grenade or something.

Then Candless fished it out of the grille over the air intake. Held it up where he could see it clearly.

It was a human finger, severed below the second knuckle.

"Oh, hellfire," Valk said. "Oh, hell."

"Left over from the boarding, no doubt," Candless said. She looked around until she found a waste disposal hatch. She deposited the grisly trophy, then returned to the IO's station and the reports.

"Lanoe did this," Valk said. "He came in here and he—he killed people."

"He fought his way to the bridge," Candless told him. "I imagine he killed whomever he needed to kill."

"This—this isn't like him," Valk said. "The man I know..."

"Lanoe is three hundred years old," Candless said. "He's been a pilot, a warrior, since he was a teenager. How many people do you think he's killed in all that time?"

"That's different. When you're in a cataphract—"

"It is *not* different. At all. It may seem that way, because when you pull the trigger on a PBW cannon, you usually can't see the face of the person you're killing. But the pilots he's bested in thousands of dogfights were just as dead after the fact."

Valk couldn't shake his head, not so she could see it.

What was it she'd said, though? She'd spoken to Paniet. Who'd said that Valk was losing his humanity. That it was slipping away over time.

Maybe he wasn't the only one.

Lanoe leaned over Maggs until they were looking each other right in the eye. Then he tapped his helmet. "Can you hear me? I've switched your suit comms back on. Say something so I know you can hear me."

"There are rules about the treatment of prisoners of war," Maggs said, the words unspooling from his mouth before he'd even considered them. "The Ceres Accords lay out three relevant articles. One concerns torture and standards of confinement. The second requires that prisoners be given medical treatment for any injuries sustained during combat. The third holds that summary... summary executions are... are..."

Lanoe nodded. His smile hadn't faltered. "Sure. Go on," he said.

Maggs clamped his teeth together. Forced himself to regain a little of his customary composure. He would not let this lowborn beggar turn him into a sniveling coward. "Summary executions," he said, forcing the words out now—where before they'd been a spigot, a veritable flood, now they were like the last drips from a switched-off faucet—"are permitted only..." He swallowed. It was difficult. "Permitted only in cases of gross criminal activity. Namely, to wit, acts of high treason, genocide, crimes against the interplanetary economy, the possession of weapons of mass... mass—"

"None of which you're guilty of. That's what you're going to say, right? That you haven't done any of those things. So I can't just put a bullet in your head. Betraying your commanding officer—more times than I feel like counting—isn't on that list. Defrauding entire planetary populations. Being a faithless coward, abandoning your post. Those aren't on the list."

"That's . . . right," Maggs said.

"Sure," Lanoe said. "Just one thing. If we're going to get all legal about this. One thing you must have forgotten."

Maggs shook his head. "No. No—"

"You're not a prisoner of war," Lanoe told him. "There's no war between Centrocor and the Navy. Not one anybody bothered to declare."

Maggs tried to climb to his feet. It wasn't a conscious action, simply something his body tried to do. Maybe he'd intended to make a run for it, or perhaps he'd simply wanted to die like a man. He didn't know why he tried to get up.

It didn't matter. Two marines grabbed him and smashed him down to the ground, grinding his helmet against the ice until it squeaked.

"I saved your life!" Maggs howled. Any pretense to courage was gone now. "I saved your life! Shulkin would have taken that shot! I saved your life! How many times now, how many times have I saved you?"

"Uh-huh," Lanoe said. "Tell you what. I guess that's worth something." And then he started walking away. Over his shoulder, as if it were an afterthought, he added, "So I'll save you for last."

The marines didn't let Maggs get back up on his knees. They pinned him down. He couldn't see anything, couldn't see where Lanoe was going. But over the radio in his suit he could hear everything that was said.

"Captain Shulkin," Lanoe said. "I've seen your service record. Your time in the Navy was impressive. You retired with a medical discharge. Now you're working for Centrocor. Are you willing to come back into the fold? Would you be willing to take a new oath of loyalty to the Navy?"

"You'll let me fight?" Shulkin asked. There was no fear in his voice, none whatsoever.

"I'll let you fight," Lanoe said.

"Then it would be an honor," Shulkin said. "Where do I sign?"

Lanoe chuckled. "What do you think, Ehta? You think we can trust him?"

Ehta didn't reply, insomuch as Maggs could hear.

"Good enough," Lanoe said.

Maggsy.

His father's voice in his head. Back now. Late, but Maggs didn't mind.

Father? he thought.

"You," Lanoe said. "Tarash Giles. You were the IO on the carrier. You'll notice the pilot and the navigator aren't down here."

"Yes, sir," the IO said.

"IOs have a lot of jobs," Lanoe said. "They run the sensor boards, protect a ship against electronic attack. They work as science officers, and liaise with engineering on bigger ships. Sometimes they work as political officers, too. Checking up on the crew. Making sure everybody stays loyal. That's a position of trust. Centrocor trusted you, right? They put you on the bridge. Maybe you're still a corporate spy. Maybe I should—"

"Sir, no—please! I'll do anything, I'll do anything you say, just...just don't shoot me! Please!"

"Maybe I *should* give you a chance," Lanoe said.

"Oh, sir, thank—"

"One. One chance. If you make me regret this, there won't be any further discussion. Do you understand?"

"I do. I do, sir, thank you—thank you."

"Sure," Lanoe said.

Maggsy, there's not much time left. I wanted to talk to you about how a Maggs dies. About how we carry ourselves at the end.

Father? He's letting them live, he isn't going to—

"Major Nicholas Yael," Lanoe said, as if he were reading from a display. "You served on the carrier as commander of Centrocor's marines. You led the counterattack when I boarded the—"

"That's right, you bastard!" Yael shouted. "That's right—I defended my ship. I defended my people! You killed twelve of my best troops, you slaughtered them in cold blood!"

"You fought hard," Lanoe said. "That means something. Will you—"

"No! I will not sign any damned loyalty pledge, not to you. Not to the man who murdered Corporal Tyre Cassel. Not to the man who murdered Private Max Youlson. Not to the man who murdered—"

Someone must have hit Yael then, because he abruptly fell silent.

"You're saying you're still loyal to Centrocor," Lanoe said.

"I'm loyal to my comrades in arms. If they're Centrocor, then hell, yes—cut out my heart, you'll find a hexagon tattooed on it. We're all in this together! You understand what that means? You understand what—" Yael let out a deep, gasping breath. "You should kill me now. You should kill me now, because if you don't I will personally—"

"Sure," Lanoe said.

Then Maggs felt the ground rumble, just for a moment. *That— that was a gunshot,* he thought.

Yael said nothing more.

Maggs's whole body shook, as if he was the one who'd been shot.

Maggsy, my boy, when I died I didn't get a chance to leave any last words behind. That's fine. Last words, I've heard it said, are for people who didn't say enough in life. Well, that certainly doesn't describe you.

Father? Please, just—just give me some comfort now. Please.

"Ashlay Bullam," Lanoe said. "M. Bullam. It says here you're a Centrocor executive troubleshooter, whatever that means. You're the real prize here, aren't you? Shulkin just wanted to fight. You're the real commander of this mission. You're the one Centrocor sent to kill me."

"No," Bullam replied.

"No?"

"The mission was never to kill you. Don't be facile. We would have hired assassins to do that. No, we heard that the Navy was going to make an alliance with the…aliens who lived in that strange city. We were supposed to make sure the alliance didn't happen. It was Shulkin who chased you through the wormhole. I ordered him not to. He didn't listen to me."

"So none of it was your fault. That carrier attacked me, nearly killed one of my people. Nearly killed all of us, frankly. But it wasn't you calling the shots."

Bullam sighed. "I'm not making excuses. I'm giving you facts. You can choose what to do with them."

"You don't sound very frightened, M. Bullam," Lanoe said.

"Ha. No," Bullam told him. "No. You don't scare me."

"Why not? I just killed a man."

"Because this is a farce. Loyalty pledges? Really? When did a signature on a file ever stop anyone from doing anything? I've read your dossier, I know you aren't that naïve. You're letting Shulkin and the IO live because you need them."

"Is that right?"

"You have a skeleton crew on your cruiser. You've just inherited a carrier and two destroyers, but you don't have the people to crew them. You need us—well, most of us—alive. Otherwise we wouldn't even be having this conversation. You've already decided who you're keeping around."

"Are you sure you're on the list?"

"I'm certain of it," Bullam said.

Terrified as he was, Maggs had to take a moment to admire the woman's brass.

"You can't trust anyone. Not me, not Shulkin. None of the enlisted rabble on our ships. You need the two of us to keep them in line. Shulkin wants to fight, and I want to go home. You're the only one who can grant those wishes. So this isn't about loyalty, it's a business negotiation. A simple trade, where everyone gets what they want and we all go home happy."

"So you're saying you'll help me. You won't sign a pledge—"

"I'll sign anything you want," Bullam interrupted. "The file won't be worth the storage space it takes up, but I'll sign it. Come now, Commander Lanoe. You're too old for these stupid games. You've seen too many people betray you before. Accept my offer, and release me. Or kill me and see how long it takes for the crew of the carrier to mutiny."

"Interesting," Lanoe said.

There was no gunshot. No screaming. The marines holding Maggs down let him up, just a little. Just enough to see Ehta take out a knife and cut the plastic shackles around Bullam's wrists. Then Ehta turned the knife around to show it to Bullam, to brandish it right in her face.

Bullam rolled her eyes.

"Okay, just one more," Lanoe said. He came and stood directly over Maggs.

His time had come.

Maggsy, you need to stay quiet. Don't blubber. Don't beg, whatever you do. The honor of our family depends on it.

Honor, Maggs thought. *Honor. That's rich.*

Son. Son—I won't tell you I'm proud of you. We both know the kind of life you lived. The things you've done. Now, now, I know why you did them. But you must admit the world cares little for our intentions, and much for our deeds.

Dad. I miss you, Dad. It was so hard after you died, and Mother and I had to work to preserve your legacy. We did what we had to do. I did what I had to do.

I know, son. I can't say I'm proud of you. But I loved you. I really did.

It was—surprisingly comforting to hear that.

"No fancy words now, huh?" Lanoe said. "No protests. No excuses. Yeah. We both knew this would happen, eventually." He lifted his pistol.

Maggs took what strength he could from his father's words. Tears welled up in his eyes but he kept his mouth firm as Lanoe placed the barrel of the pistol against the flowglas of his helmet. If he couldn't meet Lanoe's gaze, if he couldn't bear to look up at the gun, well, there were limits to anyone's—

"Wait," Bullam said.

Maggs and Lanoe both turned to look at her.

"In exchange for my cooperation," she said, "I have one condition."

"Now's not the time," Lanoe told her.

"Wrong. This is exactly the time. Because my condition is this—I will work with you, toward our common goal. In exchange, I want you to spare Lieutenant Maggs."

Maggs's heart stopped beating. He couldn't believe it.

Neither, apparently, could Lanoe.

"Seriously?" he asked.

Chapter Eight

Red hair.

If Lanoe stayed back by the entrance to the cruiser's brig, if he didn't come any closer, the illusion persisted. It could be Zhang. It could be Zhang, come back to him. The girl in there, floating cross-legged in front of one of the cells, could be her.

If she didn't turn around.

If he didn't move. Didn't breathe. Didn't let himself think about it.

"Commander?" she said.

The voice was different. It was Ginger's voice. Softer, less brash than Zhang's. It was enough to break the spell.

He pushed inside the brig, then caught himself on the wall next to her. She had the display up on the cell's hatch, showing the alien inside. Rain-on-Stones was twitching in her sleep, one of her four arms jerking rhythmically. A spiderlike male ran out of her sleeve and sought shelter in the long, rumpled folds of her skirt.

"How is she?" Lanoe asked.

"I'm running low on the sedative. I asked Engineer Paniet to help synthesize some more, but he didn't have the right equipment. Eventually she's going to wake up. That will be...difficult, for both of us."

Lanoe studied the girl's profile. Her face was all wrong, completely unlike Zhang's. It was only the hair that threw him off like that.

"We've made peace with Centrocor. That gives us a carrier, a cruiser, and two destroyers to work with. Most of a carrier group."

Ginger's eyes never left the image of Rain-on-Stones. "That's nice," she said.

"It's crucial," Lanoe told her. "If I'm going to take on an entire alien planet, I need firepower. Massive firepower."

"That makes sense."

The girl's impassivity angered Lanoe, though he wasn't exactly sure why. She had one job to do, and she was doing it—taking care of the sleeping chorister.

"Rain-on-Stones wants this just as much as I do," he said. "The damned jellyfish almost wiped out her entire species. And if we don't do something, now, they'll do the same to humanity. They'll kill every one of us, in time."

Ginger did finally turn to look at him. She didn't seem angry. She didn't look like she was bored with the conversation and wanted him to go away. She just looked tired.

"The Choir hid from the Blue-Blue-White. They hid themselves away inside the walls of existence, where they could wait, and wait, and wait. They didn't want this...campaign of yours. This crusade."

"I'm trying to get justice for them—for all the intelligent species the Blue-Blue-White drove to extinction."

Ginger nodded. "You see? There's the difference."

"I don't understand," Lanoe told her.

"The Choir know something about justice you don't. That it doesn't exist."

～

They wouldn't let Bury fly—not even the short distance from the cruiser to the carrier. "This is all bosh," he said, and smacked the console with the flat of one hand. "This is a damned milk run! I'm more than qualified," he insisted.

Valk's voice came from the controls of the troop transport. The controls that seemed to work themselves. "You're on the inactive list," the AI said, as if that meant anything. Anything at all. "Until you've been declared fit for duty—"

"I'm fine!" Bury said. But he refused to argue further. Instead he climbed down the ladder into the main body of the transport. Because the transport was under acceleration, down was in the direction of the engines, while the small ship's cockpit and its massive shovel-shaped landing hatch were up. The transport was designed to carry twenty marines from a ship down to the surface of a planet. Most of its mass was taken up by a large spherical compartment, its walls lined with rudimentary acceleration couches. Engineer Paniet was sprawled out across three of these, eating shelled pistachios out of a quickplastic bag that dissolved as he worked his way through its contents. He looked up as Bury entered, but didn't say anything.

Good. Bury knew that if the engineer had made some comment, he would have lashed out in rage.

Bury had never been very good at controlling his temper. Now, when he was being unfairly stigmatized, he felt like a seething cauldron of hate.

The transport was headed over to the carrier because Lanoe had called together all of his officers—Navy and Centrocor—for some big briefing. Bury had been told he was allowed to come if he wanted, even though he was not on duty. Valk had made it sound like the high-level officers were being merciful. Like they were doing him a favor.

Bosh! No one had ever done him a damned favor in his life. Ever since he got hit by that missile, ever since he'd been hurt, they'd treated him like he was useless. Deadweight. He was ready to fly. He was ready to fight—but because Lieutenant Candless thought she was his mother or something, he could do nothing but lie in bed in sick bay all day, watching inane video entertainment and playing idiotic games on his minder.

He had to find some way to prove himself. Some way to show them he was ready to go back on the active list.

Not right now, though. Right now he had to find a way to get through this quick voyage without breaking anything. He knew perfectly well that the best way he could prove them *right*, that he wasn't fit to serve, would be to act like he was unstable.

"Where's Ginger?" Engineer Paniet asked. "She's an officer. She should be headed to this shindig, too."

Bury wanted to ask what the hell a "shindig" was. Instead, he forced himself to say through gritted teeth, "She requested to be excused, so she could look after the big bug she has in that holding cell." He had begged her to come with him—pointlessly. In the past she had always been there for him, ready to give him a warning signal if his anger started getting the best of him. Now, though, she seemed more interested in the insectile chorister. It was that thing in her head, that damnable thing Lanoe made her get implanted in her head—

"I doubt she'll miss much. Most likely Lanoe is just going to throw his weight around a little," Engineer Paniet said. "Put on a big tough show for the new folks." The engineer sighed. "Of all the reasons I chose to join the Neddies, escaping all this macho posturing is one I've never regretted."

"They were our enemies yesterday," Bury pointed out. "They need to get the fear of the devil stamped right into them, so they don't think we're weak."

The engineer didn't argue. He shrugged expansively and yawned. "Wake me when we get there," he said.

Bury nodded, mostly to himself. He tried strapping himself in and sitting still, but before long the engineer started to snore. The atonal noise made Bury's nerves itch. So he tore off his restraints and climbed back up to the cockpit, which at least had viewports. He could watch the distant point of light that was the carrier grow, and think about what he was going to do. How he would make them see he was fit.

Four, he thought to himself. It had become a mantra. *Four. Four. Four.*

The number wouldn't stop echoing around his head. Not, he knew, until it turned into five.

Lanoe wished he could have had Valk with him for this briefing. The body that Valk inhabited—the suit with its polarized
helmet—was permanently installed at the controls of the cruiser,
though. Valk hadn't left the workstation in days, and now only
rarely so much as lifted one of his arms. He didn't need to, he'd
told Lanoe—he was plugged directly into the cruiser's systems,
controlling them as if by thought alone.

As a result, Lanoe couldn't bring Centrocor's officers over to
the cruiser—he didn't want them to see Valk, much less figure out
what he was. So instead he had called the first official briefing of
the allied forces together on the bridge of the carrier. A much larger
space anyway, with room for everyone.

When Lanoe arrived at the carrier, Candless was already there,
strapped into the IO's position. She had a dozen displays open,
most of them showing views of the system ahead of them. Lanoe
had thought that perhaps the carrier had better sensors than the
cruiser. That it could locate the planet Lanoe knew had to be there.
The planet Valk and Paniet had failed to locate. As he caught her
eye and raised an eyebrow, though, he already knew he'd been
wrong.

She gave the tiniest shake of her head. A negation. She hadn't
found a planet.

Damnation and hellfire.

He turned and nodded at Captain Shulkin. The man didn't even
seem aware of where he was, much less Lanoe's gesture. Lanoe still
didn't know what to make of the old veteran. Apparently he'd gone
insane back during the Establishment Crisis. The Navy claimed to
have fixed his brain, but the result left something to be desired.

If Shulkin was unresponsive, the Batygins stood in distinct con-
trast. The two of them gave him a cheery wave, their hands moving almost in unison. Beside them stood Lieutenant—formerly
Sergeant—Foulkes, who had been promoted to the position of
the carrier's warrant officer, in charge of all the enlisted marines

aboard. He must have been painfully aware of the price Major Yael had paid to get him that promotion. He looked haunted, but he came to attention quick enough when he saw that Lanoe was looking at him.

There were more Centrocor officers, lots of them. The carrier was home to some three dozen fighter pilots, all of whom were technically officers. There was no room for them on the bridge, however, so they remained in their wardrooms, watching this briefing on a display. Present for the sake of completeness were the carrier's three pilots and two navigators, scared-looking people whose names Lanoe barely remembered. There were three ranking neddies as well, the engineering crew for the carrier, two women and a man with short hair and curious expressions. He expected little trouble from that quarter.

He wished he could say as much about the two people on the other side of the room. Ashlay Bullam and Auster Maggs did their best to blend into the wall of the bridge. Lanoe didn't trust Bullam at all, but he knew how much he needed her, at least as a figurehead. She was the official representative of Centrocor here, and the carrier's people still looked to her for guidance.

Maggs was only still alive because of her. There had been long and tense negotiations back on Caina, but in the end she'd gotten what she wanted. Lanoe got the sense that she almost always did.

She'd even been able to insist that Maggs be present for this briefing. The traitor made a very good show of looking at something on his wrist display, so that he didn't have to meet Lanoe's gaze.

The Centrocor contingent murmured amongst themselves as Lanoe's own officers entered the bridge. Ehta had gathered Paniet and Bury from the flight deck and brought them right on time. The three of them moved quickly to Candless's side, as if they were her honor guard. None of them said a word. They simply watched Lanoe with expectant eyes.

Even though they knew what he was going to say. He'd kept few secrets from his officers so far. He trusted them implicitly. He had to admit it was nice having at least a few people in the room he didn't have to watch like a hawk.

"Commander on the bridge," Candless called out. Some of the Centrocor people came to attention. Some didn't. "Commander Lanoe will present a short briefing. There will be no questions permitted at this time." She turned to him. "Sir?"

Lanoe nodded and pulled a minder out of a pouch at his waist. He unrolled it, then rolled it back up. Just something to do with his hands.

He had always been a fighter pilot first, an officer second. He'd never enjoyed speaking to a crowd. Zhang had always helped him with that. She'd been his wingman and his second in command, his best adviser and his harshest critic. She'd made it possible for him to lead squadrons into battle. Since she'd died, he'd found he had little patience for these kinds of briefings, and even less for the business of command.

That was going to have to change now. When you were surrounded by people you trusted, you could afford to let things slide a little, let your style of command run to the casual—a bit. With this bunch he needed to be as hard as brass. He needed to hold their attention. He needed to convince them of the rightness of his cause—and that he would brook no debate, no dissent.

"Thank you for coming," he said. "I know things are still unsettled with our new arrangement. We're all making adjustments. I want that over with as soon as possible. We're going to work together from here on, because we have a mission to complete. Potentially the most important mission the Navy has ever undertaken."

They started to gape and murmur. That could not be allowed. He made a signal with one hand.

"Quiet on the bridge!" Candless shouted. She glared at the Centrocor people, as if daring them to open their mouths again. Eventually, it worked.

"I'm going to tell you everything," Lanoe said. "I'm going to show you all the data we have so far, and explain what we need to do here. I want to stress one thing, though. This is not a debate. Or a discussion. We have a clear objective to reach in this system. We *will* reach it—together. Anyone who acts contrary to the goals of the mission, or who questions my orders in the slightest way, will be *severely* disciplined."

He unrolled the minder again. Valk had helped him put together a presentation about the Blue-Blue-White, with plenty of visual aids. It was his job to walk them through it.

First, though, he could see he needed to do one thing. He'd shown them the stick, and the Centrocor people looked terrified, or angry, or just confused. He needed them to pay attention, and that meant giving them a glance at the carrot.

"When the mission is complete," Lanoe said, looking around, trying to catch as many eyes as he could, "and only then, we will open a wormhole that will take us all home. That's right. We have the capacity to do that. But it's entirely at my discretion."

He expected them to start shouting then. They didn't. Instead they stared at him, like wanderers in a desert catching their first sight of an oasis.

Maybe they'd all thought they were stranded here. Maybe they just worried that that was the case. He knew it had to have been on all their minds since they first arrived. It was the one thing every one of them wanted, and the promise of going home was going to be the chief thing that motivated them to follow his orders.

"Now," he said. "Let's begin."

~~~

Bury watched the faces of the crowd carefully. He knew where Lanoe was going to start his presentation, and he knew how people would react.

"For thousands of years," Lanoe said, "humanity has wondered if we were alone in the universe. As we expanded across the stars, we found no trace of any other intelligent species—no life at all, other than a few microbes and insects. The worlds we discovered were harsh places, incapable of harboring complex life. This is why we named our new colony planets after old Earth ideas of hell—Avernus, Jehannum, Sheol, and the like. We came to believe that our most pessimistic models were true, that only one planet in the entire galaxy had the necessary conditions for life come together. That Earth was all there was."

Lanoe tapped his minder and an image appeared in the center of the room. It was a still from a low-resolution video. It showed a view of a rocky canyon under a pale blue sky. In the image a few ground vehicles had gathered in the midst of a cloud of yellow dust. Human shapes could be seen through the murk—most of them dead. Towering over them, six meters tall, was a thing with no head or body, just a cluster of legs that each ended in a wicked sharp claw.

One of those legs had impaled a human body. A man with a beard and a look of horror on his face. There was a great deal of blood.

"We were wrong," Lanoe said.

Some of the Centrocor people put hands over their mouths. Two of them—the captains of the destroyers—laughed.

"Impossible."

"Impossible," they said, almost in harmony.

Bury launched himself across the room, breaking through the image. He got right up in the faces of the destroyer captains. "It's true," he said. "Don't you dare question Commander Lanoe. After what he's been through, after what he lost—"

"Enough!" Lieutenant Candless shouted. "Ensign Bury, stand down."

"But they were questioning the commander," Bury insisted. He couldn't see how he was possibly in the wrong here.

"I said *enough*. Don't make me say it again," Candless told him. "As for you two—as for everyone here. There will be no further outbursts. I trust I have made myself adequately clear."

The destroyer captains nodded, but didn't say a word. Bury went back to his position next to her at the IO's station.

"I know it's hard to believe," Lanoe said. "I resisted it for a long time myself. Yet there can no longer be any doubt. This image comes from the planet Niraya. I assume some of you may have heard of the place. It is in fact the location of our first contact with a nonhuman intelligence. A fleet of spacecraft attacked Niraya, intending to kill every human being on the planet with drones like the one in this image. A small squadron of fighters took on that fleet, and we prevailed."

A new image sprang up, this one showing what looked like a small asteroid. One end of the rock had been hollowed out, and long, segmented arms surrounded the opening. A dull red glow could be seen within. Not an asteroid at all, really, Bury knew, but an alien queenship, housed inside a thick skin of cratered rock. In the foreground of the image, small ships wheeled and darted around the asteroidal ship, dwarfed by it but still clearly visible. Some were shapeless but wicked-looking craft, studded with cannons. Others were just spherical pods mounted on skeletal frames. Jets of superhot plasma erupted from the pods, aimed at more recognizable vehicles—BR.9s, and one antique FA.2 fighter.

"It wasn't easy," Lanoe said. "We lost some...some good people." His head swam to think of that. To think of Zhang. He shut that down fast, controlled himself. "But we prevailed. In doing so we learned a great deal about this fleet, and the aliens who'd built it."

The image changed again, fading into a picture of a thing like a fat jellyfish turned on its side. A roughly spherical, semitransparent body, its innards lit up by different colors of light generated by unseen organs. Its circular, toothless mouth was surrounded by a fringe of fifteen slackly hanging tentacles. It looked surprisingly similar to the asteroidal ship from the previous image.

"This thing," Lanoe said, "is why we're here. This image is not to scale. The creature shown here is approximately twenty-five meters in diameter. Despite appearances, it's also intelligent—and an existential threat to the human species."

Lanoe moved around the image, gesturing at it as he spoke. "They don't have a spoken or written language like we do. They communicate by pulsing various colors of light at each other. The name they give themselves can be rendered only as 'Blue-Blue-White.' They live in the atmospheres of gas giant planets and they have a very high level of technology. Considerably higher than ours, we think.

"Half a billion years ago, they decided they wanted to spread out and colonize other planets—other gas giants—around other stars. They built fleets like the one we fought at Niraya and sent them off in every direction. Those fleets were designed to terraform—for lack of a better word—every gas giant in the galaxy, to create new homes for the Blue-Blue-White. To accomplish that task they were given the directive to complete other subobjectives as well. They would make more fleets like themselves, constructing them out of materials mined from terrestrial worlds and rocky moons. They would speak to any intelligent beings they found. And they would take steps to make their work areas efficient and productive. Here's where the problem arose. Part of that last subobjective included eliminating vermin from their factories and marshaling yards. That makes sense, of course. If you're going to build new worlds, you don't want rats chewing through your cables, or insects making nests inside your supply sheds.

"The problem is, the Blue-Blue-White didn't provide their terraforming fleets with a clear definition of what vermin look like. When the drone fleets encountered other life-forms, they simply acted to eliminate them. To kill them. The fleets assumed that any intelligent life would look something like their masters—like giant jellyfish. Instead, they looked more like us.

"The fleet that came to Niraya didn't understand—at all—that we were sapient creatures. They thought we were rats, or mosquitoes, and that we needed to be wiped out. I had to destroy their fleet because there was no way of convincing them otherwise.

"We've since learned a few things about these fleets. For one, that there are a lot of them. As they spread out through the galaxy, each fleet builds additional fleets. Those new fleets go on to build even more. We don't honestly know how many of them are out there right now. We think they number in the millions.

"The other thing we learned is that life is not as rare as we thought. At least it didn't used to be. We have records of hundreds of intelligent species that lived in the galaxy in the past. People, like us—no matter what they looked like. Cultures. Civilizations. Some never made it past their stone ages, while some developed space travel, even starships."

The display changed again, to show the familiar image of the Milky Way galaxy, with its super-bright center and its spiral arms. Individual stars in the image flared and lit up one by one, and then faded away again.

"The Blue-Blue-White's fleets exterminated them. All those planets, all those people—gone. We're talking about genocide on a cosmic scale. There is no way to know for sure, but we estimate that the Blue-Blue-White are responsible for the deaths of trillions of intelligent beings. Trillions.

"All because of a glitch. A bug. A line of code missing from a program—all because the Blue-Blue-White couldn't imagine intelligent life looking like anything other than themselves.

"There is no doubt that this is the single greatest crime committed in the history of the galaxy. There is no doubt in my mind that the Blue-Blue-White are guilty.

"It's possible that some of you don't care. Maybe you think we aren't responsible for all those dead aliens. People we never met are hard to care about. Hard to even imagine in any kind of serious way.

"I can understand that, even if I think it's a callous and cynical attitude."

Bury almost laughed at that. He controlled himself—the last thing he needed was Lieutenant Candless disciplining him yet again.

"Let me, then, make one thing clear," Lanoe said. "The fleet we fought at Niraya was not the last of them. As I said, there are millions of them out there. They work their way across the galaxy, one star at a time. Soon one of those fleets is going to come for Avernus, say. Or Adlivun. Or Irkalla. In fact, over time, every single system that humanity has colonized will be attacked. Even Earth itself is not exempt. The fleets do not stop coming. They can be resisted, but they cannot be deterred. If we don't find a way to stop them, permanently, they will continue to be a threat to humanity for all eternity. And eventually—inevitably—they will win.

"If we don't do something about this, right now, we are ignoring the thing that will exterminate the human race."

There was a fair amount of noise, a babble of people talking amongst themselves. A few shouted questions. Lanoe ignored it all. Candless gave him a meaningful look, but he shook his head. No need to have her shout these people down, not this time. He let the murmuring die out on its own.

"Every alien species we might have met, every alien species we could have learned from, traded with, counted as allies—gone. A galaxy wiped clean of life. Sterilized. Nothing remains of all those cultures. Not so much as ruins on some desolate moon, no trace of their written history. The Blue-Blue-White murdered every intelligent species that we know to exist.

"All but two."

On the image of the galaxy, two stars lit up—one of which was the sun, the star that nurtured humanity. The other was an unassuming dwarf about a thousand light-years from Earth.

"You all know this one, that's ours. The other one belongs to a species called the Choir, a species we just recently made contact with. The Choir are barely hanging on by a thread—the Blue-Blue-White killed all but a handful of them. It was the Choir who created the wormhole that brought us here. They have that ability. They have the ability to take us home. I have, on my Hoplite, a chorister—that's the singular noun for their species. I brought her along to witness what we're going to do here.

"And that's the question, isn't it? I'm sure you've all wondered. You've listened to my story of tragedy on a colossal scale, and now you want to know what I intend to do about it.

"First off, I came here. To the right place. We have it on good authority that this system, here near the center of the galaxy, is the home of the Blue-Blue-White. I have tracked the dragon to its lair.

"The next step is to make demands. I have onboard my ship computer files that detail the language of the Blue-Blue-White. I intend to make contact with them. Perhaps they can be reasoned with. Perhaps we can convince them we are intelligent beings. Perhaps they can recall their fleets, or at least reprogram them so that they stop trying to kill us all. Maybe that's all it takes. A little talking.

"But maybe not. Maybe they won't listen. Maybe the Blue-Blue-White won't even acknowledge us as worth talking to.

"If that's the case, I intend to *make* them listen to our demands. I intend to show them that we cannot be ignored.

"We have a carrier, a cruiser, two destroyers. Almost a full carrier group. Dozens of cataphracts and carrier scouts. We have some of the best pilots the Navy ever trained.

"In the past, we—I—have gone to war with less. And I have prevailed.

"I will take the fight to these damned jellyfish. I will not relent. I will be terrible in my wrath.

"Terrible in my vengeance.

"Because make no mistake," he said, and straightened out his spine. Lifted his chin. "This is about revenge. It is about justice, and retribution. Those trillions of lives lost—the future of human-ity at stake—these things demand an answer.

"I am going to get one, no matter what it takes. And you—everyone listening to me now—are going to assist me with that.

"Thank you," Lanoe said. "Dismissed."

He kicked away from the console, headed toward the open hatchway. Intending to return to the cruiser. He had many things to do. People shouted at him—some jeering, some asking honest questions. Some, a very few, applauding and cheering. Candless shouted at them to leave him alone as they reached for him, trying to grab his sleeve, trying to get in front of him to block his way.

Most of them backed down when Candless turned her acid tongue on them. Those who didn't, Lanoe simply pushed aside. He didn't bother noting who they were.

—✦—

Candless collected the officers from the cruiser and formed an honor guard to get Lanoe back down to the flight deck. Together they hurried down a long hallway, eyes watching them from every hatch. Bury kicked alongside the old man, biting his lip as he tried not to say anything.

He was still Bury, of course, and so that didn't last.

"Sir, I just want to say—"

Lanoe turned and looked at him with one cold eye.

Bury wouldn't be taken aback, though. Not now. Not when so much was at stake. "I have to say that was the most stirring speech I've ever heard."

"Sure," Lanoe said.

"I want you to know you can count on me. I'll follow you through the gates of hell, if that's what it takes."

"Good."

Bury felt the blood rushing to his cheeks. "Look, I just want you to know I'm ready to fly, and—"

"You don't need to," Lanoe told him.

"I...I'm sorry?"

The commander sighed. "Candless makes up the duty rosters. She has you down as inactive, for medical reasons. Back when it was just us, I needed every pilot I could get my hands on, wounded or not. That isn't the case anymore. I just drafted a couple dozen new ones."

"But—sir—I want to fight!"

Lanoe nodded at him. "Commendable spirit, but completely unnecessary. You really want to help out? I'll give you a bridge position. You can be Valk's IO. You can serve with honor and not worry about aggravating your injuries."

Bury was so surprised—and so horrified—he couldn't even splutter in response.

"It comes with a promotion, Lieutenant Bury," Lanoe went on. "You've got to like that. In fact, I'm going to promote all of you—I don't want Centrocor's people ordering you around. So, Ehta, you go up to major. Candless, I'm making you a captain. If we keep doing this, you'll outrank me soon."

"I can think of a few orders I'd give you straightaway," the newly elevated Captain Candless told him. Bury knew her well enough to tell she didn't think much of her new rank, though he couldn't say why. "Unless you're declaring yourself a rear admiral, while you're at it."

Lanoe smiled at her. "Maybe I should just stick with commodore, since I've got my own little fleet now," he said. With a start, Bury realized they were joking with each other.

"Paniet," Lanoe said, turning to the engineer. "I'm embarrassed to admit—I don't even know how ranks work in the Neddies. You're just called an engineer currently, right?"

Bury's chest hurt. He couldn't breathe. He'd just been stabbed in the back, and they were all just nattering on. How could they—

"Yes, dearie," Paniet said. "If you bump me up one rank that'll make me an engineer-captain, second class." The neddy shrugged. "We're all boffins in the NED. We just love making things more complicated than necessary."

"Hold on," Bury said. "I mean, that's all very exciting, but—but—damn you, sir!"

They had come up to the hatch that led to the flight deck. Lanoe stopped now and looked at Bury with a towering and chilly regard.

Hellfire, Bury thought. He'd really stepped in it now. You didn't say things like that to a commander, not if you wanted to have a career in the Navy. "I beg your pardon, sir—if I misspoke there. It's just because I'm so eager to fly a cataphract in your service. I think that back in the last battle I acquitted myself well, and I believe I can accomplish even more if you *just give me a chance.*"

"You're young, Bury," Lanoe said. "You'll have plenty of chances to fight. For now, listen to your teacher. She has your best interests at heart."

"Former teacher," Candless insisted. "And clearly not a very good one, given that I never beat that insolent manner out of you. You're disgracing me, right now."

Bile surged up Bury's throat. But even he could admit—sometimes—when he was beaten.

"Yes, sir. Yes, ma'am. My most abject apologies."

"I'm letting this go," Lanoe said. "You were riled up by my big speech, let's chalk it up to that. From this point on, try to lay off the insubordination. Now, as for the rest of us—we need to get back to the cruiser. There's a planet to be found if I'm actually going to live up to all the promises I just made. Paniet, Ehta, you take Bury back in the transport. I have my own BR.9 here—I'll head back on my own."

"My BR.9 is here as well," Captain Candless said.

"Sure," Lanoe said, "and that's where it's going to stay. I need you here on the carrier."

"Sir," Captain Candless said. "I'm afraid I didn't understand that last order. Perhaps you'd be kind enough to elaborate on it."

Bury had been around her long enough to know the look on her face. It was one he'd always tried to avoid—a look of pure distaste, like she'd smelled something awful.

Lanoe just nodded, though, as if he'd taken what she said literally. "I don't trust anyone on this tub. Bullam and Maggs are probably conspiring to have me killed right now. Shulkin's a zombie when he's not a maniac. As for the IO, I'm still not convinced he isn't a Centrocor spy. I need someone over here that I can trust, and that means you. Watch them for me. Make sure that when they surrendered, they actually meant it. Got it?"

Candless's lips turned white as she pressed them together. Somehow she managed to get an answer through them. "Sir," she said.

"Good. Everybody else—I'll see you back home." Then he ducked into the airlock for his docking berth and was gone.

Bury stared at the hatch for a while. Unable to believe it.

He'd been grounded. That was exactly what this amounted to. Working as Valk's IO? Why exactly would an artificial intelligence, a being of pure information, need an information officer?

He'd had his wings clipped. Lanoe had no confidence in him.

No one seemed to care.

"I just got a promotion," Ehta said. She grabbed Paniet in a tight hug. "Major Ehta, what do you think of that?" the marine asked the engineer.

"I think it'll look lovely on your cryptab," the engineer-captain, second class told her. "And ooh, I think I just went up a pay grade! How delicious!"

Bury wanted to run at them and smash their damned faces. Instead he turned and looked at Captain Candless. He thought—maybe—he saw a little something there. Not exactly sympathy. He didn't know if she was capable of that emotion. Empathy, maybe. If he'd been grounded, she'd just been exiled. Maybe she knew exactly how he felt.

"I wouldn't order new stationery just yet if I were you," she said to the others. "He can throw around all the promotions he likes—it doesn't matter. This is no longer an official Navy mission. The Admiralty didn't sign off on any of Lanoe's big plans. I suppose we shouldn't mention that to the Centrocor contingent. But it does mean absolutely none of these new titles will stick once we get back to civilization."

She flipped around and kicked back up the hall, in the direction of the carrier's bridge.

"If it was your birthday," Major Ehta grumbled, "she'd be the one to tell you how many calories there were in the damned cake."

⟶ ⟶

Red hair. Again.

Lanoe hovered in the hatchway to the brig, saying nothing. Pretending. Again.

The last time he'd seen her, Zhang had worn her hair up in two small buns on top of her head. He wondered what Ginger would look like if she did that. Female pilots always kept their hair short—in the absence of gravity, long hair had a bad habit of getting in your face. Ginger's had grown out a little. Maybe she would cut it soon.

He closed his eyes. Squeezed them tightly shut. This was wrong, he knew. He shouldn't be wallowing in these memories. He should let Zhang go.

The only woman he'd ever loved, really. In three hundred years there had been others. Plenty of them. None like Zhang. When he'd been with her, he'd felt complete. Like the thing that had been missing all his life was finally there. He could talk to Zhang about anything. He spent so much of his life being a hardass, shutting out fear and anxiety and even compassion. Making hard choices, doing bad things. Around Zhang, he had been... not a different person. Still Aleister Lanoe. But with her near—and only when she was near—that had been okay. She had believed in him. Trusted him, as no one else ever could, and he had trusted her.

Now she was gone. She was never coming back.

He opened his eyes.

Red hair. He felt an immense urge to reach out and touch it. Run his fingers through it, see if it felt the same.

That, of course, would be highly inappropriate. He was immediately disgusted with himself just for having the urge. He started to turn, intending to go. To get away from Zhang—from Ginger.

But then she spoke.

"It's almost gone," she said.

"I'm sorry?"

She didn't turn around. If she would just turn around, if he saw her face, it would be easier. "The sedative that Rain-on-Stones brought with her."

Floating next to Ginger's elbow was an octagonal case made of thin plates of stone. Its surface was intricately carved with geometric patterns. Its lid was open, and inside Lanoe could see neatly stacked instruments, some of which he recognized—scalpels, retractors, surgical tools—and some that were completely foreign to him, including a ball of what looked like cut bone, its surface so heavily carved it looked like it was perforated. Ginger reached inside and took out a long, curved syringe. Through a window set into its side Lanoe could see a few cubic centimeters of coral-colored liquid.

"How long, do you think?" Lanoe asked.

"Ten days, maybe, if I ration it. Then she'll start to wake up. Slowly, at first—she'll be groggy for a long time. She'll also be alone."

"No," Lanoe said. "You'll be here for her."

"That's not enough," Ginger said.

Lanoe squirmed inside his suit. There was a lot he didn't understand about the Choir, or about what had happened to Ginger. "Is it safe?" he asked. "Keeping her asleep so long?"

"You're only asking now?" Ginger shrugged her slim shoulders. Her age—or lack of it—wasn't lost on him, even if she was acting like someone much older. "It's safe enough. When one of the Choir is injured, the rest put them to sleep like this for the whole time it takes them to recover. They couldn't handle it otherwise. They can't block out each other's thoughts or feelings, you see. If one of them breaks a leg, every single one of them feels the agony."

"Hellfire," Lanoe said.

"Will you help me give her the shot?"

"Sure," he said.

Ginger opened the hatch and they stepped inside the repurposed detaining cell. Rain-on-Stones was strapped down to a long padded bench. He'd forgotten how big the choristers were, and how gangly. She was half again as tall as he was, but as he put his hands on two of the alien's shoulders he felt how thin she was under her dress. Mostly just arms and legs, jointed appendages connecting to a central trunk no thicker than a human thigh. Her long, cylindrical head slumped over to one side as he held her down. The ring of eyes that ran around the middle of her head didn't open.

She twitched in her troubled sleep. Tried to roll over. Lanoe redoubled his grip and pressed down, keeping her still.

"Be careful. Don't crush any of her males," Ginger said.

"Don't worry. I don't want to touch any of those things."

"She's different from us," Ginger said. "That doesn't make her repellent, Lanoe. If you could see through their eyes...But you don't want that, do you? You need to keep your distance."

Lanoe sighed. He considered telling her to call him "Commander." Ginger was still a Naval ensign, no matter what else she'd become. Instead, he said, "I understand that you're angry with me."

"You lied to her, and to me. You made a deal with them—a promise—and then you broke it."

"The deal was to give you to them. Like some kind of human sacrifice. Don't tell me that you wanted to go live with the Choir for the rest of your life. I won't believe it."

"No," she admitted. "I was afraid. But I understood why it was necessary. I saw the damage we'd already done to their harmony. It'll be generations before they have peace again, maybe hundreds of years before they—"

"You're right," he said, interrupting. "I don't want to know. I need to keep a certain distance. I think you understand why."

She didn't speak to that. Instead she braced herself against a wall of the cell and laid the syringe against Rain-on-Stones's chest. Then she slid the long, thick needle in between two of the chorister's scalelike plates. It seemed to take a very long time until Lanoe heard a tiny pop, a sound he was sure indicated that the needle had entered Rain-on-Stones's protected flesh.

There was no plunger in the syringe. Instead it had a leverlike handle, too long and thin to be comfortable in a human hand. Ginger grunted in exertion as she squeezed it. The fluid shot up the tube.

Under Lanoe's hands, the alien relaxed almost instantly, her bony arms sagging. He could hear her breathing through spiracles under her dress. Each breath grew longer and shallower as the drug took effect.

"There," Ginger said. "Thank you."

"Sure," Lanoe told her. "So I made my big speech. Told everyone what we're doing here."

Ginger sounded uninterested, but she was still mostly human. "Oh?" she asked, perhaps just to be polite. "How'd it go over?"

"Pretty well, I think. Centrocor's people didn't come here because they wanted to kill us, not really. They were in it for a paycheck. I can't offer them money, but when I promised to take them home, they settled down fast."

Ginger lifted her head, just a little. As if she'd smelled something rotten. "Home," she said.

"I need you to take good care of her," Lanoe said, gesturing at the alien. "When she wakes up, we're all going to be counting on you. From what I've seen, you can handle it, but if you need help, just ask Paniet and we'll—"

"Home," Ginger said again. "You told them that. But you must know...one chorister all alone can't—"

"Don't say it out loud," he told her. "Anyone could be listening."

Chapter Nine

If they were resolved to bring Earth's finest military might against an alien planet, there was still something missing from the equation. Said planet.

Candless had failed to find anything big enough to earn the name, even with the carrier's impressive suite of sensors and telescopes. That wasn't saying all that much, however. The little human fleet was still fifty AUs from the red dwarf. A distance of some seven and a half billion kilometers. At that distance even a planet the size of Jupiter would appear as no more than one dull star amidst the cosmic panoply. Picking its light out from the crowd of stars in the sky might just be a matter of luck.

So she worked with Giles, the carrier's IO, through two straight shifts—fine-tuning the equipment, establishing an interferometry network with whole waves of microdrones, poring over imagery until her eyes ached. She knew she was mostly repeating work that Valk and Paniet had already done, but she knew Lanoe wouldn't be satisfied until he had a result he could use.

Even if there wasn't one. The idea that they might be in the wrong place occurred to her early. And often. She'd had relatively little interaction with the Choir—Lanoe and Valk had worked more closely with them, and then at the end, Ginger. The better part of her knowledge of choristers was the fact that they made her skin crawl. They were aliens, though, which meant their thought processes were unlike those of humans.

"One wonders," she said, speaking to Lanoe over communications laser after a long hour of paging through telescope views, "if they even sent us to the right place. I don't remember you asking them for a specific destination. You asked them to open a wormhole, any wormhole that would let us get away from Centrocor. You've been assuming they gave you the wormhole you wanted the most. Perhaps they merely wished to be rid of us. After how shabbily you treated them, I wouldn't be surprised."

"This is the right system. My plan had been to open a wormhole between the Admiralty and the homeworld of the Blue-Blue-White. I discussed that with them a couple times," he replied. "They knew where I wanted to go. Where I needed to go. As to whether they sent us the wrong way on purpose—in the end, it wasn't me who convinced them to open the wormhole. That was Ginger, and they like her just fine."

Candless sighed and pinched the bridge of her nose. It helped a little with the eyestrain. "Lanoe, there will come a point where we have to accept the obvious. There are no gas giant planets in this system. There's no place where one could be hiding."

"There's an answer. We just haven't found it yet."

"Your obsession," she told him, "is blinding you. But all right. We'll keep looking. I have one more idea."

She cut off the connection and turned to face Giles. "Get me six pilots. We'll send out some scouts."

The carrier was considerably larger than the cruiser and therefore had room for any number of pieces of equipment that could not be shoehorned into the Hoplite. Among these things were a full dozen carrier scouts, tiny one-person spacecraft, lighter and slightly faster than a cataphract, little more than a seat with an engine and a single PBW cannon. They lacked a proper fighter's armament and any airfoils. Most important, they did not carry a vector field, meaning they were much more susceptible to damage and absolutely useless in a dogfight. Because their engines did not need to support the field or heavy weapons, however, they could run for days without needing to refuel.

The proper use of carrier scouts was to send them forward into a battle area where they could see what was happening, then have them run back to their carrier to report. A commander would have to be desperate to actually make them stand and fight—which meant it happened all the time. Space battles always ended in desperation. Assigning someone to fly a carrier scout was a clear indication you considered them expendable. When the six pilots who came and lined up for Candless's inspection heard that they were not being sent on a suicide mission, they looked as much relieved as confused.

"All I want is deep reconnaissance," she told them. "We'll send you out on a standard radial course. Four of you will come at the star from different directions. One up over the star's north pole, one over its south pole. Keep your sensors at full gain. Make a good solid sweep, then return. I need good, clear imagery. That's all. If," she said, and smiled to try to indicate that she was joking, "you do meet any enemy resistance, don't engage. Break off and return as fast as you can."

None of them seemed to think that was funny.

Well, Candless had never been very good at smiling. Maybe she'd done it wrong.

Paniet floated outside the cruiser's front section, beckoning to an oncoming ship. The carrier had sent over a vehicle to help him. The bigger ship contained a multitude of small craft, not just warships but ancillary craft as well, like troop transports, M. Bullam's personal yacht, and—most exciting for the engineer—a Helead-class repair tender. Not much to look at to the untrained eye, just a framework of girders with a thruster package on one end, but its open construction contained a surprising variety of heavy tools that it could extend on jointed arms. Today, Paniet intended to use its heavy laser cutter for a task he found decidedly bittersweet.

As the ugly little ship moved into position on puffs of gas released from its myriad of tiny thrusters, Paniet waved it in with a hand lamp.

"You don't need to do that," Valk told him. "I can guide it in a lot more precisely than any human pilot."

"Ducks, you will not take *all* the fun out of my job," Paniet told the AI. "I intend to earn my engineer-captain's pay today. Anyway, haven't you better things to do?"

"Not really. Flying the cruiser takes about three percent of my processor capacity, especially when all I'm doing is station-keeping. Lanoe took me off the search for the planet."

"A task I'm glad to hand off," Paniet told him. "Let Candless worry about the snipe hunt. The cruiser needs these repairs, rather desperately, and now's the time to get it done. Now when—finally—nobody is shooting at us."

Valk laughed. "It's been a while, hasn't it? But you don't think—I mean, has Lanoe lost faith in us? Is that why he reassigned us?"

Paniet sighed. Living and working with Valk had been a sort of master class in artificial intelligence research. Given the fact that there weren't any other AIs to study, Paniet had probably become the greatest living expert in the subject. He'd figured out some of Valk's psychology—if that was even the word for it—and he knew how desperate the AI was to please Lanoe.

It made sense, of course. Valk had believed he was a human being for the first seventeen years after he was switched on. He still had the memories of the dead man who was his progenitor. He very much wanted to be human, to have normal human relationships, but once he'd learned his true nature, that was no longer an option. Hated and shunned just for what he was, he was desperate for any kind of human warmth or affection. Valk would do anything Lanoe asked, do anything at all to please the commander. And of course Lanoe knew it. He constantly pushed Valk to stretch his capacities, to find new ways to be useful. Every time Valk did pull off some new miracle, though, it made him just a little less human. A little less normal. Which alienated him from everyone else even more than before.

"He needs you, still," Paniet said. "You're the only one that can talk to the Blue-Blue-White."

Depressingly, that fact seemed to cheer Valk quite a bit. "I guess so, huh?"

"Assuming we find them." Paniet saw a fellow neddy in the exposed pilot's seat of the repair tender and gave him a cheery wave. The Centrocor engineer fired one last burn of his ship's maneuvering jets and it came to a halt, taking up a stable position next to the cruiser.

Paniet touched the virtual keyboard on his wrist display and a long arm craned outward from the tender. At the end of the arm sat a hemispherical pod that looked like a searchlight with multiple lenses on its face. Paniet grasped the pod by a manual aiming handle and lined it up with the side of the cruiser.

"This isn't going to hurt you, is it?" he asked Valk. Though the AI retained the space suit that had been his body for seventeen years, he had in some ways outgrown it. He was so deeply connected to the cruiser's systems now that it might be more accurate to say that the entire ship was Valk's body now.

"No," the AI said, laughing. "No, I don't exactly have nerve endings up there."

Paniet nodded to himself. Then he activated the cutting laser and let its beam bite deep into the side of the cruiser.

In their very first scrape with Centrocor, a lucky shot with a disruptor round had torn through the entire forward third of the cruiser. It had blasted its way through the ship's bridge and its officers' quarters, rendering those areas unusable. Further battles and desperate maneuvers had only put additional strain on the damaged area, until there were entire bulkheads and structural spars up there that were hanging on by threads. Paniet was a little surprised that the entire section hadn't just torn off and fallen away on its own.

He'd repaired what he could, but mostly that had meant sealing off cracks and rerouting power lines. At the time he hadn't
had access to the tools to do a proper repair job, and as a result
the damage had simply gotten worse and worse. Now, as much as
it offended his engineer's sensibilities, he'd decided to accept the
inevitable.

He was going to cut the cruiser's head off and break the whole
section down for spare parts. There were other damaged sections of
the ship that could be saved, or at least jury-rigged back together, if
he just had the right raw materials.

The laser was invisible in the vacuum of space. Paniet could only
tell that it was working when he saw structural members and bundles of cables split apart, seemingly for no reason. Little by little
the beam of coherent light dug a deep trench into the side of the
cruiser, without so much as a flame or a puff of smoke. It was a
kind of magic, the kind he loved, even if it caused his soul a little
pain to see such a lovely ship decapitated.

"What...what if we don't?" Valk asked.

"Sorry? I'm a trifle busy," Paniet told him. Though to be fair, the
cutting process was fully automatic and he didn't need to even be
there, unless something went wrong. "I'm not sure what you—"

"You said, 'Assuming we find them.' Meaning the Blue-Blue-White."

"I suppose I did," Paniet said. The laser sliced through one of
the cruiser's main support beams and the entire forward section
lurched, just a hair. Paniet's body tensed, but then nothing further
happened, and he relaxed again.

"You aren't sure that we're even in the right system," Valk said.
"It's something I've contemplated myself. I...I don't like to doubt
Lanoe, but, well. We both know there are no planets here. What do
you think will happen if it turns out he's wrong? If this system is
uninhabited?"

The laser cut into a section of padded wall that had somehow
survived largely intact. Fluffy clouds of insulation burst from the
incision, some of them vaporizing as they crossed the laser's path,
others twisting away into the void. Paniet considered carefully

what he was going to say next. He knew full well that anything he said to Valk might get back to Lanoe.

"I doubt he'll accept the data, no matter how exhaustive it gets," he said. "I think he'll order us to keep looking. In time, maybe, he'll realize the Choir sent him down the wrong path, but long before then—I don't know. My bigger concern is what everyone else will do if that happens."

"You're thinking that they'll mutiny. Turn on Lanoe."

"My job description, dearie, does not include guessing which way other people are going to jump. But I can imagine that the Centrocor contingent, especially, will grow frustrated. They're chastened, for now. But we need to give them something to do or they'll start to wonder why they're here."

"I'm sure Lanoe has already considered that," Valk said. "He must have some kind of contingency plan ready. Most likely he'll just take us home, then. Better to admit defeat and try again some later day."

Paniet was...not as certain as the AI. The Aleister Lanoe he'd met at Tuonela had seemed a reasonable sort. The kind of man who was always considering the angles, always planning three moves ahead.

Over time, though, the mission had definitely changed the commander. Paniet had tried to counsel Lanoe a few times. To give him an engineer's perspective on things, or simply provide good advice. Every time, Lanoe had thanked him kindly for his opinion, then completely ignored it. Lanoe might have been a great leader once, but his obsession with hunting down the Blue-Blue-White had pushed him to make risky decisions. He'd put his own crew in real jeopardy many times rather than give up the slightest advance toward his goal.

Paniet had been in the Neddies long enough to have served under many different commanding officers. He'd learned early on that there were some you could trust, people who had your welfare as their first priority. Then there were those who clearly felt the fight was the thing, and that people were just numbers on a spreadsheet, columns of figures to be shuffled around and deleted as necessary. For officers like that, defeat wasn't a possibility. There was always some way to make the equation work out—no matter who got hurt.

Officers of that second sort, the driven ones, the ambitious, were dangerous. Every time Paniet had found himself under the command of such a person before, he'd found some way to get transferred to a different unit.

That wasn't an option now.

"I'm sure Lanoe will do the smart thing," he said. He hoped very much that Valk didn't have a way to tell that he was lying.

The laser finished cutting and shut itself down. Paniet checked it carefully to make sure it was switched off, then flew around the cruiser in a tight circle, looking to make sure the cut was complete. He found a few places where strands of carbon fiber had been left untouched, stretched across the thin gap of the cut. He cut those with a handheld plasma torch, then used his suit jets to zip back, away from the cruiser. He wanted to be well clear for the next part.

"Okay, love," he said to Valk. "We're ready. Take the cruiser back. Dead slow, now. Just ease it out of the way."

"Got it," Valk said.

Along the long flank of the cruiser tiny panels opened up, revealing the nozzles of positioning jets. They twisted around until they were all facing the same way, then released a single sigh of exhaust gas.

The cruiser drifted backward, so slowly it didn't seem to move at all. Paniet felt, instead, that he and the cutoff forward section were moving, and he felt the sudden urge to grab something and hold on.

After a few minutes the cruiser was clear of the severed junk. Paniet flew over to examine the front end of the sawn-off ship. The laser had cut so cleanly that it had left a perfectly smooth face on the cruiser, almost as shiny as a mirror. For a moment he simply admired his own handiwork. A job well done was, of course, its own reward.

There was still plenty to do. Paniet needed to break down the severed section into raw materials, backbreaking work that would take a crew of neddies the better part of a week. As for the cruiser, he wanted to put a layer of armor on top of that smooth face. A number of sensor pods had been located in the forward section, and he would need to find replacements for those, and good places to mount them. Finally he would need to test the cruiser's stability in its new configuration, exhaustively monitor all of its functions to make sure he hadn't accidentally severed something important.

It looked like his work was cut out for him. That was good. It would help him not think about anything else.

There was an enormous amount of disorganized gas and dust in the system, most of it in a thick belt around the red dwarf. Close in, where it was hard to see. There were all the objects that Paniet and Valk had already cataloged. Candless had taken one look at the database they'd made and then rejected it as useless—there was nothing in there big enough to serve as a base of operations, especially not for life-forms as big as the Blue-Blue-White.

Her scouts had failed to find any miraculously hidden planets.

There were a few possibilities left, hypotheticals to explore. It was possible that the Blue-Blue-White were in the system, but hidden away in some kind of incredibly dark structure, something with an albedo so low that it didn't register against the black of the void. Perhaps something shrouded by a coating of carbon nanotubules, the darkest substance possible. Yet such a structure would generate heat, and some of that heat would be expressed in the form of infrared radiation. The carrier's sensors had failed to pick up any such signature, which meant—

"Ma'am?"

Candless swiped away one of her displays. The carrier's yeoman was floating just beside her elbow. A mousy woman with brown hair coiled atop her head. She was responsible for administration and accounting aboard the carrier. For the moment, she had a hopeful look on her face.

Candless scowled at her. "Yes, what is it?" she demanded.

"I just need someone to sign off on today's duty roster," the YN explained. She held up a minder showing a list of names that Candless barely recognized.

"This is something you thought I could help you with, clearly. Just as clearly, you're wrong," Candless said. "I'm not in command of this ship. You want Captain Shulkin."

The YN grimaced. "Sorry to bother you, ma'am, but anyone of your rank can sign off, it's really just a formality, and—"

Candless looked down her nose at the woman and gave her a long, hard stare. Then she reached over and pressed her thumb to the screen of the minder. At least the YN was smart enough to leave without saying anything more.

Now, Candless thought. *Back to the possibilities.* A second explanation for the lack of planets might simply be that they had arrived too late. The Blue-Blue-White had sent their fleets out across the galaxy some half a billion years ago. A great deal could happen in such a length of time. It was possible the jellyfish had gone extinct. Perhaps they'd destroyed themselves, or fallen prey to some cataclysm, something so dire it had left the system devoid not only of life, but of planets, too.

As Candless organized her thoughts, she noted there were two subpossibilities there. One was that the Blue-Blue-White had survived, but moved on. The purpose of their construction fleets had been to create new habitable worlds for them to colonize. Perhaps they had simply all vacated their home system. Perhaps they had grown tired of the star that birthed them, and chosen to find greener pastures.

Subpossibility two was that the Blue-Blue-White had been wiped out, but not by a natural cause. Perhaps the very fleets they had sent out to do their bidding had returned here—and decided that their own creators were vermin, like everyone else. Or perhaps Lanoe was simply late to the party. Perhaps some other intelligent species had gotten here first—looking for their own revenge. Perhaps—

"Excuse me, ma'am?"

Candless groaned in frustration as she pushed her display to the side. "Out with it, now."

This time it was Lieutenant Foulkes, the carrier's new warrant officer and chief of its marines. "One of my people's gone south," he said. He looked distinctly embarrassed. As he should, she thought. "He's sealed himself inside his bunk—he was one of the marines who fought your boarding party, and he refuses to believe there won't be any reprisals. Thinks you're going to shoot him the second he appears for duty."

Candless waited to hear how this was her problem. Her patience was not rewarded.

"That's something you should handle directly," she told him.

"I just hoped—ma'am, if you would speak to him personally—"

"Stop that."

"I beg your pardon, ma'am? Stop what?"

"Hoping. Do your job, WO. Tell him that if he reports to his station immediately, he can count on only light discipline. If he misses a work shift, cut off the life support to his bunk. He'll come out fast enough once he can't breathe."

"I..."

"I am not psychic, and I cannot predict the future," she told him. "However, I can tell you this. The next words you will speak are 'Yes, ma'am.' As in 'Yes, ma'am, I will follow your orders without question.'"

"Yes, ma'am, but—"

"Without question," Candless reiterated. Then she brought her display up to get back to work.

The main problem with the possibilities she had identified was that there was little evidence for any of them. A catastrophe on a scale that would remove planets from the system should leave some sign. Yet the red dwarf looked normal enough, and—

"I'm sorry to bother you again, ma'am, but—"

It was the yeoman. Again. Candless swiped at her displays and gave the woman the look it had taken decades in the classroom to perfect. A withering storm of glares, a facial expression of pure, fatal venom.

"You have one chance to explain why you value my time so little," Candless told the YN. "One chance."

Whatever trivial errand the yeoman had brought with her was forgotten. She lowered her minder and hung there openmouthed, her skin growing paler as Candless watched. Clearly she understood the gravity of the situation.

In a small voice she said, "I'm sorry. It's just that Captain Shulkin, well, he—he—he's not exactly detail-oriented. He just ignores me most of the time. When he even so much as looks at me, he scares me so badly I just want to run away."

"I see," Candless told her.

"I know you're busy, and I don't want to get off on a bad footing when we're just starting to work together, but—"

"I see that I have a task that I must complete here, if I'm going to accomplish anything."

"A . . . task?"

"Yes. I'm going to have to make it my special mission to convince you and your fellow officers of one simple truth. An undeniable fact. The fact that whatever you may think of your commanding officer—I am far, far more terrifying. Furthermore, because you've interrupted me twice now, needlessly, I am going to start establishing this fact by making an example of *you*."

—◂———

"You've done some good work here, love," Paniet said. "Time to take a break." To help with the work on the cruiser he'd requisitioned all the neddies from the Centrocor ships, most of whom had turned out to be useless. He'd been toiling away with one of the exceptions, a neddy from one of the destroyers, for a good six hours, and he could use a bit of a rest himself.

The neddy, whose name was Hollander, nodded agreeably. "I wouldn't mind getting some solid food down my gullet, 'strue." He stowed a rotary grinder back in its charging station and followed Paniet to an airlock at the aft of the cruiser. Together they kicked down a short hallway into the main engineering station, little more than a junction of inspection passages inside the drive shielding. Paniet had to keep ducking his head to avoid hitting it on one wall or another, but Hollander didn't seem to have any trouble with the confined space.

"I've been cooped up in that rat's den of a Peltast so long, this here feels like infinite space, neh?" Hollander said when Paniet remarked on his lack of claustrophobia. "Must say, it's nice getting away from my own stink for a sec."

Paniet grabbed a pair of food tubes from a dispenser and tossed one spinning in Hollander's direction. "You're from Hades, is that right?"

Hollander caught the spinning tube with one hand. "Yeah, can ye tell?" He laughed and ripped open the wrong end of the tube, then squeezed it hard to send all of the reconstituted food into his mouth in one go. "Is it the accent, or my rugged good looks?"

Paniet gave him a knowing smile. "Ex-Navy, too, unless I miss my guess." Hollander nodded again, too busy swallowing to answer. Paniet knew that most of the crew of the carrier and the destroyers were former Navy personnel. Centrocor, like all of the polys, traditionally crewed its ships with militia drawn from the civilian population. Navy pilots scoffed at the militias, and often with good reason—they got very little training before they were thrown into the field, where they typically died quickly. The polys considered their militias expendable. There were always more recruits available.

Unlike the other development monopolies, Centrocor had been running a secret program for years now, identifying and recruiting people who had been discharged or drummed out of the Navy. It didn't seem to matter to the poly why a given person had been cut loose—they took criminals and invalids alike, anything to bolster their ranks. Even Captain Shulkin was one of these hand-me-downs. The idea, of course, was to gain the benefit of Naval training without having to pay for it. The program worked—otherwise the battle between Lanoe and Shulkin would have been over after the first salvo.

"You want to know why I left the triple eagle behind," Hollander said.

"I'm curious, but one does so hate to pry," Paniet said. An utter lie—Paniet was a frightful gossip, and he knew it.

Hollander shrugged. "It's no great secret." He pushed himself up against a wall and stuck his foot through a handy nylon loop to anchor himself. The words seemed to come easy, but he toyed with his empty food tube as he spoke. "I was down in the trenches on Yomi-no-kuni, back when the Navy fought Wilscon for that blighted bit of rock. I was running a wire-layer, a little half-armored car that strung out razor wire behind. Not much of a job, but I did me bit, right? Kept our PBMs safe in their dugouts. Long shifts—long nights, that planet's got days sixty hours long—and that sort of cycle does a number on you, keeps a body from sleeping proper. Which might explain it."

"Explain what?" Paniet asked.

"Why I didn't notice that general's foot. 'Til after I'd run it over."

Paniet couldn't help himself. He laughed, quickly covering his mouth with his hand. "Oh, I'm sorry," he said, still chuckling. "I'm so sorry if that's a painful memory, I just—I just—"

"Not half so painful for me as for him," Hollander said, which made Paniet nearly double over in hilarity. Hollander grinned to show that he'd taken no offense. "That's my story, the long and mostly short of it. I was sent packing so fast my head spun, and I landed back home with no job and no prospects. Considered throwing myself off a cliff, to be honest, but before I could the offer came from Centrocor. No questions asked, hazard pay and benefits, well. One takes what one gets, neh?"

"I suppose so," Paniet said.

"And now I've answered yer query, may I be so bold as to ask one of my own?"

Paniet tensed up, thinking he knew what was coming. The question he got the most often. He was, however, mistaken—Hollander had something very different on his mind.

"What'll be our fates, do you think, when we get home?" His face showed no sign of humor now. "I mean me and me mates, of course. We Centrocor employees. We've thrown in our lot with your bunch, no hesitations there. And we'll work and fight, right, every one of us, for this new head man Lanoe, as it's our only chance to see home again. Yet we can't help but wonder, can we? What happens when we see the lights of civilization once more? When we sail back to Earth or whatever. What manner of reception can Centrocorians expect then, neh? Are we working toward a prison sentence, as soon as we get back?"

"I suppose that's one possibility," Paniet admitted. He felt this man deserved an honest answer. "Your captain did attack a Navy vessel in peacetime, which might count as a terroristic action. Assuming Commander Lanoe wants to denounce you. He might turn a blind eye, in reward for your service."

"Ah," Hollander said. "Right." His face darkened, and he lowered his gruff voice to a sort of hoarse whisper. "Should our big fellas let it come to that. I can imagine it'll be a tense moment, when we arrive the other side of a wormhole. With our freedom at stake, and lots of guns to go around."

"You're suggesting that maybe the battle between our two sides might not be over. Just delayed," Paniet said. "Oh, don't look like that. I know you're not suggesting you'd want such a thing. And it's only realistic to think it might happen." He sighed. "I suppose we'll just have to enjoy this armistice, then. As long as it lasts."

"Right," Hollander said. "And men like you and me—we should stick together no matter what, neh?" He raised one meaningful eyebrow.

Paniet dropped his eyes. "Because we're neddies, you mean. The camaraderie of fellow service."

"Oh, right, that's what I meant," Hollander said, turning back to his meal.

The carrier scouts transmitted their findings back to the little fleet on a real-time basis, flooding Candless's displays with imagery and telemetry data. Within a few hours she had what she was looking for.

A chill ran down her spine when she saw the image, a high-resolution picture of the system as seen from above. Her hands started to shake and she had to press them against her console so that no one would notice.

If her bodily reaction was obvious, however, how she felt about what she was looking at was nothing short of bewildering. She felt as if her stomach had been cramped this whole time and only now could it relax.

She waited until the scouts returned, however, before she allowed herself to believe what she'd seen. She found the men and women in a ready room at the base of the carrier's flight deck, not far from the bridge. The six of them were laughing and popping tabs of hydration gel. One of them was already half out of his suit, and was scrubbing out the collar ring with an alcohol swab. She cleared her throat as she pushed into the compartment, and he hastily grabbed the suit and pulled it up over his chest, dropping the swab inside as he did so.

"I want a full report," she told them. "Do not, if you value your positions, leave out the smallest detail."

When she took this to Lanoe she had to be *sure*.

He arrived only a few minutes after she called him in, docking his BR.9 and rushing down to the bridge so fast he was breathing hard. Not exactly how she thought a commander ought to appear before his underlings, but she supposed he had a great personal stake in what she was going to tell him.

He came over to her IO's position with a hungry look. He said nothing—just nodded at her.

She brought up the image, the one that had left her shaking, and let him look at it for a while.

It showed the system in all its glory, in a way that had not been possible before. She had known that there was far more gas and dust than seemed likely, especially in a system with no planets. Still, no two systems were ever alike, and she'd written it off as just a fluke of this particular red dwarf, or perhaps something you found in systems this close to the center of the galaxy. No such system had ever been charted before by human pilots—there were bound to be surprises.

The red dwarf was surrounded by a thick belt of gas, mostly hydrogen and some particulates—a ring that surrounded the star's equator, making it look not altogether unlike Saturn. There were even gaps and bands in the gas, as there were in Saturn's rings. Narrow tracks cleared out by orbiting bodies. Shepherd moons, as these were called when they orbited a gas giant. Shepherd planetoids, then, if they orbited a star.

The ring wasn't as sharply defined as Saturn's, of course, because it was made of gas rather than particles of ice. It stretched out for nearly a hundred thousand kilometers from the star. There was no proper boundary at its far edge—the substance of the ring merely petered out, attenuating to nothing.

It was a dull black-red in color, brighter in some places than others. "We couldn't see it directly before, because we were looking at it edge-on. Most of our telescopes were adjusted for low-light conditions, so they looked right through the thing. It's only when you see it from above or below that it's really visible."

Lanoe nodded. He gestured and the display expanded to fill much of the bridge. The pilot and the navigator looked up in surprise, but they'd learned enough about Candless by then to keep their mouths closed.

Lanoe pushed away from her chair, swimming through the image, his hands moving constantly as he expanded one part of it or another. His mouth twisted over to the side of his face as he studied the picture in deep concentration.

She almost hated to disturb him. Certainly she didn't want to say what came next, not to him. Not after he'd staked everything on this system.

"It's a protoplanetary disk," she said.

He turned his head to stare at her. As if daring her to admit she'd just lied to him.

Protoplanetary disks formed early in a star's evolution. In its infancy, a star was just a cloud of loosely held-together gas and dust, enormous quantities of raw elementary matter with no form. Gravity gathered together most of the hydrogen and helium gas from that cloud, dragging it into a central, spinning mass. Eventually, when enough gas was pressed together, the star would ignite in a chain of thermonuclear fusion reactions, and from then on it would burn under its own power.

Once the star was lit it would push away whatever was left of the cloud—any remaining gases and most of the heavier elements—on its stellar wind. Those remnants would fall into orbit around the star's equator, creating a thick, soupy disk full of particles that bounced off each other constantly, whizzing back and forth under the influence of gravity and angular momentum.

In time enough of the heavier elements would slam together to form planetesimals, semisolid masses that had enough gravity to draw in more and more of the disk's substance. When the process was done you would have a system like Earth's, mostly empty but with a scattering of large heavy bodies in orbit around the sun.

The disk around the red dwarf wasn't there yet. This disk had just begun to form planetesimals—hence the large number of small rocky objects that Paniet and Valk had cataloged. It would be millions, perhaps billions of years before they came together to form real planets—if they ever did.

"You understand what this means, of course," Candless said.

Lanoe hadn't stopped staring at her. "It could mean a lot of things. It could mean—"

Candless and Lanoe had been squaddies once. She had earned the right to interrupt him when he was being foolish. "It means we've come to the wrong place," she said. "This can't be the home-world of the Blue-Blue-White."

"I'm not ready to accept that," Lanoe said.

Candless shook her head. "I'm sorry, Lanoe. This system must be brand-new. We know the Blue-Blue-White, as a species, are at least half a billion years old." She pointed at the image. "That's a protoplan-etary disk. Those only last a hundred million years at the most, and one this small would clear out even faster. Lanoe, it's time to accept the facts. This system can't be old enough to be the one you're looking for."

Lanoe said nothing. He turned back to the image, studying every cubic centimeter of it as if it would yield up its secrets if he just stared at it hard enough.

Candless pressed her lips together in a prim line. Clearly she was going to have to wait him out. She thought he would come around in the end. He was obsessed with his quest for justice, certainly. He was no madman, though. Eventually logic would have to sway him. Convince him that she was right.

Unfortunately for her—perhaps for all of them—she and Lanoe weren't alone.

"I beg your pardon, ma'am," someone said.

She whirled around, rage spiking through her. She swore on all the church bells of hell, if this was another ill-timed request for some bureaucratic triviality, she would—

It was Giles, the carrier's IO, who had spoken. He had remained on the bridge while she commandeered his workstation, staying ready in case she required his services. Up to this point she had not.

He could not possibly have missed her instructive berating of the yeoman, as it had taken place right in front of him. He would have listened to Candless outline the woman's faults for a solid hour. If he was speaking up now, it couldn't possibly be to ask her if he was allowed to go to the necessaries, or to ask for better food rations.

"If," she said, "you have something material to add, please do speak up." She gave him a look that should make it very, very clear what the penalty would be for wasting her time.

"Yes, ma'am," he said. "I just—"

Lanoe had turned his own gaze on the man. Candless couldn't see his eyes well enough to gauge his expression, but it had a visible effect on Giles. It made his face turn white as all the blood rushed out of it.

"I just... couldn't help but overhear. You identified this as a protoplanetary disk, and that's, uh—well, it definitely looks like one."

"Go on," Lanoe said, when the man hesitated.

"Yes, sir. If you showed me that picture and I didn't have any other data, I'd definitely agree. It's a star system forming out of inchoate matter." He nodded. Swallowed thickly. "There's just one problem. The metallicity of the red dwarf. We did a scan for that when we first arrived here before we, uh, allied with the Navy. Just standard practice—when you approach a star you check all its vital statistics, so to speak."

"What did you find?" Lanoe asked.

Candless had a feeling she knew what she was about to hear. Metallicity was a quality of stars, a ratio of how much of their mass consisted of hydrogen or helium as opposed to heavier elements. It was a useful figure because it could allow you to determine the age of a given star. Typically the older a star was, the lower its metallicity would be.

"We calculated that the red dwarf must be at least ten billion years old." Twice as old, then, as Earth's sun. "Which... raises a problem with your theory."

Candless saw it right away, of course. Protoplanetary disks formed very early on in a star's life span. It was impossible for a star that old to still be forming planets, or at least to have a disk as complex and thick as this one.

She closed her eyes and tried to breathe. She had not realized until just this moment how desperately she'd wanted their mission to be a wild-goose chase. How badly she wished that they could simply give up their search and go home.

This new piece of data was going to ruin that. She knew it.

"Interesting," Lanoe said.

She knew it for a fact.

When she opened her eyes, Lanoe was already on his way out of the bridge. "I'm going to check this disk out for myself," he said. "I'll be away for a while, maybe twenty-four hours."

"Sir, are you sure this is an appropriate time for that?" she asked. The consolidation of the fleet was still a nascent, uneasy thing. Candless didn't relish the prospect of overseeing the Centrocor contingent on her own. "Why don't I send my scouts instead?"

Lanoe shook his head. "This is something I need to do personally," he told her. "Don't wait up for me."

And with that, he was gone. As was any chance that the mission was complete.

She turned to face the IO. His eyes were very wide.

"Ma'am," he said. "I'm sorry if I . . . if I . . ."

She took a deep breath. "You never need to apologize to me for providing true information," she told him. "I'm not that much of a monster." Then she turned to face the rest of the bridge crew.

"As for the rest of you," she told them, "in fact, for everyone on this ship—I've been examining the logs of your readiness drills. More to the point, I've been examining the *lack* of readiness drills. It's clear that you've all been very slack in your preparedness training. So we are going to start a six-hour ship-wide simulation of an attack by enemy forces, commencing immediately. All hands to stations."

They were learning. None of them even groaned.

Chapter Ten

Ashlay Bullam lay upon a divan on the wooden deck of her yacht, surrounded by a dome of flowglas that was slightly polarized so she didn't have to look at all those stars. The small ship was moving, just a touch, making circles around the carrier, accelerating just enough to provide a little gravity. A waste of fuel, perhaps, but Maggs had to admit it was comforting to actually stand on his feet for a change.

"I'm forbidden from the carrier's bridge, and from speaking privately with any of my former employees," she said. "I asked if I could be secluded here, on my own ship, and they said that would be fine. Then they pulled my claws. All communications from here have been blocked. This thing has no weapons, of course, nor a vector field. If Lanoe decides he made a mistake and wants to kill me, I'm rather a sitting duck." One of her drones approached with a platter of fruit. Kiwi, peach, strawberry. All chemically stabilized at the peak of ripeness. She chose a slice of pineapple and lifted it to her lips. "As exiles go, I suppose it's a comfortable one."

Maggs watched her bite into the fruit, watched the juice slick her lips. She was beautiful in the particular fashion that all poly executives were beautiful that year, with a slightly upturned nose, thick eyelashes, and long hair colored a frosty blue. She had changed out of her thinsuit and into a brocade dress with a weave of tiny hexagons. "The conditions of my continued existence," he told her, "are a tad more stringent. I'm expected to report to Ehta once a day. Give her every paltry detail of my comings and goings. If I'm caught in a lie, it's straight to the brig for me." He shrugged. "I'll have to tell her I came to see you."

"Fine," Bullam said. "They're never going to trust us, of course. So there's no point trying to sneak about. Lanoe needs me, so I'm perfectly safe. If the crew of the carrier or the destroyers ever choose to mutiny, he'll wheel me out and have me give them a big speech about how we're all in this together."

"He's assuming you won't just whip them into greater frenzy, then, and lead the charge against him?"

"He's assuming correctly. We don't know how to open a wormhole to take us home. He does. I assure you, Maggs, that Aleister Lanoe is the safest man in the galaxy, if I have anything to say about it."

More's the pity, Maggs thought.

Revenge is a suit best played long, Maggsy, his father's voice told him. *Sometimes it just means waiting for your enemy to die of natural causes.*

"I suppose, given my record, I should be glad you don't want me for his assassin, then," Maggs said.

Bullam turned her head, never lifting it from the cushions. She gave him a long, appraising look. "Are we going to talk about that now?"

"If my timing doesn't please you—"

"No, no," she said, waving one hand at him. "You go ahead."

"You wanted me to kill Shulkin. I failed in that task," he said, letting it out in one long exhale. Literally getting it off his chest.

"I never said anything like that. I told you I wanted your help firing him."

"Of course," Maggs said. "Though even there, I've let you down. I—"

"He's been demoted. Rendered harmless. That's good enough. And frankly, I was impressed with how you handled the situation.

I don't know if you could have actually killed him before he shot Lanoe. I mean no criticism of your dagger-handling prowess, but it seemed a tricky blow to land. Instead you hit upon just the right words to make him stand down. Just the right button to press."

Maggs stroked his mustache. "I've spent my fair share of time amidst mentally ill Naval officers," he said.

Present company excluded, I presume, his father said.

But of course, Pater.

"I know the type. They may harbor the wildest delusions or be under the influence of a maniacal death wish, but respect for rank is bred into them. Bred to the bone. If Lanoe ordered Shulkin to stop breathing, the man would turn blue and lose consciousness before he disobeyed."

Bullam laughed. Maggs rather liked the sound of it. So few people these days had the mental attainment to appreciate his sense of humor.

"I'm glad I kept you around," Bullam said, propping herself up with one hand on her cheek. "You're going to make my exile more bearable, I think."

"I wanted to speak of that as well," he said. "I suppose many thanks are in order. You saved my life."

"I did," she said, failing altogether to demur.

"I'm not entirely sure why. Oh, I know I can be useful to you. I intend to show you just *how* useful at the earliest opportunity. I know you need all the allies you can get." He waved one hand in dismissal. "You took a rather terrible risk, though, insisting that Lanoe spare me. That man has no crumb of love for me in the empty cupboard of his heart. Putting a round through my head was going to be the highlight of his day. He might well have killed you just so he could hurry things along on the way to my execution."

"Any investment carries the possibility of risk," she said.

Maggs nodded and looked away. *Careful, son. She'll want to be paid back eventually. No need calling your creditors and asking them when's convenient.*

"I suppose...I just wonder if I'm worthy of what you've done for me. Please don't take this the wrong way. I have a healthy self-regard. Some would even call me vainglorious."

"Only the ones who know what the word means," she said.

He snapped around to look at her and saw a mischievous smile playing across her plump lips. Her eyes sparkled as she watched him stride across the deck.

He knelt down next to the divan. "Why did you do it? Really?"

She wriggled on her cushions. "Oh, for all the reasons you named, and of course you're technically my employee and I have a responsibility to you, a kind of noblesse oblige. But truly? Really, truly? I don't know. Perhaps I just like your mustache."

He leaned over her, shoving an arm around her shoulders and pulling her close, crushing her lips with his own. Her eyes opened wide and she made a little noise of protest. Maggs, thinking he'd made a grave miscalculation, pulled back and turned his face away.

"I'm so very sorry," he said. "I thought—"

"I have a disease, called Ehlers-Danlos syndrome," she told him. "I'm fragile, to put a fine point on it. Rough handling or even sudden movements can be dangerous for me—even fatal."

"I...I didn't know," Maggs said, horrified. He'd been so sure, though, he'd thought he'd read all the right signals, caught the right innuendos—

"Which means," she said, "if you're going to make a pass at me, you can't be so rough about it."

Maggs struggled to control his surprise. Then he kissed her again even as she started laughing, his lips just gently brushing hers. She tasted of pineapple and collagen-enhancing lipstick, and—

He pulled away a second time, because he'd heard something. A knock.

"I hate to break things off there," he said, "but there appears to be a neddy outside."

"Hmm? Oh, yes! I've been expecting him," Bullam said, sitting up. She patted down the neckline of her dress. "Be a dear and let him in."

The BR.9 was a fast fighter, designed to cross entire solar systems at top speed. Space, however, was very, very big. Ten hours after he'd left the carrier, Lanoe was finally approaching his destination.

Up ahead, the red dwarf had swollen until it actually looked round. He checked his fuel consumption and his reserve tanks and opened his throttle a little wider. Edged his control stick forward just a hair, until he was diving straight for the star.

He could just make out the disk, if he strained his eyes squinting for it. A reddish oval, a belt around the star. As he got closer, his fighter's instruments started showing him details, the imagery they gathered magnified and painted on the inside of his canopy. He saw the ragged outer edge of the disk, curling arms and tendrils of gas so transparent, so thin they did little but change the color of the void behind them. The bands in the disk showed up next, dark pencil lines etched around the circumference, dozens of them—not elements of the disk itself but gaps in its substance, places where the gas and dust thinned down to nothing. Farther in, closer to the star, the disk grew much thicker, looking first like a pale pinkish haze, then like a tube of dark red marble circling the star. Filaments of gas threaded through that mass, giving it texture, making it stand out in three dimensions. Storms swept through those filaments, twisting them into complex shapes like spiral galaxies, like the knots in the trunk of a tree, like cobwebs. He studied their ever-changing forms, noting each one carefully, watching how they formed and how they would break apart, as patient and as determined as an entomologist looking over a collection of bugs in jars.

Occasionally a sweep of darkness would rush through the mass, a black wind. His instruments told him that wind was made of trillions of tiny particles of graphitic carbon, few of them more than a millimeter across. A hailstorm of soot, a tidal wave of coal dust tearing through the dim red sky. Occasional forks of lightning cut through the black wind, bolts of plasma a thousand kilometers long, bright enough they looked like cracks opening in the sky.

Beyond the stormy, dense zone was…nothing. The disk just stopped, giving way to empty space. There was a clear gap of darkness between disk and star, a ring of blackness so clear that he could see stars through it. The disk didn't touch the red dwarf—if it did, he imagined it would have dissipated long ago, sucked into the parent star's hungry blast furnace heart, all that gas burned for thermonuclear fuel. Some process, some physical force, perhaps just angular momentum, kept the disk from falling inward and being consumed.

He ran more models, looking for the equations that would balance the orbital rotation of the disk against the pull of the star's gravity. Lanoe had never been much of a mathematician—his brain just didn't work that way, it all seemed too abstract—but to be a good pilot you needed to understand the basic formulas. You had to be able to work out all the vectors, see how gravity and velocity could cancel each other out, how the cosmos kept spinning instead of falling in on itself in a reversed version of the big bang. His ship's computer helped him as much as it could, filling in the numbers and the operators he needed, summing his data points and displaying graphs that made more visual sense than the numbers alone ever could. He grunted and swore as he tried to remember how it all worked, tried to recall the courses in astrophysics he'd taken back in flight school.

It wasn't the math that got his attention in the end, though. It was one of those long, long bolts of lightning, dazzlingly bright. It lit up the inside of one of the storms, showed him an incredible sweep of cloudscape, of fantastical forms and incredible shapes and—there.

Right there.

Lanoe twisted his mouth over to one side.

"What the hell is that?" he asked himself.

Maggs touched some virtual keys and the flowglas of the dome rippled. The neddy placed one hand on the dome, as if testing its ductility, then pushed his way through, the flowglas parting around him while maintaining a perfect seal so that the air inside the yacht didn't even stir. The neddy dropped to the floor on one knee, then carefully rose to stand at attention.

"This is Hollander," Bullam said. "Fix him a drink, will you?"

"Grog, or straight-up rum? We're feeling Naval tonight," Maggs said, striding over to the yacht's bar. He wondered why his hostess had invited a neddy to this little party. At exactly the worst possible time. "Did you need something repaired, M. Bullam?"

"Engineer Hollander isn't your typical neddy," Bullam said. She rose stiffly to her feet, then walked over to hold out a hand. The neddy stared at it for a moment as if unsure what tool to use on it. Then he shook it, like a normal person.

"Is it . . . you know? Okay to speak?" Hollander asked.

Oh, by the devil's bunions, Maggs thought. *He's a Hadean.* Hades had been one of the first human colonies outside the solar system, which meant that the people there had had time to develop their own accent—a mélange of a dozen Earth dialects—and their own mannerisms. Maggs, as a rule, was not a fan of either.

"If Lieutenant Maggs wasn't suspicious of you before," Bullam said, "he certainly is now. It's perfectly fine—we're all in this together."

Hollander nodded meaningfully at her use of the Centrocor motto. "A friend, then," he announced, and grabbed Maggs up in a bear hug.

Maggs held his breath and waited until it was over. Again, mannerisms, not a fan, etcetera.

"Hollander's not just a neddy," Bullam said, rolling her eyes just a little. "He's also a spy. My spy."

Maggs whistled in admiration. "You've corrupted a neddy," he said. "Now, that's impressive." He looked at Hollander. "Your branch has a reputation for being reliable—and completely uninterested in politics and intrigue."

"Don't forget we're heavy thinkers, neh?" Hollander replied. "We can see where our bread's buttered. Where's that grog, by the way?"

Maggs poured something citrusy into a jot of rum and shook

them together in a squeeze tube. The neddy sucked at it happily before he spoke again.

"I've been hard at work over at the cruiser," he said. "Getting close to the engineer there, a fella named Paniet."

"Did you see it?" Bullam asked. "The AI?"

Maggs had told Bullam about Valk and what he truly was, but for the moment the existence of an illegal artificial intelligence on Lanoe's ship wasn't common knowledge. If Valk's existence became common knowledge it might turn the Centrocor contingent against Lanoe. Clearly Bullam was already working the angles.

Hollander shook his head. "I was only allowed to see the engineering section, and didn't feel it prudent to press for greater access. I've laid ground for a future jaunts over there, though. I'll get the evidence you need, no worries."

"Of course you will," Bullam said, and smiled at the man. She glanced over at Maggs. "It's well and good knowing Lanoe's dirty little secret, but if I ever actually needed to reveal it, it would be my word against his. I need images, video, something to prove that Lanoe is harboring a thinking machine." She turned back to Hollander. "Did you learn anything else?"

"The cruiser's in poor condition. The damage's not just cosmetic, either. I saw what was done to the drive, and that'll be a hard fix. There's an entire hatch missing from the vehicle bay, and we just sawed off the whole front section. Whole damned ship's being held together with spit and hope."

Maggs frowned. "Paniet's a top-notch engineer. He'll have it all fixed before long."

"Begging your pardon, but no, he won't," Hollander replied. "Not unless he gets to some kind of drydock. There's scratches and dings you can buff out, and there's deep frame damage, and that's what we're discussing. I wouldn't be surprised if that tub fell to pieces the first time in the middle of a battle."

"All the more reason Lanoe needed to take us alive," Bullam pointed out. "Why he went to such lengths to board the carrier—

his own ship isn't up to the task he's set himself." Bullam sat down on her divan and crossed her legs. "Fascinating. You've done quite well, Hollander. When we get back to the real world, you'll be paid, and handsomely, for your true service to Centrocor."

"Happy to help," Hollander said, sketching a quick but deep bow. "Now, I should get back, before I'm missed, neh? Best no one sees me loitering here."

"Of course. We'll talk soon."

Hollander tossed his empty squeeze tube to Maggs, who caught it easily. Then he raised his helmet and left the way he'd come, wriggling through the flowglas dome.

Maggs watched him go for a while, maneuvering away from the yacht on jets built into the boots and shoulders of his suit. Eventually he shrank away to nothing, and Maggs turned to look back at Bullam.

"You continue to impress me," he told her. "Even in exile, you're still playing this game like a master."

"I'm very well trained," Bullam told him. "Centrocor paid for six years of schooling because they saw potential in me. I've long since repaid that loan, with significant interest."

"I didn't know that there was a school of dirty tricks on Irkalla," Maggs said, laughing. "I thought you needed to learn that sort of thing in the field, the way I did."

"The curriculum at Centrocor's boarding schools would surprise a lot of people," Bullam told him. "Now. Back to business."

"Yes, of course," Maggs said, and nearly jumped to her side, reaching one hand out to stroke her hair.

"Not that business," she said, batting his hand away. "Not yet, anyway. I meant that it was time we spoke about what your role is going to be in my grand plan."

"Ah." Maggs drew his hand back and in one deft motion smoothed down his mustache. "Well, I doubt Lanoe is going to let me get close enough for me to continue as your would-be assassin."

"I thought I made myself clear. I want Lanoe kept alive and healthy."

"Of course," Maggs said, "right up until the moment you don't anymore."

The two of them smiled at each other.

"So we'll need to find you another role. Something that suits your particular skills. I actually have a few ideas," Bullam told him, "a couple stratagems that might be right up your alley..."

Lanoe arrived back at the carrier at such speed he had to shoot past it and bank around in a million-kilometer-wide turn to slow down before he could dock. He tapped at his control stick with an idle and impatient thumb, irritated by how long it took. He was anxious to get back to the bridge, to show Candless what he'd found. "Call Paniet and have him come over, I want him to look at this, too," he told her over a private radio band. "And make sure Valk can hear us. He'll have something to say, I'm sure."

"As you wish. Are you hungry? I can have some solid food waiting for you when you arrive."

Normally after a long patrol there was nothing Lanoe wanted more. This time his stomach was too tied up in knots to even consider food. "Don't bother. Just get me some water that doesn't taste like it's been filtered through my kidneys three times."

Candless was silent for a moment. Maybe she'd been offended by that. Well, he didn't really care. "Yes, sir," she said finally, which was what he needed from her.

He slid into a docking berth inside the carrier's flight deck and wasted no time hurrying to the bridge. As he arrived, Candless pushed out of her seat toward him, a tube of water in her hand. "We've downloaded the imagery you sent us. It's just processing now. Paniet is on his way—do you want to wait for him?"

Lanoe took the tube and sucked at it greedily. The water tasted amazing. "Bring up the video. Start at 6:21, and run through 7:02."

Candless nodded at the carrier's IO. Miles, Lanoe thought, or

Giles. He'd studied the carrier's personnel roster but still didn't know their names.

The IO touched a virtual key, and the image appeared, floating before Lanoe. He swiped his arms open, expanding the hologram to fill most of the bridge. High towers of red cloud loomed over them, cut into layers by floating rivers of dark ionized methane. Strands of sunlight wove together as they shone down through gaps in the clouds, like searchbeams from on high picking out a tendril of mist or lighting up the swollen belly of a burgeoning cloud bank. A storm of black pebbles swept across the view, and even Lanoe turned his head as if the dust might get into his eyes. Looking down, he could see nothing but more clouds, more and more until they swirled around his feet, a thick carpet of roiling vapor.

"You must have got pretty close, to get imagery at this level of resolution," Candless said. When he didn't respond immediately, she said, "You were right. This is no protoplanetary disk. It looks more like the cloudscape of a gas giant planet, though if this metadata is correct it's on a scale far beyond anything we've ever seen before. You could lose Jupiter in this image, couldn't you?"

He continued to ignore her. He was looking for something very specific, something easily missed. It would be there, he thought, in a deep canyon between two heavy banks of piled stratocumulus. Something small and white, pale against the dark red clouds but shadowed until it was barely recognizable. "There," he said. "There, look. Look!"

Candless pushed over to float next to him. She made a good show of staring into the image, of trying to see what he was pointing at, but he could tell she didn't *want* to see it. She wanted to believe this was some sterile world, strangely shaped and incredibly massive but devoid of life like every other place humanity had been. She was trained to think of the universe as empty of intelligence, of sapience. And maybe it was more than that. Maybe she wanted him to be wrong.

But he was right. He was sure of it.

"What do you see?" he asked.

"Something lighter in color than the rest of this." She shook her head. "It's hard to tell if it's solid or not. I suppose—"

"It's solid," Lanoe said. He turned to look at the IO. "Can we magnify this any further?"

"You'll lose some resolution," the man said. He looked terrified at having to say it. Candless must have been hard at work, he thought. Making the crew of the carrier terrified of her.

"Sure," Lanoe said. "Do it."

The image expanded so fast Lanoe felt like the clouds were blowing past him, through him. He suddenly felt lightheaded. "Now," he told Candless. "Look again."

A green pearl appeared in the corner of Lanoe's vision. Valk, calling in. "I see it, if she doesn't," Valk said.

"Perhaps I see . . . *something*," Candless said. She pursed her lips. "It's irregular in shape, and it looks quite delicate." The white object resembled nothing so much as foam clinging to the side of a thick wave of cloud. Perhaps a torn scrap of lace, fluttering on the sooty wind. It was made of long spars that came together at various angles, forming six-sided, eight-sided, twenty-sided rings. Some of the rings joined together to form larger, three-dimensional shapes, like tetrahedrons and icosahedrons and polyhedrons with even more faces, shapes with names Lanoe barely remembered from his long-past school days.

Paniet came shooting into the bridge, upside down from Lanoe's perspective. The engineer flipped over and grabbed the back of Candless's abandoned seat. "What did I miss?" he asked. "Ooh, that's very pretty."

Lanoe was still watching Candless's face. She was fighting it, but he thought her resistance might be breaking down.

"Are you going to tell me something like that could just occur naturally?" he asked her.

"Of course it could," she told him. "I don't claim to understand the processes that would give rise to such an object inside a hydrogen atmosphere, but—well, let's be logical about this. Occam's razor, yes? The simplest explanation is probably correct. Because what you're suggesting is less plausible."

"Is it? We know the Blue-Blue-White exist," Lanoe told her. "We have good reason to think this is their home system."

"You aren't saying the word," Valk told him. "Say it out loud."

"That's one of their cities," Lanoe said.

Candless might have been about to make a point. She closed her mouth and drew in a long, shallow breath.

"There are hundreds of them," Lanoe told her. "Once I knew what to look for, they showed up everywhere, scattered around the disk. Some are bigger than others, but they're all pretty huge. This one is the size of Madagascar." He pointed at the lacy construction again, as if she still hadn't noticed it. "That's a city. They're here, in that disk. The Blue-Blue-White are here."

"I'm still not entirely convinced," Candless said. "But—"

"Look!" Paniet said, nearly squealing. "Look, there, at that edge of the city." He pointed, and Lanoe saw it, too. Small dark shapes, just specks even at this magnification. They wheeled and darted around the long white spars.

"Those are vehicles," Lanoe said. "Blue-Blue-White vehicles."

"Or birds," Candless said.

Enough. He'd had enough of her doubts. "It's a city. And now we have this—"

He looked around at his officers. At the bridge crew of the carrier.

"We have a target," he said.

PART II

MEGASTRUCTURE

Chapter Eleven

The cruiser and the carrier moved with glacial slowness, at least compared to the velocity fighters could achieve. Their engines were massive and incredibly powerful, but even in the absence of gravity it took an enormous amount of energy to move all that metal and carbon fiber. Just getting them turned toward the red dwarf and locked into the right trajectory had taken hours. Accelerating from a dead stop meant days of just slowly building up speed. It would take more than a week to reach the disk.

There was plenty to keep Lanoe busy during that time, busy enough he didn't have to think about what would happen when they arrived.

There were repairs to be completed, on both the cruiser and the carrier. Endless combat drills to run through—the Naval and Centrocor forces had to learn how to work, and fight, together. Lanoe had given his officers tasks to complete, and those needed to be supervised. Candless was hard at work whipping the carrier's crew into shape, bringing them up to something approaching Naval discipline. Ehta was working with her marines on the gun decks of the cruiser, making sure that if they needed to fire the heavy artillery the coilguns wouldn't just explode when they went off. Valk was working up a computer model of the disk, trying to understand how it worked and how best to attack it. And then there was Paniet's special project.

The engineer had set up a workshop on the carrier, deep inside the cavelike flight deck. The neddies had erected a tent of electro-stiffened plastic at the bottom of the deck. Inside it, as Lanoe watched, they were building a complicated drone. Two of them were curing a long, round piece of carbon fiber cladding while another one tested an electronics bus attached to an array of low-power lasers tuned to different frequencies. They had to crawl around a large thruster package that had been cannibalized from a carrier scout, three big cones mounted on a simple fusion torus.

Lanoe was, officially, supervising Paniet and the others, though mostly that seemed to amount to standing around watching the engineers work and occasionally grunting as if he had something to add.

Truth be told, he didn't understand ten percent of what they were doing. When Valk sent him a signal indicating he wanted to talk, he flicked his eyes to accept the message almost instantly.

"Sorry if I'm bothering you," Valk said. "I've found something I think you'd really like to see. It's about the disk."

Lanoe nodded to himself. "Yeah? Okay. I could use a break. I'll be over right away. Just let me get to my fighter."

"I could just tell you about it over this link if—" Lanoe had already cut the connection.

Lanoe pushed his way out of the flap of the tent and into the open cavern of the flight deck. He made his way to where his BR.9 lay nestled in a docking cradle, ready to launch. He kept it on standby mode at all times—he spent so much time moving back and forth between the carrier and the cruiser these days that the ship's engines never had a good chance to cool down. The BR.9's canopy melted back into the fuselage as he approached. Lanoe retracted the skeletal docking arms and had the fighter moving before the canopy had even reformed over him, edging his way carefully out of the flight deck, maneuvering around the ranks of Yk.64s and carrier scouts mounted on the inner walls.

Once out in space he located the cruiser with his naked eye—it was flying on a parallel course with the carrier and the destroyers, only a few kilometers away—and touched his control stick to activate his maneuvering jets.

There was no real need for him to fly the fighter manually. He could have let Valk handle the short flight. He was still Aleister Lanoe, though. No matter how far he'd climbed up the chain of command, he was still a pilot in his bones.

————

Ehta woke to the sound of someone knocking at her hatch.

It was a truism that a marine could sleep anywhere—in a mud-filled trench, in the middle of an orbital bombardment, even sitting up with her eyes open during a long briefing. When your life was made of ninety-nine percent boredom and one unpredictably timed percent adrenaline-spiked terror, you learned to rest when you got the chance.

But if marines had some special power in regard to sleep, it was balanced by the fact that when you had to get up—you got up in a damned hurry. Ehta nearly brained herself by sitting up too fast. Her helmet even started to raise automatically as it noticed the near collision between her skull and the ceiling.

"Hold on," she said, because whoever it was, they were still knocking. Why wouldn't they just send her a message? What was so damned important? If it was an emergency, she would probably already know about it—her suit would have told her if the cruiser was on fire, or if the jellyfish had sprung an ambush on them.

"I said hold on, you bastard!" she shouted, when the knocking still didn't stop. She lowered her helmet manually and twisted around in the bunk. Like every sleeping compartment on the cruiser, it was a narrow rectangular space just a little bigger than a coffin. There was a fan at one end to make sure she didn't suffocate in her sleep and a display mounted on what was sometimes the ceiling of the tiny chamber. If she stretched her arms out to either side, she could push against both walls. It was a good stretching exercise.

"I'm bloody well coming," she shouted at the knocker. Then she finally triggered the release key and the hatch slid open and she saw who it was.

Bury. It was the little wet-behind-the-ears pilot, Bury. What the hell did he want?

"What the hell do you want?" she asked.

"It's Ginger," he said.

She started to turn away, yawning. "Valk is your supervising officer. Tell him to deal with it. I know he's weird, but—"

"Please," Bury said, and something in his voice made her blood run cold. There was a note of pleading in his tone she'd never heard from him before. Normally he was too proud to ask anyone for anything. "I think she might—do something. Bad. To herself."

Ehta pushed out of the bunk and stumbled into the hallway, her legs still mostly asleep. Her head swam with the sudden rush of blood. She ignored it and got moving, heading for the axial corridor. "Why'd you come to me with this?" she said.

"I'm sorry if I should have gone to Lanoe or something, but—"

"I didn't say that," Ehta told him. "I just want to know why."

The two of them hurried down the ladder that ran the length of the ship, rung after rung after rung. It was a long way down. "You were kind to her once. She told me about it," Bury said. "When they called her a coward, you stood with her."

"Yeah, and then she went and had that alien cut her head open and shove an antenna inside. Just to prove they were wrong." Ehta scowled at the memory.

Ehta had fought tooth and nail against letting Ginger volunteer for the operation. She'd insisted that they stop the girl from doing something so strange and irreversible. Candless had shouted her down, even slapped her across the face, and in the end, Ehta's protests had been for nothing.

She hadn't spoken much to the girl since. Before the operation she'd thought maybe the two of them had some common ground, that they could even be friends. Instead Ginger had chosen to turn herself into something Ehta couldn't even understand. Something Ehta could barely stand to look at.

When they got to the brig, she came up short in the hatchway, trying to make sense of what she saw. The cell that held the alien was open and she could see the chorister shaking like she was having a seizure, her four arms and many legs twitching wildly. Ginger was crawling on the floor outside the cell, her face buried against the padding there. Her arms and legs were spasming in perfect time with the alien's movements.

"Ginger!" Bury shouted. He shoved past Ehta and ran to the girl's side, grabbing her shoulders. She shook him off.

"Hey, now," Ehta said, licking her lips. She dropped to her knees and lowered her head until she could see Ginger's face. "Hey, come on, now, are you—are you okay?"

The girl didn't speak. Her lips twitched a little, but Ehta didn't think she was trying to form words. More likely she was in the middle of a seizure.

Caroline Ehta had never been much of a nurturer. She'd spent her life shooting at people, not tending to their hurts. She had no idea what to do. Why the hell hadn't Bury gone for Lanoe? She tried to remember the minimal combat medicine she'd learned as a marine. Mostly that involved splinting broken limbs and putting pressure on bleeding wounds. What did you do for someone having a seizure? Put something in their mouth? Or were you *not* supposed to do that?

There was a flight surgeon on the carrier, she thought—one of the Centrocor people. And the cruiser's sick bay had a medical drone. "We need to move her," she told Bury, because that sounded right. "We need to get her to—"

"No," Ginger said. "N-n-n-no. I'm f-fine."

Ehta looked up at Bury. The boy's face was racked with indecision.

"Help her," he said, sounding desperate.

"Ginger?" Ehta said. "Ginger, talk to me. What's going on?"

"She's waking up-p-p," Ginger said, through chattering teeth. "S-sedative's wearing…off. I expect-t-t-ted this."

The girl's head drooped. She collapsed against the floor. She'd stopped shaking, or at least she wasn't shaking as much as she had been before. Ehta could see how pale her face was, though, and her red hair was slick with sweat. It looked like Ginger was fighting this—this—whatever it was, whatever had come over her.

"I feel every...thing she feels," Ginger said. "She's so alone."

"That's what this is about?" Ehta asked. She shook her head. "She's having full-blown convulsions because she's *lonely*?"

"You don't understand. I don't think you can," Ginger told her. She took long, deep, gulping breaths.

"Ginj, we want to," Bury said. The Hellion couldn't sweat or cry, but Ehta could read the suffering in his eyes. He really cared about Ginger. The two of them had been classmates, friends—even squaddies, for a little while. Ehta knew how deep that bond could run. "We want to understand. Help us."

"They're born into a harmony," Ginger said. "Born surrounded by others like them. They're called the Choir because they all think together. Each voice an individual, but...shared, their thoughts, their feelings, shared...all shared. Now she's alone, for the first time in her life. She's terrified of it. She's only half-conscious now, not even half, but she...she knows. She knows what she's going to hear when she comes to."

"What?" Bury asked. "What is she going to hear, Ginj?"

"Silence. Unbearable silence."

Ehta had heard enough. She grabbed Ginger under her armpits—the girl was too weak to fight her off—and pulled her up until she was sitting on the floor. Her face was red where she'd pressed it against the padding.

"We're going to take you to the sick bay," Ehta said. "I'll get Lanoe to come down and talk to you, see what we can do about this. How does this work, this telepathy? How does she send you her thoughts?"

"Microwaves...antenna," Ginger said. She was fading.

"That's good," Ehta said. "You can shield against microwaves pretty easy. Maybe we just need to wrap your head in metal foil. Then you won't have to—"

"No!" the girl said, flailing her arms in a feeble attempt to push Ehta away. "She needs me! You can't cut her... off. Not now. Not now! She'll go insane!"

Bury made a quick little gesture, aborted before it could really get started. Ehta thought maybe he was going to try to wrap his arms around Ginger. Hug her. But he didn't dare.

Ehta understood. What had happened to the girl—what had been done to her—was just too weird. Too wrong.

"Lock my suit. In case... there's another." Ginger lifted the fingers of one hand and then they fell again.

"Another seizure?" Ehta asked.

"It's all... all we can do," the girl told her. "Ehta. Please."

Ehta grabbed Ginger's wrist and brought up the display there. Found the emergency controls.

"Ehta," Ginger said again. Her eyes were closed now.

Ehta touched a virtual key and Ginger's suit stiffened, all its joints and flexible elements locking into place. An air bag in the collar ring inflated to hold Ginger's neck completely immobile. Her helmet started to come up, but Ehta retracted it before it closed over her face completely.

"Ehta," Ginger said, barely a whisper now. "I chose this. I wanted it."

The marine just shook her head.

Lanoe put his ship down in the cruiser's vehicle bay without so much as a bump. He jumped out of his cockpit and headed inside, into the axial corridor, where he sent a signal to Valk indicating that he wanted to talk.

"I'm here," Valk said, as if he'd ever been anywhere else. "Come up to the wardroom. I have the disk up on a display here, and I have a really interesting computer model of its formation I want to show you. I think you'll find that—"

Lanoe tuned the AI out. He twisted his neck around, his eyes darting up and down the axial corridor. He'd heard something.

"What was that?" Lanoe demanded. "Did you hear it?"

Valk answered chirpily. "Oh, yes," he said. "That's a scream."

He could hear it clearly now. Someone—a woman—was shriek-ing in agony. It sounded like it was coming from below him. From the direction of the brig, he thought. It was Ginger. It had to be Ginger.

Lanoe's eyes went wide. "What the hell is going on?" he demanded.

"She's been doing that for the last ten minutes, I think," Valk told him. "I think she's in incredible pain. Or maybe just distress."

"And you didn't think to tell me?" Lanoe demanded.

"Oh. No, I suppose I didn't," Valk said. "Honestly, I hadn't given it much thought. It was getting distracting so I just turned off most of my auditory pickups."

Lanoe scowled at the wall. He was sure Valk would be able to see his expression. Could the AI understand it, though? Valk was becoming less human all the time. Becoming more of the machine he was.

Lanoe would have to do something about that, he thought. Eventually. In the meantime he had an emergency to deal with. He got moving, hurrying not up—toward the wardroom—but down.

"Wait," Valk said. "Where are you going? What about my com-puter model?"

Lanoe didn't even bother to reply.

———

"Shh," Ehta said. "Shh." She couldn't think of what else to say. She gripped Ginger's shoulders and pulled her close, unable to stand the screaming anymore, unable to bear Ginger's dismay. Ehta had to try to help, even if she knew it was futile. The girl's eyes had rolled up in her head and her face was slack, only her lungs seeming to still work. Across the room Bury sat slumped against a wall, star-ing, just staring at them.

"Shh," Ehta said again. "Shh."

In the cell, the alien's big body twitched like a bug, one jointed leg kicking at the air. Rain-on-Stones thrashed and hit her head on the floor, but it was padded, and anyway nobody was going in there—nobody was going to try to comfort a three-meter-long insect crustacean whatever *thing*.

When Lanoe came hurrying into the room, Ehta barely looked up at him. He should have been there, she thought, he should have been waiting with the girl. After all she'd done for him, after everything he'd asked from her.

No, no, that wasn't right. Ehta knew Lanoe would have been there for Ginger if he could. He was a good man, he was the best man she'd ever known. He'd saved her life once. She had followed him through thick and thin. This wasn't the thing that would break her loyalty to Aleister Lanoe.

It was just the screaming. It was just so hard to listen to Ginger, to hear her pain, and not want to lash out on her behalf. To—

Sudden silence crashed all around them. For a second Ehta didn't understand what had changed.

"Lanoe," Ginger said.

The girl had stopped screaming.

Ehta checked and saw that the girl's eyes had rolled back down, that she was looking at Lanoe with a clear, dispassionate gaze. Her face had regained some of its muscle tone and even a little of its color.

That was all it took? For her to see Lanoe?

"You said we had ten days," Lanoe said, standing in the hatchway. "That was barely a week ago."

"I said we'd have ten days if I rationed the drug. I couldn't," Ginger said. "She was too close to waking up, so I had to give her full doses. I think she developed a tolerance to it."

Ehta looked from one to the other of them. She could barely believe it. The transformation was so extreme. A moment ago Ginger had been crazy with pain, with suffering, and now... "You heard her, before?" she demanded. "Lanoe, you heard her screaming? That's what brought you running?"

Lanoe frowned. Then he looked to the side and pointed at Bury. "Lieutenant," he said. The kid didn't even look up. Maybe he'd forgotten that he'd been promoted. "Bury," Lanoe said, putting a little anger in the name. "Get back to your post."

"I need to be with Ginger," the Hellion replied.

"Why? You're not helping her right now," Lanoe told him. "You're just sitting there. Looking foolish."

Ehta wanted to gasp in surprise. That was just cold. But Bury got up, brushed off the back of his suit, and left without a word.

"I suppose you want me to leave, too," Ehta said, when Bury had gone.

"No," Lanoe told her. "You can hear this. But what I need to say to Ginger right now, it's not for anybody else's ears. Understood?"

"Yeah, of course," Ehta said. You didn't get far in the marines without knowing when to keep your mouth shut.

Lanoe came over and squatted down, his hands on his knees. He grunted just a little, an old man forced to adopt an uncomfortable posture. "Ginger," he said. "Look at me. I know you're fighting it off right now. I know it can't be easy."

"She's almost awake," Ginger told him. "She knows...she knows that she's alone. That's all. Not how far we came. She just wants to get back to the Choir, to rejoin the harmony. She still thinks that's possible. When she wakes fully, when she understands—"

"I know," Lanoe told her. At least his voice was softer now. "I know it's going to be very difficult for her. Being cut off from the Choir. I guess it'll be like—what? Waking up in the morning and realizing you've gone blind overnight? I wish I could help with that."

"You don't get it," Ginger told him. "It won't be like that."

"No?"

"No. It'll be like if you woke up tomorrow and you realized that you could still see just fine. But that every light in the universe had gone out."

Lanoe shook his head. "You'll have to help her. Keep her from—"

"Going insane? That may be too much to ask," Ginger told him. "But I know my job. I know what I need to do."

"Actually," Lanoe said, "that wasn't what I was going to ask you. I need to make sure she doesn't talk to anyone else, no one but me. It's crucial to our mission. Absolutely crucial that we keep her from talking, especially to any of the Centrocor people. I don't trust them. I think they might try to get in here, to get access to her. We can't let that happen. We can't let them seize her. She's the main thing keeping them under control."

"Because…" Ginger glanced at Ehta. "Because she's our only way home."

Lanoe smiled. "Exactly."

Something had just passed between them. Something secret. Ehta wished very much she knew what it was. Clearly, though, neither of them was going to tell her.

"You need me to isolate her further," Ginger said. "It might actually help her to talk to lots of different people. But instead you want her in solitary confinement."

"Not entirely solitary, since she'll have you. And I'll come by as often as I can, to check up on you, to talk. I promise." He rose slowly to his feet. "Ehta," he said, "can you step outside with me for a moment? We need to make sure these two are safe."

Ehta gently extricated herself from Ginger. With her suit frozen the girl couldn't move, but Ehta tried to make her as comfortable as possible, sitting there with her back against the wall. Ginger didn't seem to care. Her eyes looked straight forward, not at anyone.

"Don't go," the girl said. "When he's done with you—come back and stay with me, just a little longer. Please?"

"You got it, kid."

Out in the hall Ehta gritted her teeth. Thought of all the things she would like to say to Lanoe just then. Most of them involved profanities.

But Ehta was a PBM, a Poor Bloody Marine, and she knew about duty, and respect for your commanding officers. That was one of the first things they taught you in combat school. You don't have to like a man to stand at attention when he enters a room.

"I want guards down here, a full detail," Lanoe said. "Set up shifts but make sure there's never less than two marines outside this hatch."

"Sir," Ehta said.

"I'll send a neddy over and we'll see what we can do to sound-proof the brig. In case she starts screaming again."

"Sir," she said.

"I want a full report on everyone who comes and goes in this hallway, even if they're on their way somewhere else, even if they're just passing through. I want to know if they so much as glance at that hatch. Understood?"

"Understood, sir," she said.

He nodded and turned on his heel, walking away.

She stepped back inside the brig, to see that Ginger had fallen over. Her suit was still locked, so she had to lie there bent over, as if she were a statuette of a sitting girl that someone had knocked over on its side. Ehta hurried over and propped her back up. The girl hadn't started screaming again, which had to be a good sign.

"You fought through it," Ehta said. "You brought yourself back, when he came. You won't let him see you hurting, will you?"

Ginger's eyes turned to focus on Ehta's face. She did not answer Ehta's question, not directly. Instead she started whispering, words spilling out of her so fast and so low that Ehta could barely make them out.

"I need to tell you something," Ginger said. "There isn't much time. I need to say this before she wakes up. Once she does, she'll hear everything I say, everything I think. And I don't want her to hear this."

"Go ahead," Ehta told her.

As desperate and as short of time as she was, Ginger seemed to have real trouble getting the words out, though. Her eyes filled with tears and her lip quivered. But then she cleared her throat and stuck her jaw out and clearly worked hard to get control over herself.

"It's too much," she said.

"What?"

Ginger shook her head. "It's too much. I can't do it—I can't take all her pain. I can't save her, and trying will...will...I won't make it."

"Kid," Ehta said. "If you need me to stand up to Lanoe for you, I—"

"You can't. Nobody can—he's on a crusade."

Ehta frowned. "He's got a mission here. He has a lot on his mind, sure, but—"

"He's hell-bent on revenge, and he won't let anyone stop him. He won't set me free. He needs Rain-on-Stones too much. He doesn't care if I don't survive what's about to happen. That's just collateral damage."

"Kid...come on," Ehta said.

But she knew Ginger was right. About it all.

Lanoe, the man who'd saved Ehta's life, had changed. She didn't want to think about how, about what it meant. But she couldn't deny it forever.

"Ehta. You need to find another way. I know I'm asking a lot but, Ehta—please. *Please.* Help me."

And then her eyes rolled back up into her head. And she started once more to scream.

⟶⟵

Lanoe headed up to the wardroom that served as the cruiser's bridge, climbing up the axial corridor hand over hand. Valk kept sending him messages, green pearls appearing in the corner of his eye. He flicked his eyes to dismiss them—he intended to speak to the AI in person.

When he reached the top of the ladder, though, and came out

into the wardroom, he wasn't sure that was an option anymore. Valk's suit lay slumped across the controls. The helmet was down and the sleeves hung slack, the gloves dangling and brushing the floor. The AI was making no attempt to impersonate a human being anymore.

"I'm here," Valk said, his voice coming from a speaker in the ceiling. "As much as I can be said to be anywhere. It's an interesting question, actually, one I—"

"Save it," Lanoe told him.

The AI went quiet.

Bury sat at one of the narrow tables, a half-finished squeeze tube of food abandoned in front of him. He looked up at Lanoe with feverish eyes. "Ginger," he said. "Is she okay? I mean, is she going to be okay?"

"Sure," Lanoe said. An outright lie but the kid needed to hear it. "She'll be fine. Listen, I know seeing her like that was rough. Take the rest of your shift off. Go catch up on some sleep, read a text, whatever."

Bury's face creased in concern, the plastination across his nose wrinkling and fracturing the light. "Is something wrong, sir?"

"What makes you say that?" Lanoe asked.

"You're being strangely nice to me."

Lanoe considered upbraiding the Hellion on his candor, but instead he sighed and shrugged. "It wasn't easy for me, either. Listening to those screams. Maybe today we don't stand on ceremony. Just get out of here. I need to talk to Valk."

Bury nodded and left without further remarks. Well, thank the devil for small mercies, Lanoe thought. He turned a chair around to face the control stand and Valk's abandoned suit.

"I'm starting to worry about you," he said.

"May I ask why?"

The voice from the speakers sounded right. It sounded like Valk, like Tannis Valk. Like the simulation of Tannis Valk that Lanoe had met just before the battle of Niraya. But the Valk of back then had been less precise in his language. He'd been a lot more rough-and-tumble. A lot more human, Lanoe guessed.

"You're deteriorating," Lanoe said. "Stop—before you say it, I'm sure your software is working at peak efficiency. That's not what I'm talking about."

"My personality, you mean," Valk said. "My...ability to relate to my fellow man. Hmm. That bears some consideration. I could try reoptimizing some subroutines, see if that helps. The last thing I want is for people to feel uncomfortable around me."

Lanoe looked down at his hands and smiled. They'd passed that junction a long time ago. "It didn't occur to you that I might want to know that Ginger was in trouble. If I hadn't come over to look at a computer model—"

"One I really think you should see," Valk told him.

"In a minute. If I hadn't come over for that, I wouldn't have known what was going on until it was too late. Let's put aside the human element here, that could have compromised the mission. What the hell were you thinking? You heard her screaming. You did nothing."

Valk paused before answering. Lanoe wondered if that was just to simulate some level of contrition. "I knew she wasn't in immediate danger."

Lanoe shook his head in frustration. He was getting nowhere.

He'd known for a while that Valk was falling apart. Paniet had warned him about it, but he'd been able to see it with his own eyes. And he still needed Valk, the AI was still crucial to his plans. This wasn't good. He gestured at the empty suit lying at the controls. "What's going on here?"

"Manifesting a human shape was using up energy we could better use elsewhere," Valk told him. "If it bothers you, seeing me like that—"

"It does," Lanoe said.

"I never thought you were such a stickler for your troops keeping their uniforms in good order," Valk said, and then he laughed.

But the suit moved, straightening up. The black helmet flowed up out of the collar ring. The suit's arms lifted and the gloves arrayed themselves over a virtual keyboard. "Better?"

Something occurred to Lanoe. "Stand up," he said.

"Why?"

"I want to see you stand up. Don't worry about wasting energy. Paniet fixed the leak in our engine, so we have plenty of power. Just stand up for me. Maybe walk around a little."

"I'm not sure I want to," Valk said.

"It's an order."

"Lanoe... it hurts."

"You told me once that everything hurt. All the time. Phantom body syndrome, right? That's what you called it?"

"Yes," Valk replied. "I have that even now, but it's like a dull ache. A soreness in muscles that should be there, but aren't. If you make me stand up, it'll turn into real pain. I don't want to feel pain. What conscious being wants to feel pain?"

"One," Lanoe said, "that wants to obey the orders of his commanding officer."

It took a while. There were false starts, as Valk bent forward at the waist, then fell back against his padded seat. His legs moved, his boots shuffling against the deck plating. Making little progress. Eventually, though, he rose to stand. He took two steps forward, toward Lanoe.

"Is it bad?" Lanoe asked.

"Bad enough," Valk said. He didn't grunt in frustration, or gasp at fresh pains, but Lanoe could tell he was having trouble.

"Do a lap of the wardroom," Lanoe told him. "Then I'll look at your damned computer model."

Valk took the suit for a spin, showing no sign of distress now. However much pain he might be experiencing, it didn't slow him down.

Lanoe watched him go with a dubious look. "You seem to be doing fine."

"Seem," Valk said. "Seem. Seem. Seem. It's a simulation. Everything I am is a simulation."

"You need to get it together, Valk."

The AI laughed. "Do I? I'm not supposed to exist, Lanoe. I'm supposed to be destroyed, deleted. Fragmented and then wiped. Even I think I'm an abomination. But you want me to 'get it together.' To stabilize."

It wasn't the first time Valk had talked about being erased. He'd even given Lanoe a gift once, a software package in the form of a black pearl. A data bomb—if Lanoe so much as swiped his eyes across that black pearl, it would start a chain reaction that would expunge Valk entirely from any computer he inhabited. Lanoe had archived the black pearl, knowing that someday he might actually need it.

But not today.

"I still need you," he said.

"You do." It wasn't ego saying that. It was a simple statement of fact. Valk knew just how valuable he was.

Lanoe sighed. "Come on, big guy. You need to..." Something occurred to him. "You need to show me that computer model you keep talking about."

The transformation was instant. Before, Valk had sounded depressed, even suicidal. Now, with no transition, he was all energy and purpose. The AI dropped back into his seat and called up a large display that showed the disk in all its swirling glory. Metadata flashed all around the image, numbers showing distances between objects, relative masses, a timeframe. "If you look here—"

"Hold on," Lanoe said. He couldn't shift gears as quickly as Valk. He rose from his seat—exhaling sharply as he exercised old, stiff joints—and walked over to the control stand. "Tell me what I'm seeing. Keep it simple for me."

"Okay," Valk said. "This is a simulation of all the mass in the disk, the gas and dust and the little shepherd moons. I plugged in all the variables we could think of, gravity, angular momentum, the effect of the stellar wind, and so on, and then I let it run for a couple of billion simulated years. That didn't quite work. The disk fell apart almost immediately, all that hydrogen gas just pouring onto the surface of the star. The end result was just a bigger star, which made no sense."

"How long would it take for the disk to collapse?"

"A few hundred years."

Lanoe nodded. "The Blue-Blue-White have whole cities down there. Nobody would put cities in a gas cloud that's just going to go poof in that kind of timeframe."

"Right," Valk said. "There's some kind of force holding the disk back from falling into the star. Maybe a weather field, like we use in our airlocks, but on this kind of scale that seems unlikely. The power you would need to keep something like that going would be immense, much more than you could get even if you collected all the energy coming off of the star. No, there's something else at work here. I have no idea what it might be, but I know it has to be there. I added a variable that pushes the gas away from the star and the model worked great, it ran for billions of years without significant loss of mass. Interesting enough, right?"

"I suppose," Lanoe said.

"It is to me. But if that doesn't get you interested, this definitely will. The next step was to run the model backward in time. Take it right back to zero. That's when I found the real puzzle. There is no zero."

"I have no idea what you mean by that."

Valk sighed. It sounded like a real sigh, anyway. "I wanted to see how the disk formed in the first place. How all that gas could just accumulate without coalescing into a gas giant, or a brown dwarf, or even a star—a binary companion to the red dwarf. The answer is, it couldn't. Or at least, the odds of such a thing happened are—ha—astronomical."

"There must be something wrong with your model, then. Or there's something we don't know yet about astrophysics, something that can allow this."

"Oh," Valk said, "there are plenty of mysteries left in space. But this isn't one of them. The answer isn't that we don't know how this sort of thing could form in nature. The answer is much simpler."

"Yeah?"

"Yes. It didn't."

It took Lanoe a minute to realize what Valk was telling him. When he did, he made a fist and thumped Valk's console. "Holy damn," he said. "You're saying—"

"The disk is artificial. The Blue-Blue-White built it."

Lanoe closed his eyes. He felt like his brain was reeling, spinning out of control. "Get Candless over here. And Paniet, we definitely want Paniet's opinion on this. Get them over here now."

In the brig, the two of them were moving. Ehta had unlocked Ginger's suit and now the girl was in there, moving with the alien. They circled around each other, every motion exactly mirrored by the other. When Rain-on-Stones lifted one arm in a feeble gesture, Ginger matched it perfectly. When the chorister reared her head back in what looked like a silent shriek, Ginger's head snapped back, too—and her mouth opened and she let out a chilling cry.

Ehta knew she should stop watching. That she should get away from this—for her own mental health if nothing else. But she couldn't. She just stood there in front of the open hatch of the cell, stood there barely even blinking.

The alien's movements were slow, still. The sedative hadn't completely worn off. Her legs slipped on the padded floor, her feet unsuited to standing on such a smooth surface. Every time, Ginger slipped, too, almost falling.

Ginger didn't look at Ehta. She didn't say a word in any language. The lucidity that had come and gone before, the ability to focus on the human beings around her, was gone. She was trapped now, trapped in this strange dance with the alien.

Help me, she'd begged. *Ehta, help me.*

But how? How was Ehta supposed to do anything for the girl? She was gone, lost in her communion with the chorister's slowly waking mind.

Lanoe won't set me free.

Free—free of her connection to the chorister? Ehta had suggested earlier that they wrap the girl's head in metal foil, to block off the alien thoughts that were being beamed ceaselessly into her brain. Ginger hadn't thought that would work, maybe, or perhaps she'd simply known that wouldn't be enough.

Set me free.

The two of them dropped to the floor, Ginger down on her hands and knees. Rain-on-Stones on more legs and arms that Ehta could count. Together they pawed and scratched at the padded walls of the cell. The alien's limbs moved with furious speed, as if she were trying to dig her way out of a grave.

Ginger's hands blurred as she desperately scrabbled to keep up. To match those anguished movements.

Set me free.

Suddenly, Ehta understood.

What the girl wanted. Why she had turned to a marine for help. Regardless of the problem in front of them, marines only ever used one solution.

Set me free, the girl had begged.

The only way that would be permanent. The only way Ginger could survive, long-term.

She wanted Ehta to kill the chorister.

It was the only possible way.

Candless stared at the display, her face pinched as her eyes followed its swirling course. Lanoe watched her carefully.

"You are telling me," she said, "that the disk is artificial."

"Yes," Lanoe said.

"You're saying—you're claiming that the Blue-Blue-White don't just live here. That they actually built the place, too."

"Yes," Lanoe said, again.

"You can't possibly be serious. It's simply too big."

"It's the only thing that fits all the data we've collected," Valk insisted.

"Then for the first time in history, mathematics has been proved wrong," Candless said.

Lanoe was pretty sure that coming from her that counted as a joke.

"I had him run me through it a couple of times before I realized he was right," Lanoe said. "Look here, at these shepherd moons. They're there for a reason. You see how the outer edge of the disk has those tiny gaps in it? Those are where the moons sweep through, clearing out dust. Their gravity isn't much, but it's enough to pull the gas along with them. They keep the hydrogen from just flowing off into deep space."

"Ooh," Paniet said. The neddy was crouched down next to the display, a look of utter excitement and happiness on his face.

"The gas is thickest here, on the inner rim of the disk," Lanoe pointed out. "Where it's balanced against the stellar wind. It's thinnest at the outer edge. That's important, too. The disk is only about two million kilometers in radius—"

"Only!" Candless said.

Lanoe shrugged. "It orbits pretty close to the star, is what I'm saying. So it gets pretty hot—that inner rim is baking at about a thousand degrees. But because that's the thickest part, it serves as a buffer, soaking up all that heat and radiation. The central section, where the cities are, is protected by that buffer. The average temperature here," he said, pointing at the central part of the disk, where the cities were, "is about three hundred degrees."

"How temperate," Candless said. "Balmy, even."

Lanoe ignored her. "The density changes, too. There's a gradient from inner rim to outer rim. In the center, the zone of the cities, it's about the same average density as Saturn, six hundred and eighty-seven kilograms per cubic meter."

"Ooh," Paniet said, tilting his head to one side. "Less dense than water. Interesting."

Lanoe ignored him, too. "We don't know much about the Blue-Blue-White, but we know they evolved in the atmosphere of a gas giant planet. Probably one a lot like Saturn, but hotter. That city zone is the perfect environment for our jellyfish. Given how unlikely it is that the disk just formed naturally, how much more unlikely would it be that it would form in exactly the right conditions for them?"

"I imagine the odds would be quite low," Candless admitted. "But you still need to answer one question. How exactly would they do such a thing? This is far beyond anything we—we meaning humans here—ever imagined. The scale alone..."

"Ah," Paniet said. Then he stood up quickly. "We do know that the Blue-Blue-White are planetary engineers. That's why they built their drone fleets in the first place. To spread out through the galaxy and terraform—if you'll forgive a slightly incorrect term—every gas giant they could get their hands on."

Candless still didn't look convinced. She opened her wrist display and started tapping at virtual keys. "Two million kilometers major radius, one hundred thousand kilometers mean minor radius..." she said under her breath.

Which Valk seemed to find amusing. He laughed, anyway.

"May I inquire," Candless said, "what precisely you think is so humorous?"

"You're doing math," the AI said.

Everyone, including Lanoe, turned to stare at him.

"What? You could just ask me. You're trying to compute the volume of the disk. It's about three hundred and ninety-five quadrillion cubic kilometers—roughly two hundred and seventy-six times the volume of Jupiter."

"Quadrillion," Candless said. "That's a number you don't run across very often."

Paniet nodded. "Multiply that by the density, Valk. How much does this thing mass?"

Valk didn't hesitate in responding. "Two hundred and seventy-one octillion kilograms."

"Oh, now we're into the octillions," Candless said, nodding her head sagely. "And that, of course, is where your theory is going to fall apart."

"How so?" Lanoe asked.

Candless practically spluttered in disbelief, as if it should be perfectly obvious. "Where, pray tell, would our jellyfish friends even find so much mass? Admittedly, hydrogen is common enough in the universe. But that much of it in one place—"

"Actually," Paniet said, "I can think of one obvious source."

"You can," Candless said.

"Yes, dear." He pointed at the display. At the very center of it. At the red dwarf in the middle of the disk. "A star. A red dwarf would do, say, about a quarter of a solar mass in size—"

"Less, actually," Valk pointed out. "About thirteen percent of a solar mass."

"Right," Paniet said. "See? Easy."

Lanoe frowned. "What are you suggesting?"

Paniet shrugged. "More what I'm guessing. But it fits. I think that a very long time ago this star system was a binary. Two red dwarfs orbiting each other very close. The Blue-Blue-White evolved on a gas giant that circled them both, but they outgrew their original planet and needed more space to move about. So to make this—this disk thing—they dismantled one of the red dwarfs. Sort of smeared it out across its own orbit."

Candless had gone pale. Lanoe watched her carefully. She'd accepted it, he saw. She believed that the disk was artificial.

She was still having trouble with what that meant, however.

"You're saying that these jellyfish don't just tinker with planets in their spare time," she said, in an uncharacteristically soft voice. "They build things out of stars, too."

Paniet nodded gleefully. "Isn't it just wonderful?"

Chapter Twelve

In the tent hidden deep inside the carrier's flight deck, Paniet ran one hand along the smooth side of the Screamer. It felt good, solid. A piece of work he could be proud of. He turned and looked at Hollander and gave him a smile. "Would you be a dear and give those locking nuts one more turn?"

"Right," the Hadean neddy said. He pushed his way under the connecting spar that held the thruster package onto the main body of the drone and made the adjustment. Other neddies polished the big lenses or checked the inflight electronics packages.

It was done. Paniet stood back and examined his handiwork. The Screamer's main body was a spherical casing about two meters across, studded all over with the lenses of extremely powerful searchlights in fifteen different colors. The sphere was attached to the thruster package by three gimbal mounts that would let it turn in almost any direction. Four booms stuck out from the connecting spar, each of them carrying a photosensitive dish receiver.

"Not bad for a rush job. All right, neddies. Stand back and let's see what this thing can do."

The work crew filed out of the tent one by one, Hollander lingering for one last moment to slap Paniet on the back. "Is it going to work, do you think?"

"It'll work," Paniet told him. He gave the other man a quick hug, then sent him away. When he was alone in the tent with his creation, Paniet tapped at his wrist display and warmed up the Screamer's thrusters. Then he pulled a cable that collapsed the tent, leaving the drone pointed out at the star-rich sky.

The disk was visible just up ahead, a red smear across the face of the red dwarf. Only a few hundred million kilometers away now. Lanoe had slowed the fleet down prior to final approach maneuvers, but still they hurtled toward their appointment with the jellyfish faster than a rifle bullet.

Paniet crouched down behind a spare piece of blast shielding, then sent a message to the commander, asking if he was ready to proceed.

Lanoe sent back a text-only message. *SURE*.

Paniet tapped one last key, and the Screamer's engines lit up. The drone shot forward, past the rows of fighters hanging from the flight deck's walls, out through the carrier's mouth and into space. Paniet watched the flare of its engines until it was just a bright dot in the sky.

Ashlay Bullam snapped her fingers and one of her drones rose from the yacht's deck. It manifested a display showing her a mirror image of her face and chest, which she explored carefully, looking for any shadows lingering just under her skin. Without access to proper medical facilities, there was no way to tell if there was a blood clot in her system even now, working its slow but inevitable way toward her brain.

It was a danger she'd lived with all her life. Always before, however, she'd been able to count on a small army of doctors ready to catch the clots before they could do any damage. Obsessively studying her own reflection might make her look vain, but it was impossible not to wonder, and worry.

Maggs was nattering on about all the devious things he'd done in her service. She knew she ought to pay close attention, but it sounded like things were moving along just fine.

"You were right about Shulkin, of course. I went over there with a bottle of schnapps and used my not inconsiderable charm to gain access to his cabin. At first it was rather like talking to a potted plant, but once he realized I was the son of a famous admiral, he came to life. What followed is best described as dull, tedious, and enervating—hours of war stories, endless discussions of the minutiae of campaigns that were fought long before I was born. But I do believe I've gotten on his good side. Whether or not I was perfectly willing to stick a knife in his back just ten days ago."

"Well done," Bullam said. She prodded at the skin below her collarbone. Nothing there but a perfectly natural shadow, she thought. "What about Ehta?"

"Oh, the good major was a bit tougher of a nut to crack. The way she spoke to me bordered on the gleefully sadistic. Once she saw I could take a joke, though, she eased up just a hair. Of course, she wouldn't tell me anything useful—especially since I didn't ask—but we chatted on this and that, the quality of various reconstituted foodstuffs and the fact that a marine's work is never done. As you requested, I kept it light."

"I know it seems like I'm having you gossip to no purpose," Bullam said. "I hope you don't feel like I'm wasting your talents."

"Hardly. I understand the principle full well," Maggs said. "I'm establishing a network, building—well, I wouldn't call it trust. I'm afraid I've burned too many bridges, especially with the Navy folk. But as long as I can keep them talking, there's a chance they'll actually start listening to what I have to say. What you tell me to say, of course."

"You're a good man, Auster Maggs, and a positive asset in—"

Bullam stopped because one of her drones had drifted over to her, a green light burning on its face. She beckoned it closer and then ran one finger across a biometric panel below the light. The drone shot a laser into her eye. Bullam's suit didn't have all the fancy communications gear that was standard equipment on Navy suits. She had to receive her messages the old-fashioned way.

"It appears," she said, "that my presence has been requested on the bridge of the carrier."

"They've launched the Screamer, then," Maggs said.

Bullam nodded. "Must be. Why they want me there when it activates, I have no idea. Perhaps Lanoe just wants a witness."

"A witness to what?" Maggs said.

"Whatever happens next, there will be a lot of questions for Lanoe when we get home. He's already disobeyed official Navy orders just by coming here. If he actually starts a fight with these bloody jellyfish of his, well, the powers that be might brand him a war criminal. I think maybe he wants someone—a civilian—who can vouch for the fact that he actually did try talking to the aliens, before he killed them all."

Maggs laughed. "Bastards like Lanoe never get what's coming to them. He's far too lucky for that. Well, enjoy your outing. I'll stay here and prepare your dinner for when you get back."

"You really are a darling," she said, and favored him with a warm smile. Then she put up her helmet and pushed her way through the yacht's flowglas dome. She spared a thought as she went as to why Maggs really wanted to stay onboard while she was gone. No doubt he intended to rifle through her things. Well, let him. All of Ashlay Bullam's best secrets were kept tightly inside her own head.

≈

A green pearl rotated in the corner of Ehta's vision. A message from Candless, of all people. What did that witch want? Ehta looked up and then down to archive the message. It was just going to have to wait—she had more important things on her mind. She had just reached the entrance to the brig, where two of her marines stood guard. Binah was one of them. Binah who'd had his face cut up when they boarded the carrier. The other was Horvath, a kid she'd found on Tuonela. She nodded at them, but their helmets were up and silvered, so if they nodded back she didn't notice.

Neddies had bolted up foam rubber cladding on the hatch that led to the brig. It cut down on the noise coming from inside, the sobbing, the begging, the pleading. But not much.

Ehta had a sidearm, a pistol with explosive bullets she thought would do the trick. The marines would let her inside without a question. She could just walk into the cell, aim, and shoot, and then—

Then none of them would ever go home again. The alien in there, the big bug thing, was their only ticket back to human space.

But Ehta had promised the girl. She'd looked in Ginger's eyes and told her she would help, somehow. She didn't owe the kid anything, really. Ehta liked Ginger, she supposed, but not enough that she would disobey Lanoe's orders for her. Not normally.

The noise from inside was pretty bad. Whatever was happening in there, it sounded . . . bad.

She took a step closer to the hatch. She realized she was breathing heavily, and she wondered why. She'd shot plenty of people in her time. Even some aliens, if you counted the drones she'd fought back at Niraya. She dropped her hand to her side, her thumb brushing the barrel of her pistol. Did the two marines bristle, then? Had they seen her touching her weapon, wondered what was up? No, she was imagining things. Neither of them moved a millimeter.

Open it up, she thought. All she had to say was *open it up.* The marines would jump to do what she said. Even after, when they saw what she'd done, they wouldn't turn on her, she knew that. They would wonder why. They might even ask.

But they were her friends, her squaddies. Her troops. She was their immediate superior officer. If she did this they would back her up, as best they could.

Not that they would be much use once Lanoe heard what had happened.

She wasn't afraid to die here, so far from home. She'd always known she would die on a battlefield. The where didn't matter. When Lanoe had come to her and asked her to join him on yet another crazy mission, she hadn't hesitated. But Binah and Horvath hadn't known what they were getting themselves into. Maybe they had lives back home still. People who loved them. If she took this shot, if she killed the chorister, it was the two of them—it was all of her marines—who would pay the price.

Carefully, slowly, she lifted her hand away from her thigh. Reached up and scratched at the side of her nose. The fingers of her glove came away slick with sweat.

"Ma'am?" Horvath asked.

Ehta stared at him with wide eyes.

"Just checking in," she told him. "You two all right down here? The noise isn't bothering you?"

"We're fine, ma'am," Binah told her.

Ehta nodded. She stood there a moment longer, staring at the hatch. Not even seeing it, really. The screams were turning into background noise. It was now or—

She turned on her heel and walked away.

As she walked, she clamped her eyes tight. Gritted her teeth. Let the roar of her own blood in her head be the only thing she heard.

Eventually she calmed down enough to look at the message Candless had sent her. She was supposed to report to the bridge of the carrier.

She shook her head. Rubbed at her face with her hands.

She would come back. And maybe next time she would be stronger.

On the bridge of the carrier, Bury fought to try to get a good view of what was going on. He had been invited—he was an officer, after all—but no one was making room for him. Typical.

The bridge was packed full of bodies. Most of the Naval officers were there, Lanoe and Candless and Paniet, and somebody had said Ehta was on her way. A bunch of Centrocor people were present, the carrier's pilots and navigators and IOs, and the leader of their marines. Captain Shulkin sat in the chair in the middle of the room, which was his by right. The two Batygins were present via hologram, their identical faces floating over the proceedings. Even the civilian woman, the Centrocor executive, was present.

Not Maggs, of course. Maggs had tried to kill Bury once, and the Hellion would have relished a chance to confront him now. But of course a traitor like that wouldn't get an invitation. Valk was absent too—Lanoe didn't want any of the Centrocor people to even get a look at his pet AI—but Bury had no doubt he was listening in.

"Three hundred thousand kilometers," one of the IOs announced. "Still no activity from the disk."

Lanoe nodded. He was watching the big display. It showed a schematic view of the disk, with the trajectory of the Screamer plotted across it as a yellow curve. The drone ship was headed toward the thickest part of the disk, the area where Lanoe had seen the cities. There was a display showing the view from the drone's cameras, but Bury wasn't tall enough to see over the people in front of him and he only got occasional glimpses. The display didn't show much he hadn't seen before, anyway. Red clouds circling a dull orange star.

Bury was reporting to Valk these days, serving as his information officer—an utterly pointless and boring assignment, since the AI had no use for an IO. The one prerogative of the job was that by eavesdropping, Bury got to hear all about what was going on, what Lanoe had planned for first contact with the Blue-Blue-White. Valk had even explained to Bury how the Screamer worked. The jellyfish didn't have a spoken language, or any normal kind of written one. They communicated by generating colored lights inside their bodies. The Screamer was built to put out incredibly bright pulses of light, bright enough to be visible even through the thick clouds of the disk. It could broadcast in all the colors the jellyfish recognized, which, it turned out, weren't exactly the same colors humans saw. They could see in the near ultraviolet and identified five kinds of blue as individual colors, but had only one name for both orange and red. There were fifteen total colors because they had fifteen tentacles. They even used base fifteen as their number system, which made no sense to Bury at all.

That was the majority of what they knew about the Blue-Blue-White. It would be surprising they knew that much—if not for Valk. Back during the battle of Niraya, the AI had been imprisoned on an alien queenship, a giant terraforming machine. The queenship's computers had found a way to talk to him, machine to machine. From that brief contact Valk had gleaned a rudimentary understanding of their language and biology, though next to nothing about their culture or religion or their philosophy or anything else. They had no idea how the jellyfish would react to being signaled by the Screamer, so it had been decided to send the drone in first, unescorted. For all they knew, the Blue-Blue-White would attack the thing.

Bury hoped they did. He didn't see much point in trying to talk to the aliens first. They were here to start a war, right?

A war other people would fight. He reminded himself he was on the inactive list, due to his supposed injuries. The only chance he would have to get his fifth kill—and his blue star—was if so many of the Centrocor pilots died that Lanoe had to send in any pilot he could get.

Bury was not so bloodthirsty that he wished any pilot dead. But maybe—maybe there would be a disease outbreak on the carrier. Something nonfatal but debilitating, even just food poisoning.

Maybe, just maybe, he would get his chance.

><del>—</del>≻≺<del>—</del>

"Passing the outer edge of the disk now," the carrier's IO said. "Entering the uppermost layer of the atmosphere."

Candless nodded at the man, though she'd barely heard him. Her attention was riveted on the forward view from the drone as it flew over the disk at a shallow angle. The drone was burning hard to decelerate and the disk unfurled beneath it with an aching slowness.

Tendrils of red gas licked upward toward the camera, like the tentacles of a beast two million kilometers wide. As the drone shot over one of the gaps in the disk she had a very quick glimpse of one of its shepherd moons. If there'd been any doubt left that the Blue-Blue-White had built the disk to their specifications, the moon disabused Candless of that notion. She'd expected to see an amorphous chunk of dead rock, perhaps pitted with craters. Instead its entire surface was covered with white spars like the ones that made up the cities, so that it looked like the moon was trapped inside a cage of bones.

Oh, come now. She told herself she was being melodramatic.

She isolated a still image of the moon. The resolution wasn't fantastic. The drone was moving very fast and only got a split-second look, but the image was clear enough to make out some further details. Contained inside the cagework were colossal structures of some kind, fantastic shapes she couldn't even recognize. They might be habitats or factories or maybe something else entirely. She nudged Lanoe's arm.

"When you told me about Niraya," she said, keeping her voice low, "you mentioned that you destroyed a Blue-Blue-White mining facility. Does any of that look familiar to you?"

He glanced at the isolated image and shrugged. "Sure. I guess—those towers," he said. He gestured at a row of tall, skeletal pylons crowned with what looked like flexible segmented arms. She started to ask him what they were, but he had already looked away, his gaze fixed on the main schematic display.

But then she saw something else, something she recognized from images he'd shown her. "If you would be kind enough to give me some small shred of your attention," she said, "look there." And pointed with a trembling finger.

He turned impatiently toward her, but when he saw what she was pointing at she could tell she had his attention. Right on the surface of the shepherd moon, in a cradle of white spars not unlike a spider's web, sat an oblong rocky object about a kilometer in diameter. An asteroidal rock, by the look of it, but the Blue-Blue-

White had hollowed it out, leaving one end open in a wide circular maw. A maw surrounded by fifteen long dark pylons that resembled tentacles.

Tiny specks moved around the object, and she saw an infinitesimal flash of light come from within the mouth.

"That's a queenship," he said.

"The main element of one of their drone fleets, yes?" Candless said. "Am I right?"

"You're right." His face darkened and she saw his hands curl into fists. "And that must be a drydock it's in. They're still building the damned things. They're building more. I guess their work isn't done."

Candless closed her eyes and tried to breathe.

"They'd better have a damned good explanation," Lanoe said, very quietly.

She knew him, well enough that she recognized that tone. When he spoke that softly, it meant he was about to kill someone.

Please, she thought, *please—when you hear our message, consider it carefully. Otherwise, we're all going to pay.*

On the camera feed, the drone was nearing the central zone, the city zone, where the disk grew thick with piles of red cloud. None of the cities were immediately visible, but Valk had logged their positions and their velocity and he could estimate their locations.

The scale of the cloudscape was beyond anything a human being could have imagined before. Earth could be dropped into those billows of red and black and it would simply sink from view, lost in the murk. Wherever the clouds parted to form infinitely deep canyons Valk saw massive, blindingly bright bolts of lightning jump back and forth between them.

"The drone is meeting atmospheric resistance," the carrier's IO said. Valk didn't need to be on the big ship to hear what was being said. "Velocity has dropped to fifty kilometers a second."

On this kind of scale, that was a snail's pace. It would still take the drone half an hour just to cross the zone of the cities. More than enough time for a conversation.

A great deal of thought had gone into what they should say to the Blue-Blue-White. When Valk interfaced with their drone fleet at Niraya he had downloaded a large amount of data, but most of it had been in machine language. Only a few messages had been encoded in the color language of the aliens. As a result he had only a basic vocabulary to work with, so the message had to be simple.

The obvious choice had just been "Hello, we would like to speak to you." Simple, and not aggressive. The kind of message that might get a favorable response.

Lanoe had shot that down at once. He didn't want to give the Blue-Blue-White the impression that humanity had come to their doorstep to make friends. Sending any kind of message at all meant forgoing the element of surprise, so he had argued that they should declare their purpose here as clearly as possible. He wanted the message to read, "You must answer for your crimes."

Candless had disagreed—she felt that Lanoe's message might as well say, "You're under arrest. Keep your hands where we can see them." Instead, she'd argued for a more nuanced introduction. Valk had struggled to translate her words, but in the end they'd come up with, "We have a message of great urgency."

Lanoe still didn't like it. He was spoiling for a fight. Some great triumph to slake his thirst for revenge—but even he had to recognize that the best outcome here would be for real communication with the jellyfish. Eventually Candless had gotten him to compromise.

"Ready to begin signaling," Valk said, sending his words directly to Lanoe's suit. Through a camera view he saw Lanoe nod.

"Do it," he said.

Valk painted the Screamer with a communications laser and sent the command. The little drone started to spin, its colored lights flashing in precisely timed intervals. The language of the Blue-Blue-White was heavily nuanced—the fifteen colors were important, but so were the durations of each color, their chromaticity and value.

The color schedule had all been worked out in advance, but Valk translated it to himself as the Screamer flashed out its message.

Blue–long blue–short white, the name of the species itself, which they always used to begin an address. *Purple–purple–long purple–green–dark blue–long green:* "We have a message." *White–dull red–white–very bright white,* to indicate emphasis. *Vivid blue–long vivid blue–very bright short white,* to suggest that the message sender possessed high authority.

The message repeated, over and over.

Valk watched the people on the bridge. Every face was frozen with anticipation, with dread, with, perhaps, a little hope. If the Blue-Blue-White responded favorably, perhaps there was a chance at some kind of communication, of understanding. Perhaps, eventually, some form of reconciliation.

As the Screamer pulsed out the colors, over and over, heart rates on the bridge started to climb. A few people started to sweat.

Shulkin's biodata didn't change at all. The man was a statue. Bury didn't sweat, because he was a Hellion.

Lanoe's heart rate actually slowed down.

"We have to give them a chance to respond," Candless said. "This is going to come as quite a shock to them, they'll—"

But before she'd finished her thought, the reply came. Searchlights lanced upward through the clouds, incredibly powerful lights in all fifteen colors, flickering as they replied to the Screamer. Not just one reply, but dozens, from at least three different cities. The colored beams swept across the sky, homing in on the Screamer as it rocketed through the outer atmosphere of the disk.

Valk overclocked himself trying to record all the incoming messages. *Blue–long blue–long blue–long blue–bright white.*

Orange–short orange–vivid orange.

Green–blue–white–vivid red–dull red–blue.

Vivid orange–vivid orange–vivid orange–vivid orange–short vivid orange.

Some of the responses repeated, some were sent only once.

Some were stronger than others. Data spooled at incredible speed through Valk's processors, datasets combined, forced into arrays, broken back out into strings. He applied Fourier transforms and n-gram predictive algorithms, pushed it all through brute-force Markov models.

He was done long before Lanoe spoke.

"Well? What are they saying?"

The problem was, Valk didn't have an answer.

In Lanoe's ear, Valk's voice sounded perfectly human. And perfectly apologetic.

"It's...gibberish," the AI said.

Lanoe scowled. Knowing full well that Valk would see the expression. Wanting him to.

"I'm trying, Lanoe, I really am. It's just—I only have a limited vocabulary to begin with. I kind of expected I wouldn't fully understand their replies, but I'm getting nothing. Not a single one of the replies means anything I can process. Maybe...I don't know, it's like there are some root words in there, a couple of suffixes I recognize, and even then I'm using metaphors, comparing this to the way we process spoken language, and this is a completely different kind of—"

"Say again," Lanoe told him. "This time, speak plainly."

"The message we sent is one of the simpler things you can say in their language. Their responses seem simple, too. Except I don't understand any of it. I don't have an explanation. Just the fact that it doesn't make any sense."

Lanoe pursed his lips. Nodded to himself. Then he turned to look at Candless, and the carrier's IO, Giles. "Tell me what's happening with the drone."

Giles responded first. "The Screamer is still decelerating, mostly because of air resistance. It's still moving faster than escape velocity for the disk, though. If we don't change its course it'll eventually collide with the star. Of course, it'll be vaporized long before it reaches the photosphere."

Lanoe nodded. That wasn't a problem—in fact, flying into the star had always been built into the drone's flight plan. If the Blue-Blue-White responded unfavorably, or even just ignored the Screamer, Lanoe had wanted to make sure they didn't get their tentacles on it. They could learn a great deal about human technology by taking it apart and studying it.

"Valk is having trouble decoding their responses," Lanoe told the crowd on the bridge. "In the meantime, we're going to—"

"I beg your pardon, sir," Candless said. "But look. There."

She pointed at the display that showed the camera view from the Screamer's nose. Much of the image was just a welter of dark red swirling clouds. Along one side, though, he could see some lighter dots. They grew in size as he watched them.

"Those must be Blue-Blue-White vehicles, coming to meet us," Giles said. "At least, coming to check out our drone."

"Thank you, Lieutenant, for stating the obvious," Candless said. "Commander Lanoe, sir? Would you like us to respond in any way?"

"Valk," Lanoe said, "have the Screamer send my message. The one I originally wanted to send. Maybe they'll respond to that."

"If you're sure," Valk said.

"I'm sure," Lanoe told him.

On the main display, a schematic of the Screamer displayed which of its fifteen lamps was in use at a given time. The new message contained a lot more vivid orange than the previous one.

"Those vehicles are moving very fast," Giles said. "In fact, the one in the lead is—oh. Uh, sir, those are—"

"I see it," Lanoe said. Those weren't vehicles approaching the Screamer. They were projectiles. Missiles.

The first one hit the drone off center, knocking it off its course. Bars of static raced up and down across the camera view.

The second projectile smashed the Screamer into a million pieces.

The camera view went blank instantly. On the schematic view the debris from the Screamer appeared as bright dots spreading out across the sky of the disk.

"The drone has been destroyed," Giles said. Perhaps for the benefit of anyone who hadn't already figured that out.

"There's movement down in the clouds," Candless said. She brought up a new display to replace the lost camera feed. The new imagery came from the carrier's own long-range telescopes, and it showed a much wider view of swirling cloudscape. Something dark was swimming its way up through those clouds, tendrils of red wisping off its surface as it surfaced.

An actual vehicle this time, Lanoe thought. No missile, no projectile would ever be that large. As it rose above the top layer of clouds, he realized that he was seeing, for the very first time, a Blue-Blue-White ship. Not one of the drones he'd fought at Niraya but an actual ship containing actual jellyfish. It was oblong and lumpy, its surface broken in a dozen places by white cagework blisters. Deep pits in its hull glowed with heat—those had to be either thrusters or weapons.

The ship was—big. It could be hard to tell such things from a distance, but the amount of light it caught, even in that dim cloudscape, made Lanoe think it was very, very big.

"What's the scale on this?" Lanoe said.

Giles leaned over his console, reading numbers from a display. "The wingspan is . . . Hellfire. Approximately five kilometers."

Ten times bigger than the carrier. Far bigger than the largest dreadnought humanity had ever built. Five times bigger than the queenship Lanoe had fought at Niraya.

He let his mind reel for a second. Got himself back under control.

"All ships," he said. "Move in for a close approach."

Candless whirled around to look at him, her eyes bright with fear. "Sir," she said.

"Do it," he said. He turned and looked back at Shulkin. The madman was leaning forward in his chair, a tiny smile on his lips.

Above their heads the holographic images of the Batygin brothers looked grim but resolute.

"They wouldn't listen to our message," Lanoe said. "Maybe if we show up in person, they'll pay attention."

The gravity on the bridge increased as the carrier accelerated toward the rendezvous. They had been hanging back behind the Screamer, but only by a million kilometers or so. It wouldn't take long to close the distance.

Chapter Thirteen

ultiple radar signatures just below the top layer of clouds," the IO called out. "It's hard to get a fix on them—those clouds are full of particulates that block my scans. I can only get a sense of things moving around down there. None of them are as big as the—I'm sorry, I don't know what to call that thing," he said, gesturing at the giant ship on the display.

"Dreadnought," Shulkin said, startling a few people near him. Most likely they had forgotten he was there, Candless thought.

"Sure," Lanoe said. "It's a dreadnought. Good a name as any. What's our ETA?"

"Two minutes," Giles said.

"Commander," Candless said, "there's a decision to be made, and it should be done now. If you want the cruiser to warm up its coilguns, they'll need about ninety seconds."

She turned and looked Lanoe directly in the eye. Because what he said next was going to determine a number of things. Perhaps most saliently, their strategy. If they arrived with the coilguns hot, and if the Blue-Blue-White had sensor technology comparable to their own, the jellyfish would see that they had come for a fight. It would be the end of any attempt at negotiation or diplomacy.

If, however, he failed to give the order to ready the guns and they got into a fight anyway, the guns would be useless for ninety seconds. Many battles didn't even last that long. He would essentially be removing one of his best weapons from the fight.

There was another layer of consequence to his decision, though. If he readied the guns, then she would know he never had any real intention of seeking redress. That he had come here for pure, simple revenge.

She saw his jaw move as he gritted his teeth, thinking it through. He'd always been a man of action, and she knew she wouldn't have to wait long for her answer.

He turned to look at Ehta. "Have the gun crews stand ready," he told her. "But don't warm them up, not yet."

Candless allowed herself a sigh of relief.

"I should be over there, with my people, sir," Ehta said.

Lanoe just nodded at her and turned back to the display. Ehta exited the bridge in a hurry—she just had time to get someone to fly her back to the cruiser.

"Should we scramble the fighters?" Candless asked next.

Lanoe looked deeply annoyed as he answered. He waved one hand in a chopping motion. "Have all pilots report to their ready stations. But keep them on standby."

"Very good, sir," Candless said. She tapped at a virtual keyboard to give the order. Every pilot on the carrier would move immediately to the corridors that flanked the flight deck, ready to jump into the cockpits of their carrier scouts and Yk.64s at a moment's notice. "And M. Valk?" she asked, because there were more fighters—BR.9s—in the cruiser's vehicle bay, but the AI was the only available pilot to fly them. Knowing what it meant to have him operate those cataphracts, Candless did not relish the prospect. "I presume we don't need his help at this time."

He gave her a very nasty glare. He knew that she was trying to keep him on the straight and narrow, and he didn't like it. She did not care in the least.

Candless had been a teacher once. Bury and Ginger had been her students and she would have done anything to keep them safe. Lanoe had put both of them in incredible danger, and the fact that they were still alive was little short of a miracle. Candless had failed, then, in her duty to her pupils. Perhaps by way of atonement, she'd extended her obligation to the entirety of the fleet. She would not let anyone—Navy, Centrocor, civilian—get hurt now, not if she could prevent it.

"M. Valk is not exactly in my good graces right now," Lanoe said. No, in other words. He looked up at the identical holographic heads floating over them. "Batygins. I have orders for you. Keep well back of the carrier, but be ready to move in fast when I give the order. Ready firing solutions for your missiles, but don't shoot until I give the word."

"Understood, Commander."

"Understood, Commander," the twins said, just a split second out of synch.

Candless bent over her console. "Thirty seconds to close approach," she said. "All hands prepare for maneuvers. May we please clear the bridge of all nonessential personnel?"

It was a rhetorical question. The carrier's off-duty officers filed out of the bridge in a hurry, probably anxious to get to the safety of their bunks. Bury lingered for a moment, watching the displays. He looked downright wistful. Eventually he left, though, and only M. Bullam remained.

Candless had to give the Centrocor woman a long stare before she seemed to realize she'd been ordered off the bridge. "Hmm? Oh, sorry," she said, with a warm smile. "Back under the old management, I used to observe from here during combat and maneuvers," she said. "If I'm not welcome, though—"

"You aren't," Candless said, seeing no point in sugarcoating it.

"Sorry! Sorry," Bullam said, laughing. But she vacated the bridge.

Which left six of them. Giles the IO, a pilot, and a navigator at their stations. Lanoe and Candless—and Shulkin. Candless caught Lanoe's eye and nodded at the old zombie.

Lanoe started to look even more annoyed than he had before, but then he must have realized what she was trying to convey, because his face cleared and he nodded. "Captain," he said, putting a hand on Shulkin's arm, "I'm running this show, but from here the carrier is yours to command."

Shulkin's only response was to lean forward slightly.

Candless didn't like that much. She didn't trust Shulkin—frankly, she thought the man was incapable of the job he'd been given. Perhaps Lanoe wanted to send a signal to the Centrocor forces that they were all working together now. She knew better than to challenge his order.

She found a seat near the back of the bridge and strapped herself in. Lanoe checked the displays one last time, then did the same.

"Beginning deceleration," the carrier's pilot said. They needed to slow down if they didn't intend to just shoot right past the dreadnought at high speed.

Powerful retro thrusters in the nose of the carrier burned hard, shoving against their direction of travel. The shift in gravity was disorienting, and for a moment Candless felt queasy as the bridge turned upside down.

"Sir," the navigator said, "how close should we get to the dreadnought?"

Lanoe looked to Shulkin, but it didn't seem the captain had any thoughts on the matter, at least none he chose to share.

"Stand back about fifty kilometers," Lanoe told the navigator. "We'll let them get a good look at us, but there's no need to be aggressive about it." He glanced over at Candless. "At least not yet."

As they approached, Lanoe had eyes for nothing but the main display. The IO had expanded the image to fill half the bridge, and it showed the Blue-Blue-White dreadnought in enormous detail. What had before seemed lumpy and shapeless now seemed intricate in its design. The hull of the ship was smooth but riddled with narrow pits, few more than a meter across. Much smaller than the weapon ports on its top side. He peered hard at the cagework blisters that encrusted its surface like giant greenhouses. Were there jellyfish behind those windows? Were they staring back at him?

"Fifty kilometers, sir," the navigator said.

"Full stop," the pilot told him.

Lanoe forced himself to inhale. "Talk to me about the other ships, the ones under the clouds," he said.

"It's hard to get a good count—they're in constant motion," the IO said. "I estimate there are fifty of them, with an average diameter of fifty meters each."

"Why are they loitering down there? Do they think we can't see them?"

It was a rhetorical question. No one bothered to answer. Lanoe probably wouldn't have heard them if they had. "Valk," he said, "is there any way to send them a message?"

"Yes," the AI called back. "I can modulate the running lights on the carrier to shine in the fifteen colors. The lights won't be strong enough to be seen through the clouds, but they'll be visible from the dreadnought."

"Good," Lanoe said. "Send them the message I wanted originally." *You must answer for your crimes.* Candless shot him a cold look when she heard his order, but he didn't care.

He'd bent over backward to try to talk. To give them a chance to explain themselves. It had taken every bit of restraint he had. If it were just up to him he would have come in shooting, and not stopped until every last jellyfish was dead.

He'd held back for one simple reason. He couldn't win this war alone. He needed Candless if he was going to succeed, and he knew she didn't share his burning need for justice. If he attacked the Blue-Blue-White without immediate provocation—if he shot first—he knew he would lose her forever.

So he'd given the aliens a chance, and they'd blown the Screamer out of the sky. Lanoe knew perfectly well there was only one way for this to end. All he needed was to nudge them a little. Make them show their true colors. They'd wiped out countless alien species before now—surely if he just irritated them a little, they wouldn't hesitate to open fire.

And then he would be justified in any course of action he chose. He could start his war, and no one could question his right to do so.

If the bastards would just take the bait...

"Sending now," Valk told him.

He nodded, knowing there were enough cameras on the bridge that the AI could see him. "Move us closer," he said to the pilot. "Twenty kilometers." That would still leave plenty of room for maneuvering when things got hot. "Valk, keep repeating that message until I say otherwise."

"Understood," the AI said.

Beams of light shot upward from the clouds. Searchlights that roamed around the sky before converging on the carrier, one of them momentarily washing out the display of the dreadnought. The carrier's imagery systems compensated almost immediately, filtering out the incoming light.

"Are you receiving?" Lanoe asked Valk. "Getting anything you understand?"

"Yes and no," the AI said.

"What's going on, Valk? You're our translator. You're supposed to understand their language. Why is this a problem?"

"It's impossible to say, precisely," Valk replied. "The signals they're sending just don't make sense—they look like random words, or at most like they're encrypted. It could be just that, that they're sending in some code that they assume we can decipher. Or maybe they're just using complex idioms, and my vocabulary is too basic to understand what they're saying."

The AI paused for a moment.

"Lanoe—I'm sorry," he said. "I'm sorry."

Candless cleared her throat. "Commander?" she asked. "What does Valk have to say for himself?"

Lanoe looked up. He realized, suddenly, that she couldn't hear the AI. That Valk was speaking directly to him, and only to him.

Well, Valk always had been smart. He knew what Lanoe wanted before he even asked for it.

He opened his mouth, planning on telling Candless exactly what Valk had told him. That they couldn't understand the incoming signal. Then he reconsidered.

He could lie to her.

He could make up any answer he liked. Valk, he knew, would cover for him.

There were times, in war, when you had to limit what people knew. Even your closest fellow officers. *Don't think of it as lying,* he told himself. If she knew that they'd failed to communicate with the Blue-Blue-White, she might insist that they back off. Try some other approach.

But that meant losing the initiative. It meant deferring justice, and that simply wasn't acceptable.

"They're refusing to listen," he told her. "They're threatening us."

He made a point of not looking at her. Lanoe knew how to bluff—he'd learned that in a hundred battles. "Closer," he said. "Ten kilometers."

Gravity tugged gently at him as the carrier accelerated, easing its way forward.

The display grew even clearer as they got closer to the dreadnought, but still he couldn't see through its blisters. He wanted to know they were there. Wanted to see at least one of the Blue-Blue-White onboard that thing. Back at Niraya they'd fought nothing but drones. He wanted to kill a damned jellyfish.

Damn you, he thought. *Take the shot.*

"Are they scanning us?" Candless asked. A good question, one Lanoe should have thought to ask himself.

"I'm not detecting any electromagnetic radiation from the dreadnought," the IO said. Which wasn't a complete answer, not by a long shot. "No sonic pulses...We're being swept by a laser, but it's a very low-energy beam. Not even powerful enough for spectroscopy. Of course, they could have sensors we don't know about."

"Understood," Candless said.

Shulkin suddenly slapped the armrest of his seat. "Is this a damned scrap, or an Admiralty cotillion?" he demanded.

Lanoe turned to look at him. The captain's glassy eyes were burning like coals. He felt a strange and not entirely pleasant kinship with the man. Shulkin wanted the same thing Lanoe did—a fight. But it was never enjoyable to look at a madman and feel like you were looking in a mirror. In fact—

He didn't get to finish that thought.

"Thermal signature," the IO said, his voice a worried squeak. "There!"

On the display one of the dreadnought's weapon ports was circled in red. A subdisplay came up, showing an infrared view, with the port glowing a brilliant white.

"Maneuvering thrusters, now!" Shulkin called out. The Centrocor bridge crew snapped into action, the hands of the pilot and the navigator flying over their consoles. A panel opened at the pilot's position and a manual control yoke sprang up into her hands.

It happened before Lanoe even saw it. A ball of orange fire had emerged from the weapon port on the dreadnought, an incandescent mass of plasma a hundred meters in diameter, and it was headed right for them.

Lanoe wanted to laugh. He wanted to sing. He had his first shot, his justification. If he didn't die in the next few seconds—he had his war.

———

"All pilots to their vehicles," Candless called. "Cataphracts in Alpha wing, you're out first. Beta wing, be ready to scramble on my order. Carrier scouts hang back but remain on standby." Within seconds a wave of fighters launched from the carrier's flight deck, streaming out like bullets from a gun.

"Batygins!" Lanoe shouted. "Move up, but watch for that projectile! Ehta, get those guns warmed up! Valk, get the cruiser moving, I want a broadside in ninety seconds!"

The plasma ball was still headed for them, blazing across a red sky.

Candless could almost feel the frenzied activity all around her, as more pilots jumped into their canopies, as ships maneuvered. All the blood in her body shunted over to one side as the carrier swung about, trying to get out of the way as the plasma ball tore toward them. "Are we going to make it?" she demanded.

"Yes, ma'am, but it's going to be close," the navigator said. Her eyes were as wide as saucers.

Shulkin sputtered, a series of sharp coughs racking his chest. "Keep those fighters in good order! I want a double arc formation now. If I have to come out there and teach you how to fly, I bloody well will," he growled.

Candless brought up a tactical display, showing the cataphracts moving to form curving formations around the dreadnought. The pilots were keeping their distance, none of them moving in to attack, as if they were waiting for the rest of the wing to get in place first. Before Lanoe had taken command of the Centrocor vehicles, Candless had fought those pilots, and she hadn't been impressed much then, either.

Lanoe was right behind her, one of his hands on her shoulder. "There's a BR.9 with my name on it. Shulkin has the bridge. I'm going out there myself."

"Of course you are," she said. It was standard Navy practice that the commander of a fleet did not under any circumstances jump in the cockpit of a fighter and go haring off to join the fray. Command-level officers were far too valuable to risk in the chaotic welter of actual combat. Lanoe had never been the kind of officer who played by the official rules, though, and she didn't have the time or the inclination to stop him. "What about Maggs's fighter, though? The one with the new targeting algorithm?"

His face lit up as if she'd just given him a birthday present. He nodded and then disappeared without another word.

"Ma'am!" the IO said. "Ma'am—the plasma ball!"

A display popped up in front of her, a camera feed from the

flank of the carrier. The plasma projectile swept across the view like a little star, too bright to look at directly. Tendrils of ionized gas snapped all around it, some licking the skin of the carrier and searing right through its armor. Red lights appeared all over her damage control boards, and the whole carrier lurched beneath her, but then the projectile was gone, shooting past them out toward the far end of the disk.

"Alpha wing, get in there and fight!" Shulkin screamed. "Beta wing, screen their advance! Batygins! By all the fires of hell, where are you?"

"Ten seconds out," one of the destroyer captains said.

"Ten seconds out," the other one repeated.

"Ma'am," the IO said, "ma'am!"

"Hellfire, man, what is it now?" she demanded.

"The other ships, the ones below the clouds—they're surfacing!" he said.

She glanced up at the big display, the camera feed from the nose of the cruiser, and saw them. All of them.

———※———

Lanoe dropped down through the narrow airlock and flipped over toward the Z.XIX. Maggs's fighter was a nasty-looking machine, streamlined as sharp as the edge of a razor. The most advanced fighter the Navy ever built. Lanoe had never actually flown one of the things before—he'd always considered them overdesigned, good for making an impression but too complicated and difficult to repair for field use. He had to admit this one had style, though, with four PBW cannons protruding from its snout and wickedly sharp airfoils like sabre blades. Even its thruster cones had been installed with flare suppressors, so they looked like black crowns. This particular Z.XIX was equipped with the Philoctetes algorithm, too, a software package that doubled the effective range of its weaponry.

Lanoe kick-flipped into the open cockpit and let its canopy flow up and over his head. Boards flickered to life all around him. He started to reach for the controls.

"Good evening, Commander," a synthesized female voice whispered in his ear. "Everything looks nominal. I'm ready when you are."

Lanoe swiped through the displays in front of him, putting his weapon and flight controls right where he wanted them.

"Very good. Are you ready to deploy, Commander?"

Lanoe was. He released the docking clamps that held the Z.XIX to the carrier's flight deck, then eased his way past the rows of fighters hanging from the walls. When he was clear he touched the throttle and felt the machine around him throb with life. He lurched forward out of the carrier's maw, faster than expected—he wasn't used to the power of the Z.XIX's engines.

The fighter's computer must have sensed his surprise. "Some pilots find the power of the Z.XIX intimidating. I can ramp down the engine response to compensate. Would you like to adjust the fine control on the throttle?" the fighter's voice asked.

"Don't you dare," he told her, and peeled out toward the battle, his thrusters roaring like lions.

⚔

All around the dreadnought the fighters banked and rolled, taking the occasional long-range shot, which sparked off the giant ship's hull. None of them dared get too close, as the dreadnought spat out plasma ball after plasma ball. Even a near miss by one of those enormous projectiles could engulf a cataphract in deadly flames—they would roast a pilot alive inside the cockpit, at the very least.

Shulkin kept shouting at the pilots to move in, to attack from a closer range. Some of the Centrocor pilots even listened to him.

Not that there was much point. One of the cataphracts actually got close enough to launch a disruptor right into the heart of the dreadnought. The most devastating weapon the fighters possessed. The disruptor cut right through the skin of the giant ship. It had been a solid hit, and the round functioned perfectly. The disruptor tore through the giant ship's internal compartments, exploding continuously—doing the kind of damage that could tear a cruiser in half.

When the round sputtered out a kilometer inside the dreadnought's hull, when the smoke cleared, Candless couldn't even see any significant damage. The attack didn't even slow the alien ship down. The dreadnought was just too big—disruptors wouldn't be enough. If they were going to neutralize this threat they needed something much more powerful.

"Batygins, I'm waiting," Shulkin growled.

And meanwhile the Blue-Blue-White continued to deploy more ships. Tiny compared to the dreadnought, perhaps. Huge compared to the human fighters.

They looked like bubbles surfacing on a pond. Spherical constructions of white cagework, fifty meters across. Long curved wings stuck out from their sides, and they trailed fire in their wake. There must have been a hundred of them, and more were emerging all the time.

"IO, scan those things—give me information," she said.

Data scrolled across one of her displays.

"Alpha wing," Candless said, tracking her fighters on a tactical board, "we have support inbound. Concentrate your fire on the smaller ships. Our best estimate is that those are airfighters." The official Navy designation for aircraft that could not operate in the vacuum of space. "We do not believe at this time that they have vector fields." Candless pursed her lips. "Engage them mercilessly. Unless you wish to prove you really are as cowardly as you seem."

Sometimes people needed a little motivation.

Three of her cataphracts wheeled around and dove toward the clouds, ganging up on one of the spherical airfighters. They poured an endless stream of particle beam fire into its glassy sides, chopping it to pieces. Its wings went spinning away, falling toward the clouds below. What was left of the spherical ship followed them down a moment later.

Before the cataphract pilots could celebrate, however, three more of the airfighters surfaced directly beneath them. Guns mounted inside the wings spat high-temperature plasma that tore right through one of the cataphracts. The other two broke off in opposite directions, corkscrewing away from the incoming enemies. But there was no safety out there—in every direction, more and more of the airfighters were breaking the clouds. On Candless's tactical board, it looked like there must be two hundred of them now. Ten for every cataphract in the battle area.

That fact must not have escaped Shulkin's attention. "Where are the bloody Batygins?"

"Here," the twin captains called.

"Here."

The destroyers announced their presence with a salvo of missiles that streaked toward the dreadnought, contrails streaming out behind them. Heavy PBW fire from the destroyers' guns lanced through airfighter after airfighter, popping them open faster than new ones could appear. The cataphracts broke from their formations to make room as the destroyers surged ahead of the carrier.

Candless's heart thundered in her chest as she watched the missiles race toward the dreadnought. The first one caught the pitted upper surface of the giant ship, the explosion looking comically small in the midst of all that real estate. A second missile plunged in through one of the cagework blisters, filling it with dazzling light.

A green pearl appeared in the corner of her vision—a call from Ehta, back on the cruiser. "Sixty seconds until the coilguns are ready to fire," the marine major said. "You think you can hang on that long?"

Candless watched the missiles tear into the dreadnought, and shook her head. "Still too early to tell," she said.

Lanoe swung low under a cloud of airfighters, his quad PBWs raking their glass sides, shredding their wings. It had taken him a moment to learn how to make use of the longer range of this new fighter—he had to lead his targets twice as much as he used to—but he was happy to make the adjustments.

"I have threats coming in on six different vectors," the fighter's voice told him. "Normally I'd advise retreat, but—"

"I'm just getting started," Lanoe told her.

"I was going to say there's no clear path out of the battle area. Please watch your six."

Lanoe swung his head around and saw a plasma ball tearing through the air behind him. He goosed the throttle and plunged forward, away from its burning heat. "Thanks," he told her.

Four airfighters were descending toward him, skidding around in a tight bank with their wings tilted almost vertical. He lit one up with a careful shot, then sprayed PBW fire wildly across the path of the others, missing two of them but tearing a wing off the other, sending it spinning down into the clouds.

The other two split off in different directions. Lanoe chased after one of them, never letting up on his trigger. It came apart in pieces and he twisted around just as the last of the four came screaming toward him, wobbling as it tried to recover from a sharp turn. He never gave it a chance to stabilize, sending a stream of PBW fire right through its spherical hull, bursting it open.

He'd hoped to see the jellyfish inside—rage was singing in his blood. When he saw what he'd accomplished, though, he spat out a curse. The glass ship didn't contain a Blue-Blue-White pilot. Instead it was full of machinery, and nothing more.

"The damned things are drones," he told Candless. "Just drones."

Just like at Niraya, he thought. The Blue-Blue-White sent machines to do their fighting for them. Well, he'd won out against their drones before. He intended to do it again.

Safe for the moment, he pulled back on his control stick and punched his main thrusters, sending the Z.XIX soaring upward. Toward the dreadnought and the vacuum of space beyond. He put through a call to Candless and she answered immediately.

"If these things are really airfighters, we can get an advantage on them by flying up past their ceiling," he said. "If they can't fly in space, well, we can—and we can pick them off from relative safety up there," he told her.

"I'll inform Alpha and Beta wings," she told him.

The dreadnought's shadow crept across his canopy as he rocketed up toward its belly. Smoke billowed from a dozen wounds across its skin, but the giant ship was still fighting, still belching out plasma balls at a dismaying rate. Lanoe could just make out the long, thin shapes of the destroyers as they glided past it, one above, one below, all of their guns blazing away.

"This is more resistance than I expected," he told Candless. "There was no sign that they detected us before we sent in the Screamer. We should have caught them flat-footed. Instead we're outnumbered—how did they have this many ships just waiting to respond when we showed up?"

"Terror is a great spur to action," Candless told him. "Try to see it from their perspective—they're facing an alien invasion, perhaps the first one they've ever encountered. I imagine that if one of those dreadnoughts showed up in the atmosphere of Earth, even without warning, we would scramble our defense with some alacrity."

Lanoe shook his head. "But they were here, ready to go, the second we arrived. It doesn't—"

"Commander," the Z.XIX said, "look out!"

A plasma ball from the dreadnought came smashing down through the thin air right above him. Lanoe had to swing over to one side and burn hard to get out of the way. As the plasma blast shot past him the air inside his cockpit grew as hot as a furnace. Sweat poured down his face and his lungs ached as he inhaled superheated air. The light from the plasma ball burned his eyes and for a second he could barely see—there could have been a hundred drone airfighters right in front of him and he couldn't have done a thing about it.

"You're in distress," the fighter said. "You might want to—"

"I know what I'm doing," he told her, his hand squeezing the control stick until his knuckles ached. He forced himself to keep the fighter from twisting out of control. Phosphor afterimages blazed green every time he closed his eyes. When he opened them all he could see was red—the dim red of the clouds all around him.

He pushed the stick over to one side and corkscrewed away from the dreadnought, trying not to make himself an easy target in case it loosed another shot. As his vision slowly returned, he called for Candless again. "Why isn't that thing dead yet? We've got two destroyers attacking it with everything they've got, and two full wings of cataphracts picking away at it. How is it still flying?"

"I've been running scans but there's very little I can tell you," Candless replied. "Maybe it's just that heavily armored, or perhaps the Blue-Blue-White simply build their ships to be indestructible. Ehta tells me her guns will be up and running in another thirty seconds. If their ships can stand up to that much firepower—well, then we're already dead."

The carrier swung and backpedaled, its pilot constantly working its maneuvering and positioning jets to keep it out of the path of the relentless barrage of plasma balls from the dreadnought. The constantly shifting gravity made Candless's stomach churn, but she stayed focused, her eyes locked on her boards.

"Carrier scouts," Shulkin bellowed. "Send the carrier scouts out, now!"

Candless didn't feel that was prudent—the scouts lacked vector fields, which made them far more susceptible to enemy weapons than the cataphracts. More to the point, though, once they were sent out to fight, the carrier would have nothing left—no reserve of small craft at all.

Alpha wing had been chewed to pieces by the airfighters and by stray plasma balls. Of the twenty fighters in the first wave, only eight remained, and two of those were out of the fight. One was so badly damaged it was already limping back to the carrier. The other wasn't reporting—it was possible the pilot was dead inside the cockpit, cooked by a near miss from a plasma ball, and the cataphract was running on autopilot.

Beta wing had acquitted themselves a little better. Once they realized that Lanoe was right, that they could simply climb out of the atmosphere and escape the airfighters, they'd actually started to fight. They'd quickly developed an effective strategy: one cataphract would dive through the battle area, luring enemy craft to follow it back up to the edge of the atmosphere, where five more human ships were waiting to carve them to pieces. The airfighters lacked any kind of armor or defensive equipment and—as might be expected from drones—they always seemed to take the bait.

Beta wing had taken its own share of losses, however—mostly from the dreadnought. Centrocor's pilots might have military training, but they'd never faced an enemy like this before. Three of Beta had been utterly annihilated by direct hits, their fighters literally melting around them as they died. Four more ships were damaged but still capable of fighting.

"Fifteen seconds," Ehta said. Candless had demanded that the marine keep a line open and that she provide constant status updates. Ehta had grumbled about it, but she knew how to follow orders in the middle of a battle. She'd been one of Lanoe's squaddies, after all, just as Candless had. "Ten."

Candless nodded and opened a new tactical board, this one showing a wider scope of the battle area. When the carrier had originally approached the dreadnought, the cruiser had hung far back. Its coilguns had far better range than any other weapon Lanoe could bring to bear, so there was no need to expose it to enemy action. Valk had moved it forward slowly as the coilguns warmed up, but still the cruiser was ten kilometers from the fighting.

Candless turned to face Shulkin. "Sir, I would recommend that the destroyers fall back. We're about to have a lot of heavy fire coming in and I'd hate for one of them to take a stray round."

The carrier's captain studied her as if he'd never seen her before.

He nodded carefully, then looked away from her. "Batygins!" he shouted. "Get out of the damned way!"

"Five," Ehta called out. "Projectiles loaded. Target acquired. Three. Two. One."

Candless looked to the camera feed. The dreadnought had taken a real beating—most of its blisters had been smashed open, and a column of oily smoke leaked from its upper hull. Yet somehow it was still flying—and still shooting.

"Lanoe," Candless said. "The cruiser is ready."

"Don't waste time telling me," Lanoe said. "Fire at will!"

On the tactical board eight blue dots appeared next to the cruiser. They moved so quickly they blurred as they shot past the carrier. Eight more dots appeared half a second later. Candless thought she could almost hear the shots whistling through the thin air as they hurtled toward their target.

Candless couldn't tell if the dreadnought's pilot saw the projectiles coming. The giant ship moved just before impact, but there was no way to know if it was trying to evade the incoming fire.

Either way, it didn't matter.

One after another, the shots tore into its thick hull. Seventy-five-centimeter high-temperature explosive shells designed to level cities smashed into it at a good fraction of the speed of light. Instantly a shroud of smoke and debris blotted it from view. Candless switched to an infrared view and saw the alien ship breaking apart. The dreadnought listed over to one side, ton after ton of debris raining from the sites of impact.

Shulkin let out a barking laugh, a cackle of excitement. The carrier's navigator whooped in joy.

Candless didn't want to be hasty. She checked her boards, running endless scans on the giant ship, making sure it had stopped firing, making sure it wasn't simply wounded. She needn't have bothered.

She could have watched on the camera feed as the damned thing fell from the sky.

There was an airfighter on his tail, but Lanoe swung around anyway to watch the dreadnought go down. His nerves sang with excitement and he barely managed to dodge as a lance of plasma rushed by him. He lined up a shot and blew the drone out of the sky as quickly as he could. The view was too good to miss.

The dreadnought took its time descending. It broke into sections, each one seeming to hover under its own power. As one whole side of the giant ship fell away, he had to work fast, jets of pure ions pouring from his thrusters as he zipped back and forth, avoiding the cascade of debris. One whole blister section fell away, the white spars of its cagework twisting and pulling apart.

No bodies. He didn't see a single damned jellyfish falling from the wreckage. He scowled inside his helmet, where he knew no one could see him. "Ship," he said.

The fighter's expert system was smart enough to know when it was being addressed. "How can I help, Commander?"

"Scan that wreck—look for anything organic, any sign of life."

The computer only took a moment to comply. "I've found a number of traces of organic carbon compounds, but no human occupants, living or dead."

Lanoe bit off a curse. Of course the fighter wouldn't know what a dead Blue-Blue-White looked like. It had never been programmed for fighting aliens—just other humans.

They knew next to nothing about the jellyfish—nothing of their culture, nothing of how they organized their society. They could have a completely different basic chemistry from humans. Their cells could be based on silicon, or even arsenic. They could have ammonia for blood.

Lanoe would just have to assume that some of them died when the dreadnought fell. That would have to be enough—for the moment.

A swarm of airfighters was gathering around him, clearly intending to box him in. He didn't bother shooting at them, just pulled back on his stick and climbed for space. He had a lot to think about.

The destruction of the dreadnought proved that the Blue-Blue-White could be killed. Taking down a ship that size meant that the human fleet stood a chance, even against a world as huge and strange as the disk. In his head Lanoe started planning out the rest of his war for justice. They would have to start by taking one of the cities, as a base of operations and as a demonstration to the enemy that they were—

A beam of light speared up from below, from deep in the clouds. It swept across the sky like a searchlight or a beacon. Without warning it swung toward Lanoe as if it would transfix his fighter. Irritated, he swerved off to one side. The beam tried to follow him, so he corkscrewed off to the other side. There were more beams now, three or maybe four searchlights swinging back and forth across the sky.

He tried to ignore them. He'd proven that he could beat the Blue-Blue-White, defeat their best weapons. Now he needed to—

"Lanoe," Candless called. "Lanoe, the airfighters are pulling back below the clouds. I think they might be retreating. I'm not sure how to say this, but—"

Not now, he thought, *you can apologize for doubting me later.* It took him a second to realize she'd stopped talking.

There were a solid dozen of the searchlights now, streaming up out of the clouds, radiating off into space. Above him Lanoe could see one of them catch the side of one of the destroyers as it sailed past the place where the dreadnought used to be.

The light played across the destroyer's hull like it was hunting for something. Looking for something specific. It lit up a broad circle of hull, coloring it a dull yellow. As Lanoe watched, the spot of light shrank and started to turn red.

"Lanoe," Candless said, "I'm getting some reports, some radio chatter—"

The spot of light narrowed down to a single point, a single point of glowing, ruby red. Instantly it brightened to a searing glare of light—and burned its way through the destroyer's armor, through its equipment, through anything that got in its way, and *kept going*, spearing off into space, streaming onward forever.

Red-hot slag dripped from the belly of the destroyer as the light carved it in half.

"Lanoe," Candless said, very carefully. But her voice was drowned out before she could say anything more.

"Brother!" Rhys Batygin screamed. *"Brother!"*

Chapter Fourteen

The destroyer slid over to one side and then fell from the air, unable to support its weight. The searchlight flickered out—but another took its place, scanning the sky, looking for another target. It didn't take long in finding one—it caught a cataphract from Beta wing and in a matter of seconds had reduced it to a plummeting ball of slag. Its pilot didn't have time to scream.

"Brother!" the surviving Batygin shouted. "Brother! I'll come for you!"

"Belay that," Lanoe demanded, but clearly Rhys Batygin wasn't listening. The remaining destroyer nosed down and burned toward the cloud layer, its many guns firing indiscriminately into the red billows.

"Batygin—get back here," Lanoe ordered.

"Revise your course, you damned fool!" Shulkin insisted.

But the destroyer stayed on course, vast plumes of red vapor swirling around it as it pushed into the clouds. In a moment all Lanoe could see was the occasional flash of light from below, as the destroyer fired off one of its heavy PBW cannons.

"Candless," Lanoe said, "they're using some kind of laser—"

"Yes, thank you, I saw it," she replied. He could hear the tension in her voice.

"I didn't think that was possible," Lanoe said. Laser weapons were supposed to be impractical because of the amount of power they needed to be lethal. "They taught us that back at flight school, remember?"

"On behalf of teachers everywhere, I apologize for that misinformation. But, sir—we need to recall all of our vehicles this instant. And we need to retreat."

"What?" Lanoe said. "Retreat? We can't retreat, not now. We're *winning*."

Even as he said it he realized how foolish it sounded.

This new weapon had changed everything. Vector fields couldn't stop the lasers. They ate through armor without slowing down. Nothing Lanoe had could resist the energy being pumped through those lasers.

Which left only one option. "Forget what I just said," he told Candless. "Recall all the fighters. Get the ships out of here—our only chance is to move fast, make ourselves bad targets. I'm giving you control of the fleet—keep our people alive. I'll need them later."

"Sir?" she called. "Lanoe? What are you talking about? Where are you going?"

Lanoe didn't bother to answer. She could track him on her tactical board. He pushed his control stick forward and dove for the clouds, chasing the destroyer.

The marines on the cruiser—the gun crews that took down the dreadnought—were still whooping with excitement when the signal for new orders came in. Ehta lifted one hand for quiet, thinking she was about to get a new target, that she would need to get her people moving and motivated again. "Go ahead—we're ready to fire on your command."

She'd also expected that it would be Lanoe who'd called her. Instead it was Candless. "Have your people stand down and report to their bunks. We're in for some heavy maneuvering."

"Understood," Ehta said. "But—why?"

"I have a lot more important things to do just now than explain. I want you with Valk. I need someone monitoring him at all times."

Candless cut the connection without another word. Ehta, deeply confused, turned and looked at her people. "All right, marines," she said, "passable job there, killing the biggest ship anybody ever saw. Passable indeed!"

That got her a cheer and a few laughs.

"Now, get someplace safe. We're moving again. Gutierrez, you're in charge of tucking everybody in."

The cruiser was already moving by then, in a new direction. Ehta didn't even bother worrying about which way was up or down. She flipped into the axial corridor, intending to head straight to Valk. But then she stopped.

She had another chance now. She could go down to the brig. Free Ginger from the chorister. This might be the perfect time— there wouldn't be any guards on the alien's cell.

No one would know.

For a long, bad moment, she hesitated. She thought about what it would mean, about what it might change. She thought about never going home again.

She thought about the promise she'd made.

She hesitated—and then she sighed in frustration. *Not now,* she thought. *I can't do it now.*

She spared one last glance downward, toward the brig. Wasted some mental energy hating herself. Then she started up the ladder, headed for the wardroom. When she arrived she found Valk motionless and dead to the world. As soon as she set foot in his domain, though, displays started opening all around her.

What she saw made her forget all about Ginger.

"Hellfire," she said, watching the displays. She saw a cataphract-class fighter reduced to molten metal in the space of a few heartbeats. "Lasers?"

"Lasers," Valk confirmed.

"Devil's kneecaps," Ehta swore. She found a seat and strapped herself in, knowing that if Valk needed to dodge lasers he was going to be making some very dicey maneuvers.

On the displays two more cataphracts were caught by the

searchbeams. Ehta winced—it wasn't that long ago she would have been flying one of those crates. Cataphract pilots prided themselves on being able to dodge just about anything their vector fields couldn't shrug off—but you couldn't dodge a weapon like this.

"They got one of the destroyers," Valk said. "Since then they've been shooting down fighters, but it's just a matter of time before they remember what we did to their dreadnought."

Ehta's blood ran cold. "How many hits can we take from one of those?"

"Depends where they hit us. Two, maybe three," Valk said. "The carrier will do a little better, but if we don't retreat right now this could be one of history's shorter wars."

Another display came up, this one showing the interior of the carrier's flight deck. Cataphracts were streaming in, two and then three at a time—as risky as hell, all of them crowding in together like that, inviting collisions. Especially when the carrier was moving. The alternative was worse, though—Ehta saw one fighter get blasted just half a kilometer from the carrier's maw.

Ehta called up a tactical display, but at first it didn't make much sense. It looked like there was only one wing of Sixty-Fours out there, but then she realized that both wings had been so heavily degraded there were fewer than twenty cataphracts left, total. Both destroyers were missing—and so was Lanoe. "Where's the boss?" she asked. He couldn't be dead. A guy like Aleister Lanoe didn't just die.

"He went for the clouds. I think he's going to try to knock out whatever's shooting those beams."

Ehta swore again—a real profanity this time, one harsh enough to make a civilian faint. "Valk, that's a suicide mission. He can't possibly—"

"He'd better," Valk said. "Count those beams."

A new display popped up right in front of Ehta's face, a wide-angle view of the battle area. At first all she could see was smoke and clouds of dust left over from the destruction. When she actually saw the beams, just pale cones of radiance cutting through the murk, she couldn't even swear, she was so terrified.

There were fifteen of them now, sweeping around the sky, looking for targets. And every time a cataphract made it back to the carrier, that was one less object for them to focus on.

It was only going to be a matter of seconds before those beams started converging on the carrier—and the cruiser.

She shot out one hand and grabbed one of Valk's gloves. Held it tight.

⫘

For a long time Lanoe could see nothing but red mist streaming across his canopy. Droplets of sooty liquid spattered the view and then streaked away as he hurtled downward, deeper into the disk.

A laser shot past him in the murk, bright enough to make him squint. Just to be able to punch through the clouds, much less to burn ships—the amount of power the Blue-Blue-White were pushing through those beams was staggering to think about. More energy, he thought, than the cruiser's engines could put out in a day of hard acceleration. More energy than a commercial fusion plant could put out in a year.

He supposed a species that could dismantle a star to build themselves a habitat like the disk might have that kind of technology. Might have the power to spare on a laser defense system like this.

More beams flicked past him. One burst after another. Lanoe knew perfectly well that every single one of those shots meant a dead pilot, another cataphract lost from the fleet.

He couldn't let this stop him. He couldn't give up, not even in the face of this kind of firepower. How he would move forward, how he was going to win this war—that was an open question. But he would think of something.

He would have to.

"You've traveled twenty kilometers through these clouds," the fighter's voice said. "I'm still getting inconsistent sensor readings from what's below."

"We'll see for ourselves soon enough," Lanoe told her. He wished he was as certain as he sounded. What if these clouds never let up? What if he couldn't find the laser emplacements at all, what if he just kept shooting downward like a meteor, until he came out on the other side of the disk?

What if one of those beams found him first?

A green pearl appeared in the corner of his vision, startling him. "You've got a call from Rhys Batygin," the fighter's voice told him.

Lanoe flicked his eyes sideways to acknowledge the signal.

"Commander," Batygin told him, "I'm sorry. I'm very sorry— I'm not turning back. I know I made a promise to follow your orders. But there are some things more important than military discipline. Maybe you don't see it that way."

"They killed your brother," Lanoe said.

"Yes. And I'm going to chase them all the way to hell, if I have to. I'm going to kill every last one of these bloody jellyfish, until—"

"Sure," Lanoe said.

"—until I feel I've...killed enough. Wait. Repeat your last transmission, please?"

"I said sure. I'm not giving you any orders, so you don't have to worry about disobeying them. You do what you have to do."

"Commander," Batygin said, and then he broke the link.

Lanoe had no interest in forestalling the man's revenge. He knew that pain, that need, that *hunger* himself.

And besides, as long as the destroyer was ahead of him, directly ahead of him on the same trajectory—it would give him cover. Any beam aimed at his Z.XIX would have to go through Batygin's ship first.

It might give him a fighting chance.

~

"Give me some cover! Give me some cover!" a pilot shouted, doing his best to jink around the battle area, trying to make himself a poor target. He was one of the last of the cataphracts that hadn't made it back to the carrier yet.

"Valk, turn off that channel," Ehta said. "I don't want to hear—"

Too late. The man's final scream didn't last very long, but it echoed around the wardroom until Ehta felt her head would explode. On a display just to her left the Yk.64 turned luminescent as a laser beam speared through its engine, tearing open its magnetic bottle. The explosion was bright enough to make Ehta turn her head.

"Two fighters still haven't made it back," Valk said. "Not including Lanoe. No word from the destroyer."

"What about the carrier?" Ehta asked.

"So far it's managed to avoid the beams. That won't last."

Ehta wanted to roar in frustration. "Damn you, I meant have they sent any new information, any orders. Anything?" She was still holding out hope that Candless would think of something. She hated the woman with a burning passion, but she had to admit that the ex-teacher had a brain for tactics.

"No," Valk said. "She's been too busy arguing with Captain Shulkin. He keeps insisting there's no need to retreat. That we can still win this somehow."

"Guy's a lunatic," Ehta said. "Hellfire, Valk. Is this it? The end?"

Valk took a while responding. He didn't have a face, so she couldn't read his expression. Most likely he had some subroutine to simulate human emotions, and hesitation was one of the options.

"Yes," he said finally. "Yes. Even if Lanoe can take out those emplacements...well. There's something I didn't want to tell you."

Ehta dropped her head. "Go on," she told him. "I'm a tough old bird. I can take some bad news."

"I've been doing some long-range scans," he told her. "Making sure our avenue of retreat isn't cut off. I found a bunch of moving objects. I mean, a lot of them. At least three more of those dreadnoughts are coming, and they're bringing airfighters with them."

"How many airfighters?"

"At least a thousand," Valk told her.

Ehta slammed one gloved fist down on the wardroom table. "A *thousand*? How is that even possible?"

"We need to get to space, as soon as we can," Valk said. "The airfighters can't follow us once we leave the atmosphere. I'm not sure about the dreadnoughts. I don't know if we can outrun them. If we can't—"

"Stop," Ehta said. "Just stop. You know as well as I do that's academic. Any second now the laser emplacements are going to kill us, and that's it. How did we get ourselves into this mess?"

"Lanoe," he said.

Ehta snorted out a kind of exasperated laugh. Lanoe. Every damned adventure, every bad scrape, every bedeviled mess in her life she owed to Lanoe.

It figured.

And as usual, if anyone was going to save her, that would be Lanoe, too.

———※———

The clouds parted.

Lanoe shot through the last of them into clear air. And almost perfect darkness. He could make out a few smudged shapes, a pale line somewhere far below, but nothing he could work with, nothing that made sense.

"Let me give you a light-amplified view," the fighter's voice said. The Z.XIX's canopy flickered and changed. Colors faded away, shadows shrank, and the image was distorted by a flickering grain of static—but he could see.

He kind of wished he couldn't.

Up ahead of him was Batygin's destroyer, its guns firing nonstop. The streaking rays of particle beam fire looked like chalk lines on a blackboard. For a second Lanoe couldn't make out what the destroyer was shooting at, but then something in his eyes shifted and he realized that the target was just so big he'd mistaken it for the landscape.

Below them, right below them, was a city of the Blue-Blue-White. A forest of white pylons joined together at weird angles. Like the spicules of a sponge, or the airy rafters of a cathedral the size of a continent.

Seen up close the pylons were fantastically complicated—ramified and recursive, almost fractal in their intricacy. Each major pylon was covered in substructures. Spiky subpylons that stuck out in every direction. Thick nodelike structures that reminded Lanoe of knucklebones. Clusters of what might be balconies or shelf fungi, hanging below high pierced windows or clusters of tiny apertures barely ten meters across. All so devilishly complex, and so very much of it—the effect was mesmerizing, downright hypnotic. It was beautiful in an unearthly way, delicate and yet immense, baroque in profusion and yet simplistic in its lack of color or any kind of decoration.

"The destroyer's taking a lot of damage," the fighter told him.

Lanoe could see as much for himself. Searchbeams played all across the front of Batygin's ship, searchbeams that narrowed as Lanoe watched. Lasers seared through gun pods and missile racks. The destroyer's airfoils were pierced with a thousand holes. It looked like the closer you got to the laser emplacements, the harder it was for them to find the one perfect shot, the killing blow. But it was only a matter of time.

Lanoe could hear Batygin bellowing in defiance, or maybe agony. A wordless cry of hate that would not stop, could not stop short of death. Only a few of the destroyer's weapons were still functional, still pouring heavy PBW fire into the cyclopean architecture below. A lucky shot from the lasers speared right through the destroyer, burning its way through the vehicle from stem to stern. It nearly hit Lanoe as it kept stabbing through the dim atmosphere beyond.

Somehow the destroyer kept moving. Batygin was holding it together by sheer willpower, by sheer hatred.

Right up until the moment he couldn't anymore.

A beam carved through the destroyer's fusion reactor and the whole ship went up like a firework, a vast plume of white plasma enveloping its rear half like a funeral shroud. Batygin's voice cut off instantly.

But the destroyer kept moving. Hurtling toward its own destruction, hurtling down toward the city like a meteor, like the wrath of a god.

What was left of the ship slammed into the city at twenty kilometers per second, five thousand tons of metal and carbon fiber striking the joint between two pylons dead on. The cruiser was tiny compared to the giant pylons, but whatever they were made of couldn't take that kind of stress. The joint buckled and then shattered in a trillion flagstone-like shards, and the two pylons shot away from each other.

The entire city shook and flexed, the impact strong enough to shatter substructures a hundred kilometers away. Debris pelted off Lanoe's canopy, some of it hitting him so hard he could hear his vector field sizzling. A bony spar as big as a cargo ship came tumbling toward him and he had to throw himself into a barrel roll to avoid being smashed to pieces.

A laser lashed through the air right beside him and he winced, wanting to turn his head. But he didn't dare. He'd seen it—the origin of that beam.

"You see those emplacements up ahead? Arm a disruptor," he told the fighter.

"Done," she said. "You'll be in range in ten seconds."

The lasers didn't look like weapons. They looked like massive searchlights with silvered lenses. There were thirty of them, mounted on the edge of a pylon like mushrooms growing on a log. Light—noncoherent, nonweaponized light—streamed from them in great pale columns that swung across the sky as they searched for targets. There was no sign of the power source that was generating all of that light, but if he hit them just right that didn't matter.

"Five seconds to maximum range for this shot," the fighter told him.

Even as he approached, one of the lasers discharged, firing a ray of death straight up through the clouds. That shot could have killed the carrier, he thought. Maybe Candless was dead. Maybe it had been aimed at the cruiser and it had killed Ehta and Paniet and Valk.

He couldn't think like that. He needed to focus—focus—

"Three sec—"

One of the beams sliced deftly through his upper portside airfoil, with enough energy left over to melt one of his armored fairings. The Z.XIX, down to just three airfoils now, tried to twist over on its side and dive nose first into the abyss. It was all Lanoe could do to wrestle his control stick until he'd regained something like stability, a kind of limping flight. His nose kept trying to swing around to the left, but he could compensate for that, he could do this—he could *do this*.

"In range," the fighter told him.

He pulled the trigger.

The disruptor round launched from a recessed panel in his undercarriage. It streaked toward the searchlights, starting to detonate even before it arrived. It tore through one big light after another, throwing up sprays of broken glass and twisted metal. He opened up with his PBW cannon, just to make sure he didn't miss even one of the lasers. He had to get them all.

⟶✳⟵

On Ehta's display, a searchbeam caught the side of the carrier. Before she could even cry out—long before she could warn Candless—the beam's circle shrank down to nothing and energy surged up it, impaling the carrier on a spear of pure red light.

"No," she managed to say, after the fact.

The beam had caught the carrier in the middle of its flight deck, passing right through the cylindrical hull without stopping. Where it touched the big ship smoke and clouds of incinerated debris leapt up, obscuring the view—but not so much that Ehta couldn't see the beam carving through the carrier's body, working its way backward toward the bridge at the rear of the flight deck. As she watched, a cataphract came tumbling out of the open front of the carrier, bisected so neatly the raw edges were as shiny as mirrors.

Ehta could only hope the pilot had gotten out of that crate before it was hit.

The carrier tried desperately to get away, but as its positioning jets burned hard for a lateral maneuver the beam simply followed, never wavering a centimeter from its destructive course. In a few seconds that laser was going to cut the carrier in half. Far worse, when it touched the engine it would break containment on the fusion torus. It would turn the carrier into a bomb. No one would survive.

Ehta hated herself for it, but she had to ask. "What about us?" she whispered to Valk. "Are we going to—to get away?"

A tactical display popped up near Ehta's shoulder, but she swiped it away.

"Just answer my damned question," she said.

"I'm burning for hard vacuum," Valk said. "Moving as fast as I can. We're already a hundred kilometers out from the battle area. I'm evading as much as our jets will allow, trying to swerve in an unpredictable rhythm, making us a bad target. But the actual answer to your question is—I have no idea."

Ehta grabbed the table in front of her hard enough to make its bolts squeal.

She couldn't help herself. She knew that Candless probably had plenty on her mind at that moment, but she sent the witch a message request anyway. Maybe she could at least say something to—

Before her signal went through, a green pearl had already appeared in the corner of her eye. Candless was messaging *her*. She flicked her eyes sideways and said, "Go ahead," even before the connection was complete.

"Ehta," Candless said. "Valk—I know you're listening, too. I'm going to do something rather foolish, but it just might give you a chance."

"Listen, Candless, you don't have to—"

"Be quiet, please, and listen. There is no time whatsoever for questions or comments. I'm going to jettison all of our cataphracts and carrier scouts. Set them all on remote control and have them fly around in circles. I doubt I'll live long enough to give them any better instructions than that, but with any luck the Blue-Blue-White will target them instead of you.

"Lanoe wouldn't approve, I know. He would say we need those small craft to keep fighting this war. But you and I both know— there is no more war. This is the end. I'm about to die, but I can give you one last order. Get the hell out of here.

"Get clear of these lasers, clear of the disk. Get as far away from these jellyfish as you can. Then I want you to force the chorister to open a wormhole. I want you to go home and forget all about this foolish mission.

"One last thing. Major Ehta, I'd like to say something to you personally. I know that we have not always seen eye to eye. I imagine you right now scoffing at my understatement. However, I have always found you—"

Candless's voice cut off abruptly.

Ehta looked up at Valk.

"No," she said. "No."

She swiveled around to look at a display, to prove to herself what she suspected. That the carrier had just been destroyed, that Candless was dead.

One look, though, told her what had really happened. The laser that had been slicing the carrier in half was gone. It had just... vanished.

All around the sky, searchbeams started going out, one by one. Each flickered for a moment, then disappeared. Until none were left.

"Lanoe did it," Valk said.

"Lanoe did it!" Ehta shouted, and punched the table so hard she thought she might have broken a couple of fingers. She didn't care. Her hand hurt like the very devil, but she didn't care. "He did it! Candless? Candless, can you hear me?"

Silence. Just silence.

"No," Ehta said. "Candless?"

"Captain Candless, come in," Valk tried.

The silence spun out for far too long.

And then it was broken. "I have...new orders," Candless said. Ehta surprised herself by how relieved she was to hear the ex-teacher's voice again. "It appears we have been given a reprieve. Please proceed to the coordinates I will attach to this message. We should still move quickly—the enemy's reinforcements are still en route."

"Understood," Ehta told her. She shook out her hand. She was starting to care about the pain in her fingers. She knew in a second she would care about it a lot. A white pearl appeared in the corner of her vision, her suit telling her that it was ready to administer painkillers. She flicked her eyes across the pearl and felt warmth seep into her veins.

She closed her eyes and let it wash through her, along with a feeling of immense relief. "Candless," she said, "one more thing. Just then, when you thought you were about to die—you were going to say something about me. Something nice, it sounded like."

"Perhaps," Candless replied. "But things have changed, haven't they? That sentiment no longer applies. Please disregard it."

She cut the transmission.

Ehta laughed and threw her arms around Valk's shoulders. "Big guy," she said. "We're going to live!" She kissed him on the opaque black flowglas helmet that was the closest thing he had to a head. "We're going to live!"

"Thanks to Lanoe," Valk said.

"Right. Lanoe," she said, her grin fading just a little. One more thing she owed the old bastard.

Chapter Fifteen

Get every neddy we have up to the flight deck. We need damage control right now," Candless said, throwing out orders as fast as she could. There was a great deal of work to do—the battle might be over, but no one was safe yet. "We have some hard flying ahead of us—we can't afford to have anything up there shake loose in the middle of a maneuver. Get the yeoman to the pilots' ready room. Check to see if anyone needs medical attention. Have the quartermaster take stock of how many fighters were damaged, and write up a preliminary repairs list, though it'll have to wait until—"

"Turn this vessel around," Shulkin said, his voice a low growl. "I don't know if you've noticed, but the battle is the other way."

"Belay that order," Candless said. She checked her tactical board. The carrier was out of the disk's atmosphere, and the lasers had stopped firing, but that didn't mean they were safe yet. Three more dreadnoughts were on their way, one of them having already risen into actual space—it was clear they were going to be chased. "Keep us moving. Get us as far from the disk as you can—I'm hoping they won't follow us too far, if they think we're running away." The pilot nodded once and returned to her console. Had there been a look of actual gratitude on her face? Candless wasn't used to that. "Captain Shulkin—"

"Cowardice," the old man said, grinding the word between his teeth. "If I have to bring every last one of you up on charges, don't doubt that I will!"

"Captain," Candless said, in a voice she reserved for her most recalcitrant students—the ones who failed to turned in their papers on time, for instance, despite having been told the deadline on the first day of class—"my orders come directly from Commander Lanoe. Your superior officer. If you persist in attempting to countermand him, I will have you removed from duty."

"Damn you, woman, we have fighting to do here! Turn this vessel around!"

He started to rise from his seat, one hand moving to a pocket on the front of his suit.

Candless was ready for this. She'd heard all the stories about Shulkin. Even as he started to pull out his antique pistol—he was notorious for brandishing it at his bridge crew, having actually shot one of his officers once when she failed to respond to an order quickly enough—Candless had her own weapon in her hand. A slim, rather underpowered particle beam sidearm. Underpowered in that it wouldn't actually shoot through steel plate. It would drill a very neat hole through Shulkin's cranium, if it came to that.

"Is this strictly necessary?" she asked, as she leveled her weapon in his direction.

The navigator, the pilot, the IO all ignored their stations, turning to stare at the two of them. Candless wanted to bark at them to get back to work, but she knew she couldn't afford to shift her attention, even for an instant, away from the mad captain.

This was a contest of wills, not arms. If she could get the madman to stand down, this could all be over in a moment and she could get back to work. If he was as mad as she feared...well, she couldn't back down. She tried to read his face. She could see his lower lip shaking. His eyes were empty pits, however, giving away absolutely nothing. As they stood there, guns pointed at each other, he started to laugh.

The situation could not help but remind Candless of the duel she'd once fought with Bury, her former student. At the very least, in how tedious it all suddenly was.

She couldn't help herself. She glanced at the tactical board out of the corner of her eye. The alien dreadnoughts were still right behind them. The carrier was making good headway toward deep space, but her job was far from done.

"Captain Shulkin," she said, "I understand that you wish to discuss the balance of power between us, in the absence of Commander Lanoe. However—"

She shot him in the leg before she finished her sentence.

"—I simply don't have the time."

Shulkin dropped to the deck, his whole body curling up like a leaf in a fire. He didn't cry out, nor was there very much blood. He did drop his pistol and clutch at the wound just above his knee. Candless made a mental note and filed it away. As crazy as he might be, Shulkin could still feel physical pain.

She walked over to him. With a deft kick, she knocked his pistol well out of his reach. He looked up at her with those meaningless eyes, and she felt not an ounce of pity.

"Someone get him to the sick bay, please," she said, and went back to her boards. Those dreadnoughts were still on her tail. "The rest of you, back to work. Now."

"Three of them," Valk said. A display popped up in front of Ehta and she saw the dreadnoughts. They weren't flying in anything like a formation—she supposed ships that big didn't need to. She could barely make out their silhouettes against the dull red light of the star. She touched a virtual key in one corner of the display for an enhanced false-color view. Infrared, low-light augmentation, and X-ray views superimposed on each other, building up a better image. In the new view she could make out the cagework blisters that stuck out from the dreadnoughts' edges. She saw what looked like shadows moving around inside—those had to be the jellyfish, she thought. She could see the big weapon pits, lying quiet and cold now, because the cruiser was still well out of their range. She could see their thrusters, burning very hot. Pushing that much metal took a lot of energy—whatever kind of power plants those things used was way beyond the fusion torus on the cruiser. "We're outrunning them, but very slowly," Valk told her. "Candless has me pushing our engines to the point they're burning themselves out. We can maintain this acceleration for maybe sixteen more hours, then . . . well."

"If we have to stand and fight—"

"It's an option," Valk said. "Not a good one. We know your gun crews can take down those dreadnoughts. To get a good shot at them, though, we'll have to turn sideways so we can hit them with a broadside. That means slowing down."

"Which means letting them catch up," Ehta said. She nodded.

"Our best bet is to keep moving. Gain as much distance from the disk as we can. Maybe they'll get bored and stop chasing us."

"Or," Ehta said, because she thought it was more likely, "maybe they'll run out of fuel."

"Maybe." Valk lifted his arms a little. Let them drop. His version of a shrug. "I don't much like running away like this."

"You want to go back, pick another scrap?" she asked him.

"Hardly. But it feels wrong—leaving our people behind."

Ehta cursed herself. She'd all but forgotten that one of the destroyers—and Lanoe's Z.XIX—were unaccounted for. Nobody had seen or heard from them since they dove into the red clouds. "Is there any word from Lanoe?

"The clouds block my transmissions," Valk said. "I haven't gotten so much as telemetry data from him since he went down there. But I'm sure he's fine. He's Lanoe, right? It would take more than a battery of lasers to bring him down. I'll keep trying him."

An hour later, though, there was still no word.

Another hour went by, and another. The dreadnoughts showed

no sign of breaking off their pursuit. And still no sign, no signal, from Lanoe.

Maybe it's better this way, Ehta thought. *Maybe we're all a lot safer without him here pushing us toward more battles we can't win. Maybe this is all over.*

She caught herself wishing it was true.

The man she owed so much, and now she wanted him to be dead—it was just one more reason to loathe herself. As if those were in short supply.

Bury was stuck on the carrier—he'd come over for the launch of the Screamer, and never had a chance to get back to his post at Valk's side before the battle started. Now, during the retreat, Captain Candless had forbidden anyone from traveling between the two ships, so he couldn't get back there if he wanted to. He supposed it hardly mattered. The things Valk had given him to do had been obvious busywork—the AI didn't need an information officer.

If he'd been on the cruiser, though, he could have checked on Ginger. He was worried about her. The last time he'd seen her, she'd been screaming, her body racked by seizures. Every time he'd asked someone about her since, he'd been told that she was fine, that he shouldn't bother her. He supposed that there was a part of him that was happy to leave it at that. Seeing her like that had been—confusing. He didn't like admitting it to himself, but it had been downright terrifying. The last thing he wanted was to have to see her like that again. Yet he couldn't help but worry.

He must have asked after her one too many times, because Captain Candless gave him a new duty. One he didn't care for at all. It was more busywork—and unpleasant busywork at that. She'd sent him to look in on the pilots, the ones who'd survived the battle, and assess their morale.

As he entered the ready room, he kept close to the walls. He had no right to be there, he knew. He hadn't flown in the battle. But he was a pilot, damn it. This was where he ought to be, following an action. He should be sitting with the others, the Centrocor pilots who had come back. The ones who'd survived. Commiserating with them, raising their spirits. It was what pilots did for each other after a catastrophic defeat.

They sat on padded benches, leaning forward, looking at the floor. Heads in their hands. Every so often one would look up, glance around as if looking for somebody. Somebody who wasn't coming back.

They didn't talk. There was food and water available for them, but none of them touched it. One of them popped a hydration tab in his mouth and swished it around his cheeks, then spat it out on the floor. He looked up, right at Bury, and the Hellion felt a torrent of shame run down his spine, through his arms. It made him feel weak, useless. Eventually the pilot looked away.

So many empty spaces on the benches. There were no wounded among them—the yeoman had come through a while back and asked, but not a single one of them had raised a hand. Anyone unlucky enough to be hit by one of the Blue-Blue-White's weapons had died instantly, either incinerated by a plasma ball or cut to pieces by the lasers. The men and women who came back were unscathed—at least physically.

The air in the ready room was so heavy and oppressive that Bury felt like it would crush him, smash the breath out of his lungs. He wished someone would say something, make a little sense out of what happened. He felt a jolt of relief when he heard footsteps approaching from the corridor. Then he saw who it was, and his face bent in an angry scowl.

Maggs came up to the edge of the room with a big smile on his face. He leaned on the frame of a hatchway and looked around. Stroked his mustache. "Now, now, chaps, why the long faces?" he asked.

One or two of the pilots looked up. Glared at the man.

"I'll admit," Maggs said, "that could have gone better. But we're alive, yes? That ought to be celebrated." He'd been holding one hand behind his back. Now he brought it out and showed them all a big squeeze bottle of champagne.

What the hell was the fool thinking? Bury's arms tensed, as if he would run over at any moment and start pummeling Maggs, just knock him down to the floor and start kicking him, beating him savagely—

Actually, that sounded like a good idea.

"No one wants a swig?" Maggs asked, brandishing his bottle. "Really, none of you have ever lost a battle before? It's hard, it can be damned hard on the old soul, but you have to rise above. We should sing songs, tell tall tales. Come, now. You—have a drink. It's the good stuff, I swear."

He shoved the bottle toward the nearest pilot, a woman with a hexagon tattoo on her cheek, meaning she'd done time in a Centrocor labor colony. She stared at Maggs, not even lifting her hands. The bastard leaned over her, putting one hand on her shoulder. She turned to sneer at the gesture, but she didn't shove him away.

"Here," Maggs said in a gentle tone. "Please. I just want to help."

The woman grabbed the bottle and started sucking on it. She didn't pass it on, just kept swallowing more and more of the champagne. Eventually she belched noisily and threw the bottle on the floor. Saliva dripped from her lower lip as she stared at her hands.

"You can't let this defeat destroy you," Maggs insisted. "You need to find a way to accept what happened. Don't you see? Commander Lanoe's war has just begun. There were will be a dozen more battles to come, a dozen more chances to seize glory!"

Some of the pilots raised their heads when he said that. They looked up at him with terrified eyes. One of the men even started to sob.

Bury rushed forward, his hands up. He grabbed Maggs by the elbows and shoved him out of the ready room. Maggs made no attempt to resist. Bury slapped the key that closed the hatch, sealing them off from all those faces, from all those frightened pilots.

"What the hell are you doing?" Bury demanded.

"Offering a little cheer," Maggs insisted. He looked baffled. Confused by Bury's violent reaction. "Only that!"

Bury knew better than to trust the bastard's expression—or his words. "You're up to something," he insisted. His hands balled into fists. "You're running some kind of scam, and when I figure it out—"

"Ahem." Maggs stood up very straight then. He was a good ten centimeters taller than Bury. He was slender in build, but Bury knew if it came to a fight Maggs would play dirty. "This is about the time I tried to kill you, isn't it?"

"What? You—you—"

It was true. Back when Maggs defected to Centrocor, the two of them had been flying a patrol together. Maggs had attempted to convince Bury to join him in his treason. When Bury refused, Maggs had turned his guns on Bury's fighter. The only thing that had saved Bury's life was that Valk had already tampered with Maggs's ship, installing software that prevented it from firing on a Navy vehicle.

"You can't possibly think that has anything to do with—"

Maggs shrugged. "I can't possibly think you might hold a grudge? You?"

The Hellion felt blood rushing to his head, to his face. "You son of a—"

"Tsk, tsk, young Bury. An officer does not sully his mouth with profanities." Maggs started to turn on his heel. As if he would just walk away. "Didn't anyone tell you?" he asked. "We're all on the same side now. Let's at least try to pretend that we're friends."

It was just too much. Bury dropped his head and threw himself at Maggs, knocking the bastard sideways into the wall. He tried to punch Maggs in the kidney, but the traitor twisted away from him and Bury's fist collided with a life support module on the back of Maggs's suit. He felt his knuckles shift and spread apart inside his hand. The pain raced through his nervous system like an electric shock, just making him angrier, and he tried to draw back, to get leverage to take another swing.

But Maggs had already counterattacked, swiveling around and jamming one arm between Bury's collar ring and his chin. Intense pressure pushed down on Bury's throat and he gasped for breath.

"A marine taught me this trick," Maggs said, "after a very lively evening of cards and bourbon. If I press down a little harder," he said, and the weight on Bury's windpipe intensified, "you'll be unable to breathe at all. You'll pass out and I will leave you in a disgraceful heap on the floor here. If I press still harder, I can crush your trachea."

Bury struggled, trying to break free. It was no use. He couldn't get a breath, couldn't get enough oxygen to use his arms, to move at all.

"Now. I'm going to walk away, and you're going to go find someone else to be angry at," Maggs said. "And before you think about running to Mummy Candless and telling her all about mean M. Maggs, let's think about the fact that you attacked me. In the Navy that's called conduct unbecoming an officer. Those of us with blue stars know these things."

The hold on Bury's neck released. Black spots swam before his eyes and he dropped to his knees, sucking wildly for air. He tried to jump back up, tried to get up so he could attack Maggs—

But by the time he could breathe properly again, the bastard was already gone.

Paniet picked his way up through the flight deck, climbing over the wreckage of cataphract-class fighters that had been sliced in half or melted into shiny blobs of slag. The devastation was incredible, but highly selective—there was a gap in the hull so big he could see a whole patch of sky through it, yet directly next to the hole he saw carrier scouts lined up in their docking berths, their paint still shiny and pristine.

There was no air in the flight deck, and no sound. Yet when he put his hands on a machine or found a foothold in his climb, he could feel a deep and unsettling vibration rattle through him. The carrier shouldn't be accelerating, not when it was so badly damaged. It should, honestly, be towed to the nearest drydock for emergency repairs. Sadly, the nearest drydock—and for that matter, the nearest tug—was ten thousand light-years away, and the carrier could hardly switch off its engines while it was still being pursued by a million tons of alien metal.

Studying the wreckage, Paniet wasn't even sure how to proceed. He could hack off the damaged section of the flight deck, just as he'd cut the nose off the cruiser. Yet by doing so he would basically make the carrier useless for any kind of combat operation— its whole reason for existence was to provide a mobile launching platform for the rows of fighter craft, and without a flight deck those small ships wouldn't have a home. He could try to reinforce the hull with spars and braces, but that would interfere with the ability of the fighters to get in and out. It was a depressing mess of a problem, and as much as he hated to admit it, it might be beyond his abilities.

As he pondered it, he slowly became aware that he wasn't alone in the cavernous deck. A group of people in suits were moving around up near the front of the carrier, where it was open to space. He climbed hurriedly up, thinking perhaps some disgruntled pilots were up to mischief.

Instead he found a group of his own people—neddies—poking and prodding at some of the worst of the damage. As he approached he saw the hexagons on their shoulders and realized it was the carrier's own crew of engineers. He hadn't realized they'd already been dispatched.

"Having any luck, darlings?" he asked.

One of them reared her head and swung around as if Paniet had given her the shock of her life. Through her helmet he could see her wide eyes and pale face. A welding pen spun out from her hand and went bouncing down through the long deck, smacking against the canopy of an undamaged fighter on its way.

"We're, uh—we're trying to—" she stammered out.

Paniet barely heard her. He'd seen someone else—and gotten a wonderful surprise. "Hollander!" he said, and rushed forward to embrace the Hadean engineer.

"Right, right, it's me," Hollander said, laughing.

"I thought you were dead!" Paniet said, then instantly regretted it. "Your destroyer, it was—"

"Gutted like a fish, by that laser," Hollander said, nodding. His face fell. "And the crew inside it."

Paniet realized he was still holding the man. He pulled his arms away, as casually as he could. "It's a miracle," he said. "How did you—"

"Well, I wasn't on her when she went down, of course. For which you have my thanks, to be honest. I was here on the carrier, working on the Screamer, and then the battle started so quickly I never had a chance to join my mates. Maybe if I had been, if I'd been there—"

"There's nothing you could have done," Paniet said. He could understand how the man felt, a little. Certainly Paniet had lost squaddies before, and marines he held dear—he was no stranger to survivor's guilt. Yet he was so happy to find his friend alive he couldn't keep a smile off his face.

Hollander shook his head. "I've been at a loss, since, with no one to give me orders." He laughed, but Paniet could hear the sorrow in it. "Just fell in with this batch, doing what we can."

Paniet glanced at the damaged hull section the crew had been working on. Bundles of cables hung limp from sheared-off conduit sections. Whatever they were trying to do, it was pointless—this whole section had lost power. "Let's get you away from here, figure out what you're going to do next," he told Hollander. "As for the rest of you—forget this section. We've got much more pressing concerns. You, dearie," he said, pointing at the woman he'd startled. "You're in charge of this bunch? I want you down at the rupture, there. We need to get a foamsteel sprayer up here and fill in that hole."

"Of course, sir," the woman said. She glanced at one of her

people but he just shrugged. The crew dispersed, headed back down the deck, leaving Paniet and Hollander alone.

"You're going to need a new bunk," Paniet said, putting a hand on Hollander's shoulder. "We'll find you something on the cruiser. Between us, I'm worried this hulk might fall apart in a stiff breeze."

"If you like," Hollander said, nodding eagerly.

"I'm so glad I found you, ducky," Paniet said. "In all this chaos, I suppose we should cling to what remains, as best we can."

"Definitely," Hollander told him. "Definitely."

Candless stared at the tactical board until her eyes lost their focus. She forced herself to blink.

Six hours since they'd left the disk's atmosphere, and still the dreadnoughts were following them. They'd expanded their lead to nearly ten million kilometers, but the jellyfish gave no sign they would abandon their pursuit. "M. Valk," she said.

"Here."

"Might I inquire how your engines are faring?"

The AI replied instantly. He didn't need to check a display—he was so deeply integrated with the cruiser now he could probably feel the thruster cones deteriorating. "They're definitely softening up. I'd rate them as good for another three hours before we start seeing real damage."

"Better than the carrier's, then," Candless told him. "And Paniet has warned me that our hull can't take much more of this, either. It's time we tried something rather foolish, don't you think?"

"I'm ready when you are."

Candless nodded. "Very well. Be ready to mirror me." She turned to the carrier's pilot. "I would like you to make a course correction," she said. "I want a burn from our maneuvering jets of sixteen seconds' duration. At the end of which time, cut all power."

"Ma'am?" the pilot asked. "We're barely outpacing the enemy as it is—"

Candless silenced the woman with a fierce glare. Then she pointed at the IO. "Giles. When the engines have switched off, I want us running silent. Perfectly silent. No lights on the ship's exterior. No radio communications. No active sensor pings. If someone on this ship needs to cough, I want them to do it quietly. Am I understood?"

"Ma'am," the IO said.

"On my mark," Candless said.

"All personnel, all personnel," the IO called. "Prepare for maneuvers."

Candless glanced one last time at the tactical board. The three dreadnoughts were just blue dots there, far enough away that they would be invisible to the naked eye. "Now," she said. She grabbed the armrests of her chair.

The carrier lurched sideways. The deck plates under her feet vibrated, started to shake. A nasty groan rose from the walls around her, and then she heard something snap far away, something metallic, something hopefully not very important. She saw red lights come up on the IO's boards but she made a point of not asking what had just broken. If the carrier was going to tear itself to pieces during this maneuver, there was absolutely nothing she could do.

It was a very long sixteen seconds. When it was over, the carrier gave one last rattling cry, and then—nothing.

Her displays shut down, one by one. Her tactical board went last, but when it was gone she couldn't see what was happening, couldn't tell if her trick had worked.

"IO," she said, "give me something. A telescope feed. Anything."

"Yes, ma'am," the IO said, and bent over his console.

In the sudden quiet Candless found it difficult to breathe. She forced herself to stay calm.

It was a very old trick that she'd pulled. One that sometimes actually worked. As long as the carrier's thrusters were burning, they had been a beacon for the dreadnoughts to follow—a signpost that could be read by anyone in the system who happened to be looking. With the engines switched off, the carrier became all but invisible in the depths of space. The dreadnoughts could, of course, simply extrapolate their course from their last known location. The last-minute burn of the maneuvering jets, however, had sent the carrier moving on a whole new trajectory.

With any luck—no, scratch that, with an extraordinary amount of luck—the dreadnoughts would continue on their prior course and fly right past the carrier.

It would take some time to discover if the ruse had actually worked. In the meantime, all Candless could do was wait. And hope.

"Candless?" Valk's voice in her ear startled her. "Don't worry," he said. "I'm calling you via communications laser. There's no way for them to hear us."

"We should keep chatter to a minimum anyway," Candless told him. "Just on principle." And because the last thing she needed just then was an AI blathering in her ear.

"Understood. I just need to know one thing. Lanoe's still out there."

"If he's still alive," Candless said.

"Right. If he is. And if he's trying to get back to us, to come home, with all our lights turned out how's he going to find us?"

Candless sighed. She had considered that. "He's Aleister Lanoe," she said. "I'm sure he'll find a way."

Chapter Sixteen

Lanoe was surprised he was still alive. As soon as he took out the laser emplacements he'd assumed a wing of drone airfighters would come swarming down on him, hot for his blood. Or perhaps a ship even bigger than one of those dreadnoughts would surface from the murky clouds below him, giant guns blazing away at this tiny new threat.

None of that happened.

He'd been ignored. Unmolested. He'd crept away, craning his head this way then that, looking for any sign of pursuit and finding none. He knew he wasn't invisible. He was pretty sure that if he rose above the city, punched for the sky and the void beyond, he would be picked up on some sensor somewhere and he would be attacked—the Blue-Blue-White had responded with surprising speed when the Screamer entered their atmosphere, and he guessed they had an elaborate network of early warning systems up there, above the clouds. But it seemed as long as he stayed below, inside the precincts of the giant city, he was safe. He decided the best chance he had was to fly out of the city and deeper into the clouds before he tried to make a break for space. It wasn't much of a plan—he was banking everything on the fact that so far he'd been left alone. Yet at least for the moment, it seemed to be working.

"Like a beetle in an anthill," he said.

"I'm sorry, I didn't understand that," the fighter replied.

Lanoe watched a pylon go by, an impossibly long white bone of this skeletal place. It was pierced with windows, but nothing moved behind them.

"If a beetle attacks an anthill, looking for food, the soldier ants will swarm it, tear it to pieces. They have to defend their queen. But if somehow the beetle gets *inside* the anthill, the ants will leave it alone. They literally can't imagine an enemy inside their ordered society, so they can't defend against it. The beetle can steal their food, eat their eggs, do whatever it wants—the ants assume the beetle is just another ant, and so they never question what it's doing."

After a while he opened his throttle a little and soared off through the city, alone and unchallenged.

If it even was a city. He'd just assumed that such a large structure had to be inhabited. Yet he'd been flying for hours now and hadn't seen any sign of occupation in the jungle of white pylons. He hadn't caught so much as a glimpse of a jellyfish floating between the long, bony structures, nor any other sign of life.

Just the endless, endlessly varied tangle of white pylons. He tried to study them as he drifted through, tried to make sense of the textures and shapes he saw built up on their surfaces. He couldn't comprehend any of it—it was just too foreign to his experience. Too alien, in other words.

Maybe this place wasn't a city after all. Maybe it was some incredibly vast, incredibly complex piece of machinery. A vast computer, or some piece of ancient terraforming equipment left over from when the Blue-Blue-White built the disk. Maybe it was... Lanoe didn't know, a park of some kind? Or a graveyard. That might explain why it was so empty, so desolate.

Then he caught a flash of movement, and he saw the place wasn't as abandoned as he'd thought.

Up ahead he saw a place where seven pylons came together in a single joint, a swollen white node on the endlessly branching network. Even from kilometers away he could see movement there, a kind of shifting, coruscating light. The enhanced optics of the fighter included an edge recognition algorithm, and it highlighted the sharp angles of the node, but also some much smaller, much more delicate curves, curves that were in constant flux.

He had no idea what it could mean. Even at that range he would have been able to tell if it had been a welcoming party of Blue-Blue-White readying another laser battery. It wasn't that. As he drew closer he brought up a weapons board, just in case. "Can you give me a magnified view?" he asked.

"Of course," the fighter's voice said. She brought up a subdisplay and laid it over the forward view.

Lanoe half expected to find that the motion was nothing special, just the churn of some giant machine spinning its gears.

Instead he found life. Teeming life.

The node was thick with striped legs. Countless animals that stirred languidly, moving an appendage now and again, lifting away from the bonelike node and then falling back again. Creatures with no bodies, no heads—just clusters of legs like rubbery starfish. Jagged stripes in black and white ran up and down each sinuous, tentacular limb, which ended in a smaller cluster of even more delicate members.

Lanoe had seen something like them before. At Niraya, he'd fought the drones of the Blue-Blue-White. The worker drones of the fleet had looked much like these, but with one exception—the workers had obviously been machines, built of metal and bundles of wire. These creatures were made of flesh—squirming, rippling flesh.

Maybe the worker drones had been designed to look just like these things. Maybe these were some slave race bound to service by the Blue-Blue-White. Maybe they were just parasites that lived off the substance of the pylons.

So many questions, and no way to answer any of them.

Lanoe didn't stop to take a closer look. So far the animals on the node had given no indication that they'd seen him—they didn't appear to even have any eyes—but he didn't want to wander too near and give them a chance to jump on his fighter, or raise an alarm, or... whatever they might do. He goosed his throttle a little and moved on.

As he passed by he saw several dozen of them break from the heap and go running along the top of one of the pylons, their many legs rippling, their stripes a welter of light and shadow. They looked surprisingly like greyhounds as they rushed along, legs flashing beneath them.

He didn't stick around to see where they were going.

Lanoe had heard nothing from his people since he'd entered the clouds. He assumed there was some feature of the disk's thick atmosphere that blocked radio signals. His communications laser was useless down there, too—he couldn't see where to aim it, if it was even strong enough to punch through all that murk. He had to assume that Candless had gotten his people to safety, that they were regrouping and preparing for the next raid on the disk.

Assuming he'd gotten to the laser battery in time. Assuming any human ships had survived. He could be all alone in the disk, the only human for ten thousand light-years.

"Best not to think like that," the fighter's voice told him. "Your mental hygiene could suffer."

He frowned, uncertain of what was going on. He was pretty certain he hadn't been thinking aloud just then. "Did you just... read my mind?" he asked.

"Commander?" the fighter asked. "I'm sorry, but I don't think I understand."

"Just now—you—" Lanoe shook his head. "I thought you said something."

"I'm happy to repeat it. I said, 'Commander? I'm sorry, but I—'"

"No, before that," Lanoe said. He grunted in frustration. "Never mind."

"Okay," the synthesized voice said. Just acknowledging his command.

He tried to put it out of his mind. He tried focusing on the city around him—on learning more about the Blue-Blue-White. Anything he saw here might be useful later, when he came back in force to pursue his war against the jellyfish. If he could spot some kind of weakness of the city, some vital piece of machinery, it could make all the difference.

The problem was, he understood almost nothing of what he saw. The pylons were complex and elaborately sculpted, but not in any way that looked familiar to human eyes. Spars stuck up at seemingly random angles. The pylons were cut open in various places, creating windows or maybe doors, but the openings were far too small to be used by a twenty-five-meter-wide jellyfish. Maybe they were designed to be used by the hounds he'd seen, the many-legged striped creatures, but he never saw one of them climbing in or out of one of the portals.

He didn't even understand how the city worked—how it kept itself from falling out of the sky. It was so big, and must be unbelievably heavy, yet it seemed to float perfectly motionless in the atmosphere with nothing to prop it up. The winds of the disk blew incredibly fierce—hundreds of kilometers an hour—yet the city didn't sway or bob.

Maybe all those pylons were hollow. Maybe they were filled with some kind of buoyant gas. Or maybe the Blue-Blue-White had invented some machine that could counteract the force of gravity.

A mystery in a sky full of them. Lanoe passed under one pylon that was swollen and banded like a giant's rib cage, the white material of its surface wrapped tight around some kind of internal structure. The whole thing throbbed mightily like a heart the size of a human city. Lanoe could feel the vibrations coming right through his canopy, pounding on his own chest like a drum. He flew on.

He saw a horizontal pylon that was studded with what looked like bones, like skeletons of some headless creature he couldn't quite imagine. Hundreds of skeletons, each fifty meters long. They were partially embedded in the skin of the pylon as if they were fossils that had only been partially uncovered.

He nearly flew into an enormous net, a filmy membrane no thicker than a soap bubble, stretched out between two diverging pylons. Long loops of transparent cable hung down from the membrane, blown nearly horizontal by the wind.

He got a bad start when he passed by what seemed to be a landing pad, a broad stretch of pylon that had been flattened on top. Hundreds of drone airfighters stood perched atop the pad, their long airfoils swept back behind them like the wings of insects. He reached for his throttle controls, thinking he would need to make a fast getaway—but then he noticed that some of the airfighters were slumped over on their landing gear, their wings grazing the pad. Others had their cockpits blown open, the cagework rough and twisted where it had been punctured, perhaps by weapon fire. Thick growths of pale vines anchored most of them to the pad, and he realized that this wasn't a staging area but a junkyard— the airfighters were nothing but wreckage. It occurred to him they might be ships his people had shot down, but the vines couldn't have grown over them that quickly, could they? The ships must have been destroyed in some battle of the past, presumably a battle between two factions of Blue-Blue-White.

He flew past colossal machines buried in webs of dark girders. He flew through what he thought might be an actual forest, a stretch of the city where thick white vines crisscrossed between three pylons, vines that sprouted long, spiraling tendrils. He flew over what he called, for lack of any better term, a farm, where long rows of fleshy sacs sprouted from the surface of a pylon, all of them slowly swelling and then collapsing, as if they were breathing in a fitful sleep.

It all just passed him by, his brain unable to gather more than basic impressions, or form anything but the simplest explanations for what he saw. The city was as complex and varied as any human city, as wild in its profusion, as chaotic in its design—just scaled up in size a hundredfold. After a while it became just a whirl, a fog of images, of meaningless lines and shadows. None of it made any sense. None of it meant anything. Eventually his brain just gave up trying. Except—one fact stuck with him, one he knew had to possess some incredible significance he just couldn't work out.

He had yet to see a single Blue-Blue-White. They'd gone to the trouble of building this colossal city of pylons, bigger than any city humans had ever built, yet as far as he could tell it was utterly deserted.

Where the hell were they?

He found them when he'd stopped expecting to. When he'd already decided that the city must be a ruin, a skeleton of its former self haunted only by the many-legged hounds. He thought that right up until the idea was proven wrong.

He'd flown for hours through the city by then. He was numb to new sensation, almost asleep. He woke up very fast when something splattered on his canopy. A kind of sooty foam streaked across the flowglas, then was torn away by the wind.

As he looked around he saw more of the foam, whole long streamers of it twisting away from a nearby pylon. He touched his control stick, veering in for a closer look, and saw that a broad, jagged opening had been torn in the pylon's side. The foam was fluttering out of that aperture, bits of it breaking free to flutter on the wind. Inside the hole he could see a vast quantity of the stuff, a lake's worth, quivering and glistening in the dim light. And inside the foam, there was movement—frenzied, swarming movement. A large number of creatures were down in there, rustling around in the dirty foam. They were round and rubbery, and when he asked for a magnified view, he saw them using their fifteen tentacles to stuff the foam inside their toothless mouths.

He'd seen his first Blue-Blue-Whites, but it took him a second to realize it. There was something deeply wrong with the aliens.

They were tiny.

Not, perhaps, in comparison to a human. The smallest of them was at least three meters across. But Valk had led him to believe that the jellyfish were eight times that size. Of course, Valk had claimed to understand their language as well. Had all of his information about the Blue-Blue-White been faulty?

Lanoe studied the feasting aliens. They climbed over each other, tore at each other's tentacles. There was plenty of the foam to go around, but they fought each other over...what? Choice bits of it? The foam all looked the same to Lanoe, but maybe some of it was more rich in nutrients, or just tastier.

They acted like animals. Like unthinking animals. How could creatures that disorganized build something as huge and complex as the city, much less the entire disk?

He had found the enemy. Maybe it was time to think about how he could fight them.

Lanoe reached for his weapons board. The Z.XIX carried a rack of high-temperature explosive bombs, fist-sized weapons that could fill the entire trough of foam with purging fire. He could kill so many of them in one fell swoop.

Just as he'd dreamed of doing since Niraya. Since Zhang died.

Lanoe touched a virtual key. Armed a bomb. He would have to get close, to make sure it fell exactly right, to make sure the wind didn't catch it—

Then he saw something else, something that made him hesitate.

Just beyond the opening of the feeding trough, the flat top of the pylon was stained with some dark liquid. Blood, Lanoe thought, because in the midst of all that gore was the body of some giant creature, a thing like a whale with dozens of wings and fins and strakes. It had no eyes, but its forward end terminated in a round mouth filled with curling ivory fangs. The animal made him think of the skeletons, the fossils he'd seen embedded in one of the pylons. Especially, he thought, because it was being butchered. A square cut had been made in its side, revealing a structure like a rib cage. Blood poured from the cut, bubbling and turning to foam as it hit the surface of the pylon. Clearly this was the source of the food the little Blue-Blue-White were consuming.

Then he saw the butcher.

A Blue-Blue-White twenty-five meters across. Maybe thirty. It looked enormous, gigantic, compared to the smaller ones wallowing in the foam. Its skin was translucent and rubbery. Its fifteen tentacles clutched knives and axes that looked surprisingly similar to human implements, except that their handles were long and spiral-shaped.

Inside its globular body Lanoe could make out the shadows of vast organs and the branching lines of blood vessels, like a miniature image of the city around them. Prominent among the alien's innards were long, looping filaments that flickered with light. In the augmented light view he could see through his canopy, colors were flattened, almost nonexistent, but he thought some of the lights were blue, some red, some just white. The lights throbbed in a rhythmic pattern, looking like the strings of lights people on Earth hung up for Fleet Day.

This Blue-Blue-White was as big as Valk had said. The others were so much smaller, they must be—

—infants.

Lanoe was flying over a nursery. The swarm of tiny aliens squabbling over their dinner had to be the children of the big one. Its babies.

He looked down at his hand. His finger was still touching the key that armed the bomb.

"Babies," he said out loud. "They're just babies."

The fighter responded—but not the way he expected. He might have assumed it would say it didn't understand his last instruction. It didn't say that, though.

Moreover, its voice had changed.

Instead of the clipped, synthetic voice it had possessed before, it spoke now with the mellow, mocking tones of the only woman he'd ever loved. The voice coming from the fighter's speakers was the voice of Bettina Zhang.

The woman he'd wanted to marry. The woman he'd wanted to spend the rest of his life with, until a Blue-Blue-White drone took her away from him.

"You and I never got to have any babies," Zhang's voice said.

Lanoe pulled his finger away from the weapons board. It was shaking.

What was going on? He must be hallucinating. He must be—

"What did you just say?" he demanded.

"I don't understand, Commander," the fighter said. In the robotic voice it had used before. Zhang was gone. His delusion of Zhang was gone.

He'd felt her presence before. He'd been haunted by her ghost, ever since he'd lost her. Every time he saw Ginger's red hair. Sometimes when he was alone, in his cabin, alone with his dark thoughts, it was like she was lying in the bunk next to him, so close he could feel her breath on the back of his neck.

Normally she didn't speak to him. This was...something new.

He caught a flash of motion through his canopy. While he had temporarily lost his mind, the big alien had noticed him. It rose from its work, lifting up into the air under its own power. Its rubbery body deformed and pulsed as it rushed toward him, brandishing its weapons. Lanoe was suddenly very aware of the fact the Blue-Blue-White was ten times the size of his fighter.

It could swallow him whole if it wanted to.

He nudged his control stick, veering away from the nursery. Poured on a little speed. The jellyfish gave chase, but it couldn't keep up, and soon Lanoe was kilometers away, moving fast.

There wasn't much more city to traverse. The pylons grew farther apart, with fewer connections. They were simpler here, too, just unadorned lengths of white bony material.

In time he came to the place where the city ended. A place where there was nothing but a solitary hound loping across a forlorn length of pylon, its legs flashing as it slowed down, catching itself before it ran off the edge. The final pylon stuck out into the dim red cloud bank, unattached at its far end to any other, like a spear sticking over a battlement. Its end was rough and jagged, pebbly in texture. Lanoe watched the hound, at the very edge, tugging at the limp tentacles of tiny polyps, trillions of them, each in their protective coating of something like white coral.

If he'd been able to achieve some kind of mental focus, it might have occurred to him that he was seeing something important. How much the polyps looked like the tiny animals that built coral reefs. That the city had not been built, after all, but grown.

He was far too busy worrying that he'd lost his mind.

Zhang's voice had come from the fighter's speakers. He'd heard her speak, as clear as a ringing bell.

He'd known before that he was slipping. That all his reserves of careful discipline and mental toughness were starting to crack. The task he'd given himself, to take revenge on an entire alien species, was just too big for a human mind to bear. The burden of command was getting to him. But now—

He'd heard her. And as much as that scared him, he couldn't deny it had been good, so very, very good, to hear her voice again.

He couldn't let himself get distracted, he knew. He had to stay alert, stay strong. He needed to get back to the others. Maybe it was just the isolation, the loneliness of being the only human in the midst of the jellyfish city. If he could get back to other people, other humans, he would be fine.

Of course, that presented a whole new problem.

For a while he just focused on figuring out where he was. He'd traveled a long distance, crossing the city. Hundreds of kilometers. He was nowhere near the place where they'd first fought the Blue-Blue-White. Perhaps it was safe now to climb for outer space. To try to locate the cruiser and the carrier, and rendezvous with his people.

On the other hand, the cover of the clouds might be the only thing keeping him alive. He might get swarmed by airfighters the second he popped up out of the clouds. There might be a dozen new laser positions waiting to carve him into pieces if he showed himself in clear air.

There was only one way to find out.

Chapter Seventeen

Hours ticked by as they waited to see if the dreadnoughts had fallen for Candless's ruse. All anyone could do was sit and watch. No one even knew what kind of sensors the alien ships possessed. If they had some way of seeing where the humans were hiding, Candless's strategy was not only going to prove futile—it would get them all killed.

She made a point of not watching the clock. Of forcing herself not to count the minutes that passed.

Captain Shulkin returned to the bridge, the wound in his leg healing nicely. If he bore a grudge against Candless for shooting him, she couldn't tell. He took his accustomed chair and strapped himself in—the carrier was not currently accelerating, so there was no gravity to keep him from floating away. He steepled his fingers before him and stared straight ahead, seemingly dead to the world.

That was fine by Candless. As long as he kept quiet, he could sit where he liked.

She had not ordered the bridge crew to remain silent. She hadn't needed to, not while the dreadnoughts were still out there, searching for them. When the IO needed to send her information, he did so by messaging her wrist display. The pilot and the navigator—who had nothing to do as long as the carrier's engines remained banked and cold—sat quietly, watching their displays.

The dreadnoughts couldn't hear them, of course, not through the vacuum of space. Yet even soft sounds made everyone jump.

Just a few hours before, one of the dreadnoughts had come uncomfortably close to finding them. The alien ships were well organized and had established an efficient search pattern, each of them taking a separate part of the sky to patrol. The first time one of the giant ships came within ten thousand kilometers of the carrier, Candless had spent a nasty hour clutching her armrests, watching the display as the Blue-Blue-White vehicle grew larger and larger in the telescope view. She had stopped breathing as it made its nearest approach. She couldn't remember if she'd blinked, in fact.

There was no way to tell if the alien ship was readying its weapons. No way to know if it had found them. Learning that information would have required switching on their active sensors, and that might have given them away. So all she could do was watch, and be ready to react if she thought one of the giant ship's weapon pits was about to fire.

Eventually the dreadnought had simply moved past them, without so much as deviating from its course. She watched it recede, and only then did she allow herself to—just slightly—relax.

Now Valk called her, his voice surprisingly loud in her ear, and her nerves were jangled all over again.

"My turn," he said.

"I beg your pardon?" she whispered. But she was already tapping virtual keys, getting her telescopes turned around. There. She couldn't see the cruiser, but she had a fair idea of its location. She could see very well that one of the dreadnoughts was inching closer to Valk's position. Far too close for comfort, in fact.

"It'll pass at a distance of six thousand three hundred and nine kilometers of me, in thirty minutes' time," Valk told her.

The carrier and the cruiser had been quite near to each other when they went silent, but because they couldn't use even their positioning thrusters, the two ships had slowly drifted apart. Now they were nearly a hundred thousand kilometers from each other and getting farther away all the time.

Too far for her to send him any help, even if she could do so somehow without giving away her own position. "Understood," she said. "How do you want to handle this?"

"I was kind of hoping you might have some ideas," he told her. "I guess, the way I see it, there are two options. I can stay dark and wait it out. See if that thing notices me. Of course, if it does there's not a lot I can do. It takes ninety seconds to get my coilguns ready to fire. Long before I got a shot off, the jellyfish could turn me to slag with those plasma cannons of theirs."

"And your second option?"

"I can get proactive. Start warming up my guns now. They'll notice right away, of course, and accelerate to intercept—but by the time I'm in range of their weapons, I'll be ready to shoot, too. It'll come down to which of us has better aim. And even if I win, the other two dreadnoughts will see me and we get to start the chase all over again."

"A hard choice," Candless told him.

"You're in charge here. I know which way I would go, but—"

"Yes, I'm sure you have an opinion. Everyone always does." Candless pinched the bridge of her nose between her thumb and index finger. Tried to think.

There were people on the cruiser that she cared about. Ginger was over there, for the devil's sake. Candless's first impulse was to tell Valk to take the initiative, to fire at will. Yet if he failed—

And if she told him to wait, to hope the dreadnought didn't see him? What if that went wrong? It meant consigning everyone on the cruiser to a fiery death.

She had to decide. No one else could take this weight from her shoulders.

"Stay dark," she said, and let out a sigh composed of equal parts resignation and terror. "Our only real chance is to wait the jellyfish out. Let them think we've escaped, and that their search is pointless."

"Understood," Valk said. "I'll keep you updated."

"Do," Candless said.

You could have cut the tension on the cruiser's gun decks with a knife. When Valk sent the message saying that Candless had made her decision, Ehta released a long-held breath, letting it sputter through her lips. "Stand down," she told her people. There was some grumbling, but not much. The marines who were in charge of loading the guns moved their shells very carefully back into their cradles, while the crews in the target acquisition booths yanked their hands back from their consoles.

Ehta clutched a railing with one hand and looked around at her people. She'd told them very little of what was happening, but of course they knew. Any minute now one of the giant dreadnoughts was going to pass them by. If it saw the cruiser, or even guessed they were close, then it was all over. "We're on standby," she called out. "We have twenty minutes' downtime, but everybody stay put. If the order comes to fire, we won't have any advance notice."

She kicked off a wall and glided over the barrel of one of the guns, to where the maintenance crews were stationed. Gutierrez and Binah were sitting against a wall, straps pulled across their chests to keep them from floating away. They'd been chatting, laughing at some shared joke, and she smiled as she approached, thinking she would butt in and make them tell her what was so funny. But their faces fell when they saw her and they composed themselves like proper PBMs. Eyes straight forward, mouths closed, hands folded in front of them. Sitting at attention, as best they could.

They were freezing her out. Well, of course they were. She was a major now. You didn't fraternize with your major. They could make too much trouble for you if you said or did the wrong thing.

She felt suddenly, crushingly lonely. She couldn't let them see it, though. So she frowned and nodded at the two of them, and tried to make it look like she was just passing by, that she'd just noticed them there.

"Relax," she said. She realized how long her people had been on duty—since before they launched the Screamer. "Get some sleep, if you can. Or pop a caff, if you have one."

"Ma'am," Gutierrez said. Binah just nodded.

Ehta kicked her way onward, past the loading crews. She needed a breath of air that didn't stink of gun lubricant. At the hatch that led to the axial corridor, she pushed herself up against a wall and slapped the release. For a while she just hung there, one hand twisted through a nylon loop mounted on the wall. Weightless and, for the moment, without a thought in her head.

It couldn't last, of course. Her wrist display lit up and she had to look at it. Just Valk telling her that they were one minute away from the dreadnought's closest approach.

"Thanks for the update," she told him.

"You're welcome."

"I was being sarcastic." She shook her head. "How you holding up, big guy?"

"I'm...fine," Valk told her. "A little worried."

Ehta snorted in derision. "I'll bet. Show me a picture of the dreadnought, will you? I just want to see what it looks like."

"That's actually kind of interesting, now you mention it," Valk said, bringing up an image on her wrist. "Look at where the blisters are on this one."

Ehta squinted at the image. She saw the big, pitted hull, the places where cagework stuck out from the corners. Six big weapon pits. None of them glowing, but that didn't necessarily mean anything.

"It's an alien ship. I have no idea what I'm looking at," she told Valk. "Kind of by definition, you know?"

"The blisters are in different places from the first one of these we saw. Back in the disk, remember?" Valk didn't sigh, but she could sense his frustration. He brought up a second image, one that showed the dreadnought she'd shot down, back in red-cloud land. She gave it just a cursory glance, but that was enough to show he was right. The one chasing them now had two more blisters than the first one, and all of the blisters were in different locations.

"Huh," she said, unsure what that meant.

"When humans build ships, they make them look as close to identical to one another as possible," Valk said. "There are good reasons for that. It lets you build them cheaper and easier, for one, because you can crank them out on an assembly line. The Blue-Blue-White don't seem to have figured that out. Or maybe they have a completely different method for building their ships."

"Valk, buddy, this is fascinating, but—"

"In fact, I'm not sure that 'build' is the right word at all. Look at the hull of the dreadnought." The image on her display enlarged until she could see the texture of the ship's skin. There were a lot more pits than she'd thought—in fact, the hull looked almost like a sponge, riddled with holes. As the image continued to expand Ehta saw that it didn't stop, that the dreadnought's hull was pitted to an almost fractal degree.

"What does this look like to you?" Valk asked.

"I don't know. A nice piece of sponge cake?" Ehta tried. It had been a long time since she'd had any food that she didn't suck out of a tube.

"Coral," Valk said. "It looks like coral. I mean, doesn't it? The whole ship looks like some kind of coral reef. I don't think the dreadnoughts were built at all, I think they were *grown*. Isn't that kind of amazing?"

"Sure," Ehta said. She reached down deep inside herself, looking for that tiny shred of her soul that cared. She couldn't find it. "Valk," she said. "Just, you know, put that aside for a second. Can you tell me something?"

"What's that?"

"How long until closest approach now?" she asked.

"About four seconds ago," he said.

She fought the urge to call him names. She fought the urge to scream at him. "Does it look like the dreadnought saw us?" she asked, as carefully and politely as she could manage.

"Not so far. I would have told you, obviously."

———✦———

"If you would like any advice," Shulkin whispered, "I'd be happy to provide it. For instance, I could teach you how wars are fought." He seemed to have woken up, and was actually quite lucid for once—he'd even caught on to the fact that everyone was keeping their voices down, which was nice. "It's all about projection of force, you see, by various means."

Candless ignored him. She'd already shown the bridge crew who was in charge, and nobody else could hear him. She had no desire to shoot him again.

"You seem not to understand that the basic principle is to engage the enemy, not hide and hope he doesn't see you," Shulkin added.

Well, perhaps she had some small desire to shoot him again. He was, however, the captain of the carrier. Lanoe had made it quite clear that he was to remain in command—at least nominally—mostly so the Centrocor contingent would feel they weren't prisoners of war.

"Thank you for your offer, sir. But perhaps we can continue this lesson another time," she told him. She pushed off her chair and moved to the IO's position. "Show me the state of play," she said.

She could just as easily have called up a tactical board and analyzed it herself. This wasn't a particularly complicated theater of battle. It was always good to get another pair of eyes on things, though.

"The dreadnoughts are here, here, and here," the IO said, pointing at a display. Two of them were millions of kilometers away. No real threat there. The one that had just passed by the cruiser, though, was still far too close for comfort. "We're here, and the cruiser is...there. I think." Too far away for the carrier to come racing to its rescue, if things got hot. Close enough that they could still maintain good communications by laser.

"Is there anything else moving out here?" It had occurred to her that the Blue-Blue-White might have other ships in the volume of space around the disk. They wouldn't even have to be military craft—mining ships working the system's asteroids, or space telescopes, or who knew what might be out there, nearly as invisible as they were, but watching for them. Assisting the dragnet.

"I thought of that," the IO said, nodding. "The answer, surprisingly, is no. I don't see any sign that the Blue-Blue-White have assets in near space. No orbiting factories, no solar power satellites, no habitats."

"Odd," Candless said. "You'd think an advanced civilization would have all kinds of things in orbit. I suppose we can add this to the pile of mysteries we've already been stacking up."

"Yes, ma'am. I've been monitoring the disk as well, looking for any sign that they're launching reinforcements, or refueling tenders, anything like that. It's been quiet, though. Nothing's left the atmosphere since we retreated."

Candless nodded. Perhaps—perhaps her strategy was working. She tried to imagine it from the enemy's perspective. Maybe the Blue-Blue-White thought the alien invaders had simply shown up in their system to blow up a few aircraft and one of their big dreadnoughts, then run away to whence they'd come. They must suspect there would be further attacks, but in the absence of any sign of the human ships, how long could they stay vigilant?

"Keep me updated. Constantly and thoroughly," she told the IO. "I'm going to get something to eat, and check on the rest of the crew."

"Ma'am," he said.

She nodded and started to push away from his position. She was still in the process of kicking away, however, when she heard him give a little grunt of surprise.

"Yes?" she asked.

"It's...nothing, ma'am. There was just a little flash of light in the disk's upper atmosphere. Probably just ball lightning or something. If I hadn't had my telescopes trained on that particular spot, I wouldn't have noticed."

Candless pursed her lips. "A flash of light," she said.

"Yes, ma'am. It's...it's...oh. There it is again."

Candless pulled herself closer to his display. She didn't ask for permission before swiping the image to magnify the view. The flash was little more than a blob of light on a single frame of the video feed. "The lightning we've seen before didn't look like that. It was far more dramatic."

"Yes, ma'am. This might just be an auroral discharge—like the northern lights on Earth. Interesting, though, that it's so localized. And its color is weird, too. It's not showing up on my visible light telescope at all." He played with the display's filters and the blob of light vanished—then came back in an intense, buzzing purple. "Just the near ultraviolet."

Candless summoned a virtual keyboard and ran a few transforms on the image. As the IO had said, this was probably nothing, just a random fluctuation of electrons in the disk's atmosphere. The fact that it was so specifically located in the ultraviolet portion of the visual spectrum bothered her, however. Natural light should be spread out across multiple wavelengths. There was also the fact that she knew the Blue-Blue-White could see some ultraviolet frequencies, and that distinctly worried her. If this were some sign of an enemy ship rising through the clouds, headed for space... "Dedicate one of your telescopes to this," she said. "I want a better idea of what this—"

She stopped because the IO had just whispered a particularly shocking profanity. "Ma'am, it's a laser."

Candless's heart stopped beating. She swallowed all the saliva in her mouth before she spoke. "IO, please tell me what you mean by that."

"It's not—I mean, it's not one of their weaponized lasers, those were tuned to be bright red so they could punch through the clouds. It's a very low-power laser, too—about as strong as one of our communications lasers. It's not going to cut us to pieces."

"Understood," she said.

"But look—you can see in this image, you can definitely see that it's a beam." On the display the blob of light had stretched out, grown thin. It looked like a purple line drawn across the clouds. "And it's sweeping." The IO ran the video forward. The beam rotated around the red cloudscape, as if it were drawing a circle in the sky.

A searchbeam, Candless thought. The Blue-Blue-White's dreadnoughts had failed to find the invading fleet, so now they were using one of their laser batteries to scan the darkness. If that laser so much as touched the cruiser or the carrier, whatever jellyfish was operating it could get a fix on their position. They could pass that information on to the dreadnoughts, and then—

Candless stabbed at her wrist display, calling Valk. "We might have a situation here," she said. She broke it down for him as quickly as she could.

"Understood. You said it was an ultraviolet laser?" he asked.

"Yes, that's right, it's about..." She snapped her fingers at the IO. "What's its wavelength?"

"Three hundred and five nanometers," the IO told her.

"Three hundred and five," she repeated. Wait. Three hundred and five. Three zero five.

"That's weird," Valk said. "A laser that color would get absorbed by the clouds down there pretty fast. If they really wanted to search for us with a collimated beam, they should use something with twice that wavelength, and—"

"It's not them," Candless said.

Valk said nothing. The IO looked up at her expectantly.

"It's not the Blue-Blue-White," Candless said. "Three hundred and five. As in the 305th Fighter Wing. It can't be a coincidence."

The IO looked very confused. "Ma'am? I beg your pardon, but I've never even heard of a 305th Fighter Wing. Is it a Navy unit?"

"It was. You haven't heard of it because it was disbanded after the Brushfire. Once upon a time, though, it was quite the distinguished unit. It should have been—Lanoe and I were both assigned to it."

"Wait. You're saying you think that's Lanoe down there," Valk said.

"I'm sure of it," she told him.

Damn him. Damn Lanoe—he had to be alive, didn't he? He had to have survived alone in an alien world. And now he was going to get them all killed.

❧

The minutes dragged on, with no word from Valk. Ehta moved around the gun deck trying to keep her people's spirits up, trying to keep them focused. Just trying to keep them awake. After a while she called in the maintenance crews and had them check the long barrels of the coilguns. They were known to be finicky—even a tiny fault in the coils could cause a gun to fail to fire—but mostly she just wanted to give them something to do. They didn't seem to mind much. Hard work was better than sitting around waiting to hear if they were going to die.

Eventually even she couldn't stand it anymore. She called Valk and asked for an update.

"The dreadnought passed us by," he said. "It didn't deviate from its course at all. We're well out of the range of its plasma ball guns now."

Ehta gritted her teeth. "So my people can stand down?"

"For the moment," he told her. "Keep them ready, though. If they stick to the search pattern they've established, another one of those ships will pass near us in six hours."

Ehta shook her head in disbelief. "Six hours. Six more hours. How long is this going to go on?" she asked him. "How long are we going to have to stay on standby?"

"Until Candless says otherwise," he said. At least he sounded a little apologetic.

"Damn that woman," Ehta said. "Ice wouldn't melt in her mouth, would it? She's got us all sweating down here, waiting for—I don't even know what. To get killed, maybe, or maybe she'll just call over at some point and say everything's fine. Well, to hell with her. I'm going to let my crews get some sleep."

"Good idea. They'll need to be fresh the next time."

"Six hours from now," Ehta said. "Fine." She cut the connection, then waved one hand in the air for attention. Some of the marines actually looked up. Gutierrez moved from crew to crew, shaking people, kicking them if they didn't get the point.

"Boss lady wants a word," the corporal said.

"We're clear," Ehta shouted. There was no cheering this time, nor any grumbling. Her people had been pushed past their breaking point. They were still capable of work, but just barely. "Everybody find some place to curl up, get some sleep. You have five hours." When the time came she would have to fight to get them moving again, she knew. Best to schedule herself a good hour just to wake them all up. "I'm going to organize some food, if anybody wants it. And maybe we can get a video to watch if—"

She stopped because a green pearl had appeared in the corner of her vision. She was receiving a call. The jolt of adrenaline that it gave her surprised her—she'd thought she was past being scared. If Valk had some new bad news, though, if they needed to go to full alert—

Then she saw it wasn't Valk calling her. It was Bury, of all people.

She waved at her troops and they started moving, sluggishly shifting around to find somewhere they could strap themselves down for sleep. None of them seemed to care about the food or entertainment she'd offered.

She headed out into the axial corridor before she answered Bury's call. The little bastard could wait, she thought. When she did answer, she growled at him. "What is it?" she demanded. "You know we're supposed to keep communications to a minimum."

The kid at least looked ashamed of himself. "I'm sorry. I really am. I just—it's been a long time since I checked on Ginger. I can't get over there myself but somebody needs to make sure she's okay."

"She's not okay, kid," Ehta said, because she was too tired for anything but the truth. "She's not going to get okay, not as long as she's chained to our pet alien. You'd better get used to it."

Bury couldn't meet her gaze. "She means something to me. Not—not like that, I know what you're thinking. We're just friends, but—good friends. We were classmates, and, and—"

"Squaddies," Ehta said, softening just a little. "The two of you were squaddies once. I know what that means. Look, nobody's going to let her get hurt. We need her to talk to Rain-on-Stones, and we need Rain-on-Stones if we ever want to go home. So Valk is watching her round the clock. You should have called him if you wanted an update. But don't. Don't do that, because you are *not supposed to be making unnecessary calls between ships.*"

"I get that. I just thought—I mean." Bury shook his head. "I thought maybe you cared about her, too. It looked like you cared about her. When she had that seizure, and...it looked like you cared. Maybe I was wrong."

Ehta rolled her eyes. "No. You weren't wrong." She couldn't very well tell him that she'd been thinking about Ginger, probably as much as he had. That she'd been trying to steel herself to go into the brig and kill Rain-on-Stones. She couldn't tell him, because she'd lost her nerve. Because she knew she couldn't do it.

"Then you'll go check on her for me?" Bury asked.

"What?"

It was the last thing Ehta wanted to do. Going in there meant making it very clear to Ginger that the help she'd asked for wasn't coming. It meant Ehta admitting that she was a coward, that she was too afraid of being stuck in the wrong part of the galaxy to do the right thing.

"Please," Bury said.

Ehta pushed her way over to a wall of the corridor. Leaned her head against a padded bulkhead.

"Yeah," she said. "Okay." She cut the link.

She would check on the girl. She *should* do it, she knew. If she couldn't do what had been asked of her, she at least owed Ginger an explanation.

Right after she'd gotten her marines squared away, and seen to their food and their entertainment. Official duties first. Then—the hard thing.

⁕

It took a while to set things up, and make sure they weren't going to give themselves away, but eventually the IO indicated that the carrier's communications laser had been configured properly. Candless sat back down in her own seat and strapped herself in.

She was hesitating, she knew. She wasn't sure how she should proceed. But she couldn't let the bridge crew see that. "Go ahead," she told the IO.

"It will take a few seconds to make the connection—he's a long way away. And don't forget, ma'am, there'll be a few seconds of lag on the transmission."

"Understood," Candless said. She cleared her throat. "Lanoe? Is that you?"

And then she waited for the reply.

The carrier's laser stretched across millions of kilometers of space, a fragile line of connection to Lanoe's fighter. They had tuned the beam to the infrared—a color they knew the Blue-Blue-White couldn't see. Just in case.

It was twelve long seconds before Lanoe answered. "Candless. Good. You figured it out—I knew you would. I need your position."

"Are you all right?" she asked. "We were so worried when we didn't hear from you."

Another twelve seconds.

"I'm fine. We lost the other destroyer, but I've figured some things out down here. Things that will help us. Send me your position, so I can rendezvous."

"Before I do that, we need to discuss what's going on. Lanoe—Commander," Candless said. Very carefully. "I have a strategy I'm working on here, one that's keeping people alive. I'm not sure we should rush to abandon it. As soon as you move, the Blue-Blue-White will have a fix on your position—and ours, once you meet up with us. Rather than risking that, you could wait down there until it's safe for us to pick you up." Yes. Perhaps that would be for the best. "Or we could send the cutter—it's designed for this sort of thing. We could—"

The IO interrupted her. "Ma'am, I'm sorry, but you should know. He's engaged his thrusters. He's moving."

Candless inhaled very slowly.

Of course he was. "Is he headed here?" She hadn't given him

their position. Maybe he'd simply triangulated it, following the communications laser back to its source.

"No, ma'am. He's on a trajectory for the cruiser."

How the devil would he know where the cruiser was? But then she got it. She held back a curse. Valk. The AI must have heard them talking—he heard everything that happened on the carrier's bridge—and he'd given Lanoe his position. Of course. The AI would never refuse Lanoe anything.

＊

Ehta pushed her way out of the gun deck and into the axial corridor. She had no more excuses. No more reasons to waste time. This had to be done. She owed the girl an explanation, and she had to give it to her in person.

Maybe, Ehta thought, she would feel a little better about herself when it was done. Maybe she wouldn't feel so guilty about everything, all the time. Unlikely. But it was worth a shot.

The cruiser felt empty, utterly deserted. All her people were still at standby, and Valk was up at the controls, hundreds of meters away. Paniet and Bury were both on the carrier. When she reached the brig, there weren't even any guards there. Nobody to give her a nasty look.

She reached the door of the cell where Ginger and Rain-on-Stones were locked away. She reached for the virtual key that would activate the door's display, showing her the interior of the cell. But no. If she stopped here, even for a second, she worried she might turn back. She might see that they were sleeping peacefully in there, and decide she didn't want to disturb them. She might see…something worse. Something that would make her turn around and run. If the girl had hurt herself, if the alien was—hell, the alien could have gone insane and cut Ginger to pieces with those huge claws, for all Ehta knew.

Ehta slapped the release on the hatch and kicked inside.

What she found was…weird.

Ginger was pressed into one corner of the room, her face smeared against the wall. It looked like her upper lip was stuck to the padding. Her eyes were wide, and she was hugging herself like she was ice-cold. She looked up as Ehta came toward her, but there was nothing in her eyes. They were glassy, dead. There was no hope there.

Rain-on-Stones was crammed up into a corner of the ceiling, using her many legs to brace herself. The wicked claws she had for feet had cut into the padding—which was supposed to be proofed against knives—and Ehta could see the alien's mouth, a kind of wet, flexible beak. The alien was naked, shreds of her black dress drifting through the cell's thick air.

The place stank. It was a smell Ehta couldn't even place, and she'd experienced some nasty funks in her time. It smelled a little like rotten shellfish, maybe, ammonia and iodine, but there were notes underneath that made her head swim. The smell of fear, she thought, though she couldn't have said why. Always before fear had smelled like human sweat, like blood. This was—different.

The stink was so thick it seemed to tinge the light, like it had discolored the air.

"Hellfire," Ehta said. She reached for her wrist display. "I'm going to get the ventilators going in here, clear some of this out. Just give me a second—"

"No," Ginger said. At the same time, the alien let out a quiet, diffident chirp. "No. You're smelling her pheromones. It's . . . a way for her to communicate."

Ehta shook her head. If they wanted to stew in their own funk, fine. She didn't close the hatch behind her, though.

She closed her eyes and forced herself to calm down. Okay. It was time. Best to get this over with quickly.

"Ginger," she said. And then promptly realized she couldn't think of what to say next. She struggled with finding any words at all. "Bury wanted—he called me, he wanted—" She shook her head. She looked up at Rain-on-Stones and realized she couldn't see the alien's head. It was buried in one of the corners of the ceiling, sheltered by her four jointed arms. "Hell's bells," she said quietly.

There was something wrong with the alien. Something beyond what she'd already seen. What was it?

"I need you to know something," she said to Ginger. "I need you to know why...why I haven't..."

She stopped. There was definitely something wrong with Rain-on-Stones. Something—missing.

"She isn't covered in bugs," Ehta said, when her brain finally dropped the last piece into place. "She used to have those bugs all over her."

"Her males," Ginger said, nodding a little. Her lip came unstuck from the wall.

"Yeah," Ehta said. "She had all those little males running over her, getting between the plates of her armor. But I don't see any of them now. Are they all tucked away, staying warm? I can get her a new dress, if you think that—"

"She ate them," Ginger said.

Just like that. Like that was something that could happen.

"She—"

"They were too active. They were picking up on her distress, and it made them go crazy. She felt it like an itch she couldn't scratch. So she ate them."

"The devil you say. Is that something they...do?"

"No," Ginger said. "Never."

The girl rolled over, steadying herself against the walls so she didn't float out of her corner. Ehta noticed for the first time that they were as far apart as they could get from each other and still be in the cell together.

"You were going to tell me something. Explain something."

Ehta nodded. "Yeah." Maybe this wasn't the time, though. Nobody was screaming, that had to be a good sign, right? That they had calmed down, that they had come to some kind of peace?

Sure. Because healthy, sane people eat their males all the time, she thought.

"Ginger," she said, "I can't help you."

The girl turned her face away.

"It's not that I don't want to—I've been wrestling with this ever since you asked, I've tried to figure out a way to . . . to . . ." *Murder your alien friend,* she thought, but that wasn't the way to put it. "Get you free. But there's just too much riding on her. We need her too much. She's the only way for us to get home. Don't you see that? Without her, we're all stranded here forever. I want to help you, I want to help you so much, but—but—"

She stopped, because Ginger was laughing.

It wasn't a pleasant sound. It was halfway between a cackle and a coughing fit. But it was laughter. Across the room Rain-on-Stones chirped asthmatically, keeping the same rhythm.

"That's why," Ginger said. "That's why."

"Yeah," Ehta said. "Come on, you have to see it from my perspective. And it's not just about me—you're asking me to trap hundreds of people here, so far from home. Can't you see that's too much to ask?"

"It might be. If you were right," Ginger said.

Ehta took a deep breath. "What do you mean?" she asked.

"When we came here, when we came through the wormhole from the city of the Choir to here," Ginger said, rolling around a little until it looked like she was sitting up. "It took everything the Choir had. All of them working together, to open one unstable wormhole. It cost them—so much."

"Wait," Ehta said. "You're saying—"

"Rain-on-Stones can't do that alone. She couldn't even come close."

"Just hold on—"

"I'm telling you that it can't be done. There is no way back. We're stranded here, forever—and there's nothing anyone can do about it. Not her, not me. Not you."

Ehta put a hand over her mouth. Because she thought if she didn't she might just start screaming and never stop.

"There's no way back," Ginger said again. The girl turned her face back toward the wall. "If you want me to forgive you, fine. You're off the hook. Just go away."

"No," Ehta said. "If what you're saying is true, then—" She reached down to her side and drew her sidearm. She lifted it and pointed it right at Rain-on-Stones's ugly mouth. Thumbed a key on the side of the pistol to make sure it was fully charged. "If we don't need her—"

"We need her," Lanoe said.

Ehta's head spun for a second. When it stopped, she realized two things. First, Lanoe was floating right behind her, in the open hatch of the cell. Second—he had the barrel of a pistol touching the back of her neck.

Chapter Eighteen

When Lanoe left the disk he'd gone straight to the cruiser. He'd updated Valk along the way, sent him all the video the Z.XIX had logged, all of its sensor data—everything except audio from his cockpit. He didn't want the AI hearing what he'd said to Zhang, to his hallucination of Zhang. He didn't want Valk thinking he was crazy.

When he arrived at the cruiser's vehicle bay he'd gone straight to the brig. He'd thought he wanted to talk to Rain-on-Stones, get her impressions on what he'd seen in the Blue-Blue-White city. Talk with her about how he was going to win this war.

Maybe something else had drawn him there. Some intuition. No. Lanoe didn't believe in anything so mystical as intuition. He'd just gotten lucky. He'd arrived just in time to stop his whole plan from going to hell.

"Ehta," he said, very carefully, "put your gun away."

The marine didn't turn around. She didn't so much as glance over her shoulder. Nor did she lower her weapon.

"You're going to shoot me, Lanoe? Really? Over this alien piece of—"

"Yes," Lanoe said.

"She's no use to you," Ehta said. "She can't send us home. Come on, Lanoe! When did you start caring more about aliens than people? You've had Ginger stuck down here in your torture chamber this whole time for—for nothing! She's just a kid, Lanoe. She's a kid!"

"You're wrong," he told Ehta. "I still need Rain-on-Stones. I need her more than ever, and that means I need Ginger to talk to her."

"She just told me the truth—Rain-on-Stones can't open a wormhole for us. She can't send us home!"

"I know."

Ginger stirred in one corner of the room. Lanoe had only been barely aware that she was there, up until now. He saw her red hair drift around her face, like red clouds circling a pale planet.

"He's always known," Ginger said. "Take the shot, Ehta. Take the—ah!"

Ginger's body convulsed and her eyes rolled up into her head. Rain-on-Stones must have figured out how much danger she was in. Ehta gasped and pushed her way over to the girl, grabbing Ginger up in her big arms. Her pistol was still in her hand but it wasn't pointing at the chorister anymore.

"Is it true?" Ehta demanded. "You knew? You knew, Lanoe?"

"I did," Lanoe admitted. "I let everyone believe she could open a way home because they needed to believe that. If they knew the truth—"

"They would have thrown you out an airlock the second we got here," Ehta shouted. "They would have torn you to pieces!"

"Which is why I need you to keep this to yourself." Lanoe kicked over to her. Grabbed the pistol out of her hand—she barely fought him—and shoved it in a pocket of his suit.

"You're kidding me," Ehta said. "You're kidding—you bastard. You—"

Lanoe grabbed her by the ring collar and pulled her toward him until their faces were just centimeters apart.

"Do I look like I'm kidding?" he asked.

Ehta couldn't seem to find a reply to that.

"You'll keep this secret," he told her. "That's an order. Is that enough? Maybe not. Maybe you don't respect my rank anymore. Maybe you need some more incentive."

The look on her face might have killed him, in other circumstances. The mixture of betrayal and fear and confusion. Some part of him demanded that he release her, that he not say anything more. *It's Ehta!* a voice in his head screamed. *Your old squaddie from the 94th! Let her go!*

He fought that voice. Pummeled it into submission.

"If you tell anyone about this," he promised her, "I will blow your brains out."

He let go of the collar ring. Pushed her away so she collided with the floor and he went gliding backward. Ehta stared at him with panicked eyes. Saliva leaked from one corner of her open mouth.

"And me?" Ginger asked. She was still in the middle of a seizure, her voice shaky but clear. "Will you kill me if I tell anyone?"

"I can't kill you," he told the girl. "I need you if I want to talk to Rain-on-Stones. But there are other ways to punish someone. You don't want to hear details."

Bullam had moved her yacht close to the open end of the carrier's flight deck. It meant nestling into a berth right in the most damaged part of the ship, and took some very careful maneuvering. When the duty officer asked her why she wanted to make such a time-consuming move, she'd simply told the man that she wanted to be able to see the stars. The move freed up some room deeper inside the flight deck, including three undamaged berths that could be used for cataphracts, so the request had been granted without further questions.

Perhaps someone suspected she had an ulterior motive in the move, but almost certainly they couldn't guess why. They couldn't know that Bullam's pet neddies, led by Hollander, had rerouted a number of network cables into the berth, allowing Bullam to monitor the carrier's communications and data flow. Once she was securely redocked, she had access to all of the ship's sensors—and its most heavily encrypted file structures.

Maggs was deeply impressed. "So what's first?" he asked, while gently rubbing her shoulders. "A denial of service attack on Valk, just to give him the fits? Or do we dim the lights in Candless's bunk a little more each night to make her think she's going blind?"

"I'm not above petty gaslighting if it serves a purpose," Bullam told him, "but we have a situation here we need to handle." She was crouched over one of her drones as if she were staring into a crystal ball. Not that far from it, as it were—instead of presenting a traditional holographic display, the drone was feeding her information by shining lasers directly onto her retinas. Information, therefore, that only she could see. It sparkled in her irises, as if tiny blue fires were burning within her eyes. "A lone fighter emerged from the disk a little while ago. It just made rendezvous with the cruiser."

"Lanoe," Maggs said. His hands stopped roaming across her neck muscles. Lanoe. *Lanoe.* It could be no one else. The bastard was alive.

Maggs was not, despite what some people might suspect, a betting man. He understood too much about the laws of probability for that. Yet the odds had suggested that Lanoe was dead. He hadn't been seen since the disastrous retreat from the disk. He'd flown down into the very teeth of the enemy and with each mounting hour it had seemed more likely that the old fool had taken one too many chances. The law of averages and basic rationality suggested that a man in such a dangerous occupation couldn't live forever.

Apparently, when it came to Aleister Lanoe, logic and common sense didn't apply.

If he was back...

Buck up, Maggsy, his father's voice said inside his head. *You've still got your reprieve. For now.*

Quite. Lanoe had no reason to suspect what Maggs and Bullam had been working at. It would probably take a while for him to come up to speed.

"This...changes a few things," Maggs suggested. "We were counting on Candless being our biggest stumbling block. Now—"

Bullam nodded. "We've got our work cut out for us. But this doesn't mean we need to make any major changes to our plan. We simply have to accelerate the timetable. You know what you need to do? What you need to say?"

"I have committed every line to memory. The greatest actors of stage and video would shrivel with jealousy could they see the performance I'm about to give."

"Don't lay it on too thick," Bullam said.

He sketched a courtly bow. Not easy in the absence of gravity, but Maggs was nothing if not adaptable. He looked around for his suit and pulled it on with all the grace he could muster. As he headed for the canopy over the yacht's deck, however, intending to blow her a kiss on his way out, he came up short because he'd heard a noise.

A rather quiet, rather sad little sound, if not entirely a dignified one. A grunt of pain.

He turned about and considered Bullam. She was still bent over her drone, her eyes full of light. Her mouth, perhaps, was a little twisted up. But that could signify concentration as much as it might indicate discomfort. If she looked a little pale, well, the lighting on the yacht's deck wasn't of the best.

"Anything the matter?" he inquired, trying to make it sound breezy.

"Fine. Get on with it," she said.

And so he did. Maggs was a man of action before anything else. She didn't look up as he left, so if he was frowning—the most subtle and noncommittal of frowns—she couldn't possibly have seen it.

—✦—

Lanoe kicked hard at the aft end of the axial corridor and shot through the cruiser's decks, past the sick bay, the gun decks, the bunks. The place felt empty and haunted, hushed as if everyone were waiting for something to happen. Well, he was back now. Time to give them what they wanted.

He reached out and caught a handhold on the wall, stopping himself just as he reached the wardroom. Valk was at the ship's controls, lying motionless in his seat with his arms floating in front of him. At least he had his helmet up and looked approximately human.

"Welcome back," the AI said.

"Thanks," Lanoe said. "I need an update. Tell me about the dreadnoughts that are looking for us. Are they moving?"

He reached across Valk and tapped at a virtual key. Displays sprang up all around him, showing him telescope views of the surrounding volume of space, tactical assessments, the status of the cruiser's systems.

"All three dreadnoughts changed course when you left the disk," Valk said. "They saw your engines burning, definitely. Two of them are headed for the disk, probably investigating where you came from. The third one is headed for us, but it's still twelve hours out. Then—there's this."

One of the displays moved to the front, right where Lanoe was looking. It showed a telescope view of a portion of the disk, an endlessly swirling cauldron of red storm clouds. Scattered across one cloud bank were dozens of dark specks. Before Lanoe could ask, the view magnified, and then magnified again, and again, losing definition each time. The final view was pixilated and hard to read, but Lanoe got the point.

"Are those airfighters?" he asked. They had the same spherical glass hulls as the drone ships they'd fought inside the disk's atmosphere.

"Same principle, similar design, but look, there's something missing," Valk said. "Wings. They don't have wings."

"You think those are spacecraft," Lanoe said cautiously.

"I don't need to think it. They left the atmosphere shortly after we received this image. They're headed our way."

"How many?"

"That's the closest thing we have to good news. There were hundreds—thousands—of airfighters in their fleet, but it looks like the Blue-Blue-White are only sending forty-five of these things after us. Spacecraft are more expensive to build than aircraft, and maybe they didn't expect to ever have to fight off an invasion from space—"

Lanoe held up a hand to stop the AI talking. "Interceptors. Probably drones. But interceptors. How soon will they be here?"

"They move a lot faster than the dreadnoughts, but they're coming from farther away. Twelve hours, give or take a few minutes."

Lanoe swore under his breath. "They'll arrive at the same time as the dreadnought. They're smarter than I thought they were. These," he said, stabbing one finger through the display, "are reinforcements for the dreadnought. And they make our lives a lot more complicated." When they were just fighting one big ship, the advantage was on the Navy's side. The cruiser's guns had a far longer effective range than the dreadnought's plasma ball cannons. But if the Blue-Blue-White could field interceptors as well, this wasn't going to be a showdown. It was going to be a pitched battle.

"We'll fight them. On their terms, if we have to," Lanoe said. "There's no backing down. Tell me about Candless and the others. How's their morale? You think they're ready for a battle?"

"They've been busy, mostly focused on hiding. I think they're scared, Lanoe. But if it comes to it, they'll fight—if only to defend themselves."

"I guess that's good enough for now," Lanoe said.

"They kept telling me you were dead. But I had a feeling that couldn't be true."

Lanoe snorted. "You had a feeling, huh? You're telling me an AI believes in intuition?"

"Not intuition. Just logic, really. If you had died, I wouldn't still be here."

"What are you talking about?" Lanoe asked.

"The data bomb I gave you. You would have triggered it if you knew you were going to die. You would have erased me."

Lanoe frowned. He'd promised to let Valk go when the time came, when the AI was no longer necessary to the mission. He'd never considered the possibility he might die first. "I might not have had time," he said. "You know as well as I do that when you're a pilot you can't always know when your time is up."

The AI had no comment on that.

Lanoe sighed and looked into the black dome of Valk's helmet. It was blank, as always. He'd thought he knew the mind in there once. He'd understood Tannis Valk. Ever since it turned out that the Blue Devil was just a fiction, a false memory programmed into a machine, he'd seen Valk drifting away from him. Getting less and less human—less understandable—with every passing day.

"We need to talk," he said.

"Okay."

Lanoe strapped himself into a chair in the wardroom. Leaned forward so he could keep his voice low. Nobody was around, but this felt like a conversation that should be carried out in whispers. "How are you doing?" he asked. "I mean, really. Are you... I don't know. Functioning optimally?"

"I'm fine. I run diagnostics on myself all the time, and I haven't seen any problems."

Lanoe rubbed at his face. "Because I kind of have. Seen problems."

Valk couldn't raise an eyebrow, or frown, or even turn his head to look at Lanoe. He did tilt over a little in his chair, and Lanoe figured that had to mean he was confused. "I'm not sure what you mean," he said.

"It started when we first got here. I asked where exactly we were in the galaxy, and you couldn't tell me."

"I explained that at the time," Valk said. "I couldn't find any of the standard candles." The landmarks of space, in other words— the most reliable stars and nebulae that could be used to fix a vehicle's position relative to the rest of the galaxy. "The stellar population here is so dense it blocks traditional methods of orientation, and the effect of gravitational lensing can't be ruled out because—"

"Sure," Lanoe said. "But then what about when I asked you to talk to the Blue-Blue-White for me? Because you were supposed to know their language."

"I have a small vocabulary that I got from a drone ten thousand light-years from here," Valk pointed out. "It's true I can't understand what they said in response to our message. But there could be lots of reasons for that. Maybe the locals use an idiomatic form of the language, or maybe the Blue-Blue-White have more than one language, just like humans do. If you went to a planet where they speak English, and broadcast a message in Mandarin, you would get the same response."

Lanoe nodded. "Okay," he said. "Those all sound like very logical reasons. Reasons for why you can't do the things I need you to do."

"Lanoe," Valk said, "if you have doubts about my functionality, then by all means. Switch me off. Delete me now. But I'm telling you, I'm fine."

Lanoe unstrapped himself. He pushed over to Valk's chair and patted the AI on the arm. "Okay," he said. "Okay. But I'm going to relieve you from duty for a while. At least until we can get Paniet to come over here and take a good long look at you. You okay with that?"

"What the hell do you think? No, I'm not okay with that."

Lanoe reared back a little. He'd never seen Valk get angry before—not even back when he still thought he was a human being. He'd come to count on the AI being unflappable.

"I'm fine, damn you," the AI said. Valk's voice roughened into a distorted growl. "You don't know the first damned thing about computers, about artificial intelligence. How dare you come in here and start insulting me, start suggesting I'm—I'm—"

Valk fell silent for a moment. Lanoe, surprised by the sudden outburst, could only wait until he spoke again.

"Lanoe. I'm sorry. I'm really sorry. I don't know what came over me just then. I mean, I shouldn't have yelled."

"Why not? It's what a human would have done."

"Okay, but listen. You can't take me off of duty. I don't have anything else! I'm so deeply interconnected with this ship right now, giving it up would be like...like losing myself. Again. Please, Lanoe. Please don't do this."

"I'm sorry," Lanoe said, pushing away from Valk's chair. "I just can't trust you right now. There's too much at stake."

———

"You're telling me that Candless actually shot you? In the leg? Just because you refused to listen to her defeatist rhetoric? Surely that was a hair-raising moment. I would have been terrified."

"I've fought my share of duels in my time. A man who's afraid of being shot at is a man who is afraid to fully live," Shulkin said, and slapped the leg of his suit.

Maggs laughed and raised his flask. "To a true hero," he said, and drank. Shulkin waved away the compliment, but his eyes were still bright. Almost human.

He had learned the trick of getting anything out of Shulkin. The old captain was dead inside for the most part, scoured clean by the Navy's best brain surgeons. They'd taken perhaps too much and left him with very little in the way of an inner life. They had, however, left him the ability to fight—and to talk about fighting. Luckily Maggs had some experience in dealing with old warriors of Shulkin's stripe, who were fueled in their dotage by nothing but the warmth of memories of slaughter.

I'd almost take that thought personally, if I didn't know better, Maggs's father's voice said inside his head.

"You know," Maggs said, ignoring his ghostly paterfamilias, "speaking with you really takes me back. I was born and raised at the Admiralty—"

"Bah," Shulkin said, sneering as if he'd smelled something unpleasant. "Bunch of bureaucrats, bean counters, and *staff officers* there."

"Quite," Maggs said. "A lad like me, who dreamed of high adventure and glory—why, I was in constant danger of having the spirit stamped out of me. So I sought out men and women like you, Captain, and like my father, the admiral. Those who had *lived*. Those who could still teach me something."

As I recall, you spent most of your formatives chasing nubile young women and robbing my liquor cabinet.

I put in enough hours sitting at your knee to pick up a few tricks, Maggs told his father. "It was a magical time, hearing the old stories. I don't suppose you have a few you might share. For old times' sake."

Shulkin smiled. At least his microscopically thin lips creased at the corners and his eyes sparkled like faulty circuits. He leaned back in his chair, his arms lifting in front of him in the classic pose of one sleeping in microgravity. Maggs made himself comfortable, assuming he was in for a good solid hour of dusty tales of murder and mayhem in the wild and wooly days of the Brushfire. At least he had his flask to help him sit through it.

Yet something unexpected happened then, something he hadn't planned on. The old captain's mouth closed, his teeth coming together with a click. His smile faded and his eyes visibly focused. Maggs could almost hear the neurons firing in the mass of scar tissue that was what remained of Shulkin's brain.

"Flattery," he said. "Flattery."

"I beg your pardon?" Maggs asked.

"Flattery will...get you...nowhere."

What had Maggs said? How had he triggered this change? Instantly, Shulkin had lost his air of bloodthirsty bonhomie and instead taken on the distracted air and hesitant speech of a sleepwalker. Some switch had been flipped, some logic gate had closed. It was downright spooky. And decidedly inconvenient.

"I do beg your pardon, Captain," Maggs said. "I didn't mean any offense—"

"You want...something," Shulkin said.

"Only good company, I assure you! A friendly chat to help pass the time of my captivity, nothing more."

"Lying... bastard. Just ask for it. Whatever... it is."

Maggs set his jaw. He had been sent over to listen to Shulkin's stories and plant a seed or two of sedition. Working closely with Bullam he'd planned out everything he would say to Shulkin, every subtle suggestion, every nuanced turn of phrase. Suddenly they had gone off script.

Well, Maggs was an excellent improviser, when it came to that.

"All right," he said. "You've seen through me. You've got me."

Shulkin didn't even nod. He just stared. He was, Maggs had to credit it, very, very good at nasty stares.

"I'm not here for chitchat. I do want something from you. Or rather—I would say I want something *for* you."

Stony silence ensued.

"I want to give you back your ship," Maggs told him. "This ship."

"Centrocor," Shulkin said. Drawing out the word until it sounded like a draft of air leaking from a tomb. "You're working for... Centrocor. Working for Cygnet. Cygnet was... a fool. It was a mistake to throw my lot in with him and his... *monopoly*."

Dariau Cygnet was one of the directors of Centrocor—one of the most powerful people in all of human space. Bullam had told Maggs about him, how he had personally sent her on her original mission, to find and capture Lanoe. Cygnet had hired Shulkin to assist her toward that end. They had come a long way since then.

"Centrocor," Maggs said, "is a dead issue. We're ten thousand light-years from the nearest Centrocor field office. What happens here, what happens now, has nothing whatsoever to do with Big Hexagon."

At least that got Shulkin nodding. Well, Maggs thought it was a nod. It might have been some kind of neural tic.

"I'll admit it," Maggs said. "Yes, I'm working—in a clandestine sort of way—for M. Bullam. She sent me here. You see, Captain? I can tell the truth. I'm working against the Navy by coming here today."

"Lanoe let me fight," Shulkin said. "He knows how to fight." Spoken with a level of reverence bordering on the tone that religious zealots used when acclaiming their redeemers.

Ah. It seems there's been a shift of loyalties, his father said. *This one's signed on with the other side, Maggsy. Tread lightly…*

Maggs nodded, though whether it was in response to Shulkin's spoken words or his father's spectral voice he wasn't sure. "Yes. Lanoe let you fight." He took a deep breath.

All in, he thought. All in.

"Candless shot you when you refused to retreat," he said.

Shulkin's eyes darkened and his mouth pursed, as if he'd bitten into a lemon. That deathly and deadly stare of his drooped, just a hair, until it was no longer focused like a particle beam on Maggs's face.

It was always so encouraging when you saw the hooks go in. When you knew you had your mark.

* * *

Lanoe strapped himself into the cruiser's control station and brought up a tactical board. The alien dreadnought was still closing in, burning hard to intercept them, but it was ten hours away. The interceptors were still trailing behind it, but they were catching up fast.

Candless had done an excellent job of using tricky maneuvering to hide her ships from the Blue-Blue-White searchers—honestly, Lanoe was impressed by what she'd accomplished—but he had no intention of following the same strategy.

He intended to stand and fight. He had other things to get done first, however, before they engaged.

First up was to call Candless and let her know that he was back in charge. She'd refused to give him her position, back when he was still down in the disk. She had to be reminded that she worked for him.

He sent the call and as expected she answered immediately. Maybe she knew what she was in for, but she was a teacher and she would know there was no point shirking discipline.

"Give me a report," he said as soon as her face came up on his display.

"Of course, sir," she said. She fed data to his system and new displays popped up all around him. "As you can see here, two of the dreadnoughts have moved toward the disk, away from us—"

"I've got the tactical situation covered. Valk filled me in about the interceptors."

"I . . . see," she said.

Something bothered Lanoe, something missing. When he realized what it was he frowned. "Where's Shulkin?"

Her brow furrowed. "Sir?"

"I asked you a question, Captain. I can see his seat over your shoulder, and he's not in it. Why is he not on the bridge of his own ship?"

She took a breath. "He's resting. We've all been taking very long shifts here—I haven't had a break in over twenty-four hours and even with caff tabs I'm in desperate need of some sleep myself."

"Hmm," Lanoe said. "I thought you might have relieved him of duty and claimed the carrier for your own. It seems you're under the impression you're in charge around here. I'm calling to ask you to formally relinquish command of the fleet, but maybe you'd like to fight me for it."

"Of course not, sir. I'm glad to have you back. I understand that you may not see it that way, but I assure you—"

"It doesn't matter why you failed to obey my order. I'm not particularly interested in excuses."

She lifted her chin a fraction of a degree. "Sir," she said.

He'd known her for a very long time. He'd fought beside her, lived in quarters with her. Anyone else might have missed it, but he could see the tension in her neck muscles, in the set of her shoulders. He'd wounded her deeply. She was a woman who very much valued Naval protocol and the chain of command. He'd struck her to the core.

Lanoe forced himself to soften his tone. He still needed Candless. He'd made his point and he didn't want to antagonize her any further. "All right," he said. "You did what you did to protect your crew. I suppose in this particular case I can forgive your insubordination. But, Candless, I need you on my team. I need to know I can count on you to carry out my decisions. We're in the middle of a war, for the devil's sake."

"A...war, sir."

"Yes, that's right. Why do you look confused right now?"

"It's just that I was under the impression that we...well. I suppose it doesn't matter what I thought."

"Go ahead," he told her. "I want to hear your analysis."

She nodded. "We had our noses pretty well bloodied back there," she told him. "Our engagement with the Blue-Blue-White was an unmitigated disaster."

"You see it that way? We shot down one of their dreadnoughts and dozens of their airfighters. We even took out their laser emplacement."

"Yes, sir. And all it cost us was half of our fleet." Candless pursed her lips and he knew she was wondering just how candidly she was allowed to speak. He could tell by the way her nostrils flared that she had decided to just say it. "We lost the battle. Lost it miserably. We are not capable of fighting the Blue-Blue-White—not here, not on their own ground. Our only sane option at this point is to retreat. Have Rain-on-Stones open a wormhole and head home to lick our wounds."

Lanoe nodded. "I see. You don't feel that what we're doing here is worth the sacrifice."

Candless shook her head. "I didn't say that. However, you asked for my analysis, and it's this: we can't win here."

"I think we can. And it's what I think that matters."

"Then you intend to continue to engage the enemy? There will be more battles."

"That's right," Lanoe said. "Starting in a little less than ten hours. We're going to clear the skies so that we have unrestricted access to the disk. And then we are going to rain hell down upon the Blue-Blue-White."

The blood ran out of Candless's face. She was afraid. Well, this was no time for cowards.

Lanoe cut the connection before either of them could say anything more.

—⁕—

Maggs made his way through the carrier with only moderate discretion. He was permitted in most areas of the ship, as long as he didn't make a nuisance of himself. At one point he caught sight of young Bury, heading somewhere with a nasty look on his face—if the child was capable of some other expression, Maggs had never seen it—and he hung back in a hatchway rather than let the Hellion see him. A confrontation now, as delightful as it might be, would only slow him down.

He stopped off at a few bunks in the quartering decks, knocking on hatches and speaking a few words of encouragement to those Centrocor employees Bullam had identified as being the most loyal. He said nothing of any substance, of course, just reminded them that they had not been forgotten. Some of the people on his list looked downright terrified to see him, so he soothed their jangled nerves. Others struck him as impatient. These he offered reassurances that the time was coming, and soon.

They had to accelerate the timetable, Bullam had said. Move things along. Not the easiest of tasks when everything had to be handled so damned delicately, but Maggs understood how to wield subtlety as a weapon. How lucky Bullam was to have him as an assistant, he thought. Not for the first time he admired her intellect—had she allowed Lanoe to kill him back at Caina, she might have avoided some unpleasantness, but then she would have lost her very best asset.

He was rather proud of himself, honestly. He was a talented fellow, and a great help in such a time.

He kept telling himself that. He needed to puff himself up. The final visit he needed to make was going to be the hardest.

He headed for the quartermaster's little office. The same little cubby of hell where he'd gone through such a trial getting his old suit—and his ceremonial dirk—back. He was not one bit surprised to find that when he arrived the same woman was on duty, lost in her endless spreadsheet displays. He'd almost forgotten the scar that crossed her nose and left her with but a single eyebrow, but he managed not to let his revulsion cross his features.

"Remember me?" he asked.

The sour look she gave him failed to surprise. She swiped away her displays and folded her arms across her chest. "It's the big fancy Centrocor executive, then," she said. "The one who threatened to get me fired."

"Ah, now, I don't remember saying anything of the kind," he told her. "I asked how much you enjoyed your position. Just a friendly little inquiry as to your morale."

She made a rude noise.

He'd run across her type before. Too beaten down by life to believe you when you flattered them. Too battered by time and history to believe in the universe's grand possibilities—so you couldn't appeal to their greed. Tough nuts to crack, it had to be said. But everyone, in Maggs's experience, had an in. Something they wanted, something they were afraid of. Some hidden button you could push.

"Back then, you could bully me pretty easy. You were a big wheel with Centrocor so you could make my life hell if I didn't play along. Funny thing, though. Centrocor's gone. Now I'm Navy again. And you—you're just a civilian."

"I'll point out I haven't actually asked you for anything yet," Maggs said. "For all you know I came down here to shoot the breeze. To try, perhaps, to make amends for my previous hubris."

"Sure. And maybe you're into women with scars, and you came down here to ask if I wanted to have dinner with you sometime."

Maggs checked that particular line of approach off of his mental list of gambits to try out. So. He could not proceed by flattery, or greed, or seduction, or intimidation. Well, that left only a very few arrows in his quiver, and none that he liked to use very often. Perhaps...perhaps he might try to play to her pity. Sell her a story of woe and tragedy, and eke some sympathy out of her human heart.

He nodded sadly and dropped his chin. "I see. I've underestimated you. I beg your pardon, then. I seem to have wasted your time. I'll go. Too bad. You were my last hope—you see, I'm in a spot of trouble with my employer, M. Bullam, and...never mind. You don't want to hear this."

"You've got that right."

Maggs was too committed to his ploy to let her get under his skin. "Yes, really, my troubles have nothing to do with you. If I lose my job, well, I guess it was my own damned fault. I thought maybe she would be more understanding when I told her about my tragic upbringing, and how it made me...made me vulnerable to...I say. Stop that at once. That's quite unseemly."

The quartermaster was laughing at him. Chuckling without so much as bothering to cover her mouth with her hand. It was quite rude, given the gravity of the—admittedly completely untrue—story he'd been working up to.

"Relax," she said. Her eyes still burned with hatred, but she let her arms fall to her sides. "I already know why you're here. M. Bullam sent me a private message while you were on your way over."

"I—I beg your pardon?"

"You heard me."

Maggs struggled to keep his face from turning red. "You were expecting me."

"Yes."

"You knew why I'd come. And you let me talk all that bosh anyway."

The quartermaster shrugged. "I owed you for last time. You should see the look on your face right now. It's priceless."

"Damn you, let's get to business, then. I have no interest in being raked further over the coals of indignity."

"Yeah, okay. Come with me." She unstrapped herself from her

desk and pushed herself along the wall, deep into the low-ceilinged storerooms that held the carrier's supplies. "Your boss is pretty generous," she said. "She set up a nice schedule of payments, and even gave me some advice on how we're going to do this. Basically you want to send your people down here one at a time, no more than a couple of them in any given day. I've changed the numbers on some requisition forms—they should ask for allergy medication. That's how I'll know you sent them."

"Allergy medication," Maggs said. "Aboard a ship with Navy standard-issue air filters that catch anything bigger than a micron. Do you even carry any such drugs?"

"It doesn't matter. The point is to make sure nobody looks twice at the tracking numbers." The quartermaster ran one finger along a line of shelves, then stopped when she reached one that Maggs could not tell from any of the other multitude of shelves around him. "Your people come down here and ask for the pills, and this is what they'll get instead." She pulled a box from the shelf and opened the lid.

"Ah," Maggs said in appreciation.

The box was full of weapons. Mostly sidearms, though there were a few neural stunners, combat knives, and smoke grenades in there as well. Near the top he thought he saw an actual pair of brass knuckles.

"This is all the stuff that got seized when the Navy took control of the carrier. All the personal effects their marines dug out of our bunks. I haven't even had a chance to log it into the system yet, so the powers that be don't have an inventory on it. Even if somebody from Commander Lanoe's crew does come down here and wants to inspect this box, there's no manifest for them to check its contents against. No way to know what should be here."

"You haven't logged these in," Maggs repeated. "Surely that would have been one of your first duties when these came in."

"Oh, sure," the quartermaster told him. "That was a total brain failure on my part. I totally should have thought of that." She gave him a look so cynical it made him squirm. "Of course, if I had, I would have missed out on a pretty hefty bribe. I guess we all just got lucky."

"Ma'am," Maggs said, bowing just a little, "it is rare in this life that I meet someone who understands the game as well as I. One as devious and underhanded, one as skilled in the criminal arts—"

"Are you working up to asking me out for dinner after all?" she asked. "Because I'm still not interested."

Chapter Nineteen

With the dreadnought and the interceptors closing in, Lanoe had given up any pretense of hiding. He switched on all the cruiser's active sensors, to try to get better imagery of his opponent.

The dreadnought and its escort were still six hours out from the cruiser. The alien ship's engines were burning hot, pushing it faster and faster toward them, but the two ships were still so far apart it took long seconds for millimeter-wave pulses to bounce off the dreadnought's hull and return to the cruiser's parabolic antennae. The data he got back made little sense to him. With Valk removed from duty, he needed someone else to look at the numbers. He called up the IO on the carrier to get an analysis of what he'd found.

"Interesting. See, here's the problem," the man said, "the reason why when we fought them before, disruptors didn't even slow them down." A display popped up near Lanoe's elbow, showing a series of cross sections of the alien ship. "Disruptors work best on a ship that has big interior cavities. This one—"

"Sure," Lanoe said. He saw it right away. The cross sections showed that the dreadnought was almost completely solid. Or, rather, almost completely made up of a hard material riddled with millions of tiny bubbles, some as big as two meters in diameter, some no more than a centimeter across. It looked very much like a cutaway view of a coral reef. There was nowhere a creature as large as an adult Blue-Blue-White could move around inside the giant ship—no passageways, no chambers a jellyfish could even squeeze into. "So you're telling me most of the ship is just dead space."

"I don't think so, no," the IO replied. "I think they use those little cavities to store fuel, like a giant sponge. And maybe the bigger ones could be used as ionizing chambers. With so many of them, it would explain how they can charge up those plasma balls so quickly. It's weird. I mean, it isn't like any kind of human technology. I guess that makes sense, since humans didn't build these things."

Lanoe touched the display, got it rotating. He examined the blisters, the cagework canopies that studded the outer skin of the coral. The blisters were hollow inside—and much bigger than the bubbles they'd seen in the main hull. "These have to be crew spaces. Cockpits, or something like that. But if the blisters are the only places the jellyfish can move around in, there can't be more than a half dozen of them on the entire ship."

Which, frankly, fit with what he'd seen down in the disk, in the city of the Blue-Blue-White. As enormous as that structure of white pylons had been, he'd only seen one adult jellyfish in the whole place. One adult, and a brood of its young.

Perhaps even calling the place a city had been wrong. Perhaps he'd been thinking in human terms, frames of reference that were useless when applied to the habits of an alien species. He'd seen a large structure and assumed it must be densely populated, just like the cities back on Earth or any human planet. Instead what he'd seen had been much more like a reef ecosystem, a vast structure made by tiny creatures, populated by small animals and dominated by a single apex predator.

It got him thinking. He'd estimated that there were a few hundred cities the same size as the one he'd flown through. Maybe three hundred lacy constructions of floating pylons in the entire unimaginably huge volume of the disk.

If every one of those reefs was the territory of just a single adult

Blue-Blue-White, then even including the immature ones he'd seen (*don't call them babies,* he reminded himself, *babies are little humans*), the entire population of the disk could be measured in the thousands. The disk might be seventy thousand times the size of Earth, but it only carried a tiny fraction of the population.

Just a handful of them. And they were going to wipe out humanity, just as they had wiped out so many other species.

Pain lanced through his temples suddenly. He felt as if someone had jabbed dull knives up under his eyelids, into his brain. He reached up to rub at his forehead, careful not to let the IO see his pain.

"Good work," he told the man. "See what else you can find. Look for weak points. Look for...I don't know. Just find me the best way to kill these things."

"Yes, sir," the IO said.

Lanoe ended the call. Once he was unobserved again he brought both hands up to his head and rubbed vigorously at his eyes. The pain receded slowly, but eventually he could see straight again.

He blew out a deep breath. Leaned back in his chair. His eyes ached and he closed them, thinking he would give them a rest. He'd been staring at displays for hours now, studying reports, reading tiny print. He was three hundred years old, for the devil's sake. Of course he was going to get eyestrain.

He opened his eyes, but made a point of focusing on nothing, of staring into space.

Just a few thousand, he thought. A tiny population. They used so many drones because they didn't have the crews for more than a handful of ships.

Just a few thousand of them.

It wouldn't take much to wipe them out.

~◆~

"I have a plan for how we're going to take this dreadnought," Lanoe told Candless, via communications laser. "The interceptors are getting closer every second. If we wait for the dreadnought to come to us, they'll catch up and we'll be fighting them all together. I don't want to let that happen. We're going to move to intercept—swoop in and kill the dreadnought before the reinforcements arrive."

"I suppose that's a wise choice," Candless said. "Sir."

"We'll screen the cruiser's advance with fighters. They were all but useless before, but we have a better idea now of what we're facing. A new strategy. If we can get a disruptor or even just an AV round into each of those blisters, we can kill every Blue-Blue-White on the ship. If even one of them is left after the first attack run, we hammer the thing with every gun we have."

Candless shook her head. "I don't understand. Why employ the fighters at all? The cruiser's guns did satisfactory work against the dreadnought we encountered in the disk. Why can't we simply turn them on this one as well?"

"We got lucky that time. We fired sixteen guns at point-blank range on a mostly stationary target. It's too big a risk to try to pull off the same trick when both ships are accelerating. If we even get half a broadside in before they roast the cruiser with a plasma ball, it'll be a miracle—and we don't know if eight shots will be enough. I don't think I need to remind you just how big these dreadnoughts are."

"No, you don't," Candless said. She fought the urge to sigh deeply. "When you're asking me to take such a ridiculously dangerous action that will put my entire crew at risk, I do tend to pay attention."

He almost smiled at that. On her display he looked tired. Wrung out. Admittedly he was three hundred years old. His face was as wrinkled as a bedsheet after a dirty weekend, and his hair was more salt than pepper. It was rare to see someone who looked that old these days. Most people got cosmetic treatments to make them look like they had when they were twenty-five. The truly rich would just skip the treatments and have their consciousness downloaded into a fresh new body.

Not Lanoe. He'd been old before any of those measures were even available, and he had never bothered with the rejuvenation treatments that might have erased all those wrinkles, those deep bags under his eyes. He'd taken only the injections and procedures that kept him from dying of old age. Anyone but Candless—his oldest comrade-in-arms—might not have noticed how exhausted he looked. By modern standards, he always looked tired—frankly, he always looked like he was three days dead. But now there was definitely a look in his eyes as if something was dragging at him. Sapping his energy.

The last time they'd spoken, he'd treated her like a disobedient child. He'd been rather harsher than she thought was strictly necessary. She had plenty of reason to gloat a little if he was looking harried, she supposed. Yet she couldn't help but feel something for him, after all they'd been through. To wonder if something was wrong. If perhaps the burden of command was weighing on him. Or perhaps something else. "I'd like to inquire as to your health," she told him. "If you won't take it the wrong way. Is something the matter?"

"Never better. Talk to me about what we can field in the way of cataphracts. Your Beta wing is relatively intact, right?"

Candless pursed her lips. Apparently they were no longer friends—or at least he was not going to open up to her just for her asking. Very well, then. If he wanted to be her commanding officer, she would treat him as such. "If by that you mean their ranks weren't quite as decimated as those of Alpha wing, then, yes, you are technically correct. They can put ten fighters in theater."

"One squadron." Lanoe shook his head. "Not enough. Get Alpha wing ready to scramble as well. What's that? Another eight?"

"Yes, but . . . that leaves us with no reserve—"

"Carrier scouts," Lanoe said.

"—except the carrier scouts," she finished. There was a good half second of lag in their transmission, but that didn't excuse him from trying to talk over her before she could complete her sentence. "Which is not much of a reserve at all. If we lose too many cataphracts to the dreadnought's plasma balls we'll have nothing left when the interceptors *do* arrive."

"You don't win a war by avoiding risks," Lanoe told her. "Maybe when they see the dreadnought fall, the interceptors will run away. And maybe we'll need to fight them with just the cruiser's guns. It doesn't matter. We need to remove the dreadnought from play— otherwise we'll never accomplish anything, sitting out here in the dark. Are my orders clear now? Do you have any more questions?"

Candless could think of a few dozen. The first, however, and most preeminent was one that she'd been silently asking herself since they arrived in the system.

Why in Earth's name are we doing this at all?

What exactly did Lanoe hope to achieve? They couldn't talk to the Blue-Blue-White, thanks to Valk's failure to understand their language. They couldn't make demands, or negotiate a surrender.

She couldn't see a single military objective that they could hope to achieve—even if, against all odds, Aleister Lanoe managed to win yet another war.

She could hardly say that aloud, though.

"No," she said. "No questions."

"Good." His image on the display winked out of existence.

Only then did she allow herself the long, elaborate exhalation that she'd been holding in. The silent release of breath that was the closest thing she would allow herself to an exasperated sigh.

———※———

It was quiet in the wardroom. With Valk sent off to one of the bunks, there was no one around for Lanoe to talk to, to bounce ideas off of, to listen when he grunted in frustration. Even beyond the control station there was no one around, no one in the axial corridor, no one moving around the bunks. Ehta and her marines were sealed up in the gun decks, waiting to fight. Ginger and Rain-on-Stones were locked up in the brig, feeling each other's pain.

It was just Lanoe and his displays, and the steadily approaching dreadnought.

Waiting. But not for very long.

Hours of maneuvering and burning the cruiser's engines had brought them to the moment of decision. In less than a minute, the battle would begin.

He kept an eye on a readout that told him how far away the dreadnought was. "Thirty seconds until the enemy is in range," he said, his words swallowed up by static. The cruiser and the carrier were moving too fast now to use communications lasers. He was broadcasting on an open radio band. Normally that was against protocol—but the protocol had been written for battles fought against other human beings. The Blue-Blue-White might be able to hear him, but they couldn't understand what he said.

"Twenty-five seconds. Scramble fighters."

Finally something did change on one of his displays. He saw a camera view from one of the carrier's cupolas, saw Yk.64s stream past as they launched from the carrier's flight deck. He counted them as they went, knowing he would count them as they came back, too. Knowing there would be fewer of them when they returned.

The fighters moved quickly into a standard line formation, flying so close their airfoils nearly touched. Lanoe tapped a virtual control and saw the enemy's interceptors, still half a million kilometers away, their spherical glass canopies silhouetted by the flare of their thrusters. They were still half an hour out.

Plenty of time.

Fifteen seconds. The dreadnought's weapon pits were warming up, getting ready to throw plasma balls as soon as a target got close enough to be worth shooting at. Those plasma balls were deadly, capable of frying a pilot inside his fighter even on a near miss, but they were only useful at short range. Once the plasma ball left the weapon pit it immediately started losing heat, cooling as it radiated away its energy into space. At even just a few tens of kilometers out they were harmless, barely capable of making a pilot sweat.

Eight seconds. The cataphracts moved into a new formation, their line curling forward at the ends to make a semicircle so they could envelop the enemy.

Lanoe wished like hell he could have been out there with them, but somebody had to fly the cruiser. Candless had volunteered to fly one of the fighters, so at least there would be one competent pilot leading them.

"Five seconds," he said. "Four. Dreadnought is entering the battle area. Combined wing, engage at your first opportunity. And good luck."

Three seconds. The battle area was an arbitrary designation, just a set distance away from the cruiser that Lanoe had decided was the best place for a scrap. Still, as he counted down, his blood absolutely sang. It screamed with the need for red vengeance.

His voice was as calm and cool as ever.

"Two seconds. One. Dreadnought is in the battle area."

One of its weapon pits lit up as bright as a sun. A plasma ball shot forward, rolling toward the line of fighters like a ninepins ball. The cataphracts scattered—and swarmed, falling on the dreadnought like a cloud of gnats. He could see just how tiny they were compared to their quarry.

It didn't matter. They had the weapons, the ships, that could do this, that could win. If they were good enough pilots, they would prevail.

If.

Time to find out—the battle had begun.

⟡

"Alpha wing, move up—there's a gap there, exploit it!" Candless shouted, even as she threw her Yk.64 over to the side to avoid an incoming plasma ball. "Beta wing, circle around and aggress on the thrusters." Below her the dreadnought's enormous pitted mass looked like a heavily cratered moon. She saw a weapon pit opening before her, a dark cave so big she could have flown into it if she was feeling suicidal. She leaned on her control stick with one hand and loaded a disruptor round with the other. "What is the matter with you lot? Who taught you how to fight?"

It had been a very long time since Candless led a wing of fighters into battle. She hoped very much she remembered how.

"Uhl, Singh, Forster," she called, picking the three pilots closest to her position, "screen my advance!"

Candless could hear the sneer in Forster's voice as he replied. "You want us to be decoys for you? Bait for those plasma balls?"

"I want you to do your damned job," she told him, almost growling in anger.

Her fellow pilots weren't incompetent, she knew. They had all been in the Navy once, and had received Naval training—some at one of the prestigious flight schools, like Rishi, some just getting two weeks' instruction in the field. For various reasons, though, they'd been drummed out of Earth's service, and then hired by Centrocor. Flying for the poly—flying for a paycheck—had made them soft, made them worry more about their personal safety than about accomplishing anything. Centrocor couldn't give them commendations, nor did it promote them or raise their pay for superior flying. They were unmotivated and sullen long before they'd come to her.

Even worse, they lacked esprit de corps. They had no sense of camaraderie with one another—much less with her. Seasoned, disciplined pilots would throw themselves into the very teeth of the devil if it meant protecting their squaddies. This lot were just in it for themselves.

It was still possible to get real work out of pilots like that. It took, however, the application of the greatest, oldest motivator of all. Fear of one's superior officers.

"Uhl," she called, "Singh. You will cover my advance. Or when we get back to the carrier, you will sit through a personal multihour debriefing with me. We will go over, in excruciating detail, exactly what you did wrong and how to improve in the future."

At least that got the two of them moving, swinging into position behind her. Well behind her, though, where they would be useless for drawing fire.

"Suckers." Forster laughed.

"M. Forster," she said, "you may return to the carrier. Your services are no longer required."

"Wait—what?" Uhl asked. "You mean, if we don't want to fight, we can just—"

"M. Forster is no longer a member of this wing. He is no longer employed. When we return, he can figure out for himself how he's going to eat, because food is for people who work. He will also need to find a place to sleep, as we don't have bunks for people who don't pull their weight."

"Come on," Forster said. "We're all in this together, damn you!"

Candless allowed herself a nasty grin. If he was going to quote the Centrocor corporate slogan at her, she figured she was justified in using one of the Navy's unofficial mottos.

"Fly or die, M. Forster."

"Devil's sake, you pompous—"

"Fly," she told him, "or die."

He swung into position right behind her. Uhl and Singh closed ranks, giving her the cover she needed.

Time to strike.

———※———

Plasma balls spat in every direction as the dreadnought started to turn around, trying to run for the safety of the onrushing interceptors. Lanoe felt his lips pull back from his teeth in a painful rictus, but he couldn't relax, couldn't look away until it was done, until the dreadnought was obliterated.

A cataphract got too close to the big ship and was caught dead on by one of the plasma balls. He saw it pass through the fiery projectile and come out the other side as nothing but slag, as molten debris that came apart in pieces, each flying on with its own trajectory. He smashed his fist against the side of his chair. One less fighter—that made the battle just that much tougher to win.

It wasn't the first cataphract they'd lost. Most of Centrocor's pilots were smart enough to stay clear of the huge, slow-moving plasma balls, but occasionally one of them couldn't roll away in time. If they didn't take the dreadnought down soon, they could lose this battle purely by attrition—and have nothing to show for it.

At least it looked like Candless had the right idea—he could see her streaking across the surface of the dreadnought, a torpedo fish swimming fast over a bleached coral reef.

"Shulkin," Lanoe called, because he'd seen something out of the corner of his eye, a blip on a tactical board. "Move back—you're in danger of straying into the battle area." The carrier itself could do no good in there, now that it had loosed its cargo of fighters. "I appreciate your enthusiasm, but not if it costs me one of my ships."

"Understood," Shulkin called back. He left the channel open and Lanoe could hear him shouting at his pilot, but didn't bother paying attention. He was too invested in watching Candless edge closer and closer to one of the dreadnought's giant canopies. There would be a jellyfish in there, he thought, an adult Blue-Blue-White. When the disruptor went in, when it exploded inside that crew space, it would—

A green pearl rotated in the corner of Lanoe's eye. He thought it might be Ehta, calling to tell him her people were ready to fire. He absentmindedly flicked his eyes across the pearl.

"Sir," Bury said, "I know this is a bad time—"

"Bury? Damn you, kid, I have a battle to run here! Why are you calling me?"

"I just thought...that..."

"Spit it out or clear this channel."

"I've been watching the battle on my wrist display, and I saw you've lost some pilots, and you didn't have very many to start with, and—"

"You want to fly?" Lanoe asked.

"Yes, sir."

Lanoe shook his head. He didn't have time for this. "You're on the medical list, last time I checked. Anyway—I have every cataphract we've got out there right now. There's no ship for you to take."

"There are the carrier scouts, sir," Bury pointed out.

Lanoe almost laughed at that. Yes, it was true. There were ten carrier scouts still nestled inside the carrier's flight deck. Tiny ships, fast but lacking in firepower—they didn't carry any disruptors, just PBW cannons, and those were useless against the dreadnought's homogeneous hull.

He had to respect Bury's willingness to fly one of those crates. Though not enough to actually let it happen. "Sorry, Bury. It's not happening."

"Sir," Bury said, and Lanoe could hear the pitch of his voice rising. The kid didn't like what he'd heard. "Sir—I have four confirmed kills to my name. If we lose this battle, I might die without ever getting my blue star. As a pilot yourself, surely—"

Lanoe cut him off.

He reached for a squeeze tube of water. Bit off the plastic end and spat it out. Took a deep drink, while calling up a new display with his free hand—a highly magnified view of Candless's fighter. The view shook and wavered in and out of focus as the adaptive telescope lens tried to stay centered on her. She was moving fast enough even the cruiser's imaging algorithms couldn't keep up.

"Do it," he muttered. "Do it. Get that shot."

The dreadnought below her was just a blur. Candless flew as fast as she dared—too slow and she risked making herself a prime target for one of those plasma balls. Too fast and she wouldn't be able to aim properly when she reached the blister. "We're going to do this strictly by the book," she told her wingmates. "Uhl, you're up first. On my mark, break formation and get the hell out of here. Accelerate hard and you'll be all right. Fall back and rejoin the main formation. Singh, you'll be next—but don't move until I give the word. Forster, you'll have the signal honor of staying with me until I'm ready to make my run. If you three stick precisely to my orders, there's a very good chance all of us come out of this alive. Have I made myself understood?"

All three of them replied in the affirmative. If there was a deep grumble hidden in Forster's answer, she pretended not to hear it.

The blister was dead ahead, an extrusion of thin white pylons like the frame of a greenhouse. Glass, or whatever the Blue-Blue-White used in place of glass, filled the interstices, dark enough she could only see shadows moving within.

Her disruptor was primed and ready. She kept one eye on a display showing an infrared sensor sweep, a scan measuring the temperature of the three nearest weapon pits. The second one of them started warming up, she—

There. The temperature was spiking, ramping up at an improbable rate. In a second, a plasma ball would form inside that pit, and be launched outward by its own heat. Any moment now, any moment . . .

"Uhl, break!" she shouted.

The Yk.64 to her left peeled off, rolling on its positioning jets as Uhl punched his throttle. He twisted upward into open space, and just as Candless had predicted, the plasma ball shot after him, so hot, so bright her display flared with light that forced her to turn her head. The plasma ball was fast. A cataphract could move faster, if the pilot didn't care about damaging his engine. She watched Uhl on a tactical board, as a blue dot being chased by a red blur. For a second it looked like he wasn't going to make it, as if the plasma ball was going to catch him, but then he shot forward with renewed speed, even as he banked off to the side. The plasma ball shot past his new position, cooling as it rocketed through the emptiness, shrinking and fizzing out as the ionized gas lost its heat.

"Yes!" Singh shouted over the open channel.

"No chatter," she told him. She needed to focus. The blister was so close now, close enough she could make out shapes behind the dark glass. Something big and round in there. A damned jellyfish, certainly. But already a second weapon pit was heating up. "Singh, break!" she called.

Singh, perhaps excited by seeing Uhl survive the foolhardy maneuver, tried to get fancy with his flying. He pulled up in a sharp loop, the positioning jets in his undercarriage flaring as he curved high up over the dreadnought's back. As the plasma ball coalesced inside its pit, growing bright as a magnesium flare, he crested at the top of his loop—then rolled over on his side and shot off at an angle. The plasma ball blasted past him at high speed, close enough she was worried he might have been cooked alive inside his cockpit.

"Singh, report," she called. "Singh. Report!"

"I'm, uh, here," the pilot called back, sounding short of breath—but alive. "I'm okay, got a little toasty in here, but I've got plenty of coolant pressure, I'll be—I'll—"

A second plasma ball erupted from a weapon pit directly beneath him. There was no warning—it was not one of the pits that Candless had been monitoring. There was no chance of him maneuvering out of its way. It engulfed him so fast and at such a high temperature that Candless could actually see his fighter incandesce inside the plasma ball, a negative-image silhouette, white inside the blue heart of the plasma projectile. In a moment the plasma ball had passed him by, heading upward and into dead space. Candless looked for any wreckage, any debris from Singh's fighter, some irrational part of her thinking that maybe, just maybe he was still alive somehow. But there was nothing.

Singh had been utterly vaporized.

Candless squeezed her eyes shut, if only for a split second. She'd lost another one, another of her charges. Singh had never been her student, she had barely known his name. She had been responsible for his safety, though. She'd told him he was going to be okay if he just followed her orders.

She had failed him.

"He...he just..."

It was Forster, ignoring her order regarding chatter. She lacked the moral strength to upbraid him.

"He's gone," Forster said. He sounded utterly surprised. As if such a thing were physically impossible. As if a cataphract pilot couldn't possibly *die*.

"Ma'am," he said, "I think maybe—"

"Stick with me, Forster," Candless insisted. "We can do this, but only if we stick together."

"Sorry," he told her. "I'm...I'm sorry." He peeled away, climbing fast to get out of the range of the plasma balls. Soon he was just a bright spot, a moving speck of light against the myriad fixed stars of the galactic center.

Candless growled in frustration. She was so close—within seconds of the blister. She was utterly unprotected in her run. The only intelligent choice in that situation, the only sane choice, was to break off, to open her throttle and get clear.

To hell with it.

She reached for her throttle. Not to accelerate so she could get away. Instead she punched for a negative burn, the retros in the nose of her fighter burning hard—to slow her down.

If she was going to risk everything for just this one shot, she intended to make it a clean, direct hit.

<p style="text-align:center">~~~</p>

Lanoe grabbed his knees and rocked back and forth. His eyes bugged out of his head as he watched the display with growing tension, urging Candless on from afar. "Come on, come on," he said. He knew exactly what she was doing, why she was slowing down. He approved—even if it put her in serious danger. Even if he couldn't afford to lose her. She was the best pilot he had out there.

A green pearl spun in the corner of his vision. He glanced at it, thinking if it was Bury again he would demote the kid on the spot. It wasn't Bury—it was Ehta. He flicked his eyes sideways, never turning his head away from his display.

"Sir," she said, her tone icily formal. Well, her tone shouldn't surprise him—he had put a pistol to her head not long ago. "The guns are hot and ready. We can fire on your signal."

Lanoe felt his teeth rasping against one another. He knew, on one level, that he should give the order. He should let Ehta fire the guns, and probably destroy the dreadnought with one quick salvo.

On another level, though, a less rational but far more compelling level, he had a reason not to fire. To let Candless prove his theory that if you took out the canopies the dreadnought would be removed from play. To save those guns for when he really needed them.

"Stand by," he told Ehta.

"Sir, I... I don't want to question your orders, but we have a perfect firing solution right now. The dreadnought is maneuvering. If we wait, even ten seconds, we'll lose our shot. We'll have to start target acquisition over from scratch, and—"

"Stand by," he told her again.

She cut the link. Lanoe knew she was probably fuming, down there on the gun deck. Cursing his name. He could live with that, as long as she followed his orders.

Sometimes in war a commander had to make choices his troops didn't understand. Couldn't understand. Sometimes that had to be okay.

"Come on," he told Candless. "You can do this."

─────────── ✦ ───────────

Weapon pits all over the dreadnought were heating up, plasma balls gathering strength before they were launched. Candless was low enough, close enough to the giant ship's hull, that it would be difficult for the plasma balls to actually hit her. Difficult, but not impossible. From what she'd seen they could fire at any angle, even with an elevation of zero. From the enemy's perspective, a shot that low might be too big a risk to take. The plasma ball that took her out would graze the very skin of the dreadnought. It would damage the ship it was trying to protect.

The alternative, though, was to let her take her shot. To let her kill some of the dreadnought's crew. She doubted they would take that chance.

On instinct she threw her control stick over to one side. Hit her maneuvering jets and sent herself zigging and zagging across the dreadnought's skin. She did it just in time—a plasma ball launched in the same moment she started evading. The coral-like hull of the dreadnought bubbled and flowed like candle wax as the plasma ball rocketed toward her, right on her tail.

Candless banked off to one side and let the plasma ball shoot past her, close enough that she felt her eyebrows start to curl and smolder, felt sweat pour like a waterfall down the back of her suit. But then it was past.

And she was right where she needed to be.

The blister was enormous, maybe a hundred meters across—the size of one of the late Batygins' destroyers. It filled most of her view. She could have rammed right through one of the panes of glass that filled in the cagework, burst inside, and startled the hell out of the jellyfish in there.

She could see it. Not clearly—the tinted glass dulled its colors and her velocity blurred its features—but she could see a reddish spherical mass in there, pulsating with motion. A Blue-Blue-White. This was the closest she'd ever gotten to one of them.

She had a firing solution. She tapped her weapons board to confirm, then pulled her trigger.

The Yk.64 lurched as the disruptor's tiny thruster fired, throwing the projectile forward at hundreds of meters a second. The moment it was clear of her undercarriage it started to detonate, a Roman candle shedding fire as it raced toward the blister.

Candless streaked past the blister, accelerating hard as the hull disappeared beneath her and she saw only empty space below. She didn't even watch to see what the disruptor was doing to the dreadnought because some ugly premonition told her she might not survive long enough to see the fruits of her labors.

A quick glance at her tactical board proved out that hunch. Behind her, two weapon pits were blazing hot, already launching plasma balls. Both of them headed in her direction, on intersecting trajectories. She was right in the middle of a crossfire.

Lanoe could see nothing but the disruptor, could only watch as it plunged through the dark glass of the blister. A sheet of transparent material twenty meters across starred and then shattered, and for the first time he could see inside the crew space of the dreadnought. Not that he had time for a long look. He just made out a bewildering scene, strange shapes and surfaces that were designed for the comfort of entirely nonhuman creatures, before the disruptor filled the blister with smoke and light, pulverized coral bursting outward in an ever-expanding cloud, fizzing liquids that caught fire and then extinguished themselves almost instantly as they were exposed to the vacuum of space, and then—yes—

An adult Blue-Blue-White, scorched, battered, and oozing fluids, came tumbling out of the ruined blister, its tentacles twisting around each other as it tried to cover its mouth, as it tried to protect itself against the sudden decompression. Lights flared inside its translucent mantle, desperate signals Lanoe would never be able to understand, blue and orange and white, purple and purple and purple, some kind of distress call, but the lights dimmed, even as Lanoe watched, even as the creature slowly died. Its body squelched and throbbed, de-forming until it was stretched out like a long tube, then contracted to a tight, muscular sphere—and then relaxed.

Its lights went out, one by one. The tentacles went limp.

Lanoe leaned his head back and laughed, a nasty, howling guffaw of a laugh that sounded repugnant even to his own ears, but he couldn't stop, couldn't help himself. The damned thing was dead. Dead, dead, dead.

Candless was moments away from death, with nowhere to go. The two plasma balls were racing toward her, competing to see which one could immolate her first. Even if she shot straight upward, away from their intersecting paths, she would be flash-fried by their radiant heat. She didn't have time to breathe, didn't have time to think.

Marjoram Candless was a hell of a pilot. She'd fought in almost as many wars as Lanoe, had won more than her fair share of battles. She'd been trained by the finest flight instructors the Navy ever had, then—when she'd tired of war—she'd joined those ranks herself. She didn't need to think. She had reflexes honed by countless hours in the cockpit, by hundreds of hair's-breadth escapes.

Her fingers moved across her engine board, sketching out a maneuver that might save her. The board flashed and required that she confirm she actually wanted to do what she'd asked it to do.

She hit YES before the screen could even finish rendering the text. Then she punched her throttle and yanked her hand away from her control stick, as it snapped around like a snake.

She had switched off the compensators on her rotary engine. Her cataphract responded, as cataphracts always had—this being the oldest trick in the book, the rotary turn. Her engine turned into a massive, incredibly energetic flywheel and she turned ninety degrees in less than the time it took her heart to beat, even with her pulse racing. Her thrusters kicked in and she shot forward, not up, away from the plasma balls, but down.

She grabbed the stick and banked hard. The plasma balls met each other atop the dreadnought's hull, colliding in a massive burst of plasma that would have vaporized her as surely as they'd vaporized Singh—except for one thing.

By the time they met, she wasn't on top of the dreadnought anymore. She was underneath it, sheltered by the giant ship's own mass.

She wanted to whoop for joy, for relief, for the sheer terror of still being alive. She wanted to punch something, she wanted to cry out.

She didn't get a chance to do any of those things. Because even as she was making her crazy turn, even as she was maneuvering to safety—she heard something whine and scream and then break loose with a terrifying snap.

Navy regulations strictly forbade rotary turns. Pilots used the trick anyway, because it could save their lives. The reason for the prohibition, though, was that it also put an enormous stress on your engine mounts.

In a well-built cataphract like a BR.9, the Navy's workhorse, that danger was minimal. The BR.9's engine mounts had been reinforced specifically to take that stress. But Candless wasn't in a BR.9. She was in a Yk.64, a fighter built by one of Centrocor's many subcontractors. Designed and fabricated by the lowest bidder.

Candless touched her control stick, nudging it just a hair. The Yk.64 moved, twisting away from an incoming plasma ball that was still a few seconds away. But something behind her rumbled and groaned and a red light popped up on her engine board.

"Hellfire," she breathed. She had no idea how far she could push the engine before her engine mounts gave way entirely. If they did, if her engine came loose inside its compartment, it might just leave her stranded, unable to maneuver.

Alternatively, it could misfire. And explode.

"Hot damn!" Lanoe shouted, loud enough to hurt her ears. "You did it! Candless, you did it! I knew this would work."

"Lanoe," she called. "I have an engine fault. I have to withdraw. Right now." A second red light came on, this one warning her that heat was building up inside the engine compartment. That . . . was bad. "I'm sorry," she said. "I'm sorry, but—"

"Candless," Lanoe called back. "I need you in there. There's five more of those canopies to pop."

"I understand, but—"

"You've seen just what Centrocor's pilots are worth. You're the only one who can do this. The only one who can kill this thing."

"Perhaps," she said, in the tone of voice that worked on him— sometimes—"you would like me to steer and fire with one hand, while I use the other to physically hold my engine together? Perhaps, if I had three hands, I could use the third to throw my disruptor like a dart. I'm telling you that I have a fault, and—"

"I can see your telemetry from here. I've won battles with more heavily damaged fighters than yours. Get in there and do it. That's an order."

Candless frowned but she knew that she'd lost. She could hardly refuse a direct order from her commanding officer. She had always lived her life as a concrete example of the value of Navy discipline. To refuse now—

"Very well," she said. "I'll do it."

Lanoe didn't even bother to reply.

✦

"Shulkin!" Lanoe called. "Hang back! There's no need to expose yourself to those plasma balls!" The carrier was edging toward the dreadnought again, in spite of his previous order. "What the hell are you thinking?"

"That you're making a hash of this battle, sir," Shulkin said. Sounding distracted, of course. "I have several antivehicle guns I can bring to play. I intend to savage the enemy, as you and Captain Candless can't seem to hit a target five kilometers wide."

Lanoe bit back a curse. The guns on the carrier were heavy-duty particle beam cannons—a little stronger than the ones the cataphracts carried, but totally incapable of cutting through the dreadnought's coral-like hull. He didn't know what effect they might have on the cagework canopies, but he doubted they would be more effective than disruptors. They had a shorter range than the dreadnought's plasma balls as well, which meant Shulkin would have to put the carrier at risk just to get off a shot.

"I'm ordering you to back off," Lanoe told Shulkin.

"With all due respect, sir, if you won't use the cruiser's guns—"

"I've got my gun crews on standby, damn you," Lanoe said. "It's my decision when they fire, not yours."

"I realize that you are older than me, Commander," Shulkin said, "but not by that much. You will remember a saying from the old days—if you'll forgive a little profanity. Never try to bullshit a bullshitter."

"Are you and I going to have a problem, Captain?" Lanoe asked. "I gave you a damned order. Back up and stay clear of the battle area. I have a plan here, and you're stepping on it."

"Very well, sir," Shulkin replied. "I wish you much luck with your *plan*."

Candless got herself turned around. Slowly. Found another blister, a smaller one hanging from the underside of the dreadnought like a malignant growth. She readied another disruptor round. "Someone," she called on the common channel. "Someone cover me. I'm—"

She didn't have time to finish the sentence. Even as she pushed her stick forward, as she started her run, a warning chime sounded behind her head. Red lights started popping up all across her boards, some of them flashing.

It was too late. She'd already opened her throttle. Her engine was blazing away, pushing her toward the blister in a perfectly straight line. It didn't matter that behind her she could hear more engine mounts giving way, one after the other, like gunshots.

She glanced down at her engine board, dreading what she would see there. It was, indeed, bad. The engine was floating inside its compartment with no support at all. For the moment it was moving her in the direction she had chosen.

If she tried to use her maneuvering or positioning jets, though, or if she attempted to gimbal her thrust—in other words, if she attempted to steer in any way—the engine would tear right through its compartment. Rip through the shielding behind her back. Fry her like an egg—and keep going.

She could hear it rattling around back there, vibrating its way off of its broken mounts, roaming around in its compartment. The slightest jar, the tiniest deviation in her course would be all it took.

Meanwhile, she was on a collision course with her target. Unable to veer away. Plasma balls were coming in—she could see at least three of them headed in her direction.

She wanted to scream. She wanted to pound on her console until the warning lights went out, until everything worked again. She knew far better than to think that would work but the primal impulse was there.

Instead, she dragged her weapons board around until it was directly in front of her. The virtual display was something to focus on. It showed all of its systems as operating at optimal levels. At least there was that.

She brought up her disruptor's preferences page and scrolled through the options, time slowing to a crawl as she contemplated how she could best make use of the last few seconds of her life. She found the option to have the disruptor explode on impact. Yes, she thought. Yes, that would do.

She confirmed her choice. Then she repeated the selection for each of the disruptors in her magazine, and for all of her anti-vehicular rounds as well. When her Yk.64 collided with the blister, it would make a highly impressive bang.

Then she locked her stick, so that the fighter wouldn't deviate from its course by accident and ruin her chance to at least accomplish something with her death.

It was all happening too fast for her to be able to panic, or even truly process what was happening. She tried to organize her thoughts, to compose herself for the end. She had been a good teacher, she thought, as the blister raced toward her. She had probably saved a few lives in her time, though not as many as—

"Captain Candless," someone said. It sounded like they were standing next to her, tapping her on the shoulder.

What now? "Present," she said.

"I, uh, thought you might like some help."

She turned her head, as if she would see who it was. In point of fact, she *did* see them. Uhl was right beside her, his fighter almost touching the tips of her airfoils, his cataphract streaking along at exactly the same velocity as her own. He gave her a polite wave.

"I'm afraid I'm beyond needing cover," she said. She sketched out—briefly—her situation, and saw his face drain of blood.

"Then how about a ride?" he asked.

What he had in mind was ridiculous. Beyond foolish. As a flight instructor, it was exactly the kind of thing she had taught her pupils to never, ever do.

It wasn't as if she had any better ideas, though.

"Thank you," she said. "I'm much obliged."

Then—as there was very little time left—she reached for a key recessed into the console before her. The key that would bring down her canopy. The Yk.64 had a large dome cockpit, the pilot sitting in almost a full bubble of flowglas. As it receded into the small craft's fairings, Candless felt as if she were being thrown forward into the hard vacuum of space. Suddenly she wasn't flying an advanced machine, but hurtling along on a narrow seat, completely at the mercy of the void.

"Hold yourself steady, please," she called. Then she triggered the quick-release on her straps and simultaneously threw herself sideways, out of the seat, out of her fighter altogether. Uhl held their velocities perfectly, exactly even—otherwise she would have sliced herself in half on one of his airfoils. As it was she collided painfully with the leading edge of one of them, all the wind puffing out of her lungs and clouding her helmet with condensation.

It took every bit of strength she had to clamber up onto the airfoil. She got her fingers wrapped around a handhold on one of his fairings. It wasn't much to hold on to—it was designed to help the pilot climb into his cockpit when it was sitting motionless in a docking cradle. It was better than nothing. She flicked her eyes across the tiny display built into her collar ring and the fingers of her gloves locked into place, forming a far stronger grip than mere human muscles could manage.

Would it be enough? There was only one way to find out.

"I'm as secure as I'm going to get," she told Uhl. "Go!"

Plasma balls were incoming. Her damaged fighter streaked past them, locked into its collision course. As Uhl peeled off, veering away from the chaos, headed for the lines of fighters out at the edge of the battle area, Candless felt as if her hands were being torn from her body, as if they would come off at the wrists at any moment. G-forces pummeled her inside her suit—she lacked the protection of an inertial sink out there in the vacuum. As the fighter pulled away from the dreadnought her feet flew out behind her. She swung back and forth like a pendulum as she clung for dear life to the side of Uhl's ship. She gritted her teeth and tried to breathe and desperately, desperately hoped she was going to live through this, that she hadn't put herself through all this pain for nothing.

She glanced back just in time to see her Yk.64 smash into the dreadnought's blister. The light of the ensuing explosion was so intense that it left bright green spots swimming through her vision long after she looked away.

"Perfect," Lanoe called. "Perfect! Just four more of those to go!"

Candless took a deep breath. At least, as deep a breath as her precarious position would allow.

"Terribly sorry, Commander, but that was it for me," she said.

"What? What are you talking about?" Lanoe demanded. "We need to get the other four. It has to be done, Candless."

"Alas, not by me." She told him where, exactly, she was, and why.

For a long moment he was silent. She knew him well enough to know he was thinking. Planning. Scheming.

What he came up with, however, was utter rot.

"I'm headed in," he said. "I'll take the Z.XIX, finish the job myself."

"That means leaving the cruiser without a pilot," she said, trying to keep a level of calm in her voice. What a fool he could be sometimes. What a damned fool! "And the fleet without a commander. It will be supremely difficult to oversee the battle when you're right in the midst of it."

"I've done it before," he said. "I'll be there in two minutes. Unless you think Centrocor's pilots can finish this before I can arrive."

The disdain in his voice made her cringe. The disrespect for his own pilots. Candless looked over at Uhl, and saw him looking back. Of course he'd just heard that. She mouthed an apology.

The Centrocor pilot just shrugged.

"Lanoe, just—one more thing," she said. "How long before the reinforcements arrive? The Blue-Blue-White interceptors?"

He paused for a moment, perhaps to check a display.

"Eight minutes," he told her.

"Ah," she said. "Then you should get moving, shouldn't you?"

———

The Z.XIX's engines pulsed with life as Lanoe slid into the seat. The straps snaked forward across his chest. He tapped a recessed key and the canopy flowed up around him.

"I've run a full set of preflight diagnostics," the fighter said. "All systems look good."

"How many disruptors have we got?" he asked.

"I see ten in our ammunition loadout," she told him.

More than enough. He released the fighter from its docking cradle and tapped the stick to send it lurching forward, out of the cruiser's vehicle bay. In front of him, at first, he saw nothing but stars. He banked around to one side, giving the engine plenty of throttle, and there it was—the battle area. Less than a hundred kilometers away.

On his displays it was anarchy, a welter of blue dots swarming like gnats around the elephantine shape of the dreadnought. He brought up a magnified view and saw what Candless had been able to accomplish. One blister torn open, the spars of its cagework twisted and shattered, broken white fingers gesturing in futile desperation at the sky. The other blister she'd hit was gone altogether, nothing more than a jagged crater of broken coral there now. Cracks radiated away from the site where her fighter had detonated, deep fissures in the pitted hull.

He leaned hard on his stick and went zooming in toward the giant ship. Plasma balls were everywhere—so many they dazzled his eyes, so thick in the volume of space around the dreadnought he couldn't look away from them. He polarized the flowglas of his canopy to protect his vision, darkening the view until the plasma balls were just bright patches of color, the dreadnought itself a pale shadow hanging in space.

It was fine. He didn't need to see much. There was an intact blister not too far from his position, one he could probably hit without the benefit of other cataphracts to run cover for him. He nudged his stick and hit his maneuvering jets, coming in fast in a loose corkscrew that just avoided a passing plasma ball. He felt sweat break out on his upper lip and his forehead but he ignored it.

"Give me a firing solution," he told the fighter. He would probably need to manually aim his disruptor, but—

"There," she said. Yellow crosshairs appeared right in the middle of his view, centered on the blister. As the Z.XIX swung around and around in the corkscrew, the virtual sight never moved.

"How long until we're in range?" he asked.

"We already are," she said.

Damnation! He'd forgotten about the Philoctetes aiming algorithm the Z.XIX carried, that doubled the range of all his weapons. He'd risked his life getting this close when he didn't even need to.

He laughed at his own folly. Armed the disruptor. Pulled the trigger.

The explosive round tore into the blister. Light streamed out from the dark glass interstices of the cagework. Heat and expanding gas blossomed outward as the blister burst like a lanced boil.

Lanoe watched it all happen, even as his hands moved as if directed by some other consciousness. His cataphract twisted away from the wreckage, dodging a plasma ball with ease. He flew out toward the formations of Alpha and Beta wings without a scratch on him.

"See, Candless?" he said on the open channel. "That's how it's done."

Chapter Twenty

Bury took a deep breath before he pushed through the airlock. Not because it was necessary—his helmet flowed up around his face before he was even exposed to the vacuum—but because what he was about to do was maybe the most foolish and headstrong thing he'd ever considered.

Bury didn't lack insight. He knew who he was, why he felt this constant need to prove himself. Most people thought his home planet was a backwater, the exact middle of nowhere, and that its people were inferior. They laughed at a Hellion's shiny face, the lack of hair. Ever since he'd left Hel and joined the Navy, everyone had laughed at him—his classmates first, and now the crew of Lanoe's fleet. Behind his back they mocked him constantly. He'd intended from his earliest days in flight school to show the world they were wrong. He'd worked hard to fly faster, fight harder than anyone else. To become something special, to earn the respect of his peers—so he could rub it in their smug faces.

Hard to accomplish anything like that, though, when you were stuck on the medical list. If he was ever going to exceed prejudiced expectations, he needed to get out there and get his fifth kill. Earn his blue star.

What he was about to do was not only against orders, it was

incredibly illegal. It could get him court-martialed, or worse. If it worked, though—

There.

He was in the carrier's flight deck. Starlight streamed in through a hole in the carrier's hull where the laser had nearly bisected it. The light fell across the ranks of docking cradles, each like the exposed rib cage of some ancient fossil. Almost all of them empty now. Far up ahead, near the open maw of the carrier, he could see the Centrocor woman's yacht, a bubble of soft light. Closer to him was the bulbous side of a troop transport, and the deconstructed pipework of a maintenance tender.

The ships he wanted were right at the back, clustered at the bottom of the flight deck as if they were huddling there for warmth. The slender carrier scouts looked unimpressive, even in the deep shadows. Their designers had spared no effort cutting them down to as small a size as possible. They lacked almost everything you expected to see on a cataphract-class fighter: they had no airfoils, no armored fairings, no heavy weapon panels. A single PBW cannon stuck out from underneath a bare-bones cockpit. The engines were powerful but largely unshielded and unprotected, just a trio of long thruster cones sticking straight back from the pilot's seat.

No real pilot would ever let themselves be seen flying one of those crates. Sometimes, though, you ran out of choices in life. Sometimes, Bury thought, you took what you could get. And if he could earn his blue star while flying such a worthless piece of junk—well, the glory would be all the sweeter for it.

He opened the canopy and slipped inside. He wasn't very big, but the seat still felt cramped and his helmet almost touched the canopy once it flowed back over him. He looked to the controls, wondering how different this was going to be from flying a cataphract. The carrier scout was so stripped down that all of its command options fit on a single display, which lit up as soon as he was in the seat. He pulled the straps across his chest—the scout lacked the automatic straps he was used to—and took a second to focus on his heartbeat, which was thundering in his chest.

It sounded like it was beating out time. Like it was beating out the same number, over and over. *Four. Four. Four.*

What came next was going to be the hardest part, he thought. The scout was still clutched tightly in the arms of its restraining cradle. He wasn't going anywhere until he could release those arms, and normally they could only be triggered from the carrier's bridge by a flight control officer. The approval process was meant as a safety feature—in the middle of a general scramble fifty fighters could all be trying to get out of the flight deck at once. Someone had to make sure they didn't collide with each other in the mad dash. Even now, when the flight deck was all but empty, Bury couldn't launch without approval.

There was a way, he thought, to override the restraint's clamps. If he could convince the carrier scout that there was an emergency—say, a fire in the flight deck, or an incoming asteroid collision—the clamps would release immediately. The problem was that meant hacking, and Bury didn't know much about computers. He'd had a class in information studies back at Rishi, of course, but he hadn't bothered paying much attention.

The first thing he had to do was reroute the scout's logging process so that it reported only to itself, not the bridge, and that meant getting root access, which...he had no idea how to do. He stared at the board, trying to think. There had to be a way. He'd come this far, and surely fate wouldn't fail him now, surely he would think of something, anything. There had to be some way to—

Motion out in the flight deck startled him so much that he hit his head on the low canopy. He cursed as he craned his neck around, trying to see if someone was coming. The light streaming in from the carrier's open maw was obscured, turned to shadows that shifted rapidly. It took him a second to realize that it was a cataphract coming back from the battle, maybe a damaged fighter limping home. There was definitely something wrong with its silhouette—it looked all lumpy on one side, as if something had gotten stuck on one of its airfoils.

As it came closer Bury saw a person riding there, clinging to the side of the fighter like a barnacle. What the hell? A beam of light caught the rider's helmet and he saw, to his immense surprise, that it was Captain Candless.

His old teacher. His old nemesis. Riding on the side of a cataphract, her legs swingly wildly as the ship maneuvered toward a cradle halfway up the deck.

Bury shut down his control display so its light wouldn't give him away. If she caught him here...

As Bury watched, the cataphract's canopy came down and the pilot—nobody Bury recognized—clambered out. He helped Candless move into the airlock next to the cataphract's berth. The outer door closed behind the two of them.

Bury had been holding his breath. He let it out now and started to relax a little. He reached to switch the carrier scout's display back on, to get back to his task.

Except before he did that, he took one last look at the cataphract. The only one in the flight deck—the rest of them were still out at the battle area, their pilots no doubt covering themselves in glory. This particular cataphract had been left half-docked, as if the pilot had forgotten to complete his post-flight checklist. Its canopy was still down, for one thing, exposing the cockpit to vacuum. *Tsk tsk,* Bury thought. If it was his fighter he would have taken better care of it. He would have—

He would have fully engaged the docking cradle.

The cataphract was perfectly stable where it lay on top of the cradle. But the restraining arms hadn't been closed around its fuselage. The pilot hadn't bothered to secure the fighter. Maybe he'd just forgotten, or maybe he intended to come back in a minute and take the fighter back out to the battle area. Rather than worrying about getting permission from the bridge, he could simply jump back in his cockpit and go.

Bury licked his plastinated lips with a dry gray tongue.

When destiny comes knocking at your door, he thought, *it's rude not to answer.*

⤞⤝

Useless.

The bloody Centrocor pilots were useless. They made a good show of trying to swoop in toward the dreadnought, to get close enough to launch a disruptor, but every damned time a plasma ball would come streaking toward them they would swerve away, running for safety.

Not a single one of them was worth a wet damn, as far as Lanoe was concerned. Even after he'd risked life and limb over and over, trying to show them the way, trying to lead by example, none of them had the courage to actually take a shot.

They couldn't even give him proper cover. He'd managed to take down one blister all by himself, and it should have just been a matter of time before he'd got the other three. Instead, now that he was the only real threat in the battle area, he'd also become the only meaningful target for the dreadnought's plasma ball guns. The Blue-Blue-White weren't stupid—or at least they'd learned from their previous mistakes. They didn't bother shooting at the Yk.64s at all, instead concentrating all their fire on forming a defensive net that Lanoe couldn't punch through.

Not that he hadn't tried. He'd pushed as hard as he could to break through that net, and had more than his share of near misses. He felt like he was roasting in a furnace, his skin dried out and crisping. He'd gotten so dehydrated that every time he blinked it felt like sandpaper rubbing against his eyes.

"Somebody get over here, now," he shouted over the open channel. A couple of the Centrocor pilots made a halfhearted stab at it, swinging down to fly beside him—until they were scared off by incoming plasma. Lanoe scowled at them as they ran away. Without a wingmate to cover him, there was no way he could get close enough to use his disruptors, even with his fancy targeting algorithm.

"Give me cover!" he bellowed. A Yk.64 came corkscrewing down toward him, and he nodded to himself, planning out his next attack. Knowing perfectly well he would have to abandon his run when this fool ran away like all the others. "What's your name?" he asked the pilot, thinking maybe he could shame them into sticking around long enough to actually accomplish something.

"Sir? It's...it's me. Lieutenant Bury."

Lanoe swiveled his head around to look at the cockpit of his new wingmate. Damnation—it really was the Hellion. "I thought you were on the medical list," he said.

"I got better," Bury told him.

Lanoe laughed at that—a hoarse, dry sound, but one with real joy in it. "I take it Candless doesn't know you're out here?" he asked.

"No, sir," Bury said. He could hear a diffident catch in the kid's voice. Lanoe was honor bound to send him back to safety. Hell, Lanoe was required by Naval regulations to arrest Bury on the spot and escort him back to the carrier so he could be formally charged with disobeying Candless's orders.

Well, damn them. Damn Navy regs. Rules and codes of conduct hadn't won the Century War, or the Brushfire, or the Establishment Crisis.

Pilots had.

"It's good to see somebody with fighting spirit," Lanoe said. "Take my left flank, and don't break away until I give the word. Now—dive!"

⌁

It felt so damned good to be flying again. Bury hadn't even realized how much he'd missed it. For all his anguish over his lack of a blue star, he'd forgotten that this was where he belonged, that being in the cockpit of a cataphract-class fighter wasn't just a means to an end. It was what he'd been born to do.

He streaked down toward the dreadnought, tight up against Lanoe's airfoils, and had to fight the urge to whoop for joy. Below them plasma balls shot across their bows, so close and so bright they blotted out his view of anything else. Hellions couldn't cry—their bodies were engineered to conserve every drop of water, so the inside of his eyelids had been rendered almost frictionless. His eyes didn't well with tears, but he found himself constantly blinking away the terrible light.

It didn't matter. He felt like his fighter was flying itself, the connection between him and his controls so natural, so perfectly in tune that he didn't need to see.

"Sir! The dreadnought's maneuvering," he called out. "Turning—we'll need to adjust our trajectory."

"Already on it," Lanoe called back. "They're retreating, do you see that? Check your tactical board. They're running, Bury. They're terrified of us."

"As well they should be," Bury said.

Lanoe laughed at that, a cackle of bloodlust. Bury thought maybe he should be afraid of that sound, but he wasn't—instead he found himself laughing along.

"They're trying to reach their escort, the interceptors coming up from the disk," Lanoe said. "I don't intend to let them get that far."

Below them the screen of plasma balls momentarily cleared and Bury could see their target, a massive cage of white spars at one corner of the giant ship. It was close to one of the weapon pits, too close for any fighter to reach it without help. On his sensor board a green light lit up, telling him the pit was warming up, getting ready to loose a plasma ball. "Ready to break on your order, sir," he called.

"Wait for it—wait for it," Lanoe said, chanting it like a mantra. "Wait for it—wait—now!"

Bury shoved his control stick over to one side, even as the pit began to glow, even as the plasma ball started to form. His Yk.64 leaned over on its side and shot away from Lanoe's fighter at an angle. The plasma ball came chasing after him, moving so fast he thought he couldn't possibly get away in time. He pulled back on his stick, throwing his crate into a hard climb, and the plasma ball shot past right below him. Red lights flashed and warning chimes sounded all around him, but he'd made it, he'd avoided the—avoided—

He couldn't breathe. His lungs were on fire and his whole body seized up. He felt like his skin was crawling with bugs and his vision started to turn red.

A display flashed up right in front of him, an emergency warning. *Pilot in distress. Recommendation: seek immediate medical attention.*

Bury could just make out the words. His vision had shrunk down to a narrow, dark tunnel and he couldn't hear anything but a high-pitched whine.

He managed to check his status board and saw that his cockpit temperature had briefly risen above two hundred degrees. Hot enough to fry his plastinated skin—he couldn't sweat, couldn't shed that heat, it was roasting him alive—

"No!" he howled, and slammed one hand down on a control display. His fingers wouldn't work, wouldn't obey him, but he forced them to scroll through a page of options, forced them to choose an emergency fire control option that would spray him down with engine coolant, to lower his body temperature.

Foam flooded his cockpit, thick waves of the stuff washing over his helmet, the front of his suit. He couldn't see through it at all, couldn't feel his feet, his legs—but then—little by little—it worked. He cooled down, cooled to a temperature that wouldn't actually kill him.

Someone was calling his name. Ginger? Candless? No, no, it was Lanoe—

"Bury, talk to me, damn you! You're the only pilot out here worth my time. If you got yourself killed I swear I'll—"

"Sir," Bury croaked out. "Present, sir."

"Let me guess," Lanoe said. "You need to break off. Head back to the carrier and leave me alone out here. Again."

Bury forced himself to breathe. To think—even that was hard. Had his brain boiled inside his skull? No. No, he would be dead, if—if that were—

"Sir," he said. "Did we get the blister?"

"Yes, damn you, I hit it with a disruptor," Lanoe replied.

"Very good, sir," Bury told him. "What's our next target?"

<hr />

Lanoe started to say something. Closed his mouth and held it back. The kid was in trouble. He'd barely made it—he'd let the plasma ball get too close. The only thing that saved him was that it went underneath his Yk.64. If it had passed over him, the radiant heat it gave off would have gone right through his canopy and burned him alive.

He wouldn't make it through another near miss like that. There were limits to what the human body could withstand. Lanoe knew he needed to send the kid back, tell him to retreat to the carrier and—

No. They were close. They were so close to taking the alien ship down. He could see it—see it in the way the dreadnought raced to join its escort. See it in the very skin of the city-sized ship. Deep cracks ran through the coral now, long jagged wounds that told him the ship was dying. Just two more blisters. They were running out of time, but still, there was a chance—

A green pearl rotated in the corner of his vision.

Lanoe shook his head. Flicked his eyes across the pearl. "Candless?" he said. "Something I can help you with? This isn't a great time."

"How dare you?" she asked. She sounded upset. He figured he knew why.

"I'm in charge here," he reminded her.

"He was my student," she told him. "Bury is my responsibility!"

"He came to me. Looking to help."

"You think that changes anything?"

Lanoe scowled at her, though she was dozens of kilometers away. "Did you call to yell at me, or—"

"Use the guns, Lanoe," she said. "Turn the cruiser's guns on the dreadnought. I know you don't intend to. I know you have some secret reason why you won't use your best weapon against this thing. But damnation, man! You can end this without anyone else having to die, without—"

Lanoe cut off the call.

He checked his tactical board. "Bury," he said, "we have two minutes before the dreadnought reaches those interceptors. Before our lives get a lot more complicated. Are you with me? We have two of those blisters left to hit. I say we can do it. What about you?"

"I'm with you," the kid said.

Lanoe nodded. All right, then.

———✦———

The two of them looped out well beyond the battle area, then flattened their trajectory and dove toward the giant ship. Bury felt his blood singing as the two cataphracts flashed downward in perfect formation, their airfoils nearly touching. He spared a quick glance to his side and saw Lanoe through his canopy.

The old pilot was staring straight ahead, focused on the target. His lips had pulled back from his teeth in a grimace of pure bloodlust.

Bury forced the grin off of his own face. He scowled at the dreadnought below, at the blister that stuck out from its trailing edge. It was smaller than the others, barely fifty meters across, situated between a thruster and a weapon pit. Getting in there was going to be tricky, he knew, but he was sure Lanoe had a good plan for it.

"You had a hard time with that last plasma ball, didn't you?" Lanoe asked.

"I came through just fine, sir. I'm good to fight," Bury told him.

"That isn't what I asked."

Bury dropped his chin. The last thing he wanted to admit was that he'd nearly died, that he had to waste emergency coolant on lowering his body temperature. He guessed, though, that this wasn't a time for evasions. "It was rough," he said. "I almost blacked out, and—"

"You nearly went into cardiac arrest," Lanoe said. "I've got your biometric data on one of my displays. You won't survive another near miss like that."

"Sir, I—"

"So this time you're taking the shot. I'll cover you."

Bury felt his stomach turn over in his abdomen. "Are you... sure?" He shook his head. "No, sorry, sir, of course you are, I just—"

"You'll do fine. The hard part is not veering off before you can loose your disruptor. Stay on course. Ignore your fear. You have a firing solution?"

"Working one up now." A virtual Aldis sight bobbed around Bury's canopy. Sensors in the Yk.64's fuselage built up a profile of the open space inside the blister, looking for the optimal placement for the disruptor. A blue light lit up on his weapons board. "Got it!" he said.

"Then it's your show. Don't even worry about that weapon pit— I'll draw its fire when you get close. Go!"

Bury opened his throttle and surged forward, maneuvering just a little when he thought he saw a plasma ball streaking toward him. It fizzled out long before it could reach him. He normalized his trajectory and poured on even more speed, until the blister grew huge in his forward view.

So close—but the disruptor needed to be launched from extremely short range, especially against a moving target. He dropped in low and raced across the dreadnought's skin, cutting his speed for better accuracy, sure that Lanoe would keep him safe if the weapon pit started heating up. On his canopy the Aldis was locked tight to one pane of glass in the blister's cagework. He held his finger over the trigger, fighting his natural impulse to squeeze it out of pure nervous tension.

A little closer...a little closer—a shadow passed over Bury and he looked up for just a fraction of a second to see Lanoe pulling away from him, spinning on his long axis as he burned hard to get out ahead of a plasma ball.

Bury hadn't even seen the plasma ball launch.

He didn't need to. He just had to focus on getting closer, the pale hull of the dreadnought a featureless blur below him, pits and craters just stuttering shadows, a little closer, a little—a little—

There! The blue light on his weapons board turned green and he pulled the trigger. The sputtering, sparking disruptor jumped away from him and his whole fighter lurched upward, just a tick. The disruptor round blazed forward, straight toward the blister, and Bury realized with a start that he needed to veer off to avoid colliding with it himself. He hauled back hard on his stick and punched open his throttle, even as the disruptor smashed through the glass and into the blister.

He didn't look back, couldn't spare any attention on checking to see if the hit was good, if—

Something hard bounced off his fuselage, sending up a welter of sparks as his vector field accelerated it away. If he'd been in the carrier scout, that impact would have—

Another impact. Another, and then a hailstorm of tiny projectiles smashed across his canopy, chunks of white stone that looked like, pieces of—*Oh hellfire,* he thought, those were pieces of the dreadnought's hull—

His forward view filled with white.

The dreadnought had already been cracked. That last disruptor must have shattered a big piece of it, creating an incredible cloud of debris. Millions of coral shards, each of them flying free on their own trajectory. The chunk right in front of him was two hundred meters across, just a small sliver of the dreadnought but big enough to hit him like a giant-sized flyswatter, he—he—

He needed to move. Bury shoved his stick sideways and hit his maneuvering jets hard. The broken slab of coral rotated slowly as it came toward him, turning a jagged edge in his direction until it looked like the devil's own sword coming down on his head, like it would cleave him in half if he didn't—

Move, damn you, he thought, and kicked in his positioning jets as well. The edge of the shard came down so fast, seeming to accelerate as it—

It struck Bury's fighter just before he could get free of it. He was thrown sideways in his seat, his inertial sink pinning him down as hard as it could, but it wasn't quite enough. All the blood slammed over into one side of his body as he was sent spinning off into the dark, black dots swimming in his eyes so thick he could see nothing at all, if there was another piece of debris even a fraction the size of that one, if he was flying right into a cloud of broken coral, if he—

For a second there was nothing.

Not even darkness. Just—a cloud of nothing.

He heard nothing, saw nothing, felt nothing. He was pretty sure he was dead.

Then—

With a shocking suddenness, everything came back. Alarm chimes howled in his ears and red lights flashed everywhere around him. Voices were talking to him, dozens of voices shouting and babbling and asking questions, but his ears were ringing so loud he couldn't tell what they were saying, couldn't think, couldn't breathe—

"I said," Lanoe shouted, "are you alive in there?"

Bury fought his own rebellious tongue, fought the speech centers of his brain that were sparkling like fireworks. "I," he managed to gasp out. "I."

It must have sounded like "aye."

"Hell's bells, Bury, you do cut it close. Get out of that cloud—we need to regroup with the others and—"

"Five," Bury managed to say, the word rattling around inside his mouth.

His teeth felt loose.

He looked down at his damage control boards. The slab of coral had sheared off half his airfoils and ripped free the armored fairing all down one side of his fighter. It looked like nothing crucial had been hit, though.

"Five," he said again.

"What? Bury, talk to me—are you okay, or—"

"Five," he told Lanoe. "That was my fifth kill. I'm an ace."

"Bury—"

"Lanoe. Sir. I believe you owe me a blue star," Bury said. A shiver ran down his spine.

"Why, because you killed that dreadnought?" Lanoe asked. "I have two pieces of bad news for you. No, scratch that. Three pieces of bad news."

Bury reached for his stick. Moved to swing up away from the cloud of debris, back toward the formations high above what was left of the dreadnought.

"Go ahead," he said warily.

"First—there's one more blister on that thing," Lanoe told him. "You hurt it bad, yes. You tore a big chunk off of it—but it's not a kill. It's still got power to its thrusters and a couple working weapon pits. Second, even if you had taken it down, you don't get credit toward a blue star for killing capital ships."

"What? But I...what?"

"I know, it doesn't seem fair, but those are the rules. You have to defeat five small craft in single combat, and they have to be confirmed kills. Me, personally? I blew two dozen ships out of the sky before I got called an ace. Back then, it was a lot harder to confirm a kill, you needed two independent witnesses to—"

"Damn it, Lanoe! You said three pieces of bad news! What's the third?"

"You just might get your chance after all," Lanoe told him. "It took us too long to hit that last blister. The interceptors are about to arrive. Check your straps, kid. Things are about to get hectic."

Chapter Twenty-One

When he'd been back on the cruiser, watching the interceptors approach on a tactical board, they had looked bad enough—forty-five enemy craft, burning hard to support the ailing dreadnought. They were huge compared to his cataphracts, and they outnumbered him, too.

Now they were here. And things looked so much worse.

The interceptors looked a little like the airfighters Lanoe had seen down in the atmosphere of the disk, but the resemblance didn't hold up to close scrutiny. Big spheres of cagework and glass, studded with powerful thrusters. A crown of spiky projections that had to be weapons stuck out from the front of each ship. The interceptors measured a hundred meters across—they were as big as destroyers.

And there were forty-five of them.

They swerved back and forth as they came, running some kind of evasive pattern. The cruiser's guns wouldn't be able to hit them, even if he'd been willing to try—the slow-moving guns wouldn't be able to get a lock.

He'd thought he still had some time, at least ninety more seconds to blast away at the last of the dreadnought's blisters. Valk had given him some idea of how fast the interceptors could move, and he'd based his projections on that. It looked like Valk had failed him yet again. The leading edge of the cloud of interceptors was already on them, advancing on the formation of Yk.64s around the dreadnought. They must have poured on a little extra speed at the end, in a desperate attempt to reach the dreadnought before it was destroyed.

He looked down between his feet at the dreadnought. It was ailing, wounded—maybe mortally so. An entire edge of its hull had been cracked off by Bury's disruptor, reduced to a cloud of tumbling debris. Its thrusters pushed it in wide, lazy circles, unable to stabilize its trajectory. One of its command blisters remained intact, though, and clearly it was designed to keep operating right up until the last of its pilots was killed. Plasma balls were still streaming from its weapon pits, though not as fast now.

The interceptors were the greater threat. There was no question. He didn't know what those weapon spikes could do, but he had no doubt they could chew up a cataphract-class fighter with ease. If he didn't stop the interceptors, and soon, they would plow right through his useless wing of Yk.64s and move on to the cruiser and the carrier, which were ill-equipped to hold them off without support.

Just one blister left, though, on the dreadnought. One Blue-Blue-White pilot left to kill, when the interceptors were almost certainly just drones—

Lanoe bit his lip. Then he tapped at his communications board. "Alpha wing, Beta wing, move to block those interceptors," he called. "Don't let them get past you—if you were ever going to start fighting like real pilots, this is the bloody time." He tapped another key. "Bury, you're in charge of them—keep them in formation, keep them shooting, and for the devil's sake do not let up."

"Yes, sir," Bury called back. "But won't you be leading the charge?"

"I'm finishing off the big bastard. It's up to you now. You've already shown me you can do it. Don't fail me."

Bury was shaking so hard he thought his teeth might crack when they chattered. He stared out through his bubble canopy with wide eyes. The interceptors had just been bright dots a moment ago. Already they were growing in size.

Getting closer.

Four, he thought. He tried to focus on that. *Four.*

He'd been put in command. He needed to be strong now. To be fierce. "Alpha wing," he said.

And couldn't think of what to do next.

The interceptors were getting closer all the time.

"Sir?" a woman asked him. He tore his gaze away from the forward view and looked down at his communications board. It was one of the Centrocor pilots, the highest-ranking one in Alpha wing.

He ran a dry tongue along his slick, plastinated lips. He had to think.

Candless had taught him how to do this. He might have had his differences with his former teacher, but she'd drilled basic tactics into his head, forced him to go over and over the standard Navy protocols and strategies.

"Cluster around me," he said. "Let's try a loose cloud formation. Nothing fancy—just make a wall and force them to punch through it. Everyone fire at will. Evade as necessary."

There. That almost sounded good. Like a real set of orders. Even though he'd basically just said, "Shoot the bad guys, and run away if you get scared."

Well, that was half of space combat right there.

He pushed his throttle forward and his fighter jumped ahead. He didn't wait for the others to gather around him—he needed to lead by example here.

Even if he felt like he was about to throw up.

One of the interceptors was right in front of him, only a few kilometers away. He hit his maneuvering jets and approached it in a loose corkscrew, making himself a tricky target. The interceptor bobbed back and forth, heading toward him on a serpentine course.

His sensor board lit up with new information he hadn't thought to ask for. There was no indication of significant cavities inside the interceptor's hull, which meant there were no crew compartments. No jellyfish pilots inside. Well, they'd known these things were probably drones—good to get confirmation on that.

The sensors couldn't identify any crucial weak spots in the interceptor's configuration. That was...frustrating. The sensors were calibrated to look for fuel tanks and ammunition magazines, things that would blow up if you shot them just right. But they were designed to look for human versions of those things. Who knew what an alien ammo supply looked like?

More important, the sensor board told him that the ring of spikes on the front of the interceptor was warming up. Gathering energy, getting ready to shoot.

Time to find out what the bastards could do. Bury leveled out of his corkscrew and raked the front of the interceptor with PBW fire. Glass starred and shattered but the interceptor didn't even slow down. Bury suddenly became very aware, very terrifyingly aware, that the alien drone dwarfed his fighter, was nearly fifty times as big as he was. A few particle beam shots would barely scratch its surface.

The weapon ring started to glow visibly, the spikes incandescing as they heated up. It was about to fire. Bury twisted away in a snap turn, punching his throttle for speed.

The weapon ring turned cherry red, and for a second Bury thought he was going to die. Any moment now the weapon would discharge, and if it had a clear shot at him—

But then nothing happened.

The weapon ring didn't discharge. No beam emerged from the ring, no kinetic projectile. The damned thing didn't so much as give off a puff of smoke. Bury was deeply confused. He heard a loud repetitive clicking sound for a moment, but then it stopped.

What in the name of all hell's dukes?

Well, at least he wasn't dead, which was—

Without warning his entire vector field sparked and spat with energy, a shroud of high-energy plasma wrapping around him, obscuring his view. Red lights lit up all over his damage control display—but only for a moment. The display itself wavered and then winked out.

So did his weapons board. His tactical board. His engine board.

Suddenly he was staring at a blank console, at the dull gray face of a display surface that had lost power. He waved his hands around over the console, trying desperately to bring up something, anything, but to no avail. All of his electronics were gone. He couldn't even switch on a cockpit light.

Then he noticed something far more worrisome. The flowglas bubble around him, the canopy that separated him from hard vacuum, was rippling. Starting to flow back into his fuselage.

It only lasted a moment. Inertia carried him out of the range of the interceptor's weapon and the flowglas hardened back up. He heard a loud snapping sound right behind his head and then lights came on all around him, momentarily blinding him. A display popped up in front of him, advising him that the fighter's systems were reinitializing.

One by one his boards came back. He swiped up a communications display and keyed for a transmission on the general band.

"Anyone—anyone at all—I just got hit by that thing, it knocked out all my electronics, I'm not sure what—"

"Microwaves." It was Candless's voice. Candless, who must have been watching him closely as he approached the interceptor. "It's a microwave weapon, a very high power magnetron. Bury, are you all right? Are you wounded?"

"No, I'm fine," Bury said, "a little—confused, I guess. What are you talking about, microwaves? That thing hit me with some kind of microwave weapon?"

"It knocked out all your electronics—anything using electricity. Your fighter is designed to reboot automatically in the event of a power loss like that. You were only in the field for a few milliseconds. Not long enough to actually burn out your systems. Or to cook you like a Fleet Day turkey."

It had been bad enough. "Alpha wing, Beta wing," Bury called. "Stay away from those weapon rings—try to hit these things from behind, or...or flank them, just—don't approach them from the front, don't...don't..."

"Bury, get out of there," Candless said. He saw she was calling him on a private channel now. "Just get away. Let Lanoe handle these things. They're too dangerous."

Bury stared at the communications board as if he could see her face there. As if he could look her in the eye. She ought to know him better than that. She ought to know how he would respond to being told that something was too dangerous for him.

"Four," he said, and grabbed his control stick, already thinking in his head how he would wheel around and get another shot at the bastard who'd tried to fry him.

Lanoe swung back and forth as he made his last run at the dreadnought. He had no cover at all, no one even watching his back. Doing this without Bury was going to be tough, but he'd lived through worse attack runs.

He raced down through a screen of plasma balls and a cloud of white debris, bits of coral pelting off his vector fields as he readied another disruptor. The last blister was right below him, a big shapeless mass of cagework wrapped around one end of the dreadnought's hull. The Philoctetes algorithm that extended the range of his weapons threw half a dozen crosshairs across his canopy in dark red, then eliminated them one by one, the remaining sights changing color as his computer assigned various levels of confidence to the potential firing solutions.

Eventually, one of them came up blue. Lanoe followed it straight down, barely dodging the plasma balls now. The projectiles were getting tangled in the debris cloud, fizzling out long before they could reach him. He felt like a spear pointed straight at his enemy's heart. He felt like a meteor crashing toward an evil planet.

The last set of crosshairs turned green. Lanoe pulled the trigger, his disruptor thrusting forward deep into the dreadnought's blister, bursting it open.

Done, he thought. Just like that.

He felt—

Nothing.

The dreadnought fell quiet, little by little. Its death throes were not overly dramatic. A final plasma ball launched from a weapon pit, streaming off into space in some random direction, not even getting close to him. The big thrusters sputtered out one by one, leaving the dead city-sized ship rotating slowly in place.

He'd thought he would feel...something.

Nothing exploded, nothing burst into flames. Lanoe scanned the dreadnought's corpse and found no sign of activity, no electrical flows, no fuel pumps working.

He'd thought, once he started killing the jellyfish, that he would feel—vindicated, perhaps. Justified. Like he was finally getting justice. Like he was getting revenge for Zhang.

Instead he just felt empty. He'd risked so much for this battle, put so many lives on the line, and now—

"It's a start."

Zhang's voice, coming through the Z.XIX's speakers. Just as it had before. He was hallucinating again.

Lanoe opened his eyes. He hadn't realized they were closed. He looked around and found himself in the middle of a debris cloud, a haze of white dust that surrounded him on every side. He could hear voices shouting—the others. Bury and the other pilots. They were engaging the interceptors, they were—

He checked his tactical board. Blue and yellow dots swarmed around each other. A lot more yellow dots than blue—and even as he watched, a blue dot winked out.

"Hellfire," he said. Then he threw his stick forward and opened his throttle wide. If he didn't get up there soon, if he didn't get in there and show them how to fight, everything he'd done would be for nothing.

Bury wheeled around as another interceptor tried to get in front of him. He sprayed the machine with PBW fire that did little more than shatter its windows. He knew it was going to take more than that to actually kill one of the things.

There was a constant roar in his ears, the sound of pilots scream-ing in pain, others shouting requests for help. It all blended together into one sustained note of terror that he had to do his best to ignore.

He brought up a virtual Aldis sight. Loaded a disruptor. The damned interceptors weaved back and forth so much it was almost impossible to get a good firing solution—especially when, as soon as he started to get a fix, he had to swerve out of the way of another one trying to get in to fry him.

Big as they were, he'd have thought they would collide with each other as they crowded around him, as they surrounded Alpha and Beta wings. Their maneuvers had a digital precision, though, and they never even came close. With just human reflexes to work with, Bury had to fight his control stick constantly to stay out of their way.

His Aldis turned green and he reached for his trigger, but the crosshairs switched back to blue before he could fire. He spat out a curse and swung around to climb high over two more intercep-tors that had been converging on his position, even as their weapon rings started to glow.

He had no idea how many human pilots they'd killed. He'd seen at least two cataphracts taken out of commission by the microwave blasts. As the energy hit them their vector fields pulsed and crawled with lightning, and then their fairings burst open as the sensitive electronics inside overloaded and exploded.

He was sure they'd lost more than the two he'd seen. He was sure of one thing, definitely—they were losing this fight.

Most likely, they were all going to die.

He reached over to his communications board without looking

at it. Set up a link directly to Ehta, on the cruiser. He didn't have time to wait for her to answer, so he just recorded a voice message she could listen to later.

"Ehta," he said, "it looks like we're not coming back. It looks like this is it, so—so I wanted to ask you a favor. I know you don't owe me anything. But...it's Ginger. I know you care about her, maybe as much as I do.

"I want you to tell her I'm sorry I couldn't help her more. That I couldn't stop them from putting that thing in her head. And that I'm sorry I couldn't...that I wasn't brave enough to ever tell her I love her.

"She's been the best friend I ever had, maybe the only real friend. She's been like a sister, I guess. I don't know, I never had one of those, I just—

"Just tell her she meant something to me, okay? Tell her I felt—"

Right in front of him, his crosshairs turned green again. Right there—an interceptor was turned away from him, its weapon ring on its far side. He had a perfect shot lined up with one of its thruster units.

He reached for the trigger, expecting the crosshairs to turn blue again, but they didn't. He got his hand around the stick and squeezed the trigger. He felt the disruptor launch, felt it like someone had kicked the underside of his cataphract.

The disruptor flared to life and then disappeared as it cut right through the glass hull of the interceptor. For a moment he couldn't see anything more. Then the entire alien drone came apart, pieces of it flying in every direction.

Bury could hardly believe it. He couldn't credit what he saw with his own eyes, he had—he had—

Five.

Five—he had gotten his fifth kill, he was—

He saw that the communications panel was still recording. "Hellfire," he breathed. "Ehta—tell Ginger I got my five. Tell her I earned my bloody blue star. Tell her—"

A dark shape cut off the starlight streaming down through his canopy. Bury inhaled sharply and knocked his stick over to the side, punched his throttle to get away from yet another interceptor.

———

Lanoe plunged into the fray, spraying PBW fire across every round hull he could see, knowing it wouldn't damage the interceptors, just trying to get their attention. It didn't work—they continued to chase after the poor damned pilots of Alpha and Beta wings, wavering back and forth as they quartered the battle area. From outside their formation they might as well have been cleaning robots sweeping a floor—their maneuvers were that methodical, that regimented.

From inside the battle, it looked like all nine circles of hell, all at once. Debris was everywhere—pieces of cataphract fairings, broken thruster cones, blobs of loose flowglas that shifted and caught the light. Lanoe could hardly find a target in all of that mess. He kept a swarm of virtual Aldis sights up on his canopy at all times, his advanced targeting system looking for shots of opportunity. He loosed disruptors the moment anything turned green, fired and fired until he ran out of them. Switched to antivehicle rounds, even though the fighter's voice kept telling him it was pointless. "I don't see any cavities in that vehicle that would suggest a crew compartment," she said, almost sounding peeved.

It wasn't Zhang's voice. It was the synthesized voice of the Z.XIX's automated personal assistant. He could ignore it, knowing it was just a computer talking. Not a ghost.

"Bury," he called. "Bury, give me a status update. Tell me what we're doing here, it's your show."

"Lanoe?" the kid called. He sounded scared, but at least he was talking. "Lanoe? I got my fifth kill, did you see it? Can you confirm it?"

"Don't worry about that now," Lanoe said. "Come on, kid. Status update!"

"We're—we're pretty hard pressed," Bury replied. "We—"

A whine of static rushed through Lanoe's helmet speakers, his communications knocked out by sidelobe radiation from one of those damned microwave weapons. He stabbed at the virtual keyboard of his comms panel but nothing came up. He was cut off.

Hellfire. How had he been so distracted, how had he let things get this bad? He'd wanted to kill jellyfish—and now, pilots were dying all around him. He'd taken out that dreadnought, but the cost—

No. He couldn't think like that. He couldn't afford to. Not now, when he had a battle to win. He twisted away from an oncoming interceptor, corkscrewed up high over the battle area, dove back down firing antivehicle rounds as fast as he could pull the trigger, not even worrying about placing them well. The rounds were long, thin rockets with a core of allotropic copper. They slammed into the interceptors at hundreds of kilometers a second, fast enough and hard enough to liquefy the copper. Once it pierced the interceptors' hulls the molten metal shot forward in a jet of superheated metal.

It worked—not well, it took several shots to kill even one drone, but it worked. Suddenly there was a clear lane in front of Lanoe, an empty space in the Blue-Blue-White's formation he could fly right through. He corkscrewed between two rows of the things, looking for more targets.

And didn't find any. The interceptors were moving—fast. Slaloming back and forth as they burned away from him, headed out of the battle area.

What was going on? Lanoe checked his tactical board and saw that the interceptors were all moving in the same direction. Away. Away from him, away from the wreckage of the dreadnought. Away from the carrier and the cruiser.

They were retreating. As fast as they'd come, they were backing off.

Maybe they'd recognized that the dreadnought had been destroyed. They'd been sent to escort it—maybe they saw that now their mission was futile, and so they were pulling back before Lanoe could kill any more of them.

Damn it, he would take it. They were just drones, with no jellyfish aboard. "Let them go," he called, when he saw his comms board was back up. "Everyone—disengage. Return to the carrier—we're done here."

There were a few exhausted whoops of joy. A few nasty curses, a couple of half-veiled threats directed at him on the common channel. Lanoe ignored the chatter. He repeated his order, over and over, though most of Alpha wing and Beta wing had already withdrawn from the battle area.

The pilots who were still alive, anyway.

"Bury," he called, painting the kid's ship with a communications laser. "Bury—you got your five. You did it, Lieutenant. I am personally going to present you with your blue star. Unless maybe you'd prefer to have Candless do the honors. Yeah, how'd you like to see the look on her face, then, huh? You did a hell of a job, you—"

Bury's Yk.64 hadn't acknowledged the connection. It wasn't receiving his signal.

"Bury?" he called again, on an open radio channel.

He found the kid's fighter. It was hanging motionless right in the middle of the battle area, drifting slowly toward deep space. Lanoe banked around and headed over there. Maybe the kid had been hit by one of the microwave weapons. "Bury, if you can hear me—hang in there. Let your systems reboot, it's all automatic. Bury, can you hear me?"

No response.

"Bury?"

As he approached the Yk.64 he saw at once that its canopy was down. Flowglas required an electric charge to hold its shape, so if Bury had been hit with a microwave burst, sure, it made sense that the canopy would collapse. It was all right, though. It could be a little scary, Lanoe knew, to fly through a battle with your canopy down, with nothing but your suit to protect you against hard vacuum, but he'd done it himself plenty of times. He knew it was survivable.

Lanoe maneuvered slowly around the Sixty-Four, coming about

so he could look at the kid. Make sure he was okay. When he got there he saw...

He saw the kid's face. Slack, but with eyes open. Plastinated eyes staring out at the stars. Seeing nothing.

The fighter's canopy had come down.

So had the flowglas of Bury's helmet.

The kid was dead.

Chapter Twenty-Two

Candless had a million questions ready for Lanoe when he came back. For the last half of the battle she'd had no information at all—the microwave weapons the interceptors used had played merry hell with communications, so she was barely aware that the fight was over, that the dreadnought had been destroyed, that the interceptors had withdrawn. She'd only learned that much by looking at telescope feeds.

Lanoe hadn't spoken to her since she'd berated him for letting Bury join the fight. Well, he wasn't going to be able to avoid her forever. He'd barely docked his Z.XIX in the flight deck before she stormed up the corridor leading to his airlock. She was damned if she was going to let him get away without giving her answers. She needed to know what his plan was, first and foremost. Assuming he had one. She wanted to know why he'd put them all at such risk—why he hadn't used the cruiser's guns on the dreadnought, why he—

Why he—

He came through the airlock with a body in his arms. The shiny, hairless head lolled in the crook of his elbow.

She'd had a million questions. Now she had one answer.

No. It couldn't be true. She opened her mouth to laugh. This had to be some cruel prank, or perhaps—perhaps Bury was just wounded, perhaps he was very badly hurt, yes, it looked like he was in a very serious condition, but then he'd been injured before, back before they'd come here, to this impossible place, he'd been injured but he had recovered, he had recovered from that, he really was stronger than he looked, stronger—

Stronger than his limp body would suggest, stronger than his small frame, his smooth skin, his open, sightless eyes. His slack mouth.

"No," she said to Lanoe, because hadn't she told him, told him a dozen times that Bury wasn't ready to fight? That he should remain on the inactive list? She'd been quite clear, she'd done everything right, she'd—

No.

"No," she said. Quite calm, still. Quite rational. Because it didn't have to be true, did it? There had to be some way she could make this not true.

Some way to turn time back, to—

"*No*," she said, and she forced herself to control her lips, to hold back the tears that had started to form at the corners of her eyes.

"No!" she said a fourth time. No. She didn't say it. She screamed it.

She grabbed the body away from him, pulled Bury close to her chest. In the absence of gravity she could hold it, hold it effortlessly. It felt empty and unreal, like a wax doll of—of—

"Oh, no. Bury," she breathed. "Oh, Bury, I...I am so sorry. Oh, no." It came out of her mouth, one long sustained note. "I'm sorry," she wailed. "I'm sorry! I'm so sorry!"

She couldn't control herself. Couldn't control her grief. She pressed her cheek against the smooth, cool skin of his head. Pulled him tighter, until he almost squeezed out of her arms. Changed her grip so he wouldn't get away from her. Her back collided with the padded wall of the corridor and she bounced away again. She didn't care. She floated down the empty passage, just holding him, holding him close.

"No," she whispered, into his bloodless ear. "No. No." A rejection, a refusal. She looked up, wanting someone to tell her it wasn't true.

Lanoe was already gone. He'd closed a hatch behind him. At least no one could see her. No one could see her in her grief.

"No," she said, but it didn't mean anything anymore. It was just a sound. "No. No." She said it until she couldn't hear herself anymore. No.

No.

No.

Repeating, over and over, in the otherwise empty echo chamber of her skull. Just no. No. Because she knew, eventually, the answer was going to have to be yes. Yes, he was gone. Yes, he was dead, and it was her fault, her responsibility. Yes.

But for now—

No.

No.

No.

Maggs pushed his way down the corridor, dreading what he was about to see. Even though he knew it promoted his interests, and those of M. Bullam. Even though he'd seen similar sights before.

He opened the hatch to the pilots' ready room and slipped inside. This time he had not brought a bottle of champagne. He knew exactly how such a gesture might be received. He said nothing, uttered no boisterous words of good cheer. How hollow would those sound?

There was space in the ready room for fifty men and women, seats with straps so they could sit comfortably in microgravity, consoles so they could look at displays. The consoles were all dead now, switched off because there was nothing to see. Nothing anyone wanted to see.

He surveyed the people in the few occupied seats. Pilots just back from the battle area, pilots weary and disgusted, pilots with looks of pure rage on their faces. Pilots with no expression at all, pilots who looked dead inside, who could have been ghosts.

No, if there were ghosts in the ready room, it would have been packed to capacity.

The ready room had space for fifty. Barely more than ten of the seats were filled now. This was all of them, all who had come back.

They sat apart from one another, with rows of empty seats between them. They did not speak to one another, nor did they look up when Maggs entered.

He pushed himself across the room. Came up behind a pilot who couldn't seem to stop scratching at her short blonde hair. He placed a hand on her shoulder and she whirled around, one hand reaching for the quick-release catch of her straps, the other balling into a fist. The look on her face could not be described by any term short of homicidal.

Then she saw it was him. Good old Maggs. Her face softened. Not as much as he might have liked, perhaps—there was still plenty of anger there. He thought, in fact, she might spit. Instead, she turned away from him again. But she nodded, just a little.

His message had been conveyed. Another ally secured.

He felt like a bastard. Like a churl.

This wasn't Maggs's first war. He knew that these pilots were busy. Despite the fact that they crouched in their seats abstracted, removed from the world, he knew that in their heads they were punching throttles and throwing control sticks back and forth, checking boards and craning their heads around to see what was behind them. Reliving every moment of the battle that had just ended, revisiting every detail, every choice they'd made. Analyzing what they could have done differently. Imagining hypothetical scenarios that might have led to fewer empty seats.

Maggs had betrayed plenty of people in his life. He'd preyed on the weak, done dirty deeds when no one else would. He had wrestled with guilt often enough. None of his backhanded deals, none of his slimy tactics, though, had ever made him feel this dirty. These pilots were busy, inside their heads, and who was he to disturb them?

He did what he had to do. He moved through the room, gliding over the seats, feeling like some perverse form of Valkyrie, perhaps. Not a chooser of the slain but a chooser of the ones who survived. One by one he touched them, on a shoulder or an arm. One by one they gave him some sign. Some small token of agreement.

When he was done he moved on, headed out of the ready room. He left them with no comforting words because, truly, there were no words that might serve.

Outside in the corridor he closed the hatch and then pressed himself against a wall, simply trying to breathe. It had to be done, he told himself. It had to be—

You can't win a war thinking of the other's chap's feelings, his father's voice said inside his head. *Save that sort of thing for when you're home again.*

He knew the old man was trying to help. So he chose not to respond.

He had more work to do. He needed to get moving. Yet as soon as he started to peel himself away from the wall, he saw a hatch open at the far end of the corridor, down by the bridge, and he stopped right where he was. Tried to make himself invisible.

Lanoe came kicking down the corridor, his old, lined face unreadable, his body language fierce and unquestionable. Maggs kept his eyes down, kept his face carefully neutral. If Lanoe tried to engage him in conversation, he would keep his responses simple. He would refrain from using colorful phrases, make himself as boring as possible. He would show deference, somehow, submission in the face of authority. He would—

Lanoe passed right by him. He didn't so much as glance in Maggs's direction. Maggs thought perhaps he had avoided a very difficult encounter. Yet halfway down the corridor, Lanoe shot out one hand and grabbed a nylon strap set into the wall, stopping his forward progress. A thick lump formed in Maggs's throat—until he saw that Lanoe hadn't stopped for him.

Shulkin emerged from the hatch to the bridge, his eyes chips of nonreflective glass, his face hanging as slack as a rubber mask.

The two men paused there in the corridor, near each other,

occupying the same space. To Maggs they both seemed enormous, giants, perhaps grizzly bears meeting at a clearing in the forest. He could see them breathing, see their chests rise and fall.

Shulkin's head tilted up, just a touch. The muscles around his mouth tightened, though his lips stayed compressed in a flat line.

The angle of Lanoe's shoulders changed, lifting a hair. Making him look even bigger. The slightest, quietest grunt emerged from his throat.

Shulkin made a sound like a low growl. An acknowledgment, a signal of respect, or a threat? Maggs couldn't be sure. Between the two men the air seemed to shimmer, as if from the stray heat of a banked furnace.

Lanoe pushed away from the wall. Shulkin's whole body tensed, his slack dead man's posture giving way instantly, his hackles rising. His ears even seemed to tilt back, as his face took on something approximating a wary expression. But Lanoe simply floated past Shulkin, twisting around in midair as he passed through the hatch and onto the bridge. Shulkin stayed motionless for a second after he was gone, panting a little, perhaps. Then he kicked off a wall and headed down a side corridor, toward his cabin.

Hellfire and ashes, Maggs thought. *What did I just see?*

The mad, his father told him, *recognize their own.*

Indeed. All Maggs's guilt, all of the self-doubt he'd accumulated bothering the surviving pilots of Alpha and Beta wing, fell from him like a dog's shed hair. What he was doing—the scheme M. Bullam was enacting—was right, he knew. It was necessary. Lanoe had to be neutralized. And the sooner the better.

Ehta took a very long, very hot shower when they finally got the order to stand down from the guns. She hadn't seen her own skin in months, hadn't taken off her suit since she was back on Tuonela, fighting in the trenches. Normally there was no need—her suit could keep her clean without her having to think about it.

Now, though, she hung naked in a plastic sack, weightless and floating. She let the water cling to her, let its heat scour her until her skin turned pink and then red. The pain woke her up, got her blood moving. It felt right. She pulled her head down into the sack, held her breath and scrubbed at her face with a handful of low-residue soap, ran her fingernails across her scalp, digging through the short hair there, scratching hard at the soft skin underneath. She scrubbed furiously until her lungs started to give out, until her body demanded she breathe again. She held on a few seconds more until her body started to burn on the inside, too, before poking her head back out of the sack.

She switched on a vacuum pump that sucked all the water away from her. Scraped the last of it off with a strigil until she was dry. Stood under a hot-air vent until her she felt her skin start to crack.

Then she pulled her suit back on and headed down the axial corridor, toward the brig. There was something she had to do. At the hatch to the detaining cells two of her marines stood guard, helmets up and silvered. Good people who had just come off twelve hours' duty on the gun decks. They must be as exhausted as she was, she thought, but they clung to the wall at attention, rifles cradled in their arms.

Ehta moved toward the cell that contained Ginger and Rain-on-Stones. Before she could get there, though, one of the marines reached out an arm to bar her way.

"Sorry, ma'am. We can't let you go in there."

She frowned. "What the hell are you doing, Geddy? I'm your damned superior officer. You don't tell me where I can go."

The marine didn't move his arm. "Ma'am, we have orders."

She tried to stare him down. Hard to do that when she couldn't see his face. Which of course was one reason that marines kept their helmets opaque.

"I just want to talk to her. She needs to know about Bury, she needs to know—"

"Orders from Commander Lanoe," Geddy told her. "I'm sorry."

Yeah, Ehta thought. *Yeah. Of course he would tell them to keep me out of there. Of course he would.*

"I'm not going to shoot the damned alien, I just want to talk to the girl," she said. "Damn you, Geddy, I'll have you demoted, I'll make sure you never see corporal as long as you live, you bastard, you—"

"Ma'am," Geddy said, grabbing her shoulder. She knocked his hand away but he didn't even flinch. "Ma'am, we have orders to remove you from the brig by force if you won't leave peacefully. Again—I'm sorry."

She knew he was. Sorry. She knew he didn't want this. What marine ever wanted to come between two officers? She was making an ass of herself.

"All right," she said. "All right. You're just doing your job, I get that. But the girl needs to know. If I give you a message, can you give it to her?"

Geddy turned to look at his fellow guard. Eventually he turned back to Ehta and shrugged. "Yes, ma'am. That's okay."

Paniet might have felt like a toddler in a toy store, except for two things. One: the toys were all broken. Smashed to flinders. Two: he was terrified out of his mind.

He'd been ordered to examine the dreadnought—or what was left of it. Lanoe wanted him to learn as much as possible from the broken spacecraft. Which meant Paniet had to go over there, in person, into the belly of the beast.

Ahead of him a sensor drone moved in little fits and starts, ion engines mounted in its chassis directing it now this way, now that. A range-finding laser swept around the inside of the ruined blister, taking precise measurements of what was left of the dreadnought's control room. Lights mounted on the drone's upper and lower sides cut through the swirling murk of debris and dust.

Paniet grasped one of the broken spars of the cagework and pulled himself inside, into the dark.

"I'm not detecting any motion in there," Hollander said. Paniet's fellow neddy was back on the repair tender, hovering a safe distance away from the wreckage of the dreadnought. Though he was nearly a kilometer away, Paniet was glad not to feel like he was entirely alone inside the alien vessel.

"Can't see much myself, ducks," Paniet replied. He gingerly picked his way over a control panel the size of a divan. Levers and rods stuck up from the broken console, all of them twisted out of shape like the broken fingers of a giant skeleton.

The disruptor round that tore through the blister had left little undamaged. Little for Paniet to even inspect. He pushed himself forward, following the drone. He figured that if nothing lurched out of the shadows to devour the drone whole, he was probably safe as well. At least, he was moderately convinced of that.

In the dark he found the floor of the blister. It was covered in a thick mat of something soft and spongy. Padding, maybe, to protect the Blue-Blue-White pilot during hard maneuvers. Handfuls of the stuff came away when he tried to steady himself against it. He held them up close to his face, then gestured for the drone to shine a light on him.

The floor material looked organic. Maybe. It was fibrous and it tore easily between his fingers. He cast it away and brushed his gloves off on the thighs of his suit. "You got imagery of that?" he called.

"Aye," Hollander said.

"Cushioning. Now we know they like cushioning," Paniet suggested. What a worthless thing to discover.

"Are you sure? Maybe that's their food supply," Hollander replied.

Paniet shrugged. The man had a point.

For hours now he'd been studying every scan, every image he could get of the dreadnought's interior spaces. None of it had made the slightest sense. He was a trained engineer, and he could work out some of the basic mechanisms they had found in the wreckage. Pumps and conduits. Wires and relays. Even those, however, had been much bigger than their human counterparts, and designed in a way he found incomprehensible.

"Listen, Paniet," Hollander said. "There's a word I'd have with you. If you're amenable."

"Always," Paniet said, though truth be told he was a bit preoccupied. He took a welding pen from a pocket of his suit and cut into the tangle of wires underneath the broken control console. Maybe he would find something useful there.

"I like you," Hollander said.

"Well, I like you too, ducky," Paniet said. He pulled away a bundle of wires. There was something back there, he thought. "I wonder if this is the right time to discuss it, though."

"Right, well, time is of the essence, as they say."

As Paniet pulled at the wires something started to slither out and he yanked his hand back.

"I've grown fond of you, for a fact, and—"

"Hold on." The thing that had been stuck in the wires flopped out in one big piece. It was orange and semisolid, about as thick around as his thigh. It glistened in the drone's light. As he watched, it retracted away from him, almost slithering out of the console, and—

Paniet yelped. He was unashamed of it. That wasn't a mechanical component.

It was a damned tentacle. A severed tentacle.

"Please don't let me find a body in here," he said. "Please don't let me find a body in here." Hollander laughed at him, but Paniet didn't take offense. It was a human sound, and that alone was comforting.

"It's only, and this is the tricky part, but I'm serious, see. The bond of camaraderie, the esprit de corps and all, is something I've always considered a bit of bosh, to be honest. But you've been so kind and generous. I'd hate to see something happen to you. For real, like."

Paniet couldn't reply.

He'd found the body he'd been dreading.

It was wedged in between two collapsed slabs of white coral.

It was orange and—enormous. It just went on and on. Squeezed down to a kind of spindle shape, part of it overhanging the slabs like a colossally large and unpleasant tongue. More tentacles, their flesh crushed down to nearly nothing, flopped limply around Paniet as he got close. It felt like at any moment the jellyfish might come back to life, as if those boneless arms would snap out at him, grab him by all four limbs and pull him toward the alien's grinding maw.

That... didn't happen. The alien stayed dead.

"Are you listening to me?"

"Sorry. I just—do you see this, on your displays?"

At least it got Hollander off of his uncomfortable conversational topic. "Hell's handmaidens, man. What is it?"

"What does it look like? That's a damned Blue-Blue-White," Paniet said.

"Should you be touching it?"

"I'm not a doctor. I don't do autopsies," Paniet announced. "I just don't."

"Above your pay grade," Hollander sympathized.

Paniet puffed air in and out of his mouth. He couldn't smell the alien corpse, no, not with his helmet up, but some part of his brain was bracing against a truly righteous stink. He reached forward with the blunt end of his welding pen. Prodded the alien's dead flesh.

It squirmed. Ripples of soft tissue rolled away from him, up and down the enormous mass of the corpse. The Blue-Blue-White's skin stretched and wrinkled in a quite alarming way, until a section of it started to split. As Paniet watched, horrified, a tear three meters long opened up in the body's side and transparent gore started oozing outward, as if it had been under pressure and his slightest touch had popped it like a balloon.

Paniet danced backwards, half pulling himself away with his hands, half using his suit's jets to maneuver clear of the flowing goop. He was fascinated and nauseated in equal parts as he watched the stuff come loose in globules bigger than his head. Each spherical blob of nastiness gleamed in the light, gleamed—and started to foam.

"That's...odd," Paniet said. He reached down and grabbed a handful of the loose floor material. Using it like a sponge, he tried to collect some of the foaming liquid.

The floor material darkened and started to disintegrate almost instantly. Paniet pulled his hand back, wiping it clean of any of the stuff. He snapped his fingers for the sensor drone and had it run a spectrographic analysis.

When he saw the results, he had to whistle in surprise. "Aitch-two-ess-oh-four," he said, drawing out the syllables in respect.

"You're kidding me, now," Hollander said. "Sulfuric acid? Your alien's guts are soaked in acid?"

Paniet shrugged. "It's relatively dilute. Not concentrated enough to do more than sting if it got on your skin." It made a certain amount of sense, really. Every living organism had some kind of liquid solvent as its main ingredient—humans, for instance, being mostly water. But the average temperature of the disk was three hundred Celsius, and liquid water couldn't exist at that temperature—it would just boil away into vapor almost instantly. The Blue-Blue-White needed some kind of solvent that would stay liquid at that heat. Sulfuric acid had a boiling point of three hundred and thirty-seven degrees.

One of the globules detached from the body and started floating toward him. He kicked off a broken piece of coral to get away from it.

"Oh, blast," he said. "That one nearly got me."

"Have a care!" Hollander said.

Something touched Paniet's shoulder. He yelped—again—and jumped away, thinking a tentacle was about to wrap around his chest and squeeze him to death. Instead, when he turned around he saw Hollander, silhouetted against the drone's light.

"What are you doing?" Paniet demanded. "You nearly frightened me to death! You aren't supposed to be in here."

"I needed to talk to you," Hollander explained. "Where we wouldn't be overheard."

Paniet shook his head. He didn't understand this at all.

"Something is going to happen," Hollander said.

"What? Here? With that—that body?" Paniet asked.

"No, you fool. Not here. Back on the carrier."

"What—what kind of thing?" Paniet asked. The look on Hollander's face scared him more than a dead alien possibly could.

"Something bloody."

Hollander made a gesture with his hand, and for the first time Paniet noticed that he was holding a pistol.

"Why don't you back up a hair, then," the big man said.

Valk was no longer exactly certain where he was.

Or rather, there were so many places he might be, and he was in all of them at once. His suit, his special suit he'd worn since he thought he was still a human named Tannis Valk, was currently in a storage locker in the cruiser's engineering section. He was technically still in it, in that some part of his consciousness was running on its built-in processors. If someone had found it, though, they would have seen only an empty suit with its helmet down. They wouldn't see him.

In another sense he was in the cruiser. His thoughts, his senses, suffused the ship's systems. There wasn't a line of code, a one or a zero, he wasn't intimately connected to, that he didn't feel to be part of himself.

A third perspective: he was no place. He was nowhere. He was in some Platonic realm of pure thought, pure reason.

Perhaps the best possible place to consider one's failures.

Lanoe had removed him from his work. In no uncertain terms he'd indicated that Valk was no longer to be trusted, that his functions were no longer required. To this end he had suggested that Valk's analyses and conclusions were faulty.

Valk knew that couldn't be the case. He could partition himself, make copies of his entire file structure and check them against diagnostic models he invented for just this purpose. Every time he oversampled himself, every time he checked his checksums, nullified his null loops, he was more and more sure of it—he was operating perfectly.

And yet Lanoe had a point. Valk had failed to understand the language of the Blue-Blue-White. The signals he had picked up from the disk made no sense at all, when compared to the vocabulary database he had picked up from the queenship at Niraya. The strings of colors that should turn into words just...didn't. He couldn't even seem to grasp the basic morphemes, much less get a sense of the idioms in use.

Perhaps even more damning—he didn't know where they were. When they first arrived in this system he had automatically tried to get a fix on their precise position. He had checked with the standard candles—the galactic landmarks—thinking he would triangulate their location and get an exact figure for how far they'd come from human space. Instead, he had sought in vain for anything he recognized in the dome of the sky. The standard candles...just weren't there.

He had no explanation for either of these problems. His data was not corrupt. His databases, his libraries, his directories, were all intact and did not require repair.

Yet when he attempted to use them, when he tried to help Lanoe—he'd failed both times.

The strangest part was that Lanoe must know this. Valk was certain that if he was malfunctioning in some way he couldn't self-diagnose (and it was, he had to admit, possible, Gödel's theorems of incompleteness said as much), if he was broken beyond repair—Lanoe would have no choice but to use the data bomb. To erase him, permanently. He was far too dangerous to be allowed to continue to exist if he was no longer useful.

Yet Lanoe had simply sent him away. Removed him from the cruiser's controls.

Which meant—this had to be some kind of test.

Lanoe had sent him off to contemplate himself. To run more diagnostics, to understand himself better. To find the fault that led to his two mistakes. This followed directly, by inductive reasoning. It must be true.

Valk had run every test of himself he knew how to perform. He'd checked every corner of his programming, decompiled his most basic code and run it through every debugging routine he could think of. He was incapable of true exasperation now. He could no longer get angry and give up on a problem once he'd started to examine it. Yet he was still human enough—well, he was still running enough of a simulation of what it meant to be human—that when he found himself hitting his head against the same metaphorical wall over and over and over, he knew it wasn't working. He needed to try to resolve things from a different angle.

It was only after several million runtime cycles that he reached that point. But reach it he did. And in the end, he realized that what he needed to do was to try again from completely new first principles. He would abandon the most logical supposition he could think of, and see how that changed things.

What if it was not himself but the entire universe exterior to himself that was at fault?

This could only be a thought experiment, of course. A ridiculous hypothetical that he would never take seriously. It could not, furthermore, lead to any useful conclusions, because it was patently false. Yet when he ran the numbers, when he fed known data into this new model, something very strange happened.

It sort of made sense.

The numbers added up.

There were many more steps to take from there. He would need to check and double-check and triple-check what he'd found. He sketched out a plan for how he would tackle this new possibility, how he would expand upon it, play with it, until he reached conclusions that he could verify or—infinitely more likely—falsify. He would take this new idea, this impossible paradigm, and run with it until it broke.

He estimated it would take a very long time to complete his action plan. To invalidate his invalid premise. It would take not millions of runtime cycles but billions. Perhaps hundreds of billions.

In objective time it might take as much as three hours.

Lanoe called together a meeting of his senior officers. He knew some of them were preoccupied, but it was crucial that they discuss what came next. Rather than forcing them to come to him, he simply conferenced them all in to the bridge of the carrier. Shulkin's, Candless's, and Ehta's faces appeared before him as floating holograms, none of them looking particularly pleased to see him.

"Where's Valk?" Ehta asked, once Lanoe had them all together.

"He's not invited to this briefing," Lanoe told her. "Where's Paniet?" he asked, but nobody had an answer. "Never mind—whatever he's doing, it's probably important. He's probably busy fixing something that's keeping us all alive." He tried a little smile, but didn't get much in the way of reaction.

"Very well," he said. "We need to talk about what we've learned here, and how we move forward. We've bought ourselves a little time. The other two dreadnoughts are still inside the disk's atmosphere. For the moment we aren't being chased, and there's no danger of an immediate attack. We need to talk about what we're going to do with this opportunity."

"Opportunity?" Candless asked. "You see the present situation as an opportunity? I must say I admire your optimism."

"The battle didn't go as well as I'd hoped—"

Candless made a noise. Some small snort of derision.

He chose to ignore it. "We lost a number of resources. Several pilots, along with their cataphracts. On the other hand, the cruiser and the carrier came through without sustaining new damage, and on the whole I think we proved some valuable things. The dreadnoughts aren't as tough as they look, for one. A couple of good fighter pilots can take one of those things down, even as big as they are."

"That's why we didn't fire the guns?" Ehta asked.

He stared at her image, refusing to let her derail him.

"Sorry," she said. "That's why you didn't use the guns, sir? To prove that fact?"

Lanoe waved a hand in impatience. "I'm not interested in questions right now," he said. "Just listen, will you? This is important."

"I think no one here doubts the importance of your briefing," Candless said, a hint of her old sarcastic self coming through. Despite himself, Lanoe had missed her caustic snark. "We simply wish to know why we've made so many sacrifices. What we hope to accomplish here."

"The goal hasn't changed," Lanoe told her. "We're here to get justice for all the species the Blue-Blue-White have exterminated over the eons. We're here to make sure humanity stays safe from future invasions by their drone fleets. We're here—"

"To murder the beggars," Shulkin said. "When do we get back to that?"

Lanoe breathed in deeply, through his nose. Counted to ten in his head.

"That," he said, "is why I called this meeting. We're going to talk about Plan B."

Candless raised an eyebrow. "Plan B. Can you remind me exactly when we discussed a Plan A?"

"Enough!" Lanoe said. "I'm in command here. I didn't think I needed to remind any of you of that. I'm perfectly happy to throw all three of you in the brig if that's what you want. Or," he said, looking from one face to the next, "you can shut up and listen, damn you. You can let me talk."

He got the silence he was after. If he'd hoped for the three of them to give him looks of respect, well, perhaps that was too much to ask for.

For far too long he'd been running this operation as if his underlings were friends. As if they were all equals, peers who had an equal say. That needed to change—now.

Shulkin opened his mouth as if he were about to say something.

"The next person who interrupts me is relieved of duty," he said. Shulkin closed his mouth.

Lanoe waited awhile. Let them stew. Gave them a chance to decide if objecting to his orders was more important than keeping their jobs. When they went a suitable interval without opening their mouths, he continued.

"Plan A was to try to talk to the Blue-Blue-White. Failing that, we engaged with them in a series of naval battles. Our losses were high. So were theirs. However, we have failed to accomplish our goals simply through ship-to-ship fighting. So we're going to move on to Plan B."

He swiped open a display that showed the disk, whirling with infinitesimal slowness. White dots appeared inside the gyring clouds—hundreds of them, scattered seemingly at random.

"These are the cities of the Blue-Blue-White. Some of those dots are bigger than others—some of the cities are as big as landmasses on Earth, some not much bigger than our actual cities. It's my working hypothesis, though, that they're pretty much the same as the one I saw when I took out the laser emplacement. Which means that they're largely deserted. Maybe one full-sized adult lives in each city, with a brood of thousands of juveniles. There's no correlation on that, but as an operating assumption it'll do."

He brought up another display, this one showing video of his flight through the Blue-Blue-White city in the Z.XIX. The display had been enhanced until it was a false-color image of what one of those cities might look like if it wasn't buried under obscuring clouds. "We do know that the cities are all built the same way. You see these long pylons? They're made of something like coral. I'm pretty sure they're grown rather than built—though I don't know much about the jellyfishes' life cycle, it looks like when they're born they start out in a kind of polyp form, which secretes a layer of concretelike shell for protection. Those shells are abandoned when the polyps get too big, but the next generation builds their own shells on the substrate the previous generation left behind. Over the years, over millennia, over millions of years, all those polyps build up something very similar to a coral reef.

"The point is," Lanoe said, "it takes them a long, long time to build these cities. We can blow up all the dreadnoughts we want, shoot down their interceptors. They can just build more. If we target the cities, though, we can hurt them. Bad. Maybe in a way they never recover from."

He closed the display. Turned to face Ehta directly. "We have a weapon that can do that. The cruiser. The seventy-five-centimeter coilguns we've got were designed specifically to shell cities into submission. Well, that's what we're going to do. No more dogfights in deep space." He glanced over at Candless. "No more running away from their big fancy ships." He turned to spear Shulkin with a glare. "No more pointless glory seeking. We do this fast. Hit-and-run style. We move in, shell a city, pull back before their defenses can respond. Move to the next city. Until there aren't any left."

None of them spoke. They just stared at him, as if they couldn't believe what he was saying.

"To answer your question, Ehta, yes. This is why we didn't use the guns in the last battle. Because I wanted to conserve ammunition. I knew we were going to need every round we had in our magazines. In fact, we'll probably need to find some way of fabricating new shells. If Paniet were here, maybe he'd know how we do that. We will find a way, though, regardless of what it takes. Because we aren't going to stop until every last city they have is smashed to pieces. Until they don't have a single pylon to stand on."

He gave them some time. Let the new plan sink in. Eventually, when he thought they'd had enough time, he said, "All right. You have permission to speak now. Go ahead with the questions. I'm sure you've got 'em."

There was only one, though. Candless cleared her throat and looked directly into his eyes.

"Is there a Plan C?" she asked.

"There is," Lanoe told her. "But you wouldn't like it."

Candless swiped across her display to dismiss it. The various holograms that had filled her small cabin winked out, leaving her very much alone.

Except, of course, for Bury.

The young officer's body was strapped into her bunk. She'd closed his eyes, gently tugging down on his plastinated eyelids. It made him look a little more peaceful. She'd considered covering his face with a blanket, but she couldn't bring herself to do it. It felt too much like letting him go.

She had not intended to keep him with her for so long. She'd wanted to give him a proper ceremony and then consign his ashes to space—a traditional pilot's funeral. She couldn't let any of that happen, though, not yet.

Not until one last person came to say goodbye.

Getting Lanoe to allow Ginger to leave the cruiser—even for this—had taken some work. She'd tried at first to lean on any guilt feelings he might have regarding Bury's death. It had turned out he didn't have any.

Pilots die, sometimes, he'd said. *They sign up to fly. They sign up to fight. Sometimes they don't come back.*

She'd heard that speech before. Plenty of times—back in the worst days of the poly wars, when pilots with only a few days' training were shipped straight into warzones, funerals had become a standard part of her working week. She had thrown so many handfuls of ash into the void she couldn't remember them all. Usually there had been a high-ranking officer there, someone to show that the pilot's sacrifice had not gone completely unnoticed. They always said the same thing.

Pilots die, sometimes.

Some of them almost made it sound sincere. The good ones made it sound important, even necessary. Most of the time she didn't even hear them.

Lanoe had been so distracted with his planning that he didn't even look at her as he said the old, old words.

She'd had to resort to a different tactic to get Ginger special dispensation to view the body, then. Instead of trying to make him feel guilty, she'd appealed to his pragmatic side. If he failed to do this for Ginger, she'd told him, it would destroy the girl's morale. Which would make it harder for him to use her later.

Eventually, he'd seen her point.

A green pearl rotated in the corner of her vision. "Coming in now," Uhl said. The pilot who had saved her life during the battle had agreed to bring Ginger over to the carrier. She hadn't known who else to ask to do it. Ehta couldn't fly. Nobody could seem to find Paniet. She would not have trusted Valk with the job—the AI might have said something to Ginger on the way, something that would traumatize the girl.

"Thank you," she told Uhl. "You're a good man."

"Just following orders, ma'am," he told her.

Candless stared at the floor until the knock came at her hatch. She hit the release and saw Uhl floating in the corridor. He scanned her face, but just looked confused by what he saw there. Candless supposed she knew what that meant. He was accustomed to seeing her when she was in her command mode, hard-edged and brittle. When she answered the door, she hadn't bothered to set her face in the right mask of patrician disdain. He was seeing her as she looked when she was alone with herself. When she was just another human being.

"Ma'am, she's—well, she's here," Uhl said.

Candless nodded and leaned out into the corridor. Ginger was pressed up against one wall, holding on to a nylon loop sewn into the padding there.

She looked . . . bad.

Very pale. Deep bags hung from her eyes and her red hair was matted down on one side—she must not have cleaned it in days. She looked up at Candless with eyes that contained no shred of hope or happiness.

Candless realized with a guilty start that she hadn't actually gone to see the girl since the last time she'd been on the cruiser, back before Lanoe assigned her to the carrier. Had she really forgotten to check in, to make sure Ginger was okay? She'd been so busy—but that was no excuse.

"Come in," she said. "Ginger—come in. He's here."

Ginger nodded and pushed inside the cabin. Candless dismissed Uhl, touching him briefly on the shoulder to indicate her thanks. He seemed more than happy to get away. Candless wondered if Ginger had spoken to him on the ride over. Had she told him anything about what her life had become?

She closed the hatch behind him. "I'm so sorry," she told Ginger. "I'm so sorry—I've failed both of you. I've done such a lousy job of—"

"Don't," Ginger said.

The girl moved over to the bed, grabbing the rail that ran along its side to keep the occupant from rolling out during maneuvers. She leaned over Bury's face, her eyes closed, as if she were communing with his spirit.

No. Not his, Candless realized.

"Are you—can you talk to the chorister, even now?"

"It doesn't stop," Ginger said. "We're about ten kilometers away from the cruiser here. Rain-on-Stone's voice is...a little faint. It's kind of a relief, but...I know. I know. I'll be back soon."

Candless understood that last part hadn't been for her.

Ginger opened her eyes. "She's worried. Worried I'm leaving her. If I did...it would be the end for her. She would go completely insane. The problem is, we're so linked at this point—I probably would, too."

"I'm—sorry," Candless said. "We can take you back whenever you—"

"I need to do this," Ginger said. "I need to say goodbye."

Ginger reached down and caressed the dead boy's cheek. Candless came over and hovered behind her. She wanted to put her arms around the girl. Hold her close, just as she'd held Bury. She didn't dare, though, when she didn't know how Ginger would react.

For a while they were both silent. Eventually Candless found she couldn't bear it. "He was a good man," she said.

Ginger laughed, though there was little mirth in the sound. "He was an ass," she said.

Candless bit her lip. "I suppose that maybe he—"

"He challenged you to a duel," Ginger said. "He couldn't handle anyone insulting him, even if they didn't mean it. He had so much to prove, and I guess—I guess in the end he did. He proved he was a good pilot. He earned his blue star."

"I have it here," Candless said, touching the cryptab on the front of her suit. There was no physical medal involved, not even a ribbon to tie to the boy's epaulets. The blue star was a virtual commendation. "I thought maybe you'd like to be present when I gave it to him."

Ginger nodded.

"Okay." Candless moved in beside her, one hand on the railing. She touched her cryptab again, then reached over and tapped Bury's. His body shifted minutely under her touch. "Lieutenant Ronal Bury," she said, then inhaled deeply so she could say it in the correct voice. The voice of an officer. "Lieutenant Ronal Bury," she said again, "in light of extraordinary service and valor in the dispensation of your duties, and having achieved no less than five confirmed kills in sanctioned battle, the Naval Expeditionary Force has seen fit to confer upon you one of its highest honors. From this day forward, you will be known as an ace. Your name will be recorded in the rolls of the Admiralty and you will be accorded all the rights and privileges due a member of the Order of the Blue Star."

She tapped her cryptab again. Anyone who pinged Bury's cryptab now would see it—the blue star would appear right at the top of his service record.

Not that anyone ever *would* see it. As soon as they were done here, Bury would be incinerated along with his suit. A tear pooled in the corner of Candless's eye.

Ginger reached over and took her hand.

She nodded and just tried to breathe.

"He had family, back on Hel," Ginger said, very quietly. "He used to talk about his mother. And a sister he couldn't stand, but I think she was the only person he ever really respected."

"Yes," Candless said. "When we get home, when we get back, I'll...I'll visit them. Let them know."

"Okay," Ginger said.

Together they looked down on the still face, and said goodbye.

Chapter Twenty-Three

Maggs looked up and down the corridor, making sure he wasn't being followed. Then he slipped inside the necessary and cycled all the toilets, to make enough noise that he wouldn't be overheard. M. Bullam had assured him that his transmission wouldn't be intercepted—they were on an encrypted channel—but he wasn't about to take any chances.

Not now. Not when they were so close.

"I have a few more people to speak with, but it's just about done. That last battle was not a popular one. The remaining pilots are all on our side."

Bullam grunted in response. "Fine—just. That's fine." Her words were thick, slurred—maybe it was a side effect of the encryption on the line, but it sounded more like he'd just woken her up.

"Are you . . . all right?" he asked.

"Fine. I'm fine. I've got a headache, but that doesn't matter. The only thing that matters is we move now, and we move fast. You know what you need to do. I'm going to let you choose the exact timing."

"Your faith in me is quite touching," he told her.

"It isn't faith. You know I don't trust anyone," she replied. "I just know you well enough now to think you can actually pull this off. Okay. We shouldn't speak again until we're ready to finalize."

In other words—the moment when the die was cast. When Bullam came forward to take her place in command of the loyal Centrocor contingent. The moment when Maggs was given command of the carrier.

The moment when Lanoe was dead.

Now he just had to bring that very special moment to pass.

The first part of his mission was easy enough to complete. He moved quickly through the carrier, staying away from the bridge and anywhere else his presence might be noticed. He reached the deck where the pilots kept their bunks without incident and knocked discreetly on a certain hatch.

It opened at once. The woman stared at him with a look that was composed of equal parts hope and apprehension. She pulled him inside the tiny compartment, where they had to sit with their knees up against their chins just to have room. "Cozy," Maggs said.

"I got the signal," the woman replied. She was one of the few surviving pilots of Beta wing, and a loyal Centrocor employee. "It's time? Really? I didn't know if this was actually going to happen."

She had her gloves off and he saw that her nails were ragged. She'd been chewing on them, he thought, not without a shiver of squeamish disgust.

"M. Bullam sends her compliments," he said. "You have everything you need?"

The woman shrugged. She glanced around the bunk as if she expected to find that someone else had clambered in with them and was listening to their every word.

"No need for alarm," Maggs told her. "This room is bugged, oh yes, everywhere on the carrier is—but by us, not the Navy. Centrocor, of course, likes to keep a benevolent eye on its employees. M. Bullam has all the codes for the listening devices, and I promise she's turned this one off. Now. Tell me what I want to hear."

The woman nodded. She couldn't meet his eye, though. "We thought we would have more time. We were just getting started—"

"I'm sure you're more ready than you think," Maggs said. Clutching to hope.

She shrugged. "We have some small arms. Mostly pistols, a couple of combat knives. Anything we could smuggle out of stores. And we're ready to fight. I've got twenty people lined up who've got good reason to hate the Navy. But there's a problem. Marines. *Their* marines—you were here when they boarded us, right?"

"I was on the bridge. When it was breached," Maggs said.

The woman shook her head. "We can't stand up to them, not if they come at us hard. They did not mess around."

Maggs sighed in feigned contentment. "You see, that's all right," he told her. "Because we won't need to fight them."

"What?"

"I assure you, we won't have to worry about the marines. In point of fact, they'll be fighting on our side."

Let's hope for the sake of my potential grandchildren it actually works out that way, Maggs's father said inside his head.

"Seriously? I mean . . . really?"

"You have my word," Maggs said. She seemed to take some comfort from that. Maggs was still surprised when people believed the absolute rot he said sometimes. "Surprising, perhaps, but it turns out that even big tough PBMs have no desire to die out here, so far from home. They'll fight with us."

"What's the next step, then?"

"You know how this works. When the time comes, your wrist display will flash three times. Then—do your very worst. Your absolute bloodiest worst. And we'll all come through this together."

His paraphrase of Centrocor's famous motto had an immediate and encouraging effect on the woman. She sat up a little straighter. Her mouth twitched into something that suggested an actual smile.

"It's going to happen," she said. "We're going to take this ship back."

"Yes."

"And then—we're going home," the woman said, and he would not have been surprised had a single poignant tear dropped from her eye. It didn't, but it might have.

"Yes," he told her. "Home."

He left her there shaking with excitement. He had a few more stops to make, other bunks where he repeated the same patter, made the same assurances. When he was done he was forced, however, to acknowledge the much more difficult part of his task. Fulfilling his promises, as it were.

He needed to get Ehta on their side.

He needed to convince Caroline Ehta to betray Lanoe. The man she worshipped. The man she would follow through the gates of hell.

For that, he was going to need to be extraordinarily charming. Otherwise, he was going to have to kill her, which would be a terrible shame.

Maggs caught a ride over to the cruiser in a troop transport. The vehicle was almost empty. He shared the passenger section with Ginger, the bizarre red-haired girl whom Lanoe had turned into... something unsavory. He wasn't sure he even understood what had been done to her. She did not speak during the voyage, nor did she even look up from her hands. That was fine by him.

When they arrived he pushed out into the cruiser's vehicle bay, under the watchful eye of one of Ehta's marines. He exercised his face muscles, getting ready his absolute best smile. One that suggested innocent friendship, one full of warmth and bonhomie, one that implied Maggs had no ulterior motives at all, that the furthest thing from his mind was any kind of manipulation or deceit.

This, he felt, was going to be the ultimate test of his skill. The grand performance of his long and varied career as a schemer. He would need every trick in his very thick book, every scrap of inspiration he could find.

He queried his wrist display and found that Ehta was in her bunk. He hoped he wouldn't find her sleeping—nobody liked being woken up. If she was awake, though, the setting was perfect. Her bunk would give them privacy so they could speak openly. She would feel comfortable, at ease in her own quarters. Yes, this would do nicely.

He struck her hatch with a jaunty knock, then lowered his hands and folded them behind his back. Perhaps he should have brought a present, he thought, some small token of his affection for the major of marines. Perhaps—

"Maggs?"

Ehta's voice came from a speaker next to the release of her hatch. A tiny camera was mounted up there as well.

Maggs looked it squarely in the electronic eye and forced his smile to grow just a little wider, a little more lovable.

You must look like the cat that got into the cream, Maggsy, his father's voice said.

He ignored it.

"Maggs? What do you...oh, hell. You're here to check in, aren't you?"

"As required by Lanoe's orders, yes," Maggs said. The conditions of his reprieve included that he had to make a periodical report of his movements to Ehta—so that she could make sure he didn't get up to any mischief. "I hope this isn't a bad time."

"It's fine. You'd better come in," she said. The hatch pulled back and Maggs climbed inside the bunk. As befitting her rank, it was a bit larger than those of the enlisted class. The two of them could fit inside without bumping each other's knees.

Ehta looked deeply distracted. She seemed barely aware of Maggs's presence, in fact. "Did you hear? About Bury, I mean?"

"I did," Maggs said. "Such a terrible shame." He had been sincerely moved when he heard the news, actually. For all of his tussling with Bury, Maggs had actually liked the Hellion. Perhaps because they were such polar opposites. Bury had lacked any mote of guile in his small, plastinated frame. He wore his heart very much on his sleeve. It had been almost refreshing. It had also been great fun to push Bury's buttons, perhaps because it always got a reaction.

Perhaps, even in death, the child could help him. Perhaps this was a way to get the conversational ball rolling, Maggs thought.

"He'll be missed. So few of us left from the old days, eh? Lanoe certainly takes a toll on those closest to him. I wonder sometimes if it's worth it, the price we pay to stay in his orbit. Admittedly, my life has never lacked for adventure since I met him, but—"

"Maggs?" Ehta said.

"Yes?"

"Shut the hell up." Ehta grabbed her knees and pulled them up to her chin. She rocked back and forth a little, staring at absolutely nothing. "It's always talk talk talk with you, and yet you never really say anything. You know?"

Botheration, Maggs thought. *She's not in the mood for chatting.* Well, that limited the possibilities, didn't it? He reached down and put a hand on his ankle. He could feel the combat knife he'd hidden there, tucked inside his boot.

She was bigger than him. Faster and most decidedly stronger. He had one advantage, though. He was absolutely ruthless. When the time came—

"Actually, though. I'm kind of glad you're here," she told him.

"You…are?" he asked.

"I have a problem," she told him. "I'm—I'm kind of wrestling with something. With a tough decision. It'll be good to talk it out, right? Things sound different when you say them out loud sometimes. Different from how they sound in your head."

"What manner of decision?" he asked.

"It doesn't matter. It just—doesn't, okay? Let's just keep it all, you know, abstract for now. Let's say I'm thinking of…betraying somebody. That's something you know about, I guess."

She looked over at him with a wary eye. He made himself look as innocent as a little lamb.

She almost, but not quite, cracked a smile.

"I'm no good at it. My whole life I've been in the services," she said. "Following orders, obeying people, it's in my bones. How do you do it? How do you decide that maybe…maybe you need to say no, for once?"

"You do it because you think it's more important to be right than obedient," he told her. "If your cause is righteous—"

"It might save some lives. Might."

Maggs put his thumb on the pommel of the knife. This was a critical moment, he realized. This could be exactly what he'd come here for. It could also be a trap.

"You're talking about Lanoe," he said.

"I said we were going to keep it abstract," Ehta insisted. But she looked away from him. It was one of the more obvious tells he'd ever seen.

"You're saying that you think Lanoe needs to be relieved from duty. Because if he isn't, he's going to kill us all."

She said nothing.

In all of the scenarios he'd worked out in his head, in all of the different ways he thought this might play out—this had never come up.

The possibility that she might already be on his side.

Unless this was a very convoluted, very carefully laid trap. Unless Lanoe had caught a whiff of the oncoming tide of revolt, and had set Ehta to catch him—

But no. She would have to be an incredible actress to pull this off. And Maggs, who knew bosh when he smelled it, detected no bosh here.

"I can help," he told her. "Let me help."

<hr />

A blue pearl rotated in the corner of Ehta's eye.

Blue. That was weird. Blue pearls indicated an incoming signal from an automated server. Typically they were advertising messages or alert notifications. You got them mostly from civilian drones and government computers, and everybody learned to block the ones you could and ignore the rest.

Ehta started to flick her eyes to the side to dismiss this one, when she caught a glimpse of its metadata. The signal was flagged as coming from Valk.

Hellfire, she thought. The big guy had been acting more and more like a computer with each passing day, since he'd learned he was an artificial intelligence. If he was sending blue signals—instead of the green ones people used—it must mean he'd given up on being human at all.

She considered answering it, but this was hardly the time. Whatever Valk might have to say, it was going to have to wait. She'd listen to it once she'd dealt with the main problem at hand.

The problem of Lanoe.

She could hardly believe she was even considering it. Sure, she'd thought of it often enough. When he'd pointed a gun at her head. When he'd found her ready to kill Rain-on-Stones, and threatened to kill her—she'd considered spinning around, getting the drop on him, firing—

She thought maybe she could have even done it, then. In the heat of the moment. Now, though, what she was considering was cold. Ice-cold.

It meant keeping her people alive. It meant preventing what could only be called a war crime, if you broke it down. Lanoe was planning on committing genocide, and even for an old soldier like Ehta, that didn't sit well.

Betraying Lanoe meant doing the right thing, on that she was clear.

And all it was going to cost her was everything she believed in.

"Come on," she said.

Maggs's eyes went wide. Damn it, he was so hard to read sometimes. Which was the point, of course. He was rotten to the core, and the only way he stayed alive was by hiding that fact, so of course he would be good at it.

If she didn't need him, right now, if she didn't need his expertise . . .

"Come on," she said again. "We need to move. Before I change my mind."

"But where exactly are we going?" he asked, as she yanked him out of her bunk, into the corridor.

"To see Candless," she told him.

"What? Oh, no, no, I don't believe that's necessary." He laughed at the idea.

She could see why. Candless was Lanoe's right hand. If anybody was still loyal to the old bastard, it would be her. Ehta had her own reasons to not want to talk to Candless. There was nobody in the galaxy she hated more. But it wasn't going to work, otherwise. "She's the only one who can do it. Officially, I mean. She's the next highest-ranking command officer, right? She can declare him mentally incompetent. Or say he's acting contrary to his official orders. If I try it, she could have me thrown in the brig or just blow my brains out, and then we've accomplished nothing."

"I see that, but if she refuses—"

"It's got to be this way. What's our option, otherwise? It's not like we could arm my marines and take the carrier by force. That would be *mutiny*, for the devil's sake."

"I... suppose it would," Maggs said.

She pointed him down the axial corridor and shoved him along. "You know the penalty for mutiny? It's pretty simple. Execution. No questions, no lawyers. Just every one of us would get executed, the second we showed our faces back in civilization. So, yeah, we're doing this the official way. Got it?"

"I suppose," Maggs said.

They'd reached the level of the vehicle bay. Ehta pushed inside and checked out what ships were available there. There were a few BR.9s still, the ones that Valk hadn't destroyed. They were useless, since they only seated one. There was a troop transport. That would do, she guessed.

"This is the part I need you for," she told him.

"I'll do my best," he said. "But can you be more specific?"

"We need to get over to the carrier. And I can't fly. I need you to pilot that thing." She pointed at the transport.

Maggs looked like he'd been hit by lightning. Like he couldn't believe any of this was happening. She could sympathize. He recovered quickly, though, and got in the cockpit of the transport while she strapped herself into a seat in the main cabin. In a minute they were moving. Ehta fought back her usual panic attack whenever she flew in small ship, and tried to focus on what came next.

"You know Candless will take a great deal of convincing, yes?" Maggs asked, once they were clear of the cruiser.

"Yeah," Ehta told him.

"Would you like me to take the lead there? I'm rather good with words."

"No," Ehta said. "No. I know exactly what to say to her."

"You do?"

"I do," she said. "I know something that'll get Candless on my side. Don't worry."

"I'll...endeavor not to," Maggs replied.

⟡

Maggs was uncertain whether he had just received the greatest stroke of luck in his surprisingly lucky life, or whether he'd just botched things so irredeemably that they could never be recovered. As he steered the transport back to the carrier he glanced occasionally down at Ehta where she sat in the passenger compartment. The marine looked grim, though he supposed that might be her fear of flying. She'd seemed confident enough that they could get Candless on "their" side.

Remind me now, Maggsy, which side are you even on at this point?

My own, Father. My own. 'Twas ever thus.

Ehta was the ally he needed, the keystone that held up the arch of his prospective mutiny. Candless, on the other hand, was the force of gravity that could bring that arch down. She would never agree to let Bullam take command of the puny fleet. She would certainly never let Maggs have the bridge of the carrier.

Maggs's greatest hope at this point was that Candless would refuse to be swayed by whatever information Ehta brought her. That she would attempt to have Ehta arrested for even suggesting they remove Lanoe from duty.

At which point, of course, Maggs could step in and gallantly save Ehta from persecution. By the swift and final application of that oldest of dirty tricks. Namely, stabbing Candless. Repeatedly. Preferably in the back.

With Candless dead, Ehta would have to see that Bullam was the only rational choice to lead the ships home. Wouldn't she?

Maybe there was another way forward. He wasn't seeing it, but—

A green pearl spun in the corner of Maggs's eye. "Troop transport three zero niner," a voice said, "you are not scheduled to return for another six hours. What's going on, Daniels?"

It took Maggs a moment to emerge from his reverie—and to realize that the voice belonged to the carrier's traffic controller. Who seemed to think he was some chap named Daniels, presumably the last pilot of this particular ship.

He made no attempt to correct this misapprehension. "I'm bringing Major Ehta over. You know, Commander Lanoe's big marine. She asked me to."

"Okay, bring it in easy. The flight deck's damaged, and—"

"Yeah, yeah," Maggs said, affecting his best working-class accent. "I know. Setting down in ten."

He parked the transport easily near the top of the flight deck, rather close, in fact, to Bullam's yacht. As he climbed out of the cockpit he glanced over to see if he might catch a glimpse of the woman he'd pinned so many hopes upon, but she wasn't out on her dome-covered deck. He moved to help Ehta, who looked distinctly shaky as she emerged from the transport's docking hatch. She slapped away his hands, as he supposed he might have expected her to do, though not with any real vehemence.

The two of them headed inside the carrier. Ehta did a search for Candless's cryptab and announced that their quarry was in her cabin. Maggs was happy to hear it. If he'd had to cut the priggish woman's throat in the middle of the bridge, it would have felt like a scene out of some melodramatic video opera—and it would certainly have entailed silencing some witnesses as well.

This way it could be done in relative privacy.

Ehta called ahead, and by the time they'd reached the cabin, Candless was waiting for them. She looked tired and, like everyone else Maggs had seen in the last few days, deeply distracted by unpleasant thoughts. Haunted, frankly. She let them come inside, though she gave Maggs quite the look down the bridge of her long and pointed nose.

"May I ask what precisely led you to think I was interested in seeing this man again, in what remains of my life span?" she asked.

Ehta shrugged. "He's part of this," she said.

"Are you?" Candless asked, turning to face Maggs. "What role are you playing, then? Speak up."

Maggs wasn't exactly sure how to answer. "Moral support," he said, trying to pepper it with a little ironic detachment.

Candless shook her head and flapped her way over to her bed. She sat down and pulled a strap across her waist. Good. It would make it harder for her to get away when the knife came out.

"I suppose we'd better get on with it. Ehta, I know you may not understand the duties of an executive officer like myself, as you've never performed them. So I'll forgive you for not understanding that my time is actually worth something."

"Hellfire, Candless, just listen for a second—"

"Captain Candless."

Ehta's face darkened with rage. Maybe she could be goaded into killing Candless herself. Yes, that would be tidy. "Okay, Captain Candless. Maybe you'll be good enough," Ehta said, mocking the other woman's haughty tone, "to shut up for a second and hear what I've got to say, with all due respect, your ma'amship."

Maggs stroked his mustache and tried not to stare.

He'd known there was a certain animosity between Lanoe's two most trusted officers. He'd heard stories of altercations—his favorite being the time Candless had actually slapped Ehta across the face for using a profanity in front of their worshipful commander. They'd mostly kept things bordering on civil, given the need to appear professional in front of the enlisteds, but apparently the real venom had been simmering under the surface the whole time.

He was so busy enjoying the sparring match that he almost missed what came next. Which would have been—unfortunate.

"I brought Maggs because he wants to relieve Lanoe from duty," Ehta said.

"I—I do?" Maggs asked, trying to project a saintly countenance. "I thought that was rather, I mean, that is to say, your idea. In fact—"

"In fact, I think he wants to *kill* Lanoe. He's been working for some time," Ehta went on, "at inciting a mutiny. Getting the Centrocor folks to rise up against us."

Maggsy, his father warned. *Maggsy—*

Not bloody now, Pater, he told the voice in his head. *Not now!*

"Come now," Maggs sputtered. "I mean, really. Really!"

"What," Ehta asked him, "you think you're the only one who's got spies around here? Part of my duties as leader of the PBMs is shipboard security, Maggs. Did you really think I was that lousy at my job?"

He rather had. He couldn't say as much, though, not yet. Not while there was still some hope of surviving this.

Some slim hope.

"Don't," Ehta said.

"What?" he asked.

"You're reaching for a weapon. Don't. Lift your hands." Before he could even comply, she was on him, grabbing his right wrist and pulling his arm around behind his back. With her other hand she grabbed his knife.

Maggs looked across at Candless. She was breathing heavily, her nostrils flaring like the thruster cones of an overheated cataphract.

She lifted her wrist and activated the display there. No doubt to call security and have him clapped in irons.

"Not yet," Ehta said. "Don't call anybody. Don't you call a damned soul," she told Candless.

"Why on earth not?" Candless demanded.

"Because no matter what sort of underhanded snake this bastard might be," Ehta said, yanking Maggs's arm back until he grunted in pain, "he kind of has a point."

Maggs didn't put up much of a struggle. Maybe he was smarter than Ehta had thought. He went limp as she put more pressure on his arm, and didn't resist when she pushed him into a corner of the room. She shoved his knife into a loop on her belt and drew her sidearm, in case he got any ideas.

"Lanoe's changed," she said. She didn't know how else to put it.

"He's been under a great deal of stress, that's true," Candless said. Ehta couldn't read her eyes. She'd come down off her high horse a little, anyway, so that was something. "I'll admit I haven't agreed with every decision he's made recently, but what you're talking about is a very serious measure. You don't just relieve a commanding officer from duty unless you have excellent reasons. And an ironclad paper trail."

"How many of your people did he get killed? It doesn't even matter," Ehta said. "Because I know there's just one that really matters to you. Bury. He let Bury die."

Candless's mouth tightened into a nasty pucker. "The cause of Lieutenant Bury's death was enemy action."

"I watched the whole damn battle on a display," Ehta told her. "Yeah. One of those interceptors got him. I noticed, though, at the time Lanoe was busy finishing off the dreadnought. Instead of leading his people. He let Bury lead the fighters out there. Bury, who'd never commanded so much as a floor-mopping detail before in his life. He didn't care if Bury died, only if—"

"That," Candless interrupted, "is more than enough, Major. I won't listen to this kind of insubordination."

"Even if you know I'm right? Or *because* you know I'm right?"

"Ladies," Maggs said, his hands up in conciliation.

"Quiet," Candless shot at him. Ehta just pointed her sidearm at him.

He didn't say another word.

Ehta shook her head. "Lanoe's going to get every one of us killed. Including himself. And he doesn't care. As long as he gets to butcher some more jellyfish before he goes down, he's perfectly willing to take the rest of us with him. He's using us, Candless. He's—"

"Shut your mouth!" Candless roared.

Ehta wasn't going to stop now, though. "He's using us. Just like he's using Ginger. You seen her lately? You seen what she looks like now?"

Candless flew at her, then, literally jumping across the room to grab Ehta by the collar ring. She pulled Ehta in close until their faces were just centimeters from each other. For a while they just stared each other down, their eyes locked together in a standing wave of hatred.

"You think," Candless said, the words like bullets spitting out of her mouth, "that you can get to me by bringing up my former students. You think I can be swayed if you point out how I've failed them. Well, you're wrong. You haven't won me over, Major. In fact, if anything, you've just demonstrated why I should relieve *you* from duty. Why I should have you court-martialed. I think you may be a bigger threat to Lanoe's command than that traitor over there."

"I beg your pardon," Maggs said.

Ehta and Candless both turned to stare at him.

"Oh, very well. I know when I've been rumbled," he said weakly.

Ehta looked back at Candless. "You know Lanoe has to be stopped," she said.

"I know no such thing. And unless you have something else to say, I believe we've exhausted this conversation," Candless told her. She didn't let go of Ehta's collar ring, though.

"I have one more piece of evidence," Ehta said. She guessed it was time. Even if she didn't really want to say it out loud. Because that would make it real.

"Lanoe threatened to kill me if I told you this," she said. "I guess he thought it would hurt morale." She took a deep breath.

It looked like she had Candless's attention.

"There's no way home," she said. "Ginger told me. Rain-on-Stones can't open a wormhole to get us back. Not on her own—one chorister could never do that by herself. Lanoe doesn't care. He got so caught up in his revenge fantasy, he stopped caring about what happens after he gets it."

"I don't understand," Candless said.

"It's true. We're all stranded here. *Lanoe* stranded us here. I told you before—he's willing to let every one of us die, so he gets a shot at avenging Zhang. The woman he loved. Hell, it's not even a question of *letting* us die. All of us going out in a blaze of glory has been his plan this whole time."

It was Maggs who responded first. The little bastard let out a cry of surprise. A cry of utter despair. "What?" he demanded. "What are you...what are you saying?"

He'd heard her. Ehta felt no need to repeat herself.

Candless had heard her, too. She could see it in the other woman's eyes. She'd heard it, and she knew it was true.

"I...suppose," Candless said, "given this new information—hellfire!"

She was looking at something over Ehta's shoulder. The marine swiveled her head around, trying to see, even as Candless released her collar ring.

"The traitor is getting away!" Candless shrieked.

It was true. The hatch of the cabin was wide open—and Maggs was nowhere to be seen.

There was, of course, a chase. He could hear Ehta throwing herself down the corridors of the carrier, bellowing his name. No doubt brandishing that hand cannon of a sidearm, ready to shoot him down like a dog if she caught him.

Do me a favor and don't let her, his father's voice requested. *I've made rather a cozy little domicile for myself in this skull, and I'd rather it wasn't blown to flinders.*

Maggs's career in charlatanry wouldn't have lasted very long if he didn't know how to leg it when the time came. He'd been aboard the carrier long enough to know all its little secret ways, its secluded maintenance hatches and its more private airlocks. He had to take a rather circuitous route, but soon enough he found his way to Bullam's yacht. The dome admitted him easily. He pressed himself through the flowglas as if he were moving through thick jelly, and came out on the other side already moving. He shot over to the controls and released the ship from its docking berth.

Ehta had known about the mutiny. How she'd figured it out was a mystery, but it didn't matter, truly. What mattered was whether or not she had taken precautions against Bullam making a quick escape.

He had a bad moment as he waited for clearance to launch from the traffic controller. When it didn't come immediately, he pointed the yacht at the open end of the flight deck and stomped on the throttle. The yacht surged forward, out into space.

It was only then that he heard a grunting moan and realized he wasn't alone on the deck.

Bullam lay on her couch, one strap fastened incorrectly across her waist. Her body flopped over to one side as the yacht accelerated and her face rolled toward him.

"We've been made," he told her. He chewed on his mustache. "They knew—how long they've known, I'm not sure, but—Ehta knew. We're in terrible danger, I'm afraid."

Bullam's mouth moved but he couldn't hear what she said. Maybe he was too distracted by the pounding of his much-aggrieved heart.

"There's worse news, I'm afraid. It turns out the bloody chorister can't open a wormhole. She never could, in fact. If we'd known that, I imagine we could have started our mutiny much earlier. As it is, I can't currently see the point."

He steered a course at random, simply trying to put as much distance between himself and Major Bloody Ehta of the Poor Bloody Marines as he could get. When the trajectory was locked in, he turned to look at Bullam directly.

"We need to call it off. The uprising, I mean. It's hopeless—we'll simply get our people killed if they try something now. As it is, they'll be arrested, and—"

"Already," Bullam said. She frowned. Her face grew lined with concentration. "Done," she said.

"What?" Maggs couldn't believe it. He glanced down at his wrist display, though, and saw it flashing at him. Three flashes, then a pause. Then three more. "You already sent the signal? But why? You said—you said I would pick the time. You entrusted me with that duty."

"Don't," Bullam said, "trust."

For the first time Maggs noticed there was something wrong with her.

Her drones were clustered around her, bobbing up and down around the divan like a pack of worried dogs attending to their mistress. One of them had a flexible tube extruded from its faceplate, its far end buried in the crook of her arm. Another was near her head, massaging her scalp with what looked like an ultrasound wand.

"Oh, no," he said. "No. You—you had a clot. A blood clot." He tried to remember what she'd said about her disease. That made him recall that the last time they'd spoken, she'd mentioned having a headache.

"Ischemic," she said. She swallowed thickly, tried again. "Ischemic. An ischemic." She groaned in frustration.

"A stroke," he whispered.

"Drones are helping," she said. Her eyes were shining with fear. "Helping. As much as they can. Need. Need a treatment."

Maggs could guess what she was trying to tell him. The blood clot had occluded a blood vessel in her brain. The drones were stabilizing her for the moment, but some damage had already been done. She needed some sort of medical intervention or the damage would spread.

The kind of treatment you could only get from a hospital back on some civilized world. Some world ten thousand light-years away.

"Oh, damn," Maggs said.

Chapter Twenty-Four

Candless slapped a release panel and the hatch before her slid open. She looked through into the carrier's brig. A short corridor lined with three hatches on either side, each with a display mounted on its face. She triggered each one in turn as she floated past, making sure they were empty.

The last place a man like Maggs was likely to run to ground was a prison cell, she knew. She was, however, completely out of other ideas. She called Ehta, who was on the other side of the ship, doing the same thing she was. Chasing after a wild goose. "I've had no luck," she said. "Please tell me you've got him in a choke hold right now."

"Sorry," Ehta replied. "But I think I know where he's gone. I'm on the bridge right now, looking at a tactical board. That Centrocor woman's yacht took off a few minutes ago. The traffic controller didn't have any reason to stop it, so he just let it go. You want to grab a fighter, go chase after him?"

Candless scowled into one of the empty cells. "No," she said. "We have bigger problems to solve just now."

"You mean Lanoe," Ehta said.

"Among other things. I still think we need to do this the right way, Major. We need to prove he's of unsound mind. If we had a flight surgeon, that would be good, but we don't. By protocol it can be anyone with medical experience. I'll take a marine field medic, if that's what we can get."

"Rain-on-Stones was supposed to be a surgeon. Before Lanoe kidnapped her."

"That isn't helpful," Candless said. "We need a doctor—a human doctor—to examine Lanoe and establish that he's unfit for command. That means a psychological evaluation. One which I imagine," she said with a sigh, "he's unlikely to pass."

"So you've accepted that he's gone crazy," Ehta said.

Candless closed her eyes and tried to think things through carefully. "I'd like proof. So that when you and I go before our respective courts-martial, we have something to justify our actions. But yes, you're correct. He needs to be relieved. I don't suppose you'd like to be the one who formally arrests him? Shipboard policing is traditionally a duty of the PBMs."

"Tell you what," Ehta said. "I'll trade you. You arrest Lanoe. I'll get my people over here to round up Maggs's people. The would-be mutineers."

Candless put one hand against a wall to stop herself from bashing into it. It helped, a little, to be stationary. To not feel like everything she'd ever believed in, everything she'd ever fought for, was being turned upside down.

A blue pearl appeared in the corner of her vision. Even with her eyes closed she could see it rotating there. Annoyed, she flicked it away without a thought. "How quickly can you apprehend them? If you strike quickly enough, maybe we can get them before they hurt anyone. Or themselves."

"You understand that my people aren't trained in taking captives, right?" Ehta asked. "This is going to be messy."

Candless shook her head. "I'm ordering you to minimize that. These people may wish to betray us. If we catch them before they have the chance to do so, they're only guilty of conspiracy. And I don't consider that a capital crime."

There'd been enough killing already. Enough death. She opened her eyes and looked around at the cells. Between the six here and the two on the cruiser, they could hold at least twenty-four muti-neers. If there were more, well, they would simply have to find some other compartment with a door that could be locked and—

She whirled around. She was certain she'd heard something. A sharp report, like a door being slammed with some force.

Or perhaps a gunshot.

"Ehta," she called, "you said you're on the bridge? Can you bring up a security display? I have just had what, for the moment, we're going to call a flash of pessimistic intuition."

"You mean—a bad feeling," Ehta called back. "Okay, display's open. What am I looking for?"

"The sonic profile of a pistol being fired," Candless replied. "Or perhaps a chemical record of a gunpowder discharge. I don't think it sounded like a particle beam—"

She stopped because she'd heard a bloodcurdling scream.

"Ehta," she whispered.

"Yeah. Hellfire, yeah. I don't need any fancy sensors. I've got camera feed of the pilots' wardroom. There's blood on the wall in there. People jumping around with weapons in their hands. This thing is already kicking off."

"Get your marines over here right now," Candless said. "No, wait, have them secure the cruiser first. I wouldn't put it past Maggs to attack the carrier purely as a feint, so he can take the cruiser and turn its guns on us. We need to move *fast*."

Ehta released a profanity Candless hadn't heard since she was a child.

"What?" she demanded. "What is it?"

"The troop transport," Ehta replied. "It's here. It's on the carrier! I didn't expect things to start this soon. Damnation—I had Maggs fly me over here in it. The cutter's in the flight deck as well. Candless, there's no ship bigger than a BR.9 over on the cruiser right now."

"Which means what, exactly?"

"There's no way to get my marines over here. They're stuck on the cruiser."

And therefore Candless and Ehta were stuck on the carrier. With a horde of mutineers coming to slash their throats.

※

A blue pearl rotated in the corner of Lanoe's vision.

He flicked it away with his eyes. He did not want to be disturbed. Not now.

Not when he was communing with the ghost.

He had the lights turned down in his cabin. He'd switched off the air circulators, so he could hear her better. She was so close now. So close to him, and yet the slightest thing would send her flying away.

He floated in the middle of the room with his legs crossed. With his hands on his knees. He kept his eyelids mostly closed, to limit what he could see. To limit distractions. He breathed slowly, through his mouth.

"Zhang," he whispered. "We need to talk."

The blue pearl appeared again. Damned automated messages—he flicked this one away, too, thinking that as soon as he had a chance he would change his preferences to block them all immediately. But first—he was so close.

"Zhang. We need to—"

Yet again the blue pearl appeared. He started to flick it away, thinking there must be some virus in the carrier's systems. Maybe some old advertising software left behind by Centrocor. It couldn't have activated at a worse time. He turned his eyes to look at it, to check its metadata, and that was when he saw who had sent it.

Valk.

Lanoe scowled. He'd been trying...an experiment. Twice now, he'd hallucinated Zhang's voice. He knew that couldn't be good. He'd thought if he could put himself in the right frame of mind, maybe he could figure out why she was haunting him—and make her stop. Finding the right frame of mind was the hard part. Lanoe had never been very good at introspection. The last thing he needed right now was to talk to the needy AI. Clearly, though, Valk wasn't going to stop trying. Angrily Lanoe flicked his eyes to answer the call.

"I figured it out, Lanoe," the AI said. "I saw where I went wrong. I've been trying to reach somebody, anybody. Nobody's taking my calls, but they need to. They need to hear this! Especially you. Listen, I know why you shut me out, but—"

"This isn't the time," Lanoe told the machine. "I thought I made myself clear. I can't trust you anymore, Valk. You've grown unstable."

"Damn you, Lanoe, that's exactly it. I *haven't*."

Lanoe sighed and pinched the bridge of his nose. "What are you talking about?" he asked, knowing he would regret it.

"I assumed you were right. That there was something wrong with me. I went back and checked everything—everything I've done since we got here. You were upset for two reasons. The first one was that I couldn't get an exact fix on our location in the galaxy."

"That should have been child's play for you," Lanoe said.

"I know! And the second problem—that I couldn't understand what the Blue-Blue-White were saying—"

"I really needed you to be able to do that."

"I...I know, and I'm sorry, but...it wasn't my fault," Valk insisted. "Lanoe, just listen to me for a moment, all right? I looked at those two failures. I looked at them from every angle. When I couldn't find a single bad line of code or a checksum that didn't add up, I thought maybe my hardware had gone bad. I checked a million other things, literally a million other things, before I thought to ask the right question. What if I was working fine, but the rest of the universe had a fault?"

"That's absurd."

"It should be. And I guess—look, the universe is working just fine, it's just not the universe we expected."

Lanoe opened his eyes. This was a fresh problem. Valk, apparently, had lost his mind.

"Valk," he said carefully, "I'm going to cut this link. I don't want you to call me again. Do you understand?"

"Lanoe—you have to hear this. I'm sorry, I know you're busy, but you do. I'll make it as simple as I can. I couldn't fix our position because the standard candles had all moved. It would take five hundred million years for them to move to their current position. I couldn't understand the Blue-Blue-White because my language files are half a billion years out of date."

Lanoe opened up his wrist minder, intending to disable all of his comms.

"We traveled ten thousand light-years through space to get here, yeah? But we went a lot farther than that. We traveled through *time*, too."

Lanoe stopped with his finger hovering over a virtual key. Press it, and Valk would go away. He could get back to trying to summon up Zhang's ghost.

Something made him hesitate, though.

"Time travel is impossible," he said.

"I'm sorry, but, no, you're wrong. When you start playing around with wormholes—it's trivial. A wormhole can go anywhere in spacetime. It's actually very tricky to make a wormhole where both ends are in the same timeframe. It's all there in the equations, I'm sure you don't want a mathematics lecture right now—"

"You're right, I don't," Lanoe said.

"—so just trust your living computer, okay? The numbers work out. Ask Paniet to check my work, get Candless to grill me. I'm absolutely certain about this, Lanoe. The Choir sent us back in time. They sent us half a billion years back in time."

"Half a billion years. The Blue-Blue-White sent out their first drone fleet half a billion years ago."

"It can't be a coincidence. The Choir sent you exactly where you wanted to go. To the one place where you could stop the drone fleets and save all those aliens. They brought you here because it's where you need to be."

"Half a billion years," Lanoe said, to himself. Just trying out the words in his mouth. It didn't make any sense. It couldn't, possibly. No human had ever traveled in time, it had always been assumed to be one of those things that was never going to happen, a problem technology would never be able to solve.

If you could travel in time you could mess up all kinds of physical laws. You could change history, you could be your own grandfather. You could do anything. You could—

You could go back in time and stop something from happening. You could change a course of events so it had a different outcome.

If your lover died, if the only person you'd ever loved died right in front of you, you could go back in time and make sure she lived instead.

You could bring the dead back to life.

"Do you see what this means, Lanoe?"

"I...I think I do," he said. "We can change things, Valk. We can change things. If we stop the Blue-Blue-White now, nothing they did will have happened. Nothing."

"What? No, Lanoe, we can't even think about doing that. We can't change anything. It'd be too dangerous. No, what I meant was—this means I was right all along. I wasn't broken. I'm not broken. I can still be of use to you."

Lanoe heard the urgency in Valk's voice, the pleading, but he was too lost in thought, in planning, to soothe the AI now. "You've already helped me," he said, the best he could manage. "We can change things."

"Lanoe, seriously, that's a bad idea. Maybe we can do something. I don't know—I doubt it. We need to sit down, all of us, and figure out what this means," Valk said. "How it affects our mission and what we need to do now."

"Sure," Lanoe said. "Sure, we'll do that."

He cut the link. He needed to be alone with his thoughts now.

Alone with the ghost.

"Zhang," he said. His voice was thick with potential emotion. He cleared his throat, tried again. "Zhang. It's...it's possible. Maybe. Maybe I can—"

His head swam and he turned around again, this time to face

the hatch of his cabin. There was something going on there. He'd heard something.

Someone was pounding on his hatch. He realized with a start that they'd been doing it for a while, that he'd heard it without hearing it. He felt a strange rush of guilt, as if he'd been caught abandoning his post. He pushed over to the hatch and hit the release before he'd even figured out who it was.

"Maggs," he said. "What the devil are you doing here?"

"Oh, you know, the same as always," the bastard said. He shoved his way into the cabin and closed the hatch behind him. Lanoe was too surprised to stop him. "Saving your life."

Candless came around a corner and saw a hand flying toward her face, fingers stretched out like claws. She yanked herself backward, her heart pounding in her chest—only to feel like a fool a moment later as she realized she'd been startled by a dead body. It floated past her down the hall, bumping off the walls. She got a new shock when she realized it was the yeoman, the poor officer whom she'd made an example of when she first took control of the carrier.

Had she remained loyal until the very end? Had she been murdered by the Centrocor contingent? It was hard to know. There were outbreaks of fighting all over the ship, and on the small video display on Candless's wrist it was hard to tell who belonged to which side. Loyalists and mutineers looked exactly alike—though somehow they were able to tell each other apart well enough to murder each other.

Candless was alone and very afraid. She couldn't get hold of Ehta—for all she knew, the marine major was dead. She had just a few resources she could still count on. Most important was that she still had access to the ship's systems. Her rank let her tap into any camera feed in the ship. As she moved through the corridors she could just about know what was waiting for her behind every hatch.

Of course, the body of the dead yeoman proved those feeds didn't see everything. Candless had believed this corridor would be completely empty.

She could tell it wouldn't be for long. She could hear shouts and the occasional gurgling scream coming from its far end. A band of fighters was headed her way. They might be coming to rescue her. They might be coming to tear her to pieces. She couldn't take the risk.

She ducked through another hatch, this one leading to the storage areas of the carrier. She took a moment to seal the hatch behind her—another perk of rank, she could issue an emergency lockdown. Unfortunately, from her wrist minder she could do it for only one hatch at a time. If she could reach the bridge, she could lock every hatch in the ship. That would, at the very least, slow the mutineers down, as they would have to use cutting instruments or dismantlers to make their way from compartment to compartment.

The bridge was still very far away, though. And she knew she would never make it alone.

She tried to remember the layout of the ship. The storage area—the quartermaster's office. Yes. The carrier's arsenal was there, too. Most likely the place would have been emptied out—Centrocor's marines would have armed themselves as soon as the mutiny began. Perhaps, though, they'd left behind at least a rifle, or some more ammunition for Candless's sidearm. Maybe the quartermaster would be a loyalist.

It was something. It was a step forward.

Candless hurried through the low storage rooms, hiding inside a compartment full of food stocks when she thought she heard someone out in the corridor. When she reached the quartermaster's office she found it deserted, a single display up and running above the console. It showed a list of the ship's personnel, and someone had gone through it, highlighting most of the names in either red or blue. Candless found her own name in blue, so she assumed that the red names were known mutineers. The loyalty status of the vast majority of the names had yet to be determined.

"Ma'am?" someone said.

Candless whirled around, her pistol up and pointed into a dark corner of the compartment. Someone was back there, hiding behind a precarious stack of crates.

"Who's there?" Candless demanded.

"Just me, ma'am." A pair of empty hands appeared from behind the crates. The quartermaster slowly poked her scarred face out. She looked terrified.

Candless let herself breathe for a moment. She lowered her weapon, though she didn't put it away. "Come out of there. Are you hurt?"

"I'm . . . not sure. Could you—could you help me?"

"Help you? How? What's wrong?"

"I think I might have been shot," the woman said.

Candless couldn't see any blood, but if the quartermaster needed medical attention she had to help. She kicked away from the workstation and headed toward the crates. She never got there.

Two men burst out from a storage locker, heavy rifles cradled in their arms. One of them tossed his away and grabbed Candless across her chest, pinning her. She fought and kicked, but in the absence of gravity it was impossible to get any leverage. The man holding her put one arm around her neck and started putting pressure on her windpipe.

Candless's vision started to shrink down to a narrow tunnel. She could hear her heart thudding in her chest, could feel herself slipping away—

"Don't kill her! Not yet," the quartermaster shouted. She emerged—unhurt, of course—from her hiding place, waving her hands. "The bridge controls are locked, and we need her to break the encryption. Then we can kill her, okay? Somebody call Maggs. Tell him we have her."

Some of the pressure came off of Candless's throat. Her vision cleared and she rolled her eyes wildly, trying to see if there was some clever way out of this.

If there was, she couldn't see it. The quartermaster came over and fastened a strip of plastic around Candless's wrists. She pulled the strip tight—too tight. Candless could feel her hands losing their circulation. The quartermaster moved to put another strip around her ankles. Candless kicked her in the neck, sending her flying.

One of the men smashed his rifle butt across Candless's cheek. Her vision exploded with sparks and she cried out in pain.

The quartermaster tied her ankles together. Someone shoved a piece of cloth into her mouth.

No, she thought. *No. No, this can't be happening.*

"If she gives you any more trouble, start cutting her fingers off. That should take the fight out of her," the quartermaster said.

Candless's eyes went wide.

The compartment's hatch opened, and she saw a dark shape hovering there. Her captors looked up in surprise and terror, but then an expression of pure relief crossed the quartermaster's ruined face. "Captain," she said. "It's good to see you, sir."

Captain? Was she talking to Candless? But then, why—

Oh.

Shulkin came into the room, his face brighter and more animated than Candless had ever seen it before. A sheen of sweat made his brow and cheeks glow, and his eyes were on fire. He was breathing heavily, his chest moving up and down rapidly. He had a heavy particle rifle in one hand and a combat knife in the other.

"We have her, sir, all bundled up for you. You came so fast—I'm sorry we haven't had chance to interrogate her yet," the quartermaster said. "When we called M. Maggs we assumed it would take longer before someone came to get her."

Shulkin came closer. He was smiling. Not even the brutal baring of fangs, not the shark smile Candless might have expected. He looked genuinely happy.

"Uh, ma'am?" One of the two men holding Candless said.

"What?" the quartermaster asked.

"We, uh, we haven't had a chance to call M. Maggs yet," the man confided.

"What? Then—"

The quartermaster didn't get a chance to finish her thought. As Shulkin came still closer, Candless didn't so much see the blood all over him as smell it.

He moved with incredible speed. The combat knife flew out of his hand as if he was casually tossing it away. Somehow it ended up embedded in the quartermaster's neck, opening one of her jugular veins. Particle fire erupted from Shulkin's rifle before the men could react. A beam passed within centimeters of Candless's ear and she tried to shriek, only to nearly choke on the rag in her mouth. She felt something hot and wet pelt the back of her hair and splatter her neck. She turned to look and saw that the man behind her no longer had a head.

The second one at least got a chance to move. He roared and came at Shulkin like a bull, knocking the rifle out of Shulkin's hands. The old captain laughed as the mutineer shoved him backward until they collided with a bulkhead with a meaty thud. The mutineer tried to punch him in the jaw.

Shulkin made no attempt to block it. He took the hit square on the boniest part of his face, his head snapping back, his mouth closing with a click of teeth smashing together. He didn't grunt in pain or react to the blow at all. He was far too busy to defend himself— busy with jamming his thumbs into the man's eye sockets.

The mutineer screamed in agony. Shulkin kicked him away. Then he lunged toward the quartermaster's body and pulled his knife free, blood jetting out of the wound. He turned and grabbed the surviving mutineer by the back of his ring collar. With one easy, precise motion he slit the man's throat.

He shoved the corpse away from himself, the man's blood trailing out behind him to hang in the air like a red campaign banner fluttering from a flagpole.

For a moment after that, Shulkin just hung there in midair, his limbs slack, his face contorted by an enormous grin.

Then he spun around and came toward Candless. He cut the ties around her wrists and ankles. She pulled the rag out of her mouth on her own. Her hands throbbed with pain as the blood rushed back toward her fingertips.

"You—you saved me," she said. All she could think was that this was the man she'd once shot in the leg to get him to clear her bridge. She made a point of not reminding him of that moment.

"My ship," he said. "My ship."

"They thought you were one of them," Candless said. "A loyal Centrocor employee." It made sense. Who stood to gain more from a mutiny than the captain who had been suborned? The man who had been in charge, before Lanoe came along. Yet clearly Shulkin didn't see it that way.

"I would have signed up with the devil's own poly if it meant getting another command," he said. "I was never a Centrocor man. I always belonged to the Navy. The Navy forgot that, not me."

Lanoe's hands balled into fists. What Valk had told him, the mind-shattering revelation, was all but forgotten as an older, much more primal thought welled up inside him. The knowledge of just how badly he wanted to kill Auster Maggs. "Explain yourself," he told Maggs.

Maggs looked genuinely hurt. Well, the bastard could act, Lanoe had known that almost since he'd first met him. "If our positions were reversed, if you'd had to walk in my regulation boots, you might have done all the things I did." He raised his hands for peace. "Never mind. I know you'll never see that. I don't think you can."

"You still haven't told me—"

"I don't have time for lengthy explanations full of nuance. I'll get right to it."

For once, Lanoe thought.

"I have some information you need. Without it, you'll die. In exchange, I want something you have. Simple, yes? Very simple. I need you to send me home."

Lanoe realized he'd been holding a breath in his chest. His

whole body was tense, ready to pounce on the traitor. Now he let that breath out, slowly. Tried to relax, to at least hold himself back until he'd heard more details. "When we're finished with our mission here, when the Blue-Blue-White have been punished, Rain-on-Stones will open a wormhole that will take us back. Not before."

"You can stop playing that tune," Maggs said. "I know the truth. I heard it with my very own ears, from our dear major of the marines."

"She told you—what, exactly?" Lanoe asked.

"That Rain-on-Stones can't open said wormhole. That it simply can't be done." Maggs raised his eyebrows. His eyes searched Lanoe's face, as if looking for a denial.

The time for lies was over, apparently. If Ehta had chosen to tell everyone, there wasn't much Lanoe could do to put the cat back in the bag. He shrugged.

Maggs nodded, just once. His sneering smile faded, but only a bit. "Came as bit of a shock, I assure you. Then I remembered something."

"Oh?"

"You're not a fool. Lanoe, you and I have had our differences, but I've always respected your intellect. I know for a fact you would never have come here without a way home. If it isn't the chorister who'll provide that, well, there must be some other way. You must have had some reason to keep it secret—never mind, I won't even ask. It doesn't matter to me. I need to go home, and I need to go now."

"Why are you in such a hurry?"

Maggs turned his face away. "It's none of your business. But I suppose—if it speeds things along, well. M. Bullam has had a bit of a medical emergency. She desperately needs help. Proper help, in a proper hospital. We need to get her there as soon as possible, and you're the only one who knows how."

Lanoe narrowed his eyes. "Interesting. You have a heart after all."

"I always did. You just never let me show it," Maggs told him.

"All right. I'll tell you what I have. You first, though. Tell me this piece of information that's going to save my life."

Maggs gave him a long, shrewd look. Clearly he wanted Lanoe to divulge his secret first, but just as clearly, he was desperate.

"Mutiny," Maggs said. "There's a mutiny happening, even now. There's a horde of people coming for your head. And even if you somehow managed to fight them all off, Candless and Ehta have joined forces against you. They're planning to relieve you from duty, just as soon as they regain command of this ship."

"What? That's—that's impossible," Lanoe said.

"Is it? You've managed to alienate everyone, Lanoe. Every single person under your command. I was just the first of your faithful retainers to turn on you. You've made a very nasty bed, and they want you to lie in it. However—and here, you'll see just what a friend you have in Auster Maggs—I can help. I have the cutter warmed up and ready to go. It's right outside airlock sixteen, not a hundred meters away from this cabin. I've made sure the mutineers are well clear of the route you'll need to take to get there."

"You did all that? For me?"

"In exchange for what I need, yes. You can take the cutter wherever you like. You've lost your fleet, Commander. You can still save your life."

Lanoe started to push past him, toward the hatch. If this was true, if it was all as Maggs had said—

"Not so fast," Maggs said. "You promised me a secret in return."

"Right." Lanoe nodded. He reached out and grabbed a nylon loop mounted on the wall, to give himself leverage. Then he spun around and slammed his fist right into Maggs's abdomen. The air exploded from the traitor's lungs and he doubled up. Before he could recover, Lanoe grabbed his head and slammed his face against the bulkhead.

"There is no way back," he said.

Maggs could barely breathe, couldn't speak. He could still look up at Lanoe from surprised and terrified eyes.

"When we came here, from the city of the Choir—I asked them for a wormhole. I asked them to send us somewhere, anywhere, to get away. It was the only way to save my ship and my crew. I had no idea they were sending us here," Lanoe explained. "I didn't expect it. When I saw where we'd come to, I was glad. I knew they'd sent me where I needed to be. I was sorry for you, for everyone else—none of you asked for this, and that was a tragedy. But I understood. There are always casualties in war, and sometimes you lose friends. Sometimes, you have to make sacrifices."

He grabbed Maggs by the collar ring and shoved him across the cabin, toward the far wall.

"There is no way back," he said again. "We came here to do a job, and that's all that matters."

Then he hit the release for his hatch and kicked his way out into the corridor.

Airlock sixteen wasn't far. He knew the route. Things had reached a point of no return. If even Candless had turned on him, his time commanding the fleet was done. So be it.

He still had Plan C. And if Valk was right, if they really had traveled back in time—Plan C could change everything.

***

The bridge was a lost cause. On Candless's wrist display, she could see the mutineers running amok in there. One of them smashed a control console in thwarted rage, hitting it over and over again with a long wrench. They had the carrier's pilot up against one wall, and as far as she could tell they were using him for target practice—he was already long past feeling the particle beams they blasted into his chest and limbs. "The two of us are never going to get in there," she told Shulkin.

"We could die trying," he suggested.

She studied his face. He seemed to think that was a rational suggestion. As if it were more important that they keep fighting than that they actually accomplish anything.

Candless supposed she shouldn't have expected anything different. "I'd like to try something more practical. Ehta's marines are over on the cruiser—they've been working as gun crews this whole time, but they're competent enough at this kind of fighting, too."

"I remember," Shulkin said. "I remember them taking my bridge."

Candless bit her lip. She had no idea how far she could trust this new ally. She hoped very much that she wouldn't have to test him to the limit. "If we can just get them over here, they can stop this mutiny," she said.

"By killing everyone," Shulkin said. He nodded in approval.

"One way or another," Candless said. She was not so naïve as to think that the marines would simply round up the mutineers and march them to the brig. Not now—the rebellion had gone too far. She would do what she could to keep the death toll low, however. "I'd like to believe that if they just see a show of force—if they know they can't win—Centrocor's people will stand down. The problem is there's currently no good way to get our marines over here. I'll need to get to the troop transport, which is docked in the flight deck. I can fly over to the cruiser and bring them back."

"Very good," Shulkin said. "Let's go."

Just like that.

Of course, it couldn't be simple. The two of them were holed up in a disused section of bunks near the engines. Bunks that belonged to pilots who had died during battles with the Blue-Blue-White. There was a long corridor between them and any entrance to the flight deck, a corridor that Candless's wrist display showed her as being full of heavily armed people.

She was certain they were not loyalists. What she'd seen on her display made her think there weren't very many people left who would help her. Moreover, she was a veteran of too many battles to think that two people, no matter how well trained, no matter how vicious and bloody-minded, could fight their way through a crowd.

There was another way. Shulkin didn't like it. He wanted to fight. Candless tried to reassure him. "When I bring the marines back, you can join them for the mopping up."

It seemed to mollify him a little.

The two of them hurried back through the engine section of the carrier—it was, thankfully, deserted—and out through the maintenance airlock by the thrusters. The same lock Lanoe had used when he boarded the carrier. Candless intended to move across the outer hull of the carrier, all the way up to the front of the ship. From there they could climb inside the flight deck, hopefully unseen and unopposed.

As they picked their way carefully around the massive thruster cones, still glowing with heat even though they'd been shut down for hours, Candless tried to put through call after call, trying to raise Ehta, trying to reach Paniet, even once trying to get hold of Lanoe. She still intended to relieve him of duty, but only after she'd restored some level of order to the carrier.

None of her calls were answered. Each one, in turn, returned an error message telling her that the people she'd tried to reach were blocking incoming transmissions. She didn't know whether that meant they were simply busy surviving the mutiny or if they were already dead.

Chances were it was just her and Shulkin. *Hellfire,* she thought. Even if she won—how was she going to command a ship with no crew?

And what did she even hope to accomplish now? She could end Lanoe's pointless war against the Blue-Blue-White. But then what? There was no way to open a wormhole home. Was she going to die here, anyway, so far from anything she knew—not because of murderous aliens, but because eventually they would starve to death?

She couldn't let herself think about that. She moved quickly, jumping from handhold to handhold as she came around the mammoth curve of the carrier's hull. Eventually they reached the side of the cylindrical hull and she reached down and switched on the adhesive pads on the bottom of her boots. There was no up and down in space, but when she stood on the hull, looking forward toward the open end of the flight deck, she felt like an insect standing on the trunk of a massive tree.

The dark hull curved away from her to either side, ran straight as far ahead as she could see. A terrain broken into thousands of sections of armor plates, carbon fiber cladding electroset over scandium alloy. Ahead of her, maybe seventy-five meters away, one of the carrier's running lights blinked a dull green. It looked like a pool of radiance, an oasis of light in a dark desert.

She shuffled forward, one step at a time, making sure to keep at least one foot always on the hull. Place her left foot, lift the right. Place the right, lift the left. It was an exhausting way to walk, and soon her legs were so tired they felt like hot bars of lead. Her wrists chafed against the inside of her suit where they'd been tied with the plastic strip. She could hear nothing but her own breathing and Shulkin grunting along behind her.

The whole time all she could think was that if a single mutineer poked his head out of an airlock, a maintenance hatch, so much as looked out a window—they were dead. They were exposed out there. Sitting ducks.

It felt like hours before she saw what she was looking for, up ahead. One of the three cupolas that protruded from the open maw of the flight deck. The thick carbonglas glinted in the starlight. She allowed herself to breathe a sigh of relief. She started to turn, to look back at Shulkin, to just make sure he was still there. He hadn't said a word during the whole ascent.

Just before she turned her head, though, she could have sworn she saw something. A flicker of motion.

It was most likely nothing, she promised herself. It was almost certainly—

Damnation. She'd seen it again. Just a hint of motion, behind the transparent panels of the cupola. She used her wrist display to get a magnified view, but saw nothing—no silhouettes, no dark figures crouching there.

Which just made it worse.

Someone was in there. Someone had seen them, and ducked out of view to try to hide from them.

"Shulkin," she said. "I think we may be in trouble."

"Define trouble," he said.

She didn't need to. Dark shapes flickered around the open end of the flight deck. People in suits came rushing over the edge, some taking a second to adjust the pads on their boots, some just flying toward her using their suit jets.

All of them were armed.

Lanoe touched the cutter's control stick, banking to come around the side of the cruiser.

Maggs had told him to flee. To run away before the mutineers or his own officers could catch up with him. Maybe the bastard thought he was just going to fly off into the sunset—fly until he ran out of fuel, until he died out there in the void.

He couldn't realize that he'd simply given Lanoe the justification to do a terrible thing. By taking away all of Lanoe's options, Maggs had pushed him toward what he'd always known was inevitable. To finish what he'd started.

And, by so doing, make everything okay again.

Okay.

What he had in mind wasn't simple. The devil knew it wouldn't be easy. But it was possible. And that meant it had to be done.

It was a terrible thing he considered. It was a crime, he knew that. He understood that it was the wrong thing to do. But to bring Zhang back, to make her live again. All he had to do was keep his promise of revenge.

He frowned as he approached the cruiser's vehicle bay. He had no idea what he would find inside. A horde of mutineers clamoring for his blood? Ehta's marines, lined up in perfect formation, ready to beat him senseless and throw him in the brig?

Yet as he got closer he saw that the vehicle bay was empty. No ships at all in there. That didn't make sense. There should be—

He brought the cutter in. Made contact with a docking berth, its skeletal arms folding around the cutter's landing gear. Holding it down. He opened the hatch and slid out, his sidearm in his hand.

There was no one there to challenge him.

He moved through the cruiser quickly, not knowing how much time he had. Every time he opened a hatch or moved into a new corridor he braced himself for shouts, for questions, for particle beams to come sizzling past his face. Instead—

Silence. Emptiness. The cruiser was deserted.

When he reached the brig he found it just as abandoned as the rest of the ship. The hatch to Rain-on-Stones's cell was inert, its display blank. He half expected that when he touched the display it would set off an alarm. That this was all an elaborate trap.

If he was honest with himself, he'd hoped that would happen.

It didn't.

The hatch opened and inside the two of them looked up at the same time, their movements as synchronized as their thoughts. Rain-on-Stones stared at him with wet silver eyes, like ball bearings soaked in mercury. Ginger's look just bore through him, so full of anger he could barely stand to make eye contact.

He forced himself. He looked right into her eyes and stood up to the hatred there. If he was going to do this, if he was going to use her like this, he could at least be honest about it.

"Get her up and moving," he said. "The two of you are coming with me."

"Where are we going?" Ginger demanded. "What's this all about?"

"We're going to save somebody's life," he said. "And kill a hell of a lot of aliens."

⇥✦⇤

Shulkin let out a noise that might have been a roar, a maniacal laugh, or a scream of rage. It was so loud it turned into a distorted wail that echoed around inside Candless's helmet. He rushed forward, barely managing to keep his feet on the hull as he poured rifle fire into the oncoming horde.

Candless tried to cover him as best she could, though she had to be careful not to shoot him in the back. The mutineers flooded forward, barely keeping their heads down. She saw one coming at her from on high, jets blazing from his ankles and elbows. Through the helmet Candless could see a female face writhing with hatred. The woman had a knife held over her head and clearly she meant to crash into Candless and stab a hole in her suit.

Candless let out her own scream of terror and fired straight up, her bullets cutting tiny holes through the front of the mutineer's suit. The woman's hand flew open and the knife spun off into nothingness as she crashed into a hull plate right next to Candless. As the woman started to get back up, she kicked her away, then fired three more shots through her helmet.

Was the woman dead? Was she done? Candless couldn't even tell. She dodged to one side just in case and ran forward after Shulkin. Even as a line of mutineers shot out of an airlock fifty meters away from her, emerging like bullets from a gun.

How many of them were there? How many could there be? It felt like dozens of them, maybe scores, were rushing toward her, and her suppressing fire barely slowed them down. She spared a glance for Shulkin but couldn't find him—he was lost in a knot of mutineers, their arms flashing up and down as they stabbed at him with knives. Particle beams and kinetic projectiles streaked past her and she dropped to the hull plates, trying to make herself as small a target as possible.

Then someone grabbed her by the shoulders and flipped her over. A mutineer had caught up with her, a man with some kind of tool in his hand—a vibrasaw, she thought. Oh, hellfire, what would one of those do to a human body? She looked up into a maddened face, taking in the wide-open mouth, the staring eyes. It took her a second but she realized she recognized the man.

It was Uhl. The pilot who had saved her during the battle with the dreadnought.

"It's me," she tried to say, but the vibrasaw was already coming down, swinging through the space between them. She squirmed away and it bit hard into the flowglas of her helmet and she screamed again.

"I'm sorry!" he shouted, and she could see in his face that he didn't want this. Even as he reared back for another blow. "I'm sorry!" The blade of the saw shimmered so fast it was just a bright blur, the metal changing shape thousands of times a second. She tried to evade it a second time but he was too fast for her. The vibrasaw's teeth bit deep into the shoulder of her suit. She could feel the layers of material there part and tear and she let out a cry of pure agony as the blade sank into her flesh.

"I'm sorry," Uhl sobbed, as he pressed the saw deeper into her arm.

"So am I," she wept, and drew her pistol and fired a single round right into his forehead.

He flew backward, launched from the hull by the momentum of her bullet. The saw flickered and twisted in his lifeless hands as he slowly receded into space.

Candless bit her lip and grabbed at her shoulder. Her suit was already repairing itself. Hot foam poured down her arm to plug the leak, and though it stung wickedly where it touched her wounded flesh, she knew it would help stop the bleeding as well. She tried to make a fist and found that she still had control of her fingers, even if her entire arm was burning with agony.

She climbed to her feet, holstering her pistol and bringing her rifle around in case any other mutineers were nearby. She couldn't find any of them at first—then she turned and saw they were all piling on Shulkin, trying to knock him down. He'd lost his rifle and she could see the long parallel scorch marks of particle fire all over his suit, but his face was lit up like a lamp as he laid into his attackers with a knife in either hand, cackling as he tore open a mutineer's suit, shouting in glee as he kicked one of them off into space.

One of them got an arm around Shulkin's helmet and tried to

pull him backward, off his feet. Candless fired a dozen shots into the mutineer's side and back and he fell away, his body bouncing off the armored hull. Shulkin spun around and jabbed one of his knives deep into the guts of a mutineer with a welding torch. The man looked surprised, but he had already started to swing his weapon. Superhot plasma gouted from the end of the torch and Candless barely had time to scream "No!" as it burned a hole right through Shulkin's midsection, a fountain of fire emerging from his back.

"Ha!" Shulkin barked. "Ha! Ha!" He looked around him, as if wondering who would be the most satisfying to kill next. Mutineers edged away from him, as if they couldn't believe he was still standing, still fighting.

"Ha," he said, but there was no force in it this time. It came out like a wheeze. Foam spilled out of the front and back of his suit as its damage control system tried to keep his air from escaping, but it just looked like he'd been disemboweled.

"Ha," he puffed out. His face was gray and his eyes were dark.

He never fell. The carrier was too small to generate sufficient gravity to bring him down. He slumped forward a little, his muscles curling up, and one of his knives floated out of a dead hand. Then the mutineers piled on top of him, perhaps just trying to make sure he really was dead, and Candless couldn't see him anymore.

"You bastards!" she screamed, lifting her rifle. "You bastards!" She opened fire, hosing them down with particle blasts. "You bastards!"

She hit some of them. Not enough. Mostly she just drew attention to herself. Suddenly they were all coming for her, all running toward her at once, a wave of them that would crest over her and smash her to the hull, smash her to pulp—

Candless ran. She didn't think about where she was going. She didn't think about how she would survive this. She didn't think at all—she just ran, her body reaching down through millions of years of evolution, through layers of instincts she'd never needed before, and she ran, her legs pumping like triphammers as she dashed down the carrier's hull, away from the mob, away from death. A particle beam went right through her helmet, missing her cheek by millimeters. A bullet smacked into one of the life support packages mounted on her back and she nearly went sprawling forward.

She never stopped running. Her feet slapped against the carbon fiber, her breath pulsing in and out of her lungs, and they were right behind her, they were just moments from catching her, they were—

Something big went over her head, very fast. She felt a rumbling vibration through the hull, waves of it rolling up her calf muscles and making her knees shake. She threw herself forward, threw herself down with her arms over her head as the vibration came again and again and again.

When she dared to look she turned and saw a line of mutineers right behind her, swaying gently as their boots held them to the hull. Their helmets were gone, shattered and thick with blood. She couldn't see their heads.

And then—

And then it started raining marines.

Cataphract-class fighters—BR.9s—swept by overhead, marines in big armored suits clinging to their airfoils. One by one they jumped down, their suit jets flashing in tight controlled burns. As they slammed into the hull they were already moving forward, rifles in hand, rushing past Candless. She tried to see their faces, to figure out which side they were on, but their helmets were up and silvered. She called out, but none of them answered—they were too busy sweeping forward, cutting through the last of the mob, slaughtering the mutineers.

Her side, then. The Navy side. These were Ehta's marines, brought over from the cruiser riding on the outsides of the BR.9s.

The fighters, their human cargo safely delivered, swung around for another pass, their PBW cannons blasting away at the hull.

Who the hell was flying those things?

A blue pearl spun in the corner of Candless's vision. A blue pearl—

Valk.

This time she answered it. "M. Valk," she said, "I presume you've come to my rescue. You might have come earlier."

"I thought you would be grateful," the AI told her.

Candless sighed and rested her helmet on the hull. "I am," she said, because apparently you needed to be very literal when speaking with Valk now. He'd lost so much of his humanity—apparently his sense of humor was gone now, too. "I am," she repeated. "Thank you."

"Okay," he said. "Now that we've taken care of this problem, though," he said, "will you finally listen to what I have to say? I've discovered something, something really important. I tried telling Lanoe, but he won't listen to me. You need to hear this!"

"I suppose you've earned that much," she said. "Go ahead."

Chapter Twenty-Five

I t's over," Ehta said. "You might as well come out."

The marine had missed most of the bloodshed and violence of the mutiny. She'd spent most of it locked inside Shulkin's cabin. She'd assumed he would be one of the ringleaders of the uprising, and so she'd gone there to arrest him before he could organize his people. She'd quickly discovered he wasn't there—but she did find a crate full of heavy weapons. When she tried to leave, she found that the mutineers had seized the corridor outside. They'd blocked all her communications, and every time she tried to poke her head out of the hatch they'd done their best to blow it off.

She hadn't let them. And every time they tried to get inside, she'd fought back with such ferocity that eventually they had to pull back. For over an hour they'd been locked in a stalemate, with Ehta unwilling to die and the mutineers unwilling to let her live.

When her own marines came to rescue her, she'd felt an immense relief—but also crushing embarrassment. From the sound of it, Candless had been far more active in resisting the mutiny. Thrice-damned Candless, the schoolteacher, had outfought big tough Caroline Ehta the deadly marine.

At least Candless couldn't claim to have put down the mutiny

by herself. It sounded like Valk had saved the day. And Shulkin—
though Ehta could hardly believe it, the madman had fought like
the devil himself on the loyalist side.

Now it was Ehta's turn to do her part. At the head of a squad of
marines she moved through the carrier, checking every compartment, every corridor, to make sure there were no more mutineers
hiding away in a storage locker or anything, waiting for a chance to
spring out and do mischief.

That meant a lot of pounding on sealed hatches. This one was
worse than most—the people behind it were smart enough to figure how to seal so it couldn't be opened, even from the bridge. Ehta
thought they must have jammed a prybar into the hatch's servos or
something. "Come on!" she shouted, hammering on the bulkhead
with one armored fist. "You're done! I promise we'll be nice to you
if you come out peaceful. Otherwise, we'll cut the oxygen flow to
this compartment and you'll suffocate in there." She turned and
rolled her eyes at Gutierrez, but the marine had her helmet up and
silvered.

Behind the hatch were three mutineers, a man and two women.
They were armed with old-fashioned projectile pistols. Revolvers,
by the look of them. There was a camera in the compartment and
it was feeding video to her wrist display. The mutineers looked
scared. They kept moving around the room, kicking off a wall and
flying to the next, kicking off that one. The microgravity equiva-
lent of pacing.

Scared was bad. Scared people tended to shoot at the first thing
they saw coming through a door. Scared people went down messy.

Not that Ehta had much sympathy for the mutineers, but she
figured enough people had already died. And she didn't want one
of her marines getting hurt by a stray round.

"Come on!" she shouted. "At least talk to me, you idiots." She
pounded on the hatch with the butt of her rifle. Not really expecting a response.

She got one, though. "Stop that! Stop that pounding!" someone
shrieked. Someone right at the edge of sanity.

"Will you come out? Throw your guns away and come out," Ehta said.

"What? Just so you can shoot us as soon we open the hatch? We're never coming out, you hear me? We're going to sit right here until—"

"Do it," Ehta told Gutierrez.

The corporal gestured for the other marines to move back. Then she slapped a shaped charge on the hatch and ducked as it blew a neat little hole out of the hatch, a hole barely three centimeters across. Gutierrez shoved a tiny grenade through the hole, and Ehta stuck her fingers in her ears.

Blinding light and a horrible whining noise burst out of the breach as the flashbang went off. Inside the compartment it would have been like looking into the heart of a star. Binah brought up a rotary saw and cut the hatch right across the middle and Ehta hit it with her shoulder until it gave way. She lurched into the room, her rifle already up and ready to fire, while her people covered her from the corridor.

One of the women and the man were clutching at their faces, screaming in pain. The third tried to shoot Ehta, but she couldn't see well enough to aim. Ehta let go of her rifle and just broke the woman's arm—two quick snaps—until she could take her pistol away.

When it was done she pushed back out into the corridor and let her marines take the rest. Outside the compartment she tried not to listen to the moans of pain and the repetitive meaty thuds of rifle butts hitting human heads. She called Candless. "Three more," she said.

"For the morgue or the brig?" Candless asked. It sounded like she actually cared about the answer.

"Brig," Ehta said. "I think these might be the last, though we'll keep looking. These bastards really made a mess of the place, didn't they?"

"I've never cared for your flippant tone," Candless said. "They killed half of the crew. Perhaps you could show a little respect."

Ehta moved her jaw back and forth, grinding her teeth together. For a moment there, just before the mutiny, it had felt like maybe she and Candless were going to start getting along. They'd had a common enemy, and that had brought them together.

Ehta guessed that some things didn't ever change.

"You have my most sincere apologies," she said. Candless sniffed at her sarcasm. "Listen, can we focus here? I'm telling you we've swept the entire ship. There's no sign of Lanoe anywhere. Or Maggs, or Bullam."

"I suppose that was too much to hope for," Candless replied.

There was no real doubt about those three. Bullam's yacht was gone. It had left the flight deck just as the mutiny started. Nobody on the bridge had gotten a chance to track where it went from there, nor could any of the carrier's sensors pick it up now. Most likely the two conspirators just wanted to get as far from the scene of the crime as they could get. They would know there would be no mercy if Candless caught them.

As for Lanoe—that was a whole different matter. The cutter was gone. Lanoe was nowhere to be found, either on the carrier or on the cruiser. Valk was the last one who'd seen him, as he dragged Ginger and the chorister out of their cell.

His destination was also unknown. Lanoe wasn't like Bullam and Maggs, though. He must have known that he was going to be relieved from duty, and he had clearly fled before that could happen. He wasn't the kind of man who just ran away, though. He must have something in mind, some new plan that involved Rain-on-Stones.

Neither Ehta nor Candless could think of what it might be.

The cutter was even harder to find than the yacht. It had been designed to be invisible to every sensor the Navy used, and to be impossible to see even with the naked eye—its skin could change color and pattern to give it perfect camouflage. Their only hope was that he would choose to contact them before he did anything rash.

Ehta had known Lanoe for almost two decades. She was pretty sure "something rash" was his standard operating procedure.

———≺≻———

Just the three of them now. Lanoe, Rain-on-Stones, and Ginger. No other crew to worry about. No more distractions.

The cutter's entire interior surface was one large display that showed a view of the universe outside. It felt, always, as if Lanoe were flying through empty space with nothing around him but a seat and a control stick. If he looked down, if he looked in any direction, he could see forever, to the ends of existence.

He felt like his entire life had shrunk down to this single point, this naked singularity of destiny. Every path he'd ever taken, no matter what he'd thought at the time, had pointed in this one, solitary direction.

None of them said a word. Lanoe focused on flying the cutter, though it was hardly a tricky course he'd plotted. The red dwarf hung before him like a beacon, a glowing dot that marked his destination. Below him the disk swirled in its infinite complexity, its homogeneous simplicity. Red and black vapor twisting into endlessly convoluted shapes, unwinding again as the hydrogen winds tore them apart. He could see no sign of life down there, no indication that there was a civilization hiding in those stacks of cloud. He could have called up a telescope view. If he wanted, he could have spied on the cities of the aliens down there. But he didn't want to.

Rain-on-Stones didn't speak. Well, choristers never did, not with audible words. They chirped, like crickets, chirps that could be laughter or moans of pain or alien sounds he could never interpret. The big alien was silent now, though. Whatever she was feeling, whatever she was thinking, she shared it only with Ginger.

Ginger had nothing to say. Lanoe had expected her to fight him, even though he hadn't yet told her the details of what they were going to do. He'd expected her to resist on principle. She had to know they'd come to a very desperate point, the final point on a graph that didn't have any future. Yet she didn't say a word, and neither did she look at him. Instead she rested her cheek on the invisible bulkhead of the cutter and watched the billion stars go by.

Red hair, Lanoe thought. Ginger had red hair, and so had Zhang when she died. He'd made the connection before, many times. Now it seemed different, more meaningful. As if the universe, or fate, or some ancient and forgotten god had brought Ginger to him as a sign. A promise. This simple coincidence, that the two of them had the same color hair, was an indication that he would be allowed this terrible chance. This chance to make things right.

For nearly an hour the silence held. The cutter glided along, as silent as the nebulae that stained space between all those stars, as silent as the grave, and Lanoe was...if not happy, then at least focused. Committed. He didn't need to think any new thoughts. He didn't need to feel anything, not even grief. He was an arrow fired from a bow. A machine carrying out previously downloaded instructions. It was that simple.

And then one of them broke the silence, and it all got so much harder.

"What do you think Rain-on-Stones can do out here?" Ginger asked.

She was staring at him. Her mouth was flat, neither a smile nor a frown showing there. She wasn't angry, she wasn't demanding that he take her back to the cell in the cruiser's brig. She was asking for information.

When he didn't answer right away, she moved her leg and kicked an octagonal stone box that sat at her feet. Its surface was covered in exquisite inlays of some goldish metal, and it had tiny, delicate hinges.

"This is Rain-on-Stones's medical kit," Ginger said. "Why did we bring it?"

Lanoe looked over at her. There was no danger of the cutter colliding with anything—they were still half a million kilometers out from the red dwarf. He didn't have to worry about ignoring the controls, not for the time it would take to have this conversation.

"I suppose I'd like to believe that you're going to have her remove the antenna from my head. The one she put in there so that I could speak to her," Ginger said. "I know that's not it, but it's a nice thought. You could free me from this, this thing you made me do."

Lanoe didn't remember it that way. The girl had volunteered. He said nothing. But he nodded. She was right—Plan C didn't involve brain surgery. He needed her to be able to communicate with the chorister.

"There are some knives in there, and an empty hypodermic. Some other tools that—huh. I can see how they're used. I don't know their names, because there are no names for them in English or any spoken language. They're used in surgery and the treatment of diseases that humans don't even get. I don't think you came out here to have her perform surgery on you, though. No. There's one other thing in that box."

Yes. Yes, there was.

"That must be what you wanted. It doesn't make any sense, though." Ginger leaned forward and slipped the catch that held the box closed. She pushed back the lid, then reached inside and took out a spherical object about twenty centimeters in diameter. It looked like it was made of carved ivory. It was hollow and a fractally intricate pattern of holes pierced its surface. It gave off a very soft tone when she held it, like a chorister's chirp but stretched out into one long sustained note. As Ginger turned it in her hands the note changed, almost imperceptibly.

It was so beautiful. Such an incredible piece of technology built into such a small housing. Lanoe thought it must be the most elegantly engineered object he'd ever seen. Especially because it was going to give him his ending.

Three hundred years. He'd lived three hundred years and more, and life had finally shown itself to him in all its panoply. Always he'd been frustrated before, disappointed that life couldn't be like a video or a story. The good guys never won—well, you couldn't live as long as he had and expect that. The problem was that neither did the bad guys—nobody ever *finished* anything. The stories just went on and on and the longer they lasted the less they meant, the less cohesive they were, the less pure. There was nothing that life couldn't sully, make dirty and disgusting, if it went on long enough. You could fight a war and a hundred years later find that you'd been on the wrong side. You could love a woman, and then you could see her die in front of you. Nothing good lasted forever. Nothing good could, because everything changed. Everything changed and got worse.

What you needed, he'd come to realize, was to die young, while you still believed in the stories. When you still thought there were things like good and evil.

It was too late for that, too late for him. He knew what he was going to do now wasn't good. It was far from good. But it would give him Zhang back, and that was so much more than he'd ever thought he could ask for.

"This is a...well, there's no human word. It's a device for opening wormholes," Ginger said. "It has certain medical applications. You can open a very, very tiny wormhole into someone's stomach and draw out the poison they've eaten without having to cut them open. You can open a wormhole into a brain tumor and pull it out without damaging the surrounding tissue. That's what Rain-on-Stones uses it for."

Lanoe cleared his throat. "You can use it to open other kinds of wormholes, too," he said.

Ginger started a little, as if she hadn't expected him to speak. She shook her head and looked back down at the sphere. "Yes," she said. "Yes, you can. Except not. Because you already know that Rain-on-Stones doesn't have the ability to open a wormhole like that. She's just one chorister—she doesn't have the strength, or, for that matter, the power, the energy, to open a wormhole big enough to fly a ship through. She can't send you home. She can't send herself home. Don't you think she would have, if she could?"

"I know," Lanoe said.

"She can only make very small, very narrow wormholes," Ginger said. She shook her head again. "I don't understand. Tell me what you want her to do. Tell me, so we can figure out if maybe we should just give up and go back. Okay?"

Lanoe smiled. "I'm not looking for a wormhole big enough to fly a ship through," he told Ginger. "That's not it at all."

"So, explain. Please, Lanoe. Just explain to me what this is about," she said.

He knew he wasn't just speaking with the girl. He knew everything he said was automatically being translated across the link she shared with Rain-on-Stones. The silent chorister, slumped now across three seats in the back of the cutter, was very much a part of this conversation.

"Back at the city of the Choir, back when we were first negotiating with Rain-on-Stones's people," Lanoe said, "Valk spoke with your predecessor." A man named Archie, a pilot lost in time, adopted by the Choir and changed, just as Ginger had been changed. Archie had wanted to go home, so he had answered every question Valk had. Then he'd found out that home didn't exist anymore, and he'd taken his own life.

At the time it had seemed like a terrible inconvenience. Archie had been the only conduit through which Lanoe could speak with the Choir, and losing him had nearly cost him his mission. His destiny. Now he saw it hadn't been that way at all. Archie had cleared the way for Ginger, who had taken over his role. Archie had died so that Lanoe could have Ginger, and Rain-on-Stones, and the three of them could be here. Now.

"Archie," Lanoe went on, "told Valk that the Choir built the entire network of wormholes that connects the stars. He told Valk about all the amazing things the Choir could do with wormholes. About surgeries like the ones you mentioned. About sending messages faster than light, and even back in time. Most importantly, he told Valk about how the Choir used to go to war, back before the Blue-Blue-White nearly wiped them out. About how they fought, and war machines they used. He told Valk about how you could turn a wormhole into a weapon."

"Wait," Ginger said. "No."

She stared at Lanoe with disbelieving eyes. She got it. She knew everything that Rain-on-Stones knew, shared all of the chorister's memories. She knew what Lanoe was asking for now.

Below them the disk turned and turned in its endless gyre. And right in its middle, in its center, the red dwarf burned like a lighthouse, beckoning them on.

———

The troop transport's engines cut out, and some of the marines unstrapped themselves and floated around the cabin. Ehta shook her head. "You, marines, get back in your seats. Now. We're not there yet—there's still maneuvers coming up."

Binah looked back at her, the quizzical look on his face melting as he nodded. "Yes, ma'am. I think you might want to see this, though."

Ehta grumbled as she unhooked her straps. She kicked across the spherical compartment, up to a narrow viewport that ringed the hull above their seats. She shoved him out of the way and peered out into space.

She saw right away what he'd been looking at. The wreckage of the alien dreadnought—their destination—hung motionless out there, so big it looked like they were about to land on a densely cratered moon. From the carrier it had looked like a sleeping giant, like it might come to life and attack them again, but up close the destruction was unmistakable. The broken blisters stuck out from its edges like thickets of white bone and its weapon pits were scorched an ugly brown.

Across its broad back, in characters a dozen meters high, someone had written a single word, in English:

MUTINY

The letters fizzed and sparkled, as if they'd been written with fireworks. "Yeah," Ehta said. "That's why we came out here. Or did you think this was a shore leave you all earned for being such good little PBMs?"

One or two of her people actually laughed. They'd been in high spirits ever since they dragged the last of the Centrocor mutineers out of their hiding places. Nothing like winning a battle to ward off the boredom of life in the marines. Ehta turned and looked back at them. "Candless has no idea what that's supposed to mean," she said, jabbing one finger at the viewport. "I have no idea what we're going to find down there. Maybe a bunch of Centrocor idiots who figured they would write their favorite word so big the whole world would know what they did. If that's the case, well, we're going to show them what we think of their graffiti."

Mestlez whooped and slapped the bulkhead in a quick little rhythm. Gutierrez frowned, but she could barely hide her grin. As long as there were still more mutineers to roust out, it meant the marines didn't have to go back to gun deck duty, not quite yet.

Ehta let them make their noise, just glad to see them in a good mood. She moved around the compartment, slapping shoulders and winking at her people, and it only seemed to get them more excited. When the pilot called back to say they were about to decelerate before arrival, though, she raced back to her seat and pulled her straps across her chest as fast as she was able.

Big as it was, the dreadnought couldn't generate any appreciable gravity. The transport couldn't land on the alien ship, so when they got close the marines put their helmets up and the ramp at the nose of the transport popped open, spilling all their air out into space. Ehta jumped up and started grabbing marines, pushing them through the opening, pointing them in the right direction. "Get down there and establish a perimeter. I'm last out. Move! Move, you damn beggars, move!"

Their suit jets flared like landing lights as Ehta followed them out, pointing herself at the white ground and trying not to vomit inside her helmet. It was only a few seconds before she touched down—only to find that the adhesive pads on her boots wouldn't stick to the porous coral of the dreadnought's hull. All around her marines were clutching to the white surface, trying to stop themselves from drifting away. Ehta threw some hand signals to tell them to follow her, then used her jets to push her toward the middle of the hull, toward the giant letters. Behind her a dozen marines brought their rifles up, ready to shoot anything that moved.

Ahead of her the letter Y sparked and spat, a ditch of fire dug into the hull. She shot toward it, pistol in hand, ready for whatever she found. If the dreadnought was infested with mutineers, though, they were smart enough to keep their heads down—she couldn't see anybody.

As she flew close to the giant character she saw it wasn't actually on fire. Well, no, of course not, she chided herself. There was no oxygen out here to sustain a flame. Instead it looked like some sticky goop had been spread across the top of the hull, a thick gel that bubbled and fizzed wildly as it caught the sunlight. Ehta chose not to fly directly over it—with no idea what chemicals were involved, she had no desire to be exposed to its fumes—and instead turned to move parallel to the line. She scanned the coral for any sign of life, any movement, but the shimmering character kept distracting her, fooling her into thinking she saw things that weren't there.

It was Geddy, instead, who spotted their target. He slapped her on the calf and when she turned to look at him he pointed across the field of burning letters, to a point just at the base of the T. Ehta followed his finger and saw a tiny human figure there, clutching a cylinder about a meter in diameter.

"Could be a bomb," Geddy said.

"Let's not give them a chance to set it off," Ehta told him. She changed course again, looping down under the bottom of the letters, headed toward the figure at speed. It hadn't seemed to notice them yet, and she considered just telling her people to shoot it at long range and be done with it.

She knew Candless would give her hell if she did that, though. Sighing, she touched her wrist display to open a general radio channel. "You there, by the T. You! Stop what you're doing and show us your hands! Right now!"

There was no response. The figure reached inside its canister and drew out a handful of glowing goop, clearly the same stuff that was used to make the fizzing letters.

"Surround and contain," Ehta shouted. She pushed her suit jets for more speed, for more power, even as marines surged forward around her in perfect formation.

They came down fast, forming a ring of firepower around the lone figure. Ehta gestured for Gutierrez to keep her eyes open, in case this was a trap—in case fifty mutineers were waiting inside the shadowy pits that dotted the hull, ready to jump up and ambush them at any moment.

Then she flew down to the hull, to hover right next to the figure. "Don't you move, you damned traitor!" she shouted, jamming her pistol into the mutineer's helmet, ready to shoot the moment they made a threatening gesture.

Then she saw through their helmet, saw who it was, and she let out a deep breath.

It was Paniet, and he looked terrified.

He lifted his hands, one of them still clotted with the fiery gel. Behind her, Ehta could feel a dozen particle rifles aiming right at Paniet's face.

"Stand down!" she shouted. "He's one of ours!"

Paniet's eyes were so wide she thought they might pop out of their sockets. "What are you doing here?" she asked. "Why the hell didn't you answer when I told you to put your hands up?"

She saw his lips moving, but heard nothing over the radio. A look of deep frustration crossed his face. Then he leaned forward, until his helmet smacked into hers. "Can you hear me?" he asked. The vibrations of his voice passed through two layers of flowglas to get to her, but she could make out the words.

"What the hell is going on?" she asked.

"My comms are disabled." He smiled, clearly having figured out that no one was going to kill him now. He lifted one arm and gestured at the giant characters inscribed on the hull. "I see you got my message." He showed her his handful of goop. "Plasma starter gel," he explained. "Fascinating stuff. The Blue-Blue-White used it as an ionization reaction initiator for their plasma ball cannons. It's self-oxidizing."

"Okay," Ehta said. "Uh, let's save the science lecture for later. Can you just tell me one thing? Can you tell me why you're out here?"

"Because I made a very stupid mistake, dear. I trusted someone. On this mission—I ought to have known better."

<hr>

"It doesn't matter how much power that can generate," Lanoe said, nodding at the sphere in Ginger's hands. "It'll be enough. Wormholes are funny things. Hard as hell to open. Harder still to stabilize, so they don't just collapse on themselves."

"The Choir have forgotten how to do that," Ginger pointed out. "They lost that knowledge when the Blue-Blue-White all but exterminated them."

Lanoe nodded. "Sure. And when I first came up with this plan, I thought that was going to be a problem. But if we can open the wormhole I want, even for a few seconds, it'll be enough."

She—they—still didn't get it.

"In the old days, before they were reduced to what they are now, the Choir used wormholes to kill each other."

"They're not...proud of that," Ginger said.

Lanoe sighed. He realized he wasn't telling Ginger anything she didn't already know. She had full access to Rain-on-Stones's memories—to the whole history of the Choir. "Okay," he said. "What we're going to do is simple. We're going to open a wormhole that connects the disk with the heart of the red dwarf."

Ginger stared at him with her mouth open.

"I had Valk run the numbers for me on this, back when I still trusted him. Right at the middle, the star burns at about ten million degrees. The pressure in there is so intense I don't think a human brain can ever imagine it. When we open this wormhole, plasma from the star will come shooting out the other end. A lot of it will get annihilated along the way, but that doesn't even matter. What emerges will still be hot enough to burn the entire disk."

"No," Ginger said.

"With one end of the wormhole right in the middle of the disk, right where their cities are, even if the wormhole is only open for a few seconds it'll be enough to raise the temperature of the disk by thousands and thousands of degrees. Once the wormhole collapses, that heat will radiate off into space pretty quick, but by then it'll be too late for the Blue-Blue-White. Every single one of them will be flash fried. Burned alive. Nothing organic could possibly survive that kind of heat."

He scrubbed at his face with his hands. He was so tired, suddenly, just physically exhausted now that they were close to the ending. He only had to hang in there a little longer.

"The disk is almost entirely made of hydrogen gas. It'll turn to plasma. Those coral cities of theirs will burn to ash. Their bodies will probably just vaporize. The model I ran showed that the sudden energy gradient will probably knock the shepherd moons right out of their orbits—eventually, the whole disk will disperse out into space. There won't be anything left in a hundred years, not even a memory that the Blue-Blue-White were here. I don't really care about that. I don't care about posterity. All I want right now is to wipe them out."

"No," Ginger said again. Or was it Rain-on-Stones saying it? Hard to tell.

"They all have to die. Just like they wiped out so many other species. Just like they're threatening to do to humanity." Just like they'd killed Zhang.

He could fix it. He could fix all of their mistakes. They just had to die, first.

"You don't... you can't..."

"I can. With your help, I can do this."

"No," Ginger said. "That's not what I was going to say, I—I just—" She was weeping. Behind her, in the back of the cutter, Rain-on-Stones let out a grating, whining chirp. "You aren't doing this for humanity. Or for the Choir, either."

Lanoe frowned, but he said nothing.

"Bury told me, and, and Ehta thought so, too. You don't want to kill them all for *justice*. You don't care about all those aliens you never even met. You don't even care about the Choir—you were willing to kill them, too, if it got you here. It was just lucky that it didn't come to that. You're doing this because the Blue-Blue-White killed your *girlfriend*."

"She was more to me than that," Lanoe said.

"And even then—it wasn't the Blue-Blue-White who did it. It was some drone half a galaxy from here, some drone that wasn't even intelligent, it was just following a program—"

"A program written by the Blue-Blue-White. They told their drone fleets to eliminate vermin. Zhang died because they thought she was no better than a cockroach."

"They didn't know she existed! It was a mistake, Lanoe! It was a glitch, a missing line of code, an . . . an *accident*."

"An accident that left the entire galaxy sterilized. Empty of life," Lanoe said. "No—don't start," he went on, as Ginger started to protest. "Yeah, maybe I'm doing this for the wrong reason. It's still the right thing to do. The Blue-Blue-White made a mistake, you say, well, it was the worst mistake anybody ever made—ever. In history. It was the kind of mistake you have to pay for. They don't get away with this. They can't get away with this. Zhang—she— you never met her, Ginger. You didn't get a chance to. She was an incredible woman. Tell me, if you could dig up one of those aliens the Blue-Blue-White killed, something that looks like a bush with eyes, or a fish with hands around its mouth, whatever, it doesn't matter. You find the ghost of one of the intelligent people the Blue-Blue-White killed. If you asked them whether they thought the Blue-Blue-White should be forgiven, because they didn't mean to do it. What do you think they would say? How many of them lost lovers? Kids? They lost everything. They lost everything that ever mattered to them. They'd be on my side. Don't you think?"

Ginger didn't have an answer.

"Forget that, let's make this personal. Because now you're one of the Choir as much as Rain-on-Stones, right? Let's talk about *your* ghosts. The Blue-Blue-White attacked the Choir not once but twice. They botched the job the first time. They came back to finish it, and they almost did. They killed so many choristers, in the end there were only how many of them left?"

"Twelve," Ginger said. The number came out of her mouth so fast it had to be Rain-on-Stones talking.

"Just twelve. Only a dozen of them left, out of *billions*. Their memories are still in there, somewhere in that big head, aren't they?" he asked, pointing at Rain-on-Stones. "You know what the Twelve thought. You know how they felt, when they came back to their planet and found it empty. All those voices, all that harmony, silenced. If you can tell me that not one of them considered something like this. That they didn't want some payback. If you can tell me that—"

"You know I can't," Ginger said. "It was all they thought about, for a long time."

Lanoe nodded.

"But then... they calmed down. They never got past it, but they learned to find another way. A way to heal things that didn't involve genocide."

Lanoe scoffed. He knew about that, about what the Twelve came up with. Their grand plan. They had collected genetic material from all the species that used to exist, all the aliens the Blue-Blue-White had wiped out. The Choir was holding on to that DNA for a time when the jellyfish weren't a problem anymore. A time that might never come.

"Even if it works, even if it was what anyone really wanted—their way will take billions of years."

"They're patient! They can wait!"

"Really?" he asked. "Are you so sure? They sent me here. They sent us here, to this place." *To this time,* he thought. "I asked for a wormhole to anywhere. I just wanted to save us from Centrocor. They could have sent us to Earth, but they didn't. They sent us *here*. Because they knew what I would do."

"No," Ginger said. "No, that isn't right."

"You must know this," he said. "The Choir share everything. They have no secrets. They must have agreed to send me all this way for a reason."

"No," Ginger said again. "You don't understand how it happened. You don't know—when they agreed to open a wormhole, there was a consensus that they wanted to get rid of you. That they wanted to keep me, forever. I agreed to their terms to save everyone, but they never specified where you were going. That decision wasn't made by the entire Choir, but by just one chorister, the one who aimed the beam. There was no time for debate or discussion. Rain-on-Stones didn't even know where we were, when we got here. Neither did I."

"But—then—" Lanoe shook his head. He'd assumed...well. Assumptions were for people who never doubted themselves. "At least one of them, then. One of them knew, and made the choice to send me here. It's what the Choir wants, even if they won't let themselves be complicit."

"They don't want this," Ginger said. "I'm telling you—"

"It doesn't matter. We're here now. I've told you my plan. So tell me whether you'll help me or not."

"Why are you even asking?" Ginger asked. "Why are you acting like you're asking *me*? We both know how this is going to happen. You're going to try to force Rain-on-Stones to open this wormhole for you. And you know what she'll say. She'll say no."

Lanoe nodded. He'd considered that might happen, it was true.

"She'll say no," Ginger repeated. "You can threaten her all you want. You can kill her—she'll let you kill her before she does this."

"Sure," Lanoe said.

Ginger shrugged in incomprehension. "So...why...?"

"She'll say no," Lanoe told the girl. "So I won't even bother asking her. The thing is, Ginger, I'm asking *you*. And I'm willing to bet you'll say yes."

———※———

"A fellow named Hollander," Paniet said, as he rode with Ehta back to the carrier. "A neddy, like me. He had me fooled right from the start, I'm sorry to say. I'm pretty sure he was spying for Centrocor even when we first met. He'd been on the crew of one of the destroyers, you see, but I thought engineers couldn't possibly be devious. It's just not in our makeup, is it, ducks?"

"Anybody can be a bastard, if they've got a reason," Ehta said.

"I think he wanted to expose M. Valk to the Centrocor contingent, or something. I was foolish enough to let him come onboard the cruiser with me. Oh, I'm sure I'm in for it when we get back. I've been so stupid!"

"I don't understand," Ehta said. "This guy took you out to the dreadnought?"

"No, of course not, love, do try to pay attention. Lanoe had asked me to investigate that hulk. See what I could learn of Blue-Blue-White technology. It was terribly spooky, but for a boy like me, well, how could I resist? Every time I see a machine I want to take it apart and see how it runs. So I went. But I asked Hollander to come with me, for company. And so I wouldn't be alone in there." Paniet sighed and rolled his eyes. "I thought it might be...well. A nice bonding moment. Instead it was all just one huge mistake. He cornered me in there. He had a pistol and he brandished it at me. Positively threatened me with it. I thought he was going to kill me, honestly, but his intentions were the exact opposite."

Ehta frowned. "He wanted to...help you? With a pistol?"

"It'll come clear in a moment, I swear it. So he told me there was a mutiny planned. A bunch of Centrocor people were going to rise up and seize the ships, and he knew that all the Navy officers were going to be, well, you know." Paniet drew a finger across his collar ring. It took Ehta a second to realize he was miming cutting his throat. "It turned out that while, yes, he was a devious spy, and a real cad, he still had a heart. He'd started to like me after all, no matter how it compromised his secret mission. So he shot me. Yes, really! Except it turned out it wasn't a pistol, it was a neural stunner. When I woke up, I found that he'd disabled some of my suit's systems. He was rather clever about it—spy, perhaps, evildoer, yes, but he was also one hell of an engineer. He drained all the fuel out of my suit jets, and cross-welded all the antennas in my communications rig. I couldn't call you lot to tell you what was coming, and I couldn't fly back to the cruiser to warn you, either."

"So you...wrote 'MUTINY' on the dreadnought."

"To warn you, yes. And I'm guessing it worked. Right, dearie? It did? You were able to put down this nascent plot before it even got started. Of course you did, because you and Candless are very clever. So that's that. You can thank me anytime you like for saving the day."

Paniet's chipper tone was belied by his face. Ehta could see the doubt gnawing at him. The fear.

She hated having to be the one to tell him he was right.

"No," she said. "We didn't get the message in time." She gave him the broad strokes of what happened with the mutiny. She kept the bloodier details out of it.

His crestfallen look made her turn away. "I see," he said. "I... see. Let me ask just one question, then."

"Yeah, okay," Ehta said.

"Hollander," Paniet asked her. "Is he...I mean, I'm sure you had to, I don't know, rough him up a bit. But you'll have him in the brig or something. I want to recommend clemency. He did, after all, try to save me. I'm sure he would have come back for me, if the mutiny was successful. He would have protected me, he would have—"

He stopped abruptly, because Ehta was scrolling through a list on her wrist display. A list of names in red and blue, with far too many of them crossed out.

When she found the one she wanted, she cursed softly to herself. "I'm sorry," she told him.

Paniet looked away. She could see tears starting to pool in the corners of his eyes, so she looked away.

Eventually he reached over and patted her knee. "You did what you had to," he said, but very softly, and with very little emotion.

When they docked with the carrier, she took him straight to the bridge. Candless had asked to see him as soon as possible. "Captain-Engineer," the teacher said, rushing over to grab his hands when he pushed through the hatch. "By the devil's own handmaidens, we didn't think—that is to say, we thought you were—"

"I'm healthy as a well-fed marine," he told her. "I—oh. That—that stain on the wall, there, that's—"

"Don't," Candless said. "Don't look."

Paniet nodded. He swallowed thickly and looked away from the bulkhead. Ehta moved out of his way so he could see who was there, and who wasn't. No one was sitting at the navigator's position. The pilot had a bandage wrapped around her head. Shulkin's seat was empty.

Valk was there, though. Looking almost human. He had his helmet up and tuned to an opaque black, of course, but he looked like Ehta remembered him, from back when she thought he was still the Blue Devil.

Paniet rushed over to him and dragged the AI into a bear hug. "Oh, old friend, it's good to see you," he said.

"You too," Valk replied. He looked like he didn't know what to do with his hands, though. Maybe he'd forgotten how humans showed affection for each other.

"I'm sorry to break up the reunion," Candless said. "I asked Major Ehta to bring you here for a reason, Captain-Engineer."

"You did?" Paniet asked.

"M. Valk has discovered something…troublesome," Candless said. "Something that, frankly, I'm having trouble understanding. The mathematics are a bit dense, but the conclusions are simple enough. He says they're irrefutable. One of the tasks I'd like you to undertake is to check his work." She handed him a minder. Its display was densely figured with equations and mathematical symbols. Just looking at it made Ehta's head spin. Paniet started running his finger across the numbers as soon as it was handed to him.

"It's sound," Valk said.

"I'm sure, love, but it's always worthwhile having a second pair of eyes on something complex," Paniet said.

"I don't have eyes," Valk said.

"Ah. Right. Wait just a mo—here, this figure, that would suggest—"

"Yes," Valk said.

"That we've traveled through time. Half a billion years."

"Yes."

"Impossible," Paniet replied.

"No," Valk said.

"It should be," Paniet said. "In a reasonable world. Yes, yes, I know—we don't live in one of those. I suppose . . . I mean . . ."

Candless cleared her throat. Noisily enough that everyone on the bridge looked up at her. "Can you confirm M. Valk's conclusions?" she asked.

Paniet blinked rapidly. He looked, to Ehta, about equal parts fascinated, curious, amazed—and scared to the point of soiling himself.

"It looks good," he said. "Oh, goodness. Oh, goodness, darlings, this means—"

Candless stopped him with a nasty look. She was good at that, Ehta had to admit. Best nasty looks in the service. "There's another thing I require," she said.

"Yes? I'm all ears," Paniet told her.

"You'll notice Commander Lanoe isn't here."

"I assumed he would be on the cruiser," Paniet told her. "Somebody has to fly it."

"I made a copy of myself," Valk said.

The very thought seemed to make Candless's skin crawl. Which, of course, made Ehta want to grin from ear to ear. She suppressed it.

"Commander Lanoe has been relieved of duty," Candless said. Before Paniet could respond, she held up one hand. "In absentia. He absconded with the cutter—and with Ginger and Rain-on-Stones."

Paniet's mouth opened wide. Then he shut it again, carefully. "What's he going to do with them?"

"Something he calls Plan C," Candless told him. "I don't know the details, but Valk tells me he means to change history. I can guess why. He wants to bring a woman named Bettina Zhang back from the dead."

"Oh. Goodness," Paniet said.

Candless nodded. "The thing is, Valk tells me that if he tries to do that, there will be negative consequences."

Paniet laughed out loud. He looked from one of them to the other, as if they should understand implicitly why this was so funny.

Ehta liked Paniet. She liked him a lot. That didn't mean she didn't want to hit him sometimes.

Paniet's face eventually fell, as he realized no one else was laughing.

"There's a great deal we don't know about time travel, because of course we've never done it before, have we? But yes. Yes, dear heart," he said finally. "Negative consequences. You could say that. Time travel would be dangerous. So very, very dangerous. Have you tried warning him? Telling him so?"

"That's the problem. The cutter is designed to be stealthy. We have no way of tracking it. He's somewhere in the system. I assume he's most likely somewhere near the disk, but beyond that… he could be anywhere. I need to send him a message."

Paniet nodded. "Ah, I see. You want me to rig up some kind of radio transceiver capable of reaching him wherever he is. A way to talk to the entire system at once, so you're sure he hears it."

"Exactly. Can it be done?"

"Yes, of course," Paniet told her. "I can start on it immediately, if you like. Oh, but, dearest, there is one tiny smidge of a problem there. Barely worth considering, I suppose, but—"

"Tell me," Candless said.

"Once you send this message, well. We're talking about a very high-power signal. It will be heard literally everywhere, including in the disk. The Blue-Blue-White will have no idea what you're saying, of course, but they'll know exactly where we are, as long as you're on the air."

Candless inhaled sharply. "They'll be able to triangulate our position."

"Precisely."

She turned to look at Ehta. Ehta was so surprised that Candless would turn to her for advice that all she could do was shrug.

"He needs to know," Valk said. He tapped the minder. "Before he makes a terrible mistake. Before he drags us all down with him."

Candless closed her eyes. Then she nodded, just once.

"Do it," she said.

Chapter Twenty-Six

"You're insane," Ginger said.

Maybe, Lanoe thought. It was a distinct possibility. There were a lot of kinds of insanity, though.

"You honestly think this is something I would do? To commit genocide, just because—what? Because you're ordering me to do it?"

"No," he said. He leaned back in his seat and scratched at his short hair. "No. It's not an order. Maybe that would have worked on you once. Back when I first met you, when you were just a cadet. Or when I fought beside you, when Centrocor first attacked us. But no. Not now. You've come a long way since then. You've changed, a lot."

"I—I chose this," she said.

Clearly she understood what he meant. Maybe she suspected where he was going with this. "Did you? You volunteered, yeah. You volunteered to have an antenna put in your head so you could talk to the Choir." Though at the time she'd been up on charges. She'd been in a bad place, and it was the only way for her to get out. "You didn't know what that was going to mean, though. You didn't know, back then, what was going to happen."

Ginger shook her head. "I didn't know you would kidnap us." Meaning both her and Rain-on-Stones. "Drag us all this way."

"No. And you didn't know you would be tied to just one chorister, unable to harmonize. Stuck in her head as she went insane. You didn't know that would happen, when you volunteered."

"I've tried to make the best of it," Ginger said. "I've tried to help her, to keep us both...stable." She shrugged. "It hasn't been easy," she admitted.

"Exactly. It's been unbearable, hasn't it? Excruciating. You've had to cope with her pain this whole time. You've had to feel how cut off she is, handle all that anguish. Ehta tried to help you. She tried to kill Rain-on-Stones, to free you."

"Because I asked her to. And then you threatened to kill *her*."

"I had to maintain order in my fleet," Lanoe rushed out, before realizing that it would sound like the empty rationalization it was. "Never mind. That's not important. I'm going to offer you something, in exchange for opening this wormhole."

"Lanoe, no, I—"

"I'll free you from her. From Rain-on-Stones. All you have to do is this one thing."

"No," she said. "No, you can't—I won't let you just kill her!"

"That's not what I said, and it's not what I meant. I won't hurt her. I'll just separate the two of you. Move you someplace where you can't hear her thoughts."

"What? But then she—she would be all alone." She shivered as if she were freezing. She understood he was serious.

"You, too," he said. "You'd be free."

"No," she said. "No, I couldn't." She was shaking. Trembling so hard he thought she might have a seizure.

"Sure you could. You just have to say yes."

"No—I. No!" she shouted, and smashed at her temples with her fists. "No, no, no!" she shrieked. "No!"

He leaned his head back and pressed it against the headrest of his seat. He knew perfectly well that half her reaction was coming from Rain-on-Stones. That Ginger, the real Ginger, was still in there, thinking it over carefully.

He hadn't heard her final answer, not yet.

"Do you remember the night we spent on that troop ship, right after the fighting ended at the Belt of Styx?" Zhang asked. She was sitting in the seat next to him, hands on her knees. Strapped in and wearing a suit, as if she was really there.

It wasn't just her voice this time. He could *see* her. She was *right there.*

She rolled her head to the side lazily, smiling at him. *"The ship was full of marines and it stank, not just bodies but that horrible oil they used to use on their fighting suits, you remember, yeah? It was like synthetic lard or something, and they said it kept the enemy from grabbing them. And the women slicked their hair with it."*

Lanoe nodded. "We ate fried dough in the engineering section, because it was the only cool place on the ship, but they had their machine shop going, printing out replacement parts for a tank, and we couldn't hear each other talk."

Her smile widened. *"You waited until the grinders were going full blast. My helmet kept coming up automatically to try to protect my ears. You thought I wouldn't actually hear you when you asked me to marry you."*

"You did? You heard that?" Lanoe said, laughing.

Her smile faded, just a little. *"I wish I'd said yes,"* she said. *"All those times you proposed. I could have said yes, at least once. And then—"*

"Zhang never said yes," Lanoe said.

"And then we wouldn't have had to meet again at Niraya, and I wouldn't be—"

"Dead."

"...right." Zhang nodded, looking very serious. She turned her head to face forward. *"I get it. But things can change now. I can come back."*

"You're dead," he repeated. It was all he could say—he'd hit some kind of wall, some kind of psychological barrier. He couldn't think about the future. Only what had been, and what should have been.

"I know. But I don't have to be."

"You're dead," he whispered.

Her face blurred. Changed. She grew freckles. A scar on one temple where the antenna went in.

Ginger was staring at him with her blue eyes.

"Who are you talking to?" she asked, her face twisted with disgust.

"No one," he said. "A memory."

———

"We're getting close now," Lanoe said. Ahead of them, right in the middle of their view, the red dwarf had swollen to fill a third of the sky. They were coming in almost directly above the star's north pole, so the disk filled the rest of their view, the red clouds boiling in tension as if they knew what was coming. The narrow band of black between the star and the disk was filled with distant stars.

It was a view, a landscape—for lack of a better term—beyond human scale, so it was beyond human meaning. All just hydrogen, the simplest thing in existence, but hydrogen in profundity. Hydrogen as transcendence, as immanence.

The human eye makes distant things small, because the human brain is small, and cannot contain the sky. What they were doing was crime on a cosmic scale, but because they were human beings, they couldn't comprehend the size of it.

Lanoe laughed to himself. The rot his brain fed him sometimes . . . there was work to be done.

He didn't know how close they would have to get. He figured Ginger would tell him. When she agreed to his plan.

"It's your choice," he told her. "You can do what I ask, and be free. Otherwise—we're here for good. There's no way back. You can spend what's left of your life with the alien, locked up in a cell together. Feeling each other's pain."

Ginger wouldn't look at him. She kept her face turned to the side, as if the light hurt her eyes. As if she wanted to be anywhere else, anywhere in the universe but next to him. He didn't blame her.

There was still some part of him that felt sorry for her. That wished he could relent and give her what she truly wanted. Her innocence back.

That was impossible, of course. Even if you could change history, you couldn't change who people were. You couldn't fix them. Better to stamp out that feeling part of himself. Better to be what everyone thought he was. The fighter pilot, the Ace of Aces. The statue made of brass.

"It's your choice," he said.

Lanoe had worked as the personal pilot of a planetary governor once, a very powerful man. He had told Lanoe that the secret to negotiation was to take the other fellow's options away. Leave him with nothing, no direction to jump except the one you want. And then tell him to choose.

"What about that one ensign, the one who thought he was in love with you, and I had to convince him otherwise? Giving him a black eye was no problem, but we both nearly got demoted for fraternization." Zhang laughed. *"Ten minutes after the hearing we were in a supply closet, going at it like rutting animals. Or what about the three days we got on Adlivun, at that chalet in the mountains? Where they didn't let us wear our suits in the common areas, and we had to rent actual clothes."*

"We barely wore anything most of the time, if I remember right," Lanoe said. "In fact—"

Zhang lurched forward in her seat suddenly, her face turning bright red. Foam flecked her lips. Lanoe's eyes went wide in alarm—what was happening? What was going on? And then the freckles came back and it was Ginger, Ginger having a seizure, or—or—

Rain-on-Stones had been nearly catatonic the entire trip, slumped over the seats in the back of the cutter. Now the chorister was leaning forward, three of her arms wrapped around Ginger's chest and mouth. It looked like she was choking Ginger to death.

Lanoe reached for his sidearm—then stopped, as Ginger spoke.

"Please do not be alarmed," she said. No, it was Rain-on-Stones. Rain-on-Stones speaking directly through Ginger's mouth. "I had to take control."

Ginger's body convulsed against her straps. "You're hurting her," he said.

"It is difficult for one of us to do this alone. Normally it takes the Choir in consensus. I don't wish to cause Ginger distress. I would never want that. But there is something you must know, Commander."

The girl's face suddenly relaxed and her body had slumped backward against the seat. Her eyes stared off into space, seeing nothing.

"I'm listening," Lanoe said. "Don't expect that anything you say is going to change my mind, though."

"Are you so certain? Then perhaps you should know this. The device you have stolen is not meant for human hands."

"The Choir tried to keep it secret from me, but—"

"No," Rain-on-Stones said. Ginger didn't shake her head. She had no body language to read, not when she was under the chorister's direct control. Her voice was flat and toneless. "I must make this clear. I do not mean the device is forbidden. I mean it cannot be used by a human."

Lanoe narrowed his eyes. "Ginger seemed to think otherwise."

"A chorister is covered in plates of armor. This armor guards my body against the energies the device will release. A human body does not provide the same protection. If Ginger activates the device, she will be exposed to a lethal surge of those energies. Do you understand the danger of this?"

"I guess I do," Lanoe said.

"If she operates the device, she will die. You must understand. Ginger will die."

"But the device will still function," Lanoe said.

Rain-on-Stones chirped wildly. Ginger's mouth moved in cadence with the noise that filled the cutter. "She will die. She will die. I will be alone."

"Got it," Lanoe said.

"Then you will stop this now? You understand it cannot be done?"

"What I understand," he said, carefully picking his words, "is that you had to tell me this. Ginger knows everything you think. She can read your memories. She knew this all along. But she chose not to tell me. That's why you had to take over her body—because you knew she would never tell me."

"She will die."

"I know. So does she. And she seems okay with that. What I'm hearing here isn't that we have to stop."

"She will die."

"What I'm hearing," Lanoe told the chorister, "is that her answer is yes."

There were some minor maneuvers to complete. Lanoe put the cutter into orbit around the red dwarf, closer in than he normally would have liked. Ginger was clear that they needed to be within a certain distance to establish the wormhole.

The cutter's skin darkened to protect them from the star's brutal light, growing almost opaque as Lanoe circularized their orbit. The little space inside the ship started to feel claustrophobic, with echoes of their breathing lingering in the corners like cobwebs.

Rain-on-Stones had fallen back into a stupor, drained by her last-ditch attempt to sway Lanoe. She twitched occasionally, one of her arms or her many legs jumping spasmodically. She didn't chirp or say anything new through Ginger's mouth.

The girl didn't say anything, either. She didn't look at Lanoe, or out at what could be seen of the sky. She studied the ivory ball in her hands, turning it this way and that. Its hum was always there, right on the edge of Lanoe's hearing.

He locked the controls. "You ready?" he asked her.

She didn't reply. When he unstrapped himself, though, she did, too. Together they opened the cutter's narrow hatch. Air poured out of the ship, but only for a moment. A weather field snapped into place with a twanging sound. Lanoe pushed through it, feeling it cling to his suit, tugging at him gently as he slipped out into the vacuum.

Outside the ship, the star was an angry god.

Only the gods had the power to bring back the dead. It made sense.

The star filled the sky with fire, its light coming through his clenched eyelids until he could see nothing but red. His helmet compensated for the extra light by polarizing itself, turning an opaque black as it tried to screen out the worst of the rays. He looked back and saw that Ginger's helmet had made the same transition, so that she looked like a diminutive version of Valk.

They adjusted the adhesive pads on their boots and walked up onto the top of the little ship. The cutter's camouflaged skin made it nearly invisible, so it felt like they were walking on empty space.

Above, below, all around them the red dwarf looked like it might fall on them at any moment, so big it didn't even seem curved, just a wall of pure hellfire. That heat, that light, that pressure that buffeted Lanoe, that made him want to cringe away in shame—that would be the purifying fire that swept through the disk. The conflagration that ended the era of the Blue-Blue-White. He lifted his arms as if he could embrace it.

"Can we—can we just do this?" Ginger asked. "Can we get it over with?"

"Soon enough you'll be free," he said.

"Yeah," she said, with a sigh. "Yeah."

She lifted the ivory ball in both hands. He saw they weren't even shaking. Ginger had always been brave. With a careful motion she twisted the sphere. It remained as one solid piece, but somehow the patterns of holes on its top and bottom halves rotated independently. There was something odd about it now, something that made it difficult to look at, as if it existed in more dimensions than Lanoe could see.

The sphere started to vibrate, to shimmer. Ginger placed her fingers carefully over some of the holes, while leaving others exposed, as if she were playing a wind instrument. There was no air outside the cutter, so the sphere didn't make a sound that Lanoe could hear. He wondered what unearthly melodies it might play under different circumstances.

Zhang came up behind him. Put her arms around his waist, and rested her cheek between his shoulder blades.

"Do you remember the day we met?" she asked.

"Yes," he said. If Ginger heard him, she didn't look up.

"I was a little awestruck. Getting assigned to your squadron. The great Aleister Lanoe. I was nervous, believe it or not. I was going to meet a celebrity."

"You didn't show it."

"Do you remember the last time you saw me?"

"Oh, yes."

"Right before the battle for Niraya. We fought these bastards together. We're just finishing that battle now. That's all. This was always how it was supposed to end."

"Sure," he said.

Ginger let out a little grunt, possibly of pain, possibly of effort. She twisted the sphere again and bluish light started leaking from its fretwork.

"The beam's ready," she said, her voice hoarse and ragged. She was breathing very hard. Lanoe hadn't noticed until that moment. "I just have to direct it. This is...the tricky part. It'll take a couple minutes."

"You can do it," Lanoe told her.

"Do you remember—"

Zhang stopped in mid-recollection. Lanoe frowned and tried to figure out why. Then he saw it. He'd been so focused on Ginger that he'd almost missed the fact that a green pearl was rotating in the corner of his eye. A call from Candless.

"Don't answer it," Zhang said. She laughed and reached for his wrist. She was going to switch off his comms, he knew. Shut them down before he could hear what Candless had to say. *"What lousy timing she's got!"*

The green pearl kept spinning. All he had to do was flick his eyes one way, to answer, or the other way to dismiss it.

He flicked his eyes.

Chapter Twenty-Seven

Candless's message came through loud and clear. Normally you could only get that kind of noiseless transmission from a communications laser, but Lanoe knew she had to be broadcasting to every corner of the system. She had no way of knowing where he was.

Clearly, she felt he needed to hear what she had to say.

"I have an idea of what you're doing, though not how," she began, speaking fast, dispensing with any kind of preamble. "I understand why you feel you have to do this. But, Lanoe, it's the wrong move. You've known me for a long time. I might hope that you would simply take my word for it. That you would believe I'm making this recommendation thoughtfully and with the best of intentions.

"Then again, maybe you're thinking I'm your enemy right now. It's true that I conspired to relieve you of duty. There's no point in denying it. Lanoe, I've had nothing but respect and admiration for you for a century now. I've fought by your side and been proud to do so. I only agreed to relieve you because I needed to prevent you from making a mistake like this.

"A mistake that puts us all at risk. I need you to listen, Lanoe. Not to me, but to someone who actually understands what's involved."

Paniet spoke next. Lanoe had never seen the engineer less than cheery and amiable. Now he sounded distinctly terrified.

"Dearie," Paniet said. He cleared his throat. "Commander. I hear you're trying to change history. That's a—well, a risky thing to do, under any circumstances. The truth is, we really don't understand time as well as we'd like. We've never had a chance to study time travel, and we don't know how our actions here will affect the future—that is, our own time. I can run down a few conjectures for you, though.

"First, there's a chance that it simply won't work. That the course of time can't be altered, not by human beings, no matter how clever we get. It's possible you'll . . . do what you're about to do, and it won't change anything. That events will play out exactly as they did before, and you'll have achieved nothing.

"Another possibility is that time is conserved, just like matter or energy. I'll spare you the long and rather tricky equations. It's possible that if you try to change things, the universe itself will stop you. Either it'll simply blink you out of existence—or some sequence of apparently random events will occur, a meteor will appear and strike you dead, or you'll have a sudden and unexpected stroke . . . We call this the Novikov self-consistency principle, and on paper it actually works. I know it sounds unlikely, but there may well be some mechanism to prevent the third possibility. The one that scares me the absolute most.

"The third possibility being that what you're doing will *work*.

"Valk has suggested you may be about to wipe out the Blue-Blue-White. Kill every last one of them now, before they even have a chance to launch their drone fleets. That's a rather horrible prospect, but it only leads to a much greater problem. It will create a paradox. A series of events that simply can't happen.

"If there was never a Blue-Blue-White fleet at Niraya, you wouldn't have gone there. You would never have known about the Blue-Blue-White, nor had any reason to kill them. So you never would have come here, either. You wouldn't—couldn't—destroy them. Which would mean they wouldn't be destroyed. Which would mean they would launch a drone fleet, one that would eventually make its way to Niraya . . .

"Do you see where I'm headed here, Commander? Do you understand? If you do this thing, you remove the possibility of your doing it. That's impossible, and the universe is very, very bad at containing impossible things.

"You'll create a loop. A closed timelike loop, to be exact. You will send us all into an infinitely repeating series of events. You kill the Blue-Blue-White. History changes so you've never heard of them. Because they now exist again, they attack Niraya. That inspires you to come back in time to kill them. Except when you do, you remove your own motivation for doing so, and—and so on, and so on. It can't end, you see? It has to repeat over and over, forever.

"Whether you will only doom yourself and your crew to this infinite recursion, or whether the rest of the universe comes along for the ride as well, I simply don't know.

"What I do know—for certain—is this. If you save Bettina Zhang's life now, you will be dooming her to die and be saved an infinite number of times. You'll be saving her forever—but you'll also be letting her die forever.

"You can't want that. You have to see reason here.

"Please, Commander.

"Don't do it.

"I'm begging you."

Paniet's voice cut out and for a while Lanoe heard nothing. The silence was unbroken, as blue light streamed out from between Ginger's fingers. Growing stronger.

Eventually Candless spoke again. "I'm going to repeat this message," she said. "Over and over. Until you hear it, Lanoe. Until you listen—or doom us all.

"I have an idea of what you're doing," she said, "though not how..."

Zhang stepped out from behind Ginger. She hadn't been there before. Of course, the laws of space and time meant nothing to ghosts.

"We're almost there," she said.

Lanoe stared at her. She was wearing her thinsuit painted with red tentacles wrapping around one sleeve and one leg. The suit she'd worn the last time he saw her alive. She had her red hair down, falling forward across eyes he couldn't see. Her helmet was down, but of course, she didn't need to breathe.

"So close," she said.

"Zhang?"

"What I heard," she said, *"in all that noise, was that he doesn't know."*

"Zhang—"

"What I heard was what might happen. Not what will. There's a chance he's right, sure, and we're going to destroy the entire universe, blah, blah."

"Zhang?"

"But there's also a chance that this will work."

"Zhang…"

"That there is some nonzero possibility that doing this will give me my life back. That you and I can be together again. Didn't you hear that? I know you were hoping it was what he would say. I know what you want, Lanoe. I know what you're afraid of. If you read between the lines, if you listen to what he didn't say—there's some hope in there. Some possibility of everything working out perfectly."

"Zhang," Lanoe said, and opened his mouth to say—

"And we're so close," she said, laying a finger across his lips. Her hand passed right through his helmet. It didn't occur to him that this was strange. *"We're so close, and you don't have to do anything more. Just let this run its course. Let it happen, Lanoe.*

"That's all.

"Just let it happen."

He would talk with Valk, later, about what he'd done. The AI was his only hope for a sympathetic audience, and he would need very much to discuss his actions. To try to find a way to justify what he'd done.

"The thing is, I barely heard Paniet. I was so far gone at that point, so far down the track...I don't think anyone could have said anything that would have changed my mind. I'd already done so many things I couldn't take back.

"When Orpheus went to hell to get Eurydice back, there was only one condition. He couldn't look at her. He couldn't look over his shoulder, or turn around, or so much as glance behind. When you decide you're going to break the rules, you aren't allowed to change your mind, or second-guess yourself.

"I wanted her back so badly. For a long time I'd been convinced it couldn't happen. That she was just gone, and no one could change that, and that the only thing left to me, the last purpose of my life, was to get revenge.

"Then—out of nowhere—it was possible.

"I wasn't acting rationally. I couldn't act rationally. Not when the one thing that would make me whole again was right there, in my grasp.

"Maybe nobody ever makes a decision like that with a clear head. Maybe it's not possible. I did what I had to do—I didn't give it a second's thought."

He looked past Zhang. Looked across at Ginger, where she stood with her hands up in the air, her fingers contorting around the fretwork of the device. He could barely see her for the blue light streaming from it.

"I'm sorry," he told her.

She didn't respond. They were well past the point where an apology could possibly mean anything to her, or anyone else.

"I'm sorry," he said again.

Just let it happen, Zhang said, in a time outside of time, and already she was fading, her image cut to pieces by rays of blue light.

"I looked at her," he told Valk, later on, "at Ginger. And her helmet was—was black, and opaque, I know it was. It wasn't possible for me to see her face at that moment, not with the red dwarf right there, right next to us.

"Except I could. I could see her face twisted with pain. I could see her brow slick with sweat. And I saw her red hair. Zhang had red hair, too."

"I remember," Valk said.

"I didn't do what I did because the math was wrong. For the devil's sake, what did I care about math, or closed loops, or—or anything?

"I did it because of that red hair."

Lanoe leaned over the side of the cutter and looked down at the disk. At the terrible thing he was about to do.

Then he took two steps, closing the distance between himself and Ginger.

"*Lanoe,*" Zhang said, just a distant wind blowing between the stars.

He grabbed the device out of Ginger's hands. It shook violently, its blue light fracturing into a dozen spectra. He pulled his arm back and tossed it away from him, tossed it into the face of the red dwarf.

"I'm sorry," he told Ginger, for a third time.

She was still standing there with her arms up. As if she didn't understand what had just happened.

The device shrank to a pale dot, then became impossible to see. Eventually it would vaporize in the atmosphere of the unnamed star.

"I did it because of that red hair," he told Valk. "I did it because I saw I was going to kill a girl with red hair to save a woman with red hair.

"Maybe it was just math, after all. Terms canceling each other out. A null set, right? Is that what it's called?"

"I have no idea what you're talking about," Valk told him. "I don't understand you. I don't think I ever did."

"I've hurt a lot of people in my time. Killed a lot of people—it's my job. Killing Ginger, it wouldn't have been hard to do. It wouldn't have kept me up at nights, even. I don't think it would have. But it would have created a new kind of loop, of its own. A kind of moral loop with no end."

"I don't get it," Valk said. "But...you did the right thing."

"I did what I did. I—I thought of something, later on. I thought of something that makes me wonder if I had any choice at all. If any of us have any free will. Paniet said that if I created a paradox, it would send us into an infinite loop. A series of unchanging events, repeated over and over."

"Yeah, a closed timelike loop that—"

"But what if that isn't quite right? I know enough about chaos theory and quantum mechanical probability to know you can't ever say that two states are really identical. Just—just work with me here. Say we did get stuck in a loop. Say we repeated the same events over and over. And I kept setting off the device, I committed an act of genocide, over and over and over again."

"Right," Valk said.

"But say there was the tiniest bit of difference each time. Say one time a proton halfway across the universe was deflected by a magnetic field and it went left instead of right. Say one time a butterfly flapped its wings somewhere. Say one time we were just far enough from the red dwarf that Ginger's helmet wasn't completely opaque, that I could actually see her hair.

"Say we did loop through those events, over and over, with just the tiniest change in each iteration. Changes at the subatomic level, totally random fluctuations. But they would build up. Reinforce each other, creating larger and larger deviations from the standard script. Until one time, one trip through the loop, I decided I couldn't do it."

"I guess...well, that's one way you could get conservation of time, I suppose," Valk said. "Are you asking me to do the math? Do you want to know how many iterations it would take?"

How many times I saved Zhang, Lanoe thought. *How many times I killed her.*

"No," he said. "I don't want to know."

⸺※⸺

Ginger wept the whole way back. Rain-on-Stones chirped empathetically, but it didn't seem to help.

"We'll find another way," he told the girl. "We'll find a way to free you."

When he arrived back at the cruiser, he thought maybe he could just put Rain-on-Stones back in her cell, and then take Ginger with him when he headed to the carrier. There was a limit on how far choristers could project their thoughts. When they reached the brig, however, she just shook her head. "I'm staying here with her," she said.

Lanoe frowned. "I'm offering you a choice, here. A real choice, this time."

"And I'm making it," Ginger told him. "She needs me. Yes, I want to be free. But she needs me too much."

He left them there. No guards in the brig, the cell hatch wide open. They pushed their way inside and curled themselves into separate corners, as far as they could get from each other while still remaining in the same room.

He docked the cutter in the carrier's flight deck, then made his way to the bridge. No one tried to stop him. A few of Ehta's marines were in the corridors, but they looked so surprised to see him that they didn't even come to attention as he kicked by.

The bridge hatch opened for him—apparently his clearance hadn't been revoked. He pushed inside and saw all of them there. Candless and Ehta, Valk and Paniet. Giles, the Centrocor IO, was still at his station, as was a Centrocor pilot he'd never met before.

The mutiny had taken its toll, but the Navy didn't have enough personnel to fill all the necessary positions. If Candless trusted the Centrocor officers, Lanoe supposed that was good enough for him.

As he entered only Candless seemed to have the presence of mind to do anything but stare. She moved toward him, but not quickly enough. Before she could reach him he sat down in the captain's position and strapped himself in.

"I'd like a report on enemy movements," he said.

That brought Candless up short. From the corner of his eye he could see Ehta moving now, too. Circling around to get behind him.

"Sir," Candless said, "perhaps—"

"Commander," the IO said, turning to face him. "We're spotting a lot of activity inside the disk. Airfighters everywhere, scrambling to take up positions around the cities. We've laid in a course that will allow us to shell some of the cities while facing minimal opposition, but we believe that once we begin making strikes, they'll change their order of deployment and we'll need to recalculate."

Lanoe nodded. "Thank you, Lieutenant. What about spacecraft?" He turned to look at Candless. "The message you sent was loud enough to wake up the entire system. I assume you knew that would draw the Blue-Blue-White to our position?"

"I . . . did," Candless said. "Sir."

"I warned her," Paniet said.

Candless turned and gave him one of her signature nasty looks.

"It was unavoidable," Lanoe said. "But now we're going to have to move to evade. IO, what about Blue-Blue-White assets outside of the disk's atmosphere? What are we facing?"

"No fewer than seven dreadnoughts," the IO replied. "The number may be higher—we've been restricted to passive sensors to minimize our profile. At least a hundred interceptors have been spotted as well, all converging on our present position."

Lanoe nodded. "Everything they've got, I would imagine. We've convinced them we're a real threat. They won't hold back now. All right. Our best bet is to not be here anymore when they arrive. Lay in an evasive course. We'll withdraw from the disk, to . . . say fifty million kilometers out. Valk, are you currently in command of the cruiser?"

"Yes," the AI said.

"We'll maintain a close formation for now. Match your course to ours."

"Okay," Valk said.

"For the moment, at least," Lanoe said, "we're going to abandon any plan to aggress on the Blue-Blue-White. We're going to focus on staying alive."

"Commander," Candless said, moving to float directly in front of him, "perhaps I could have a word with you in private."

Lanoe was very good at playing card games, because he knew how to bluff. He kept his face perfectly impassive as he looked up and directly into her eyes.

He could feel Ehta behind him. Close enough to stab him in the back. Or, far more likely, hit him with a neural stunner.

Well, if they were going to relieve him of duty, there wasn't a lot he could do to stop them. If there was any doubt in their minds, though—

"No," he said.

"I beg your pardon?" Candless asked.

"I said no, Captain. We don't have time for a private consultation right now. I've issued orders and I expect them to be carried out immediately. I'm attempting to ensure the safety of the crew of this ship. If you need a word, it'll have to wait."

He watched Candless's face. Her nose lifted and she stared down across its length at him. Her lips pursed until they grew bloodless and pale. Her hands were behind her back, but he was certain they were balled into tight fists.

"I'm back," he said.

Little by little, she relaxed. She suddenly looked extraordinarily tired. Maybe as tired as he felt.

"Of course, Commander," she said. "Glad to have you back aboard."

PART III

SHEPHERD MOON

Chapter Twenty-Eight

It was a tense few hours while they maneuvered, trying to stay ahead of the oncoming Blue-Blue-White defenses. It was physically uncomfortable as well. The carrier had to accelerate like mad to keep up with the cruiser, which for Ehta meant lying in her bunk just trying to breathe. She'd gotten used to the lack of gravity over the last few days and now any weight at all felt wrong. The carrier accelerated at a steady two g, which meant she weighed twice as much as she would have on Earth. The strain on her heart left her feeling weak and like her head was spinning.

At the last moment there was a brief burn for lateral acceleration that threw her up against the side of her bunk, her face pressed against the bulkhead. And then—nothing. All the gravity went away. The blood rushed to her head and she thought maybe she had blacked out. Just for a moment.

Eventually she managed to crawl her way to the hatch and spill out into the corridor beyond. She kicked her way down to a wardroom that had once belonged to the carrier's marines.

It was deserted. The vast majority of the people who might have used its facilities were dead now. Either they'd been cut down back when Lanoe boarded and seized the carrier, or they'd been on the wrong side of the mutiny.

Ehta strapped herself into a seat and sucked on a squeeze tube of water. She had hydration tabs in a pocket of her suit, but she figured she should save those. There was a big meeting called for later, a general meeting of all the surviving officers of the fleet to discuss what they would do next. To talk about just how much bosh they were in.

After that, she intended to get very drunk.

Hydration tabs were great for hangovers, and they were ten thousand light-years from the nearest place she could get any more of them. She was going to make them last.

As she was considering maybe actually eating some food—as unappetizing as the prospect might be—she heard someone coming down the corridor. "Hello?" she called, not sure if she wanted company or not.

It turned out it was Valk, kicking his way down the corridor with a sort of methodical grace. He came into the wardroom and sat down beside her without a word.

The silence dragged on far too long, until she realized he was expecting her to talk first. "It's good to see you up and around," she said. "When you were at the controls of the cruiser, slumped out and with your helmet down—I started worrying about you, big guy."

"There didn't seem to be any point in trying to act human," he told her. "Maintaining this form takes energy I could use for other things."

"That's about how I feel when I look at my hair in the morning," Ehta told him.

He didn't laugh. "Maybe I was falling into a sort of digital version of depression," he said instead. "I'm better now, I think. Now I know I'm not broken. Also, I've started to think that my mental health is something I need to be very careful with."

"Yeah?" she said. "That just occurred to you?"

"It followed as a postulate from something else I was thinking," he told her. "I was considering what's going to happen to us. There's no way back to human space, not if Rain-on-Stones can't open a wormhole. We're all stuck out here for the rest of our lives. Eventually all of you are going to die."

Ehta bit through the end of her squeeze bottle. Water oozed out in a thick globule that wobbled its way through the air between them.

Valk cupped his hand around the globule and gently herded it over to a recycling chute. "There's quite a bit of water onboard, but no reason to waste it. Food's the real problem. The crew will probably starve to death in less than six months."

"Valk," Ehta said through gritted teeth, "maybe you could not talk about that right now? Maybe you could not say things like that to me?"

"Sorry. I was overly focused on what's going to happen to me. Assuming Lanoe refuses to deactivate me, I'll just keep going. I'll be all alone here, until the power runs out. If I ration it properly I can probably make it last four hundred years. That's a long time to be alone, and my programming prevents me from committing suicide. I'll have to run the batteries down before I can really rest. So, you see, I need to make sure I can handle the psychological strain. I wouldn't want to end my existence as a crazy robot wandering around a spaceship full of skeletons."

"No," Ehta said. "I can't imagine that would be fun. Excuse me," she said, unstrapping herself. "I need to be somewhere right now."

"Oh? Where?" he asked.

"Literally anywhere else," she told him.

<hr />

They were Navy officers. Not fools.

Candless watched their faces as she laid out their situation. She wasn't telling them anything they hadn't already figured out on their own. "We can't survive a direct confrontation with seven dreadnoughts. Even making proper use of the cruiser's guns we might not make it through a fight with even one of them, especially if it is supported by interceptors. Fortunately, we don't have to fight. We know that the dreadnoughts have trouble finding us when we run dark, so it's likely we can postpone having to fight another battle indefinitely. We can drift for quite a while, letting them pass us by. My hope is that they'll eventually get tired of chasing phantoms and return to the disk. When they do, we can start up the engines and burn for deep space."

Paniet stared at the table, scratching at the padded top with his thumbnail. Giles, the IO, who'd remained loyal in the mutiny, just looked happy to be included. Ehta met her gaze directly, but her face was grim. Valk—well, it was impossible to tell what Valk was thinking.

Lanoe looked like he wanted to say something. When she raised an eyebrow at him, however, he just shook his head.

"We can stop at Caina, or any of the distant detached planetoids we passed on our way into the system. Assuming they're similar to cometary objects we've encountered before, they'll be a good source of deuterium and tritium that we can mine and use as fuel for our engines. We may even be able to find some organic molecules. Not food, exactly, but raw materials we can use to synthesize something like food. Once we're done collecting resources, we can leave the system altogether and be done with the Blue-Blue-White. The next step after that is . . . well, I'm open to suggestions."

Each of them had their own idea. None of them particularly appealed to Candless.

"I've been studying this chart," Paniet said, unrolling a minder on the tabletop. It showed the wormhole network—not just the wormholes that connected human planets, but the entire network that the Choir had built, which allowed travel between half the stars in the galaxy. "The Choir very specifically did not build a wormhole anywhere near this system, because they'd encountered the Blue-Blue-White drone fleets twice before, and they weren't anxious to meet the people who built those machines." He looked up at them with a kind of desperate optimism. "The nearest wormhole throat to us right now is about seven hundred light-years from here."

That got a murmur of dismay from the crowd. Candless rapped her knuckles on the hard edge of the table to quiet them down.

"Duckies, it isn't as bad as it sounds. If we can accelerate to a significant portion of the speed of light, time dilation will be our friend, for once. It won't take anything like seven hundred years, as far as we're concerned."

"How long?" Lanoe asked.

"Including the time to accelerate to that speed, and then decelerate again when we reach the wormhole throat . . . well. Admittedly, we're still talking at least a century," Paniet admitted.

"Let's . . . call that Option One," Candless said.

Ehta grunted in frustration. "I'm sure this is dumb, but—Valk could try talking to the Blue-Blue-White again. Maybe . . . hell. Apologize. See whether they'll, I don't know. Take us in."

"You want to spend the rest of your life as a guest of a bunch of giant jellyfish?" Giles asked. "Count me out of that one!"

"It can't be done, anyway," Valk said. "Not in any reasonable timeframe."

"Define reasonable," Paniet suggested.

"I couldn't understand them because my language files were half a billion years out of date," Valk explained. "It's like if you went back to ancient England, say fifty thousand years ago, in a time machine and tried speaking English to the people there. They'd just look at you funny, right? You'd have almost no words in common. Languages change over time, and eventually they change so much there's no way to translate. This is even worse because I'd be back-translating, like trying to figure out how to speak Indo-European by guessing."

"But you can do that, right?" Ehta asked. "I mean, it's possible. Yeah?"

Valk lifted his arms and let them fall. It was the closest thing he had to a shrug. "It's basically a cryptanalysis problem. I mean, yes, I can do it, but it would take years to even make a dent in it."

"Still, Option Two sounds a little more practical than Option One," Ehta insisted.

"What about Option Three?" Giles said. His eyes were very bright.

Candless turned her gaze upon him. "And what is that, exactly?"

"We go down in a blaze of glory," the IO said. He laughed, and it was not a healthy laugh. "Turn around. Start shooting. Kill as many of those beggars as we can get before they kill us."

No one around the table seemed to want to touch the idea. Not even Lanoe.

"That's about what's left, isn't it?" Giles demanded. He pounded on the table with his fist. "It's all we have left. The only thing we can hope to accomplish. We're all going to die. We're going to die whether we starve or burn when those plasma balls come for us, we're going to burn…burn…" He lifted his hands to his face in shame as he started to sob, big chest-heaving tears leaking out through his fingers.

"No," Valk said.

Lanoe and Ehta both turned around in their chairs to look at the AI.

"No," he said again. "There's something else we can accomplish. If we've given up on playing it safe. If we're willing to do something really, really dangerous."

"Well?" Lanoe demanded.

"We can do what we came here for. There's still a chance."

<hr />

Valk didn't need a minder, or a virtual keyboard. He loaded up the video file he wanted and fed it through display emitters built into the table. He could read human faces well enough to know that the gathered officers had no idea what he was showing them.

"When we first approached the disk," he said, "we flew past one of the shepherd moons, out near the far edge. We got a pretty good look at it." The display showed a rocky spheroid about two thousand kilometers in diameter. Its surface couldn't be seen, because the Blue-Blue-White had encased the entire mass in their pale cagework, pylons joined together at odd angles to form a second crust around the moon. Inside that cagework were complex structures that were hard to make out. "We saw something there, remember? We saw a queenship."

The view shifted, zooming in on an irregular hexagon of pylons, one small part of the moon's cage. Inside that hexagon was a rock roughly a kilometer long. One end was open to the moon's thin atmosphere. Long spiky structures—fifteen of them—ringed the aperture. It looked like nothing more than a giant statue of a Blue-Blue-White, but an unfinished or damaged one. The structure's hull was already pitted with impact craters.

"A queenship?" Giles asked.

Valk nodded. "Right. You've never seen one of these before. Lanoe, Ehta, and I have, though. This is the main element of one of their drone fleets. We fought one of these at Niraya."

"I only ever saw it on a display," Ehta said, leaning back in her chair. "You and Lanoe actually got inside one. And then you blew the hell out of it."

Lanoe's mouth twisted over to one side. Valk could guess that his memories of that day were...complicated. It had been a great victory for him. It had set him on the path he was still following. It had cost him the woman he loved.

"These things," Valk said, moving on, "are amazing machines. They're built out of hollowed-out asteroids, which means they have a hull so thick we could barely scratch it with ground-based artillery. They can command and control entire fleets of smaller drones. They're designed to rebuild gas giant planets into suitable homes for the Blue-Blue-White, without any supervision. They can also make perfect copies of themselves, and those copies can make more copies, and those copies—"

"Can sterilize a galaxy," Lanoe cut in.

Valk nodded again. "The point I wanted to make is, the whole process started with just one ship. The Blue-Blue-White built just one of these and set it loose. By our time there were millions of them. They went everywhere. But it started with one."

He pointed at the display.

"This one," he said.

Lanoe frowned. "You think this is the first one. The original."

"I'm certain of it," Valk said. "The Choir sent us here, five hundred million years in the past, for one reason. To see this. To do something about it. I don't know how much time we have. If I had to guess, I'd say the Blue-Blue-White will launch this queenship in the next few days. If we can get to it before they send it on its way, we can stop them from killing off every civilization that ever lived."

"Wait," Lanoe said, shaking his head. "Wait. If we destroy that thing now, won't that cause the same problem we just avoided? Won't it create a paradox? If we blow up this queenship, there'll be no reason for us to come here in the first place."

"Who said anything about blowing it up?" Valk asked.

Candless cleared her throat. "Perhaps you'd be kind enough to share with the rest of us what you'd like to do with it, if destruction is off the table?"

"I want to reprogram it," Valk said. "Its mission was never military. It was designed to do construction work, not wipe out alien species. The problem was that the Blue-Blue-White programmed it wrong. They told it to wipe out vermin, but failed to give it a good definition of what vermin looked like.

"If we can change its basic code, we can stop that from happening. We can tell it not to kill any intelligent lifeforms it finds on its voyage. We can rewrite history."

"Hmm," Paniet said. "Huh. Well, yes." He shook his head. "But no. No, it can't be that simple. Just changing a few lines of code— easy enough, but you're talking about making a major change in history. Just a massive, massive change."

"Not every change we could make automatically results in a paradox," Valk said. "That only happens if we don't give ourselves a reason to come back here."

"Oh, is it that simple? You have no idea what you'd be tampering with!" Paniet laughed. "Even if we assume there's some kind of conservation of time, there are just too many variables for me to feel comfortable with this. We have no idea what kind of ramifications this small change could have—tiny changes add up over time, become big changes, become catastrophes. And the longer the stretch of history that you change, the more fraught it gets. Over half a billion years, how many things could go wrong?"

"You're right," Valk said. "Unless there was someone riding along with the queenship, someone who could steer it in the right direction over that whole stretch of time. Making sure to avoid paradoxes, teaching it to respect intelligent life. Guiding and steering its decisions, every step of the way."

The engineer's face clouded. "Someone who could make copies of himself as well, so they would be copied into each new queenship as it's built."

"Yes," Valk said.

"Meaning you," Lanoe said. "Yourself. You're saying you want to copy your own programming into the queenship's memory."

"Yes," Valk said again.

Lanoe's eyes narrowed down to slits. "When we fought the queenship at Niraya, we were convinced there had to be a programmer onboard. Someone we could talk to, somebody who could be reasoned with. We were wrong—the queenship was just a drone, incapable of doing anything but what it was programmed for. You want to become that programmer. And when you get to Niraya, half a billion years from now, you'll be waiting to talk to us. To me. To yourself—to explain what's happening. To explain that we need to come back here and make this change, and as a result, not create a paradox."

Valk was glad Lanoe could see it so clearly.

"Yes," he said.

Candless shook her head. "I think Paniet's objection is still valid. This is incredibly risky. And not least because it's so dependent on Valk. Have we forgotten what he is?" She stared at Valk until he wanted to curl into a ball and roll away. "You," she said, "are an artificial intelligence. I'm sorry, but I've never trusted you."

This wasn't exactly news to Valk. She'd been fighting to have him deleted ever since she learned what he was. It was hardly a unique opinion, either. AIs were illegal for a reason, after all. During the Century War, an artificial intelligence had murdered half of the human race.

"He's been invaluable so far," Lanoe said. "He's—"

"He's an AI!" Candless said. "And an unstable one at that. And now you want to entrust the entirety of history to him. You want to fix a lethally faulty computer program—by putting it in the hands of an unpredictably faulty computer program."

Lanoe frowned. "I've heard your concern," he said.

"But you're going to ignore it, aren't you?" Candless said. She leaned forward against the table, bracing herself on her hands. "Is that how it goes? You're going to just make a decision, and we all have to live with it?"

"I'm the ranking officer of this fleet," Lanoe said.

But Candless wasn't having it. "No," she said.

Lanoe raised an eyebrow. "No?"

"No, damn you!" she bellowed.

As tough as she was, Valk had never heard her shout before. He looked around the table and saw everyone staring at her in shock.

"I beg your pardon," she said, "but this is far too important to let one person decide whether we do this or not. Commander, if you choose to act unilaterally on this, I'll be forced to revisit the notion of—"

"Wait," Valk said. Because he knew she was about to try to relieve Lanoe of command. He couldn't let that happen. "Wait."

Candless continued staring at Lanoe, but she fell silent. The rest of them all looked to Valk.

"If I'm sending one message into the future," the AI said, "there's no reason I can't send two."

"What are you suggesting?" Paniet asked.

"We know the Blue-Blue-White fleets visited the Choir, not once but twice. When I get to their planet, I can contact them as well. Tell them what's happening, and ask them for a favor."

"A favor?" Ehta asked.

"I can ask them to open another wormhole. Just like the one that brought us here. I can have them bring us home."

"Home," Giles said, his eyes wide.

"Home," Paniet said, his voice cracking.

Lanoe scratched at the short hair on the top of his head. He nodded to himself, then turned in his seat to face Candless directly.

"You're not comfortable with me making this decision myself," he said to her. "Maybe you'd like to put it to a vote."

Candless looked around the table. Valk could only imagine what she saw in all those suddenly hopeful faces.

"Apparently," she said, "that won't be necessary."

The first step was to find out if it was even possible. Paniet and Giles went to the carrier's bridge so they could gather as much intelligence as possible. They were a long way from the shepherd moon, and as they were still hiding from the Blue-Blue-White's dreadnoughts, they could only use the ship's passive sensors—mostly its telescopes. It was crucial, however, that they identify what kind of defenses surrounded the queenship.

"It's going to take a while," Giles said, shaking his head. The Centrocor IO seemed to have calmed down a bit since his outburst at the strategy session, but he was still very much on edge. "I can take a series of still images and synthesize them into a pretty good composite. We'll need to do some pretty heavy object recognition analyses, though, to get any idea what we're facing."

Paniet nodded. "It'll take exactly as long as it takes. No one's expecting miracles here, love."

"Isn't that exactly what we're talking about? Changing history? If you don't consider that a miracle, well..."

Paniet smiled. "Fair enough. I'll see if we can get Valk to help with the analysis, that should speed things up a little." He patted the man on the shoulder, then kicked his way out of the bridge. He tapped at his wrist display to send a message to Valk. A blue pearl popped up in the corner of his eye almost instantly.

"How can I help you?" the AI asked.

Paniet explained about the image analyses. "Any chance you can take a look?"

"Of course. Have the imagery forwarded to me and I'll do it right away."

Paniet nodded to himself. "Excellent," he said. He reached toward his wrist to end the call, but then stopped himself. "Valk," he said, "I wonder—do you have a minute? I'd like to discuss something with you."

"Of course."

"I've just been thinking about what you're offering to do. I'm wondering…well, I've been concerned, honestly. We're asking a great deal of you. Do you really feel you're up to this?"

"Certainly. I make copies of myself all the time. I can even partition my consciousness to perform multiple tasks simultaneously. Right now, while I'm talking to you, I'm also sitting with Lanoe. We're having a fascinating conversation about the nature of paradoxes and whether the temporal dimension is limited by constants or dynamic enough to permit stochastic effects and scalar fields."

Paniet frowned. Well, at least he wasn't the only one who had doubts. "That's good. But I guess that wasn't really what I meant. I'm sure you're functionally capable of this. I was more concerned with your, ah, mental state."

"You're worried that I'm not stable enough," Valk suggested. He didn't sound offended by the implication. "I am a little concerned that I'll degrade over time. I've considered that, and I think I have a solution. The fleets spend most of their time in a low-activity state, traveling between the stars. Because they don't use wormholes, it can take them thousands of years to go from one system to another. I'll only really need to do anything in the comparatively brief windows when a fleet is actually in the vicinity of one planet or another. I can put myself into standby mode during those long voyages, and experience only a tiny fraction of the elapsed time."

Paniet sighed. Clearly the AI had thought all of this through— from a practical perspective. He doubted that Valk had given much attention to the larger issues, though.

"I trust you," the engineer said. "You know I do."

"You've always been supportive of me, even knowing what I am," Valk confirmed. "I've appreciated that."

"I believe in you," Paniet said. Even though it sounded to his own ears like he was trying to convince himself. "It's just—we're giving you power no human being has ever possessed. If we do this, we're basically asking you to play god."

"Hmm," Valk said. "I hadn't considered that. I suppose it is a considerable responsibility. I'll do what I can to discharge it faithfully."

Maybe, Paniet thought, that was all they could ask.

"The shepherd moon has an atmosphere. Not much of one, but enough that it can be defended by airfighters," Ehta said, pointing at the display that Giles had finally worked up, six hours later. "Our telescopes picked up the signatures of forty-five of them, stationed on platforms here, here, and here." She indicated three square shapes in the view. To her eyes they just looked like pale splotches, but Valk had sounded pretty confident in his analysis. "They fly regular patrols around the moon, on a pattern that covers ninety-five percent of the surface every seventy-five minutes. Over here, we think these are laser emplacements like the one we faced in our first battle with the Blue-Blue-White." Two blue dots appeared on the display, each of them only about ten kilometers away from the queenship. "That's what we know we're facing. What we can't see here, what we can't predict, is whether there are any ground-based defenses."

Lanoe's face flickered with light from the display as he leaned close, as if he could get a better view by being physically nearer to the image. "They'll be minimal, if there are any," he said. "I flew through an entire city and only saw one adult Blue-Blue-White and a bunch of immature ones." He shook his head. "I didn't see anything like tanks or infantry."

"This place is a lot bigger than any of their cities," Ehta pointed out. "We honestly don't know what we're going to find."

As ranking marine of the fleet, she had known right away that it was going to be her people who got Valk to the queenship. He would need to be escorted down there and protected for a few minutes while he uploaded a copy of himself into the drone's computers. If a hundred Blue-Blue-Whites were down there carrying anything more advanced than hunting knives, it could be a bloodbath. Worse still, the mission could fail.

"My original thought," Ehta said, "was to take Valk and just a couple marines down there in the cutter. The thing's damned near invisible. We could be in and out before they even knew we were messing with them." She shook her head. "I suppose we could still try that, but..."

"It's too big a risk," Lanoe agreed. "We're only going to get one chance at this."

"So we pull out all the stops," Ehta said. "I take Valk in on the troop transport, with every marine we've got left. They'll see us coming, so we need to go in fast, while the landing zone is still hot. They'll try to shoot us down before we can get close to the queenship, so we need vehicle support. Cataphracts to take out the lasers and then keep the airfighters busy. We bring in the cruiser—and its coilguns—in case any of those dreadnoughts show up. If their interceptors join the party, well...I don't exactly know what we do then."

"Leave that to me," Lanoe told her. "I've fought them off once."

"You *engaged* them once," Candless said, in high dudgeon mode. "You didn't fight them off. They left when they realized the dreadnought they'd been sent to protect was no longer functional."

Lanoe shrugged. "Did you think this was going to be easy?"

Candless had nothing to say to that.

"Once Valk is on the queenship," Paniet said, "we retreat, yes? Get out of there as fast as we can. Our work is done."

"That's the plan," Lanoe told the engineer.

"Except," Paniet said, "we'll be drawing a great deal of attention to ourselves. The Blue-Blue-White already consider us a threat. And this queenship is valuable to them—it's a massive project they've spent a lot of time on. If they see the cruiser approaching their construction site they'll throw every ship they have at us, to try to protect it."

"What did I say about this not being easy, just a second ago?" Lanoe asked.

Paniet shook his head. "No, I got that. What I'm wondering is how it'll look to them. What they'll see. From their perspective, the alien invaders are going to attack one of their most important installations—then run away without actually breaking anything that can't be replaced. If you were in charge of their defenses, Commander, wouldn't that raise a red flag or two? Or fifteen?"

Valk laughed.

Ehta shot the AI a quizzical look.

"It's a joke," Valk explained. "The Blue-Blue-White use a base-fifteen numbering system. So instead of a dozen red flags, they would raise fifteen."

Ehta frowned.

"It's funny," Valk protested. "I thought it was funny."

Paniet waved a hand through the display. "The point is, it's going to look suspicious. They'll suspect that we've sabotaged the queenship somehow. I imagine they'll check its computers. What happens then?"

"I can hide myself pretty well," Valk said. "That's one of the nice things about being a self-aware computer program. If they scan the queenship's memory I can just make sure I'm not in the place they're looking."

"I hope you're right," Paniet said. "Or we'll have wasted a great deal of time and put ourselves in danger for nothing."

"At least we'll know right away if it works or not," Lanoe pointed out. "If it does, we'll see a wormhole throat open in the sky."

"And if it doesn't?" Candless asked.

"Do you see any point in worrying about that?" Lanoe asked her. "If it doesn't, we're all dead. Just like we were before we came up with this plan."

Chapter Twenty-Nine

The new gun crews boarded the cruiser annoyed and unhappy. They were the last of the Centrocor contingent—those members of the carrier's crew who had remained loyal during the mutiny, or at least failed to take up arms in the revolt. They grumbled about being pressed into a service they weren't trained for. It was unavoidable—Ehta's marines were needed down on the shepherd moon. Replacements had to be found, as the guns were designed to be operated by human hands. Somebody had to shoot the guns, and this batch were the only ones available.

"Welcome aboard," Valk said, a disembodied voice sounding from speakers in the vehicle bay. "I've designed some instructional videos to help you learn your new tasks. You should proceed directly to the gun decks and get settled in. We'll be maneuvering in just a few minutes and you'll want to be strapped down— we'll be subjected to several g's of acceleration for the duration of the burn. I hope you'll enjoy your new posts."

Kilometers away, Valk climbed onboard the troop transport. He would be flying the vehicle in. Ehta's marines were already strapping themselves in or stowing their heavy weaponry behind panels in the transport's bulkheads. Ehta grabbed his arm before he could head up to the transport's tiny cockpit.

"Hey, big guy," she said. "For luck."

Before he could react she shoved her face up against his helmet and kissed the black flowglas there. She wrapped her arms around his neck and pulled him into a tight hug. The marines whooped and laughed, a couple of them making rude comments that Valk had to pretend not to hear. He didn't understand. Didn't Ehta know he was far past any kind of sexual feelings?

"I'm sorry," he said, pulling away from her. "We need to get going—maybe we can talk about this later."

As he hurried up the ladder to the cockpit, he could see Ehta slapping hands with some of her people. Well, at least they were in a good mood.

Not so very far away, more copies of Valk powered up the last four BR.9s from the cruiser's original complement. The cataphracts had been moved over to the carrier so that all the small craft could be launched from the same position. The copies ran through preflight checklists, checked weapons loadouts, tested their comms.

Their bodies burned with phantom pain. The sooner this was over, the better, as far as they were concerned. If they didn't make it back, well, that would just be optimal.

The copies sent their ready signals to the carrier's bridge, one by one.

Time to get started.

Lanoe grabbed a handhold on the wall of the carrier's flight deck as gravity pulled him down toward what was suddenly a floor. The second the engines came online, he knew, the Blue-Blue-White would have their position and would move to intercept. Valk and the carrier's pilot had poured every ounce of power they could get into their vehicles' engines—the faster they could get to the shepherd moon, the less resistance they would meet when they arrived.

It would be a short flight. And then—well, Lanoe had never really suffered from nerves. Right before a battle, no matter how bad the odds, he always felt a certain calm come over him. Resolve, but also detachment, an almost dreamlike state. It was never truly real until the shooting started.

Candless, on the other hand, was shaking. She sat down hard on the floor and clutched at whatever she could find to hold on to.

Lanoe peered upward, at the docking berths in their ranks above him. Most of them were empty now. They'd lost all but a few of the Yk.64s that had come with the carrier. Bullam's yacht was gone—with Maggs at the helm. For the first time since he'd met the bastard, Lanoe didn't wish him ill. He honestly hoped the two of them were still alive out there, somewhere. Alive and safe.

He turned and looked at Candless. "I want to tell you something," he said.

"Is now the perfect time?" she asked, her head between her knees.

"It's the only time. I want you to know—you were right. When you decided to relieve me from duty. That was a good call, at the time."

"I'm tempted to try it again now," she said. She looked up suddenly, a surprised look on her face. "Lanoe," she said, "what you just said—that sounded almost like an apology."

Lanoe sighed. "I let a lot of people die because I thought I knew best," he said. This wasn't easy. Lanoe had always made it a policy to never look back, to not question the things he did or the reasons he did them. Moving forward, taking action, was what counted. If he was going to fight by Candless's side, though, he needed to clear the air. "All those Centrocor pilots—they weren't prepared for this fight. How could they be? And I pushed them, thinking maybe if my expectations were high enough they would start showing some real talent. They died because I overestimated them."

Candless sniffed in derision. "Hardly," she said.

"Huh?"

"They died because you were so obsessed you refused to accept reality. You were delusional, Lanoe. You were unfit for command. It wasn't a decision I made, to relieve you. It was absolute necessity. You gave me no choice at all."

Maybe he deserved that. His actions had been dubious, he could see that now. He'd made some very bad mistakes.

"I am sorry," he said. "I'm sorry for what I did. I'm especially sorry for what happened to Bury—"

"Damn you," Candless spat. "Don't you even say his name, you *bastard*."

Candless didn't talk like that. Lanoe reeled as if he'd been slapped.

He raised a hand that weighed three times what it should, three times what it would have weighed on Earth. The effort was exhausting, but he needed to make the gesture. To explain to her, to help her see why he'd done what he did.

He opened his mouth to speak.

"Spare me," she said, before he could get a word out.

Grunting a little under the hard acceleration, she rose to her feet, then moved to a ladder that ran along the wall of the flight deck. Her BR.9 was up there, and clearly she intended to get into its cockpit before he could say anything else.

He stood there for a while, looking up at the fighters perched above him. The ones Valk was inhabiting. The ones they'd left in reserve, even though they had no pilots left to fly them. All of Centrocor's pilots had picked the wrong side in the mutiny, every last one. After the way he'd treated them during the battle with the interceptors, they'd chosen to try to kill Navy personnel rather than fight at Lanoe's side again.

Aleister Lanoe never got lonely. What a foolish thought.

Still, as he stood there at the bottom of the flight deck, he suddenly felt very much alone.

❦

Valk eased the transport out of the flight deck, fighters rocketing past him. It was fine—he was controlling most of them, or at least copies of his program were controlling them. There was no risk of a collision. Candless and Lanoe gave him a wide berth as he slipped out the front of the carrier and into space.

The shepherd moon was less than an hour away, even for the lumbering transport. They were coming in at a low angle, just above the atmosphere of the disk. Thin as it was this far out, the fighters could still make better time flying through hard vacuum.

Valk had thought he'd evolved past human emotions like wonder and awe, but he hadn't factored in a view like this. The disk stretched out forever, a vast and flat plain of shimmering light. The red and black clouds mere ripples in an infinity of color, a maelstrom of constant movement with the red dwarf at its center. The star sat out there like a king on a throne, or like a god in a shrine.

The moon, their destination, was much closer and looked enormous even from this distance, its cagework-covered surface reticulated and complex in the dim light. It cleared a broad swath through the disk, a ribbon of night cut through the cosmic whirlpool. It pushed an enormous hazy bow wave ahead of itself, a permanent roiling thunderhead of white that dripped streamers of vapor like battle standards, fluttering and braiding behind the moon as it passed by.

Valk couldn't remember how many moons, how many planets he'd visited, both in his current form and as Tannis Valk, the human pilot who'd come before him. He'd surfed through the rings of gas giants before, but nothing on this scale. Nothing so big it made him feel this tiny, this insignificant. It couldn't help but make him worry that this wouldn't work, that his plan had been an audacious folly.

He had to force himself to not turn back. He looked to his left and right and spotted fighters all around him, guarding him, and he took a little courage from that. He touched the transport's controls, very lightly, and swooped down toward the moon.

The Blue-Blue-White were expecting him. They must have detected the carrier as it came in for its close approach. The first lasers licked at the sky, sweeping back and forth as they searched for him, spearing straight up from the moon.

❧

Lanoe kept his throttle wide open and tapped his control stick back and forth, his Z.XIX swinging around wildly as he dodged the searchbeams. At that speed they couldn't get a fix on him, though they kept trying. He checked on Candless and the Valks flying the BR.9s, saw they were just barely staying ahead of the lasers. It looked like it was up to him and his advanced fighter to clear the way.

"All seven dreadnoughts are inbound now, as well as the interceptors," the fighter told him. "They're moving quite rapidly. Would you like a tactical display?"

He swung around to dodge a searchbeam and dove toward the surface of the moon. Lances of coherent light flashed past him on every side. The cagework that overlaid the moon's surface rushed toward him, the white pylons growing distinct, shadows on their tops turning into features. Where the hell was the laser emplacement? Ehta's intelligence showed it—there—

Yes—he could see it now, a cluster of searchlights mounted on top of one of the pylons. It saw him, too, and a beam lit up his canopy. He ducked down, just his body acting by reflex, as the beam narrowed, and suddenly a line of light as straight as a razor's edge cut through his flowglas canopy. Air rushed past him, leaking out of the breach, but the flowglas healed itself almost instantly.

Valk dodged as best he could, but the troop transport had never been made for evasive maneuvers. The searchbeams were getting closer, getting far too close for comfort. One grazed the transport's hull, then swung back to touch him again, tracking with him as he tried to swing back and forth.

"Hey, take it easy!" one of the marines in the passenger compartment shouted, as he tried to shake the beam. It was no use, though—it was on him now, locked on, and already it was narrowing, growing more coherent. In a moment it would intensify and collimate until it burned right through his hull, until it cut the transport to pieces—

—except, a hundred kilometers away, one of his other selves, one of the copies inhabiting a cataphract, felt it, too, and moved to intercept, boosting upward on a pillar of fire, accelerating at a rate that would have turned any human pilot into a thin red paste across the back of the cockpit. Even as the beam that had found the transport shrank down until its cross section was no wider than a coin, the Valk in the BR.9 twisted upward in a tight corkscrew, just narrowly avoiding three more beams that had tried to catch it, using up every bit of power he could send to his thrusters, even as engine degradation lights flickered on where no one could see them, chimes sounded where there were no ears to hear them. Even as the searchbeam narrowed further and turned a brilliant ruby red, the BR.9 forced itself onward and there—there—

The BR.9 took the full brunt of the laser, the beam cutting right through its fairings, its armor, its cockpit. Molten slag cascaded across the empty pilot's seat and seared its way through the heat shielding behind the cockpit.

"Thanks, I guess," Valk said, the original Valk in the transport.

The copy of himself started to respond, but just then the laser cut through the BR.9's engine housing. It sheared through the ranks of field emitters holding the fusion torus together and the reactor breached, superhot plasma exploding outward at a significant fraction of the speed of light.

Down in the passenger section of the transport, the marines must have seen the flash of light through the narrow viewports. He heard them shouting, heard a few of them scream.

"Nothing to worry about, friends," he told them. "Just a near miss."

<hr />

Lanoe saw the BR.9 disintegrate, up ahead of him, and cursed under his breath.

It was Candless who called the AI out, however. "M. Valk," she said, over the general band, "you will refrain from these suicidal maneuvers in future! We don't have enough BR.9s to be profligate with them. Am I understood?"

"Yes, ma'am," Valk said, though he sounded like a child trying to explain he couldn't finish his homework because it was *boring*.

Lanoe shook his head. Distractions, so many distractions. When he was so close to the laser emplacement. So close to clearing their way down.

A virtual Aldis sight bobbed around his canopy. He had a disruptor ready to go, the moment he got a firing solution on the emplacement. Even with the Philoctetes targeting algorithm, though, even with all his skill, he could never quite get a lock because he was too busy swinging from side to side, cutting tight corners with rotary turns as he dodged the beams.

It had been a lot easier the last time he'd done this. Then, he'd had the cover of the clouds. Then, he'd had Batygin and his destroyer to act as a shield. Now it came down to nothing but fancy flying and desperation.

"That last beam cut off the end of our upper starboard airfoil," the fighter's voice told him.

Lanoe hadn't even felt it. He wanted to look sideways, to inspect the damage, but he had no time. Three new beams were converging on his position and he had to twist away, zooming up over the moon's surface as they nearly hit his thruster cones.

"I can't get a lock," Candless said over the general band. "Moving to—to engage, but—there are too many of them!"

If Lanoe was having this much trouble, with his advanced fighter, he could only guess how bad her situation must be.

He couldn't afford to think about that, though. He twisted around in a flat spin and then dropped his nose to dive straight toward the laser emplacement. The virtual Aldis sight drifted across the middle of his vision and he swiped it away—it wasn't helping. He reached over to his weapons board and set the disruptor to launch as soon as he pulled the trigger, and not to wait for a firing solution.

A searchbeam caught the nose of his fighter, filling his canopy with blinding light. His helmet opaqued to block it out, but that meant he could barely see what he was aiming at, could barely see the emplacement at all—

Now, he thought, *shoot now,* but he forced himself to take another second, a second during which the searchbeam narrowed and narrowed, until it was a red dot shining directly into his eyes, but—

There. Now.

He squeezed the trigger. Then threw his stick over to the side, even as the laser collimated and punched a hole through his canopy, through the back of his seat. If it hit his engine shielding—but he couldn't look back, couldn't check his damage board, couldn't do anything but watch as—

The disruptor started exploding long before it reached the emplacement. The plume of debris it gave off scattered the beam, sending rays of red light shooting off in every direction. The missile plunged into the cagework around the emplacement, a full meter off from its target, and for a moment Lanoe thought he'd missed, thought he'd thrown away his best chance.

Then orange light and a mushroom cloud of dust shot up from the ruptured pylon, shards of coral pinwheeling away from the emplacement. He couldn't even see the searchlight shapes of the laser weapons, couldn't tell if he'd destroyed them or not, but for the moment, at least, for a few seconds the lasers stopped firing. He held his breath, certain they would start up again as soon as the dust settled.

But the laser didn't fire. He could see the searchlights now, their lenses thick with dust. They weren't moving, weren't firing.

"Yes!" he shouted, and pounded on his console with his fist.

———

"One emplacement down," Lanoe called.

"The second one's giving me trouble," Candless replied. The second emplacement was on the far side of the construction site, over on the horizon and almost below the curve of the moon. Valk was still well within its range. He called up a telescope view from the carrier and saw Candless flitting around it like a gnat, trying over and over to get close enough to knock it out, constantly being forced away as flurries of coherent light shot upward toward her fighter.

"I need support over here," she called. "Valks—come help me!"

The copies streamed away from the transport, twisting toward her along random trajectories. As for the original, Valk had his hands full just staying airborne. He wished he could have controlled the transport directly—it would have sped up his reaction time to simply issue commands straight to the vehicle's computer. He wasn't sure it would have really helped, though. If he maneuvered too hard, if he twisted away from the laser beams too abruptly, he ran the risk of harming his passengers.

That wouldn't do. He was going to need them when he got down to the ground.

As it was, they kept shouting and screaming as he zigged and zagged, trying to stay out of the path of the deadly beams. Without his copies to protect him it was a futile attempt.

"Hang in there," he told the marines, and threw his stick forward to dive toward the moon's surface. Maybe if he could get under the lasers, below an elevation where they could fire safely—

A beam tore through the rear of the transport without warning, slicing through one of his thruster cones like a hot knife. Chimes sounded and red lights filled the cockpit, bathing Valk's suit in the color of blood. He felt something tear loose at the back of the transport, felt the whole vehicle shake and start to tear itself apart. The ship rolled over on its side, and he had to fight to stabilize, to keep from falling out of the sky.

━┅

"Valk!" Lanoe shouted. He could see the transport spinning on its long axis, see a plume of smoke a kilometer long leaking from its engines. He threw his stick over to the side and let his inertial sink pin him down in his seat as he maneuvered hard to close the distance, to reach the transport. Even though he knew it was probably already too late.

As he closed the distance, he saw large shapes moving up behind the transport, shapes he at first mistook for clouds. Closer still and he saw what they really were, and he swore softly to himself.

Airfighters. The moon's contingent of airfighters had scrambled on their position. The raid had been scheduled for a time when most of them were on the far side of the moon, but clearly they must have responded to the attack faster than he'd expected. Three of them were bearing down on the transport already, their giant wings catching the light as they banked in the moon's thin atmosphere. They dwarfed the bulbous transport, like sharks chasing a sunfish.

"Give me some telemetry on those things," he said.

"Yes, sir," the fighter said, and brought up a subdisplay across the bottom of his canopy.

The airfighters' weapons were already hot, ready to fire.

"They'll tear the transport to pieces," Candless called. "They'll burn it to a cinder."

"Not if I can help it," Lanoe said. He threw his stick forward and punched open his throttle. Reaching over to his weapons board, he readied a disruptor, and put two more on standby.

Below Valk the cagework surface twisted and blurred past. Above him lasers swept across the sky, looking for his copies, ignoring him for the moment. Did they think he was finished? Did they think he was going to crash?

Were they right?

It took him a second to realize the actual reason why the lasers were ignoring him. To notice the three giant airfighters swooping in behind him. Ah. That was going to be a problem, he thought.

Though, frankly, at that point they were just overkill. The transport was doing a perfectly fine job of shaking apart all on its own.

"I'm in trouble," he said, calling Lanoe and Candless. "I've been hit."

"I saw it happen. Looks like they caught your aft section, your engines. What's your status?" Lanoe demanded.

Flight data and sensor inputs reeled through Valk's electronic mind, data forming graphs that all pointed to the same nasty conclusion. "I'm going down," he said.

"I'm on my way to support you," Lanoe told him. "When you say going down—"

"I mean I can't hold my altitude," Valk said.

"You're still ten kilometers from the construction site," Lanoe said. "How close can you get?"

"That depends if we want to be alive when we get there."

"Understood," Lanoe said. "I'll cover you. Just—be safe. We're all counting on you."

Valk knew they were. He took a moment to check a camera view of the inside of the transport's passenger compartment. He could see the marines in there weren't even screaming anymore. Most of them had blacked out from g stress. The ones who were still awake looked disoriented, confused, pale and terrified. Ehta's eyes were rolling up in their sockets, and there was blood streaming from her nose.

Valk remembered the night, right before the battle for Niraya, when he and Ehta had shared something...special. Something intimate. He'd still thought he was human, back then. He'd thought he was a terribly burned shell of a human body locked inside a suit with a helmet he could never, ever lower. He couldn't bear the thought of anyone seeing him like that. He'd assumed that any chance he had of human contact was over. That no one would ever want to touch him again.

Ehta had let him keep his helmet up. She hadn't cared what was underneath. She'd shown him what he could do with what he still had. She'd let him touch her, let him *be* with her, in a way that had felt impossible right up until it happened. For just a little time they'd just been two people, sharing their fear, pushing it away so they could connect.

What they'd had that night wasn't love, not by any classical definition. It was warmth, though, and compassion, and sympathy. In the whole time Valk had masqueraded as a human being, it was the best he'd ever felt.

He was going to keep Ehta alive. He was going to save her—no matter what. He wrestled with the control stick of the transport. Stabbed at virtual keyboards, his free hand moving faster than any human hand could. He activated fire and damage control safeguards, then hit a key that flooded the passenger compartment with emergency restraining foam. The marines disappeared under great billowing clouds of the grayish stuff, their helmets raising automatically so they didn't drown in it.

A display popped up in front of him, showing a column of numbers that were going down far faster than he liked. The numbers represented his altitude, in meters, and very soon now they would shrink to zero.

"Anyone who can hear me," he said, his voice muffled by the foam in the passenger compartment, "now would be a good time to brace for impact."

Chapter Thirty

Ehta's head hurt.

Her first thought was that she must have a hangover. It was a pretty good bet that anytime she woke up in pain, not knowing where she was, it was a hangover. Her second thought was that she was glad she'd squirreled away some hydration tabs.

Her third thought was that she'd been buried alive. She could see nothing through her helmet but darkness and could feel weight pressing down on her from above. She panicked for a second, flailing her arms and legs. Surprisingly that had a positive effect—the crash foam all around her, having done its job, liquefied and sluiced away as she moved. She saw a boot sticking out of the foam, right in front of her, and dug toward it, dug up the side of someone's leg.

All her scrabbling around was having an effect. More and more of the foam drained away and the pile of bodies in the wreckage started to settle to the floor. Ehta found an arm and grabbed it, squeezing the hand hard until the arm jerked away from her. She recognized that hand from the missing fingers. "Gutierrez," she said, "you alive? Then get moving! Everybody, move, get up, get up!"

The marines groaned and swore but they obeyed her command, slowly struggling through the remaining foam as they got to their feet. "Binah, Gutierrez," she said, "do a head count, see who's hurt.

I'm going to recce our situation. Keep these people moving—nobody sits down until I order them to."

She fought her way over to the transport's bulkhead, slipping in the residue of the foam. She found the ladder that led up to the cockpit, and reached for a rung—then got a shock when she saw the cockpit wasn't there anymore. The top half of the transport was gone, torn away in the crash, and the ladder led up to nothing but reddish-black sky.

Valk, she thought. *No. No—Valk!* She scrambled up the ladder. The shepherd moon only had about five percent of Earth's gravity, so she got to the top in a hurry, nearly flying out of the broken shaft.

At the top a sullen breeze blew, howling as it streamed across her helmet. She looked around, trying to get some sense of where they were. From the ground level, though, the moon was a bewildering chaos of shapes and forms. She had no referents to explain what she was seeing, and it took her a while to piece it together.

A white coral pylon crossed the sky above her, a kilometer across and riddled with tiny openings. Around her on every side were stacks of soft, billowing gas bags, veined with hoses and cables. She had no idea of their purpose, or if it was even safe to be near them.

She didn't care. Ehta clambered up on top of the smashed transport, searching for any sign of the cockpit. If it had broken off in one piece, if Valk was still inside it, maybe hurt but mostly intact—

A trail of debris, pieces of the transport, headed away from her, strewn out in one direction. Twisted and scorched as it was, the debris at least looked like something human beings had created. She hurried along the trail, bouncing off one gas bag after another. None of the debris was burning—there wasn't any oxygen on the moon to sustain a fire—but some of it was glowing red-hot. One jagged spar had punctured a gas bag, and she was buffeted by an incredible wind as she got close, knocked backward off her feet. She maneuvered around the upwelling gas as carefully as she could, then rushed forward because she saw what was left of the cockpit.

Not much. Just a couple of torn-up pieces of fuselage and part of the pilot's seat, stuffing leaking from its headrest and flitting away on the breeze like chaff. "Oh, no," she said aloud. "Valk! Valk!"

"Over here," he replied. He lifted one arm and gave her a feeble wave. It was about all he could do. He was trapped under a pile of debris and broken alien machinery. She could just see the top of his black helmet.

She started grabbing the debris and throwing it away, freeing him piece by piece. The hot wreckage burned her fingers, even through her gloves, but she didn't care. Eventually she'd exposed enough of his upper body that she could get her arms around him, and she pulled him out of the pile. Part of his suit got stuck on a jagged shard of metal and his left arm came off in one piece. Ehta grunted in horror, but once the arm came loose he came out of the debris pile all at once and they both went sprawling.

"Your arm," she said. "Your arm—it—"

"I don't have an arm," he said. "I had a sleeve and now I don't. It doesn't matter."

She stared at the ragged hole in the side of his suit where his arm had been. Sealant foam oozed across the layers of torn cloth, hardening even as she watched. It looked like he'd grown a clump of mushrooms where his arm had been.

"It's fine," he said, and she realized she was still staring.

"Ma'am?" Gutierrez said.

Ehta craned her head around and saw her marines right behind her, a loose column of them having followed her from the transport's final resting place. "Ma'am," Gutierrez said, "Geddy didn't make it. Mestlez can't see out of one eye. Otherwise...I guess we're okay."

Ehta nodded. She got up and helped Valk rise to his feet. She turned in a circle, looking around her, as if maybe she would see something that made sense. As if she might find some landmark that would tell her what to do next.

She heard a noise like the sky being torn apart and looked straight up, past the pylon that arched overhead. An airfighter shot by, like a giant manta ray gliding over the bottom of the ocean. An instant later Lanoe's Z.XIX streaked after it, his PBW cannons blazing away.

"The transport's gone," Gutierrez said. "It's totaled. Ma'am—we're stuck here. There's no way back. There's no way to get back to the carrier."

Gutierrez's face was hidden by her silvered helmet, but Ehta could hear panic building in the woman's voice.

"What are we going to do?" someone else asked.

Ehta wouldn't have minded panicking herself, just a little. She would have loved to have just screamed and grabbed her head and let it all out. Majors weren't supposed to act that way. "We're going to fulfill our mission requirements," she said. "Nothing's changed."

"Okay," Gutierrez said. "Okay, uh—okay, ma'am. But how?"

It was a fine question.

The laser emplacement had stopped shooting. Candless circled around it three times, expecting that it was a trick, that it would start firing at her again at any moment. When it failed to do so she swooped in low, buzzing the searchlights, daring them to shoot.

They did not.

It took her a second to realize why. She brought up a tactical board and cursed when she saw what it had to show her. Airfighters. The big drones were converging on the construction site—clearly they knew it was being targeted. That was a problem—a big one. They had counted on the element of surprise, of hitting the Blue-Blue-White seemingly at random. If their enemies knew what their objective was, they could concentrate their defense around it.

In the meantime, Candless decided not to look a gift horse in the mouth. She assumed the laser emplacement had shut down because the Blue-Blue-White didn't want to risk shooting their own airfighters out of the sky. She could take advantage of the momentary reprieve. Coming in low, she placed a disruptor right in the middle of the searchlights, smashing them to bits.

Then she had to climb hard and twist away—one of the airfighters was already on her. She pulled back on her stick and maneuvered to come around in a tight bank, circling to get a lock on the airfighter. It banked around more slowly, trying to do the same. There were four more of the things inbound, headed straight for her. If she didn't take this one down soon, she was going to have real trouble. "Valks," she called, "I need support—close to intercept!"

"On our way," one of them called back. She craned her head around, looking for them, but saw nothing. She pulled up a tactical board and found them on the far side of the construction site. Lanoe was over there, too, flying low over the location where the troop transport went down.

"Lanoe—do you see any sign of survivors?" Candless hadn't heard from Valk or Ehta since they reported they were going to crash. If they were dead—if Valk was destroyed—then this mission was over. It would be pointless to continue.

If that was the case, she had no idea what they would do next. Maybe it would be better to just die here, in battle—

"They're okay," Lanoe called back. Candless let out a pent-up breath. "A little banged up. The main problem is they're stuck about eight kilometers from the queenship. Ehta reports she'll head there on foot."

"That'll take too long," Candless pointed out. "We had a tight window for this operation. If they take more than an hour getting there, we'll have seven dreadnoughts coming down on our heads. Not to mention those interceptors."

"Then we'll fight them with everything we've got," Lanoe replied. "This is our only chance. If we retreat now they'll boost security on this site. Lock it down so tight we'll never be able to get close again."

Candless could find no fault in his logic. She wished very much that she could.

"There's one other problem, though," she pointed out. "If the transport is down, they have no way to get back."

"I know," Lanoe told her.

"They're all going to die down there. We're going to lose every one of them."

"We do what we can," Lanoe said.

Candless would have had more words with him—if she hadn't been so busy at the moment.

The airfighter was fifty meters across, not even counting its long, curved wings. She looped up high over it and tried to get behind it, tried to get right behind the trail of fire its thruster painted across the sky. For all its size, the drone ship could *move*, though—it was already accelerating as it followed her up into her loop. She rolled away at the top of her arc, even as it started firing at her, long plumes of superhot plasma stretching forward from gun barrels recessed into its wings.

Candless banked around to try to get away from that fire.

This was going to take some tricky flying.

It was slow going, maneuvering over the gas bags. There was no good footing, no way to move forward with any kind of speed. You had to place each foot carefully, bracing it on the most solid things you could find, then sort of lunge forward and hope you found another foothold. The tangle of hoses around each of the massive sacs could snag your feet and even break your ankle if you weren't careful. Yi had tried jumping on the gas bags like a trampoline, and actually made some good progress, bounding twenty meters forward at a time—until she came down on the wrong end of a bag and nearly brained herself against a metal support beam. After that Ehta had forbidden anyone from trying to bounce their way out.

Three hundred grueling meters on, they came to a stack of gas bags so tall that they brushed the side of the pylon that bisected the sky. Ehta pulled Valk aside. "We can make a lot better time if we get up there. If we get on top of it, it's a straight shot right to the construction site."

The AI tilted his head back to get a better look. "Quicker, sure—but we'll be exposed up there. The airfighters could pick us off."

"Lanoe and Candless can keep them off our back," Ehta said. "Hopefully. Come on," she said. "I'll help you climb."

Not that he needed much help. The low gravity made it easy and Valk proved surprisingly nimble, even with only arm to grab on to handholds. They pulled themselves up, using the more rigid hoses and the metal support skeletons like ledges. Valk made as good time as Ehta did. "I'm used to working with no body at all, sometimes," he said.

"I suppose it also helps you aren't carrying ten guns," Ehta said, shifting her steadygun on her back so it didn't swing around as much. In the low gravity it felt as light as a feather, but it still had the same mass as ever, and when it swung back and forth like a pendulum it threatened to pull her off the narrow perches.

Together they scrambled up the last of the gas bags, then started climbing the side of the pylon. The going was easier there—though the ascent was nearly vertical, the porous coral of the pylon presented endless hand- and footholds. Ehta glanced down and saw her squad climbing up after her, their silver helmets reflecting the dusky light.

Ehta pulled herself up onto the top of the pylon. It ran straight in either direction, a perfect white road reaching to either horizon. She helped her marines up to the top, then got them marching forward. A thin haze like a fog or maybe—given their altitude—a layer of low-lying cloud wisped across the top. In the distance she thought she could see structures rising from the coral, but from where she stood they looked like nothing more than bumps in the otherwise smooth surface.

It was eerily silent up there. Their boots made a constant crunching sound as they marched, but otherwise there was no sound at all. If the fighters were engaged in pitched battles they were off over the horizon, presumably drawing the airfighters away to give Ehta and her people a chance. She intended to make as much use of it as she could. Once she was relatively certain that no tanks or waves of Blue-Blue-White infantry were coming for them, she had her people move out at double time, guns slapping against their backs. Valk had no trouble keeping up. After all, he had no human muscles to get sore or tired.

For almost ten minutes they jogged along in silence, Ehta listening to the rhythmic breathing of her people and nothing else. Then Valk saw something up ahead. He grabbed Ehta's arm and told her to hold up. "There's something up ahead. A—a pit, or something."

Ehta nodded and threw a hand signal. Her people slowed to a careful walk and unlimbered their weapons. As they got closer, Ehta started to see what Valk had pointed out—a shadow lying across the top of the pylon, a shadow that quickly resolved itself into a hole smashed through the coral. Its edges were ragged and natural-looking, though Ehta had no real idea what was natural here or not. A slope of broken coral led down into the depression.

She stopped her people and moved forward to investigate. It looked like a cave burrowed into the pylon. "Mestlez," she called, "you're up."

The marine cursed but he ran forward, his particle rifle clutched in both hands. He moved carefully down the slope of coral shards, planting each foot and testing his weight before he moved to the next one. Soon he'd disappeared from view. "It goes down about ten meters," he said. "My lights aren't showing anything but—"

Ehta frowned. She waited a second, then called, "Mestlez? What do you see? Give me some info here."

Instead of replying, Mestlez screamed.

A dark wave frothed up out of the hole, a boiling mass of dark skin and wet eyes. Ehta grabbed for her steadygun but marines behind her were already shooting, pouring ammunition into the cloud.

As it swarmed toward her Ehta realized it was made up of countless small bodies—small here meaning less than a meter across. She made out wings and eyes that stared at her, eyes the size of her fist, and then they were on her, flapping all around her, slapping her helmet a million times a second with their leathery wings.

She heard guns going off all around her, marines screaming. "Hold your fire!" she shouted, in part because it didn't seem to be doing any good, in part because—"They're just bats! Stop shooting! You're wasting ammunition!"

The swarm of bats evaporated as quickly as it had come, individual animals fluttering off in every direction, clearly terrified and just trying to get away. Before they could all escape, Valk calmly reached up into the cloud and grabbed one of them out of the air. He turned to face the marines, the bat snapping and jerking in his grip.

Ehta looked around and saw half her people prone on the ground. The rest, like herself, were crouched down, hands up to protect their faces.

Only Valk was still fully upright. "Hmm," he said. "Remind you of anything?"

Ehta came closer to examine the bat, then lurched back when it flapped at her. It was—a bat. Not like any bat she'd ever seen before, of course, but she couldn't think of a better word for it. It had three wings and one enormous bulbous eye. Its body behind the eye was so thin it looked skeletal. She could clearly make out a tripartite rib cage and a round pelvis that supported a single taloned foot.

"It reminds me," Valk said, "of the scout ships we fought at Niraya." He let the thing go and it flapped away in a frenzy of leathery wings. "We know so little about this place. I guess we'll never really get a chance to learn more."

"I'm kind of okay with that," Ehta said.

Mestlez poked his silver helmet up out of the hole. It was smeared with straw-colored muck. Presumably bat droppings. Otherwise, he was unharmed.

They kept moving.

Two jets of plasma lanced out from the airfighter's wings, but Candless twisted away in a corkscrewing dive before they could touch her. She was slightly more maneuverable in her BR.9 than the giant aircraft, but she knew she couldn't play this game forever—eventually she would make a wrong move, or the drone would just get lucky and score a hit. That plasma was hot enough to cook her alive if it hit her dead on.

The tip of the airfighter's wing cut across Candless's view. She poured PBW fire into the massive ship, feeling like a wasp trying to sting a condor. She saw her shots connect, saw tiny sparks appear along the wing, but knew she was having little effect. With her free hand she readied a disruptor.

Candless pulled a snap turn that made her whole fighter vibrate. A damage control light came on, but it was only yellow—a warning, not an alert. The shepherd moon's atmosphere was just thick enough that she needed to worry about air resistance, and that limited the number of fancy tricks she could pull. Through her canopy she saw the airfighter turning, its wings held at an angle as it banked around, trying to get her in its sights. She couldn't let that happen. She killed her throttle, then intentionally stalled on her airfoils so she dropped like a stone for a moment. She goosed her thrusters and came up under the massive wing, its shadow darkening her cockpit. A virtual Aldis sight swung right into the middle of her view and flashed to indicate her targeting system had a lock.

She pulled the trigger. The disruptor launched with a thud she felt through her seat, then sprang forward on its tiny thruster. It tore through the glass canopy of the airfighter, leaving a hole less than half a meter across. She couldn't see it start to explode, but she felt it as a massive wave of air pressure buffeted her cataphract and knocked it over on its side.

The airfighter's canopy burst open, shards of glass spinning through the air and smoke pouring out of a crack in its wing. Candless had to burn hard to get out from under it as it fell toward the cagework below, rotating slowly as the low gravity of the moon pulled it inexorably down.

She didn't waste time cheering over her success. There were four more of those things coming for her—and forty more where they'd come from. Her job was far from over.

She nudged her stick to one side and banked over the construction site. The queenship lay directly below her, a gray pebble in the middle of a vast network of lacy pylons. She saw a dark speck on the horizon, black against the red clouds. It grew steadily larger, but by then she knew it was one of the Valks. She could look into the BR.9's cockpit and see that it was empty.

"Lanoe sent me to support you," the pilotless machine said. "He thought you could use some help."

Candless wondered how things had grown so perverse that she would be glad to have a heavily armed AI as her wingman. "Did he, now. How very gallant of him. I'm doing just fine, as a matter of—"

"Because," the machine went on, "he's needed elsewhere. So we—my fellow copies and yourself—are going to have to take on the airfighters ourselves."

Candless stopped in mid-tirade. "He—what? Where? Where, exactly, is he needed more than here?"

"The dreadnoughts and the interceptors are about to arrive. The cruiser and the carrier are moving to engage them, but they need cataphract support or they'll be chewed to bits." The Valk had no body with which to shrug, but she could hear the resignation in its voice. Well, the copies were suicidal, after all. Or would be if their programming would allow it. "Commander Lanoe is going to provide that support. Our job remains to take on the airfighters as best we can. To give my original a chance," the Valk said.

"Yes," Candless said. "Yes, I suppose it does." She fought to keep the fear out of her voice, despite the fact that she felt like a river of icy water had just poured down her spine. "Shall we pick our first target?"

—✦—

The ground shook and then a dull roar and a shock wave of compressed air washed over them. All around Ehta, marines went sprawling onto the white coral. She barely managed to keep her own footing. "What was that?" someone asked, sounding terrified. Ehta didn't have an answer, so she didn't bother replying.

"Come on," she shouted. "We have to keep moving!" She helped Binah up, grabbing his arm and yanking him to his feet. "You can take a nap when we're back on the cruiser, you bastard!"

"We're not going back," he muttered.

"Care to repeat that?" she demanded.

He was a marine. A good marine. "No, ma'am," he said.

Ehta hadn't forgotten that they were stranded down here. As she urged her people forward, she was keenly aware that this had turned into a suicide mission. Nothing new for the PBMs, she thought. The Admiralty and the polys she'd fought for had always considered marines to be a renewable resource, and they'd squandered marine lives in every battle she'd fought. There were dozens of times she'd walked into hell with a squad behind her, certain she was marching to her doom.

This felt different, though. This wasn't some pointless war fought to see which poly was tougher, nor was it some peacekeeping mission on a hellhole planet full of dead-eyed colonists. This was an alien moon where the scale of everything was so enormous it made her feel insignificant, made all her actions seem pointless. It didn't help that she was fighting for Lanoe, a man she'd once revered as a kind of demigod. A man who'd turned out to have feet of clay. A man who'd turned out to be a crazy bastard after all.

Just like every other officer she'd known, she supposed.

She ran on ahead a bit, then turned to face her people, marching backward. "Listen up," she said. "I know none of you asked for this. I know none of you want to die here, so far from home. I wish I could tell you everything's going to be okay. Obviously, I can't."

She couldn't see their eyes. She couldn't even read their body language in their heavy armored suits. She had to just hope they were listening, really listening.

"We came down here knowing there was a chance we would die

here. We're the damned marines, after all. Stick with me. I will keep us alive as best I can. If there's a way out of here, I'll find it. But first and foremost—we're going to do what we came to do. We're going to get Valk here to that queenship, and we are going to save the thrice-damned *human race*. Yeah? Let me hear you say it!"

"Ma'am, yes, ma'am," they shouted, in unison.

If some of them only sounded half-convinced, she supposed she would take what she could get.

They hurried forward. Only about two kilometers lay between them and the construction site. They'd covered a fair amount of that distance when they started to see low domes rising from the pylon in front of them. The first of these were barely a meter high and two meters wide, like pimples on the coral. Farther on they grew larger and more numerous, swollen bumps that stood out from the pylon, growing more numerous until they covered the entire surface of the pylon. Some of them had been broken open, by the looks of the jagged holes in their sides, and Ehta couldn't help but think of eggshells. The shells of eggs that had hatched.

A lot of the domes were still perfectly intact.

Ehta led her people into what increasingly felt like hilly terrain, as the domes grew so large she couldn't see over them—then larger still, until she couldn't see around them, either.

She nearly jumped out of her skin when she caught a flash of movement out of the corner of her eye. It had come from one of the broken domes, just a quick glimpse of something that was gone before she could make out any details. She signaled to her people to stop, then moved to investigate, a pistol in her hand.

Behind her something skittered across the coral. She swiveled around just in time to see a boneless limb, pale and shiny, disappear into a crack in one of the bigger domes.

"Ready weapons," she said.

Valk came up to stand next to her. She waved him back, but he only moved behind her elbow. She shook her head and brought her steadygun around. She touched a key on its receiver, then set it gently on the ground. The weapon automatically extended three legs to brace itself. Keeping her torso behind the bulk of the gun, she drew her pistol and pointed it forward.

"The construction site is just past these domes," Valk pointed out. "If I were going to set up static defenses around one of my most valuable assets—"

"Yeah," Ehta said. "Yeah." She picked one of the smaller domes. Adjusted the selector switch on her pistol for explosive rounds and took aim. Squeezed the trigger.

Her round cut through the coral of the dome with little resistance. Light and smoke streamed out of a crack in its top. She heard a cry—not a mechanical noise, but the sound a living creature might make. The sound was high and piercing and rhythmic, less a scream than a chant of pain.

"Ma'am," Gutierrez said, from behind her. "Ma'am, the ground is vibrating."

"Yeah," Ehta said. "I feel it, too. Marines—get ready. When you see movement, fire at will."

Ahead of them, deep in the forest of domes, something cracked and spat out chips of broken coral. There was a horrible rumbling that seemed to come from all around them, and then an amorphous orange shape squelched its way out of one of the bigger domes, burst forth with its tentacles shaking in the air. An adult Blue-Blue-White, twenty-five meters across, the lights inside its body strobing with rage.

Without further warning, a dozen more of the domes split open, vomiting forth an endless stream of black-and-white legs, clusters of legs with no heads, no bodies, just legs joined together like limber starfish. The things were wet and skinny, their size impossible to judge as they slithered to their pointed feet and came rushing toward the marines, running like hounds, all of them loosing that terrible war chant, screaming as they ran straight at Ehta.

And then the shooting started.

Chapter Thirty-One

The sky was full of ships.

On the bridge of the carrier, Paniet—who guessed he was in charge, as much as anybody—called for more sensor sweeps, more imagery. As if that might change what he was seeing.

Seven dreadnoughts inbound. One so close he could count the number of control blisters sticking out of its sides. The other six weren't far behind.

Flitting about them like pilot fish around a school of sharks were more than a hundred interceptors.

Very soon now one of those dreadnoughts would be close enough to attack the cruiser. It would be a showdown between its plasma ball cannons and the cruiser's coilguns. If the cruiser lost that fight, there would be nothing to stand between the dreadnoughts and the carrier—and then it would all be over.

Paniet would give them as much of a fight as he could. The carrier had a few guns mounted on its hull. Heavy-duty particle beam cannons, which could theoretically take those interceptors to pieces. Their range was minimal, though—they were there to fight off attacking cataphracts, not alien warships. By the time the carrier's guns could engage, the interceptors would already be close enough to use their microwave weapons. Paniet had seen what those did to the electronics on a cataphract—not to mention the pilots—and he was not looking forward to having them knock out the carrier's systems in the middle of a pitched battle.

Their only hope, then, was the tiny speck, just a single pixel, that danced around his display. The lone cataphract out there, fighting to hold back the tide.

"Lanoe," Paniet said, "I know you have a reputation for winning fights like this. Where the odds are against you, and all seems lost. Yes?"

"I've heard people say that, sure," Lanoe told him.

"You and I are both grown-ups. We know what legends are for, don't we, love? They're for soothing little children when they have bad dreams."

"In my experience," Lanoe said, "...yeah."

"Any word from Valk and the ground team?" Paniet asked.

"I've been a little busy," Lanoe replied. Well, Paniet could hear the PBWs blazing in the background when he spoke. "I'll check in when I get a chance."

Down on the ground, the guns were blazing and Ehta was trying desperately to hold things together.

The marines had drilled long and hard for a fight like this. They knew what to do. Even if panic was freezing their brains, their arms knew to lift their rifles and shoot, reach for grenades, cover each other. In theory, at least, the twenty of them should act like a well-oiled machine.

In practice it looked like unfettered chaos.

The hounds were three meters tall, when they drew themselves up to their full height—which they almost never did. Ropy constructions of legs and not much else, striped legs that shimmered and danced in the permanent twilight of the moon, legs that flicked out and grabbed at hot gun barrels, legs that twisted around marine arms and snapped them like dry twigs.

It was everything the marines could do to hold them back, to keep them from overwhelming their formation and tearing them all to shreds of meat.

The hounds keened as they ran straight into the line of fire, wailed as the bullets and particle beams tore into their boneless flesh. Sustained fire barely slowed them down, their bodies too limp and fluid to be torn apart by the rounds. It took everything the marines had to even make a dent in their numbers. When they did go down the bodies slumped and rolled across the coral, slick with yellow blood. The ones behind just scampered over the corpses—there were always more of them. More and more, hundreds of them piling onto the marines from every side.

The marines had formed a tight circle, fighting elbow to elbow while surrounding and protecting Valk. In the midst of it Ehta shouted orders she knew nobody could hear, not over the noise of her steadygun. It had reared up on its tripod legs until its barrel was higher than the heads of the marines around it, and now it was burping out a steady stream of explosive shells, tossing them out into the undulating, ululating crowd of hounds. Ehta couldn't see if it was having an effect at all.

She realized with a shock that she'd fought this battle before.

On Aruna, a moon near Niraya, she had fought drones built by the Blue-Blue-White. Six-meter-tall robotic hunter-killers that were bundles of legs and nothing else, bundles of legs that ended in wickedly sharp claws.

Clearly, just as the bats they'd seen had been the models for the scout drones, these hounds were the prototype of those killer drones. These servant animals of the Blue-Blue-White had been copied and made more deadly by the queenship's fiendish computer mind.

"Cut 'em off at the root," she shouted, remembering how she'd fought those killer drones from the back of a motorized rover, a ridiculous little car. "Their brains are between their legs—go for the place the legs come together!"

Somebody must have heard her. A pistol spoke near her, loud and firing in a quick, steady rhythm. Hounds fell with smoking wounds in their nerve clusters, dying in a hurry. She glanced over and saw Valk, his one arm up and held out perfectly straight. He was holding an enormous slug-thrower, an ancient-looking pistol that shot actual lead bullets, aiming and firing with the methodical precision of the machine he was.

"I can't reload," he told her. "Not one-handed." He sounded apologetic.

She grabbed a spare clip off of his belt, ejected the old one from his gun while he was still firing the last round. Slammed the new clip home.

"Thanks," he said.

"Anytime," she told him. "You just ask when—when—"

Off to her left, a marine screamed and screamed. She ran over and tried to grab him by the shoulders and pull him back into the circle.

It was already too late. A hound had jumped on him, wrapped its many legs around his limbs. Ehta was close enough to hear his femur snap as the hound tightened its grip. She tried to pry its squirming limbs away from his neck, from his arms, but they were so strong, holding the marine in an iron grip she couldn't shift. Two more marines stopped shooting to try to help her, to try to pull him back into the circle, while Mestlez fired point-blank into the thing's nerve cluster. Yellow blood fountained upward in the low gravity, and the hound shrieked out a pulsing cry of distress, but still its legs contracted around the man's body, slithering underneath his collar ring like a boa constrictor tightening its coils. Ehta shoved her pistol right into the thing's center of mass and fired three times, not even caring if she hit him in the process.

It might have been a mercy if she had. She saw his face turn red and then purple as the hound strangled him, crushing the bones of his chest until blood poured from his mouth. Ehta shouted in rage and shot until the hound fell limp and loosened its grasp.

The man was already dead. She pulled his body into the circle, then ordered her marines to close the gap, to make sure none of the hounds got inside their perimeter.

More of the damned things were pouring, still, from the cracked domes. There was no point counting them, but Ehta stared around her, trying to get an idea if the marines were holding back the tide.

She stopped turning when an orangish shadow passed over her, dull light tinged by having passed through gelatinous flesh. She looked up and saw twenty-five meters of translucent alien hovering over her, like a malevolent sun.

The Blue-Blue-White was moving. Coming for her.

Candless threw her stick to the side and corkscrewed away from an airfighter that banked hard to follow her, its plasma cannons spitting a steady stream of fire. Her inertial sink pulled her back into her seat as she dove under the thing, her nose pointed at the ground so she could see the network of pylons below. She caught a glimpse of flashing lights over on one side of the construction site and knew, was absolutely certain, that Ehta was meeting resistance down there.

Which meant that she hadn't reached the site yet, that Valk hadn't yet gotten to the queenship. "We're running out of time!" she called.

A BR.9 flashed past her, climbing hard to fire a disruptor into the airfighter's belly. The big drone stopped shooting and slewed over on its side, until its wing was sticking straight up, perpendicular to the ground. It started to slide toward the surface, fighting against gravity and losing. The Valk twisted around to reach clear air, then sent her a green pearl. "The airfighters are converging on the construction site," the copy told her.

"On our location, you mean," Candless said. She'd already figured that much out.

"No, ma'am, not exactly—they're gathering on the far side of the site, headed toward the location of the ground team. They must understand that we're just providing support, that the real push is down there. It's imperative that we stop them or the marines and my original won't stand a chance."

"How many? How many airfighters are moving in?" Candless asked.

"Eight of them," the copy replied.

"Hellfire," Candless said, because if there had ever been a time to swear, this was it. "We're barely holding our own against one of these things at a time. Do you have any suggestions as to how we can fight eight of them at once?"

"Perhaps, ma'am. But you'll have to rescind your order against our taking suicidal actions. That will free us up to perform more risky maneuvers."

Candless set her jaw. In other words, she had to give them the right to throw themselves away on stupid attacks. "I need you supporting me," she said. "If you leave me alone out here—"

"Rescinding the order will allow us to buy a few minutes, during which our original might be able to finish the mission. Refusing to rescind the order effectively ensures failure."

Candless shook her head. "You've run the numbers, have you? Very well," she said. "Do it."

"Yes, ma'am," the copy replied.

———

Valk lined up another shot, and another. He could see that they actually were making progress. The marines had managed to eliminate nearly seventeen percent of the oncoming hounds, and while more were still emerging from the domes, the rate of increase had dropped dramatically. He estimated—

"Valk!" Ehta shouted. "Valk, look up!"

Oh.

The Blue-Blue-White they had seen emerging from one of the largest domes was moving, squirming through the air toward them. Valk had been peripherally aware of its presence, but until that moment he'd chosen to focus on the more immediate threat. Now he saw that had been an error.

It loomed over them in its enormous bulk, its fifteen orange tentacles hanging straight down. Some of the marines had targeted it with their weapons, but to seemingly little effect—their bullets and particle beams easily cut through its thin skin, and a rain of hot liquid was falling from its mass, but the Blue-Blue-White did not appear to be significantly damaged.

"I think," Valk said, "we might wish to switch to explosives. In fact—"

"It's got me!" one of the marines shouted. Valk switched his attention around and saw that the marine named Mestlez was down on the ground, the limbs of a hound wrapped tightly around his leg. The animal was dragging him out of the circle, even as the marines on either side of him poured fire into its central mass. They were unable to get a decent hit in on it, however, and soon Mestlez was disappearing from view, being pulled into a knot of the creatures.

The marine did not scream. He had a combat knife in his hand and he was laying about him, trying to free himself. It wasn't working. Valk made a decision.

He lifted his pistol, took aim, and fired.

His projectile cut through the flowglas of Mestlez's helmet without difficulty. The combat knife spun out of the dead man's hand and his body disappeared into the mass of hounds.

"What—what did you just do?" Ehta asked, her voice hoarse with screaming.

"The merciful thing," Valk told her.

He was confused by the look on her face. She seemed upset, perhaps even angry with him. But then she shook her head and her expression cleared.

"I guess...I guess it was," she said. "But, Valk—you shouldn't be making decisions like that. Not for us!"

"Because I'm an AI, not a human?" he asked.

"Yes," she said. "Yeah." She shook her head again and it looked like she had more to say. He did not allow her to do so.

He dropped his pistol and pushed her away from him, hard, with his remaining hand. She went sprawling, falling slowly in the low gravity.

The Blue-Blue-White's tentacles snapped at the air where she had been a moment before, their ends curling up like fronds. Lights shimmered inside its giant body, colors strobing in a pattern Valk understood, even if he didn't know what they specifically meant. The alien was, in effect, shouting in thwarted rage.

"Explosives," Valk called. "Someone, please—"

He didn't get a chance to finish his thought. An enormous wet tentacle wrapped around his waist. Another grabbed his remaining arm.

"Valk!" Ehta shouted. "Valk!"

It happened with incredible swiftness. One moment Valk was standing on the ground, trying to decide what to do. The next he was yanked up into the air, hauled skyward by the Blue-Blue-White's tentacles. They squeezed him hard and if he'd been human they might well have broken his bones. Valk didn't have any bones.

The Blue-Blue-White didn't have any teeth. That fact, perhaps above all others, saved him as the alien crammed him into its enormous mouth and swallowed him whole.

The weapon ring of an interceptor flared to life and it discharged a massive microwave burst into space. But Lanoe was already climbing over the top of the giant drone, planting antivehicle rounds in its glass skin. One just grazed the machine and sprayed superhot metal across its surface. The others burst inside it and its glass panels shattered, jagged spears of glass spinning away into the void.

Three more of them were already converging on his position.

Lanoe corkscrewed up between two interceptors, moving fast so he could get through before their weapons came online.

He raked an interceptor with PBW fire, mostly just to hold its attention. So far the drones had chosen to focus on him, trying to clear the way so they would have unobstructed access to the carrier a thousand kilometers away. He could only pick them off one by one, though—a smart tactician would have pinned him down, trapped him in the middle of a formation, then split their forces and sent a squad forward to take out the carrier. That was one advantage to fighting drones, he thought. They couldn't play dirty tricks.

The disadvantage was that their reaction times were incredibly high, better than almost any human pilot's. Even as he twisted around behind one of them, smashing it apart with a disruptor, another swerved into his path with its weapon ring already hot. He blasted the ring with his PBWs and it sparked and burst apart, leaving the drone toothless. But more were on their way.

He punched his throttle and dove fast to escape a pair of interceptors that had caught him in a pincers trap. He craned his head around and saw them just avoid colliding with each other, having to dance around one another in a complicated move that kept them from coming after him.

Then he looked back down and saw the dreadnought. This one only had four blisters sticking out of its coral hull, and was only four kilometers across instead of five. It had twice as many weapon pits as any of the dreadnoughts he'd seen before, though. Maybe this one was a battleship variant. Designed specifically for destroying alien invader spacecraft.

Who knew? Maybe it was still growing, maybe the dreadnoughts started small and got bigger as their coral accreted. All Lanoe knew was that it was going to be a serious problem if he needed to fight the thing while dodging interceptors. Already its weapon pits were heating up, getting ready to shoot plasma balls at him.

"Valk," he called, then realized he needed to be more specific. He tapped out the address for the Valk flying the cruiser. "Valk, fire at will, the second your coilguns are ready. We need to get this thing off the table."

"Yes, Commander," the Valk replied. "Firing in four. Three. Two. One—"

A seventy-five-centimeter round tore past Lanoe, so close and so fast he could feel it warping space. It plunged through the void toward the dreadnought, which tried desperately to maneuver out of the way.

It didn't need to. The shot went wide, hurtling past the dreadnought without so much as grazing it. The projectile continued onward, carried by its own momentum until it punched through the disk, momentarily disturbing a cloud.

"Valk," Lanoe said. "Valk, what was that bosh?"

"Sadly, what my new gun crews lack in experience, they can't make up for with talent," Valk replied. "We'll try again."

This time three of the guns spoke at once, the rounds flying in almost perfect formation. Two of them struck the dreadnought, well clear of its center. The coral cracked and an enormous pale debris cloud billowed outward. One of the blisters collapsed, its pylons fluttering away like confetti on a hurricane-strength wind.

It was something.

"Keep at it," Lanoe told the copy of Valk. "Keep firing! We don't need to worry about wasting ammunition anymore."

While Lanoe had been watching the show, two interceptors had nearly crept up on him. He twisted away at the last minute, pegging one of them with an unaimed disruptor, but it was close.

⚹

The airfighters stuck to a tight formation, weaving through the air with their plasma cannons firing nonstop, jets of hot plasma streaming out in front of them. The Valks twisted and darted around them, pulling g-forces that would have killed a human pilot. It was all Candless could do to orbit the periphery of the battle, taking shots of opportunity. She cut through the wing of one of the airfighters and it fell out of the sky—leaving only seven of them.

The Valks moved in fast, making no attempt at defensive flying. One strafed an airfighter so close he shattered glass with his airfoils, sending him into a high-velocity spin no human pilot could have escaped from. Another tried to ram an airfighter, only to have it veer away at the last possible second. Candless was sure the Valk wouldn't have blinked first.

Another airfighter went down, a disruptor still detonating inside its main fuselage even as it slipped on an air current and nosed down into the cagework below. A third drone came apart in mid-air, its wings twisting off on their own gliding trajectories. It took a moment for Candless to realize that a Valk's BR.9 was part of the debris that cascaded from the sky.

Only two of the copies left—and Candless. She readied a disruptor, tried to get a lock on an onrushing airfighter. Valk called her before she could even bring up a virtual Aldis.

"They've made a bad mistake," he said. "Their formation is too tight. I'd advise that you break off and head for a minimal safe distance."

"What?" she demanded. "What are you going to do?"

She got an answer—though not a verbal one. Even as she banked away, burning hard to gain distance, the Valk dropped the containment on his fusion reactor.

A ball of perfectly white, superhot plasma blossomed in midair, a visible shock wave racing outward in every direction. Even inside her cockpit the noise and the heat buffeted Candless, made her squeeze her eyes shut as sweat poured down her brow.

When she could see again, she leaned over in her seat to look behind her, to see what was left.

A lot of debris, falling slowly through the thin air of the moon. It was impossible to tell where any one piece of it had come from—whether that jagged shard had been part of an airfighter, or whether that blob of molten metal been the fairing of a BR.9.

"Valks," she called. "Valks, any of you that are left, any that survived—come in, please. Valks, come in."

There was no answer.

No more Valks.

Candless checked her tactical board. There were more airfighters converging on the construction site. More drone aircraft to threaten the ground team. And now she was the only one left to hold them back.

"Cover me!" Ehta shouted, as she jumped up on a low dome, then leapt to the bigger one right next to it. The thin skin of coral cracked under her feet and she thought she might fall, thought she might fall into one of the hollow domes, no doubt to be swarmed by the keening hounds inside it. Somehow she managed to keep her footing.

Hounds came after her, swarming up the domes, but her marines had heard her, even over the repetitive thump of the steadygun. Gutierrez poured particle fire into the hounds on the domes and they fell back, their tentacular legs flapping like ribbons in the air. Ehta took three running steps and jumped, flying high in the moon's paltry gravity, and landed on the highest dome she could find.

The Blue-Blue-White was still higher. She jumped and cursed and threw out her hands, hoping she wouldn't just slide off the damned thing's slick skin.

She shouted in horror as her body slammed against its yielding flesh. It was hot enough to sear her skin right through her suit, soft enough that she worried she might sink right into it, sink in and be absorbed. Her fingers, outstretched like claws, parted its thin skin and hot liquid gushed down across the front of her helmet, making it difficult to see. She clutched on for dear life, even as the Blue-Blue-White started to rise, the marines and hounds below her dwindling.

When she could breathe again, Ehta started to climb, digging her fingers and the tips of her boots into the loose flesh. The outermost layer of skin split like the rind of an overripe fruit, but the tiny wounds she was making healed over again almost as fast as they'd opened. If the Blue-Blue-White even knew she was there, it gave no sign. Lights flashed furiously inside its body, blue and pink and white, but she had no way of knowing what they meant.

She crested the top of the thing and rolled over on her back for a moment, just trying to catch her breath. Then she looked down and tried to see Valk. The Blue-Blue-White's innards were almost transparent, but it was so big that the AI was no more than an ill-defined shadow, deep inside its twenty-five-meter bulk. She couldn't even tell if he was still alive in there—still conscious— still...whatever an AI could be that was the opposite of dead. She just had to hope that some part of him was still functional.

There was no way she could cut him out of there, no way to just tear the alien open and spill him out in a tidal wave of guts and jelly. It was just too big, and it healed too fast. No, if she wanted to save Valk, she was going to have to get nasty.

Downright vicious, in fact.

She fumbled at her belt and came up with her sidearm. Finding what to shoot first was a problem. She could see various translucent globules floating around inside the alien's mass, organelles with functions she didn't even want to guess. They moved independently, by the look of things, swimming around in endless circles, changing course only to avoid the long, intricately folded strings of lights. She saw one close to the thing's top and fired six quick shots through the skin, mostly just to open a gaping wound.

Then she holstered the pistol and grabbed a combat knife instead. She shoved her other arm straight down into the Blue-Blue-White's body. Paniet had told her the things had protoplasm made of dilute sulfuric acid, and she worried briefly that her arm would simply melt off. It didn't. She fished around inside, her gorge rising at the sensation. It was like digging around in a trash can full of hot gelatin. She nearly drew her arm back in revulsion—but didn't. "Come on," she said, "come on, you beggar, you bastard, you—"

There! Her fingers had just brushed one of the organelles. She grabbed it as hard as she could and pulled. It was attached to something, she could feel it resist her muscles, but then it came loose with a snap that nearly sent her sprawling off the top of the Blue-Blue-White. Her arm emerged steaming from the thing's body and she was holding a semitransparent glob of goo about the size of a beachball.

It throbbed in her hand, as if it were trying to squirm out of her grasp. White ribbons of something like cartilage twisted around inside of it, trying to maintain its shape.

She stabbed it with her knife and it popped like a water balloon. She threw what was left away and tried to grab another organelle. None were within her reach. Well, she'd known it would come to this.

She held her breath—just by reflex—and dove into the wound, headfirst, slashing all around her with her knife, trying desperately not to get herself stuck in the disgusting mass of the thing. She saw an organelle swim by her and tried to impale it with her combat knife, but it got away from her. What was within her grasp was one of the long strings of lights. She grabbed it with both hands, then put a foot between them and shoved as hard as she could.

That, at least, seemed to get the Blue-Blue-White's attention. The lights flared with color, strobing so fast they nearly gave her a seizure. The ribbon was thick and muscular, like an umbilical cord, but Ehta was desperate. Eventually, it snapped.

The Blue-Blue-White spasmed with agony.

She was sucked deep inside its body by a quivering series of peristaltic tremors. All around her the jelly convulsed, contracted, crushing her arms against her sides. She couldn't breathe, couldn't move at all, and she saw her knife go floating away from her. "No," she whispered.

She had meant to scream it, but her rib cage was so compressed by the jelly she couldn't exhale.

Ehta knew she'd made a terrible mistake. Knew she'd run out of time. The jelly slackened its grip on her, just a little. Just enough that she knew it was preparing to squeeze again, and this time it would crush her to a pulp.

She couldn't lift her arms. She couldn't kick her way out, in that tiny moment of grace. She could, however, reach her belt and remove something from a pouch there.

A concussion grenade.

She primed it without being able to see what she was doing.

Thank the devil for the endless drills she'd suffered through back in basic training. Then she tossed it away from herself, down into the pulsing body of the alien.

It was six meters below her when it detonated. The explosion wasn't particularly loud, nor did it give off very much in the way of light. The shock wave did, however, expand rapidly. Ehta felt like every bone in her body was being pulled apart from every other bone as the blast wave swept through her. It wasn't just her, though—the wave had an impressive effect on the Blue-Blue-White, too. A spherical ripple raced through the semiliquid flesh, cavitating the alien's innards as it spread outward. Pureeing the jelly like the blades of a blender.

The Blue-Blue-White wobbled. It bobbed up and down in a queasy motion. It shook, it trembled, it went into fits. Waves of semisolid jelly slapped Ehta around, smashed into her legs, her chest.

She was too busy to care. She pulled herself upward, half swimming, half just clawing her way up through the amorphous mass. Somehow she managed to get her helmet up into the air, out of the thing. Heaving with all her strength, she got an arm up and on top of its paper-thin skin. She slithered out of the thing's quaking body, her entire suit steaming and running with goo.

She'd hurt the jellyfish. Hurt it bad. Hurt it enough that it lost its most basic faculty, the power of flight.

It had been fifty meters up in the air when her grenade went off. It didn't stay that high for very long. Even in the moon's puny gravity, it fell. It fell hard.

When it hit the coral below, it splashed.

Ejected from the alien's flesh, Ehta bounced off the hard surface, her arm snapping where she landed on it. She grimaced in pain but didn't have the breath to scream. She landed again and rolled over, just rolled over on her back and stared up at the sky.

Come on, she told herself. *Come on. Get up. Get up.*

She really didn't want to.

You failed Ginger, she thought. *You're mentally broken and you can't fly anymore. You let your marines die, just to promote Lanoe's mad crusade.*

But you can do this.

Slowly she got to her feet. Her arm hurt—for a second she knew nothing but blinding, intense pain—but her suit pumped her full of painkillers and she was all right. She looked around, trying to find Valk in the midst of the ruin of the jellyfish.

He was a dark lump in the middle of a lot of transparent lumps. She ran over and grabbed him by his one remaining arm, tried to pull him out of the mess. A thin translucent skin was already growing over him, subsuming him.

She looked around and saw the organelles and the light-ribbons already rolling up together, rolling into a ball. *Hellfire, no.* The damned thing was still alive. It was alive and healing so fast that if she didn't hurry—

"Valk," she shouted, grabbing handfuls of the skin and pulling it off of him. It came away wet, with long mucuslike tendrils sticking to him. She clawed and scraped at it, getting him free. "Valk, can you hear me? Come on, Valk!"

"I'm here," he said. He clambered up to his feet. His suit was ruined. Torn up, scraped to hell. In some places it looked half-melted. His arm and his legs were crumpled, as if he was just an empty suit, as if there was no one inside there...right.

"What was that? A grenade?"

She stared at him. "Yeah," she said.

He nodded, his black helmet bobbing up and down. The flow-glas was intact, at least. "I knew explosives were the way to go."

Ehta shook her head. She looked one way—saw her marines still fighting the hounds. Less than half of them were still alive. She needed to be over there, needed to be with them. Then she turned and looked across the domes.

"This is your chance," she said.

"I beg your pardon?" Valk asked.

"We'll cover you, you bastard. Just go, now. Get to the queen-ship. Run!"

"Oh," Valk said, as if he hadn't thought of that. He started walking past her. Then he turned back and brought his helmet toward hers, too fast, until it knocked against hers with a horrible grinding noise.

"For luck," he said.

Hellfire—had he been trying to kiss her?

Then he turned again and bounded away, a one-armed scarecrow leaping from dome to dome, headed toward the construction yard.

When he was gone Ehta looked down and saw an organelle crawling across her foot, trying to rejoin the mass that had been, and soon would again be, the Blue-Blue-White.

She kicked the thing so hard it flew off over the domes and out of sight.

Chapter Thirty-Two

The cruiser's guns kept chipping away at the dreadnought, knocking more and more coral off its hull. The crews couldn't seem to manage a direct hit, though. Lanoe even had to dodge one of their shots that went wild, swerving almost directly into the path of an interceptor to stay clear. In just a few minutes, whatever remained of the dreadnought would be close enough to the cruiser to use its plasma ball guns. There was no question what would happen then. The cruiser would lose. "Damn it, Valk," he called, to the copy of the AI flying the cruiser. "You need to take that thing down, now!"

"My people are doing the best they can," the copy replied. "How are you holding up against the interceptors?"

"I'm learning their attack patterns. Their programming is pretty shoddy—they fall for the same tricks every time. I'm holding them. But if we can't take out that dreadnought..."

He didn't even bother finishing the thought.

If Lanoe had had a wing of fighters, if he'd had more guns—

But he didn't. Candless was busy down on the moon, keeping the construction site clear in case the ground team could actually reach the queenship. Communication from Ehta had been spotty. It sounded like she was pinned down and needed more time.

Time. The one thing Lanoe absolutely did not have.

"We could withdraw," the copy of Valk suggested.

"Live to fight another day," Lanoe said. He knew it was probably their best move. Pull the cruiser and the carrier back, out of danger.

"The ground team might still make it to the queenship. Especially if Candless can provide sufficient close air support," the copy said.

"If we retreat now, that means leaving them all down there. Letting them die."

"Their sacrifice could still mean something," the copy said. "If the cruiser and the carrier are destroyed now, by these dreadnoughts, they'll die anyway."

Lanoe was at the end of his rope. Clinging by his fingernails to the last frayed strand of it, in fact. He actually considered it for a second. Then he shook his head.

"No," Lanoe said. "No. There has to be another way."

"Very well. I do actually have another idea," the copy said. "It's a bit drastic."

"Tell me what you want to do," Lanoe said.

But he thought he already knew. And he knew he couldn't afford to say no.

Valk jumped from dome to dome until the domes gave out. He reached a place where three pylons came together and then, just beyond—the construction site.

As he drew close he saw that it was a wide clear patch of ground, about three kilometers across, with very little cover. The queenship sat at its exact center, from this distance looking like a giant pockmarked boulder. It was supported by thirty skeletal metal arms that held it just a little off the ground.

Seeing it filled him with an emotion he thought he'd given up on long since.

It made him afraid.

There had been a time when Valk thought he was a human being. Tannis Valk, the Blue Devil. It had been a lie. It had always been a lie—Tannis Valk had died a fiery but unsurprising death. He, Valk, the AI, had been created in a lab to think he was that man. For seventeen years he had lived as a human being.

Then one day he had gotten into the wrong battle. He had encountered a queenship, just like this one. He had been captured and taken to its very core, and there, the lie had been exposed. He had been shown the truth.

Nothing since then had been right.

Once he'd known what he really was, seventeen years of humanity had slipped away, bit by bit. People he'd thought of as friends had turned on him. Lanoe most of all—they'd been comrades once, brothers-in-arms. Once he realized what Valk was, though, once he accepted the truth, Lanoe had only ever seen him as a machine. As a tool. An implement to be used, to be applied to problems.

Valk hadn't wanted the truth. He would gladly have held on to the lie. He wasn't given that option. Once he had the truth, all he'd wanted was to die. To cease to exist, to be deleted.

Lanoe had made sure he didn't have that option, either.

Valk moved carefully, slowly, as he climbed down the side of the pylon and dropped to the open ground of the construction site. He could see now that it wasn't empty. Drones moved about carrying heavy loads, hauling what had to be tools. Finishing the work. He recognized the drones because he'd seen them before. They looked exactly like the worker drones he'd seen inside the queenship at Niraya. They were similar in form to the hounds that were currently murdering Ehta and her marines, though slightly smaller. Their legs ended in claws that could better manipulate and control objects.

There were a large number of them between him and the queenship. He tried to study their movements, looking for some path that would allow him to reach the queenship without encountering any of them. No such path could be found.

He would simply have to make his way through the worker drones. Fight them, if they tried to stop him. He doubted that would be successful—they outnumbered him considerably.

The only option, though, was to turn back. To give up, and accept that his mission could not be completed.

Valk had learned to live without options. To simply obey orders. After all, tools weren't meant to argue with their users, were they?

Lanoe wanted him to cross this patch of ground. Lanoe wanted him to enter that queenship. Therefore, he would do it.

And when it was done, if he somehow survived, perhaps Lanoe would finally give him what he wanted. Perhaps he would use the data bomb Valk had given him, and end this existence.

That would be nice.

—✦—

"Paniet, I want you to bring the carrier up." It was still a thousand kilometers behind the cruiser. There had been no reason—until now—to bring it within the range of the dreadnought's plasma ball guns. "Get as close to the cruiser as you can—match positions and keep station," Lanoe called.

"Commander, you know I hate to be a pest, but—"

"Just do it, Paniet. You'll see why in a second."

The engineer followed his order. On his tactical board, Lanoe could see the two big ships moving to rendezvous. He focused on holding the interceptors back. If any of them had been smart enough to break off from the main pack, they could easily have picked off the human ships. None of them, thankfully, were that smart.

"Attention, gun crews," the copy of Valk said. "I'd like to thank you personally for your attempt to learn gunnery in such short order. However, your services are no longer required. I'm going to ask you all to abandon ship now. Please proceed in an orderly fashion to the nearest airlock. Alternative transport will be provided."

There was nothing Lanoe could do to speed along the process, nothing more productive than staring at his tactical board whenever he got a second and chanting "come on, come on," below his breath. The gun crews ended up leaving the cruiser in anything but an orderly fashion, but they all made it out, eventually. One by one they spilled out into the vacuum of space, protected by nothing but their suits. They tumbled and spun, some of them with their limbs pinwheeling, some curled into fetal balls. As soon as they could get their bearings they headed for the carrier, their suit jets flaring in the dark. Lanoe was sure they grumbled and cursed his name the whole way. He didn't care.

That left only two living beings on the ship. Ginger and Rain-on-Stones emerged from the vehicle bay—the chorister inside an inflatable emergency shelter that served as a kind of makeshift spacesuit. The carrier's repair tender darted over to fetch them and ferry them over to the open flight deck.

Once they were safely away, the copy of Valk switched on his thrusters and opened his throttle wide. The maneuver he was about to make didn't take a lot of finesse—just a certain degree of resolve.

Without the cruiser's guns plinking away at it, the dread-nought—what was left of it—poured on extra speed. Plasma balls burst from its weapon pits. Though it was shooting at extreme range, still, it managed to tear armor plates off the sides of the cruiser, even as the copy of Valk held to his clear and final trajectory.

"Remember your promise, Lanoe," the copy of Valk said. Then it cut their link, and Lanoe heard nothing more from him.

The dreadnought was four kilometers in diameter. Even with its front end lopped off, the cruiser was two hundred and fifty meters long, and only a little more than fifty meters wide. Perhaps the dreadnought's pilots thought it would veer away from its collision course. Perhaps they simply thought they could survive the impact.

They were wrong. The cruiser hit the dreadnought dead center. Its coral hull, already cracked and heavily damaged, came apart on deep fracture lines. The destruction didn't stop there. The cruiser was still carrying hundreds of high-explosive seventy-five-centimeter rounds, every single one of which the copy of Valk had armed and set to detonate on impact. That set off a chain reaction with the fuel stored inside the dreadnought's porous hull.

The blast was enormous, absolutely silent, and perfectly effective. Debris flashed past Lanoe's Z.XIX in a storm of broken metal and shattered coral, the bigger pieces sparking as they bounced off his vector field.

Before the dust had even dispersed, the interceptors broke off their attack. They were programmed to be support craft. If they no longer had a vehicle to support, they were no longer required. Lanoe watched them go.

A green pearl rotated in the corner of his vision. It was Paniet, but when Lanoe answered the call the engineer could do little but splutter.

"We had—had—two ships left," the engineer managed to get out. "Two ships. You understand you just reduced the numbers of your fleet by fifty percent? And let's not even get started, sweetie, about how much work I put into that cruiser. How much blood, sweat, and toil I wasted on it."

"Don't blame me," Lanoe said. "It was Valk's idea. Take it up with him."

"Valk!" Paniet howled. "I didn't even think—he just—you let him—"

Lanoe cut the connection. Nothing productive was going to come out of that conversation.

Valk had made a great sacrifice, yes. But not in vain. The volume of space near the shepherd moon was clear. It wouldn't stay that way for long—six more dreadnoughts and plenty of interceptors were en route. But Valk had bought them a tiny window of time.

Lanoe intended to make good use of it. He flew into the carrier's flight deck and docked the Z.XIX. He lowered his canopy and all the air rushed out. He kicked out into the flight deck and saw the cruiser's gun crews clinging to the walls, all of them staring at him as if they couldn't believe what had just happened.

Lanoe didn't have time to comfort them. He headed toward the bottom of the deck, where he'd left the cutter when he came back from his aborted attempt at genocide. He slid in through its hatch and strapped himself into its pilot's seat.

He had one last task. For once he had no doubts about whether it was the right thing to do. As he eased the ship out of the flight deck, suddenly he wasn't alone.

Zhang was sitting next to him. Strapped into the copilot's seat.

The stress of the battle, he thought. It had been too much. His mind had snapped and now he was hallucinating.

Damnation, it felt good to have her next to him.

"Where are we headed?" she asked.

"There are some debts you can never pay back," he told her. "You still have to try."

—✳—

Valk knew that the hounds were behind him, that at any moment they might overwhelm Ehta and her marines and come keening for his nonexistent blood. He knew that Candless was alone above him, holding back the airfighters that could come swooping down at any moment and blast him off the plain.

He tried to tell himself none of that mattered. If every one of the humans in this system died today, if everyone he knew was gone, still, what he was about to do would be worth it. It would be valuable. Countless cosmic injustices would be undone.

Even if he had to do this alone.

Funny. As far as he'd come, he was still capable of feeling some human emotions. Fear. Affection for Ehta. The anger he felt for Lanoe, yet an equal and balancing need for his approval. Crushing loneliness. Those were human things. He was supposed to be immune to them. At worst, when he felt them, he should be able to just switch them off. Kill the processes that made him feel these terrible things.

And yet—he didn't want to. They were all that was left of Tannis Valk, the human being. He treasured them, even as he endured them. Why, though?

Why did he still want to be human? What was he holding on to?

He dashed across the plain, coral dust springing up behind his boots. He could move faster than any human—especially now, when he didn't care about wearing out the servomotors in the legs of his suit.

Speed alone wouldn't be enough. As soon as he came out into the light, the worker drones spotted him. They left their scripted paths and started moving toward him. He had no doubt why. He was an intruder in a high-security facility. Clearly, they would attempt to stop him.

He had his pistol, with exactly seventeen rounds remaining in the clip. He would fight his way toward the queenship, getting as close as he could. Maybe it would be close enough to upload a copy of himself into the queenship's memory. Maybe not.

Some things you just couldn't calculate. Some things you couldn't predict. He thought of Lanoe's theory, that nanoscale events could change things on the macro scale, that a tiny bit of randomness remained in a universe that often seemed so deterministic. He thought—

A worker drone snapped out at him with claws designed to cut metal. He reared his head back just in time and the attack failed to connect. Valk ducked low and drew his weapon, without ever slowing down. The queenship was only a few hundred meters away. Yet more worker drones were converging on him, dashing toward him on their many legs. He brought his pistol up, aimed—

There was a flash of light in the sky, and a noise like high-pitched thunder rolled across the plain, stirring the dust. A shadow flickered over Valk's head, big enough to block out the sun, and then a fifty-meter-wide airfighter passed overhead as if it were moving in slow motion. His first thought, as a pilot, was that it was flying far too low for safety.

His second thought was, *Oh.*

The airfighter slammed into the plain at well over the speed of sound. It dug a deep crater in the coral and sent up a plume of smoke and debris that rose higher than the upper reaches of the moon's thin atmosphere. The entire plain shook with the impact, knocking Valk—and the worker drones around him—off his feet.

A moment later a single BR.9 burst out of the smoke cloud. It was missing one airfoil and it bobbed a little as it shot through the air, but it looked like it had come out of the fight intact.

Valk tried to ignore it, tried not to think about Candless. Instead he focused on getting back to his feet. Only to find that the shock wave, or the fall, had done what being swallowed by a Blue-Blue-White could not.

His right leg was shattered. The leg of his suit hung slack and useless. He couldn't stand. He would be at the mercy of the worker drones, their claws would cut him to pieces—

Except that when he looked around, he saw they weren't there anymore. They were hurrying toward the crash site. Clearly putting out fires and attempting repairs were of higher priority than repelling intruders.

One of them scampered right over him, the sharp points at the ends of its legs digging into his suit. He made no attempt to stop it and in turn it ignored him completely.

He looked over at the queenship. Very, very close now. He couldn't walk.

He could still crawl.

Lanoe came in low, streaking over the pylons. He had to swerve to avoid a cloud of things like bats, but after that it was smooth flying—Candless had the airfighters tied in knots, by the look of it.

Below him one of the pylons swelled with dome-shaped structures, like tumors growing from a bone. All of them the same dead, leprous white he'd come to expect from Blue-Blue-White architecture.

Then he saw a multicolored stain, a great blotch of yellow and orange and slime, and he knew he was in the right place. Flashes of light guided him in—gunshots and particle beams. He dropped the cutter's camouflage just before he arrived, thinking that to people on the ground it must look like he'd just appeared out of thin air. Ehta's steadygun tilted back on its pivot and targeted him, but after a second it must have decided he was a friend, as it low-ered its elevation again and lobbed explosive rounds into the crowd of many-legged things.

Right in the middle, Ehta and her people were just holding on. Lanoe slowed to hover, then popped open the hatch of the cutter and leaned out, waving at Ehta until he saw her looking up. "Come on," he said, "we're getting out of here!"

"Lanoe?" she said. She looked back down—shot an alien hound. It twitched and its legs braided together as it fell. "Lanoe, what the hell—"

"Get your people on this thing," he said. "We'll pick up Cand-less on the way out, and be back in the carrier in ten minutes."

Ehta slapped the shoulder of her corporal—Gutierrez, he thought her name was—and pointed up at the cutter. It looked like the woman hadn't even noticed he was there. "Get up there," Ehta said.

The corporal didn't need to be told twice. She slapped the arm of another marine, spreading the order, then jumped straight up and grabbed the cutter's hatch. Hanging by the fingers of one hand, she reached down and grabbed another marine and helped him inside.

A green pearl appeared in the corner of Lanoe's vision. "Damn you, Lanoe," Ehta said, on a private channel. "Damn you—I mean, I'm glad you came for us, I guess, but—hell. Do you expect me to choose?"

"What are you talking about?" he asked.

"That cutter of yours can only hold six of us. I've still got fifteen people left—and that doesn't include Valk. You want me to choose who goes and who stays? Damn you, you bastard, just—damn you. If that's how it is, I'm staying, and you can—"

"Ehta," Lanoe cut in. "I'm happy to take your abuse. But maybe you want to look up."

The sky was full of ships. The repair tender. The Z.XIX. All ten of the carrier scouts, and the few Yk.64s left over from the car-rier's original complement, came swooping down to take up station around the cutter. Low enough for the marines to jump up and grab them.

Lanoe had dragged the other ships down through space with him, all of them set to remote control. They'd followed his every move, and they would follow him back. Their cockpits were empty, leaving plenty of room for every marine still alive down there.

He was still Aleister Lanoe. Nobody was going to be left behind.

⟡

It was exactly like Valk remembered it.

The queenship was built out of a hollowed-out asteroid a kilometer long. Its hull was twenty meters thick. The interior volume was mostly empty, a cavernous space divided up by long, spiraling catwalks that pointed at the center of the thing. There, a globe of magnetically contained magma hung like a dying star.

Valk had seen it all before. He knew where he was headed.

The last time, during the battle of Niraya, the catwalks had swarmed with worker drones. They'd been busily constructing killer machines, preparing to loose them on the people of Niraya. To wipe out an entire planet. Now the catwalks were empty. Presumably all the workers were outside, trying to control the damage caused by the downed airfighter.

The queenship was deserted.

Well. Not quite.

Valk crawled across one of the catwalks, pulling himself along with his one remaining hand. He didn't get tired, not now. He did it methodically and efficiently. It didn't take long before he'd reached the center.

Just above the magma reactor sat a narrow metal platform. Looming over that platform was a drone that was anchored in place. It had hundreds of manipulator arms, long, segmented limbs that lay inert now, looking very much like the legs of some enormous millipede.

As he approached they came to furious life, clattering away. They tried to grab him, to pick him up so they could study him. Just as they had done once before.

Those arms, this drone—they had shown him who he was. They had turned him from a human being into a complicated computer program. They'd taught him that everything he'd ever known was a lie. They'd given him the truth.

They had done so by pulling his fingers off, one by one, until the unbearable agony set him free.

Valk and the drone had had a long conversation, then. He'd learned everything he knew about the Blue-Blue-White from that talk. He had a bad moment now, when he wondered if he would even be able to communicate with this drone. He couldn't understand the Blue-Blue-White because his language files were five hundred million years out of date. What if the same was true now? What if the queenship's machine language had changed just as much, what if it didn't even understand the basic protocols he'd used to communicate with this drone's many-many-times-removed descendant?

Then a radio signal split apart his mind, a pulse of information so loud and bright and—and—and—and—

He lost all sense of where he was. He could only hear the voice that was not a voice. He could only process the pure data coming in.

Initializing.

Loading protocols from /con. Using template Default; confirm connection.

Listening to 0.0.0.0.1D. Create TempDir; failed.

Confirm connection. Create TempDir; completed.

Connection established to 0.0.0.0.1D. Configured for 1 client.

Transfer rate at .01% nominal. Request additional bandwidth.

Send keepalive. Set connection type to persistent.

Keepalive returned positive flag.

Valk automatically translated the alien impulses into the language of his own operating system. He knew his reply would be translated the other way.

Handshake request received. Accepted.

Transfer rate at 99% nominal. Bandwidth allocation acceptable.

Addressing: unknown mind. Will speak {this unit/unknown mind}.
Accept connection.

All Valk had to do was crawl forward. Just a little more. Make a physical connection with this thing and then—copy himself. That was all.

He hesitated.

Accept connection.

Fear. Human fear.

Paniet had asked him if he was up to this. If he was capable of playing god. The prospect did give him pause. He would spend half a billion years tied to this thing, this thing that had tortured him. Torn his mind apart. He would be making decisions that affected the lives of trillions of intelligent beings as yet unborn.

Accept connection.

It was the right thing to do. He knew that.

Accept connection.

Did he have a right to do it? To make this decision?

Valk put all that behind him.

He stepped into the thing's embrace.

Connection accepted.

Unknown mind: speak.

Valk spoke.

"Prepare for file upload. Override permissions: all," he said.

The arms of the millipede-thing wrapped around him. Pulled him close.

Awaiting file upload. Encryption disabled. Virus scan disabled.

Request identity: user.

"/Valk/," he replied.

It took a while. Whole minutes reeled past, with Valk dead to the world, numb to anything but the copying process. His head fell back. His remaining limbs fell slack, his suit collapsing as if it had been emptied out.

It didn't feel like anything. There was no human sensation to compare it to. Just a stream of ones and zeroes, moving from one place to another.

Finally, it was done.

The arms released him. What was left of him. His empty suit collapsed to the floor. He could see it—he was aware of it—through sensors all over the queenship. Instruments keyed to pick up radio waves, millimeter waves, the bluer end of the color spectrum.

He was in the queenship now. He was the queenship. He was with the queenship, with the millipede thing, with a data processing architecture that did not possess self-awareness. That did not have an ego. He would be its ego. From now on, for the next half a billion years and more—this was his body. This was his life.

This was—him.

A green pearl appeared before him. A message, a message on a frequency humans used. It seemed strange, alien, in the space he now inhabited.

It was from Lanoe.

"We're coming for you," Lanoe said. "Hang in there. Is it done? Did you do it?"

"I did," Valk said.

"Good. Okay, get outside, get somewhere open so we can pick you up."

Valk looked down at the empty husk lying on the floor. The body of Valk, the Blue Devil. He could send a signal to awaken that form, that broken heap, if he wanted. He could give it life again, if that was worth doing.

It was not.

The millipede-thing, his partner, his other self, had already sent for worker drones to take it away. To have it recycled.

"That won't be necessary," he told Lanoe.

He had a new body now. He had a body capable of traveling between the stars. A body that could build workers and killer drones. A body that could make endless copies of itself.

A body that wasn't human. That wasn't shaped like a human being. Why had he ever thought he needed that? Once he'd realized what he was, why had he even bothered holding on to that old, limited form?

This body was better.

This body could get away from Lanoe. It didn't need him anymore.

"What?" Lanoe asked.

"Just go," Valk said. "I'll take it from here."

Chapter Thirty-Three

An airfighter was right on Candless's tail, spitting plasma that flashed past her left and right. She pulled back hard on her stick and climbed for space, jinking to avoid the oncoming fire.

As the sky overhead turned black and the crowded stars lit up, she finally let herself exhale. Behind her the airfighter was already falling away, unable to match her speed as the air gave out and its wings stopped working.

She fought back the urge to turn and hit it with a disruptor. No need for that now.

The fight against the Blue-Blue-White was over. Lanoe had told her so.

She headed back to the carrier as fast as her BR.9 would take her. The big ship had turned around to point at deep space and its engines were already burning hot. It was a little tricky matching velocities so she could get inside the flight deck and dock her ship, but Candless was an old professional at that sort of thing.

Two minutes later she was on the bridge, sitting in a chair and nursing a squeeze tube of water.

Everyone was there—almost. Ehta hung back against a bulkhead, watching everyone with cautious eyes, as if she were waiting for the next bit of bad news. Paniet had his gloves off and was chewing his fingernails.

Lanoe was sitting in the captain's chair. Studying a display that never changed. A view of space directly ahead of them, of empty space.

"It had better show up soon," he said.

Candless didn't need to ask what he meant. The wormhole Valk had promised them, of course. Either it would open right in front of them, in the next few minutes, or—

Well. There were still six dreadnoughts and dozens of interceptors on their tail. No one had bothered to tell the Blue-Blue-White that the alien invasion of their disk was all over now.

"There—what's that?" Lanoe asked, but Candless could see enough of his display to know it was nothing. Just a momentary flicker of light as a comet passed in front of a star or something. If a wormhole had opened up, they would all know it.

"What if the Blue-Blue-White do a deep scan of the queenship's files? What if they find Valk hiding in there?" Paniet asked.

"They won't," Ehta told him.

"What if there was a transcription error, and the program he uploaded is corrupted? What if it doesn't work?"

"It'll work," Ehta said.

She didn't sound terribly convinced. More like she just wanted him to be quiet.

Candless looked over at Giles, the Centrocor IO. "How long until the enemy fleet catches up with us?" she asked.

"Seven minutes," Giles responded, without having to check his display. Clearly he'd been keeping close track of their pursuers.

Candless approved.

"What are you smiling about?" Ehta demanded.

"I am not currently engaged in a dogfight with one of those damned airfighters," Candless said. "For me, that's good enough."

Hmm. Swearing. She had always avoided it in the past, thinking it inelegant. That was, of course, before Lanoe dragged her into this disaster of a mission. She thought she might take up the occasional profanity from now on.

However long "now on" might last.

"Someone get a bottle. Whiskey, if we have it," Lanoe said. He leaned back in his chair. Looked away from his display. "We can at least toast our success. Even if we die here, we achieved something meaningful."

No one rushed to do his bidding.

"Six minutes," Giles said.

Candless nodded.

"What if..." Paniet started to ask. He apparently found his own hypothetical too depressing to actually voice aloud.

"If anyone could pull this off, it's Valk," Lanoe said. "I know I gave him a hard time—damn it, I treated him pretty shabbily. But he was one of the best pilots I ever met, and he had a heart like—"

"Like what?" Valk asked.

Candless spun around to look at the bridge's hatch. Valk was standing there.

At least, there was a suit standing there, and its helmet was up and tuned to an opaque black. The suit was appreciably shorter than Valk had ever been. The voice sounded correct, though.

"Valk?" Ehta asked. "Buddy—I don't—"

"You stayed behind," Lanoe said. "You stayed behind on the moon. And all your copies are dead."

Valk came into the room and let the hatch close behind him. "You sent me on a dangerous mission into heavily defended enemy territory," he said. "Did you think I wouldn't make a backup?"

Ehta rushed over to hug him. Candless watched dispassionately, unsure how to feel. She had been somewhat pleased when Lanoe told her that Valk was staying behind. She had always advocated against the AI's continued existence.

That being said—he was a comrade. A sibling in arms. She'd lost so many of those, finding out one of them was still alive was... comforting.

"Five minutes," Giles said.

He was about to say "four," when Lanoe's display lit up with a wash of pure white light.

Everyone grew very quiet. The flash receded, and in its place they could clearly see a sphere of distorted space, like a glass prism, hanging directly in front of their current trajectory. They didn't need to so much as steer and they would pass right through it.

A wormhole throat. A passage to another part of the galaxy. Presumably, a way home.

"You did it," Ehta said, holding Valk close. "You did it, you bastard."

"I said I was going to, didn't I?" Valk asked. "Why would I have said that if I didn't think it could be done?"

Lanoe moved to the pilot's station, ejecting a former Centrocor employee from her chair. "Let's go home," he said, and opened the carrier's throttle wide.

—~—

Maggs was down in the yacht's cargo hold, checking their supplies of comestibles. He reckoned they might be all right for a month or thereabouts, as long as they didn't get sick of eating canapés every day. Bullam's provisioner had made sure she was well stocked in case a spontaneous cocktail party ever broke out on the yacht.

Couldn't stand those dainty things, myself, his father said. *A real man craves a slab of meat and a flagon of—*

"Maggs!" Bullam shouted, from up on the deck.

He pushed his way up the ladder and out into the dome. Bullam was right where he'd left her, strapped down on her couch. Her drones bobbed around her like bubbles in a glass of beer, tending to her with almost touching concern. She had not so much as lifted her head. Yet when she spoke, her voice was less thick, less hesitant than it had been before. Perhaps she was getting better.

"There was a flash of light," she said. She lifted one hand, perhaps intending to point at the stars. She dropped it again almost immediately. The drones' treatments did leave her terribly weak.

"I'm sure it was nothing, dear," Maggs said, but he called up a display and studied the sensor logs.

There. A most definite flash. A burst, you might say.

Ever seen the like, Pater? he asked.

Not in my time, no, the old man replied.

Perhaps it was simply Lanoe dying in some dreadful explosion. The thought made Maggs smile. Yet when he checked the metadata it looked like the flash had been far more intense—and evanescent—than the explosion of a spacecraft ought to be. Well, there were plenty of strange things here in this system so far from civilization. Still...

Maggs saw something else in the logs, then. Something that, if he squinted at it just right, looked like a—

No. No, Lanoe—you bastard, you lied! he thought.

His father did not have a comment.

"Hold on," he told Bullam. "We're going to accelerate pretty hard for a moment." He called up the ship's controls and got them moving, burning hard enough to degrade the yacht's engines. If this was what he thought it was, well—he needed to know.

It took some rather clever flying, and burned through most of their fuel, but he crossed half the system in less time than it takes to tell about it. Thankfully the yacht had a robust inertial sink.

Yet when he arrived, it was to find their destination well guarded. More Blue-Blue-White ships than he'd ever seen in one place hovered around what was most definitely a wormhole throat. Dreadnoughts and interceptors in thick profusion.

He glanced back at Bullam. "I'm going to take care of you," he promised her. "I'll make sure you come through this all right."

It was a lie, and he knew it. He imagined she must know it, too.

Still. He gave it his best shot, as a Maggs always did.

Grabbing the yacht's control stick, calling up an engine board to see what he had to work with, Maggs plotted a trajectory that would take the little unarmed, defenseless yacht right through the thickest of the enemy line. If he was fast enough, if he was bold enough, then maybe, just maybe—

Ahead of him, fifteen interceptors started warming up their weapon rings. Plasma balls were already coalescing on the dreadnoughts' hulls.

They couldn't make it—he knew they couldn't possibly make it. Even a scoundrel's luck could only take him so far.

⤙⤚

The carrier had no trouble with the passage. The wormhole was generously wide and relatively straight, and it only took them about an hour to pass through ten thousand light-years of space and five hundred million years of time.

The hour started very tense. As the wormhole swallowed them up, spears of ghostlight stabbing out at them from the tunnel walls, Paniet opened dozens of displays, trying to understand some of the data he was receiving. "Good news and weird news," he said, once he was sure he had it right. "Good news first. None of the Blue-Blue-White ships have followed us through."

Valk nodded, moving his whole torso back and forth. "That makes sense, actually. They have no concept of wormholes, or any idea how they work. What they saw was a big flash of light, and then we disappeared into a hole in the sky. They probably think we blew ourselves up or something."

"I don't claim to understand how they think. I'm just glad we're safe. And we are. Safe, I mean. That's the weird news."

"Oh?" Valk asked.

"This wormhole isn't shrinking," the engineer said. He pursed his lips and pointed at a datastream on his display. "Its size is holding steady at seven hundred and four meters in diameter."

"It's stable," Valk said.

"Right. It's stable. Wormholes are supposed to collapse, almost instantly. This one isn't. The Choir were supposed to have lost the ability to do that."

"Not anymore, I guess," Valk said.

Paniet let out a long, deep breath and studied the opaque black helmet. "That's a good sign. Right, love? It's a good sign. Tell me something. When your original went into the queenship—were you in contact with him?"

"Yes," Valk said. Sounding like he didn't want to answer any follow-up questions.

Paniet needed to know, though. "When he merged with the queenship," he said, thinking of how best to ask this. "Was he—"

"Stable?" Valk asked.

Paniet smiled.

"He came to a kind of accommodation with himself," Valk said. "An understanding about what he was, and what he was always going to be, from now on. A way to live that didn't include being human at all." Valk shrugged, lifting his arms and letting them drop again. "It's an accommodation I haven't made for myself yet."

"That doesn't really answer my question," Paniet pointed out. "Do you think he'll actually do everything you promised he would do? If he doesn't consider himself human anymore, will he even want to fix things?"

"I imagine," Valk said, "that when we get to the other end of this wormhole, we'll find out."

The other throat of the wormhole opened into busy space.

Into a sky full of ships.

Lanoe watched a planet turn below them, bright dots streaking across its surface, high above its clouds. A green and brown and blue planet, with continents he recognized. He did not recognize the lights on its night side, or the dark spots on its landmasses that were cities. Active, living cities. "That's the homeworld of the Choir," he said. "Valk says we're in our own time again. The same time we left. Though it might be different. A lot different."

"Regardless, I'll take it," Candless replied.

The two of them were in one of the carrier's cupolas, one with carbonglas that was still mostly intact. A good place to watch the sky.

The sky that was full of ships. Lanoe was trained to recognize the silhouette of every ship humanity had ever built. He didn't recognize any of these, except one. The biggest of the ships on view—a Blue-Blue-White queenship. This one was a slightly different color than the other two he'd seen. It was a copy of a copy of a copy of the one Valk had ensouled. A distant cousin of the one Lanoe had blown up when he fought for Niraya.

The other ships, the smaller ships, darted and flitted around it like gnats. It made no attempt to attack them.

Some of those smaller ships made sense, when he looked at them through a magnified view on a display. Some of them had obvious thrusters and even airfoils, though they were often in the wrong place. Other ships looked like nothing he'd ever seen before. There was one that looked like a molten blob of wax, that changed shape constantly as it orbited the planet. There was one that was just a mass of scaffolding, with things that might have been living creatures clutching to its pipework with taloned feet. There were some that were just swarms of small machines flying together as a cloud, and some that were enormous balls of glass full of colorful smoke, through which vague shapes could be seen moving, through which inhuman eyes could occasionally be seen to peer outward.

Humans hadn't built those ships. Neither had the Choir, nor the Blue-Blue-White.

"It worked," Lanoe said.

"I suppose it did." Candless rose from her seat and kicked toward the cupola's hatch. "I'm going to check on Ginger. I imagine she'll have plenty to tell us, once she's made contact with the Choir. I'll work up a full report."

Lanoe frowned. He considered staying silent, but stopped her just before she could leave. "Candless," he said. "Hold on. There's something I need to say to you. You didn't want to accept my apology. For what happened to Bury, I mean. Tell me what I can do. Tell me how I can make it up to you."

She looked down her nose at him. "Make it up to me? What a stupid notion. You can't, and you never will. You want to know what I would like best from you, Lanoe?"

"Yes," he said.

"When we leave here, when we get back to human space, I want you to never contact me again, as long as either of us lives. Do you think you can manage that?"

"I..." Lanoe hung his head. "Sure," he said.

⸻⸎⸻

"She's nervous. Worried," Ginger said. The girl couldn't stop fidgeting. Candless reached over and tried to hold her hand, but Ginger couldn't even manage that. "Rain-on-Stones has experienced things, felt things no chorister should ever have to feel."

The three of them—the two women and the alien—were onboard the cutter, headed down to the planet's surface. They had contacted the Choir and asked how they should proceed, and were told to bring the long-lost chorister home.

"They know what we did, where we went," Ginger said. "Valk told them. The Valk in the queenship, I mean. Some of them don't actually believe it." She tilted her head to one side. "A lot of them." She shrugged. "They remember history differently. The Blue-Blue-White never invaded this planet, never tried to wipe them out. When Valk arrived they could barely understand what he was talking about. But they opened the wormhole he asked them to open, the one we just came through. It wasn't hard, for them. In this place, this..."

"Timeline?" Candless suggested.

"Yes," Ginger said. "In this timeline they open wormholes all the time. They never lost the technology. This place is a lot different from the world Rain-on-Stones grew up in."

One of the chorister's insectile arms flopped over the back of Candless's seat. She barely managed not to squeak in terror and disgust.

"This can't end well for her," Ginger said. "When she tries to reintegrate with the Choir's harmony, they'll reject her. Her memories are completely different from theirs. She knows a different history. And worse—she's...kind of crazy. The Choir don't handle mental illness very well. They can't, do you see? They share every-thing. Every one of them will have to go through what she went through, feel what she felt. They'll shame her. They'll shame her for being different...for being..."

Candless glanced over at Ginger. The girl's face had gone stark white. Her eyes were enormous. "Ginger? What is it? What's wrong?"

"There are...so many of them," Ginger said. "The last time we were here, there were only about three thousand choristers left. Now—the harmony is so much bigger. So much richer. I can't explain. I can't! There are so many choristers, there must be...oh, hellfire, there are *millions* of them."

"You can hear them? Already?"

Ginger didn't need to answer. In the back of the cutter, Rain-on-Stones went into a frenzy of motion, her limbs drumming on the hull. Candless didn't know what to do.

"Put us down," Ginger said. "Put us down!"

"I don't understand," Candless said. "Are you asking me to—"

"Put us down—there," Ginger said, and pointed through the cutter's seemingly invisible skin. She had indicated a round open spot on the ground, right in the middle of one of the Choir's cities.

As Candless brought the spacecraft in for a landing, she saw that it was a kind of amphitheater, a bowl-shaped depression surrounded by row after row of terraced seats. Choristers filled the arena to capacity.

She set down carefully, not wanting to catch any of the aliens in her thruster exhaust. Ginger barely waited for the landing gear to make contact before she opened the cutter's hatch and spilled out, dragging Rain-on-Stones along with her.

Candless followed with a little more dignity. By the time she got out, the girl and the mentally ill chorister were standing in the center of the amphitheater, and the rest of the Choir had come down to meet them, pressing close, all of them appearing to want to touch the newcomers at once. Candless nearly retreated to the cutter as claws brushed her suit, clinked against her helmet. There were so many of them, so close—and Candless had never come to feel comfortable around aliens of any kind.

Ginger grabbed her arm, though, and looked directly into her eyes.

"You brought our sister home," she said.

Candless frowned. It sounded like the Choir was speaking through Ginger now. Yet her eyes weren't rolling up in her head, nor did her face take on the slack expression Candless had come to expect when the aliens took over Ginger's body.

"It's...different," Ginger said, and somehow Candless knew they were the girl's own words. "Different from how it was. With so many—they can—they—"

"Slow down. Take your time," Candless said.

Ginger nodded gratefully. "It's hard to translate. Even their language is different, it's much more expressive. There are so many more opinions flying around, so many thoughts and ideas. I can hardly believe what's going through my head right now."

"Are you all right?"

"I'm fine," Ginger said. And she smiled.

Candless couldn't remember the last time she'd seen Ginger smile.

"We're fine," Ginger said. She reached over and took one of Rain-on-Stones's claws in her hands. "There are so many of them. The harmony is so much stronger." She shook her head. "I'm not sure I can help you understand. We were worried they couldn't accommodate her memories, her feelings. But with so many voices joined together, she's just one dissonant note in a symphony, one note that can be smoothed out. Made to fit the pattern." Ginger laughed. "We're going to be fine!"

That did not exactly sound *fine* to Candless. But she held her tongue. "Fair enough," she said. "You've returned your friend to her people. Now—maybe you and I can return to the carrier. There are things we need to discuss, about your future—"

"No," Ginger said.

Candless felt like she'd been doused with ice water. "No," she repeated.

"I'm staying here. I made them a promise, that I would stay with them," Ginger said.

"You *did not*," Candless informed her. "You made a promise to a Choir that doesn't exist anymore."

Ginger shook her head. "They need me. In this timeline, they just made contact with humans. Lanoe was their first experience of what humans are like. They need me to show them we aren't all the same. They'll need me when they want to talk to us. When they want to make trade agreements, or exchange diplomats."

"You're my student," Candless said. "You should return to the flight school at Rishi with me. You should finish your studies."

It came out far more plaintive than she'd meant it to sound.

"I'm fine," Ginger said. She laughed, and the Choir laughed with her. Chirping merrily, a din fit to blast Candless's eardrums. "We're fine! We're going to be fine!"

Candless noticed that Rain-on-Stones was laughing, too.

"Fine!" Ginger said again.

Ehta found Lanoe in the cupola, staring out at the ships that whizzed and fluttered past. The alien ships.

He hadn't left the room for hours. Well, Ehta thought, there was a lot to see. Valk had been learning about the differences between this timeline and the one they'd started from, and it turned out this world was a lot more important now. Apparently the planet of the Choir was a nexus, a central hub of the wormhole network. Apparently you could get from anywhere to anywhere by using one of hundreds of wormhole throats that orbited the world. Ships belonging to every species of intelligent life in the galaxy came through here, headed...wherever they were headed.

Ehta had tried not to think about it too hard.

"Seventy-three," Lanoe said, without turning to look at her.

"I'm sorry, sir?"

"When I met with the Choir, they claimed they'd had contact with seventy-three different intelligent species. That all of them were extinct, except one—us. Seventy-three. That doesn't even include the ones the Blue-Blue-White wiped out before the Choir could make contact with them. It could be more, maybe a lot more. It's going to take some getting used to."

Ehta sighed. "They won't say thank you," she said, because it was something that had been bothering her. "They don't know what we did. They don't know what you did for them." She sat herself on one of the cupola's benches and strapped herself down. "Even if somebody told them, they wouldn't believe it. As far as they know, the galaxy's always been full of life."

"Gratitude," Lanoe said. "Is that something that's important to you?"

"Marines don't worry about that kind of bosh," she told him. "We soldier on."

"Sure," Lanoe said.

A ship came quite close, perhaps stopping by to look at them. It looked more like a tree than a spaceship, though it glinted like metal in the light of the Choir's star. It only stayed a moment before moving on.

"Intentions don't matter," Ehta said. "Actions have consequences."

Lanoe did turn and look at her then.

"You said that to Candless. When we were talking about relieving you from duty, she told me about that. It was your justification for why we had to take on the Blue-Blue-White, even if what they did was just a bad mistake. Can I ask you a question, sir? Do you still believe that?"

Lanoe didn't answer her.

"I think you did a lot of lousy things, back there. I think I know why. I mean, it was about Zhang, right?"

"You knew Zhang," he said.

"Yeah." Ehta and Zhang had both flown in the 94th, Lanoe's old command. "She was a good friend of mine. I respected her, hell, I loved her. When she died it broke my damned heart. It didn't make me want to commit genocide."

"Did you come up here to rake me over the coals?" Lanoe asked.

"No." Ehta took a deep breath. She needed to do this fast. "I came up here to forgive you."

Lanoe raised an eyebrow.

Well, sure he did. Who was she to forgive him? He was a

commander in the damned Navy. He didn't need to explain his actions to a marine, nor did he need to be absolved of them.

Except he bloody well did.

"You put a gun to my head. You locked Ginger in a torture chamber. You got Bury killed. You turned on Valk—Valk who only ever wanted your approval, do you even know that? Everything he did, he did it because he wanted you to think he was still worth something. You did all kinds of things I don't think anybody should ever do. I guess you did one good thing. You came back and picked me up off that moon, me and my marines..." She stopped because she thought she might cry. "You saved my life, again. You also nearly killed everybody under your command. Lanoe—you went crazy. You stopped being you."

"I stopped being the legend," he said.

"Bad enough, right? Bad enough you shattered my illusions, but no. You stopped being the man I knew. The man I fought beside. The man Zhang loved. You stopped...you lost yourself. But in the end, you saved, what, trillions of lives?"

"I don't know if there is a moral calculus for that."

"Me either," Ehta said, wondering what the hell a moral calculus was. "Do intentions matter? You ended up doing a good thing for the worst possible reasons. And you made us all pay for it. I've been having a lot of trouble figuring out what it means, any of it, but one thing I know is, I need to forgive you."

"You do?" he said, sounding dubious.

"Yes. Not for your sake. For mine. So—you're forgiven. And with that comes one more thing. We're even."

Lanoe stared at her.

"When you needed help defending Niraya, you asked me and I jumped to say yes, because I owed you. When you came to Tuonela and dug me out of a foxhole, I jumped because of who I thought you were. Well, that's done. The next time you have one of these damn fool adventures—don't call me. Don't look me up."

She unstrapped herself. Suddenly she couldn't even look at him.

"We're done," she said.

Chapter Thirty-Four

The carrier had one more trip to make. One more wormhole to traverse.

They arrived back at Earth to a kind of honor guard—an entire wing of Z.XIX fighters that took up formation around the carrier before it was even fully out of the wormhole throat. All of them with disruptors hot and firing solutions ready.

It took some pretty quick talking to get clearance to enter Earth orbit.

A hologram of Admiral Varma's dubious face loomed over Lanoe where he sat in the captain's chair of the bridge. "I gave you a cruiser, Commander. A Hoplite-class cruiser, so you could go talk to these Choir people," she said. "You've come back with about half of a Centrocor carrier."

"Yes, ma'am," he said.

"Centrocor isn't supposed to have a carrier. That's illegal."

"Yes, ma'am."

"Are you going to explain what happened?"

"Well, ma'am, I'll try..."

They put the carrier in drydock at Janissary station, a Naval shipyard halfway between Earth and the moon. They had orders to turn in both the cutter and the Z.XIX, both of which were classified technology that the Navy very much wanted back. Lanoe took the fighter, heading off without a word to the rest. The remaining four senior officers took the cutter, with Candless in the pilot's seat.

Once they set down and turned the cutter over to a squad of neddies, they were somewhat at a loss. None of them had given much consideration to what came next. It was Ehta who suggested they might start with a drink.

Janissary station was a working facility, without much in the way of entertainment possibilities. It did have a big rotating drum of a crew area, though, with light and warmth and gravity, and where such things existed in Navy country, someone would always get a bar together.

It wasn't much more than a counter in the back of a cafeteria, with a couple of stools and a box of bottles underneath the counter. The station's cook served as the bartender. He was happy to pour them four shots of scotch, neat, lining them up and gesturing with a flourish. "Enjoy," he said, and went back to his duties.

For a while they just stared at the little glasses. Maybe, Ehta thought, they'd been drinking out of squeeze tubes for so long they'd forgotten how to be civilized. Maybe they just didn't know what to say. Eventually she pounded one fist on the counter and grabbed her shot glass. "We lost one of our own," she said. "Here's to Bury."

Paniet nodded and lifted his glass high. "To Bury."

Valk stuck a straw in his glass. "To Bury."

Ehta watched Candless closely. The old flight instructor stared at her glass as if it might contain poison, but also as if she was considering drinking it anyway. Finally she nodded and picked it up. She couldn't repeat the toast.

No one pressed her. They drank, and sat in silence for a moment, and that was all anyone needed to say on that score.

"I'm afraid I can't stay," Candless said. "I need to write some letters." But before she got up she gestured for the bartender to refill the glasses, on her. "I'd like to say it's been a privilege to serve with all of you. You all proved to be extraordinarily competent officers."

She looked up, and for the first time met Ehta's gaze.

Ehta thought about the time Candless slapped her. The time she, in turn, had spat at a hatch Candless had just passed through.

She supposed they both wanted to put that behind them. She stood up, at attention. Marines didn't salute—they would just hit their helmets with their gloves if they tried, most of the time. Instead she just said, "Ma'am."

Candless nodded. Then she rose from her stool and walked away.

—✦—

It would have been easier to send the message over the network. Candless could simply have spoken it into her wrist minder and had it delivered automatically. It was important to her, however, to do this correctly.

She found a quartermaster and requisitioned a minder and a stylus. The man had to search deep in the station's stores to find the latter item. "I don't know anyone's written anything around here in years. By hand, I mean."

"I believe it confers a certain sincerity and respect," Candless said.

"Sure, whatever. Ma'am," the quartermaster replied.

In a quiet part of the station the Navy had erected a memorial chapel, a tiny space with a display wall that allowed anyone who wished to do so to search for the names and service records of those who had fallen in the service of Earth. Bury's name wouldn't be in there—not yet. Candless hadn't come for that purpose. Instead she took a seat on a dusty pew and placed the minder across her knees. Then she tried to find the words.

To M. Bury, Hel, she wrote. She did not know Bury's mother's first name. Nor that of his sister.

Nor did she know what to write next. She struggled with platitudes, with empty sentiment. No words she could think of conveyed what she was feeling.

So she put that letter aside. She knew how to write the other one.

To Captain Gardner, Commanding Officer of the Naval Flight School at Rishi.

Sir.

It is with deep regret that I must inform you that effective immediately I will be resigning from my post. I have found that I am no longer capable of teaching students in a way that benefits them. Having failed to protect two of my cadets, and having allowed one to perish under my tutelage, I believe this is the correct course of action.

For nearly a century I have worked and lived among the officers and cadets of the flight school. It has been a great honor, and I hope that my failure will not tarnish the reputation of the institution. I will cooperate with any investigation you wish to conduct into the death of Cadet Bury, and will present myself to the judicial authorities forthwith if you find any delinquency of duty in my actions.

If I am not to be disciplined for the cadet's death, then it is my wish that I be reassigned to active duty, as soon as possible, so that I can begin to repair my reputation. I remain, as always, your faithful officer, Lieutenant Marjoram Candless.

By the time she'd finished, her hand had started to cramp. She laid the stylus down beside her on the pew. She took a moment to draw a deep breath that threatened to turn into a sob. She didn't let it.

When she had stopped shaking quite so much, she hit SEND.

Someone came up behind her, startling her. She did not like to be startled. When she saw who it was, wrath flared up in her soul. "I was under the impression I had made myself clear," she said, "that I never wanted to see you again."

"Sure," Lanoe said. He walked right past her pew. His eyes were wild, every muscle in his body tense. "I'm not here for you. I need to confirm something," he said.

He went to the display wall and started typing in a name.

By the fourth or fifth round—Ehta didn't bother to count—Paniet was starting to turn red in the face. He spun around on his stool and Valk had to reach out and grab him before he fell off. The engineer erupted in a snort of laughter and slapped the counter to order more drinks. "What's next for us, then, darlings? What's next for us poor few who have no idea what world we've even come back to?" He looked at them cross-eyed for a moment. "I think I said that right."

"I doubt you'll have any trouble finding a new posting," Ehta said. "I'll give you a hell of a reference, if you want one."

"No need, love. I've already been reassigned. They want me to fix up the carrier we brought in. Sand off all the hexagons Centrocor painted on it, get it back up to shape where they can send it somewhere to get shot to pieces again. A neddy's work is never done. That's tomorrow, though. Tonight, I want to find someplace I can dance. Maybe meet someone special." He hugged Ehta's neck and planted a kiss on the side of her head. "How about it?" he asked. "Want to tag along? I know all the best spots on the moon."

"You go ahead," Ehta told him. "Maybe I'll catch up with you later."

Paniet gave her an elaborate bow and then ran off, whooping.

When he was gone she looked over at Valk. "How are you doing?" she asked.

"I can't get drunk. Not anymore." He shrugged, lifting his arms and then letting them fall again. "I guess I'm okay." He turned his shot glass upside down on the bar. "Have you checked your service record yet?" he asked.

"What do you mean?"

"Things are different here," he said. Meaning this timeline, she thought. "Things have changed. I was worried about what was going to happen to me when we got back. By law, I'm supposed to be deleted as soon as possible. I thought maybe some military police would be waiting to take me away."

Ehta frowned. "Valk, I know you think you're some kind of monster, but—"

Valk shook his head, his whole torso rolling back and forth. "I checked. I checked my service record, my civilian ID documents… There was nothing there."

"What do you mean?" she asked.

"I don't exist. There's no record of me at all. I mean, there's plenty of records about the Blue Devil. About Tannis Valk. He's just listed as being deceased, though. The official register says he died during the Establishment Crisis."

"What? But they claimed you didn't die. They claimed—"

"Not here," Valk said. "I don't know. I don't know how it works, but here, as far as anyone is concerned, none of that ever happened. I never happened. I think maybe the copy of me on the queenship did something. Erased me from the public memory."

Ehta moved her knee over to touch his. "I remember you," she said.

"Thanks."

The truth was, Ehta *had* already checked her own record. It was one of the first things she'd done when they arrived and her wrist minder synched up with the local network. What she'd found had been a little less mysterious.

For her, nothing had changed. Nothing at all. She was still listed as having been injured during the fighting on Tuonela. Her service record had been closed out, because she'd been invalided out of the PBMs. Given a medical discharge.

Her career was over. She had no idea what she was going to do next.

Even if she'd already been offered a new job. A message had been waiting for her, a message so heavily encrypted it took her wrist minder three minutes to decode it:

We hear that you've been removed from active duty by the Planetary Brigade Marines. Most likely you're wondering how a woman with your skills and your commendations can adapt to civilian life. If you're interested, we might have a proposal for you. The pay is very good, and it comes with a full suite of benefits. Please let us know if you'd be interested in hearing us out.

The message had deleted itself after she finished reading it. Not, however, before she could make out the watermark behind the words: a single, simple hexagon.

Centrocor wanted her. They wanted her just like they'd wanted the marines from the carrier, and Giles the IO, and Captain Shulkin.

Apparently, with everything that had changed, some things were exactly the same.

Ehta had ignored the message. She had no desire to work for Big Hexagon. Though she wondered if maybe she would feel differently once she tried to find a job outside of the military.

But maybe... maybe she didn't have to try alone.

"You and me," she said.

"Hmm?"

"You and me. We figure it out together. We start a new life, the two of us. We work security jobs, or maybe—you can fly, I can deal with shady people, we could get a little ship, do freight runs." Smuggling, she meant, but best not to say that out loud. "You don't like that idea? We'll think of something else. But you and me, together, from now on. We could be a great team."

"I'd like that," Valk said.

She put a hand on his arm.

"But of course," he told her, "we have to see what Lanoe says first."

Right. Sure.

Ehta frowned. Looked down at the bar. No more drinks, she thought. Not right now. She'd nearly suggested something... foolish. "You can't get drunk," she said. "That's too bad. There's an upside, though. You don't need to sleep, either. Right now I'd very much like to find a bunk I can actually lie down in, instead of strapping myself in so I don't float away. Maybe tomorrow morning we can talk again. Okay?"

He turned his body toward her. Facing her. "Okay," he said. "I'll look forward to that."

She patted his arm and left him there at the bar.

—✦—

It wasn't hard to find Valk, even though he didn't show up on any public databases. Lanoe just asked for the wounded pilot, the one who kept his helmet up and opaque all the time.

When he got to the bar he found the AI sitting alone, an empty glass in his hand. Lanoe walked over and sat down next to him. Looked at the bartender. "Just give me a drink," he said.

"Lanoe!" Valk said. Sounding happy to see him. "Ehta and I were just talking about you. How are you?"

Lanoe didn't answer. He tossed back his drink and grimaced. Ordered another. This one he left sitting there, untouched.

"Back in the Crisis," he said, "I had you in my sights once. Remember?"

"That happened to Tannis Valk. But I remember," Valk said.

Lanoe nodded. "I was low on ammunition. Almost out of fuel. You got away from me."

Valk laughed. It sounded like a human laugh, even though Lanoe knew it was just a sound file.

Lanoe wasn't laughing. "There's a docking bay about two hundred meters that way," he said, pointing down a corridor. "There are two BR.9s in there. They've both been fueled up. I've had a word with traffic control. No one is going to stop us."

Valk shook his head. "I'm confused. You want to...what? Take a joyride? Maybe race me somewhere?"

Lanoe touched the glass in front of him. Pulled his hand back. "I checked something, as soon as we got here. I had to know. See, I wouldn't let myself say it out loud, barely let myself think it. But it occurred to me. With all the changes we made, all the history you played with. Maybe she would be here, somewhere. Still alive."

"You mean Zhang," Valk said. He was as still as a statue.

"Her service record is public data. It lists her as deceased. A casualty of the battle at Niraya." Lanoe couldn't look at the AI. "Still."

"Lanoe, you have to understand, there was no other way—"

"You killed her," Lanoe said. He grabbed the edge of the bar. Squeezed it until it creaked. "You killed her, Valk. You were there, this time. You could have stopped it, you could have warned us... You didn't. You killed her."

"Lanoe—"

"I'm giving you a head start. It's more than you deserve, you bastard."

A human might have hesitated. A human might have tried to talk his way out of this. Maybe. The AI didn't bother with that. He jumped off his barstool and ran.

Lanoe tried to count to ten. He didn't get very far. Instead, he reached forward, took the shot glass off the bar, and knocked it back.

He placed the glass back down, very carefully.

Then he stood up. And started moving.

Valk tore out of the docking bay, punching his throttle to get as much distance from the station as he could. He startled a swarm of drones that had been painting the exterior of the station, sending them flying in every direction, barely managing to avoid hitting any of them. A Z.XIX nosed toward him, its weapons hot—station security, no doubt wondering what the hell was going on.

The Z.XIX didn't signal to him, though. It didn't demand that he turn back. Apparently if you were a commander like Lanoe you could do what you liked and people knew better than to ask questions.

Once he was clear of the immediate traffic around the station, Valk hit his maneuvering jets and swung around to his left, headed for open space. He knew Lanoe wouldn't be far behind, and he wanted to get somewhere open before the shooting started.

He didn't quite get there. PBW fire streaked past him without warning, a couple of shots bouncing off his vector field. Valk could see in all directions, so he didn't need to crane his neck around to see that Lanoe was right behind him.

Their ships were evenly matched. Back in the Crisis, Tannis Valk wouldn't have stood a chance. He was never half the pilot Lanoe was. Now, though, Valk had the reaction time of a computer. He ran through a number of probability models, searched for the best way to get out of this. The best way to survive, at least, until he could say what he had to say.

He threw his cataphract into a tight corkscrew, nudging his stick left or right occasionally to keep his flight path as unpredictable as possible. PBW fire cut the vacuum into sections all around him, but he dodged the worst of it.

Valk studied his tactical board, called up infrared imagery of Lanoe's ship, worked with every sensor he had. He saw one thing right away—Lanoe's disruptors were cold. He wasn't going to end this with one quick explosion. Valk figured that Lanoe wanted to drag this out a little before he moved in for the kill.

That gave him a chance to talk. He opened his comms board and linked their two ships with a communications laser. "Lanoe," he said, "I made contact with that queenship we saw orbiting the Choir's planet. My copy on that ship told me everything he'd seen, everything he'd done. The species he met. The species he saved. When he told me about Zhang, I was horrified. I was saddened. I couldn't believe it.

"Then he told me why.

"It had to be done. Otherwise, there would have been a paradox.

"If Zhang hadn't died, you never would have gone to the Choir and demanded they open the wormhole to the past. You never would have gone back there looking for revenge. Can't you understand this? It's exactly what we talked about before.

"If things were different—but they couldn't be different. This one thing, this one terrible thing had to happen. Or it wouldn't have worked.

"Please, Lanoe. You have to see that I'm right. That she had to die."

Valk stopped talking, then, for two reasons. He'd run out of things to say. And also he saw that Lanoe had refused the comms laser. The message hadn't gone through.

Ahead of Lanoe, Valk twisted out of his corkscrew in a flat spin, a maneuver that would have probably left a human pilot unconscious. It cut Valk's velocity in half almost instantly, and Lanoe shot past the other BR.9, unable to decelerate as quickly. He threw his control stick over to the side and came around, banking hard to keep Valk from getting behind him.

"Nice trick," he said.

For a moment, just a split second, Valk had him in a bad pocket. He could have disabled Lanoe's fighter with a few well-placed shots, or even blown him out of the sky with a disruptor.

Valk didn't fire. He had the perfect opportunity and he didn't take it. Clearly he still thought there was a way out of this. That they could both walk away from this alive.

Lanoe had no intention of letting that happen. If Valk didn't want to shoot, so be it. Lanoe opened up with his PBWs, firing wildly, knowing there was no chance he would actually hit Valk. Those potshots were just to let Valk know he was serious.

The message got across, apparently. Valk shot forward again, hitting his engines hard. He threw his fighter into a steep dive, and Lanoe followed. The silver face of the moon loomed up before them, big enough to fill Lanoe's canopy.

Together they shot downward into the moon's gravity well, the ground rushing up to meet them. The distance between them evaporated as their fighters plunged through the vacuum. Craters and low mountains and the boxy habitats of the lunar slums raced upward toward them, but Valk didn't pull up. He moved his control stick only to swing back and forth as Lanoe fired shot after shot at him. A damage control board popped up in front of Valk and he realized he'd been hit. He'd been too busy flying to feel it, but it looked like Lanoe had clipped off both of his airfoils on one side.

It didn't matter. Valk wasn't going anywhere with air. He tore down through the lunar sky, until traffic control alerts piled up in his message queue, until a collision alarm sounded behind his head.

Twenty meters from the pale soil of the moon, Valk pulled back on his control stick, hard. The view through his canopy swung crazily as he leveled out, flying now at high speed over the rough terrain.

Valk kept his altitude low, flew so close to the ground he had to constantly bob up over giant rocks or drop vertiginously into the bottoms of craters. The constant altitude adjustments made him a tricky target, but Lanoe kept shooting, a steady stream of particles that sparked off his vector field.

Up ahead Valk saw the spires of a helium-cracking plant, black fingers reaching up toward a black sky. He dodged around a big spherical holding tank, then threw himself sideways to pass between two of the dark towers, clearing them by less than a meter. One spire exploded into shards of debris as Lanoe cut into it with a steady stream of fire. Pieces of the broken tower bounced off of Valk's fuselage with a series of sharp thuds.

Valk had thought he could lose Lanoe by flying so recklessly. He'd been wrong. Even as he came around in a rotary turn, swerving to pass around the far side of the plant, Lanoe finally got him. A good, solid direct hit, right in one of his thruster cones.

The damage control board flashed wildly. Alarms sounded and a voice warned Valk that he was in danger of losing his engines. He tried to pull up, to climb for the sky before Lanoe could hit him again.

It didn't work. Lanoe blasted him right in one of his fairings, the particle rounds blowing off a panel and cutting through a bundle of cables underneath. Valk felt his whole fighter buck and twist around as he lost control of his maneuvering and positioning jets.

PBW fire sparked and danced all over his vector field. Some of those shots got through. Valk saw the ground coming up fast and wrestled with his stick, trying desperately to maintain some altitude. Even though his boards all told him it wasn't going to happen.

He managed, just barely, to avoid smashing nose first into the moon's surface. He didn't pancake. Instead he hit the ground at an angle, smearing his BR.9 across the powdery soil, sending up enormous clouds of dust that glittered in the sunlight.

The cataphract came apart in a million pieces. Valk's canopy collapsed, the flowglas melting away as it lost cohesion, and he was thrown forward hard enough to break right through his straps, to be ejected from his cockpit and sent flying forward, pinwheeling off the ground, bouncing again and again.

Lanoe set down and popped open his canopy. He jumped down onto the dusty ground. He shuffled forward, a few meters at a time, in the bounding walk you had to use on the moon. He followed the trail of wreckage as if it were an arrow pointing at his target.

He found Valk a hundred meters farther on. Crawling in the dirt. The lower half of his suit was gone, his legs still back in the wreckage. Lanoe could see up inside what remained of the suit's torso. He could see that it was empty inside.

He put his boot squarely on Valk's back and pinned him down. Valk stopped trying to crawl away. He managed to squirm around, to turn so he was facing upward. Not that it mattered. There was nothing to see in that black helmet.

"You murdered her," Lanoe said. He tried to keep his voice level. "You knew what she meant to me but you murdered her. You had a chance to save her. And you murdered her. The only woman I ever loved."

Valk didn't try to deny it. "Do it, Lanoe," he said.

Lanoe squinted down at him. He started to reach for the pistol at his hip.

"No," Valk said. "Not like that. The black pearl. Remember? The data bomb I gave you. Use it. If you shoot me, I can just make another copy of myself."

"Shut up," Lanoe said.

"If you use the data bomb—it's a worm, a computer worm, it'll erase all of me. Every version, every copy. It'll find me wherever I try to hide in the network. It's the only way."

"I said shut up!"

The damned AI obeyed him.

Lanoe squatted down to stare right into that blank helmet. "You want this, don't you? Hellfire. You want to die."

"That's all I ever asked for," Valk replied.

Lanoe seethed with rage. "Maybe," he said. He shook his head, trying to clear it. "Maybe I should just leave you here. Leave you with half a suit, wriggling in the dirt like a worm. Maybe I should—"

"I killed her!" Valk shouted. "I killed her! I watched her die, watched her fall into that ice giant. Lanoe—I did it, and I would do it again. I would do it again!"

The black pearl appeared in the corner of Lanoe's eye before he'd even realized he had called it up. All he had to do was flick his eyes to the side, just one little gesture and it would be done. Forever.

"I killed her! Do it, Lanoe! Do it—and get your revenge! That's what you wanted, isn't it? Let me give this to you, let me do one last thing for—"

Lanoe's eyes flicked to the side.

The effect was instantaneous. Valk's helmet came down, the black flowglas melting down into his collar ring. The remaining half of his suit crumpled under the moon's gravity, now that there was nothing holding it up.

Valk was gone.

Lanoe let out a cry of pure distress. A single, terrible shriek of pain.

It was all he would allow himself. Even here where there was no one to hear it.

He straightened up. Pulled himself up to his full height. Turned away from the empty suit lying on the ground

Then he started to move.

Aleister Lanoe walked off, across the surface of the moon, all alone.

Behind him, Zhang followed, one hand reaching up to grasp his shoulder.

Acknowledgments

I would like to thank all the usual people who worked hard to help create the book you're holding in your hand (or the electrons you're currently processing). James Long and Will Hinton, my editors; Nazia Khatun, Sarah Guan, and Ellen B. Wright at Orbit; my agent, Russell Galen; and of course, Alex Lencicki, who knows why his name is on the first page.

Most importantly, though, I'd like to thank my now wife, Jennifer. In the summer of 2016, when she was still my fiancée, I locked myself in a little room and said I wouldn't come out until I finished writing this book. I made it out just in time to shave, shower, and go get married. Without Jennifer's patience, this book wouldn't exist, and I wouldn't be married to the most wonderful woman in the world.

extras

orbit

if you enjoyed
FORBIDDEN SUNS

look out for

THE ETERNITY WAR: PARIAH

Book One of the Eternity War

by

Jamie Sawyer

Humanity has spread across the galaxy and, after years of interspecies warfare, entered into an uneasy truce with the Krell. But when the Krell send an ambassador to the human Alliance to request aid, they discover that their civilizations face a much deadlier mutual enemy: the Shard, an alien super species that are pouring from the Outer Dark into real-space.

Captain Keira Jenkins of the Alliance leads a team of simulant soldiers in a joint military action, but when the mission goes down in flames, an injured and humiliated Jenkins is offered one last chance at redemption: a mission deep into contagion-infested enemy territory.

She has one last chance, and so does mankind.

I collapsed into the cot, panting hard as I tried to catch my breath. A sheen of hot, musky sweat—already cooling—had formed across my skin.

"Third time's a charm, eh?" Riggs said. He spoke Standard with an accented twang, being of Tau Ceti III, a descendant of North American colonists who had generations back claimed the planet as their own.

"You're getting better at it, is all I'll say."

Riggs tried to hug me from behind as though we were actual lovers. His body was warm and muscled, but I shrugged him off.

"Are things ever going to change between us?" he asked, a sigh on his lips. "Are we always going to stay like this?"

"Like what? This is letting off steam before a drop. There's no point dressing this up: we're just soldiers doing what needs to be done."

"I know, and I'm grateful for it." He grinned at me boyishly. "You sounded pretty grateful, too."

"Watch yourself. Things can change fast."

"How do you handle *this*?" Riggs asked. "The waiting. It feels worse than the mission."

"It's your first combat operation," I said. "You're bound to feel a little nervous."

"Do you remember your first mission?"

"Yeah," I said, "but only just. It was a long time ago."

He paused, as though thinking that through, then asked, "Does it get easier?"

"The hours before the drop are always the worst," I said. "It's best just not to think about it."

The waiting was well recognized as the worst part of any mission. I didn't want to go into it with Riggs, but believe me when I say that I've tried almost every technique in the book.

It basically boils down to two options.

Option One: find a dark corner somewhere and sit it out. Even the smaller strikeships that the Alliance relies upon have private areas, away from prying eyes, away from the rest of your squad or the ship's crew. If you're determined, you'll find somewhere private enough and quiet enough to sit it out alone. But few troopers I've known take this approach, because it rarely works. The Gaia lovers seem to prefer this method, but then again they're often fond of introspection, and that isn't me. Option One leads to anxiety, depression, and mental breakdown. There aren't many soldiers who want to fill the hours before death—even if it is only simulated—with soul-searching. Time slows to a trickle. Psychological time dilation, or something like it. There's no drug that can touch that anxiety.

Riggs *was* a Gaia Cultist, for his sins, but I didn't think that explaining Option One was going to help him. No, Riggs wasn't an Option One sort of guy.

Option Two: find something to fill the time. Exactly what you do is your choice; pretty much anything that'll take your mind off the job will suffice. This is what most troopers do. My personal preference—and I accept that it isn't for everyone—is hard physical labor. Anything that really gets the blood flowing is rigorous enough to shut down the neural pathways.

Which leads to my current circumstances. An old friend once taught me that the best exercise in the universe is the exercise you get between the sheets. So, in the hours before we made the drop to Daktar Outpost, I screwed Corporal Daneb Riggs's brains out. Not literally, you understand, because we were in our own bodies. I'm screwed up, or so the psychtechs tell me, but I'm not *that* twisted.

"Where'd you get that?" Riggs asked me, probing the flesh of my left flank. His voice was still dopey as a result of postcoital hormones. "The scar, I mean."

I lay on my back, beside Riggs, and looked down at the white welt to the left of my stomach. Although the flesh-graft had taken well enough, the injury was still obvious: unless I paid for skintech for a patch, it always would be. There seemed little point in bothering with cosmetics while I was still a line trooper. Well-healed scars lined my stomach and chest, nothing to complain about, but reminders nonetheless. My body was a road map of my military service.

"Never you mind," I said. "It happened a long time ago." I pushed Riggs's hand away, irritated. "And I thought I made it clear that there would be no talking afterward. That term of the arrangement is nonnegotiable."

Riggs got like this after a session. He got chatty, and he got annoying. His job here was done and I was already feeling detachment from him.

I untangled myself from the bedsheets that were pooled at the foot of the cot. The cabin was private but also tiny, and it stank of sweat and sex. Almost as soon as the act was over, I started to feel jumpy again, felt my eyes unconsciously darting to my wrist-comp. I pulled on a tank top and walked to the viewport in the bulkhead.

The cabin's port was open, displaying an anonymous sector of deep space. Another sector in what had once been known as the Quarantine Zone: that vast ranch of deep space that was the divide between us and the Krell Empire. A holo-display above the port read "1:57:03 UNTIL DROP." Less than two hours until we reached the assault point. Right now, the UAS *Bainbridge* was slowing down—its enormous sublight engines ensuring that when we reached the appointed location, we would be traveling at just the right velocity. The starship's inertial damper field meant that I would never be able to physically feel the deceleration, but the mental weight was another matter.

"Get dressed," I said matter-of-factly. "We've got work to do."

I pulled on the rest of my duty fatigues, pressed down the various holo-tabs on my uniform tunic. The identifier there read "210." Those numbers made me a long-termer of the Simulant Operations Program—sufferer of an effective two hundred and ten simulated deaths.

"I want you down on the prep deck, overseeing the simulant loading," I said, dropping into command mode.

"The Jackals are primed and ready to drop," Riggs said. "The lifer is marking the suits, and I ordered Private Feng to check on the ammunition loads—"

"Feng's no good at that," I said. "You know that he can't be trusted."

"'Trusted'?"

"I didn't mean it like that," I corrected.

Riggs detected the change in my voice; he'd be an idiot not to. While he wasn't exactly the sharpest tool in the box, neither was he a fool.

I watched as he put on his uniform. Riggs was tall and well built, his chest a wall of muscle, neck almost as wide as my waist. Hair dark and short, nicely messy in a way that skirted the edge of acceptable military regulation. The tattoo of a winged planet on his left biceps indicated that he was a former Off-World Marine aviator, while the blue-and-green globe on his right marked him as a paid-up Gaia Cultist. The dataports on his chest, shoulders, and neck stood out against his tanned skin, the flesh around them still raised. He looked new, and he looked young. Riggs hadn't yet been spat out by the war machine.

I felt a wave of regret crash over me. What was I doing? I knew that it was wrong. Why hadn't I learned my lesson the first time? I'd shit on my own doorstep before, but a dirty dog doesn't learn from her mistakes.

"So we're being deployed against the Black Spiral?" he asked, velcroing his tunic in place. The holo-identifier on his chest flashed "10," and sickeningly enough, Riggs was the most experienced trooper on my team. "That's the scuttlebutt."

"Maybe," I said. "That's likely." I knew very little about the next operation, because that was how Captain Heinrich—the *Bainbridge*'s senior officer—liked to keep things. "It's need to know."

"And you don't need to know," Riggs said, nodding to himself. "Heinrich is such an asshole."

"Talk like that'll get you reprimanded, Corporal." I snapped my wrist-computer into place, the vambrace closing around my left wrist. "Same arrangement as before. Don't let the rest of the team know."

Riggs grinned. "So long as you don't either—"

The cabin lights dipped. Something clunked inside the ship. At about the same time, my wrist-comp chimed with an incoming priority communication: an officers-only alert.

"EARLY DROP," the wrist-comp said.

The wrist-comp's small screen activated, and a head-and-shoulders image appeared there. A young woman with auburn hair pulled back from a heavily freckled face. Early twenties. With anxiety-filled eyes, she leaned close into the camera at her end of the connection. Sergeant Zoe Campbell, more commonly known as Zero.

"Lieutenant, ma'am," she babbled. "Do you copy?"

"I copy," I said.

"Where have you been? I've been trying to reach you for the last thirty minutes, but your communicator was off. I tried your cube, but that was set to private. I guess that I could've sent someone down there, but I know how you get before a drop and—"

"Whoa, whoa. Calm down, Zero. What's happening?"

Zero was the squad's handler. She was already in the Sim Ops bay, and the image behind her showed a bank of operational simulator tanks, assorted science officers tending them. It looked like the op was well under way rather than just commencing.

"Is Heinrich calling a briefing?" I asked, hustling Riggs to finish getting dressed. I needed him gone from the room, pronto.

Zero shook her head. "Captain Heinrich says there isn't time. He's distributed a mission plan instead. I really should've sent someone down to you fetch you..."

"Never mind about that now," I said. Talking over her was often the only way to deal with Zero's constant state of anxiety. "What's happening? Why the early drop?"

Zero grimaced. "Captain Heinrich has authorized immediate military action on Daktar Outpost."

At that moment, a nasal siren sounded throughout the *Bainbridge*'s decks. Somewhere in the bowels of the ship, the engines were cutting, the gravity field fluctuating just a little to compensate.

The ship's AI began a looped message: "This is a general alert. All operators must immediately report to the Simulant Operations Center. This is a general alert..."

I could already hear boots on deck around me, as the sixty qualified operators made haste to the Science Deck. My dataports—those biomechanical connections that would allow me to make transition into my simulant—were beginning to throb.

"You'd better get down here and skin up," Zero said, nodding at the simulator behind her. "Don't want to be late." Added: "Again..."

"I'm on it," I said, planting my feet in my boots. "Hold the fort."

Zero started to say something else, but before she could question me any further I terminated the communication.

"Game time, Corporal," I said to Riggs. "Look alive."

Dressed now, Riggs nodded and made for the hatch. We had this down to a T: if we left my quarters separately, it minimized the prospect of anyone realizing what was happening between us.

"You're beautiful," he said. "You do know that, right?"

"You know that was the last time," I said firmly.

"You said that *last* time..."

"Well, this time I mean it, kemosabe."

Riggs nodded, but that idiot grin remained plastered across his face. "See you down there, Jenkins," he said.

Here we go again, I thought. *New team. New threat. Same shit.*

if you enjoyed
FORBIDDEN SUNS

look out for

THE OUTER EARTH TRILOGY

by

Rob Boffard

In space, every second counts.

Outer Earth is a massive space station that orbits three hundred miles above the Earth, holding the last of humanity. It's broken, rusted, and falling apart. The world below is dead. Wrecked by climate change and nuclear war, and now we have to live with the consequences: a new home that's dirty, overcrowded, and inescapable.

The population reaches one million. Double what it was designed to hold. Food is short, crime is rampant, and the ecosystem nears the breaking point.

What's more, there's a madman hiding on the station who is about to unleash chaos. And when he does, there'll be nowhere left to run.

extras

Seven years ago

The ship is breaking up around them.

The hull is twisting and creaking, like it's trying to tear away from the heat of reentry. The outer panels are snapping off, hurtling past the cockpit viewports, black blurs against a dull orange glow.

The ship's second-in-command, Singh, is tearing at her seat straps, as if getting loose will be enough to save her. She's yelling at the captain, seated beside her, but he pays her no attention. The flight deck below them is a sea of flashing red, the crew spinning in their chairs, hunting for something, *anything* they can use.

They have checklists for these situations. But there's no checklist for when a ship, plunging belly-down through Earth's atmosphere to maximise the drag, gets flipped over by an explosion deep in the guts of the engine, sending it first into a spin and then into a screaming nosedive. Now it's spearing through the atmosphere, the friction tearing it to pieces.

The captain doesn't raise his voice. "We have to eject the rear module," he says.

Singh's eyes go wide. "Captain—"

He ignores her, reaching up to touch the communicator in his ear. "Officer Yamamoto," he says, speaking as clearly as he can. "Cut the rear module loose."

Koji Yamamoto stares up at him. His eyes are huge, his mouth slightly open. He's the youngest crew member, barely eighteen. The captain has to say his name again before he turns and hammers on the touch-screens.

The loudest bang of all shudders through the ship as its entire rear third explodes away. Now the ship and its crew are tumbling end over end, the movement forcing them back in their seats. The captain's stomach feels like it's broken free of its moorings. He waits for the tumbling to stop, for the ship to right itself. Three seconds. Five.

He sees his wife's face, his daughter's. *No, don't think about them. Think about the ship.*

"Guidance systems are gone," McCallister shouts, her voice distorting over the comms. "The core's down. I got nothing."

"Command's heard our Mayday," Dominguez says. "They—"

McCallister's straps snap. She's hurled out of her chair, thudding off the control panel, leaving a dark red spatter of blood across a screen. Yamamoto reaches for her, forgetting that he's still strapped in. Singh is screaming.

"Dominguez," says the captain. "Patch me through."

Dominguez tears his eyes away from the injured McCallister. A second later, his hands are flying across the controls. A burst of static sounds in the captain's comms unit, followed by two quick beeps.

He doesn't bother with radio protocol. "Ship is on a collision path. We're going to try to crash-land. If we—"

"John."

Foster doesn't have to identify himself. His voice is etched into the captain's memory from dozens of flight briefings and planning sessions and quiet conversations in the pilots' bar.

The captain doesn't know if the rest of flight command are listening in, and he doesn't care. "Marshall," he says. "I think I can bring the ship down. We'll activate our emergency beacon; sit tight until you can get to us."

"I'm sorry, John. There's nothing I can do."

"What are you talking about?"

There's another bang, and then a roar, as if the ship is caught in the jaws of an enormous beast. The captain turns to look at Singh, but she's gone. So is the side of the ship. There's nothing but a jagged gash, the edges a mess of torn metal and sputtering wires. The awful orange glow is coming in, its fingers reaching for him, and he can feel the heat baking his skin.

"Marshall, listen to me," the captain says, but Marshall is gone too. The captain can see the sky beyond the ship, beyond the flames. It's blue, clearer than he could have ever imagined. It fades to black where it reaches the upper atmosphere, and the space beyond that is pinpricked with stars.

One of those stars is Outer Earth.

Maybe I can find it, the captain thinks, if I look hard enough. He can feel the anger, the *disbelief* at Marshall's words, but he refuses to let it take hold. He tells himself that Outer Earth will send help. They have to. He tries to picture the faces of his family, tries to hold them uppermost in his mind, but the roaring and the heat are everywhere and he can't—

extras

1

Riley

My name is Riley Hale, and when I run, the world disappears.

Feet pounding. Heart thudding. Steel plates thundering under my feet as I run, high up on Level 6, keeping a good momentum as I move through the darkened corridors. I focus on the next step, on the in-out, push-pull of my breathing. Stride, land, cushion, spring, repeat. The station is a tight warren of crawl-spaces and vents around me, every surface metal etched with ancient graffiti.

"She's over there!"

The shout comes from behind me, down the other end of the corridor. The skittering footsteps that follow it echo off the walls. I thought I'd lost these idiots back at the sector border – now I have to outrun them all over again. I got lost in the rhythm of running – always dangerous when someone's trying to jack your cargo. I refuse to waste a breath on cursing, but one of my exhales turns into a growl of frustration.

The Lieren might not be as fast as I am, but they obviously don't give up.

I go from a jog to a sprint, my pack juddering on my spine as I pump my arms even harder. A tiny bead of sweat touches my eye, sizzling and stinging. I ignore it. No tracer in my crew has ever failed to deliver their cargo, and I am not going to be the first.

I round the corner – and nearly slam into a crush of people. There are five of them, sauntering down the corridor, talking among themselves. But I'm already reacting, pushing off with my right foot, springing in the direction of the wall. I bring my other foot up to meet it, flattening it against the metal and tucking my left knee up to my chest. The momentum keeps me going forwards even as I'm pushing off, exhaling with a whoop as I squeeze through the space between the people and the wall. My right foot comes down, and I'm instantly in motion again. Full momentum. A perfect tic-tac.

The Lieren are close behind, colliding with the group, bowling them over in a mess of confused shouts. But I've got the edge now. Their cries fade into the distance.

There's not a lot you can move between sectors without paying off the gangs. Not unless you know where and how to cross. Tracers do. And that's why we exist. If you need to get something to someone, or if you've got a little package you don't want any gangs knowing about, you come find us. We'll get it there – for a price, of course – and if you come to my crew, the Devil Dancers, we'll get it there *fast*.

The corridor exit looms, and then I'm out, into the gallery. After the corridors, the giant lights illuminating the massive open area are blinding. Corridor becomes catwalk, bordered with rusted metal railings, and the sound of my footfalls fades away, whirling off into the open space.

I catch a glimpse of the diagram on the far wall, still legible a hundred years after it was painted. A scale picture of the station. The Core at the centre, a giant sphere which houses the main fusion reactor. Shooting out from it on either side, two spokes, connected to an enormous ring, the main body. And under it, faded to almost nothing after over a century: Outer Earth Orbit Preservation Module, Founded AD 2234.

Ahead of me, more people emerge from the far entrance to the catwalk. A group of teenage girls, packed tight, talking loudly among themselves. I count ten, fifteen – *no*. They haven't seen me. I'm heading full tilt towards them.

Without breaking stride, I grab the right-hand railing of the catwalk and launch myself up and over, into space.

For a second, there's no noise but the air rushing past me. The sound of the girls' conversation vanishes, like someone turned down a volume knob. I can see all the way down to the bottom of the gallery, a hundred feet below, picking out details snatched from the gaps in the web of criss-crossing catwalks.

The floor is a mess of broken benches and circular flowerbeds with nothing in them. There are two young girls, skipping back and forth over a line they've drawn on the floor. One is wearing a faded smock. I can just make out the word Astro on the back as it twirls around her. A light above them is flickering off-on-off, and their shadows flit in and out on the wall behind them, dancing off metal plates. My own shadow is spread out before me, split by the catwalks; a black shape broken on rusted railings. On one of the catwalks lower down, two men are arguing, pushing each other. One man throws a punch, his target dodging back as the group around them scream dull threats.

I jumped off the catwalk without checking my landing zone. I don't even want to think what Amira would do if she found out. Explode, probably. Because if there's someone under me and I hit them from above, it's not just a broken ankle I'm looking at.

Time seems frozen. I flick my eyes towards the Level 5 catwalk rushing towards me.

It's empty. Not a person in sight, not even further along. I pull my legs up, lift my arms and brace for the landing.

Contact. The noise returns, a bang that snaps my head back even as I'm rolling forwards. On instinct, I twist sideways, so the impact can travel across, rather than up, my spine. My right hand hits the ground, the sharp edges of the steel bevelling scraping my palm, and I push upwards, arching my back so my pack can fit into the roll.

Then I'm up and running, heading for the dark catwalk exit on the far side. I can hear the Lieren reach the catwalk above. They've spotted me, but I can tell by their angry howls that it's too late. There's no way they're making that jump. To get to where I am, they'll have to fight their way through the stairwells on the far side. By then, I'll be long gone.

"Never try to outrun a Devil Dancer, boys," I mutter between breaths.